SCARECROW
and
SEVEN ANCIENT WONDERS

Matthew Reilly is the Australian-born bestselling author of four previous novels: *Contest*, *Ice Station*, *Temple* and *Area 7*. He wrote his first two books while studying law at the University of New South Wales, and now writes full-time, producing novels and screenplays and creating television series. The author still lives in Sydney, and you can visit his website: www.matthewreilly.com.

Also by Matthew Reilly

ICE STATION

TEMPLE

CONTEST

AREA 7

MATTHEW REILLY

SCARECROW and SEVEN ANCIENT WONDERS

PAN BOOKS

Scarecrow first published in Great Britain 2003 by Macmillan
This edition published 2004 by Pan Books
Seven Ancient Wonders first published 2005 by Macmillan
an imprint of Pan Macmillan Australia Pty Limited, Sydney
First published in Great Britain 2006 by Macmillan
First published in paperback 2006 by Pan Books

This omnibus first published 2008 by Pan Books
an imprint of Pan Macmillan Ltd
Pan Macmillan, 20 New Wharf Road, London N1 9RR
Basingstoke and Oxford
Associated companies throughout the world
www.panmacmillan.com

ISBN 978-0-330-50799-8

1 3 5 7 9 8 6 4 2

A CIP catalogue record for this book is available from the British Library.

Printed in the UK by CPI Mackays, Chatham ME5 8TD

SCARECROW

FOR NATALIE, AGAIN

Permissions Acknowledgements

'The Second Coming' by W. B. Yeats reproduced by kind permission of A. P. Watt Ltd on behalf of Michael B. Yeats.

The Coming Anarchy: Shattering the Dreams of the Post Cold War by Robert Kaplan. Originally published in *Atlantic Monthly*, February 1994. Copyright © Robert Kaplan 1994. Reprinted by permission of Brandt & Hochman Literary Agents, Inc.

The Death of the West: How Dying Populations and Immigrant Invasions Imperil Our Country and Civilization by Patrick J. Buchanan. Copyright © Patrick J. Buchanan 2002. Reprinted by permission of St. Martin's Press, LLC.

No Logo: Taking Aim at the Brand Bullies (Alfred A. Knopf Canada, 2000). Copyright © Naomi Klein 2000. With permission of the author.

Every effort has been made to contact copyright holders of material reproduced in this book. If any have been inadvertently overlooked, the publishers will be please to make restitution at the earliest opportunity.

ACKNOWLEDGEMENTS

I don't know about you, but when I read a book, usually most of the names on the 'Acknowledgements' page mean very little to me. They're either friends of the author, or people who helped the author with research or getting published.

But let me tell you, profound and public thanks is exactly what these people deserve.

In my previous books, I have written on the 'Acknowledgements' page these words: 'to anyone who knows a writer, never underestimate the power of your encouragement.'

Believe me, writers – indeed, all creative people – live off encouragement. It drives us, propels us onward. One encouraging word can outshine a thousand critical comments.

And so while you, dear reader, may not recognise all of the following names, each in their own way *encouraged* me. This book is the richer for their help.

So.

On the friendship side:

Thanks, again, to Natalie Freer for her companionship and her smile and for reading the book in 60-page chunks once again; to John Schrooten, my mum and my brother, Stephen, for telling me what they really thought. And to my dad for his quiet support.

To Nik and Simon Kozlina for taking me out for coffee when I needed it and to Bec Wilson for those dinners every Wednesday night. And to Daryl and Karen Kay, and Don and

Irene Kay, for being keen test subjects, hard-nosed engineers and good friends.

On the technical side:

Special thanks to the remarkable Richard Walsh from BHP Billiton for taking me on a fantastic tour of a coalmine down at Appen – the mine scenes in this book are so much more authentic for that experience! And thanks to Don Kay for arranging the introduction.

And of course, once again, sincere thanks to my amazing American military advisors, Captain Paul Woods, US Army, and Gunnery Sergeant Kris Hankison, USMC (retired). It's incredible what these two guys know – as such, any mistakes in the book are mine and were made over their objections!

And again, to everyone at Pan Macmillan, thank you for another great effort. They're a wonderful crew at Pan Macmillan: from editorial to publicity to the sales reps out on the road.

To anyone who knows a writer, never underestimate the power of your encouragement.

M.R.

TURNING AND TURNING IN THE WIDENING GYRE,
THE FALCON CANNOT HEAR THE FALCONER;
THINGS FALL APART; THE CENTRE CANNOT HOLD;
MERE ANARCHY IS LOOSED UPON THE WORLD . . .

W. B. YEATS

The Second Coming

ALL OF THE BRAVE MEN ARE DEAD.

RUSSIAN MILITARY PROVERB

PROLOGUE

THE RULERS OF THE WORLD

LONDON, ENGLAND
20 OCTOBER, 1900 HOURS

There were twelve of them in total.

All men.

All billionaires.

Ten of the twelve were over sixty years of age. The other two were in their thirties, but they were the sons of former members, so their loyalty was assured. While membership of the Council was not strictly conditional on heredity, over the years it had become commonplace for sons to replace their fathers.

Otherwise membership was by invitation only and invitations were rarely given – as one would expect of such an august collection of individuals.

The co-founder of the world's largest software company.

A Saudi oil magnate.

The patriarch of a Swiss banking family.

The owner of the world's biggest shipping company.

The world's most successful stock trader.

The Vice-Chairman of the US Federal Reserve.

The newly inherited heir to a military construction empire that built missiles for the United States Government.

There were no media barons on the Council – since it was widely known that their fortunes were largely based on debt and fluctuating share prices. The Council controlled the media simply by controlling the banks that fed the media barons their money.

Likewise, there were no national leaders – as the Council well knew, politicians possess the lowest form of power: transient power. Like media barons, they are beholden to others for their influence. In any case, the Council had made and unmade presidents and dictators before.

And no women.

It was the Council's view that there was – as yet – no woman on the planet worthy of a seat at the table. Not the Queen. Not even the French make-up heiress, Lillian Mattencourt, with her $26 billion personal fortune.

Since 1918, the Council had met twice a year, every year.

This year, however, it had been convened nine times.

This was, after all, a special year.

While the Council was a somewhat secretive group, its meetings were never held in secret. Secret meetings of powerful people create attention. No. It had always been the Council's opinion that the best-kept secrets existed out in the open, witnessed by the world but never actually *seen*.

As such, Council meetings were usually held during major international gatherings – the annual World Economic Forum in Davos, Switzerland; various World Trade Organisation meetings; the Council had even met once at Camp David, when the President wasn't there.

*

Today it met in the grand executive boardroom of the Dorchester Hotel in London.

The vote was taken and the decision was unanimous.

'Then it is agreed,' the Chairman said. 'The hunt will commence tomorrow. The list of targets will be released tonight through the usual channels, and bounties will be paid to those contractors who present to Monsieur J. P. Delacroix of AGM-Suisse the accustomed form of proof that a particular target has been eliminated.

'There are fifteen targets in total. The bounty for each has been set at US$18.6 million.'

An hour later, the meeting ended, and the members of the Council adjourned for drinks.

On the boardroom table behind them lay their meeting notes. Of the notes sitting in front of the Chairman's seat, one page lay face-up.

On it was a list of names.

	Name	Nat.	Org.
1.	ASHCROFT, William H.	UK	SAS
2.	CHRISTIE, Alec P.	UK	MI-6
3.	FARRELL, Gregory C.	USA	Delta
4.	KHALIF, Iman	AFGH	Al-Qaeda
5.	KINGSGATE, Nigel E.	UK	SAS
6.	McCABE, Dean P.	USA	Delta
7.	NAZZAR, Yousef M.	LEBN	HAMAS
8.	NICHOLSON, Francis X.	USA	USAMRMC
9.	OLIPHANT, Thompson J.	USA	USAMRMC
10.	POLANSKI, Damien G.	USA	ISS
11.	ROSENTHAL, Benjamin Y.	ISR	Mossad
12.	SCHOFIELD, Shane M.	USA	USMC
13.	WEITZMAN, Ronson H.	USA	USMC
14.	ZAWAHIRI, Hassan M.	SAUDI	Al-Qaeda
15.	ZEMIR, Simon B.	ISR	IAF

It was, to put it mildly, a singularly impressive list.

It featured members of the world's elite military units – the British SAS, the US Army's Delta Detachment and the Marine Corps.

The Israeli Air Force made an appearance, as did intelligence agencies like the Mossad and the ISS – the Intelligence and Security Service, the new name for the CIA. Plus members of the terrorist organisations HAMAS and Al-Qaeda.

It was a list of men – special men, brilliant at their chosen deadly professions – who had to be removed from the face of the earth by 12 noon, October 26, US Eastern Standard Time.

FIRST ATTACK

SIBERIA

26 OCTOBER, 0900 HOURS (LOCAL TIME)

E.S.T. (NEW YORK, USA) 2100 HOURS (25 OCT)

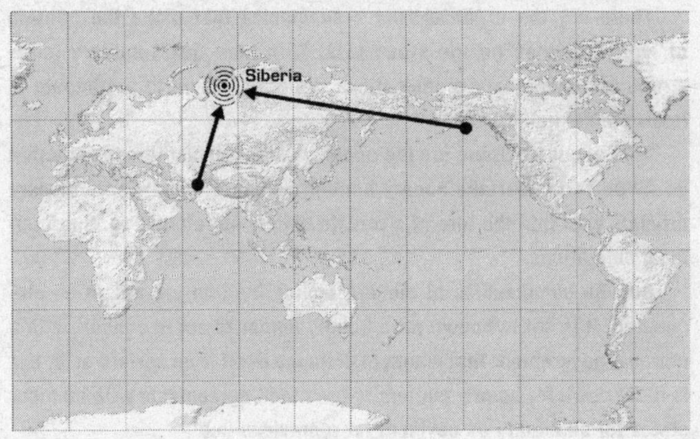

Modern international bounty hunters bear many similarities to their forebears in the Old American West.

There are the *lone wolf bounty hunters* – usually ex-military types, freelance assassins or fugitives from justice themselves, they are lone operators known for their idiosyncratic weapons, vehicles or methods.

There are the *organisations* – companies that make the hunting of fugitive human beings a business. With their quasi-military infrastructures, mercenary organisations are often drawn to participate in international human hunts.

And, of course, there are the *opportunists* – special forces units that go AWOL and undertake bounty hunting activities; or law enforcement officials who find the lure of a private bounty more enticing than their legal obligations.

But the complexities of modern bounty hunting are not to be discounted. It is not unknown for a bounty hunter to act in concert with a national government that wants to distance itself from certain acts. Nor is it unknown for bounty hunters to have tacit agreements with member states for sanctuary as payment for a previous 'job'.

For, in the end, one thing about them is clear: international borders mean little to the international bounty hunter.

United Nations White Paper:
Non-Government Forces in UN Peacekeeping Zones,
OCTOBER 2001 (UN PRESS, NEW YORK)

AIRSPACE ABOVE SIBERIA
26 OCTOBER, 0900 HOURS LOCAL TIME
(2100 HOURS E.S.T. USA, 25 OCT)

The aeroplane rocketed through the sky at the speed of sound.

Despite the fact that it was a large plane, it didn't show up on any radar screens. And even though it was breaking the sound barrier, it didn't create any sonic booms – a recent development in wave-negativing sensors took care of that.

With its angry-browed cockpit windows, its black radar-absorbent paint and its unique flying-wing design, the B-2 Stealth Bomber didn't normally fly missions like this.

It was designed to carry 40,000 pounds of ordnance, from laser-guided bombs to air-launched thermonuclear cruise missiles.

Today, however, it carried no bombs.

Today its bomb bay had been modified to convey a light but unusual payload: one fast-attack vehicle and eight United States Marines.

*

As he stood in the cockpit of the speeding Stealth Bomber, Captain Shane M. Schofield was unaware of the fact that, as of six days previously, he had become a target in the greatest bounty hunt in history.

The grey Siberian sky was reflected in the silver lenses of his wraparound anti-flash glasses. The glasses concealed a pair of vertical scars that cut down across Schofield's eyes, wounds from a previous mission and the source of his operational nickname: Scarecrow.

At five-feet-ten-inches tall, Schofield was lean and muscular. Under his white–grey Kevlar helmet, he had spiky black hair and a creased handsome face. He was known for his sharp mind, his cool head under pressure, and the high regard in which he was held by lower-ranking Marines – he was a leader who looked out for his men. Rumour had it he was also the grandson of the great Michael Schofield, a Marine whose exploits in the Second World War were the stuff of Marine Corps legend.

The B-2 zoomed through the sky, heading for a distant corner of northern Russia, to an abandoned Soviet installation on the barren coast of Siberia.

Its official Soviet name had been 'Krask-8: Penal and Maintenance Installation', the outermost of eight compounds surrounding the Arctic town of Krask. In the imaginative Soviet tradition, the compounds had been named Krask-1, Krask-2, Krask-3 and so on.

Until four days ago, Krask-8 had been known simply as a long-forgotten ex-Soviet outstation – a half-gulag, half-maintenance facility at which political prisoners had been forced to work. There were hundreds of such facilities dotted around the former Soviet Union – giant, ugly, oil-stained monoliths which before 1991 had formed the industrial heart of the USSR, but which now lay dormant, left to rot in the snow, the ghost towns of the Cold War.

But two days ago, on October 24, all that had changed.

Because on that day, a team of thirty well-armed and well-trained Islamic Chechen terrorists had taken over Krask-8 and announced to the Russian government that they intended to fire four SS-18 nuclear missiles – missiles that had simply been left in their silos at the site with the fall of the Soviets in 1991 – on Moscow unless Russia withdrew its troops from Chechnya and declared the breakaway republic an independent state.

A deadline was set for 10 a.m. today, October 26.

The date had meaning. October 26 was a year to the day since a force of crack Russian troops had stormed a Moscow theatre held by Chechen terrorists, ending a three-day siege, killing all the terrorists and over a hundred hostages.

That today also happened to be the first day of the Muslim holy month of Ramadan, a traditional day of peace, didn't seem to bother these Islamist terrorists.

The fact that Krask-8 was something more than just a relic of the Cold War was also news to the Russian government.

After some investigation of long-sealed Soviet records, the terrorists' claims had proved to be correct. It turned out that Krask-8 was a secret that the old Communist regime had failed to inform the new government about during the transition to democracy.

It did indeed house nuclear missiles – *sixteen* to be exact; sixteen SS-18 nuclear-tipped intercontinental ballistic missiles; all contained in concealed underground silos that had been designed to evade US satellite detection. Apparently, 'clones' of Krask-8 – identical missile-

KRASK-8: PENAL AND MAINTENANCE INSTALLATION
OUTER SIBERIA, FORMER SOVIET UNION

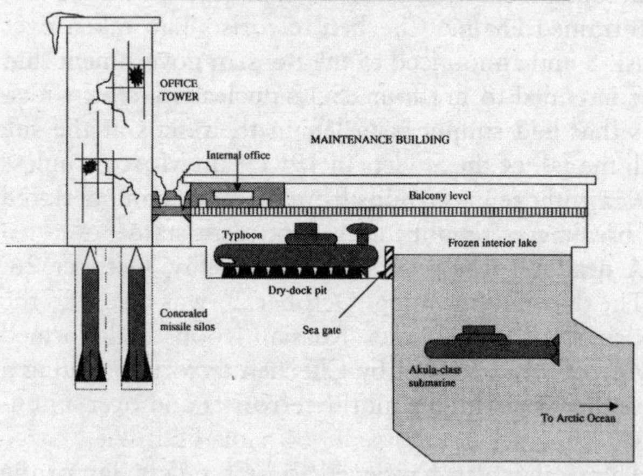

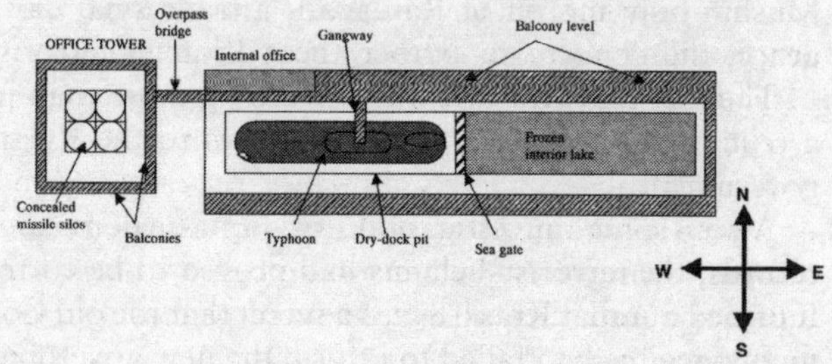

launch sites disguised as industrial facilities – could also be found in old Soviet client states like the Sudan, Syria, Cuba and Yemen.

And so, in the new world order – post-Cold War, post-September 11 – the Russians had called on the Americans to help.

As a rapid response, the American government had sent to Krask-8 a fast-and-light counter-terrorist unit from Delta Detachment – led by Specialists Greg Farrell and Dean McCabe.

Reinforcements would arrive later, the first of which was this team, a point unit of United States Marines led by Captain Shane M. Schofield.

Schofield strode into the bomb bay of the plane, breathing through a high-altitude face-mask.

He was met by the sight of a medium-sized cargo container, inside of which sat a Fast Attack 'Commando Scout' vehicle. Arguably the lightest and fastest armoured vehicle in service, it looked like a cross between a sports car and a Humvee.

And inside the sleek vehicle, strapped tightly into their seats, sat seven Recon Marines, the other members of Schofield's team. All were dressed in white–grey body armour, white–grey helmets, white–grey battle dress uniforms. And they all stared intently forward, game faces on.

As Schofield watched their serious expressions, he was once again taken aback by their youth. It was strange, but at 33 he felt decidedly old in their presence.

He nodded to the nearest man. 'Hey, Whip. How's the hand?'

'Why, er, it's great, sir,' Corporal Whip Whiting said,

surprised. He'd been shot in the hand during a fierce gun battle in the Tora Bora mountains in early 2002, but since that day Whip and Schofield hadn't worked together. 'The docs said you saved my index finger. If you hadn't told them to splint it, it would have grown in a hook shape. To be honest, I didn't think you'd remember, sir.'

Schofield's eyes gleamed. 'I always remember.'

Apart from one member of the unit, this wasn't his regular team.

His usual team of Marines – Libby 'Fox' Gant and Gena 'Mother' Newman – were currently operating in the mountains of northern Afghanistan, hunting for the terrorist leader and long-time No. 2 to Osama bin Laden, Hassan Mohammad Zawahiri.

Gant, fresh from Officer Candidate School and now a First Lieutenant, was leading a Recon Unit in Afghanistan. Mother, an experienced Gunnery Sergeant who had helped Schofield himself when he was a young officer, was acting as her Team Chief.

Schofield was supposed to be joining them, but at the last minute he'd been diverted from Afghanistan to lead this unexpected mission.

The only one of his regulars that Schofield had been able to bring with him was a young sergeant named Buck Riley Jnr, call-sign 'Book II'. Silent and brooding and possessed of an intensity that belied his twenty-five years, Book II was a seriously tough-as-nails warrior. And as far as Schofield was concerned, with his heavy-browed face and battered pug nose, he was looking more and more like his father – the original 'Book' Riley – every day.

Schofield keyed his satellite radio, spoke into the VibraMike strapped around his throat. Rather than pick up actual spoken words, the vibration-sensing microphone picked up the reverberations of his voice box. The satellite uplink system driving it was the brand-new GSX-9 – the most advanced communications system in use in the US military. In theory, a portable GSX-9 unit like Schofield's could broadcast a clear signal halfway around the world with crystal clarity.

'Base, this is Mustang 3,' he said. 'Sitrep?'

A voice came over his earpiece. It was the voice of an Air Force radio operator stationed at McColl Air Force Base in Alaska, the communications centre for this mission.

'*Mustang 3, this is Base. Mustang 1 and Mustang 2 have engaged the enemy. Report that they have seized the missile silos and inflicted heavy casualties on the enemy. Mustang 1 is holding the silos and awaiting reinforcements. Mustang 2 reports that there are still at least twelve enemy agents putting up a fight in the main maintenance building.*'

'All right,' Schofield said, 'what about our follow-up?'

'*An entire company of Army Rangers from Fort Lewis is en route, Scarecrow. One hundred men, approximately one hour behind you.*'

'Good.'

Book II spoke from inside the armoured Scout vehicle. 'What's the story, Scarecrow?'

Schofield turned. 'We're go for drop.'

Five minutes later, the box-shaped cargo-container dropped out of the belly of the Stealth Bomber and plummeted like a stone towards the earth.

Inside the container – in the car resting inside it – sat

Schofield and his seven Marines, shuddering and jolting with the vibrations of the terminal-velocity fall.

Schofield watched the numbers on a digital wall-mounted altimeter whizzing downwards:

50,000 feet . . .

45,000 feet . . .

40,000 . . . 30,000 . . . 20,000 . . . 10,000 . . .

'Preparing to engage chutes at five thousand feet . . .' Corporal Max 'Clark' Kent, the loadmaster, said in a neutral voice. 'GPS guidance system has us right on target for landing. External cameras verify that the LZ is clear.'

Schofield eyed the fast-ticking altimeter.

8,000 feet . . .

7,000 feet . . .

6,000 feet . . .

If everything went to plan, they would land about fifteen miles due east of Krask-8, just over the horizon from the installation, out of sight of the facility.

'Engaging primary chutes . . . *now*,' Clark announced.

The jolt that the falling container received was shocking in its force. The whole falling box lurched sharply and Schofield and his Marines all shuddered in their seats, held in by their six-point seat belts and rollbars.

And suddenly they were floating, care of the container's three directional parachutes.

'How're we doing, Clark?' Schofield asked.

Clark was guiding them with the aid of a joystick and the container's external cameras.

'Ten seconds. I'm aiming for a dirt track in the middle of the valley. Brace yourselves for landing in three . . . two . . . one . . .'

Whump!

The container hit solid ground, and suddenly its entire front wall just fell open and daylight flooded in through the wide aperture and the four-wheel-drive Commando Scout Light Attack Vehicle skidded off the mark and raced out of the container's belly into the grey Siberian day.

The Scout whipped along a muddy earthen track, bounded on both sides by snow-covered hills. Deathly grey tree skeletons lined the slopes. Black rocks stabbed upward through the carpet of snow.

Stark. Brutal. And cold as Hell.

Welcome to Siberia.

As he sat in the back of the Light Attack Vehicle, Schofield spoke into his throat-mike: 'Mustang 1, this is Mustang 3. Do you copy?'

No reply.

'I say again: Mustang 1, this is Mustang 3. Do you copy?'

Nothing.

He did the same for the second Delta team, Mustang 2. Again, no reply.

Schofield keyed the satellite frequency, spoke to Alaska: 'Base, this is 3. I can't raise either Mustang 1 or Mustang 2. Do you have contact?'

'*Ah, affirmative on that, Scarecrow,*' the voice from Alaska said. '*I was just talking to them a moment ago—*'

The signal exploded to hash.

'Clark?' Schofield said.

'Sorry, Boss, signal's gone,' Clark said from the Scout's wall console. 'We lost 'em. Damn, I thought these new satellite receivers were supposed to be incorruptible.'

Schofield frowned, concerned. 'Jamming signals?'

'No. Not a one. We're in clear radio airspace. Nothing should be affecting that signal. Must be something at the other end.'

'Something at the other end . . .' Schofield bit his lip. 'Famous last words.'

'Sir,' the Scout's driver, a grizzled old sergeant named 'Bull' Simcox, said, 'we should be coming into visual range in about thirty seconds.'

Schofield looked forward, out over Simcox's shoulder.

He saw the black muddy track rushing by beneath the Scout's armoured hood, saw that they were approaching the crest of a hill.

Beyond that hill, lay Krask-8.

At that same moment, inside a high-tech radio receiving room at McColl Air Force Base in Alaska, the young radio officer who had been in contact with Schofield looked about himself in confusion. His name was Bradsen, James Bradsen.

A few seconds before, completely without warning, the power to the communications facility had been abruptly cut.

The base commander at McColl strode into the room.

'Sir,' Bradsen said. 'We just—'

'I know, son,' the CO said. 'I know.'

It was then that Bradsen saw *another* man standing behind his base commander.

Bradsen had never seen this other man before. Tall and solid, he had carrot-red hair and an ugly rat-like face. He wore a plain suit and his black eyes never blinked. They just took in the entire room with a cool unblinking stare. Everything about him screamed ISS.

The base commander said, 'Sorry, Bradsen. Intelligence issue. This mission has been taken out of our hands.'

The Scout attack vehicle crested the hill.

Inside it, Schofield drew a breath.

Before him, in all its glory, lay Krask-8.

It stood in the centre of a wide flat plain, a cluster of snow-covered buildings – hangars, storage sheds, a gigantic maintenance warehouse, even one fifteen-storey glass-and-concrete office tower. A miniature cityscape.

The whole compound was surrounded by a twenty-foot-high razor wire fence, and in the distance beyond it, perhaps two miles away, Schofield could see the northern coastline of Russia and the waves of the Arctic Ocean.

Needless to say, the post-Cold War world hadn't been kind to Krask-8.

The entire mini-city was deserted.

Snow covered the complex's half-dozen streets. Off to Schofield's right, giant mounds of the stuff slouched against the walls of the main maintenance warehouse – a structure the size of four football fields.

To the left of the massive shed, connected to it by an enclosed bridge, stood the office tower. Enormous downward-creeping claws of ice hung off its flat roof, frozen in place, defying gravity.

The cold itself had taken its toll, too. Without an anti-freeze crew on site, nearly every window pane at Krask-8 had contracted and cracked. Now, every glass surface lay shattered or spiderwebbed, the stinging Siberian wind whistling through it all with impunity.

It was a ghost town.

And somewhere underneath it all lay sixteen nuclear missiles.

The Scout roared through the already blasted-open gates of Krask-8 at a cool 80 kilometres an hour.

It shot down a sloping road toward the complex, one of Schofield's Marines now perched in the 7.62 mm machine-gun turret mounted on the rear of the sleek armoured car.

Inside the Scout, Schofield hovered behind Clark, peering at the young corporal's computer screen.

'Check for their locators,' he said. 'We have to find out where those D-boys are.'

Clark tapped away at his keyboard, bringing up some computer maps of Krask-8.

One map showed the complex from a side-view:

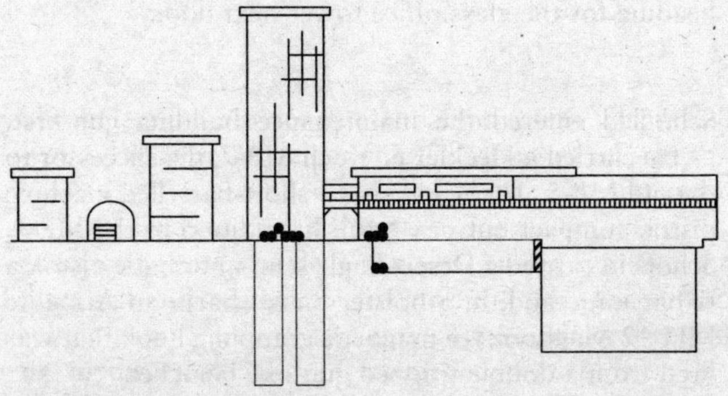

Two clusters of blinking red dots could be seen: one set on the ground floor of the office tower and a second set inside the massive maintenance shed.

The two Delta teams.

But something was wrong with this image.

None of the blinking dots was moving.

All of them were ominously still.

Schofield felt a chill on the back of his neck.

'Bull,' he said softly, 'take Whip, Tommy and Hastings. Check out the office tower. I'll take Book II, Clark and Rooster and secure the maintenance building.'

'Roger that, Scarecrow.'

The Scout rushed down a narrow deserted street, passing underneath concrete walkways, blasting through the mounds of snow that lay everywhere.

It skidded to a halt outside the gargantuan maintenance warehouse, right in front of a small personnel door.

The rear hatch of the Scout was flung open and immediately Schofield and three snow-camouflaged Marines leapt out of it and bolted for the door.

No sooner were they out than the Scout peeled away, heading for the glass office tower next door.

Schofield entered the maintenance building gun-first.

He carried a Heckler & Koch MP-7, the successor to the old MP-5. The MP-7 was a short-barrelled machine pistol, compact but powerful. In addition to the MP-7, Schofield carried a Desert Eagle semi-automatic pistol, a K-Bar knife and, in a holster on his back, an Armalite MH-12 Maghook – a magnetic grappling hook that was fired from a double-gripped gun-like launcher.

In addition to his standard kit, for this mission Schofield carried some extra firepower – six high-powered Thermite-Amatol demolition charges. Each hand-held charge had the explosive ability to level an entire building.

Schofield and his team hurried down a short corridor lined with offices, came to a door at its end.

They stopped.

Listened.

No sound.

Schofield cracked open the door – and caught a glimpse of wide-open space, *immense* wide-open space . . .

He pushed the door wider.

'Jesus . . .'

The work area of the maintenance warehouse stretched away from him like an enormous hangar bay, its cracked-glass roof revealing the grey Siberian sky.

Only this was no ordinary hangar bay.

Nor was it any ordinary old 'maintenance shed' for a penal colony.

Taking up nearly three-quarters of the floorspace of this massive interior space was a gigantic – *gigantic* – rectangular concrete pit in the floor.

And mounted at Schofield's end of the pit, raised off the floor on a series of concrete blocks, was a 200-metre-long submarine.

It looked awesome.

Like a giant on its throne, surrounded by a complex array of structures that belonged to people of a vastly smaller size.

And all of it covered in a crust of ice and snow.

Cranes and catwalks criss-crossed over the top of the sub, while thin horizontal walkways connected it to the concrete floor of the shed. A single vertiginous gangway joined the three-storey-high conning tower of the submarine to an upper balcony level.

Blinking away the strangeness of the sight, Schofield's mind processed this new information.

First, he recognised the submarine.

It was a Typhoon.

The Typhoon class of submarines had been the jewel in the crown of the USSR's ocean-going nuclear arsenal. Despite the fact that only six had ever been built, the long-nosed ballistic missile subs had been made famous in novels and Hollywood movies. But while the Typhoons looked sexy, they had been terribly unreliable, requiring constant upgrades and maintenance. They remain the largest submarines ever built by man.

This one, Schofield saw, had been having work done to its forward torpedo bays when Krask-8 had been abandoned – the outer hull around the Typhoon's bow torpedo tubes lay ripped open, taken apart plate-by-plate.

How a Typhoon-class sub came to be inside a maintenance shed *two miles* inland from the Arctic Ocean was another question.

A question that was answered by the remainder of the maintenance building.

Beyond the Typhoon's enormous dry-dock – indeed, cutting the dry-dock off from the rest of the pit – Schofield saw a large vertical plate-steel sea gate.

And beyond the sea gate was water.

A wide rectangular *indoor* expanse of partially-frozen water, held out from the dry-dock by the dam-like sea gate.

Schofield guessed that beneath that pool of water lay some kind of underground cave system that stretched all the way to the coast – allowing submarines to come into Krask-8 for repairs, away from the prying eyes of American spy satellites.

It all became clear.

Krask-8 – two miles inland from the Arctic coast, listed on maps as a forced-labour facility – was a top-secret Soviet submarine repair facility.

Schofield, however, didn't have time to ponder that issue, because it was then that he saw the bodies.

They lay over by the edge of the dry-dock pit: four bodies, all dressed in US Army snow fatigues, body armour and . . .

. . . all shot to hell.

Blood covered everything. It was splashed across faces, splattered over chests, spread out across the floor.

'Motherfucker,' Clark breathed.

'Christ, man, these were friggin' D-boys,' Corporal Ricky 'Rooster' Murphy said. Like Schofield – and maybe in imitation of him – Rooster wore silver anti-flash glasses.

Schofield remained silent.

The uniforms on the corpses, he saw, had been customised: some of the men had removed their right-hand shoulderplates, others had cut off the sleeves of their snow gear at the elbows.

Customised uniforms: the signature of Delta.

Two more bodies lay down in the pit itself – thirty feet below floor level – also shot to shit.

Hundreds of ejected shell casings lay in a wide circle around the scene. Fire from the Delta men. By the look of it, Schofield saw, the D-boys had been firing in nearly every direction when they'd gone down . . .

Whispered voices.

'How many in total?'

'Just the four in here. Blue Team reports four more in the office tower.'

'So which one is Schofield?'

'The one in the silver glasses.'

'Snipers ready. On my mark.'

One of the bodies caught Schofield's attention.

He froze.

He hadn't seen it at first, because the body's upper half had been hanging over the edge of the dry-dock pit, but now he saw it clearly.

Alone among the six dead bodies, *this man's head had been cut off*.

Schofield grimaced at the sight.

It was absolutely disgusting.

Ragged threads of flesh hung from the corpse's open neck; the twin pipes of the oesophagus and the windpipe lay exposed to the open air.

'Mother of God,' Book II breathed, coming up alongside Schofield. 'What the hell happened here?'

As the four tiny figures of Schofield and his Marines examined the death scene down on the floor of the dry-dock hall, no fewer than twenty pairs of eyes watched them.

The watchers were arrayed around the hall, at key strategic points – men dressed in identical snow fatigues but carrying a variety of weapons.

They watched in tense silence, waiting for their commander to give the kill signal.

*

Schofield crouched beside the headless body and examined it.

D-boys didn't wear ID tags or patches, but he didn't need to see a tag or a patch to know who this was. He could tell by the physique alone.

It was Specialist Dean McCabe, one of the Delta team leaders.

Schofield glanced around the immediate area. McCabe's head was nowhere in sight. Schofield frowned at that. The Delta man's head had not only been cut off, it had been *taken*—

'*Scarecrow!*' a voice exploded in his earpiece. '*This is Bull. We're over in the office tower. You're not going to believe this.*'

'Try me.'

'*They're all dead, all the Delta guys. And Scarecrow . . . Farrell's head has been fucking cut off.*'

An ice-cold charge zoomed up Schofield's spine.

His mind raced. His eyes scanned the hall all around him – its cracked glass windows and ice-faded walls blurring in a kaleidoscope of motion.

Krask-8. Deserted and isolated . . .

No sign of any Chechen terrorists since they'd got here . . .

Radio contact with Alaska lost . . .

And all the D-boys dead . . . plus the bizarre extra feature of McCabe's and Farrell's missing heads.

And it all crystallised in Schofield's mind.

'Bull!' he hissed into his throat-mike. 'Get over here right now! We've been set up! We've just walked into a trap!'

*

And at that moment, as he spoke, Schofield's searching eyes settled on a small mound of snow in a corner of the immense dry-dock hall – and suddenly a shape huddled behind the snow-mound came into sharp focus, revealing itself to be a carefully-camouflaged man dressed in snow-fatigues and pointing a Colt Commando assault rifle directly at Schofield's face.

Damn.

And with that the twenty assassins arrayed around the hall opened fire on Schofield and his men and the dry-dock facility became a battlefield.

Schofield ducked reflexively just as two bullets swooshed low over his head.

Book II and Clark did the same, diving in amongst the Delta bodies on the ground as a rain of bullets sparked against the floor all around them.

The fourth Marine, Rooster, wasn't so lucky. Perhaps it was the reflective glasses he wore – making him look like Schofield – or perhaps he was just unlucky. Nevertheless, a hailstorm of rounds pummelled his body, cut it to ribbons, making him dance even though he was dead.

'Into the pit! Now!' Schofield yelled, practically crash-tackling Clark and Book II out of the line of fire and rolling the three of them off the edge of the dry-dock pit just as it was assaulted by a thousand bullet sparks.

As Schofield and the others dropped down into the dry-dock pit, they did so under the watchful eye of the commander of the heavily-armed force surrounding them.

The commander's name was Wexley – Cedric K. Wexley – and in a previous life he had been a major in the elite South African Reconnaissance Commandos.

So this is the famous Scarecrow, Wexley thought, watching Schofield move. *The man who defeated*

Gunther Botha in Utah. Well, if nothing else, his reflexes are good.

Before his own fall from grace, Wexley had been a shining star in the Reccondos, chiefly because he had been a devoted follower of apartheid. Somehow, he had survived the transition to democracy, his racist tendencies going unnoticed. And then he had killed a black soldier in boot camp, beat him to death during hand-to-hand training. He had done it before, but this time it was noticed.

And when soldiers like Cedric Wexley – psychopaths, sociopaths, thugs – were discharged from the legitimate armed forces, they invariably ended up in the illegitimate ones.

Which was how Wexley came to be in command of this unit: a Special Ops team belonging to one of the world's pre-eminent mercenary organisations – the highly corporate, South African-based 'Executive Solutions' or 'ExSol'.

While ExSol specialised in Third World security missions – like propping up African dictatorships in exchange for diamond-mining royalties – it also, when the logistics allowed, engaged in the more lucrative international bounty hunts that occasionally arose.

At nearly $19 million per head, this was the most lucrative bounty hunt ever, and thanks to a well-placed friend on the Council, Executive Solutions had been given the inside running to claim three of those heads.

Wexley's radio operator came up beside him. 'Sir. Blue Team has engaged the Marines in the office tower.'

Wexley nodded. 'Tell them to return to the dry-dock via the bridge when they're done.'

'Sir, there's another thing,' the radio man said.

'Yes?'

'Neidricht up on the roof says he's picked up two incoming signals on the external radar.' There was a pause. 'Judging by the signatures, he thinks it's the Hungarian and the Black Knight.'

'How far out are they?'

'The Hungarian's about fifteen minutes away. The Knight is further, maybe twenty-five.'

Wexley bit his lip.

Bounty hunters, he thought. *Fucking bounty hunters.*

Wexley hated bounty hunt missions precisely because he hated bounty hunters. If they didn't beat you to the target, the little fuckers would let you do all the dirty work, stalk you all the way back to the proof-station, *steal* the target out from under you and then claim the money for themselves.

In an up-front military exchange, the winner was the last man standing. Not so in a bounty hunt. In a bounty hunt, the winner was the one who presented the prize back at base – *however* he might have obtained it.

Wexley growled. 'The Hungarian I can handle, he's a brute. But the Black Knight . . . he'll almost certainly be a problem.'

The ExSol commander looked down at the submarine pit. 'Which means we'd better make this quick. Get this Schofield asshole, and bring me his fucking head.'

Schofield, Book II and Clark dropped down the wall of the dry-dock pit.

They fell for a full thirty feet, before – *whump* – they landed heavily on the two Delta bodies slumped at the bottom.

'Come on, move! Move! Move!' Schofield pulled the

other two underneath the big black Typhoon sub, mounted on its blocks in the pit.

Each block was about the size of a small car and made of solid concrete. Four long rows of the blocks supported the massive submarine, creating a series of narrow right-angled alleyways underneath the Typhoon's black steel hull.

Schofield spoke into his throat-mike as he zig-zagged through the dark alleyways: 'Bull! Bull Simcox! Do you copy!'

Bull's voice, fast and desperate: '*Scarecrow, shit! We're under heavy fire over here! All of the others are down and I'm . . . I'm hit bad! I can't – oh, fuck – no!—*'

There was a brief crack of gunfire at the other end and then the signal cut to hash.

'Shit,' Schofield said.

Then, abruptly, there came several soft whumps from somewhere behind him.

He spun – MP-7 up – and through the forest of fat concrete blocks, saw the first set of enemy troops drop into the pit on ropes.

With Book II and Clark behind him, Schofield weaved his way through the shadowy alleyways under the Typhoon, ducking enemy fire.

Their pursuers had now entered the dark concrete maze as well – maybe ten men in total – and they were systematically moving forward, covering the long alleyways with heavy fire, herding Schofield and his men toward the sea-gate-end of the dry-dock.

Schofield watched his enemies as they moved, analysed their tactics, eyed their weapons. Their tactics were standard. Basic flushing stuff. But their weapons . . .

Their weapons.

'Who are these guys?' Book II said.

Schofield said, 'I have an idea, but you're not going to like it.'

'Try me.'

'Check out their guns.'

Book II took a quick look. Some of the white-masked men held MP-5s while others carried French-made FAMAS assault rifles or American Colt Commandos. Others still held old AK-47s, or AK-47 variants like the Chinese Type 56.

'See the guns?' Schofield said as they moved. 'They've all got different kinds of weapons.'

'Damn it,' Book II said. 'Mercenaries.'

'That's what I'm thinking.'

'But why?'

'Don't know. At least not yet.'

'What are we going to do?' Clark asked desperately.

'I'm working on it,' Schofield said, gazing up at the thick steel hull above them, looking for escape options.

With his back pressed against a concrete block, he poked his head around one of the outer corners and looked all the way down the dry-dock pit – and saw the high steel sea gate that separated the pit from the ice-covered pool of water at the eastern end of the hall.

The mechanics of the dry-dock leapt into his mind.

To get an enormous Typhoon into the dock, you lowered the sea gate, flooded the dry-dock, and sailed your sub into it. Then you *raised* the sea gate again and drained the dry-dock, lowering the sub onto the concrete blocks in the process and giving yourself a clean and dry environment to work on the submarine.

The sea gate . . .

Schofield eyed it closely, thought of all the water being held back behind it. Looked the other way: toward the bow of the sub, and saw it.

It was their only shot.

He turned to the others. 'You guys got Maghooks on you?'

'Er, yeah.'

'Yes.'

'Get ready to use 'em,' Schofield said, looking down at the great steel sea gate, three storeys high and 90 feet wide. He drew his own Maghook from his back-mounted holster.

'We going that way, sir?' Clark asked.

'Nope. We're going in the other direction, but to do that we need to blow open that sea gate.'

'*Blow open* the sea gate?' Clark gasped, looking at Book.

Book II shrugged. 'This is standard. He destroys things —'

Just then, an unexpected volley of bullets raked the concrete blocks all around them. It had come from the direction of the sea gate.

Schofield ducked for cover, peered out, and saw that ten more mercenary soldiers had dropped into the pit at that end.

Christ, he thought, now they were stuck in the pit between two sets of bad guys.

The new group of mercenaries began to advance.

'Screw this,' he said.

Cedric Wexley watched the dry-dock pit from high above.

He saw his two squads of mercenaries closing in on Schofield and his men from both sides.

A cold smile cracked his face.

This was too easy.

Schofield grabbed two Thermite-Amatol demolition charges from his combat webbing. 'Gentlemen. Maghooks.'

They all pulled out their Maghooks.

'Now do this.' Schofield moved to the port-side edge of the Typhoon, raised his Maghook and fired it at close range up into the hull of the sub.

Clangggggg!

Clark and Book II did the same.

Clangggggg! Clangggggg!

Schofield peered down the length of the submarine. 'When the wave hits, let your Maghook ropes play out, so we can move along the outside of the sub.'

'Wave?' Clark said. 'What wave . . . ?'

But Schofield didn't answer him.

He simply took the two demolition charges in his hands and selected the timer switch he wanted.

Timer switches on Thermite-Amatol charges come in three colours: red, green and blue. Depressing the red switch gives you five seconds. Green gives you thirty seconds. Blue: one minute.

Schofield chose red.

Then he hurled the two charges down the length of the dry-dock pit, over the heads of the advancing mercenary team, sending the two high-powered explosives bouncing into the plate-steel sea gate like a pair of tennis balls. They came to rest at the gate's weakest point, at the spot where it met the pit's concrete right-side wall.

Five seconds. Four . . .

'This is going to hurt . . .' Book II said, wrapping the rope of his Maghook around his forearm. Clark did the same.

Three . . . two . . .

'One,' Schofield whispered, eyeing the dam. 'Now.'

Boom.

The twin blasts of the Thermite-Amatol demolition charges shook the walls of the entire dry-dock building.

A blinding-white flash of light lit up the sea gate. Smoke rushed up the length of the pit, filling the alleyways between the giant concrete blocks as it roared forward, consuming the nearest group of assassins, enveloping everything in its path, including Schofield's team.

There was a moment of eerie silence . . .

And then came the crack – an almighty, ear-splitting *craaaack* – as the wounded sea gate broke under the weight of the water pressing against it, and 100 million litres of water rushed into the pit, *bursting* through the smoke.

A wall of water.

The immense body of liquid created an incredible sound – it *roared* down the length of the dry-dock pit: foaming, roiling, bounding forward.

The nearest group of mercenaries were simply blasted off their feet by the wall of water, and hurled westward.

Schofield, Book II and Clark were next in line.

The wall of water just collected them where they stood – one second they were there, the next they were gone. It lifted them instantly off their feet, flinging them like rag dolls toward the bow-end of the Typhoon, bouncing them along the side of its hull.

The other team of mercenaries was also taken by the rushing wall of water. They were smashed into the solid concrete wall at the far end of the dry-dock, many of them going under as the waves of roiling water crashed against the edge of the 200-metre-long pit.

Schofield and his men, however, didn't hit the end of the pit.

As the roaring body of water had collected them, they'd held grimly onto their Maghook launchers as the ropes connected to their magnetic hooks unspooled at a phenomenal rate.

When they came alongside the bow of the Typhoon, Schofield had yelled, 'Clamp now!'

He had then jammed his finger down on a button on his Maghook's grip, initiating a clamping mechanism inside it that stopped the unspooling of its rope.

Book II and Clark did the same . . . and the three of them jolted to simultaneous halts right next to the bow of the Typhoon, the rushing water kicking up blast-sprays all around their bodies.

Next to them, exactly where Schofield had seen it before, was the yawning opening of the Typhoon's port-side torpedo tubes – the tubes which had evidently been undergoing repairs when Krask-8 had been abandoned.

At the moment, the torpedo tubes lay a foot above the surface of the inrushing water.

'Get into the tubes!' Schofield yelled into his mike. 'Into the sub!'

Book and Clark did as they were told, and squirming and struggling against the rushing water, entered the submarine.

*

Sudden silence.

Schofield wriggled out of the torpedo tube last of all and found himself standing inside a Soviet Typhoon-class ballistic missile submarine.

It was a world of cold steel. Racks that had once contained torpedoes occupied the centre of the room. Rows of pipes lined the ceiling. The stench of body odour – the smell of fear, the smell of submariners – filled the air.

Two fat waterfalls of seawater now gushed in through the sub's open torpedo tubes, rapidly filling the cramped room.

It was largely dark in here: the only light, the grey daylight that crept in through the now-flooding torpedo tubes. Schofield and the others flicked on their barrel-mounted flashlights.

'This way,' Schofield said, charging out of the torpedo room, his legs sloshing through the rising water.

The three Marines bolted through the Typhoon's imposing silo hall next – a long high-ceilinged chamber that contained twenty gigantic missile silos; tall tubular structures that rose from floor to ceiling, dwarfing them.

As he ran past the silos, Schofield saw that the access hatches on some of them were open, revealing hollow emptiness inside. The hatches on at least six of the silos, however, remained closed – indicating that they still contained missiles.

'Where to now?' Book II called forward.

Schofield said, 'The control room! I need information on these assholes!'

He hit the nearest rung-ladder on the fly.

Thirty seconds later, Shane Schofield entered the control room of the Typhoon.

Dust lay everywhere. Mould grew in the corners of the room. Only the occasional glinting reflection from his men's flashlights betrayed the shiny metallic surfaces under the dust.

Schofield hurried over to the command platform, to the periscope located there. He yanked the scope up out of the floor, turned to Book II.

'See if you can get some power up. This sub would've been connected to the base's geothermal supply. There might still be some residual power. Fire up the Omnibus central control system. Then get the ESM and radio antennas online.'

'Got it,' Book II said, hurrying away.

The periscope reached its full height. Schofield put his eye to it. A basic optical periscope, it didn't need any electric power to work.

Through it, Schofield saw the dry-dock hall outside – saw the swirling water filling the pit around the Typhoon – saw a half-dozen mercenaries standing at the edge of the pit, watching it fill with seawater.

Pivoting the periscope, Schofield lifted his view, casting his gaze over the balcony level that overlooked the dry-dock pit.

There he saw more mercenaries, saw one man in particular gesticulating wildly, sending another half-dozen men running toward the gangway that connected the Typhoon's conning tower to the balcony level.

'I see you . . .' Schofield said to the man. 'Book? How's that power coming!'

'Just a second, my Russian's a bit rusty – wait, here it is . . .'

Book flicked some switches and suddenly – *vmmm* – a small collection of green lights burst to life all around Schofield.

'Okay, try it now,' Book said.

Schofield snatched up a pair of dusty headphones and engaged the sub's Electronic Support Measures antenna – a feature on most modern submarines, an ESM antenna is little more than a roving scanner, it simply trawls over every available radio frequency, searching for activity.

Voices came through Schofield's headset instantly.

'*—crazy bastard blew open the fucking sea gate!*'

'*—they went in through the torpedo tubes. They're inside the sub!*'

Then a calmer voice.

As he gazed through the periscope, Schofield saw that it was the commander-type individual up on the balcony level who was speaking.

'*—Blue Team, storm the sub via the conning tower. Green Team, find another gangway and use it as a bridge. Split up into two groups of two and enter the sub via the forward and rear escape hatches—*'

Schofield listened to the voice intently.

Crisp accent. South African. Calm, too. No sign of pressure or anxiety.

That wasn't a good sign.

Usually a commander who has just seen a dozen of his men swept away by a tidal wave would be somewhat rattled. This guy, however, was completely calm.

'*—Sir, this is radar. That first incoming aerial contact has been identified as a Yak-141 strike fighter. It's the Hungarian.*'

'*—ETA?*' the commander asked.

'*—Based on current speed, five minutes, sir.*'

The commander seemed to ponder this news. Then he said, '*—Captain Micheleaux. Send me every other man* *we've got. I'd like to finish this before our competitors arrive.'*

'—*It will be done*,' a French-accented voice replied.

Schofield's mind went into overdrive.

They were about to storm the Typhoon – through the conning tower and the forward and rear escape hatches.

And reinforcements were on their way . . . but from where?

All right, he caught himself. *Rewind. Think!*

Your enemy. Who are they?

They're a mercenary force of some kind.

Why are they here?

I don't know. The only clue is the missing heads. McCabe and Farrell's heads . . .

What else?

That South African guy spoke of 'competitors' who were on their way. But it was a strange word to use . . . competitors.

What options do you have?

Not many. We have no contact with our home base; no immediate means of escape; at least not until the Rangers arrive, and that's a minimum of thirty minutes away . . .

Damn it, Schofield thought, *a whole half-hour, at the very minimum. That was his enemies' biggest advantage.*

Time.

Aside from the 'competitors' they had mentioned, they had all the time in the world to hunt Schofield and his men down.

Then that's the first thing we have to change, Schofield thought. *We have to impose a time constraint on this situation.*

He looked about himself, assessing the constellation of pilot lights that illuminated the control room.

He had power . . .

Which meant maybe he could –

He thought of the six missile silos down below that had been firmly sealed, while all the others had been opened.

There might still be missiles in them. Sure, the Russians would have removed the warheads, but maybe the missiles remained.

'Here,' Schofield invited Clark to the periscope. 'Keep an eye on the bad guys outside.'

Clark seized the periscope, while Schofield dashed to a nearby console. 'Book. Give me a hand here.'

'What are you thinking?' Book II asked.

'I want to know if the missiles on this sub still work.'

The console came alive when he hit the power switch. A code screen came up and he entered an ISS-obtained all-purpose Soviet code that he had been given at the start of this mission.

Called the 'Universal Disarm Code' it was kind of like an electronic skeleton key, the *ultimate* skeleton key, designed for use by only the most senior Soviet personnel. It was an eight-digit code that worked on all Soviet-era keypad locks. It had been given to Schofield to overcome any digital keypads at Krask-8. Apparently, there was an American equivalent – known only to the President and a few very senior military figures – but Schofield didn't know that one.

'I can see six men on the balcony level heading for the gangway!' Clark called. 'Four more down on ground level, they're hauling a bridge into position so they can board us!'

Book II flicked some switches, brought up a screen

that revealed, yes, there were indeed some missiles still sitting in their silos in the forward section of the Typhoon.

'Okay,' Book II said, reading the screen. 'The nuclear warheads have been removed but it seems that some of the missiles are still in their silos. There appear to be, let me see, six of them . . .'

'One is all I need,' Schofield said. 'Open the hatches for the six missiles, and then open one extra hatch.'

'An extra one?'

'Trust me.'

Book II just shook his head and did as he was told, hitting the hatch switches for seven of the sub's missile silos.

Cedric Wexley's eyes widened at the sight.

He saw the Typhoon, now surrounded by an enormous indoor pool of water, saw his own men converging on it . . .

. . . and now, to his astonishment, he saw seven of the submarine's forward missile hatches slowly and steadily opening on their hydraulic hinges.

'What on earth is he doing?' Wexley asked aloud.

'What on earth are you doing?' Book asked.

'Changing the timescale for this fight,' Schofield said.

He brought up another screen, saw the exact GPS co-ordinates of Krask-8: 07914.74, 7000.01. They matched the grid co-ordinates he had employed when his team had dropped in from the Stealth Bomber earlier.

Schofield punched in the necessary information.

He set the missiles to fire immediately – programmed

them to fly for a duration of twenty minutes – and then he set the target co-ordinates as: 07914.74, 7000.01.

He didn't expect *all* of the missiles to work. The O-ring seals on their solid-fuelled rocket boosters would have degraded significantly over the past few years, possibly rendering all of them useless.

But then he only needed one to work.

The fourth one he tried did.

When its green 'Go' light blinked to life, a final approval-code screen came up. Schofield used the Universal Disarm Code. Authorisation granted.

Then he hit 'FIRE'.

Cedric Wexley heard the noise before he saw the spectacle.

An ominous deep-seated *thromming* emanated from within the submarine.

Then – with an ear-shattering explosive *shoom* – a thirty-foot-long SS-N-20 ballistic missile blasted out from one of the sub's forward hatches!

It looked like the launch of a space shuttle: smoke billowed everywhere, expanding wildly, completely filling the dry-dock hall, shrouding the giant Typhoon in a misty grey fog, enveloping the mercenaries who had been converging on its entrances.

For its part, the missile shot straight upward, blasting right through the cracked glass roof of the hall and rocketing off into the grey Siberian sky.

Cedric Wexley was unperturbed. '*Men, continue your attack. Captain Micheleaux, where are those reinforcements?*'

If, at that same moment, one had been watching Krask-8 from the horizon, one would have witnessed an incredible sight: a single dead-straight column of smoke rocketing high into the sky above the mini-city.

As it happened, someone was indeed watching that sight.

A lone individual, sitting in the cockpit of a Russian-made Yak-141 fighter jet that was speeding towards Krask-8.

In the control centre of the sub, Schofield whirled around.

'Where are they?' he asked Clark at the periscope.

'It's too cloudy,' Clark said. 'I can't see anything.'

The view through the periscope now revealed a grey misty nothingness. Clark could only see the immediate area around the periscope itself – the small standing-room-only space on top of the sub's conning tower and the narrow gangway connecting the conning tower to the balcony level.

'I can't see a thi—'

A man's face brushed up against the periscope, large and clear, wearing a gas-mask.

'Yow!' Clark leapt back from the eyepiece. 'Jesus. They're right outside. Right above us!'

'Doesn't matter,' Schofield said, heading downstairs. 'It's time for us to go and we're not leaving that way.'

Schofield, Book II and Clark raced into the missile silo hall that they had passed through before. A foot-deep pool of rising water covered its floor.

They came to one of the empty silos – its little access hatch still lay open – and hustled inside it.

They were met by the sight of the empty missile silo: a towering thirty-foot-high cylinder, at the top of which, looking very small, they could see the open outer-hull hatch – the *seventh* outer hatch that Schofield had opened. Some hand and foot indentations ascended the wall of the silo like a ladder.

The three Marines began climbing.

They reached the top of the silo, and Schofield peered out—

—and saw two mercenaries disappearing *inside* the submarine's forward escape hatch three metres further down the hull.

Perfect, Schofield thought. They were going in while he and his men were coming out.

In addition to this, the hall around the Typhoon was still enveloped in the cloudy white fog of the missile launch.

Schofield's eyes fell on the balcony level overlooking the Typhoon and on the South African commander directing the mercenary operation.

That was the man Schofield wanted to talk to.

He charged toward the hand-rungs on the outside of the Typhoon's conning tower.

Schofield and the others climbed the submarine's conning tower and dashed across the gangway connecting it to the upper balcony level.

They saw a small internal office structure at the end of the elongated balcony.

Standing in a doorway there, barking into a radio mike while at the same time trying to peer through the fog at the Typhoon, was the mercenary commander, Wexley, flanked by a single armed bodyguard.

Under the cover of the smoke, Schofield, Book II and Clark side-stepped their way down the balcony, approaching Wexley fast.

They sprang on him: Schofield yelling 'Freeze!' – the bodyguard firing – Clark firing at the same time – the bodyguard dropping, hit in the face – Clark falling, too – then Wexley drew his pistol – only to see Schofield roll quickly and fire his Desert Eagle twice – *blam! blam!* – and Wexley was hit in both the chest and the hand and hurled backwards a full three feet, slamming into the outer wall of the office structure and slumping to the ground.

'Clark! You okay!' Schofield called, kicking Wexley's gun away.

Clark had been hit near the shoulder. He winced as Book II checked his wound. 'Yeah, he just winged me.'

Wexley was largely okay, too. He'd been wearing a vest under his snow gear, which saved him from the chest-shot. He lay slumped against the outer wall of the office, winded and gripping his wounded hand.

Schofield pressed the barrel of his Desert Eagle against Wexley's forehead. 'Who are you and why are you here?'

Wexley coughed, still gasping for air.

'I said, who the hell are you and why are you here?'

Wexley spoke in a hoarse whisper. 'My name . . . is Cedric Wexley. I'm with . . . Executive Solutions.'

'Mercenaries,' Schofield said. 'And why are you here? Why are you trying to kill us?'

'Not everyone, Captain. Just you.'

'Me?'

'You and those two Delta men, McCabe and Farrell.'

Schofield froze, remembering Dean McCabe's headless body. He also recalled Bull Simcox saying that the same thing had been done to Greg Farrell.

'Why?'

'Does it really matter?' Wexley sneered.

Schofield didn't have time for this. So he simply pressed his boot against Wexley's wounded hand, twisting it slightly.

Wexley roared with pain. Then he looked directly up at Schofield, his eyes filled with venom.

'Because there is a price on your head, Captain Schofield. Enough to entice just about every bounty hunter in the world to come after you.'

Schofield felt his stomach tighten. 'What?'

With his good hand Wexley withdrew a crumpled sheet of paper from his breast pocket, threw it dismissively at Schofield. 'Choke on it.'

Schofield snatched the piece of paper, glanced at it. It was a list of names.

Fifteen names in total. A mix of soldiers, spies and terrorists.

He quickly noticed that McCabe, Farrell and he himself were on it.

Wexley's South African accent dripped with grim delight as he spoke: 'I can imagine that you are about to meet quite a few of the world's crack bounty hunters, Captain. Your friends, too. Bounty hunters do so have a proclivity to hold friends and loved ones as bait to draw out a target.'

Schofield's blood went cold at the thought of his friends being held hostage by bounty hunters.

Gant . . . Mother . . .

He yanked his mind back to the present.

'But why do you have to cut off our heads?' he asked.

Wexley answered him with a snort. Schofield simply moved his boot towards Wexley's bloody hand again.

'Wait. Wait. Wait. Perhaps I haven't been specific enough,' Wexley said nastily. 'The price on your head, Captain, is *literally* a price on your head – 18.6 million dollars to the person who brings *your head* to a castle in France. It's a worthwhile sum, the largest I've ever seen: enough to bribe the highest officials, enough to erase all evidence of a sham mission against some terrorists in Siberia, enough to ensure that your reinforcements, a company of Rangers out of Fort Lewis, *never even left the ground*. You're on your own, Captain Schofield. You're here . . . alone . . . with us . . . until we kill you and cut off your fucking head.'

Schofield's mind raced.

He'd never expected this. Something so targeted, so individual, so *personal*.

Then abruptly, he saw Wexley do something odd: he saw him look away again, only this time the South African was glancing out over Schofield's shoulder.

Schofield turned – and his eyes widened in horror.

Like the ominous precursor to an underwater volcanic eruption, a roiling mass of bubbles appeared in the ice-covered 'lake' that now extended out from the dry-dock pit. The thin layer of ice covering this body of water cracked loudly.

And then from out of the middle of the bubbling froth, like a gigantic whale breaching the surface, came the dark steel body of a Soviet Akula-class attack submarine.

While it could never attain the international sales of the smaller Kilo-class submarines, the Akula was rapidly gaining popularity on international arms markets – markets which the new Russian government was keen to exploit. Obviously, Executive Solutions was one of Russia's customers.

The Akula in the icy lake moved quickly. No sooner was it up than armed men were swarming out of its hatchways, extending exit gangways to the shore, and running across those gangways onto the floor of the dry-dock hall.

Schofield blanched.

It was at least *thirty more mercenaries*.

Wexley smiled wickedly.

'Keep smiling, asshole,' Schofield said. He looked at his watch. 'Because you don't have forever to catch me. In exactly sixteen minutes that missile from the Typhoon is going to return to this base. Till then, smile at this.'

Thwack!

Schofield punched Wexley in the nose with his Desert Eagle, knocking him out.

Then he hustled over to Book II and started helping him with Clark. 'Grab his other shoulder . . .'

They helped the young corporal up. Clark strained to get to his feet. 'I can do it—' he said just as his chest exploded in a sickening gout of blood. An involuntary bloody gob shot out from his mouth – direct from the lungs – and splashed all over Schofield's chestplate.

Clark just stared at Schofield, aghast, the life fading quickly from his eyes. He dropped to the balcony's grilled catwalk, dead – shot from behind – by the force of mercenaries now charging out of the newly-arrived sub and swarming down the length of the hall.

Schofield just looked down at his dead companion in horror.

He couldn't believe it.

Apart from Book II, his whole team was gone, dead, murdered.

And so here he was, stranded at a deserted Siberian base with close to forty mercenaries on his tail, one man by his side, no reinforcements on the way and no means of escape at all.

Schofield and Book II ran.

Ran for their lives as bullet-holes shredded the thin plasterboard walls all around them.

The new collection of ExSol mercenaries from the Akula had entered the battle with frightening intensity. Now they were climbing every rung-ladder they could find and sprinting down the dry-dock hall, with only one purpose: *to get Schofield's head.*

The mercs who had entered the Typhoon earlier were now also aware that Schofield had got away, and they re-emerged, guns blazing.

Schofield and Book II dashed westward, entering the concrete overpass bridge that connected the dry-dock hall with Krask-8's office tower.

As they had approached the bridge, Schofield had seen the movements of the Executive Solutions forces – some of them were scaling the balcony level, while others were paralleling his and Book's movements down on ground level, running along underneath them, also heading for the tower.

Schofield knew one thing: he and Book had to get over to the office tower and then down to the ground before the bad guys got there. Otherwise, the two of them would be stuck in the fifteen-storey building.

They bolted through the overpass bridge, whipped past its cracked concrete window frames.

Then they burst out the other end of the bridge, entered the office tower . . .

. . . and stopped dead.

Schofield found himself standing on a balcony – a tiny catwalk balcony, one of many that rose up and up for fifteen floors, all connected by a network of ladders – overlooking a gigantic square-shaped chasm of open space.

This wasn't an office tower at all.

It was, in truth, a hollowed-out glass-and-steel structure.

A false building.

It was an amazing sight, kind of like standing in a gigantic greenhouse: the grey Siberian landscape could be seen beyond the cracked glass windows that formed the four sides of the building.

And at the base of this gigantic crystalline structure, Schofield saw its reason for being.

Four massive ICBM missile silos, half-buried in the wide concrete floor in a neat square-shaped formation. Covered by the false office tower, they could never have been spotted by US spy satellites. Schofield guessed that three more silo clusters could be found under the other 'buildings' in Krask-8.

On the ground beside the silos, one level below him, he saw ten slumped figures – the six members of Farrell's Delta team and Bull Simcox's four-man Marine squad.

Schofield glanced at his watch, at the countdown indicating when the Typhoon's missile would return to Krask-8: 15:30 . . . 15:29 . . . 15:28 . . .

'The ground floor,' Schofield said to Book. 'We have to get to the ground floor.'

They dashed for the nearest rung-ladder, started down it—

— just as it was assailed by a volley of gunfire.

Shit.

The mercenaries had got to the ground floor first. They must have run across the snow-covered road between the dry-dock warehouse and the tower.

'Damn it!' Schofield yelled.

'What now!' Book II called.

'Doesn't look like we have much choice! We go up!'

And so they went up.

Up and up, climbing rung-ladders like a pair of fleeing monkeys, dodging the mercenaries' fire as they went.

They were ten floors up when Schofield dared to stop and take a look down.

What he saw crushed any hope of survival he'd had until then.

He saw the whole mercenary force arrayed around the concrete missile silos on the ground floor of the tower – about 50 men in all.

And then the crowd of mercenaries parted as a lone man walked into the middle of their ranks.

It was Cedric Wexley, his nose all smashed up with blood.

Schofield froze.

He wondered what Wexley would do now. The mercenary commander could send his men up the ladders after Schofield and Book – and watch Schofield and Book pick them off one by one until the two Marines ran out of ammunition and became sitting ducks. Not exactly an appealing strategy.

'*Captain Schofield!*' Wexley's voice echoed up the wide shaft of the tower. '*You run well! But now there is nowhere else for you to go! Mark my words, very soon you will run no more!*'

Wexley pulled several small objects from his combat webbing.

Schofield recognised them instantly, and stopped dead.

Small and cylindrical, they were Thermite-Amatol demolition charges. Four of them. Wexley must have taken them from the bodies of Schofield's dead Marines.

And now he saw Wexley's plan.

Wexley passed the Thermite charges to four of his men who promptly scattered to the four corners of the ground floor and attached them to the tower's corner pillars.

Schofield snatched his field binoculars from his webbing, pressed them to his eyes.

He caught a glimpse of one of the Thermite charges affixed to its pillar, saw the coloured timer switches on it: red, green and blue.

'*Initiate the timers!*' Wexley called.

The man Schofield was watching hit the blue timer switch on his Thermite-Amatol charge.

Blue meant one minute.

The three mercenaries manning the other demolition charges did the same.

Schofield's eyes went wide.

He and Book II now had sixty seconds till the building blew.

He started his watch's stopwatch:

00:01 . . .

00:02 . . .

00:03 . . .

'*Captain Schofield! When this is over, we will sift through the rubble and we will find your body! And when we do, I will personally rip your fucking head off and piss down your throat! Gentlemen!*'

With that, the mercenaries scattered, dispersing like a flock of birds to every exit on the ground floor.

Schofield and Book II could only watch them go. Schofield pressed his face to the nearest window to see them appear on the snow-covered ground outside and spread out in a wide circle, covering every exit from the building with their weapons.

He swallowed.

He and Book were stuck in this building – a building which in 52 seconds was going to explode.

It was while he was peering out the window at the mercenary troops on the ground that Schofield heard it.

A deep reverberating *throbbing* sound.

The unmistakable sound of a fighter jet.

'The transmission from before,' Schofield breathed.

'What?' Book II asked.

'When we were inside the Typhoon, they picked up an incoming aerial contact: a Yak-141 strike fighter. Flown by someone they called "the Hungarian". On his way here.'

'A bounty hunter?'

'A competitor. But in a Yak-141. And a Yak-141 is a . . .' Schofield said. 'Come on! Quickly!'

They dashed for the nearest rung ladder and climbed it – heading upwards – heading for the roof of the doomed office tower.

Schofield threw open the hatch to the roof. He and Book II climbed out – to be immediately assaulted by the bitter Siberian wind.

His stopwatch ticked upwards:

00:29

00:30

00:31

They cut a lonely sight indeed: two tiny figures on the

roof of the tower, surrounded by the deserted buildings of Krask-8 and the stark Siberian hills.

Schofield hurried to the edge of the roof, searching for the source of the engine noise.

00:33

00:34

00:35

There!

It was hovering in the air over by a low dome-shaped building five hundred yards to the west: a Yakovlev-141 strike fighter.

The Russian equivalent of a Harrier jump-jet, the Yak-141 is potentially the ugliest fighter plane ever built; indeed with its squared edges and single fat afterburning engine, it was never meant to look beautiful. But a hinged rear nozzle allows it to redirect its afterburner so that it points downward, allowing the plane to take off and land vertically, and also hover like a helicopter.

00:39

00:40

00:41

Schofield drew his MP-7 and loosed a full clip of thirty rounds across the bow of the hovering Yak, desperately trying to get the pilot's attention.

It worked.

Like a T-rex disturbed from its meal, the Yak-141 pivoted in the air and seemed to gaze directly at Schofield and Book II. Then with an aerial lurch, it powered up and approached the glass tower.

Schofield waved at the plane like an idiot.

'Over *here*!' he yelled. 'Closer! Get closer . . . !'

00:49

00:50

00:51

The Yak-141 came closer, so that it now hovered about fifty yards out from the roof of the tower.

Still not close enough . . .

Schofield could see its pilot now – a wide-faced man wearing a flight helmet and a confused frown. Schofield waved frantically, calling him over.

00:53

00:54

00:55

The Yak-141 edged a fraction closer.

Forty yards away . . .

00:56

'Jesus, hurry up!' Schofield yelled, looking down at the roof beneath his feet, waiting for the Thermite charges to blow.

00:57

'Too late.' Schofield turned to Book and with a meaningful look, drew his signature weapon. Seeing him do so, Book did the same.

'Just do what I do,' Schofield said, 'and you'll stay alive. Now *run*!'

And so they ran – hard, together, side-by-side – rushing toward the edge of the 15-storey roof.

00:58

They hit the edge, moving fast, legs pumping—

00:59

—and as Schofield's stopwatch hit 1:00, he and Book II leapt out into the clear open sky, their feet stepping off the parapet just as the whole lower section of the building exploded in a billowing cloud of concrete and the entire office tower – all 200 feet of it, the roof, the glass walls, the concrete pillars – just fell away beneath them like a gigantic falling tree.

The pilot of the Yak-141 watched in absolute amazement as the fifteen-storey building in front of him just disintegrated, crumpling to the earth in eerie slow motion, collapsing into its own dustcloud.

A stocky bear of a man with a wide round face forever set in a heavy-browed Eastern European frown, his name was Oleg Omansky.

But no one ever called him that.

A former major in the Hungarian Secret Police with a reputation for employing violence rather than brains, he was known in freelance bounty-hunting circles simply as 'The Hungarian'.

Right now, however, the Hungarian was confused.

He had seen Schofield – whom he recognised immediately from the bounty list – and Book II leap off the roof a moment before the building had collapsed.

But he couldn't see either of them now.

A massive dustcloud rose up from the wreckage of the building, enveloping everything within a half-mile radius.

The Hungarian circled the site, looking for the spot where Schofield had landed.

He noticed a force of men forming a perimeter around the fallen building – a bounty-hunting force, no doubt – saw them rush forward when the collapse of the tower had ceased.

But still he saw no Schofield.

He readied his weapons, and made to land on the roof of a nearby building.

The Yak-141 landed lightly on the roof of one of Krask-8's smaller buildings, its downward-pointed rear thruster blasting the rooftop clear of any debris.

No sooner was it down than the fighter's canopy opened and the Hungarian climbed out, his body as heavy as his face, carrying an AMD assault rifle – the crude but effective Hungarian variant of the AK-47, notable for its extra forward handgrip.

He was four steps away from the plane when –

'Drop the gun, mister.'

The Hungarian turned . . .

. . . to see Shane Schofield emerge from the underside of the Yak-141, an MP-7 held in his hand and pointed right at the Hungarian's nose.

While the glass tower had smashed down into the earth, Schofield and Book II had launched themselves into the air above it, falling in matching arcs underneath the bow of the hovering Yak-141.

Before they'd started their run, Schofield had drawn his signature weapon – his Maghook – from his back-holster. Then as he had fallen through the air, he had aimed it at the underbelly of the Yak and fired. Book II had done the same.

Their Maghooks had shot into the air, unspooling wobbling tails of rope behind their hooks. With a pair of dull *clunks*, the two powerful magnetic heads had slammed into the underside of the Yak – and Schofield's and Book's respective falls had abruptly ceased as they were yanked up by their Maghooks' ropes.

As the Yak had made its way toward the nearest rooftop, they had initiated the internal spoolers on their Maghooks which had reeled them upwards, toward the safe forward underbelly of the hovering fighter jet – while at the same time they were hidden from the eyes of the mercenary force on the ground by the billowing dustcloud below.

The landing had been a little hairy, what with all the flying debris and the deflected heat-blast from the Yak's downward thruster, but they'd made it.

The Yak-141 had touched down, and Schofield and Book II had dropped down to the roof underneath it and rolled away.

Now Schofield had one simple plan for the Yak-141.

To steal it.

Schofield and Book II faced off against the Hungarian on the roof of the low building.

The Hungarian dropped his assault rifle. It clattered to the ground. Schofield scooped up the ugly gun.

'You another bounty hunter?' he demanded, yelling above the roar of the idling fighter.

'Da,' the Hungarian grunted.

'What's your name?'

'I am the Hungarian.'

'Hungarian, huh? Well, you're too late. The mercenaries beat you here. They got McCabe and Farrell.'

'But they did not get you.' The Hungarian's voice was entirely devoid of emotion.

Schofield's eyes narrowed. 'They told me that you

have to bring my head to a castle in France to claim the money. Which castle?'

The Hungarian eyed Schofield's gun warily. 'Valois. The Forteresse de Valois.'

'The Forteresse de Valois,' Schofield said. Then he asked the money question. 'And who is paying for all this? Who wants me dead?'

The Hungarian held his gaze.

'I do not know,' he growled.

'You sure about that?'

'I said I do not know.'

There was something in his simple directness that made Schofield believe him. 'Right . . .'

Schofield headed for the Yak, walking backwards, his guns still up, but as he did so, he felt a twinge of pity for this chunky bounty hunter in front of him. 'I'm taking your plane, Hungarian, but I'm also going to tell you something that I don't have to. Don't be here in eleven minutes.'

Schofield and Book II ascended the cockpit ladder of the Yak-141, their guns trained on the Hungarian.

'You know,' Book II said, 'one day your Maghook isn't going to work . . .'

'Shut up,' Schofield said.

They climbed in.

A former Harrier pilot, Schofield had little difficulty figuring out the Yak's controls.

He keyed the vertical take-off thruster and the Yak-141 lifted into the air above the rooftop.

Then he charged up the plane's afterburners and blasted off over the barren Siberian hills, leaving the lone figure of the Hungarian staring dumbly and helplessly after him.

*

Schofield and Book II left Krask-8 disappearing in their wake.

As he sat at the controls of the Yak-141, Schofield contemplated his next move.

Sitting in the back, Book II said, 'What are you thinking? We go to that castle?'

'The castle is important,' Schofield said. 'But it's not the key.'

He pulled Wexley's bounty list from his pocket.

'This is the key,' he said.

He looked at the names on the crumpled sheet and wondered what they all had in common.

In short, the list was a Who's Who of international warriors: crack commandos like McCabe and Farrell; British spies from MI-6; an Israeli Air Force pilot. Even Ronson Weitzman was on it – *Major General* Ronson Weitzman from the United States Marine Corps, one of the highest-ranking Marines in America.

And that wasn't even mentioning the Middle-Eastern terrorists on the list: Khalif, Nazzar and Hassan Zawahiri.

Hassan Zawahiri . . .

The name leapt out at Schofield.

He was the second-in-command of Al-Qaeda, Osama bin Laden's right-hand man.

And a man being hunted right now in the mountains of northern Afghanistan by the United States, by Schofield's Marine Corps friends: Elizabeth Gant and Mother Newman.

Wexley's voice invaded Schofield's thoughts: '*Bounty hunters do so have a proclivity to hold friends and loved ones as bait to draw out a target . . .*'

Schofield pursed his lips.

His friends, plus at least one target on the list –

Zawahiri – were in the same place. It was the perfect starting point for any bounty hunter.

And so he made the decision.

He set the Yak's autopilot for south-south-west, destination: northern Afghanistan.

Eleven minutes after Schofield left Krask-8, a finger of white smoke blasted out of the clouds above the base – led by the point of the submarine-launched SS-N-20 missile that had been launched twenty minutes earlier.

It descended like a lightning bolt towards the remains of Krask-8, ready to do whatever damage it could.

The missile rushed downward at supersonic speed.

5,000 feet . . .

2,000 feet . . .

1,000 feet . . .

And then in a fleeting shocking instant . . .

. . . it *exploded* . . .

. . . a clear 800 feet off the ground.

The descending missile blasted out into a million fragments, bursting like a firecracker as it was hit by a smaller laser-guided missile from the side.

Glittering fragments of the submarine-launched missile rained down on Krask-8 harmlessly.

And when the smoke cleared, there, hovering in the sky above the mini-city, was the second fighter jet to arrive at Krask-8 that morning.

This one was far sleeker than the Hungarian's Yak-141, longer too, and it was painted almost entirely black. The only trace of another colour could be found in its white-painted nose cone. It was also possessed of rare forward-swept wings and a two-man cockpit.

It was a Sukhoi S-37 – a Russian-made hover-capable fighter that was far more advanced than the old Yak-141.

The sleek S-37 hovered like a hawk above the destroyed Siberian base, surveying the scene. The streets were deserted. The members of ExSol were nowhere to be seen.

After a few minutes of aerial surveillance, the Sukhoi landed on a stretch of open ground not far from the enormous dry-dock warehouse.

Two men climbed out of its cockpit.

One was exceedingly tall, at least seven feet, and armed with a massive G-36 rifle.

The second man was shorter than the first but still tall, well-built, about six feet. He was dressed entirely in black – black combat fatigues, black body armour, black helmet – and he wore two short-barrelled Remington 870 pump-action shotguns in thigh holsters. Both shotguns were made of glistening silver steel.

He also had one other distinguishing feature.

He wore wraparound anti-flash glasses with black frames and yellow-tinted lenses.

Drawing one of his silver shotguns and holding it like a pistol, the man in black left his partner to guard the Sukhoi while he himself strode toward the door that Schofield had used to enter the dry-dock hall earlier.

He stopped at the door, checked the snow-covered ground, touched it with a black-gloved hand.

He moved inside.

The dry-dock hall was deserted. The remnants of Schofield's smoke cloud lingered in the air. The Typhoon submarine towered in the middle of it all.

The ExSol mercenary force was long gone. Likewise its Akula submarine.

The man in black examined the Delta corpses on the ground next to the now-flooded pit – the spent ammo shells on the ground – the headless corpse of McCabe – and the still-warm body of Schofield's Marine corporal, Rooster, who had been snipered when the mercenary trap had revealed itself.

Some bodies were floating face-down in the flooded dry-dock.

Moving with calm measured steps, the man in black went over to the sea gate that had once separated the dry-dock from the lake – noticed its exploded-open side section.

A sign of the Scarecrow, the man in black thought. *After they shot one of his boys, they trapped him in the dry-dock. So he blew it open, flooding the dry-dock, killing the men who had followed him in . . .*

The man in black strode over to the edge of the indoor lake, crouched beside a series of wet footprints smeared on the concrete there: the fresh outlines of combat boots.

Different brands of combat boots. Which meant mercenaries.

And all of them stepping onto the dock from a *wet* surface.

A submarine. A second submarine.

So, Executive Solutions had been here.

But they had got here very quickly. Too quickly.

They must have been tipped off by someone behind the bounty hunt. Given a head-start to claim the American heads.

There came a sudden grunt and the man in black snapped around, gun up, quick as a mongoose.

It had come from the balcony level overlooking the warehouse.

The man in black dashed up a nearby rung-ladder and arrived at a small internal office up on the balcony.

In the doorway to the shack lay two figures: the first was the dead body of Corporal Max 'Clark' Kent; the second was another soldier – judging by his French-made assault rifle, a mercenary from ExSol – and he was still alive.

But only just. Blood gurgled from a gaping bullet wound to his cheek. Half of his face had been blown off.

The man in black stood over the wounded mercenary, gazed at him coolly.

The wounded mercenary extended a hand toward the man, pleading with his eyes, moaning, '*Aidez-moi! S'il vous plait . . . aidez-moi . . .*'

The man in black looked over at the concrete overpass that had connected this hall to the collapsed office tower.

A destroyed fifteen-storey building: *another sign of the Scarecrow*.

The wounded mercenary switched to English. '*Please*, monsieur. Help me . . .'

The man in black turned to face him, looked coldly down at the distressed fellow.

After a long moment, he spoke.

'No.'

Then he shot the wounded mercenary in the head.

The man in black returned to his sleek Sukhoi, rejoined his massive companion.

They then climbed back into their fighter, took off vertically, and blasted off into the sky, heading south-south-west.

*

After the Sukhoi had gone, a lone figure emerged from one of the buildings of Krask-8.

It was the Hungarian.

He just stood there on the deserted street and watched the Sukhoi disappear over the hills to the south, his eyes narrowing.

SECOND ATTACK

AFGHANISTAN–FRANCE

26 OCTOBER, 1300 HOURS (AFGHANISTAN)

E.S.T. (NEW YORK, USA) 0300 HOURS

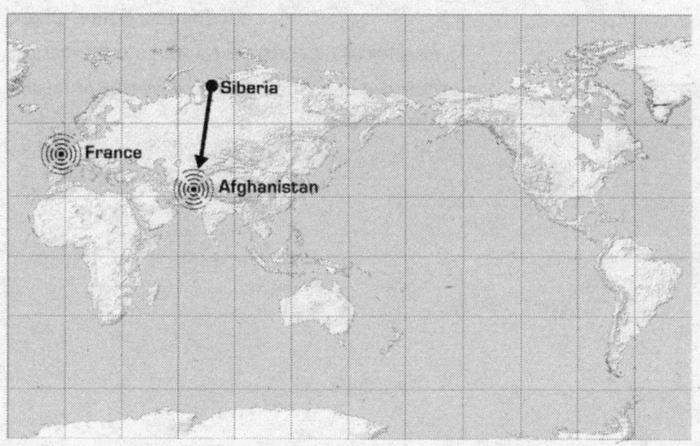

Think of a stretch limo in the potholed streets of New York City, where homeless beggars live. Inside the limo are the air-conditioned post-industrial regions of North America, Europe, the emerging Pacific Rim, and a few other isolated places . . . Outside is the rest of mankind, going in a completely different direction.

Dr Thomas Homer-Dixon,

DIRECTOR OF THE PEACE AND CONFLICT STUDIES PROGRAM,
DEPARTMENT OF POLITICAL SCIENCE, UNIVERSITY OF TORONTO

FORTERESSE DE VALOIS, BRITTANY, FRANCE
26 OCTOBER, 0900 HOURS LOCAL TIME
(1300 HOURS IN AFGHANISTAN
– 0300 HOURS E.S.T. USA)

The two bounty hunters crossed the drawbridge that gave entry to the Forteresse de Valois, a mighty castle that thrust out into the Atlantic Ocean from the rugged north-western coast of France.

Built in 1289 by the mad Comte de Valois, the Forteresse was not your typical French castle.

Whereas most fortified buildings in France put an emphasis on beauty, the Forteresse de Valois was far more utilitarian. It was a rock, a grim fortress.

Squat, fat and solid as hell, through a combination of sheer engineering audacity and the uniqueness of its location, in its time the Forteresse de Valois was all-but impregnable.

The reason: it was built on top of an enormous rock formation that jutted up from the ocean itself, about sixty yards out from the high coastal cliffs.

As they stretched downward, the fortress's colossal stone walls blended seamlessly with the vertical sides of the rocky mount, so that the whole structure stood 400 feet above the crashing waves of the Atlantic.

The castle's only connection with the mainland was a sixty-metre-long spanning bridge of stone, the last twenty metres of which was a lowerable drawbridge.

The two bounty hunters crossed the drawbridge, dwarfed by the dark castle looming above them, the relentless Atlantic wind blasting their bodies.

They carried between them a large white box marked with a red cross and the words: 'HUMAN ORGANS: DO NOT OPEN – EXPRESS DELIVERY'.

Once across the bridge, the two men stepped underneath the fortress's 700-year-old portcullis, and entered the castle.

They were met in the courtyard by a dapper gentleman dressed in perfectly-pressed tails and wearing a pair of wireframed pince-nez.

'Bonjour, messieurs,' the man said. 'My name is Monsieur Delacroix. How may I help you?'

The two bounty hunters – Americans, dressed in suede jackets, jeans and cowboy boots – looked at each other.

The bigger one growled, 'We're here to collect the bounty on a couple of heads.'

The dapper gentleman smiled politely. 'But of course you are. And your names?'

The bigger one said, 'Drabyak. Joe Drabyak. Texas Ranger. This here is my partner, my brother, Jimbo.'

Monsieur Delacroix bowed.

'Ah, oui, the famous brothers Drabyak. Why don't you come inside.'

Monsieur Delacroix led them through a garage that contained a collection of rare and expensive automobiles –

a red Ferrari Modena; a silver Porsche GT-2; an Aston Martin Vanquish; some race-ready rally cars, and taking pride of place in the centre of the showroom, a glistening black Lamborghini Diablo.

The two American bounty hunters eyed the array of supercars with delight. If their mission went according to plan, they'd be buying themselves some all-American muscle cars very soon.

'They yours?' Big Drabyak grunted as he walked behind Monsieur Delacroix.

The dapper gentleman snuffed a laugh. 'Oh, no. I am but a humble banker from Switzerland supervising this distribution of funds for my client. The cars belong to the owner of this castle. Not me.'

Monsieur Delacroix led them down some stone stairs at the end of the pristine garage, down to a lower level . . .

. . . and suddenly they entered medieval times.

They came to a round stone-walled ante-room. A long narrow tunnel branched off it to the left, disappearing into torch-lit subterranean gloom.

Monsieur Delacroix stopped, turned to the smaller of the two Texans. 'Young monsieur James. You will stay here, while your brother and I verify the heads.'

Big Drabyak gave his younger brother a reassuring nod.

Monsieur Delacroix then led Big Drabyak down the long torch-lit tunnel.

At the end of the passageway was a magnificent office. One entire wall of it was a picture window offering a stunning panoramic view of the Atlantic Ocean, stretching away to the horizon.

As they came to the end of the stone tunnel, Monsieur Delacroix stopped again.

'If I may have your case, please . . .'

The bounty hunter gave him the white medical transport box.

Monsieur Delacroix said, 'Now, if you would wait here.'

Delacroix entered the office, leaving the Texan bounty hunter standing just beyond the doorway, still inside the stone passageway.

Delacroix crossed to his desk, pulling a handheld remote from his coat as he did so, and pressed a button on it—

Wham! Wham! Wham!

Three steel doors came thundering down into the medieval passageway from slits concealed in its roof.

The first two doors sealed off the ante-room, imprisoning Little Drabyak in the circular stone room, cutting him off from both the upstairs garage and the narrow tunnel containing his older brother.

The third steel door sealed off the office from the passageway – separating Monsieur Delacroix from Big Drabyak.

Small perspex windows set into each steel door allowed the two bounty hunters to look out from their new prisons.

Monsieur Delacroix's voice came to them via speakers in the ceiling.

'Gentlemen. As you both would no doubt appreciate, a bounty hunt of this value attracts – how shall I put it – some rather *unscrupulous* individuals. You will stay where you are while I verify the identity of the heads that you have brought me.'

*

Monsieur Delacroix placed the medical delivery box on his desk, opened it with expert hands.

Two severed heads gazed up at him.

One was speckled in blood, its eyes wide with horror.

The other was in poorer condition. It had been badly burned.

Monsieur Delacroix was unperturbed.

Donning a pair of surgical gloves, he calmly extracted the blood-speckled head from the box and placed it on a scanning device beside his computer.

'And who do you claim this is?' Monsieur Delacroix asked Big Drabyak over the intercom.

'The Israeli, Rosenthal,' Drabyak said.

'Rosenthal.' Delacroix punched the name into his computer. 'Hmmm . . . Mossad agent . . . no DNA records. Typical of the Israelis, really. It is no matter. I have instructions on this. We shall have to use other means.'

Delacroix initiated the scanning device on which the severed head sat.

Like a CAT scan, the device ran a series of laser beams over the exterior of the severed head.

Once the device had finished scanning the head, Delacroix calmly opened the mouth of the blood-speckled face and exposed the head's *teeth* to the laser scanner.

Delacroix then pressed another button on his keyboard and compared the analysed head to a collection of records on his computer screen.

The computer beeped, and Monsieur Delacroix smiled.

'The cross-reference score is 89.337%. According to my instructions, a verification score of 75% or higher is enough to warrant payment of the bounty. Gentlemen, your first head has been successfully verified by cranial shape and known dental records as that of Major Benjamin Y. Rosenthal of the Israeli Mossad. You are now 18.6 million dollars richer.'

The two bounty hunters smiled in their respective stone cages.

Delacroix then pulled out the second head.

'And this one?' he asked.

Big Drabyak said, 'It's Nazzar, the HAMAS guy. Found him in Mexico. Buying M-16s from a drug lord.'

'How utterly fascinating,' Delacroix said.

The second head was blackened with burn-damage, and it appeared as if half its teeth had been blasted out with a gunshot wound . . . or a hammer.

Monsieur Delacroix performed the cranial and dental laser tests.

The two bounty hunters held their breath. They seemed to get increasingly apprehensive with Delacroix's examination of the two heads.

The skull and dental records returned a verification score of 77.326%.

Monsieur Delacroix said, 'The percentage is 77%, no doubt due to the extensive fire and bullet damage to this head. Now, as you know, according to my instructions, a verification score of 75% or higher is enough to warrant payment of the bounty . . .'

The bounty hunters grinned.

'. . . *unless* there is a DNA record of the individual at issue, in which case I am to consult it,' Delacroix said. 'And it appears from my records here that there *is* a DNA sample for this individual.'

The two bounty hunters whirled to face each other, shocked.

Big Drabyak said, 'But there can't be . . .'

'Oh, yes,' Delacroix said, 'according to my records here, Mr Yousef Nazzar was imprisoned in the United Kingdom in 1999 on minor weapons importation charges. A sample of his blood was taken in accordance with the UK's prisoner-intake DNA policy.'

As Big Drabyak shouted for him to stop, Monsieur Delacroix injected a hypodermic needle into the left cheek of the blackened head in front of him and extracted some blood.

The blood was then placed in an analyser attached to Delacroix's computer.

Another beep.

A bad one.

Delacroix frowned – and suddenly his face took on a far more dangerous complexion.

'Gentlemen . . .' he said slowly.

The bounty hunters froze.

The Swiss banker paused, as if he was *offended* by the indiscretion. 'Gentlemen, this head is a forgery. This is not the head of Yousef Nazzar.'

'Now wait a minute—' Big Drabyak began.

'Please be quiet, Mister Drabyak,' Delacroix said. 'The cosmetic surgery was quite convincing; you employed a good plastic surgeon, that much is certain. The burning of the head to remove visual identification, well, that is clever but old. And the restructured teeth were very well faked. But you didn't know there was a DNA record, did you?'

'No,' Big Drabyak growled.

'The Rosenthal head was also a fake, then?'

'It was obtained by an associate of ours,' Big Drabyak lied, 'and he assured us that it was—'

'But *you* have presented it to me, Monsieur Drabyak, therefore it is your responsibility. Let me be clear. Honesty, in this moment, may help you. Is the Rosenthal head also a fake?'

'Yes,' Drabyak grimaced.

'This is a grave offence against the rules of the hunt, Mr Drabyak. My clients will not tolerate attempts to deceive them, you do understand that?'

Big Drabyak said nothing.

'Fortunately, I have instructions on this,' Delacroix said. 'Monsieur Drabyak the Elder. The passageway in which you are standing, do you know what it is?'

'No.'

'Oh, yes. How silly of me to forget, you are American. You know nothing of world history except the name of every US President and the capital of every US state. A knowledge of medieval European warfare would be somewhat beyond you, no?'

Big Drabyak's face was blank.

Delacroix sighed. 'Monsieur Drabyak, the tunnel in which you now stand was once used as a trap to ensnare those who would attack this castle. When enemy soldiers came through that passageway, boiling oil would be flushed into it through the gutters in its walls, killing the intruders in a most painful way.'

Big Drabyak snapped to look at the walls of the stone passageway around him. They were indeed pockmarked with a series of basketball-sized holes high up near the ceiling.

'This castle, however, has been modified slightly,' Delacroix said, 'in keeping with modern technology. If you would observe your brother.'

Big Drabyak spun, and stared wide-eyed through the

perspex window in the steel door that separated him from his younger brother.

'Now. Say goodbye to your brother,' Monsieur Delacroix's voice said over the speakers.

In the office, Delacroix lifted his handheld remote again and pressed another button on it.

Immediately, an ominous mechanical humming noise emanated from the stone walls of Little Drabyak's circular ante-room.

The humming noise gathered intensity, getting faster and faster and faster.

At first Little Drabyak seemed unaffected.

Then with frightening suddenness, he convulsed violently, snapping a hand to his chest, to his heart. Then he clutched his ears – a moment before they spurted hideously with blood.

He screamed.

Then, as Big Drabyak watched, the most horrifying thing of all happened.

As the humming noise hit fever-pitch, his little brother's *chest* just burst open, his whole rib cage blurting outward in a disgusting spray of blood and gore.

Little Drabyak dropped to the floor of the ante-room, his eyes vacant, his rib cage blasted apart. Dead.

Delacroix's voice: 'A microwave defence system, Monsieur Drabyak. *Très* effective, no?'

Big Drabyak was thunderstruck.

He spun where he stood, powerless to escape.

'You little fuck! I thought you said honesty would help!' he yelled.

Delacroix laughed. 'Americans. You think you can plea-bargain your way out of anything. I said it might help. But on this occasion, I have decided that it will not.'

Drabyak glanced at his brother's grisly remains. 'Is that what you're going to do to me?'

Monsieur Delacroix smiled. 'Oh, no. Unlike you, I am an admirer of history. Sometimes, the old ways are the most satisfying.'

And with that the Swiss banker hit a third and final button on his remote . . .

. . . and 1,000 litres of boiling oil sprayed out from the wall-holes in the tunnel containing Joe Drabyak.

Any exposed flesh was burned on contact – all the skin on his face was scalded in a second. Wherever the boiling oil touched his clothes, it simply melted them to his body.

And as the oil felled him, Drabyak screamed. He would shriek and cry and wail until he was dead, but no one would hear him.

Because the Forteresse de Valois, mounted on its high rocky pinnacle overlooking the Atlantic Ocean, hanging off the edge of the Brittany coast, lay 20 miles from the nearest town.

DEEP IN THE HINDU KUSH MOUNTAINS
AFGHANISTAN–TAJIKISTAN BORDER
26 OCTOBER, 1300 HOURS LOCAL TIME
(0300 HOURS E.S.T. USA)

It was like storming the gates of Hell.

Lieutenant Elizabeth Gant's eight-wheeled Light Armoured Vehicle kicked up a tornado of dust and dirt as it sped across the 200 yards of open ground that protected the entrance to the terrorist cave system.

An absolute storm of bullets hammered the ground all around the speeding LAV as it wended its way toward the cave entrance, covered by an overhead artillery barrage of its own.

This was the Allies' fifth attempt to get troops into the cave system – a converted Soviet mine known to be harbouring Osama bin Laden's second-in-command, Hassan Zawahiri, and about 200 heavily-armed Al-Qaeda terrorists.

More than a year after the Taliban regime had been ousted from Kabul – and even though a far more public war had since been waged and won against Saddam Hussein in Iraq – Operation Enduring Freedom still raged in the darkest places of Afghanistan: the caves.

For the final annihilation of Al-Qaeda could not be

achieved until all the terrorist caves had been cleared, and that involved a kind of warfare not suitable for viewing on CNN or Fox. A down-and-dirty variety of fighting. Hand-to-hand, man-on-man cave-hunting.

And then just this week, US and UK forces had found this cave system far in the north of the country, straddling the Afghan–Tajikistan border – the most important terrorist cave base in Afghanistan.

It was the core of the Al-Qaeda network.

An abandoned Soviet coalmine once known as the Karpalov Mine, it had been converted by Osama bin Laden's construction company into a labyrinthine network of hiding caves: caverns in which terrorists lived and worked and in which they'd stored a veritable arsenal of weapons.

It also came with an extra defence mechanism.

It was a methane trap.

Coal gives off methane – a highly flammable gas – and methane levels of 5% are explosive. One spark and it all goes up. And while the inner sections of the abandoned mine were supplied with fresh air from chimney-like vents, its outer extremities were filled with methane.

In other words: invading soldiers couldn't use guns until they arrived at the core of the mine.

One thing was certain: the terrorists who had withdrawn to this cave system were not going to give up without a fight. Like Kunduz the previous year and the bloodbath at Mazar-e-Sharif, this was going to be a fight to the death.

It was Al-Qaeda's last stand.

The mine's entrance was a reinforced concrete archway wide enough for large trucks to pass through.

KARPALOV COAL MINE
SOMEWHERE ON THE AFGHANISTAN–TAJIKISTAN BORDER

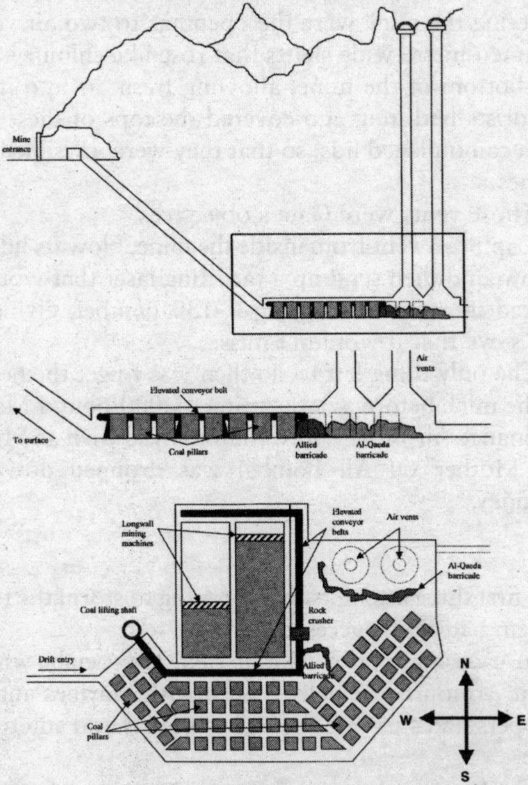

Mine entrance
Air vents
Elevated conveyor belt
To surface
Coal pillars
Allied barricade
Al-Qaeda barricade

Longwall mining machines
Elevated conveyor belts
Air vents
Al-Qaeda barricade
Coal lifting shaft
Rock crusher
Drift entry
Allied barricade
Coal pillars
N
W
E
S

The sharply-sloping mountainside above it was pock-marked with dozens of tiny snipers' nests, from which the terrorists covered the wide expanse of open ground in front of the entrance.

And somewhere up in the tangle of mountain peaks covering the mine were the openings to two air vents – twin ten-metre-wide shafts that rose like chimneys from the bottom of the mine, allowing fresh air into it. The terrorists had long ago covered the tops of these vents with camouflaged lids, so that they were invisible to spy planes.

Those vents were Gant's objective.

Capture a vent from inside the mine, blow its lid from below, and then send up a targeting laser that would be picked up by an overflying C-130 bomber, giving it a bull's-eye that it wouldn't miss.

The only thing left to do then was to get the hell out of the mine before a devastating 21,000-pound Massive Ordnance Air Burst (more commonly known as MOAB, the Mother Of All Bombs) was dropped down the chimney.

The first three attempts that morning to storm the tunnel system had been successful.

In each attempt, a pair of LAV-25s – eight-wheeled Light Armoured Vehicles – filled with Marines and SAS troopers had survived the hail of bullets and entered the cave.

The fourth attempt, however, had been a disaster.

It had ended with a terrible cross-fire of Russian-made rocket-propelled grenades – known to many as 'LAV-Killers' – slamming into the two inrushing vehicles, killing all the men inside them.

Gant's was the fifth attempt, and it had entailed sending two high-speed decoy buggies into the gauntlet first, to attract the enemy's fire, after which Gant's two eight-wheelers had zeroed in on the cave entrance under cover of mortar fire targeted at the enemy's emplacements.

It had worked.

The speeding decoy buggies caught all manner of shit – automatic gunfire, RPGs that smashed into the ground all around them – while Gant's LAV-25 had burst forth from cover, closely followed by a second eight-wheeled beast.

The mountainside above the cave entrance had erupted in mortar impacts while the two LAVs had shot across the open plain before whipping into the entrance of the cave system, disappearing into darkness, out of the rain of gunfire and into a whole new kind of hell.

Elizabeth 'Fox' Gant was twenty-nine years old and a newly minted First Lieutenant, fresh from Officer Candidate School.

Now, it wasn't often that a brand-new lieutenant was given command of a prized Recon Unit, let alone a stand-alone one, but Gant was something special.

Compact, blonde and fitter than many triathletes, she was a natural leader. Behind her sky-blue eyes lay a razor-sharp mind. Plus she already had two years' experience in a Recon Unit as an NCO.

She also, it was said in whispers, had friends in high places.

Some said that her rapid rise to Recon command had been the result of a recommendation from no less than the President of the United States himself. It had something to do, they said, with an incident at the US Air

Force's most secret base, Area 7, during which Gant had shown her worth in the presence of the President himself. But that was conjecture.

The greatest recommendation, in the end, had come from a highly-respected Marine Gunnery Sergeant named Gena 'Mother' Newman who had vouched for Gant in the best possible way: if Gant were put in command of a Recon Unit, Mother had said, then she herself would act as Gant's Team Chief.

At six-feet-two, with a fully-shaven head, one artificial leg and some of the most ruthless skills in the killing trade, Mother's word was gold. Her nickname said it all. It was short for 'Motherfucker'.

And so Gant took command of Marine Force Reconnaissance Unit 9 one month before it shipped out for Afghanistan.

There was one other thing about Libby Gant worth noting.

For almost a year now, she had been the girlfriend of Captain Shane M. Schofield.

Schofield's newly acquired Yak-141 shot through the air at close to Mach 2.

It had been nearly five hours since his battle at Krask-8, and now, spread out before him and Book II, were the formidable Hindu Kush mountains.

And somewhere in them was Libby Gant – Potential Hostage No. 1 for anyone wanting Schofield's head.

Their Yak was almost out of gas. A quick pit-stop at an abandoned Soviet airfield in rural Kazakhstan had allowed them to refuel, but now they were running low on fuel again. They needed to find Gant soon.

Since he didn't trust anyone in Alaska any more, Schofield tuned his plane's radio to a very obscure US satellite frequency – the frequency of the US Defense Intelligence Agency.

After his identity had been verified, he asked to be put through to the Pentagon, to David Fairfax in the Cypher and Cryptanalysis Department.

'*This is Fairfax*,' a young male voice came in over his earpiece.

'Mr Fairfax, this is Shane Schofield.'

'*Hey, Captain Schofield. Nice to hear from you. So, what have you destroyed today?*'

'I've flooded a Typhoon-class submarine, levelled a building, and launched a ballistic missile to destroy a maintenance facility.'

'Slow day, huh.'

'Mr Fairfax, I need your help.'

'Sure.'

Schofield and Fairfax had formed an unlikely alliance once before, during the incident at Area 7. Both had received (classified) medals for their bravery and afterwards had become good friends.

Now, as he and Book II blasted over the mountains of Tajikistan in the Yak-141, Schofield could picture Fairfax – sitting at his computer in an underground room at the Pentagon, dressed in a Mooks T-shirt, jeans, glasses and Nikes, munching on a Mars Bar and looking pretty much like Harry Potter as a graduate student. A code-cracking genius of a graduate student.

'So what do you need?' Fairfax asked.

'Four things,' Schofield said. 'First, I need you to tell me where Gant is stationed in Afghanistan. Exact GPS location.'

'Jesus, Scarecrow, that's operational information. I don't have clearance for that. I could get arrested just for accessing it.'

'Get clearance. Do whatever you have to do. I just lost six good Marines because my mission to Siberia was compromised by someone back home. It was a set-up designed to put me in the hands of some bounty hunters. I can't trust anybody, David. I need you to do this for me.'

'Okay. I'll see what I can do. What else?'

Schofield pulled out the list of names he'd taken from Wexley, the ExSol leader. 'I need you to look up the following names for me . . .'

Schofield read out the names on the bounty list, including his own.

'Find out what these names have in common. Career

history, sniper skills, hair colour, anything. Cross-check them on every database you've got.'

'*Got it.*'

'Third, look up a base in Siberia called Krask-8. Find out whatever you can about it. I want to know why it was chosen as an ambush site.'

'*Okay. And the last impossible task?*'

Schofield frowned, thinking – thinking about one of the names he had heard mentioned on the radio at Krask-8.

At last he said, 'This is going to sound weird, but can you look up a guy called the "Black Knight"? Check the mercenary databases in particular, anything ex-military. He's a bounty hunter – and so far as I know, a very good one – and he's after me. I want to know who he is.'

'*It will be done, Scarecrow. I'll get back to you as soon as I can.*'

Gant's armoured eight-wheeler skidded to a halt inside the darkened cave entrance.

Its double rear doors were flung open from within and the six-man team of Marines thundered out of it, boots slamming against the ground, guns up.

Gant stepped out of the LAV and scanned the area, the gigantic Mother Newman by her side. Both were dressed in sand-coloured fatigues, helmets and body armour, and held MP-7s and pistol-sized crossbows in their hands.

The cave here was wide and high and completely concrete-walled. A wide set of train tracks disappeared down a very steep tunnel in front of them. The tunnel was called a drift and it was how you entered the mine.

'Sphinx, this is Fox,' Gant said into her throat-mike. 'We're in. Where are you?'

A British-accented voice came in: '*Fox, this is Sphinx. Christ, it's bedlam down here! We're at the eastern extremity of the mine! About 200 metres from the drift! They're bunkered down in front of the two vents, in an air pock—*'

The signal cut off.

'Sphinx? Sphinx? Damn,' Gant turned to two of her men. 'Pokey. Freddy. Flush out those RPG foxholes upstairs. There's gotta be some internal tunnels giving access to them. Nail those suckers so we can open a safe corridor into this mine.'

'Yes, ma'am.' The two young Marines took off.

'The rest of you,' Gant said, 'follow me.'

Schofield's Yak-141 zoomed over the mountain peaks of Tajikistan.

Fairfax came on the line.

'*Okay, you listening? I found Gant for you. Her unit is working out of Mobile Command Station California-2, under the command of Colonel Clarence W. Walker. California-2 is located at GPS co-ordinates 06730.20, 3845.65.*'

'Got it,' Schofield said, punching the co-ordinates into his trip computer.

Fairfax went on. '*I also got a couple of hits on that list of yours. Seven of the fifteen names matched up immediately on the NATO personnel database: Ashcroft, Kingsgate, McCabe, Farrell, Oliphant, Nicholson and you are all mentioned in something called the "NATO Joint Services MNRR Study". It's dated December 1996. Looks like some kind of joint medical study we did with the Brits.*'

'Where is it kept?'

'*USAMRMC – Army Medical Research and Matériel Command.*'

'Think you can get it?'

'*Of course.*'

'And the other hit?' Schofield asked.

'*One of our Echelon spy satellites caught a voice transmission from an unknown aircraft flying over Tajikistan only this morning. Several of the names on your list were mentioned. I'll read you the transcript:*

'"BASE, THIS IS DEMON. WE HAVE **WEITZMAN**, ALIVE, AS INSTRUCTED. HEADING FOR THE KARPALOV MINE

SYSTEM NOW. IT'S THE MONEY SHOT – THE BIGGEST CONCENTRATION OF TARGETS ON THE LIST. FOUR OF THEM IN THE ONE PLACE: **ASCHROFT**, **KHALIF**, **KINGSGATE** AND **ZAWAHIRI**. PLUS **SCHOFIELD**'S GIRL IS THERE, TOO."'

Schofield felt his insides tighten.

Fairfax said, '*There's a notation here. It says that the voice on the intercept had a British accent, and that its owner is – whoa . . .*'

'Keep talking.'

Fairfax started reading: '*Voice identified as that of Damon F. Larkham, call-sign "The Demon", former colonel in the British SAS.*' Fairfax paused. '*He was big in the '90s, but was court-martialled in '99 because of his links with the former head of the SAS, a real bad dude named Trevor J. Barnaby.*'

'Yeah, I've met Barnaby,' Schofield said.

'*Larkham was sentenced to eleven years' jail but he escaped en route to Whitemoor Prison, killing nine guards in the process.*

'*Now alleged to be a principal in the freelance bounty hunting organisation known as the Intercontinental Guards, Unit 88, or "IG-88", based in Portugal. Jesus, Scarecrow, what the hell have you got yourself into?*'

'Something that could lose me my head if I'm not careful.' Schofield swapped a look with Book II.

'*As for that place you mentioned, Krask-8,*' Fairfax said, '*the only thing I could find was this: in June 1997, the whole town of Krask, plus its surrounding maintenance facilities, was sold to an American company, the Atlantic Shipping Corporation. In addition to its shipping businesses, Atlantic also has oil interests. It got Krask-8 when it purchased about 10,000 hectares of northern Siberia for oil exploration.*'

Schofield thought about that. 'Nope. Doesn't help me.'

Fairfax said, '*Oh, and I haven't found anything on that Black Knight guy on the regular ex-military databases. I'm running a search program now on some of the classified intelligence databases.*'

'Thanks, David. Keep at it. Let me know when you find something. I've got to go now.'

He hit the afterburners.

Nine minutes later, the Yak-141 landed vertically in a cloud of dust in a clearing not far from a large gathering of American desert vehicles and command tents.

Schofield had heard that the campaign in Afghanistan had become like Vietnam all over again – principally because Afghanistan, even in war, was one of the world's foremost producers of heroin.

Not only did the Afghan mountain-men have the uncanny ability to vanish into hidden cave systems, but every now and then, when they *were* cornered, they would try to bribe Allied soldiers with bricks of 100% pure heroin. And when one such brick was worth about a million dollars on the street, it sometimes worked.

Why, only last week, Schofield had heard of a Russian unit going AWOL. A whole unit of special forces Spetsnaz soldiers – twenty-four men in total, supposedly there as an observer unit – just stole an Mi-17 Russian-made transport helicopter and disappeared in search of a cavern reputedly filled with thirty *pallets* of heroin bricks.

Welcome to Afghanistan.

Schofield's plane was met by a ring of heavily armed Marines who didn't take kindly to an unauthorised

Russian fighter landing in their midst. But within seconds they recognised Schofield and Book II and escorted them to the tent of the base commander, Colonel Clarence Walker, USMC.

The command tent stood at the bottom of a low hill, beyond which lay the entrance to the Al-Qaeda mine.

Colonel Walker was standing at a map table yelling into a radio when Schofield and Book entered: 'Well, find a way to restore radio signals down there! Lay an antenna cable! Use fucking cups and a piece of string if you have to! I need to talk to my men down in that mine before the bombers arrive!'

'Colonel Walker,' Schofield said, 'I'm sorry to barge in on you like this, but this is very important. My name is Captain Shane Schofield and I have to find Lieutenant G—'

Walker spun, glowering. 'What? Who the fuck are you?'

'Sir, my name is Captain Shane Schofield, and I think there's more in that cave than just Islamist terrorists. There are probably also bounty hu—'

'Captain, unless you're flying a C-130 Hercules with a laser-guided MOAB bomb on board, I don't want to talk to you right now. Take a seat and take a fucking number—'

'Hey! What the hell is that!' someone yelled.

Everyone charged out of the tent and peered out into the gauntlet just in time to see a huge Russian transport helicopter swoop down in front of the mine entrance and land in the dust.

About twenty masked men leapt out of the chopper and disappeared inside the mine under fire from the terrorist emplacements on the mountainside.

No sooner were the men inside the mine than the

chopper lifted off, blasting the sniper holes with its side-mounted cannons before disappearing over a hill to the north.

'What in God's name was that?' Colonel Walker yelled.

'It was an Mi-17! With Russian insignia on its flanks!' a spotter called. 'It was that rogue Spetsnaz unit!'

'This place is nuts, fucking nuts . . .' Walker muttered. He turned. 'Okay, Captain Schofield. Do you know anything about this—?'

But Schofield and Book II were nowhere to be seen.

Indeed, the only thing Walker saw was a nearby Light Strike Vehicle skidding off the mark and speeding into the gauntlet with Schofield and Book II inside it.

The Light Strike Vehicle whipped across the stretch of no-man's-land in front of the mine entrance, kicking up a billowing cloud of dust behind it.

Gunfire erupted from the slopes above the mine entrance, smacking into the dirt next to its wheels.

A Light Strike Vehicle is like a dune buggy. It has no windscreens and no armour. It consists merely of a series of roll bars which form a cage around the driver and passenger. It is light, it is fast and it is supremely agile.

Schofield swung his LSV in a wide circle, raising a billowing dustcloud around himself, hiding his car from view. The snipers' shots began to miss by a larger margin.

Then he zeroed in on the mine entrance.

The bullet-fire became more intense—

—before suddenly there came several explosions from the mountainside above the mine's entrance, six sniper emplacements blasting outward in simultaneous showers of dirt.

And in an instant there was no more gunfire. Someone had blown up the emplacements from within the mine itself.

Schofield jammed the accelerator to the floor and zoomed into the darkness of the mine.

Six hundred metres below the surface, Libby Gant hurried on foot down a long rocky tunnel guided by flashlights attached to her helmet and MP-7.

She was followed by her three Marines, and she constantly checked her methanometer, a device that measured the levels of methane in the atmosphere.

At the moment, it read 5.9%.

That was bad. They were still in the mine's outer protective ring.

It was a maze down here – a series of low square-shaped tunnels, each about the width of a train tunnel, and all possessed of rigidly right-angled corners. Some tunnels seemed to go off into the darkness forever, others ended in abrupt dead-ends.

And everything was grey. The rock walls, the low horizontal ceilings, even the creaky wooden posts that supported the roof – all were covered in a ghostly grey powder.

Nothing escaped the powder. It was limestone dust, an inert substance designed to prevent highly flammable coal dust from flaking out from the walls and creating an even greater firetrap.

When Gant and her team had reached the bottom of the steep drift tunnel, they'd been met by an SAS commando. After the radio comms had dropped out, he'd been sent back as a verbal messenger.

'Turn left here, then go straight until you hit the conveyor belt! Then follow the belt to the barricade! Don't stray from the belt, because it's easy to get lost!' he'd said.

Gant's team had followed his instructions to the letter, jogging for about 200 metres down a bending rock-walled tunnel that housed an elevated conveyor belt.

Methanometer: 5.6% . . . 5.4% . . .

The methane levels were getting lower as they ventured further into the mine.

5.2% . . . 4.8% . . . 4.4% . . .

Better, Gant thought.

'You know,' Mother said as they jogged, 'I think he's gonna pop the question in Italy.'

'Mother . . .' Gant said.

After this mission, Mother and Gant – together with Schofield and Mother's nuggetty little husband, Ralph – were going on a group holiday to Italy. They were going to rent a villa in Tuscany for two weeks before taking in the famous 'Aerostadia Italia' airshow in Milan – the centrepiece of which were two very rare X-15s, the famous NASA-built rocket planes, the fastest aircraft ever built. Mother was really looking forward to it.

'Think about it,' she said. 'Tuscan hills. An old villa. A classy guy like the Scarecrow wouldn't miss an opportunity like that.'

'He told you he was going to ask, didn't he?' Gant said, eyes forward.

'Yep.'

'He's such a chicken,' Gant said as they rounded a bend and all of a sudden, heard gunfire. 'To be continued,' she said, giving Mother a look.

Up ahead in the darkness, they saw the beams of

helmet-mounted flashlights and the shadows of running Allied soldiers, all moving behind a makeshift barricade constructed of old mining equipment – barrels, crates, empty steel mini-skips.

And beyond the barricade, Gant saw the all-important air vents.

In this tight, low-ceilinged, square-edged world, the air vent cavern was a welcome stretch of open space. Six storeys high and lit by brilliant white phosphorus flares, it shone like a glowing underground cathedral.

The two ten-metre-wide air vents disappeared up into the roof via a pair of identical cone-shaped recesses in the ceiling.

And underneath the air vents, one of the fiercest battles in history was underway.

The members of Al-Qaeda had prepared well.

They had built a blockade of their own in this high-ceilinged cavern – a barricade that was infinitely superior to the ad hoc creation of the Allied soldiers.

It was made of the larger mining equipment that had been left in the mine: big vehicles featuring gigantic hemispherical drill bits, front-end loaders, some old white Humvee-like trucks called 'Driftrunners', and tip-trays filled with bullet-absorbing coal.

As Gant reached the Allied barricade, she saw the terrorists on the other side of the cavern: over a hundred of them, all dressed in brown leather waistcoats, white shirts, and coiled black turbans.

They were also armed to the teeth: AK-47s, M-16s, RPGs. Bathed in the fresh air of the vents, gunfire was clearly safe inside this subterranean hall.

Gant linked up with the Allied soldiers on the scene.

There were about twenty of them, a mix of United States Marines and British SAS troops.

She arrived at the side of the Allied commander, an SAS major named Ashcroft, call-sign: Sphinx.

'It's a bloody nightmare!' the English commando shouted. 'They're dug in around those vents for the long term! And then every few minutes, one of them – *shit!* Here comes another one! Shoot him! *Shoot* him!'

Gant snapped round to look over the Allied barricade.

With shocking suddenness, a bearded Arab terrorist had burst forth from a gap in the Al-Qaeda barricade *on a motorcycle*, firing an AK-47 one-handed and yelling to Allah.

Strapped to his chest were four wads of C4.

Three SAS soldiers nailed him with their automatic rifles, blasting the suicide bomber from his saddle, sending him crashing to the ground behind his speeding motorbike.

The Arab hit the ground in a clumsy puff of dust—

—and then he exploded.

One second he was there. The next he was simply gone.

Gant's eyes widened.

Madness . . .

The SAS leader, Ashcroft, turned to her. 'It's absolute bedlam, darlin'! Every now and then, the bastards launch a suicide run and we have to cut them down before they reach our barricade! The problem is they must have a supply cave somewhere back there! Generators, gasoline and enough ammo, food and water to see them through to the year 3000! It's a stand-off!'

'What if we went around?' Gant said, indicating the series of tunnels off to their right.

'No. It's booby-trapped! Trip-wires. Landmines. I've already lost two good men going that way! These rag-heads have been waiting for a fight in this place for a long time! This is going to take a frontal assault. What I need is more men!'

At that moment, as if on cue, a collection of about twenty more barrel-mounted flashlights appeared in the tunnel that led back to the mine's entrance.

'Ah, reinforcements,' Ashcroft said, heading down the tunnel to meet them.

Gant watched him go, saw him meet the leader of this new squad and shake the man's hand.

Funny, she thought. *Colonel Walker had said that the next team wouldn't be coming in for at least another twenty minutes. How did these guys get in so quickly –*

She watched Ashcroft wave his hand toward the barricade, explaining the situation, turning his back on his new acquaintance for a split second, during which moment the leader of this new group of soldiers smoothly and fluidly drew something from his belt and swiped it hard across Ashcroft's neck region.

At first Gant didn't know what had happened.

Ashcroft didn't move.

Then, to her absolute horror, Gant saw Ashcroft's head tilt at an impossible angle and just drop off his body.

Her eyes went wide with disbelief.

What—?

But she didn't have time for shock, for no sooner was Ashcroft down than the submachine-guns of this new force of men burst to life, raining fire on the Allied troops gathered behind their barricade.

Quick as a flash, Gant dived over and *into* one of the steel mini-skips that formed her barricade, just as bullets impacted all around her. She was joined a second later by Mother and her other two Marines.

The rest of the Allied troops weren't so lucky.

Most of them were caught out in the open . . . and they were pummelled mercilessly by this unexpected storm of bullets from behind. Their bodies exploded with bloody holes, convulsed horribly.

'Goddamnit! What the hell is this!' Gant pressed herself close to a mini-skip's rusty steel walls.

Now they were caught between *two* sets of enemies: one in front of their barricade, one behind.

A lethal sandwich.

'What do we do, Chickadee?' Mother yelled.

Gant's face set into a determined expression. 'We stay alive. Come on, this way!'

And with that, Gant led her team in the only direction they could go – she leapt over the *forward* side of the mini-skip and landed, cat-like, on the dusty section of open ground *in between* the two facing barricades.

At that very same moment, Schofield and Book's Light Strike Vehicle skidded to a halt in the upper entrance cave of the mine.

Schofield saw the roller-coaster-like tracks of the drift diving down into the mine, took a step toward them, just as two figures burst out from a nearby side-tunnel.

Schofield and Book whipped around together, MP-7s up. The two dark figures did the same and –

'Pokey?' Schofield said, squinting. 'Pokey de Villiers?'

'Scarecrow?' One of the figures lowered his gun. 'Man, I almost shot you dead.'

It was Corporal Paul 'Pokey' de Villiers, just returned from cleaning out the Al-Qaeda sniper holes on the mountainside with his partner, a lance-corporal nick-named Freddy.

'I need to find Gant,' Schofield said. 'Where is she?'

'Down there,' Pokey said.

Thirty seconds later, Schofield was sliding down the steep drift tunnel at the wheel of the Light Strike Vehicle with Book II riding shotgun and the two extra Marines, Pokey and Freddy, sharing the rear gunner's seat.

The LSV's headlights blazed as it rocketed down the thirty-degree slope, straddling the train tracks that ran down the centre of the tunnel.

Nearing the bottom, Schofield jammed the LSV into

reverse, causing its wheels to spin wildly backwards as the speeding car skidded *forwards* down the tunnel.

The strategy worked: they slowed, if only slightly. But it was enough and with a few yards to go, Schofield slipped the dune buggy out of reverse and the LSV blasted out of the bottom of the drift tunnel and shot into the maze, swinging left past the dead body of the SAS messenger who had been stationed there.

Gant was completely exposed.

Out on the forward side of the Allied barricade – with only thirty yards of open ground between her and about 200 murderous holy warriors.

If the terrorist forces wanted to kill her and her three Marines, then this was their chance. Gant waited for the hail of bullets that would end her life.

But it never came.

Instead she heard gunfire – from somewhere *behind* the Al-Qaeda blockade.

Gant frowned. It was a type of gunfire that she had never heard before. It sounded too fast, way too fast, like the whirring of a six-barrelled mini-gun . . .

And then she saw something that took her completely by surprise.

She saw the Al-Qaeda blockade get absolutely *raked* with internal gunfire – its walls blew out, assaulted by a million hypervelocity bullets – and suddenly a whole crowd of terrorists were leaping *over their own barricade* out into no-man's-land, fleeing some unseen force behind their own blockade . . . exactly as Gant had done herself.

Another thing was clear.

The terrorists were fleeing something far worse than Gant was.

As they leapt desperately over their barricade, they were shot in mid-air – from behind – and all but ripped apart, their limbs exploding from their bodies.

A split-second before one such Al-Qaeda warrior was ripped to pieces as he clambered over the barricade, Gant caught a glimpse of a *green* targeting laser zeroing in on him.

A green laser . . .

'Er, Lieutenant!' Mother yelled from beside her. 'What the hell happened to this fight! I thought wars were supposed to be fought between *two* competing forces!'

'I know!' Gant called. 'There are more than two forces down here! Come on, follow me!'

'Where!'

'There's only one way to solve this problem, and that's to do what we came here to do!'

With that, Gant made a break across no-man's-land, ducking underneath the overhead conveyor belt that ran up its left-hand side, and headed towards the left-hand air vent.

Gant came to the northern end of the elevated conveyor belt just as four Al-Qaeda terrorists came running out from behind their barricade, chased by gunfire.

The first three holy warriors scrambled up some boxes that had been arranged like stairs and jumped up onto the conveyor belt while the fourth hit a fat green button on a console.

The conveyor belt roared to life—

—and the three men on it were instantly whisked out of sight at tremendous speed, heading towards the Allied barricade. The fourth man jumped onto the belt after them and – *whoosh* – he was swept southward as well.

'Whoa. Fast belt . . .' Mother said.

'Come on!' Gant yelled as she dashed behind the Al-Qaeda barricade.

She burst into open space – the high-ceilinged area underneath the air vents. It did look like a cathedral here. Dim white light from electric lamps partially illuminated the area.

She also saw the reason why the Al-Qaeda terrorists had bolted from the safety of their barricade.

A team of maybe fifteen black-clad commandos – dark wraiths wearing green-eyed night-vision goggles and motorcross-style Oakley anti-flash glasses – was fanning out from a small tunnel located behind the Al-Qaeda barricade, tucked into the north-eastern corner of the cavern.

It was, however, the weapons in their hands that seized Gant's attention. The weapons which had unleashed hell on the Al-Qaeda troops.

These new soldiers were equipped with Metal-Storm M100 assault rifles. A variety of rail gun, the MetalStorm range of weapons do not use conventional moving parts to fire their bullets. Rather, they employ rapid-sequential electric shocks to trigger each round, and as such, are able to fire at the unbelievable rate of 10,000 rounds per minute. It amounts to a literal storm of metal, hence the name.

The MetalStorm guns of this new force of men were equipped with ghostly green laser-sighting devices – so in her mind, until she found out their real name, Gant just labelled them 'the Black-Green Force'.

One thing about them was truly odd. This Black-Green Force didn't seem to care about her at all. They were pursuing the fleeing terrorists.

In the midst of all this confusion, Gant slid to the dusty ground underneath the left-hand air vent and started erecting a vertical mortar launcher.

When the launcher was ready, she yelled, 'Clear!' and hit the trigger. With an explosive *whump!*, a mortar round shot up into the air vent, disappearing up it at rocket speed before . . .

. . . *BOOM!!!!*

Six hundred metres above them, the mortar round hit the camouflaged lid that capped the air vent, blasting it to smithereens. Debris rained down the vent, smacking to the ground, at the same time as a shaft of natural grey light flooded into the cavern from above.

When the rain of debris had cleared, Gant stepped forward again, and surrounded by her team, erected a new device, a much smaller one: a compact laser-emitting diode.

She flicked a switch.

Immediately, a brilliant red laser beam shot up into the vent from the diode, disappearing up the chimney, shooting into the sky.

'All units, this is Fox,' Gant said into her radio mike. 'If you're still alive, pay attention. The laser is set. Repeat, the laser is set. According to mission parameters, the bombers will be here in ten minutes! I don't care what else is happening in here, let's clear out of this mine, people!'

At the Marine compound outside the mine, a communications officer abruptly sat up straight at his console.

'Colonel! We just picked up a targeting laser coming from inside the mine! It's Gant's beam. They did it.'

Colonel Walker stepped forward. 'Call the C-130s, tell them they have a laser. And get evac crews to that mine entrance to pick up our people as they come out. In ten minutes that mine is going to be history and we can't wait for any stragglers.'

Gant and Mother and the two Marines with them turned together.

They were still behind the Al-Qaeda barricade and now they had to get back to the Allied one and then beyond it to the sloping entry shaft.

They didn't get more than a few yards.

No sooner had they started moving than they saw a stand-off taking place just in front of the Al-Qaeda barricade, at the edge of no-man's-land.

Four Al-Qaeda holy warriors stood surrounded by a six-man squad of the Black-Green Force, caught in the beams of their MetalStorm rifles.

Gant watched from behind the barricade.

The Black-Green Force's squad leader stepped forward, pulled down his ski-mask to reveal a male model's square jaw and handsome blue-eyed features. He addressed the terrorists. 'You're Zawahiri? Hassan Zawahiri . . .'

One of the Al-Qaeda men raised his chin defiantly. '*I* am Zawahiri,' he said. 'And you cannot kill me.'

'Why not?' the Black-Green squad leader said.

'Because Allah is my protector,' Zawahiri said evenly. 'Do you not know? I am His chosen warrior. I am His Chosen One.' The terrorist's voice began to rise. 'Ask the Russians. Of the captured mujahideen, I alone survived the Soviets' experiments in the dungeons of their Tajik gulag. Ask the Americans! I alone survived their cruise missile attacks after the African embassy bombings!' Now he started shouting. 'Ask the Mossad! They know! I alone have survived over a dozen of their assassination attempts! No man born of this earth can kill me! I am the One. I am God's messenger. I am *invincible*!'

'You,' the squad leader said, 'are wrong.'

He fired a burst from his MetalStorm rifle into Zawahiri's chest. The terrorist was hurled backwards, his torso torn to mush, his body all but cut in half.

Then the handsome squad leader stepped forward and did the most gruesome thing of all.

He stood over Zawahiri's corpse, drew a machete from behind his back, and with one clean blow, sliced Zawahiri's head from his shoulders.

Gant's eyes went wide.

Mother's mouth opened.

They watched in horror as the Black-Green commando then grabbed Zawahiri's severed head and casually placed it in a white medical box.

Mother breathed: 'What kind of fucked-up shit is going on here?'

'I don't know,' Gant said. 'But we're not gonna find out now. We have to get out of this place.'

They turned—

—just in time to see a crowd of about thirty Al-Qaeda terrorists *stampeding* toward them – toward the conveyor belt, screaming, shouting, their empty machine-guns useless – pursued by more Black-Green commandos.

Gant opened fire – smacked down four terrorists.

Mother did too – took down four more.

The other two Marines in Gant's team were crashtackled where they stood, trampled by the stampeding crowd.

'There are too many of them!' Gant yelled to Mother. She dived left, out of the way.

For her part, Mother stepped back onto the boxes leading up to the conveyor belt, firing hard, before she was overwhelmed by the sheer numbers of the terrorists and was herself flung backwards onto the speeding conveyor belt in their midst.

The Black-Green men who had killed Zawahiri seemed amused by the sight of the Al-Qaeda warriors fleeing desperately onto the conveyor belt.

One of them strode over to the conveyor belt's control console and hit a fat yellow button.

A mechanical *roar* filled the cavern, and from her position on the dusty floor, Gant spun to see its source.

Over by the Allied barricade, at the far end of the conveyor belt, a giant rock crusher had been turned on. It was composed simply of a pair of massive rollers that were each covered in hundreds of conical rock-crushing 'teeth'.

Gant gasped as she saw the Al-Qaeda terrorists now jumping for their lives *off* the speeding conveyor belt. She watched for Mother to jump, too, but it never happened.

Gant didn't see anyone resembling Mother leap off.

Shit.

Mother was still on the conveyor belt, rushing headlong toward the rock crusher.

Mother was indeed still on the belt – shooting down its length toward the rotating jaws of the rock crusher sixty yards away.

The problem was she was wrestling with two Al-Qaeda terrorists as she went.

While the other Al-Qaeda troops had decided to leap off the conveyor belt, these two had decided to die in the rock crusher . . . and they were going to take Mother with them.

The conveyor belt rushed down the length of the cavern, racing toward the rock crusher at about thirty kilometres an hour – eight metres per second.

Mother had lost her gun when she'd hit the conveyor belt and now she struggled with the two terrorists.

'You suicidal ratfuckers!' she yelled as she fought. At six feet two, she was as strong as an ox – strong enough to hold off her two attackers but not overpower them.

'Think you're gonna take me down, huh!' she shouted in their faces. 'Not fucking likely!'

She kicked one of them in the balls – hard – and he yelped. She flipped him over her head, toward the rock crusher, now only twenty yards away and approaching fast.

Two-and-a-half seconds away.

But the second guy held on. Tight. He was a dogged fighter and he wouldn't let go of her arms. He was travelling backwards, feet-first. Mother was now travelling forwards, on her belly, head-first.

'*Let – go – of – me!*' she yelled.

The first Al-Qaeda man entered the rock crusher.

A shriek of agony. An explosion of blood. A wash of it splattering all over Mother's face.

And then, in an instant of clarity, Mother realised.

She wasn't going to make it.

It was too late. She was dead.

Time slowed.

The terrorist holding her arms went into the jaws of the rolling rock crusher feet-first.

It swallowed him whole and Mother saw it all up close: a six-foot man chewed in an instant. *Shluck-splat!* Another blood explosion assaulted her face from point-blank range.

Then she saw the rolling jaws of the crusher inches away from her own face, saw each individual spoked tooth, saw the blood on each one, saw her hands disappear into the—

—and then suddenly she was lifted into the air above the yawning maw of the rock crusher.

Not far into the air, mind you.

Just a couple of inches, enough to take her off the swiftly moving conveyor belt, enough to stop her forward movement.

Mother frowned, snapped her head round.

And there above her, hanging one-handed from a steel overhead beam, gripping the collar of her body armour with his spare hand, was Shane Schofield.

Five seconds later, Mother was on solid ground again, standing with Schofield and Book II and their new off-siders, Pokey and Freddy. The Light Strike Vehicle was parked nearby, behind the Allied barricade.

'Where's Gant!' Schofield yelled above the mayhem.

'We got separated over at the other barricade!' Mother shouted back.

Schofield glanced that way.

'Scarecrow! What the fuck is going on! Who are all these people?'

'I can't explain it yet! All I know is that they're bounty hunters! And at least one of them is after Gant!'

Mother grabbed his arm. 'Wait. I got bad news! We've already set the targeting laser for the bombers. We got exactly' – she checked her watch – 'eight minutes before this mine is hit by a 21,000-pound laser-guided bomb!'

'Then we'd better find Gant fast,' Schofield said.

After the Al-Qaeda stampede had passed her by, Libby Gant leapt to her feet – only to find several green laser beams immediately zero in on her chest armour.

She looked up.

She was surrounded by another sub-group of the Black-Green Force, six men, their MetalStorm rifles trained on her.

One of the black-clad soldiers held up his hand, stepped forward.

The man took off his helmet – at the same time removing his protective Oakley goggles, revealing his face.

It was a face Gant would never forget.

Could never forget.

He looked like something out of a horror movie.

At some point in the past, this man's head must have been caught in a raging fire – his entire skull was completely hairless and horribly wrinkled, with flash-burned skin that was blistered and scarred. His earlobes had *melted* into the side of his head.

Beneath this scarring, however, the man's eyes glistened with delight.

'You're Elizabeth Gant, aren't you?' he said amiably, taking her guns.

'Ye— Yes,' Gant said, surprised.

Like the other Black-Green squad leader, the bald man had a British accent. He looked about forty. Experienced. Cunning.

He pulled Gant's Maghook out of her back-holster and threw it to the ground far away from her.

'Can't let you keep that either, I'm afraid,' he said. 'Elizabeth Louise Gant, callsign: Fox. Twenty-nine years old. Recent graduate of OCS. Graduated second in your class, I believe. Former member of Marine Force Reconnaissance Unit 16 under the command of then-Lieutenant Shane M. Schofield. Former member of HMX-1, the Presidential Helicopter Detachment, again under the command of Captain Shane M. Schofield.

'And now . . . now you are no longer under the command of Captain Schofield because of Marine Corps regulations about troop fraternisation. Lieutenant Gant, my name is Colonel Damon Larkham, callsign: Demon. These are my men, the Intercontinental Guards, Unit 88. I hope you don't mind, but we just need to borrow you for a while.'

And with that, one of Larkham's men grabbed Gant from behind and clamped a rag soaked in trichloromethane over her mouth and nose and in an instant Gant saw nothing but black.

A moment later, the handsome young squad leader whom Gant had seen cut off Zawahiri's head arrived at Demon Larkham's side, holding three head-sized medical transport containers.

'Sir,' the squad leader said, 'we have the heads of Zawahiri, Khalif and Kingsgate. We found the body of Ashcroft, but his head was already missing. I believe the Skorpions are here and that they got to him first.'

Larkham nodded thoughtfully. 'Hmmm, Major Zamanov and his Spetsnaz Skorpions. Thank you, Cowboy. I think we have gained more than enough from this incursion already.' He looked down at Gant's prone body. 'And we might have just added to our catch. Tell everybody to head for the back door. Time to get back to the planes. This mine has been lased for an airstrike and the bombers are on their way.'

Two minutes later, Schofield's Light Strike Vehicle slid around the conveyor-belt end of the Al-Qaeda barricade and skidded to a dusty halt.

Schofield, Book II, Mother and the two junior Marines piled out of it, guns up, searching for Gant.

'Mother. Time to the bomb?' Schofield called.

'Six minutes!'

Gant was nowhere to be seen. As was the Black-Green force. The area behind the Al-Qaeda barricade was deserted, the battle over.

Mother stood at the near end of the barricade, not far from the conveyor belt. 'This is where I last saw her. We saw a good-looking guy from that black-and-green group cut some terrorist dude's head off and then suddenly a whole bunch of Al-Qaeda chumps came stampeding at us from over there.'

She indicated the far north-eastern corner of the cavern, beyond the air vents. There Schofield saw a small tunnel about the size of a garage door.

And then he saw something else – on the floor.

A Maghook.

He went over to it and picked it up, saw the words 'Foxy Lady' written in white marker on its side. Gant's Maghook. He clipped it to his belt.

When he rejoined the others, Mother was saying: '. . . and don't forget the fourth force that's down here.'

'A *fourth* force?' Schofield said. 'What fourth force?'

'There are four separate forces in this mine,' Mother said. 'Us, Al-Qaeda, those black-and-green fuckers who took my little Chickadee, and a fourth force: that bunch of guys who killed Ashcroft and took out the Allied barricade from behind.'

'They killed Ashcroft?' Schofield said.

'Fuckin'-A. Cut off his goddamn head.'

'Jesus. It's another group of bounty hunters,' Schofield said. 'So where is this fourth force now?'

'I, uh, think they're already here . . .' Book II said ominously.

They materialised from within and around the Al-Qaeda barricade – about twenty armed troops dressed in tan desert fatigues, caramel ski-masks and yellow Russian combat boots. They stepped out of the Drift-runner vehicles and tip-trays that made up the Al-Qaeda barricade.

Most of them held sinister-looking short-barrelled VZ-61 Skorpion machine pistols: the signature weapon of Russia's elite special forces unit, the Spetsnaz. It was from this gun that they had garnered their bounty hunting nickname: *the Skorpions*.

They'd been waiting.

A man wearing major's bars stepped forward from the group. 'Drop your weapons,' he said crisply, curtly.

Schofield and the other four Marines did so. Two Spetsnaz soldiers immediately rushed to his side and held him firmly.

'Captain Schofield, what a pleasant surprise,' the Spetsnaz major said. 'My intelligence did not mention that you would be at this site, but your appearance is a welcome bonus. Your head may pay exactly the same price as the others, but there is no doubt a certain *prestige* that goes with being the bounty hunter who brings in the famous Scarecrow.'

The major seemed to appraise Schofield down his long aquiline nose. He snorted. 'But perhaps your reputation is unwarranted. Kneel, please.'

Schofield remained standing. He nodded at Gant's laser-emitting diode on the ground. 'You see that device down there. That diode is leading a 21,000-pound laser-guided bomb to this mine. It'll be here in five minut—'

'I said kneel.'

One of the guards whacked Schofield behind the knees with his rifle butt. Schofield dropped to the ground underneath one of the cathedral-like domes of the air vents.

With a sharp slicing noise, the major then withdrew a glistening sword from his back-holster: a short-bladed Cossack fighting sword.

'Really,' the major said as he approached Schofield, rotating the sword lazily in his hand, 'I am somewhat disappointed. I had thought killing the Scarecrow would be more *difficult* than this.'

He raised the sword and, gripping it with both hands, started to swing it . . . just as a pair of blue laser dots appeared on the chests of Schofield's guards. The next instant, the two guards were blown away.

Schofield snapped up—

The Spetsnaz major whirled around—

And they all saw him.

He was standing out in the open, underneath the other air vent, two silver Remington shotguns in his hands, held like pistols. High-tech blue laser-sighting devices were attached to the shotguns' stainless steel barrels.

Erected next to him on collapsible tripods were

two remote-operated FN-MAG machine-guns – also equipped with blue laser sights. One of the robot guns was now illuminating the Spetsnaz major's chest with its blue targeting laser, the other gun just roved randomly among the Russian troops.

Whoever this man was, he was dressed entirely in black.

Black fatigues.

Black body armour, scratched with battle scars.

Black hockey helmet.

And on his face – a rugged face, weathered and hard, unshaven – he wore a pair of wraparound anti-flash glasses with yellow lenses.

Schofield caught a glimpse of a thick rope hanging vertically from the air vent above the man, before – *whoosh* – it whiplashed up into the vent, disappearing like a spooked snake.

'Why hello, Dmitri,' the man in black said. 'Gone AWOL again, have you?'

The Spetsnaz major didn't look at all pleased to see the man in black. Nor was he thrilled at the blue laser dot now lighting up his own chest.

The Russian major snarled. 'It is always easier to disappear on these international missions. As I'm sure *you* of all people would know, Aloysius.' He pronounced the name: *allo-wishus*.

The man in black – Aloysius – stepped forward, walking casually in amongst the heavily-armed Spetsnaz unit.

Schofield noticed his black utility vest. It was equipped with a bizarre array of *non*-military devices: handcuffs, mountain-climbing pitons, a small handheld scuba tank called a Pony Bottle, even a miniature welding torch—

The man in black strode past a Russian trooper, and suddenly the trooper whipped his gun up.

Muzzle flash. Gunfire.

The trooper was riddled with bullets, nailed.

The roving robot machine-gun whizzed back to pin its laser sights on the other Spetsnaz troops.

Unperturbed, the man in black stopped before Schofield and the Spetsnaz major.

'Captain Schofield, I presume?' he said as he lifted Schofield to his feet. 'The Scarecrow.'

'That's right . . .' Schofield said guardedly.

The man in black smiled. 'Knight. Aloysius Knight. Bounty hunter. I see you've met the Skorpions. You'll have to excuse Major Zamanov. He has this really bad habit of cutting off people's heads as soon as he meets them. I saw the laser signal from the air – when is the bomb due?'

Schofield glanced at Mother.

'Four minutes, thirty seconds,' she said, eyeing her watch.

'If you take his head, Knight,' the Russian major hissed, 'we will hunt you down to the ends of the earth, and we will kill you.'

'Dmitri,' the man named Knight said, 'you couldn't do that if you tried.'

'I could kill you right now.'

'But then you'd die, too,' Knight said, nodding at the blue dot on Major Dmitri Zamanov's chest.

'It would be worth it,' Zamanov spat.

'I'm sorry, Dmitri,' Knight laughed. 'You're a good soldier, and let's be honest, a fucking psychotic asshole. But I know you too well. You don't want to die. Death scares the shit out of you. Me, on the other hand . . . well, I couldn't give a fuck about dying.'

Zamanov froze.

This Knight character, Schofield saw, had called Zamanov's bluff.

'Come on, Captain,' Knight said, handing Schofield his MP-7 from the ground. 'Grab your boys and girls and follow me.'

With that, Knight led Schofield and the other Marines through the ranks of Spetsnaz troops without another shot being fired.

'Who *are* you?' Schofield asked as they walked.

'Never mind,' Knight said. 'The only thing you need to know right now, Captain, is that you have a guardian angel. Someone who doesn't want to see you killed.'

They reached the eastern end of the Al-Qaeda barricade, a short distance from the tunnel in the corner of the cavern.

Knight yanked open the door to a wide-bodied Driftrunner truck that formed the end section of the Al-Qaeda barricade.

'Get in,' he said.

Schofield and the others climbed inside – under the baleful glares of the Skorpions.

Aloysius Knight jumped into the front seat of the Driftrunner, keyed the ignition.

'Now,' he turned to Schofield, 'are you ready to run? Because as soon as we leave the cover of my remote guns, those cocksuckers are gonna be really pissed.'

'I'm ready.'

'Good.'

Then Knight gunned the accelerator and the Driftrunner shot off the mark, disappearing into the small tunnel in the corner of the cavern.

No sooner was it out of sight than the twenty-odd

members of Zamanov's Spetsnaz team were moving, jumping into other Driftrunners, three men even leaping into Schofield's abandoned Light Strike Vehicle.

Their engines roared and the chase began.

Headlights in darkness.

Bouncing, jouncing, carving sabre-like beams through the dust-filled air.

The Black Knight's Driftrunner roared down the narrow tunnel.

The Driftrunner was about the size of a Humvee and essentially just an oversized pick-up truck, with a long rear tray and a partially-enclosed driver's compartment. There was, however, no dividing wall or window between the driver's compartment and the rear personnel tray: one could traverse between the two simply by climbing over the seats.

The tunnel around it was almost perfectly square, with sheer granite walls and a flat hardstone ceiling held up by wooden support beams. It was also practically dead straight, stretching away into darkness like an arrow.

And it was tightly – tightly – fitted around the Driftrunner. There were only about twelve inches to spare on either side of the speeding truck. Above the vehicle's roof the gap was about four feet.

The Skorpions were close behind them.

The three Russian commandos who had commandeered Schofield's LSV were now speeding along the tunnel right behind the Driftrunner – the smaller, more nimble little vehicle catching up to it easily. The driver drove hard while his partners fired at the Driftrunner with their VZ-61 machine pistols.

Bathed in the glare of the LSV's bouncing headlights, Mother and Book and Pokey and Freddy returned fire.

Behind the speeding LSV came three other Driftrunners, packed with the other seventeen members of Zamanov's rogue Spetsnaz unit.

A mini-convoy, racing at dangerously high speed through the tight stone passageway.

'Mother! Time!' Schofield yelled from the passenger seat of the front-running truck.

'Three minutes!'

'How long is this tunnel?' he asked Knight.

'About four miles.'

'This is going to be close.'

Book and Mother and Pokey and Freddy's guns blazed, firing at the speeding LSV behind their truck. They alternated their fire, so that while two of them fired, the other two were reloading.

Following this pattern, Mother and Book ducked to reload; Pokey and Freddy took their places – and were hit by a shocking wave of gunfire. Freddy's face disappeared, transformed to pulp. Pokey was hit in the throat and he fell, teeth clenched. Book II dived forward to stop him falling off the back of the truck, caught him—

—but that was all the Skorpions needed.

Still reloading, Mother spun to see what was happening. She turned in time to see the two passengers from the LSV leaping off the front of the Light Strike Vehicle *up onto the rear tray of the Driftrunner!*

Book had his hands full with Pokey.

The two Skorpions landed on their feet, brought their guns up to kill Book and Pokey.

Lacking a loaded gun, Mother just hurled herself into

them, crashtackling them *both*, and the three of them fell to the floor of the tray, the walls of the tunnel rushing past them in a blur of rocky grey.

Knight and Schofield saw it all.

Schofield got up to help.

'Here!' Knight yelled, tossing him one of his silver Remingtons. 'While you're back there, nail that car!'

Schofield dived back into the open rear tray of the Driftrunner.

He saw Mother on the floor, fighting – saw Book II lifting Pokey back up into the tray – saw the LSV whipping along the tunnel behind them, its headlights illuminating the confined space.

He raised the silver Remington and, two-handed, fired it at the LSV.

The recoil from the shotgun was enormous.

The effect was even bigger. Whatever shells this Knight guy used, they packed one hell of a punch.

The LSV was literally blasted off its wheels.

Hit by the shotgun shell, it was lifted clear into the air and tumbled sideways. Such was its velocity in the close confines of the stone tunnel, the speeding Light Strike Vehicle flipped and rolled and tumbled, banging off the walls and the ceiling before it came to a skidding halt on its crumpled roof.

Miraculously, its driver was still alive.

Not for long.

A split-second after it had stopped, the LSV was ripped apart from behind, blasted into a million pieces as the first Skorpion Driftrunner *exploded* right through it, followed by the second Spetsnaz truck, then the third.

Within seconds, the Skorpion Driftrunners were travelling *right behind* Schofield's truck, headlights ablaze, rushing forward in the dusty tunnel.

The first Russian truck sped up, banged its bullbar against the rear bumper of Schofield's Driftrunner.

Both vehicles rocked with the impact.

Then the Skorpions kicked out the windscreen of the first Russian Driftrunner and clambered out onto its bonnet and before Schofield could do anything about it, in the confined space of the dark tunnel, three of them leapt over into the rear tray of his Driftrunner.

They completely ignored Book II and Mother – instead they headed straight for Schofield, their machine pistols drawn.

Knight saw them in the rear-view mirror, slammed down on the brakes.

The Driftrunner lurched, and everyone was thrown forward, including Schofield, Mother, Book and Pokey in the back.

Like dominoes falling, the three other trucks in the convoy all rammed into each other, thumping nose-to-tail, nose-to-tail, nose-to-tail.

Up in Schofield's Driftrunner, the three Skorpions attacking him were all flung forward.

One dropped his gun as he reached for a handhold; another tumbled to the floor next to Schofield; the third was thrown all the way forward into the driver's compartment where he slammed into the dashboard and looked up to find himself staring into the barrel of a silver shotgun, a blue laser dot illuminating his nose.

Boom!

Knight fired.

The trooper's head exploded like a can of tomato soup.

Knight jammed the accelerator back down and the Driftrunner shot forward again.

The other two Spetsnaz guys, however, their balance now restored, only had eyes for Schofield.

The gunless one drew a Warlock hunting knife, the other brought his VZ-61 machine pistol around fast—

—and at that very same moment, Knight snapped round and saw them, and something in his eyes ignited, a look that said that Schofield could never *ever* be touched.

Schofield reacted quickly.

He parried the machine pistol away, karate-style, pushing its barrel to the side just as his enemy fired.

But he couldn't hold off the two of them.

The knife-wielding Skorpion lunged at him, swiping at his throat—

—and suddenly Aloysius Knight was there—

—and with incredible strength, Knight yanked *both* the knife-wielder and the VZ-61 man away from Schofield, down into the driver's compartment—

—at precisely the same moment as their Driftrunner was rammed hard by the truck behind it.

Knight and the two Spetsnaz commandos were hurled forward, and they smashed right through the windshield of their Driftrunner, went tumbling onto its bonnet.

Truth be told, they didn't actually *smash* the windscreen. Constructed of shatterproof glass, the windscreen just burst into a spiderweb of cracks and popped out of its frame, landing on the bonnet as an intact but crumpled rectangular mat.

The four Driftrunners continued to rocket down the narrow tunnel.

Schofield now saw that Knight had wisely wedged a steel bar against the gas pedal, keeping their Driftrunner moving down the dead-straight tunnel, its steering corrected by the tunnel's close stone walls.

Out on the bonnet of the first Driftrunner, Knight struggled with the two Skorpions.

The knife-wielder was trying desperately to get back to Schofield, while the VZ-61-armed one had lost his gun in the scramble to get a handhold.

Knight, however, had caught the worst of the smash through the windscreen – he lay with his legs dangling off the front of the speeding Driftrunner, hanging onto its bullbar for dear life.

He saw the knife-wielder clawing his way back towards Schofield, grabbed the man's boot and yanked hard on it, dragging the knife-wielder toward the front of the bonnet . . . and off it!

With a horrified scream, the Russian trooper went under the front of the Driftrunner, under its roaring tyres. He tumbled and smacked underneath the wheels of the *whole convoy of Driftrunners* before he was spat out the back of the fourth truck, crumpled and mangled and dead.

The other Skorpion saw this and started kicking at Knight's hands, but Knight got a grip on the man's belt and started pulling on it too.

'No!' the Skorpion yelled. 'Noooo!'

'You can't have him!' Knight called, dragging the Spetsnaz trooper toward the front of the bonnet.

The Skorpion came alongside Knight. He was a big guy, with a fierce angry face. He clutched Knight's throat.

'If I go, Black Knight, you go too . . .' he growled.

Knight looked him in the eye. 'Fine.'

And with that Knight kicked himself clear of the front of the Driftrunner – dragging the aghast Russian commando with him – and dropped to the dusty roadway in front of the speeding truck . . .

The Spetsnaz trooper hit the ground and rolled and – *splat!* – was flattened under the wheels of the lead Driftrunner.

Unlike Knight, he hadn't grabbed the mat-like windscreen of the Driftrunner on his way down.

As he'd fallen off the front of the Driftrunner, Knight had snatched the cracked-glass mat and thrown it to the rushing ground beneath him.

The mat hit the ground – and Knight landed on it, cat-like – and the mat slid along the dusty ground, at first sliding forward, before *whoosh* the first Driftrunner roared over the top of it, and over the top of Knight, too!

The convoy of Driftrunners – all four of them – rumbled quickly forward, *over* the tiny figure of Aloysius Knight sliding on his back on his makeshift mat.

Whoosh – whoosh – whoosh . . .

Knight shot underneath the quartet of trucks and was about to blast out behind the last Driftrunner when he drew his second shotgun, held it by the barrel . . . and hooked its pistol-grip on the underside of the rear bumper of the fourth and last Driftrunner.

The mat swished out from under him, tumbled away into the darkness of the tunnel, and Knight was dragged along behind the Driftrunner, his flailing legs bouncing on the roadway.

Then he reached up and hauled himself up into the tray of the last Driftrunner, ready to rejoin the fight.

Up in the first Driftrunner, Schofield was now sitting in the driver's seat. After Knight had gone flying out through the windshield and under the front of the truck, Schofield had kicked away the steel bar pinned to the gas pedal and taken the wheel.

In the rear-view mirror, he saw Mother and Book II fighting hand-to-hand with their two Spetsnaz assholes – saw two *more* Skorpion troopers make the leap forward from the second Driftrunner onto his one.

These two new guys charged straight for Schofield in the driver's compartment.

There are just too many of them, Schofield's mind screamed.

He saw the two new Skorpions rushing forward, guns drawn. They'd be on him in seconds.

And then he remembered something about mining vehicles. He hurriedly reached for his seatbelt.

'*Book! Mother!* Hang on to something!'

Then he reached across the driver's compartment . . . and kicked open the passenger door of the Driftrunner.

The response was instantaneous.

The Driftrunner's handbrake immediately activated itself and the speeding truck came to a sudden bone-jarring halt. It was a safety feature on all mining vehicles – to prevent miners from being hurt, if the passenger door was opened, the vehicle was instantly disabled, its park-brake initiated.

Caught by surprise, the second Driftrunner *slammed* into the back of the first one. The third and fourth trucks did the same, running into each other like a collapsing accordion.

As for the two Skorpions who had been coming for Schofield, one went flying *through* the now-empty windscreen, hurled at least fifteen feet clear of the vehicle, the other caught his chin on the roof of the driver's cabin and while his legs flew forward, his head stayed still, and with a sickening *snap!* his neck broke.

Mother and Book II, on the other hand, had done as they'd been told and instead of fighting their assailants, had grabbed onto the nearest handholds, so that when the truck stopped, their attackers had been thrown forward, smacking into the back of the driver and passenger seats.

One was knocked unconscious by the fall.

The other was only bruised, and he rose – only to be headbutted viciously by Mother, a blow that put his lights out for good.

The damage done, Schofield reached over and closed the passenger door and hit the gas and soon they were speeding again.

There was less damage and mayhem in the other Driftrunners. They sped along behind the first truck once more – still with at least ten men on board.

But then the damage came.

In the form of Aloysius Knight.

When the impact had occurred, Knight had been in the process of climbing into the rear tray of the last Driftrunner, so it hadn't really affected him.

Now that the Driftrunners were racing along again, however, he moved quickly through the last vehicle, dispatching the Skorpions in it with brutal – *brutal* – efficiency.

The Russians tried to resist, tried to raise their own weapons and kill him first.

But Knight was like a killing *machine*.

Two Skorpions in the rear tray: he shot one in the head with his shotgun, while at the same time he shoved the other one's head *above* the roof of the driver's compartment . . . allowing it to be hit by a speeding overhead support beam, an impact that removed the soldier's head from his body.

He came to the driver's compartment – levelled his short-barrelled Remington at the passenger and without so much as a blink, fired.

Boom.

The driver turned, surprised, just as Knight – ignoring him – blasted the windscreen out of its frame and climbed through it, leaping forward onto the tray of the third truck.

Zamanov was on this truck.

He dived for cover as Knight moved forward through the Driftrunner, blasting men left and right. Several of the Skorpions tried to return fire, but Knight was too fast, too fluid, too good. It was as if he anticipated their moves, even the order in which they would shoot.

On his way through the driver's cabin, Knight glimpsed Zamanov cowering under the dash, but he only saw him momentarily and since Knight's first priority was to get forward, back to Schofield, he didn't stop to kill the Russian. He was only killing anyone who was in his way.

He leapt over onto the second truck.

*

Up in the first Driftrunner, Schofield was now driving hard – with only friends not foes on his truck.

He could also now see a small white speck in the distance in front of him – the end of the tunnel.

Mother climbed into the passenger seat beside him. 'Scarecrow! Who the fuck are these people! And who is that dude in black?'

'I don't know!' Schofield yelled.

He looked in his rear-view mirror and saw Aloysius Knight step out onto the bonnet of the Driftrunner immediately behind his own.

'But he seems to be the only one around here who *isn't* trying to kill me.'

'He could be planning to kill you later,' Book II suggested from the rear tray. 'I say we ditch him.'

'I agree—' Mother began before cutting herself off.

They had reached the end of the tunnel.

Brilliant white light streamed in through a small square entryway.

It was about 200 metres away.

What had silenced her, however, was the enormous demonic object that had appeared in the air beyond the tunnel's exit.

A jet fighter.

A black Sukhoi S-37 fighter, hovering in the air just outside the tunnel.

Seen from head-on, with its sharply-pointed nose and downward-swept wings dripping with missiles, the S-37 looked like a gigantic evil hawk, *staring right at them.*

There came a loud thump from behind Schofield as Knight landed in the tray of their Driftrunner and came up behind them.

'It's okay,' he said, nodding at the fighter, 'he's with us.'

Knight pressed a button on his wrist guard, initiating a radio on it. 'Rufus, it's me! We're coming out and we're coming out hot, with three enemy vehicles on our tail. I need a Sidewinder. Just one. Aim low and to your right; arm at 200 metres. Just like we did in Chile last year.'

'*Copy that, Boss*,' a deep voice said in Knight's ear-piece.

'May I?' Knight nodded at Schofield's steering wheel.

Schofield let him take it.

Knight immediately yanked the steering wheel hard over and drove the Driftrunner up against the left-hand wall of the tunnel.

The big four-wheel-drive rode up against the wall, grinding against it until . . . *whump* . . . it jolted upwards, and suddenly was speeding along at a 45-degree angle, riding with two wheels on the ground and two on the wall itself.

'Okay, Rufus! Now!' Knight yelled into his wrist mike.

Immediately, a horizontal finger of smoke shot out from the right wing of the hovering black fighter, and with a resounding *phoom!* a Sidewinder missile streaked into the tunnel system, rocketing at tremendous speed, hugging the ground.

From Schofield's point of view, the missile stayed close to the left-hand wall, zooming fast and low before—

—*shoooooooom!*—

—it whizzed underneath his Driftrunner's 45-degree-tilted body and *slammed* into the truck immediately behind it.

The explosion ripped through the tunnel. The first Spetsnaz Driftrunner was blasted into a million pieces.

With no way to avoid it, the two mine trucks behind the first one smashed into the back of it, driving their noses into the wreck, slamming to a halt.

At the same time, Schofield's Driftrunner blasted out into glaring daylight, shooting onto a wide flat turnaround area carved into the side of the mountain. Beyond the turnaround – directly underneath the hovering fighter jet – was a sheer thousand-foot drop.

Knight turned to Mother. 'You. How long till the bomb?'

Mother checked her watch. 'Thirty seconds.'

'That'll hurt Dmitri.' Knight then spoke into his wrist mike: 'Rufus. Meet us on the next turnaround down the mountainside.' He looked over at Schofield. 'I've got three passengers with me, including our man.'

'*Any problems?*'

Knight said, 'Nah, it was pretty light this time.'

Thirty seconds later, the sleek Sukhoi landed in a cloud of dust on another turnaround area further down the precarious cliff-side roadway. Flat and round, the turnaround looked like a natural landing platform jutting out from the cliff-face.

Schofield's Driftrunner skidded to a halt beside it.

At that very same moment, guided by Gant's laser diode down in the mine, a 21,000-pound MOAB bomb was dropped out the back of a C-130 Hercules and angled in toward the mine's air vents.

The precision guidance system worked perfectly.

The bomb rushed toward the earth, hitting terminal velocity, its fins controlling its flight-path, before –

whump – the giant weapon disappeared into the mine's now-open chimney.

One, one thousand . . .

Two, one thousand . . .

Three . . .

Detonation.

The entire mountain shuddered.

A volcanic *boooom!* echoed out from within the mine.

Standing next to the Sukhoi's two-man cockpit, pushing Mother up into it, Schofield had to grab onto its ladder just to keep his balance.

He glanced up at the mountain peak above them – at the layer of snow resting on top of it – and realised.

'Oh no,' he breathed. 'Avalanche . . .'

Then he snapped round to look back up the roadway, in time to see two bent-over figures stagger out of the mine tunnel on foot – a bare moment before a *shocking* blast of air came rocketing out of the tunnel, expelling the crumpled remains of the Skorpion Driftrunners that had been left in it.

The three Driftrunners were catapulted clear off the edge of the upper turnaround – shooting horizontally out into the sky, past the two hunched figures – after which the three trucks fell a thousand feet straight down into the ravine below.

It was then that an ominous rumbling came from somewhere above Schofield.

The gigantic body of snow resting on the mountain above the Sukhoi's perch was shifting, cracking, starting to . . .

Slide.

'*Move!*' Schofield yelled, climbing up the ladder.

The sliding body of snow began to gather speed.

'Quickly! Into the bomb bay!' Knight yelled.

Book and Mother squeezed through the small cockpit and into the tight space behind it: a bomb storage bay that had been converted into a . . . holding cell.

'Just get in!' Knight yelled from behind them. 'I'll be joining you!'

Knight squeezed in with them. Schofield jumped into the cockpit last of all, climbed into the rear gunner's seat, looked up.

The vertically-sliding snowdrift had taken on the appearance of a crashing ocean wave: blasting explosions of white preceding the full weight of the avalanche.

Knight called forward, 'Er, Rufus . . . !'

'Already on it, Boss!' The large man in the front seat hit the throttles and the Sukhoi rose.

'Faster . . .' Schofield said.

The avalanche came rushing down at them, tumbling, rumbling, smashing, crashing.

The Sukhoi lifted higher, hovering for a moment before it powered out over the edge of the cliff *just as* the avalanche rushed past it, the falling wall of snow rushing by with a colossal roar, gobbling up the turnaround in a single enormous bite before rumbling past the floating black fighter jet and disappearing into the abyss below.

'Now *that* was close,' Knight said.

Three minutes later, the Sukhoi S-37 landed in a clearing on the Afghan side of the mountain, about a mile away from Schofield's parked Yak-141.

Schofield, Knight, Book and Mother all climbed out, while the pilot – an enormous bushy-bearded individual whom Knight introduced simply as 'Rufus' – killed the engines.

Schofield walked a few yards away to regather his thoughts. A lot had happened today and he wanted to clear his head.

His earpiece crackled.

'*Scarecrow, it's me, Fairfax. You there?*'

'Yeah, I'm here.'

'*Listen. I got a couple of things for you. A few facts on those USAMRMC guys on your list, and some big stuff on that Black Knight guy, most of it from the FBI and ISS Most Wanted lists. You got a moment?*'

'Yeah,' Schofield said.

'*Jesus, Scarecrow, this Knight guy is bad news . . .*'

In his office deep beneath the Pentagon, Dave Fairfax sat bathed in the glow of his computer screen. In the eastern United States, it was just hitting 4 a.m., October 26, and the office was quiet.

On Fairfax's screen were two photos of Aloysius

Knight: the first was a portrait shot of a clean-shaven young man in US Army dress uniform, smiling. The second was a blurred long-distance shot of Aloysius Knight holding a shotgun in each hand and running hard.

'All right,' Fairfax said, reading. 'His real name is Knight, Aloysius K. Knight, thirty-three years old, 6 feet 1 inch tall, 185 pounds. Eyes: brown. Hair: black. Distinguishing features: known to wear amber-tinted anti-flash glasses because of an eye abnormality known as acute retinal dystrophy. It means that his retinas are too sensitive to handle natural light, hence the need for tinted glasses.'

As Fairfax's voice came through his earpiece, Schofield gazed over at Knight, standing over by the Sukhoi with the others, with his two holstered shotguns, his yellow glasses, his all-black fighting uniform.

Fairfax went on: '*Former member of Delta Team 7 which is regarded as the best within Delta, an elite within an elite. Reached the rank of captain, but found guilty of treason against the United States in absentia in 1998 after he betrayed a mission he was leading in Sudan. Intelligence sources say that Knight was paid $2 million by a local Al-Qaeda cell to inform them of an impending US assault on their arms depot. Thirteen Delta operatives died as a result of the forewarning Knight gave.*

'*He disappeared after that, but was rediscovered eighteen months later living in Brasilia. A team of six Navy SEAL commandos was sent in to liquidate him. Knight killed them all, then mailed their heads back to the SEAL training facility at Coronado Naval Base in San Diego.*

'Now known to be working as a freelance international bounty hunter. Get this. Apparently, insurance companies keep track of these things for kidnap scenarios: he's rated by Carringtons of London as the second-best bounty hunter in the world.'

'Only second? Who's the best?'

'That Demon Larkham guy I told you about before. Wait a second, I'm not finished with Knight yet. ISS believes that in 2000, Knight tracked down and killed twelve Islamic terrorists who'd kidnapped the daughter of Russia's Deputy President, cut off four of her fingers, and demanded a ransom of US$100 million. Knight traced them to a terrorist training camp in the Iranian desert, went there, razed the whole frigging camp to the ground, grabbed the girl – minus the fingers – and returned her to Moscow without the media getting a whiff of it. In return, it says here, the Russian government gave him . . . wait for it . . . a test-damaged Sukhoi S-37 jet fighter, plus refuelling privileges at any Russian base in the world. Apparently, the plane is known in bounty hunting circles as the Black Raven.'

'*Black Raven*, huh.' Schofield turned to look at the black Sukhoi S-37 standing nearby . . . and saw that Aloysius Knight was walking toward him.

'*I tell you, Scarecrow,*' Fairfax said, '*this is not the kind of guy you want hunting you.*'

'Too late,' Schofield said. 'He's standing right in front of me.'

Schofield and Knight rejoined the others underneath the *Black Raven*.

Book II and Mother came up to Schofield.

'You all right?' Mother asked softly. 'Book told me

what happened in Siberia. Excuse my French, Scarecrow, but what the fuck is happening here?'

'It's been a tough morning,' Schofield said, 'and a lot of people have died. Any idea what happened to Gant?'

'The last time I saw her was when those cocksuckers with the green laser sights came rocking in and I was knocked onto that conveyor belt—'

'She was taken,' a voice said from behind Mother.

It was Aloysius Knight.

'Taken by a bounty hunter named Demon Larkham and his men from IG-88.'

'How do you know that?' Book II asked.

'Rufus.' Knight nodded to his partner, the mountainously tall pilot.

With his great bushy beard, Rufus had a wide smiling face and earnest eyes. He hunched slightly, as if trying to diminish his seven-foot height. When he spoke, he spoke quickly and matter-of-factly, report-style.

'After I lowered Aloysius down the air vent,' he said, 'I went to hover over by the back entrance. I dropped a MicroDot aerosol charge onto the turnaround outside the exit tunnel – just like you told me to, Boss. Then I took up a hovering pattern about a mile away – again just like you told me to.

'About five minutes before you all came charging out, a great big Chinook helicopter flanked by a couple of Lynx attack choppers landed on that turnaround. Then two LSVs and a Driftrunner came speeding out of the mine tunnel and shot straight up the ramp of the Chinook and into its belly. Then the Chinook lifted off and headed out over the hills, back toward Afghanistan.'

Schofield said, 'How do you know Gant was with them?'

'I got photos,' Rufus said simply. 'Aloysius told me

that if anything unusual happened while he was inside the mine, I was to take photos of it, so I did.'

Schofield assessed Rufus as the big man spoke. For a guy who could manoeuvre a hover-capable Russian fighter with incredible skill – something which required an almost innate knowledge of physics and aerodynamics – his speech seemed oddly formal and direct, as if he took comfort in military formality.

Schofield had seen men like Rufus before: often the most gifted pilots (and soldiers) had great difficulty in social situations. They were so focused on their area of expertise that they often had trouble expressing themselves, or missed conversational nuances like irony and sarcasm. You just had to be patient with them. You also had to make sure their fellow troops were equally patient. Direct but not stupid, there was more to this Rufus than met the eye.

Knight pulled a handheld monitor from the cockpit of the Sukhoi, showed it to Schofield.

On the monitor was a series of digital photos showing three speeding vehicles blasting out of the mine's rear entrance, out onto the turnaround and up the ramp of a waiting Chinook helicopter.

Knight flicked a switch, blowing up several of the photos, zooming in on the lead Light Strike Vehicle.

Knight said, 'See the three white boxes on the passenger seat. Medical transport cases. Three cases: three heads.'

He clicked to another photo, which showed a blurry zoomed-in image of the Driftrunner racing along behind the two LSVs.

'Check out the rear tray on the truck,' Knight said. 'Notice that all of Larkham's guys are dressed in black. One person, however . . . that one . . . the one without the helmet . . . is wearing sand-coloured Marine fatigues.'

And Schofield saw her.

Although the figure was blurred and out-of-focus, he recognised her shape, the fall of her short blonde hair.

It was Gant.

Slumped unconscious in the rear tray of the Drift-runner.

Schofield's blood ran cold.

The greatest bounty hunter in the world had Gant.

More than anything else, Schofield wanted to go after her –

'No. That's exactly what the Demon wants you to do, Captain,' Knight said, reading his thoughts. 'Don't rush into anything. We know where she is. And Larkham won't kill her. He needs her alive if he's going to use her to flush *you* out.'

'How can you be sure of that?'

'Because that's how I'd do it,' Knight said evenly.

Schofield paused, holding Knight's gaze. It was almost like looking in a mirror – Schofield with his silver anti-flash glasses masking his scars, Knight with his yellow-lensed wraparounds covering his defective eyes.

A tattoo on Knight's forearm caught Schofield's eye. It showed an angry bald eagle and the words:

SLEEP WITH ONE EYE OPEN.

Schofield had seen that image before: on posters that had come out soon after September 11. On them, the American eagle said, 'Hey terrorists, sleep with one eye open.'

Underneath Knight's eagle tattoo was another one which simply read: BRANDEIS. Schofield didn't know what that one meant.

He locked eyes with Knight.

'I've heard about you, Mr Knight,' he said. 'Your loyalty isn't exactly something to brag about. You sold out your unit in the Sudan. Why should I think you won't sell me out, too?'

'Don't believe everything you read in the papers,' Knight said, 'or what you read in US Government files.'

'Then you're not going to kill me?'

'Captain, if I was going to kill you, you'd already have a bullet in your brain. No. My job is to keep you alive.'

'Keep me alive?'

Knight said, 'Captain, understand. I am not doing this because I *like* you or because I think that you are in any way *special*. I am being paid to do this, and paid well. The bounty on your head is 18.6 million dollars. Rest assured, I am being paid considerably more than that to make sure that you don't get killed.'

'Okay, then,' Schofield said. 'So who's paying you to keep me alive?'

'I can't say.'

'Yes, you can.'

'I won't say.' Knight's eyes didn't waver.

'But your employer—'

'—is not a subject for discussion,' Knight said.

Schofield chose another tack.

'All right, then, so why is this all happening? What do you know about this bounty hunt?'

Knight shrugged, looked away.

Rufus answered for him. Released from straight reportage, his tone was simple, honest. 'Bounty hunts happen for all kinds of reasons, Captain Schofield. Catch and kill a spy who goes AWOL with a secret in his head. Catch and retrieve a kidnapper who's *been paid* his ransom – mark my words, hell hath no fury like a rich guy who wants payback. Some of those rich assholes prefer to pay us two million dollars so they can catch some kidnapper who took them for one. It ain't often, though, that you get a list worth ten million dollars in total, let alone almost twenty million dollars *per head*.'

'So what do you know about this hunt then?' Schofield asked.

'The ultimate sponsor is unknown,' Rufus said, 'as is the reason for staging it, but the assessor – a banker from AGM-Suisse named Delacroix – is experienced at this sort of thing. We've run into him before. And so long as the assessor is legitimate, most bounty hunters don't care about the reason for a hunt.'

Rufus turned to Knight.

Knight just cocked his head. 'Big hunt. Fifteen targets. All have to be dead by 12 noon today, New York time. 18.6 meg per head. That's 280 million dollars in total. Whatever the reason for staging this hunt is, it's worth paying over a quarter of a *billion* dollars for.'

'You say that we all have to be dead by 12 noon, New York time?' Schofield said. This was the first he'd heard of the time limit placed on the hunt. He looked at his watch.

It was 2:05 p.m. here in Afghanistan. That made it 4:05 a.m. in New York. Eight hours till crunch time.

He fell silent, thinking.

Then abruptly he looked up.

'Mr Knight, now that you've found me, what are your instructions from here?'

Knight nodded slowly, impressed that Schofield had asked this question.

'My instructions are very clear on this point,' he said. 'From now on, I am to keep you alive.'

'But you haven't been told to keep me imprisoned, have you?'

'No . . .' Knight said. 'I have not. My instructions are to allow you complete freedom of action – to go wherever you please – but under my protection.'

And with that a piece of the puzzle fell into place in Schofield's mind.

Whoever was paying Knight to protect him not only wanted Schofield kept alive, that person also wanted Schofield to be active, to do whatever this bounty hunt was designed to stop him doing.

He turned to Knight. 'You said you knew where Gant is. How?'

'The MicroDot aerosol charge that Rufus dropped onto the turnaround area before the Demon's boys got there,' Knight said.

Schofield had heard about MicroDot technology. Apparently, it was the Next Big Thing in nanotechnology.

MicroDots were microscopic silicon chips, each about the size of a pinhead but with enormous computing power. While many believed that MicroDots would be the basis for a new series of liquid-based supercomputers – imagine a liquid ooze filled with supercomputing particles – at the moment they were mainly used by prestige car manufacturers as tracking devices: you sprayed the bottom of your Ferrari with MicroDot-loaded paint, then the Dots, and your car, could be traced anywhere in the world, and no car thief, however persistent, could wash them all off.

The MicroDot charge that Rufus had detonated on the turnaround area had released an aerosol cloud of about a billion MicroDots over the area.

'The Demon, his men, his vehicles and your girl are all covered in MicroDots,' Knight said. He pulled a jerry-rigged Palm Pilot from his belt. It bristled with home-made attachments and antennas, and looked a little chunkier than a regular PDA, as if it were waterproof.

On its screen was a map of the world and superimposed on that map, over Central Asia, was a set of moving red dots.

Demon Larkham's team.

'We can trace them to any point in the world on this,' Knight said.

Schofield started thinking, tried to order his thoughts, to weigh up his options so he could arrange a plan of action.

Then at last he said, 'The first thing we have to do is find out why all this is happening.'

He pulled out the bounty list, analysed it for the hundredth time.

Mother and Book II read it over his shoulder.

'The Mossad,' Mother said softly, seeing one entry:

```
11.  ROSENTHAL, Benjamin Y.     ISR     Mossad
```

'What about it?' Schofield said.

'That Zawahiri guy said something about the Israeli Mossad down in the mine, before he lost his head. He was crazy, shouting about how he'd survived Soviet experiments in some gulag, and then the US cruise-missile attacks in '98, and then about how the Mossad knew he was invincible, since they'd tried to kill him a dozen times.'

'The Mossad . . .' Schofield mused.

He keyed his sat-comm. 'David Fairfax, you still there?'

'*So long as there's coffee around, I'm still here,*' came the reply.

'Mr Fairfax, look up Hassan Mohammad Zawahiri and Benjamin Y. Rosenthal. Any cross-matches?'

'*Just a second,*' Fairfax's voice said. '*Hey, got something already. A match from some US–Israeli intelligence swap. Major Benjamin Yitzak Rosenthal is Hassan Zawahiri's "katsa", or case officer, the guy who monitors him. Rosenthal is based in Haifa, but it seems that only yesterday he was recalled to Mossad's London headquarters.*'

'London?' Schofield said.

A plan was beginning to form in Schofield's mind.

And all of a sudden he started to feel alive.

He'd been on the back foot all morning, *reacting* – now he was getting *proactive*.

'Book, Mother,' he said, 'how would you like to pay Major Rosenthal a visit in London? See if he can shed some light on this situation.'

'Be happy to,' Mother said.

'Sure,' Book II said.

Aloysius Knight watched this exchange casually, uninterested.

'*Oh, hey, Scarecrow,*' Fairfax's voice said, '*I was going to mention this before but I didn't get a chance. You remember that US Army Medical Research and Matériel Command paper I mentioned earlier, the "NATO MNRR Study". Well, that thing is out of my reach from here. It was deprioritised two months ago and deleted from the USAMRMC's files. An archive copy exists in some warehouse in Arizona, but otherwise all other copies have been shredded or deleted.*

'But I did find something on the two guys who wrote it, those two fellas on your list who worked for Medical Research Command: Nicholson and Oliphant. Nicholson retired a couple of years ago and is now living at some retirement village in Florida. But Oliphant quit USAMRMC only last year. He's now chief physician in the ER at St John's Hospital, Virginia, not far from the Pentagon.'

'Is that so?' Schofield said. 'Mr Fairfax, would you like to be a field officer for a day?'

'*Anything to get out of this office, man. My boss is the biggest asshole on the planet.*'

'When you get a chance, then, why don't you go down to St John's and have a chat with Dr Oliphant.'

'*You got it.*' Fairfax signed off.

'What about you?' Mother said to Schofield. 'You're not going to stay with this bounty hunter, are you?' She shot Knight a withering glare. Knight just raised his eyebrows.

'He says I can go wherever I like,' Schofield said. 'It's up to him to protect me.'

'So where are you going?' Book II asked.

Schofield's eyes narrowed. 'I'm going to the source of this bounty hunt. I'm going to that castle in France.'

Book II said, 'What are you going to do? Knock on the front door?'

'No,' Schofield said. 'I'm going to collect a bounty.'

'A bounty?' Mother said. 'I, er, don't mean to be devil's advocate, but don't you need a . . . *head* . . . to collect the reward?'

'That's right,' Schofield said, looking at Knight's modified Palm Pilot, the mini-computer that depicted Demon Larkham's progress. 'And I know just where to get some. And at the same time, I'm going to get Gant back.'

THIRD ATTACK

FRANCE–ENGLAND–USA

26 OCTOBER, 1150 HOURS (FRANCE)

E.S.T. (NEW YORK, USA) 0550 HOURS

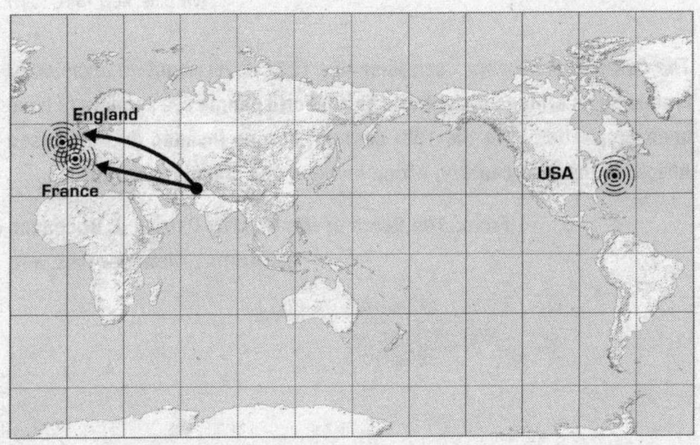

Over the next fifty years the earth's population will soar from 5.5 billion to more than 9 billion . . . 95 percent of the population increase will be in the poorest regions of the world.

From: *The Coming Anarchy* by Robert D. Kaplan

(VINTAGE, NEW YORK, 2001)

***The Camp of the Saints*, Jean Raspail's 1972 novel about an invasion of France by an armada of destitute Third World people . . . appears to have been prophetic . . . In the 19th century, Europe invaded and colonised Africa. In the 21st century, Africa invades and colonises Europe.**

From: *The Death of the West* by Patrick J. Buchanan

(ST MARTIN'S PRESS, NEW YORK, 2002)

```
10.  POLANSKI, Damien G.        USA       ISS
```

BERLIN, GERMANY

22 OCTOBER, 2300 HOURS

He liked to fuck girls from behind, pumping like a jackhammer and calling out cowboy shouts. And he was an ass man, too. He loved young twenty-somethings with tight little bottoms.

She'd discovered these facts from the prostitutes of Berlin's red light district, whose services he engaged often.

Damien Polanski's career had seen better days.

An Eastern Bloc expert during the Cold War, he was now stationed in the ISS's Berlin field office, growing older and more irrelevant every day. His daring conquests of the '80s – the defection of Karmonov, the discovery of the Soviet 'Cobra' files – long forgotten by an intelligence agency that didn't love you back.

An old dog in a new world.

She caught his eye easily enough. It wasn't hard. She was stunning to look at – long slender legs, muscular shoulders, small perfectly-formed breasts and those cool Eurasian eyes.

The Ice Queen, some called her.

She'd stood at the bar opposite his booth, dropped her purse, and bent over to get it, offering him a clear view up her black-vinyl mini-skirt. No panties.

Within fifteen minutes, he was hurriedly taking off his trousers in a hotel room, thinking, *Giddy-up, baby! Giddy-up!*

She emerged from the bathroom wearing nothing at all, her hands hidden behind her back. Polanski's eyes widened with delight. He dived onto the bed, and turned – just as the short-bladed samurai sword that she gripped in her hands sliced clean through his neck.

```
7.  NAZZAR, Yousef M.          LEBN    HAMAS
```

BEIRUT, LEBANON
23 OCTOBER, 2100 HOURS

Witnesses would say it was one of the most professional hits they had ever seen in Beirut – which was saying something.

They saw Yousef Nazzar, a senior HAMAS commander known to have been trained by the Soviets, enter the apartment building.

Not a moment later, two sedans skidded to a halt outside the lobby and eight commandos piled out of them, rushed into the building. One of them carried a white box with a red cross on its side.

One thing was common to all the witnesses' accounts: the guns the assassins used. They were either identified or described as VZ-61 Skorpion machine pistols.

And then suddenly the assassins were out and, with a squeal of tyres, were gone.

Yousef Nazzar's body was found later, spreadeagled on the floor of his apartment, the head missing.

```
8.  NICHOLSON, Francis X.      USA      USAMRMC
```

CEDAR FALLS RETIREMENT VILLAGE
MIAMI, FLORIDA
24 OCTOBER, 0700 HOURS

The front-desk nurse couldn't have known he was a killer.

When she'd asked, 'Can I help you?' he had replied politely that he was from the hospital, come to collect the personal effects of a recently transferred resident of Cedar Falls.

He was tall and thin, with deep black skin and a high forehead. More than one witness would describe him as 'African' in appearance. They didn't known that in the global bounty hunting community he was known by a very simple name: 'the Zulu'.

Dressed in a white labcoat, he strode calmly through the home, carrying a white organ-delivery box in his hand.

He found the room quickly, found the old man, Frank Nicholson, lying in his bed asleep.

Without missing a beat, the Zulu drew a machete from under his coat and . . .

The police found his car two hours later, abandoned in the long-term carpark at the airport.

By that time, however, the Zulu was sitting in the first-class section of United Airlines Flight 45 bound for

Paris, the white organ-delivery box resting on the seat beside him.

Frank Nicholson was missed at the retirement village. He'd been a popular resident, friendly and outgoing.

The management had liked him too. Since he'd been a doctor in his career days, he'd saved more than one elderly resident who had collapsed on the golf course.

It was funny, though, unlike many others, he'd never really spoken about his glory days.

If asked he would say he'd been a scientist at the US Army Medical Research and Matériel Command at Fort Detrick, 'just doing some medical tests for the armed forces' before he'd retired the previous year.

And then came that night when the assassin had come and cut off his head.

FORTERESSE DE VALOIS, BRITTANY, FRANCE
26 OCTOBER, 1150 HOURS LOCAL TIME
(0550 HOURS E.S.T. USA)

He'd always loved anarchy.

Loved the idea of it, the concept of it: the complete and utter loss of control; society without order.

He particularly loved the way people – common people, average people, ordinary people – responded to it.

When soccer stadiums collapsed, they stampeded.

When earthquakes struck, they looted.

During anarchic warfare – Nanjing, My Lai, Stalingrad – they raped and mutilated their fellow human beings.

The teleconference with the other members of the Council wouldn't begin for another ten minutes, which gave Member No. 12 enough time to indulge his passion for anarchy.

His real name was Jonathan Killian.

Jonathan James Killian III, to be precise, and at thirty-seven he was the youngest member of the Council.

Born into wealth – his father had been American, his

mother French – he had the supercilious bearing of a man who was accustomed to having everything he desired. He was also possessed of a cold level stare that could give the most combative negotiator pause. It was a powerful gift, one that was accentuated by an unusual facial feature: Jonathan Killian had one blue eye and one brown.

He was worth $32 billion, and by virtue of a labyrinthine network of companies, was the ultimate owner of the Forteresse de Valois.

Killian had always disliked Member No. 5.

While wealthy beyond measure thanks to an inherited Texan oil empire, No. 5 was of low intellect and prone to tantrums. At fifty-eight, he was still essentially a spoilt brat. He had also been a continually stubborn opponent of Killian's ideas in Council meetings. He was very irritating.

Right now, however, Member No. 5 stood in a wide stone dungeon on the lowest level of the Forteresse de Valois, deep within the castle's stone mount, accompanied by his four personal assistants.

The dungeon was called the Shark Pit.

Sixteen feet deep with sheer stone walls, it was perfectly circular; and wide too, about fifty yards across. It was also filled with an irregular array of elevated stone stages. One thing about it was clear: once a person was placed inside it, escape was impossible.

In the pit's centre, plunging vertically down into the earth, was a ten-foot-wide 'sink-hole' that led directly to the ocean.

Right now, the tide was coming in, so the water entering the Pit via the sink-hole was rising fast, spilling out into the wider pit, *filling it*, turning the irregular collection of elevated stages into a series of small stone islands – much to the horror of Member No. 5 and his assistants.

Adding to their fear, two dark shapes could be glimpsed swimming through the alleyways between the islands, just beneath the surface of the water – shapes featuring dorsal fins and bullet-shaped heads.

Two large tiger sharks.

In addition to all this, the Shark Pit came with two other features worth noting.

First, a viewing balcony situated on its southern side. Before the Revolution, the French aristocracy were known to hold gladiatorial contests in their dungeons – usually pitting peasants against peasants, or in the more elaborate dungeons like the one at the Forteresse de Valois, peasants against animals.

The second noteworthy feature of the Shark Pit could be found on the largest of its elevated stone platforms, over by the northern wall. On this stage sat a truly terrifying device: a twelve-foot-high guillotine.

Tall and brutal, the guillotine was an addition made by Jonathan Killian himself. At its base was a crude wooden block with slots carved into it – slots for a person's head and hands. A crank handle on the guillotine's side raised its steeply-angled blade. A simple release lever dropped it.

Killian had been inspired by the acts of Japanese soldiers during the sack of the Chinese city of Nanjing in 1937.

During three horrific weeks, the Japanese had subjected the Chinese to unspeakable torture. Over 360,000 people were murdered *by hand* during that time. Horror stories emerged of Japanese soldiers conducting

'THE SHARK PIT'
FORTERESSE DE VALOIS, FRANCE

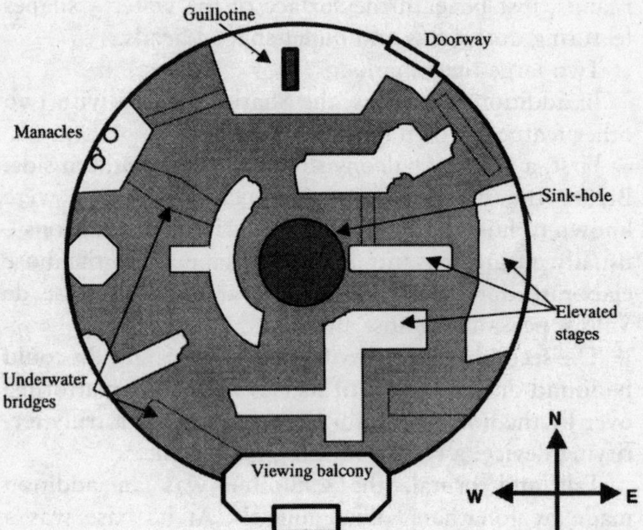

Guillotine
Doorway
Manacles
Sink-hole
Elevated stages
Underwater bridges
Viewing balcony
N
W
E
S

beheading contests; or worse, giving fathers a choice: rape their own daughters or watch them be raped; or telling sons to have sex with their own mothers or die.

Killian was intrigued. Usually, the Chinese men would take the honourable way out and accept death rather than perform such hideous acts.

But some did not.

And that was what had amused Killian. Just how far people would go in pursuit of self-preservation.

And so he'd had the guillotine inserted into the Shark Pit.

It was designed to give those who were placed in the pit a similar choice.

Die a terrifying death at the mercy of the tiger sharks, or die quickly and painlessly by their own hand on the guillotine.

Sometimes, when he had a group of people in the pit (as he did today), Killian would offer them Faustian bargains: 'Kill your boss on the guillotine, and I will release the rest of you'; 'Kill that hysterical screaming woman, and I will release the rest of you.'

Of course, he never released anyone. But the prisoners never knew that, and on many occasions they themselves died with blood on their hands.

The five people in the pit scratched desperately at the walls, the incoming water rising rapidly around them.

One of No. 5's female assistants made it a few feet up the wall – making for a tiny stone handhold there – but she was quickly pulled down by a bigger man who saw the handhold as his chance at life.

Killian watched them from the southern viewing balcony, utterly fascinated.

One of these people is worth $22 billion, he thought. *The others earn about $65,000 a year in salaries. Yet now they are all truly equal.*

Anarchy, he thought. *The great equaliser.*

Soon the water level rose five feet above the floor – chest height – and the two tiger sharks now roamed the pit more freely in a rush. At first the people cowered on the stone islands, but soon those islands also went sufficiently under the surface.

Five people. Two sharks.

It wasn't pretty.

The sharks rushed the hapless people – ramming them into the water, taking them under, ripping them open. Blood stained the churning waves.

After a male assistant went under in a froth of spraying blood, No. 5's two female assistants killed themselves on the guillotine.

So, too, No. 5 himself.

In the end, rather than face the sharks, he preferred to cut off his own head.

Then abruptly it was over and the rising water enveloped the guillotine stage, washing it clean of evidence, and the sharks gorged themselves on the headless corpses too, and Jonathan Killian III turned on his heel and headed up to his office for the noon teleconference.

Faces on television screens, arrayed around the walls.

The faces of the other members of the Council, tuning in from around the world.

Killian took his seat.

Five years previously, he had inherited his father's vast shipping and defence-contracting empire – a maze of companies known as the Axon Corporation. Among other things, Axon Corp constructed destroyers and long-range missiles for the US Government.

In each of the first three years after his father's death, Jonathan Killian had increased Axon's annual profits fivefold.

His formal invitation to join the Council had come soon after.

'Member No. 12,' the Chairman said, addressing Killian. 'Where is Member No. 5? He is staying with you, is he not?'

Killian smiled. 'He pulled a muscle in the swimming pool. My personal physician is looking at him now.'

'Is everything in place?'

'Yes,' Killian said. 'The Kormoran ships are in position all around the world, fully armed. DGSE delivered the corpses to America last week and my facility in Norfolk has been liberally stained with their blood – ready for the US inspectors. All systems are in place, merely awaiting the go signal.'

Killian paused. Took the plunge.

'Of course, Mr Chairman,' he added, 'as I've said before, it's not too late to initiate the extra step—'

'Member No. 12,' the Chair said sharply, 'the course of action has been decided upon and we will *not* deviate from it. I'm sorry, but if you raise this "extra step" matter again, penalties will be imposed.'

Killian bowed his head. 'As you wish, Mr Chairman.'

A Council penalty was something to be avoided.

Joseph Kennedy had lost two of his famous sons for disobeying a Council directive to cease doing business with Japan in the '50s.

Charles Lindbergh's infant son was kidnapped and killed, while Lindbergh himself had been forced to endure a smear campaign suggesting he admired Adolf

Hitler – all because he had defied a Council edict to *keep* doing business with the Nazis in the 1930s.

More recently, there was the impertinent Enron board. And everyone knew what had happened to Enron.

As the teleconference went on, Jonathan Killian remained silent.

On this issue, he felt he knew better than the Council.

The Zimbabwe Experiment – his idea – had more than proved his point. After decades of economic repression at the hands of Europeans, poverty-stricken African majorities no longer cared for the white man's property rights.

And the Hartford Report on global population growth – and Western population *decline* – had only further bolstered his argument.

But now was not the time to argue.

The formal business of the teleconference concluded, and several of the Council members stayed online, chatting among themselves.

Killian just watched them.

One member was saying, 'Just bought the drilling rights for a flat billion. I said take it or leave it. These stupid African governments just don't have a choice . . .'

The Chairman himself was laughing: '. . . I ran into that Mattencourt woman at Spencer's the other night. She certainly is an aggressive little filly. She asked *again* if I would consider her for a seat on the Council. So I said, "What are you worth?" She said, "26 billion." "And your company?" "170 billion." So I say, "Well, that's certainly enough. What do you say, you give me a blow job in the men's room right now and you're in." She stormed off!'

Dinosaurs, Killian thought. *Old men. Old ideas.*

You'd expect better from the richest businessmen in the world.

He pressed a button, cutting the signal, and all of the televisions on the walls around him shrank to black.

AIRSPACE ABOVE TURKEY
26 OCTOBER, 1400 HOURS LOCAL TIME
(0600 HOURS E.S.T. USA)

The MicroDots that had attached themselves to Demon Larkham's IG-88 team told a peculiar tale.

After leaving the Karpalov coalmine, Larkham's team had flown to a British-controlled airfield in Kunduz – a fact which had immediately rung alarm bells in Schofield's head.

Because it meant that Larkham was working with the tacit approval of the British government on this matter.

Not a good sign, Schofield thought, as he ripped through the sky in the back of Aloysius Knight's *Black Raven*.

So the British knew what was going on . . .

At the airfield in Kunduz, the IG-88 men had divided into two sub-teams, one getting on board an aircraft and heading in the direction of London, the other boarding a second plane and heading for the northwestern coast of France.

The aircraft flying toward London – a sleek Gulfstream IV executive jet – was pulling rapidly away from the second one, a lumbering Royal Air Force C-130J Hercules cargo plane.

Right now, Knight's Sukhoi was paralleling Larkham's planes, flying just beyond the horizon, its stealth features on full power.

'Common tactic for the Demon,' Knight said. 'Dividing his men into a delivery team and a strike team. The Demon takes the strike team to liquidate the next target while his delivery team ferries the heads to the verification venue.'

'Looks like the strike team is going to London,' Schofield said. 'They're going after Rosenthal.'

'Likely,' Knight said. 'What do you want to do?'

Schofield could think of nothing else but Gant, sitting in the belly of the Hercules.

'I want that plane,' he said.

Knight punched some keys on his computer console.

'All right, I'm accessing their flight data computer. That Hercules is scheduled for a mid-air refuelling over western Turkey in ninety minutes.'

'Where's the tanker plane taking off from?' Schofield asked.

'A VC-10 aerial tanker is scheduled for lift-off from the Brits' Akrotiri air force base on Cyprus in exactly forty-five minutes.'

'Okay,' Schofield said. 'Book and Mother, Rufus here will take you to London. Find Benjamin Rosenthal before Larkham's strike team does.'

'What about you?' Mother asked.

'Captain Knight and I are getting off in Cyprus.'

Forty-five minutes later, a British Vickers VC-10 air-to-air refuelling tanker lifted off from its island runway on Cyprus.

Unbeknownst to the plane's four-man crew, it contained two stowaways in its rear cargo bay – Shane Schofield and Aloysius Knight – whom Rufus had dropped off, under the curtain of active stealth, in the shallows three miles away.

For their part, Rufus, Mother and Book II had powered off immediately in the *Black Raven*, cutting a beeline for London.

Soon the VC-10 was zooming through Turkish airspace, pulling alongside the RAF Hercules coming from Afghanistan.

The tanker moved in front of the Hercules, rose a little above it. Then it extended a long swooping fuel hose – or 'boom' – from its rear-end. The boom was about seventy metres long and at its tip was a circular steel 'drogue', which would ultimately attach itself to the receiving aircraft.

Controlled by a lone operator, or 'boomer', lying on his stomach in a glassed-in compartment at the rear of the tanker plane, the boom angled in toward the receiving probe of the Hercules.

The Hercules' receiving probe – essentially, it was just a horizontal pipe – was located just above the cargo plane's cockpit windows.

The aerial ballet went perfectly.

The tanker's boom operator extended the boom, manoeuvred it into place, just as below and behind it the Hercules flew forward and – *kerchunk* – the Hercules' receiving probe locked into the drogue at the end of the boom and fuel started pumping between the two moving planes.

While this was happening, Knight started loading his H&K pistol with some odd-looking 9mm rounds. Each bullet had an orange band painted around it.

'Bull stoppers,' he said to Schofield. 'Every Delta man's best friend. Gas-expanding nine-millimetre rounds. Better than hollow points. They enter the target and then blow big.'

'How big?'

'Big enough to cut a man in half. Want some?'

'No thanks.'

'Here, then.' Knight placed some of the orange bullets in a pocket on Schofield's combat webbing. 'For when you reconsider.'

Schofield nodded at Knight's utility vest, at the peculiar array of devices hanging from it – the Pony Bottle, the mini blowtorch, the mountaineering pitons. There was even a very small pouch-like rollbag which Schofield recognised.

'Is that a *body bag*?' he asked.

'Yeah. A Markov Type-III,' Knight said. 'Gotta hand it to the Soviets. Nobody ever built a better one.'

Schofield nodded. The Markov Type-III was a chemical body bag. With its double-strength ziplock and poly-coated nylon walls, it could safely hold a body infected with the worst kind of contamination: plague, chem weapons, even superheated radioactive waste. The Russians had used a lot of them at Chernobyl.

It was the pitons, however, that intrigued Schofield the most. He could understand a bounty hunter carrying a portable body bag with him, but pitons?

Pitons are small springloaded scissor-like devices that mountain climbers jam into tiny crevices. The piton springs open with such force – pinioning itself against the walls of a crevice – that climbers can attach ropes to it and hold up their bodyweight. Schofield wondered what a bounty hunter might use them for.

'Question,' he said. 'What do you use pitons for?'

Knight shrugged casually. 'Climb over walls. Up the sides of buildings.'

'Anything else?' Schofield asked. *Like torture, perhaps.*

Knight held Schofield's gaze. 'They do have . . . other uses.'

When the refuelling was almost complete, Schofield and Knight sprang.

'You take the boomer,' Knight said, drawing a second 9 mm pistol. 'I'll take the cockpit crew.'

'Right,' Schofield said, before adding quickly: 'Knight. You can do whatever you want on the Hercules, but how about using non-lethal force here.'

'What? Why?'

'This crew didn't do anything.'

Knight scowled. 'Oh, all right . . .'

'Thanks.'

And they moved.

With its fifteen wraparound cockpit windows, the C-130 cargo plane provided its pilots with exceptional visibility, and right now the two pilots of the British Hercules could see the bird-like rear-end of the VC-10 high above them, the long swooping fuel hose extending out from it like a tail and attaching itself to the receiving probe directly above their cockpit.

They'd done this sort of mid-air refuelling a hundred times before. Once the two planes were connected, the pilots had switched over to automatic pilot and become more concerned with observing the fuel pumping stats than with watching the amazing view outside.

Which was probably why they didn't notice when – twenty-two minutes into the refuelling – a lone black-clad figure came *whizzing* down the length of the fuel hose like a death-defying stuntman and their cockpit windows exploded under his withering assault of gunfire.

The sight was truly spectacular.

Two gigantic planes flying in tandem at 20,000 feet, connected tail-to-nose by the long swooping fuel hose . . .

. . . with a tiny man-shaped figure sliding down the hose as if it were a zipline, hanging onto a makeshift flying-fox one-handed, an H&K pistol held in his free hand, firing at the cockpit of the Hercules plane!

The two pilots of the Hercules went down in a hail of smashing glass.

Wind rushed into the cockpit. But the plane, under automatic pilot, remained steady.

For his part, Aloysius Knight slid down the fuel hose at incredible speed, hanging onto a seatbelt that he had lashed over the hose – his face covered in a high-altitude breathing mask, an ultra-compact MC-4/7 attack parachute strapped to his back.

Since the Hercules' receiving probe was situated directly above its cockpit, Knight's slide ended with him blasting *right through* the shattered glass windows of the Hercules and landing inside its wind-assaulted cockpit.

He keyed his radio mike. 'All right, Scarecrow! Come on down!'

A few seconds later, a second figure – also wearing a breathing mask and a small attack parachute – swung down from the tanker plane, shooting down the length of the fuel hose before disappearing inside the shattered windows of the Hercules.

In the cargo hold of the Hercules, everyone turned – eight black-clad commandos, two men in suits, and two prisoners – as a terrible crash rang out from the cockpit, followed by the roar of inrushing air.

The eight commandos were members of the IG-88 delivery team. The two men in suits had no names that anyone knew but they did possess MI-6 identity badges: British Intelligence.

And the two prisoners were Lieutenant Elizabeth 'Fox' Gant and General Ronson H. Weitzman, both from the United States Marine Corps, both captured by the Demon's forces in Afghanistan.

Just before the mid-air attack had commenced, Gant had regained consciousness – to find herself seated in the wide cargo hold of the Hercules, her hands flex-cuffed behind her back.

A few feet away from her, Ronson Weitzman – one of the most senior officers in the entire US Marine Corps – lay spreadeagled on his back, on the bonnet of a Humvee parked in the cargo bay, tied down, his arms stretched wide as if he had been crucified horizontally, his wrists attached by two separate pairs of handcuffs to both of the Humvee's side mirrors.

The right sleeve of Weitzman's uniform had been torn off and a rubber tourniquet was tied tightly around his exposed arm.

Flanking the General were the two MI-6 men. Gant had awoken just as the shorter one had been removing a hypodermic needle from Weitzman's arm.

'Give it a couple of minutes,' the short one had said.

The General had raised his head, his eyes glazed.

'Hello, General Weitzman.' The taller intelligence officer smiled. 'The drug you are feeling right now is known as EA-617. I'm sure a man of your rank has heard of it. It's a neural disinhibitor – a drug that retards the release of the neurotransmitter "GABA" in your brain – a drug that will make answering our questions truthfully just that little bit easier.'

'Wha—?' Weitzman looked at his arm. '. . . 617? No . . .'

Watching the scene from a discreet distance were the members of the IG-88 bounty hunting team – led by the tall and strikingly handsome soldier Gant had seen in the caves in Afghanistan. She had heard the other IG-88 men calling him 'Cowboy'.

'All right, General,' the tall MI-6 man said. 'The Universal Disarm Code. What is it?'

Weitzman frowned, squinting hard, as if his brain was trying to resist the truth drug.

'I . . . I don't know of any such code,' he said unconvincingly.

'Yes you do, General. The United States Universal Disarm Code. The code that overrides any and every security system in the US armed services. You oversaw its entry into a secret US military project called the "Kormoran Project". We know about Kormoran, General. But we don't know the code, and the code is what we want. What is it?'

Gant was completely shocked.

She'd heard rumours about the Universal Disarm

Code. It was the stuff of legend: a numerical code that overrode *every* US military security system.

Weitzman blinked, fighting the drug. 'It . . . it doesn't . . . exist . . .'

'No, General,' the tall man said. 'It does exist, and you are one of five people in the US military establishment who know it. Maybe I will have to increase the dosage here.'

The tall man pulled out another syringe, inserted it into Weitzman's exposed arm.

Weitzman groaned, '*No* . . .'

The EA-617 serum went into his arm.

And that was when the cockpit windows had exploded under Knight's hailstorm of gunfire.

Schofield dropped into the cockpit of the Hercules, landed next to Knight.

'*Now* can I use lethal force?' Knight shouted.

'Be my guest!'

Knight pointed to a TV monitor on the cockpit dashboard – it showed a high-angle view of the Hercules' rear cargo hold.

Schofield saw about a dozen large wooden crates near the cockpit steps, one Humvee with Weitzman crucified on the bonnet, eight bad guys in black combat uniforms, two bad guys in suits and on the floor, up against the wall of the cargo hold, on the left-hand side of the Humvee, her hands cuffed behind her back . . .

. . . Libby Gant.

'Too many to take out with guns,' Schofield said.

'I know,' Knight said. 'So we take guns out of the equation.'

He pulled two small grenades from his combat webbing – small hand-held charges painted pale yellow.

'What are – ?' Schofield asked.

'British AC-2 charges. Adhesive-chaff grenades.'

'Anti-firearm charges,' Schofield said, nodding. 'Nice.'

The British SAS, experts in counter-terrorist ops, had developed the AC-2 for operations against armed hostage takers. They were basically standard flash-bang grenades, but with one very special extra feature.

'You ready? Just remember, you get one shot before your gun jams,' Knight said. 'Okay, let's rock this joint.'

At which point, he cracked open the cockpit door and hurled his two AC-2 charges into the cargo hold beyond it.

The two pale yellow grenades flew into the hold, skipping across the tops of the wooden cargo crates before landing on the floor beside the Humvee and—

—*flash-bang!*

The standard explosion came first: blinding white flashes of light followed by ear-crashing bangs, designed to deafen and disorient.

And then came the AC-2 grenades' extra feature.

As they exploded, the two grenades sent brilliant starbursts of tiny white-grey particles shooting out in every direction, completely *filling* the enclosed space of the cargo bay.

The particles looked like confetti, and after they dispersed, they floated in the air, infinitesimally small, forming a white-grey veil over the scene, making it look like a snowglobe that had just been shaken.

Only this wasn't confetti.

It was a special form of adhesive chaff – a sticky stringy compound that stuck to *everything*.

The cockpit door burst open, and Knight and Schofield charged into the cargo hold.

The nearest IG-88 commando reached for his rifle,

but received an arrow-bolt in his forehead – care of the mini-crossbow attached to Knight's right forearm guard.

A second-nearest man also spun quickly, and – *shlip!* – received an arrow from Knight's *left*-arm crossbow square in the eye.

It was the third IG-88 commando who actually managed to pull the trigger on his Colt Commando assault rifle.

The machine-gun fired – once. One bullet only. Then it jammed.

It had been 'chaffed'. The sticky adhesive chaff of Knight's grenades had got into its barrel, its receiver, all its moving parts, rendering it useless.

Schofield nailed the man with the butt of his Maghook.

But the other IG-88 men learned quickly, and within seconds, two Warlock hunting knives slammed into the wooden cargo crates beside them.

Knight responded by pulling one of the most evil-looking weapons Schofield had ever seen from his utility vest: a small four-bladed ninja throwing star, or *shuriken*. It was about as big as Schofield's hand: four viciously-curving blades that extended out from a central hub.

Knight threw the shuriken expertly, side-handed, and it sliced laterally through the air, whistling, before – *shnick! shnick!* – it cut the throats of *two* IG-88 commandos standing side-by-side.

Five down, Schofield thought, *three to go, plus the two guys in suits . . .*

And then suddenly a hand grabbed him—

—a *stunningly* strong grip—

—and Schofield was hurled back toward the cockpit doorway.

He hit the floor hard, and looked up to see an enormous IG-88 trooper stalking toward him. The IG-88 man was huge: at least 6 feet 9 inches, black-skinned, with bulging biceps and a face that bristled with unadulterated *fury*.

'Wot *the fuck* d'you fink you're doin'?' the giant black man said.

But Schofield was already moving again – he quickly jumped to his feet and unleashed a thunderous blow with his Maghook's butt at the black trooper's jaw.

The blow hit home.

And the big man didn't even flinch.

'Uh-oh,' Schofield said.

The giant black trooper punched Schofield, sending him flying back into the wind-blasted cockpit like a rag doll. Schofield slammed into the dashboard.

Then the big black trooper picked him up easily and said, 'You came in froo that window. You go out froo that window.'

And without so much as a blink, the gigantic trooper hurled Shane Schofield out through the broken cockpit windows of the Hercules and into the clear open sky.

In the particle-filled cargo hold, Aloysius Knight – charging forward, hurling throwing stars – spun around to check on Schofield . . .

. . . just in time to see him get thrown out through the cockpit windows.

'Holy shit,' Knight breathed. Like himself, Schofield was wearing a parachute, so he'd be okay, but his sudden disappearance didn't help the mathematics of this fight at all.

Knight keyed his radio mike. 'Schofield! You okay?'

A wind-blasted voice replied: '*I'm not gone yet!*'

Seen from the outside, the Hercules was still cruising steadily at 20,000 feet, still behind and below the VC-10 tanker plane . . . only now it was possessed of a tiny figure hanging off its nose cone.

Schofield clung to the bow of the speeding Hercules, his body assaulted by the speeding wind, 20,000 feet above the world but thanks to his Maghook, now magnetically affixed to the nose of the cargo plane.

His big black attacker – the man's IG-88 nickname was, appropriately, 'Rocko' – stood peering out the cockpit windows above him.

Then Rocko ducked inside and suddenly reappeared with a Colt .45 pistol which had been kept in the cockpit and as such had been unaffected by Knight's chaff grenades.

'Whoa, shit!' Schofield yelled as the first shot went flying over his head.

He'd been hoping that Rocko would just assume he'd fallen to his death and then head back inside the plane, giving Schofield a chance to climb back in through the cockpit windows.

But not now . . .

And so Schofield did the only thing he *could* do.

He unclipped Gant's Maghook from his belt, and now moving downward with *two* Maghooks, affixed it to the hull of the Hercules below him – *clunk!* – and swung down *below* the nose-cone of the massive plane, out of the line of Rocko's fire, so that he was now hanging from the underbelly of the cargo plane, 20,000 feet above the earth.

He spoke into his voice-activated throat-mike.

'Knight! I'm still in the game! I just need you to open an external door for me!'

Inside the cargo bay, Knight ducked a flying knife and threw one of his shurikens into the chest of one of the suit-wearing bad guys.

He heard Schofield's call, saw the big red control button that opened the Hercules' cargo ramp, hurled a shuriken at it.

Thwack!

The multi-bladed throwing knife hit the button, pinned it to its console and with a low *vmmmmm*, the rear cargo ramp of the Hercules began to open.

*

'*All right, Captain! The cargo ramp is open!*' Knight's voice said in Schofield's earpiece.

Schofield moved as quickly as he could along the underbelly of the Hercules, manoeuvring the two Maghooks above him, alternately magnetising and demagnetising them, and then swinging from them like a kid on a jungle gym, making his way along the sixty-foot length of the cargo plane's belly, toward its now-open rear ramp.

Wind blasted into the cargo bay, rushing in through the plane's open rear loading ramp, sending the chaff particles suspended in the air whizzing into swirls. An indoor blizzard.

Inside the cargo hold, Knight slid to Gant's side.

'I'm here to help you,' he said quickly, bringing his knife toward her flex-cuffs—

—just as two great black hands grabbed him and yanked him backwards.

Rocko.

The big IG-88 trooper banged Knight against the side of the Humvee. Knight's knife flew from his grip.

The IG-88 leader, Cowboy, stepped out from his cover position on the right side of the Humvee.

'His glasses!' he called.

Rocko let fly with a savage punch that cracked the bridge of Knight's yellow-tinted glasses, and also broke his nose. The cracked glasses fell from his face, exposing his eyes to the light.

'Ahh!' Knight squeezed his eyes shut.

Another crunching blow from Rocko knocked the wind out of him.

'Put him in front of the car,' Cowboy said, unclasping the Humvee's flight restraints before jumping behind the wheel. 'Knees in front of the tyres.'

Rocko did as he was told – lay the limp Knight in the path of the Humvee's tyres and stepped out of the way.

Cowboy fired up the engine, thrust the Humvee into gear, jammed down on the gas pedal.

The Humvee rushed forward, heading *straight for* Aloysius Knight's kneecaps.

And Cowboy felt a small satisfying bump as the big jeep ran over the bounty hunter and slammed into the side of a cargo crate.

'Damn it! Fuck!' Rocko yelled.

'What?' Cowboy called.

'The other one is back!'

None of the British men had seen Schofield re-enter the Hercules.

Not Cowboy or Rocko or the only other remaining bad guy in the hold – the surviving suited man from British Intelligence.

Hadn't seen him climb up into the hold behind the Humvee, via the rear cargo ramp, clutching onto his Maghooks.

Nor had they seen him slink down the right side of the Humvee and race across in front of it, tackling Aloysius Knight out of the way . . . while at the same time dragging the other remaining IG-88 commando to the ground in front of the speeding vehicle, causing it to bump over him instead.

Schofield and Knight fell against the side wall of the hold, right next to Gant.

Knight clutched his eyes. Schofield didn't even stop for breath.

He sliced open Gant's flex-cuffs, gave her the knife. 'Hey there, babe. Missed you in Afghanistan. Quickly, help me free the General.'

General Weitzman was still spreadeagled on the

bonnet of the Humvee, his wrists handcuffed to the car's mirrors.

Gant scooped up a set of keys from the run-over IG-88 man, found a handcuff key.

In the meantime, Schofield rose, just as beside him Cowboy emerged from the driver's door of the Humvee – while at the *forward* end of the vehicle, Schofield saw the British Intelligence guy remove a knife embedded in a wooden crate.

A bad guy sandwich.

Schofield extended his arms in both directions, raising his two Maghooks simultaneously. In the chaff-filled environment of the cargo hold, he'd only get one shot from each.

He fired.

The first shot didn't hit Cowboy – but it wasn't meant to. Rather, it hit the car door that Cowboy had been opening. From such close range, the Maghook thundered into the armoured door, banging it shut, knocking Cowboy back into the car.

The suit-wearing Intelligence man was hit square in the chest by the other Maghook. He just folded in half, his ribs cracked, and went crashing back into the crate behind him.

For her part, Gant was busy unlocking General Weitzman's left hand. The cuff around his wrist came free.

'Okay,' she said. 'Other wrist. Other side . . .'

But on the other side of the Humvee stood . . .

Rocko.

Just standing there. Towering above Weitzman's prone body.

Schofield appeared at Gant's side, locked eyes with Rocko.

'Take care of the General,' he said, not taking his eyes off the gigantic commando. 'And get ready for my signal.'

'What signal?'

But Schofield didn't answer her. He just crouched down and withdrew two of Knight's evil-looking shurikens from a dead body. Across the Humvee from him, Rocko did the same.

Then the two of them strode around to the area of open space behind the Humvee, a small space which adjoined the rear loading ramp and looked out over the wide blue sky beyond it.

They stood opposite each other for a moment – the tall and bulky Rocko, and the smaller, more evenly proportioned Schofield – each holding two four-pointed throwing blades in his hands.

And they engaged.

Flashes of silver, the clang of clashing knives.

Rocko lunged, Schofield fended. Rocko lashed, Schofield parried.

As Schofield and Rocko fought at the aft end of the cargo hold, Gant unclasped Weitzman's right handcuff, freeing the General but leaving the open cuff still attached to the side mirror. She slid Weitzman off the Humvee, rolled him to the floor.

All while the General mumbled incoherently: 'Oh, God, the code . . . the universal code . . . all right, all right, it does exist, but only a few people know it . . . It's based on a mathematical principle . . . and yes, I inserted it into Kormoran, but there was . . . there was another project involved . . . Chameleon . . .'

Schofield and Rocko danced around the back of the cargo hold, their shurikens flashing and clanging.

They came down the right-hand side of the Humvee

– towards Gant and Weitzman – Schofield leading the way, moving backwards, fending off Rocko's slashes.

'Gant!' Schofield called. 'You ready for the signal!'

'Sure! What is it!'

'This!'

And then, brilliantly, Schofield *caught* Rocko's next swing, and with lightning speed, he shifted his weight and slammed Rocko's knife-hand down into the bonnet of the Humvee, *right next to* the open handcuff that only moments before had bound Weitzman.

'Now!'

Gant responded instantly, dived up onto the bonnet of the Humvee and clasped the cuff around Rocko's knife-wrist.

Rocko's eyes boggled.

He was now shackled to the side mirror of the Humvee!

Schofield dived away from him, over toward General Weitzman on the floor.

'Sir! Are you okay?' he asked quickly, leaning close.

But the General was still babbling. 'Oh, no . . . it wasn't just Kormoran. It was Chameleon, too . . . oh God, Kormoran and Chameleon together. Boats and missiles. All disguised. *Christ* . . . But the Universal Disarm Code, it changes every week. At the moment, it's . . . the sixth . . . oh my God, the sixth m . . . m . . . mercen . . . mercen—'

A sudden whoosh. The flash of steel. And abruptly the General's head jolted slightly, a line of red appearing across his neck . . .

. . . and then, right in front of Schofield's eyes, General Ronson H. Weitzman's head tipped off his shoulders.

The head bounced on the floor, rolled to a stop at

Schofield's feet. After beheading, the human head actually lives for up to thirty seconds. As such, Weitzman's disembodied face stared gruesomely up at Schofield from the floor, eyelids fluttering for a few moments before, mercifully, the facial muscles at last relaxed and the head went still.

Schofield snapped to look up, and saw Demon Larkham's handsome young deputy, Cowboy, standing on the other side of the Humvee, brandishing a long-bladed machete, fresh blood dripping from its blade.

His eyes were wide with bloodthirsty madness, and he made to hurl the machete at Schofield—

—just as a hand gripped his wrist from behind and slammed it down on the bonnet of the Humvee, causing the machete to spring out of Cowboy's grasp, at the same time as this unseen assailant quickly snapped the Humvee's *other* handcuff around Cowboy's now-exposed wrist.

Cowboy spun: to see Aloysius Knight standing behind him, now wearing a new pair of amber-lensed glasses.

'Not bad, Cowboy. You remembered my Achilles heel.'

Then Knight grabbed the machete and smiled at the IG-88 assassin. 'And I remember yours. Your inability to fly.'

Knight then walked to the driver's door of the Humvee, leaned inside and shifted the car into reverse. He nodded to Schofield and Gant: 'Stand clear.'

Cowboy and Rocko – cuffed to opposite sides of the Humvee – stared at Knight in horror.

'Goodbye, boys.'

And with that, Knight stabbed the Humvee's gas pedal to the floor with the machete.

The Humvee shot off the mark, racing backwards, toward the open rear cargo ramp.

It hit the edge doing twenty, before it tipped off it, rear-end first, and to Cowboy and Rocko's absolute terror, dropped out of sight and fell 20,000 feet straight down.

After the Humvee had disappeared out the back door of the Hercules, Schofield rushed over to Gant and held her tightly in his arms.

Gant returned his grip, her eyes closed. Others might have cried at such a reunion, but not Gant. She felt the emotion of the moment, but she was not one to shed tears.

'What the hell is going on?' she asked when they separated.

'Bounty hunters,' Schofield said. 'My name is on a list of people who have to be exterminated by noon today, New York time. They grabbed you to get to me.'

He told Gant about his experience in Siberia and then in Afghanistan, about the bounty hunters he had met – Executive Solutions, the Hungarian, the Spetsnaz Skorpions and, of course, Demon Larkham's IG-88. He also showed her the bounty list.

'What about him?' Gant nodded at Knight as he disappeared inside the cockpit to disengage their plane from the tanker. 'Who is he?'

'He,' Schofield said, 'is my guardian angel.'

There came a pained groan from over by the wooden crates.

Schofield and Gant spun quickly . . .

. . . and saw one of the suit-wearing British agents lying on the floor, clutching his broken ribs. It was the man Schofield had hit in the chest with his Maghook.

They went over to him.

The suited man was wheezing desperately, coughing blood.

Schofield bent down, examined him. 'His ribs are smashed. Punctured lungs. Who is he?'

Gant said, 'I only caught part of it. He and the other suit were interrogating the General with some disinhibiting drug, asking him about the American Universal Disarm Code. They said Weitzman oversaw the code's incorporation into something called the Kormoran Project.'

'Is that so?' Schofield said. 'A disinhibiting drug.' He looked around the hold, saw a medical kit on the floor. It had spilled out some syringes, needles and serum bottles. He grabbed one of the serum bottles, checked its label.

'Then let's see how he handles a dose of his own medicine.'

Aloysius Knight returned from the cockpit to find the suit-wearing British agent seated up against the wall of the cargo hold, his sleeve rolled up, and with 200 mg of EA-617 coursing through his veins.

Knight touched Schofield on the shoulder.

'I've disengaged us from the tanker plane,' he said. 'We're currently on autopilot, staying on the course they already set: heading for a private airstrip in Brittany, on the French Atlantic coast. And Rufus just called. He's going to drop your people at an abandoned airfield about forty miles outside of London.'

'Good,' Schofield said, thinking of Book II and Mother heading for the Mossad's headquarters in London.

Then he turned his attention to the captured British agent.

After a few vain efforts to resist the disinhibiting drug, it soon emerged that the man's name was Charles Beaton and he was a member of MI-6, British Intelligence.

'This bounty hunt. What do you know about it?' Schofield asked.

'Nearly twenty million per head. Fifteen heads. And they want you all out of the picture by 12 noon today, New York time.'

'Who are *they*? Who's paying for all this?'

Beaton snorted derisively. '*They* go by many names. The Bilderberg Group. The Brussels Group. The Star Council. The Majestic-12. M-12. They are an elite group of private industrialists who rule this planet. Twelve of them. The richest men in the world, men who *own* governments, men who bring down entire economies, men who do whatever they want . . .'

Schofield leaned back, his eyes widening.

'O-*kay* . . .' Knight said drily.

'Give me names,' Schofield said.

'I don't know their names,' Beaton said. 'That's not my area. My area is the American military. All I know is that Majestic-12 exists and that it's bankrolling this bounty hunt.'

'All right, then. Do you know what they hope to achieve by staging this hunt?'

'No,' Beaton said. 'My job was to get the Universal Disarm Code from Weitzman and then give him to the bounty hunter, Larkham. To take advantage of this bounty hunt. I don't know about the hunt itself or Majestic-12's reasons for staging it.'

'So who at MI-6 does know?'

'Alec Christie. He's our man on the inside. He knows everything about Majestic-12 and presumably, this bounty hunt. But the problem is MI-6 doesn't know where Christie is any more. He disappeared two days ago.'

Christie.

Schofield remembered the name from the list:

```
2.  CHRISTIE, Alec P.          UK      MI-6
```

'But this Christie guy must have blown his cover,' he said, 'because Majestic-12 put him on the list as well.'

He tried a new angle. 'What are these Kormoran and Chameleon Projects that you were interrogating Weitzman about?'

Beaton winced, still trying to resist the drug. 'Kormoran is a US Navy project. Deep black. In World War II, the German Navy disguised some of their strike vessels as commercial freighters. One of these was called the *Kormoran*. We believe that the US Navy is doing the same thing but on a modern scale: building warships capable of launching intercontinental ballistic missiles, only these warships don't look like warships. They're disguised as supertankers and container ships.'

'Whoa,' Gant whispered.

'Okay. That's Kormoran,' Schofield said. 'What about the Chameleon Project?'

'I don't know about Chameleon.'

'You sure?'

Beaton groaned. 'We know it's linked to Kormoran, and we know it's big – it has the highest US security classification. But at this stage, we don't know exactly what Chameleon entails.'

Schofield frowned, thinking.

This was like building a jigsaw puzzle, piece by piece, until slowly a picture emerged. He had some pieces, but not the whole picture. Yet.

He said, 'So who does know, Mr Beaton? Where has MI-6 been getting all this top secret US information from?'

'The Mossad,' Beaton breathed. 'They have a field office in London at Canary Wharf. We managed to bug it for a few weeks last month. Trust me, the Mossad knows *everything*. They know about Majestic-12. They know about Kormoran and Chameleon. They know about every name on that list and why they are on it. They also know one other thing.'

'What's that?' Schofield said.

'The Mossad knows Majestic-12's plan for October the 26th.'

KING'S TOWER, CANARY WHARF, LONDON
26 OCTOBER, 1200 HOURS LOCAL TIME
(1300 HOURS IN FRANCE – 0700 HOURS E.S.T. USA)

Book II and Mother rode up the side of the 40-storey King's Tower inside a speeding glass elevator.

The Thames stretched out before them, brown and twisting. Old London receded to the horizon, veiled in rain.

The Canary Wharf district stood in stark contrast to the rest of London – a crisp clean steel-and-glass business district that boasted skyscrapers, manicured parks, and no less than the tallest building in Britain: the magnificent Canary Wharf Tower. While much of London was faded nineteenth-century Victorian, Canary Wharf was crystal-cut twenty-first-century futurism.

Book and Mother rose high into the grey London sky. Four other glass elevators ferried people up and down the side of the King's Tower, identical glass boxes rushing past them in either direction.

Book and Mother wore civilian clothes: suede jackets, boots, blue-denim jeans and turtleneck jumpers that covered their throat-mikes. Each had a Colt .45 pistol wedged into the back of their jeans.

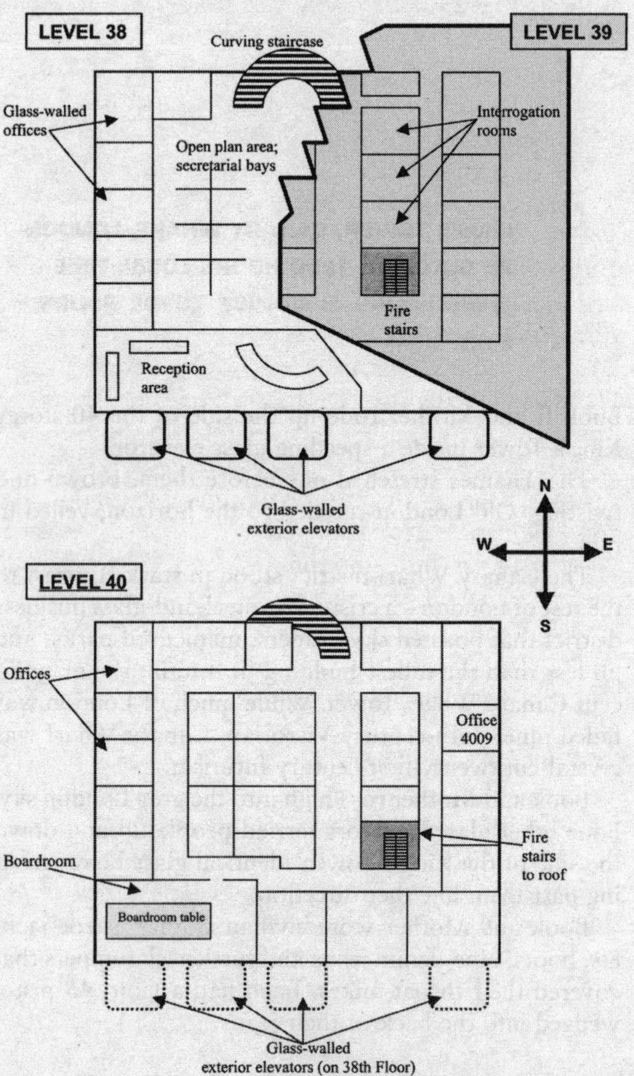
KING'S TOWER
CANARY WHARF, LONDON
LEVEL 38
LEVEL 39
Curving staircase
Glass-walled offices
Open plan area; secretarial bays
Interrogation rooms
Fire stairs
Reception area
Glass-walled exterior elevators
N
W
E
S
LEVEL 40
Offices
Office 4009
Fire stairs to roof
Boardroom
Boardroom table
Glass-walled exterior elevators (on 38th Floor)

A pretty young executive in a Prada suit stood in the lift with them, looking very small next to the broad-shouldered and shaven-headed Mother.

Mother inhaled deeply, then tapped the girl on the shoulder. 'I really love your perfume. What is it?'

'Issey Miyake,' the girl replied.

'I'll have to get some.' Mother smiled.

They'd made good time.

After entering British airspace under active stealth, Rufus had dropped them off at an abandoned airfield not far from London City Airport. From there they'd hitched a ride on a charter helicopter, piloted by an old friend of Rufus's. He'd dropped them at Canary Wharf's commercial heliport fifteen minutes later.

Ping.

Their elevator stopped on the 38th floor. Book II and Mother stepped out into the enormous reception area for Goldman, Marcus & Meyer, Lawyers. Goldman Marcus occupied the top three floors of the tower – the 38th, 39th and 40th floors.

It *looked* like the reception area of a big city law firm – plush, spacious, great view. And indeed to the casual visitor Goldman Marcus was a full-service legal provider.

Only this wasn't just a law firm.

In amongst its many offices, meeting rooms and open-plan areas, Goldman Marcus's offices contained three rooms on the 39th floor that all the lawyers were forbidden to enter – rooms that were kept for the sole and exclusive use of the Mossad, the notorious Israeli Secret Service.

*

The Mossad.

The most ruthless intelligence service in the world, protecting the most targeted nation in history: Israel.

No other nation has experienced such a continued threat of terrorism. No other nation has been surrounded by so many openly hostile enemies – Syria, Egypt, Jordan, Lebanon, not to mention the Palestinians inside its borders. No other nation has seen eleven of its Olympic athletes killed on international television.

So how has Israel dealt with this?

Easy. It finds out about foreign threats first.

The Mossad has people everywhere. It knows about international upheaval before anyone else does, and it acts according to an immovable policy of 'Israel First, Last, Always'.

1960. The kidnap of the Nazi war criminal Adolf Eichmann in Argentina.

1967. The pre-emptive strikes on Egyptian air bases during the Six Day War.

August 31, 1997. There had been a Mossad agent in the bar at the Ritz Hotel in Paris on the night Princess Diana died. He had been shadowing Henri Paul, Diana's driver.

It has even been said that the Mossad knew about the September 11 attacks on America before they happened – and *didn't* tell the Americans. Because it suited Israel to have the US enter the war on Islamist terrorism.

In global intelligence communities, there is one golden rule: the Mossad always knows.

'May I help you?' The receptionist's smile was polite.

'Yes,' Book II said. 'We'd like to speak to Benjamin Rosenthal, please.'

'I'm afraid there is no one here by that name.'

Book II didn't miss a beat. 'Then please call the Chairman of Partners and tell him that Sergeants Riley and Newman are here to see Major Rosenthal. Tell him we're here on behalf of Captain Shane Schofield of the United States Marines Corps.'

'I'm terribly sorry, sir, but—'

At that moment, as if by magic, the receptionist's phone rang and after a short whispered phone call, she said to Book: 'The Chairman is sending someone down to collect you.'

One minute later an internal door opened and a burly man in a suit appeared. Book and Mother both registered the Uzi-sized bulge under his jacket –

Ping.

An elevator arrived.

Ping.

Then another one.

Book II frowned, turned.

The doors to the two elevators opened—

—to reveal Demon Larkham and his ten-man IG-88 assault squad.

'Oh, *shit*,' Book II said.

They came charging out of the elevators, dressed in their charcoal-black battle uniforms, their high-tech Metal-Storm guns blazing.

Book and Mother flew over the reception desk together, just as the whole area around them was raked with whirring hypermachinegun fire.

The burly man at the internal door convulsed under the barrage of gunfire and fell. The receptionist took a bullet in the forehead and snapped backwards.

Demon's team rushed inside, one man lagging behind to take care of the two civilians who had dived over the reception desk.

He rounded the counter and—

—*blam!-blam!*—

—received two bullets in the face from two separate guns. Book and Mother leapt to their feet, pistols smoking.

'They're here for Rosenthal,' Book said. 'Come on!'

It was like following in the path of a tornado.

Book and Mother entered the main office area.

Men and women in suits lay draped over desks, their bodies riddled with bloody wounds, their workstations smashed.

Up ahead, the IG-88 force stormed through the open-plan office area, their MetalStorm guns blazing.

Glass shattered. Computer monitors exploded.

A security guard drew an Uzi from beneath his jacket – only to be cut down by hypervelocity MetalStorm bullets.

The IG-88 men raced up a beautiful curving internal staircase, up to the 39th floor.

Book and Mother gave chase.

They reached the top of the staircase just in time to see three members of the IG-88 team break away from the others and enter an interrogation room, where they promptly killed two senior Mossad men and dragged a third – a young man who could only be Rosenthal – from the room. Rosenthal was thirty-ish, olive-skinned and handsome; he wore an open-necked shirt and he looked tired beyond belief.

Book and Mother wasted no time. They bounded off

the stairs and took out the three bounty hunters, working perfectly as a pair – Book dropped the man on the left, Mother the one on the right, and both of them nailed the man in the middle, blowing him apart with their guns.

Rosenthal dropped to the floor.

Book and Mother raced to his side, scooped him up, draped his arms over their shoulders.

'You Rosenthal?' Book demanded. 'Benjamin Rosenthal?'

'Yes . . .'

'We're here to help you. Shane Schofield sent us.'

A glint of recognition appeared on Rosenthal's face. 'Schofield. From the list . . .'

Blam!

Mother dropped another IG-88 man as he emerged from the next room and saw them.

'Book!' she yelled. 'No time for chit-chat! We have to keep moving! You can debrief him as we run! Up the stairs! Now!'

They swept further up the internal staircase, heading for the 40th floor, running past a set of curving picture windows that looked out over London – before the view of the city was abruptly replaced by that of an evil-looking assault helicopter swinging into position, hovering right outside the windows, staring in at Book and Mother and Rosenthal!

It was a Lynx gunship, the British equivalent of a Huey, equipped with side-mounted TOW missiles and a six-barrelled mini-gun.

'*Go!*' Mother yelled, hauling them upward. '*Go-go-go-go-go!*'

The Lynx opened fire.

There came a cataclysmic shattering of glass as the

picture windows encasing the curving staircase collapsed under the weight of the helicopter's fire.

Glass rained down all around Book and Mother as they scampered up the stairs carrying Rosenthal between them, a whole section of the staircase itself falling away behind them, ripped clear from its mountings by the barrage of fire, just as they dived off it to the safety of the 40th floor.

Demon Larkham strode through the wreckage of the 39th floor, listening as reports came in over his headset radio.

'*—This is Airborne One. They're up on forty . Two contacts in civilian clothing. They appear to have Rosenthal with them—*'

'*—Airborne Two, landing on the roof now. Offloading second unit—*'

'*—This is Airborne Three. We're coming round the north-east corner. Heading for forty—*'

'*—This is Tech Team. Elevators are locked down. Four elevators are frozen on thirty-eight, the fifth is down in the lobby. No one's going anywhere now—*'

'Gentlemen,' Demon said, 'exterminate these pests. And get me Rosenthal.'

Seen from a distance, the three IG-88 Lynx choppers buzzing around the peak of the King's Tower looked like flies harassing a picnicker.

One had landed on the roof, while the other two prowled around the upper floors, peering in through the windows.

At the sound of the windows being blasted to oblivion, a few local businesses called the police.

Book II and Mother charged down a hallway on the 40th floor, dragging Benjamin Rosenthal with them.

'Talk to me!' Book said to Rosenthal as they ran. 'The list. Why are you and Schofield on it?'

Rosenthal heaved for breath. 'Majestic . . . Majestic-12 put us on it . . . I'm on the list because I know who the members of Majestic-12 are, and I can expose them when they carry out their plan.'

'And Schofield?'

'He's different. He's a very special individual. He's one of the few who passed the Cobra tests . . . one of only nine men in the world who can disarm CincLock-VII, the security system on the Chameleon missiles—'

Just then, a fire stairwell door *right next to them* burst open, revealing four IG-88 mercenaries brandishing MetalStorm rifles and green laser sights.

Book and Rosenthal had no time to react, but Mother did.

She pushed them round a nearby corner, into another corridor, while she herself dashed the other way down a long hallway, inches ahead of a wave of hypermachine-gun fire.

Book and Rosenthal ran northward down their corridor, burst into a small office branching off it.

Dead end.

'Shit!' Book yelled, racing over to the window and looking out just as a Lynx helicopter shoomed past.

And then, outside the window, he saw it.

The four IG-88 bounty hunters who had burst out of the fire stairwell had split into two pairs – two going after Book and Rosenthal, the other pair going after Mother.

The two commandos pursuing Book and Rosenthal saw them enter the side-office twenty yards down the corridor.

They approached the office's door, flanked it silently on either side. The door was marked '4009'.

'Tech Team, this is Sterling Five,' the senior commando whispered into his headset. 'I need a floor schematic. Office number four-zero-zero-niner.'

The response came back. *'It's a dead-end, Sterling Five. They've got nowhere to go.'*

The senior man nodded to the trooper beside him – and the junior trooper kicked open the door, blazing away with his MetalStorm rifle.

He hit nothing.

The office was empty.

Its single floor-to-ceiling window was *already* shattered, the pouring London rain sweeping in through it.

No Book.

No Rosenthal.

The two IG-88 men rushed to the broken window, looked down.

Nothing. Only the sheer glass side of the tower and a grassy park below.

Then they looked up – just as a mechanical whirring came to life above them – and they saw the steel underside of a window-washer's platform rising up the side of the building, heading for the roof.

Book and Rosenthal stood on the window-washer's platform as it rose quickly up the side of King's Tower.

The long rectangular platform hung from two sturdy winch-cranes that stuck out from the tower's roof.

Moments before their attackers had stormed the office, Book had blasted open the window, and with Rosenthal in front of him, leapt up and grabbed its catwalk.

He'd pushed Rosenthal up, and then hauled himself onto the platform, yanking his feet out of view just as the two IG-88 men had burst into the office.

A wave of hypercharged bullets chased Mother as she dashed westward down her hallway with two IG-88 bounty hunters on her tail.

Just as the bullets caught up with her, she dived sharply left, into an office – and found herself standing in a beautifully appointed boardroom.

It had a polished wooden floor, deep leather chairs, and the most gigantic boardroom table she had ever seen. It was easily thirty feet long.

'Fucking lawyers,' Mother breathed. 'Always over-compensating for their teeny-weeny dicks.'

It was a corner office, with floor-to-ceiling windows lining one side, providing a breathtaking view of London. The other side backed onto the exterior elevators.

Mother knew that her Colt pistol didn't stand a chance against the MetalStorm guns of the IG-88 men, so she waited behind the door.

Bang!

They kicked it in, rushed inside.

Mother shot the first man in the side of the head before he even saw her, turned her gun on the second man—

Click.

'Fuck!'

Out of ammo.

She crashtackled the second man instead, sending the two of them flying onto the boardroom table, the bounty hunter's MetalStorm rifle firing wildly in every direction.

The floor-to-ceiling windows of the boardroom took the brunt of the gunfire and spontaneously cracked into a million spiderwebs.

Mother grappled with her attacker on top of the boardroom table. He was a big guy, strong. He unsheathed a knife just as Mother did too and the two blades clashed.

Then, suddenly, as they fought, Mother caught sight of two shapes in the doorway.

Men.

But not IG-88 men.

Rather, two burly Israelis in suits, with Uzis slung over their shoulders and bloodstains on their shirts.

Mossad security men.

The two Israelis saw the fight taking place on the long boardroom table.

'Bounty hunters!' one of them spat.

'Come on!' the other yelled, looking back down the hallway. 'They're coming!'

The first man sneered at Mother and her attacker – then he quickly pulled a high-powered RDX grenade from his pocket, popped the cap and threw it into the boardroom.

Then he and his partner dashed off.

Still fending off her attacker's blows with her knife, Mother saw the grenade fly into the room in a kind of detached slow motion.

It bounced on the floor, disappearing underneath the gigantic table. Mother heard the unmistakable sound of it clunking against one of the table's tree-trunk-sized legs.

And then it detonated.

The blast was monstrous.

Despite its solidity, the corridor-end of the massive table just disintegrated, shattering instantly into a thousand splinters.

As for the rest of the table – still a good 25 feet long – something very different happened.

The concussive force of the grenade *lifted* the elongated table clear off the floor and – like a railroad car being shunted forward on its tracks – sent it sliding at considerable speed down the length of the boardroom, *toward* the bullet-cracked windows at the western end of the room.

Mother saw it coming an instant before it happened.

The table exploded through the cracked glass windows, blasting through them like a battering ram, and shot out into the sky, forty storeys up.

Then with a sickening lurch, the table tipped downwards, and Mother suddenly found herself sliding – fast, down the length of the table, rain pounding against her face – toward 400 feet of empty sky.

It looked totally bizarre: the elongated boardroom table jutting out from the top floor of the tower.

The table tilted sharply – passing through 45 degrees, then steeper – with the two tiny figures of Mother and the IG-88 commando sliding down its length.

Then – completely without warning – the falling table jolted to a halt.

Its uppermost edge had hit the *ceiling* of the 40th floor and wedged against it, while two of its thick legs had locked against the *floor* right on the precipice – causing the whole table to stop suddenly, suspended at a vertiginous angle forty storeys above the ground!

Mother slid fast, before at the very last moment she jammed her knife deep into the surface of the table – and using the knife's brass fingerholes as a handgrip, swung to a halt, hanging from the embedded knife, her feet dangling off the lower edge of the almost-vertical table.

Her attacker wasn't as quick-thinking.

In an attempt to get a handhold, he'd dropped his knife as they'd fallen. As it turned out, he hadn't been able to find a handhold, but luckily for him he'd been *above* Mother as the table had burst out through the window. As such, he'd fallen into her, his feet slamming into her embedded knife.

He now hung above her, one foot crushing her knife-hand, smiling.

Gripping the edges of the table with his hands, he started kicking her fingers, hard.

Mother clenched her teeth, held on grimly despite his blows, the brass fingerholes of her knife deflecting some of them.

And then she heard the noise.

Thump-thump-thump-thump-thump-thump . . .

The sound of helicopter rotors.

She glanced around and saw a Lynx chopper hovering *right beside her* like a giant flying hornet.

'Oh, fuck . . .' she moaned.

The IG-88 man above her waved to the chopper pilot, directing him to go down, *below* them.

The pilot complied and the chopper swung below Mother, its speed-blurred rotor blades forming a hazy white circle beneath her dangling feet.

Then the bounty hunter above her resumed his kicking, only harder.

Crack!

She heard one of her fingers break.

'You mother*fucker*!' she yelled.

He kicked again.

The rotor blades roared like a buzzsaw ten feet below Mother's boots.

Her attacker raised his foot for one last blow. He brought it down hard—

—just as Mother did a most unexpected thing.

She withdrew the knife from the table, causing *both of them* to slide quickly downward, off the table's lower edge, toward the blurring blades of the helicopter!

Her attacker couldn't believe it.

Without the knife to lean on, he rocketed downward, sliding off the lower edge of the boardroom table!

They slid off the bottom end of the table together – but unlike her attacker, Mother had been prepared. As she went off the edge, she stabbed her knife into the underside of the table, and swung in underneath it, her fall halted.

The IG-88 man shot right past her, off the edge of the table and out into space . . .

. . . and the world went slow as Mother watched his horrified face – eyes wide, mouth open – falling, falling, dropping away from her.

Then he hit the rotor blades – *splat-choo!* – and his entire human shape just disappeared, spontaneously erupting into a star-shaped burst of blood.

A wash of red liquid splattered the windscreen of the chopper and the Lynx peeled away from the building.

Mother didn't even have time to sigh with relief.

For just then, as she hung from the downward-pointing boardroom table, pelted by the London rain, *the whole table shifted slightly*.

A sudden jolt.

Downward.

Mother snapped to look up: saw that the legs pinioning the table to the 40th floor were buckling.

The table was going to fall.

'Oh, damn it all to fucking hell!' she yelled to the sky. 'I am not going to die!'

She gauged her position.

She was at the corner of the building – the south-west corner – on the western side.

Just around the corner, slightly below her, she could

see one of the glass elevators, stopped on the 38th floor on the southern face of the building.

'Okay,' she said to herself. 'Stay calm. What would the Scarecrow do?'

Maghook, she thought.

She drew her Maghook, aimed it up at the interior ceiling of the 40th floor, and fired.

Nothing happened.

The Maghook didn't fire.

Its trigger just clicked and its barrel emitted a weak fizzing noise. It was out of gas propellant.

'Oh, come on!' Mother yelled. 'That never happens to the Scarecrow!'

Then suddenly the table lurched again, dropped another two feet.

Mother started unspooling the Maghook manually – with her teeth – muttering as she did so. 'Not fair. Not fair. Not *fucking* fair . . .'

The table teetered on the edge of the 40th floor, its legs groaning under the weight, about to snap –

Mother felt she had enough rope and with her free hand, hurled the Maghook's grappling hook up at the 40th floor.

It landed on the edge of the shattered window sill, its claws catching . . .

. . . just as the table tipped wholly out of the window . . .

. . . and Mother let go of her knife, swung away from the falling boardroom table . . .

. . . and the table fell through the rainy sky, all twenty-five feet of it dropping down the side of the building . . .

. . . while Mother swung on her rope, swooping around the corner of the building, before she slammed into the glass wall of the elevator just around the corner, and grabbed hold of its roof rim.

Seven whole seconds later, the gigantic boardroom table of Goldman, Marcus & Meyer hit the sidewalk and smashed into a billion tiny pieces.

Book and Rosenthal arrived at the roof on the window-washer's platform.

They ducked behind an exhaust stack, peered out to see one of Demon Larkham's Lynx helicopters resting on the rooftop helipad, it rotors turning, veiled in the pouring rain.

'Keep talking,' Book said to Rosenthal. 'This Majestic-12 wrote the list. And they want Schofield dead because . . .'

'Because of the Cobra tests,' Rosenthal said. 'Because *he passed* the Cobra tests. Although in NATO they were called something else: Motor Neuron Rapidity of Response tests. "Cobra" was the Russian name.'

'Motor Neuron Rapidity of Response?' Book II said. 'You mean reflexes.'

'Yes. Exactly,' Rosenthal said. 'It's all about reflexes. Superfast reflexes. The reflexes of the men on that list are the best in the world. *They passed the Cobra tests*, and only someone who passed the Cobra tests can disarm the CincLock-VII missile security system, and CincLock-VII is at the core of Majestic-12's plan. That's why Majestic-12 needs to eliminate them.'

'A missile security system . . .'

'Yes, yes, but don't be fooled. This bounty hunt is but one element of Majestic-12's larger plan.'

'And what is that plan?'

'Smashing the existing world order. Creating world-wide warfare. Scorching the earth so that it can regrow afresh,' Rosenthal said. 'Listen, I have a whole file on this downstairs. The Mossad has been debriefing me on it for the last two days. It's a file on this bounty hunt, on Majestic-12, its members, and, most importantly, what its overall plan is—'

Rosenthal's head exploded. Burst like a blood-filled water balloon.

There was no warning.

Rosenthal's face was simply ripped to pieces by a lethal twenty-round burst from a MetalStorm rifle somewhere behind Book II.

Book spun—

—and saw Demon Larkham himself standing in the doorway to the fire stairs, thirty yards away, his MetalStorm rifle pressed against his shoulder.

Book looked down at Rosenthal, bloodied and broken. The Mossad man would tell no more tales – not without his face.

And so Book ran.

For the helicopter parked nearby, his pistol up and firing.

The glass wall of the elevator shattered and Mother swung inside it.

She was now on the south face of the tower, on the 38th floor. She saw the other glass elevators sitting silently in position, level with her own.

If the elevators were numbered 1-through-5 going across the face of the building, then Elevators 1, 2, 3 and 5 were stopped on Level 38. A gap existed where the fourth elevator should have been. It must have been on a lower floor. Mother stood in Number 1, on the far left-hand side of the southern face.

She hammered the 'DOOR OPEN' button.

It was like standing in a fishbowl and Mother knew that the Lynx helicopter that had terrorised her before would come searching for her soon and she didn't want to be a sitting duck when it di—

Thump-thump-thump-thump-thump-thump . . .

The Lynx.

Mother turned.

It was right there!

Hovering just out from her glass elevator, off to the western side, seemingly staring at her.

Mother kept hitting DOOR OPEN. 'Damn it, fuck! Is this button actually wired to anything?'

And then she saw the puff of smoke from one of the Lynx's side-mounted missile pods.

They were firing a missile at her!

A TOW missile blasted out of the pod, carving a horizontal line *straight at* Mother's glass elevator.

The elevator doors started to open.

The missile roared toward Mother's eyes.

Mother squeezed through the doors and dived out of the lift just as the TOW missile pierced her elevator's shattered western wall, entering it from the side, its superhot tail-flame charring the whole interior of the elevator before – *clash!* – it shot out the other side and rocketed into the next glass elevator beside it.

The sight was truly amazing.

The TOW missile shot across the southern face of the King's Tower, blasting through *all four* of the glass elevators parked there – *clash!-clash!-clash!-clash!* – causing sequential explosions of glass as it penetrated each lift's walls, one after the other – before in a final glorious shower of glass, it shot out of the last elevator and peeled off into the Thames where it exploded in a gigantic geyser of spray.

For her part, Mother landed in a clumsy heap inside the reception area on the 38th floor, the door of her glass elevator open behind her.

Lying flat on the floor, she looked up.

And saw four IG-88 bounty hunters standing in the destroyed reception area, right in front of her. They looked just as shocked to see her as she was to see them.

'Talk about out of the frying pan . . .' Mother breathed.

The IG-88 men whipped up their MetalStorm rifles.

Mother pounced to her feet and leapt in the only direction she could: back out onto her elevator.

Into the elevator, ducking behind its control panel just as a wave of hypermachinegun fire rushed in through the open doorway.

Rain and wind whipped all around Mother, the semi-destroyed elevator now little more than an open-air viewing platform that looked out over London.

Mother looked across the southern face of the tower.

The three other glass elevators faced her, lined up in a row, their glass walls all shattered by the TOW.

'Live or die, Mother,' she said aloud. 'Fuck it. Die.'

And so she ran.

Thirty-eight floors up, charging hard, across the southern face of the building, leaping across the three-foot gaps between the semi-destroyed elevators.

As soon as she landed on the second elevator, the Lynx helicopter returned, swooping in fast, now firing

with its mini-gun, razing the side of the building with a storm of bullets.

But Mother kept running, outstripping the chopper's brutal rain of fire by centimetres, hurdling over onto the third elevator platform.

The gap where Elevator Number 4 should have been yawned before her.

Mother didn't miss a step.

The gap was wide – twelve feet – but she jumped anyway, diving forward, arms outstretched, thirty-eight storeys up, hoping to catch the floor of the fifth and final elevator with her hands.

No dice.

She knew as soon as she jumped that she wasn't going to make it.

Her hands missed the floor of the fifth elevator by inches and Mother dropped below it.

But the clawed grappling hook of the Maghook in her hand didn't miss the edge of the elevator.

The damn Maghook might not have been working any more, but by holding its hook in her outstretched hand, Mother had added another twelve inches to her reach.

Which was just what she needed.

The steel claws of the hook caught the floor of the elevator and Mother swung to a halt beneath it. She had just started climbing up into it when –

Thump-thump-thump-thump-thump-thump . . .

The Lynx.

It was back. Hovering menacingly in front of her as she hung from the destroyed elevator's floor. A second IG-88 Lynx chopper swooped in behind it, checking out the action.

This time the Lynx was so close that Mother could see the pilot's smiling face.

He waved at her, then gripped his gun trigger.

Hanging from the elevator platform, dead for all money, Mother just shook her head.

'No . . .'

The Lynx's gunbarrels began to roll, just as another glimpse of movement caught Mother's eye – a grey smoketrail shooting through the air behind the Lynx – a *missile* smoketrail that seemed to come from . . .

The second Lynx helicopter.

The missile slammed into the Lynx that had been threatening Mother.

A colossal explosion rocked the air, and in the blink of an eye the Lynx was gone. In the face of the blast wave, it was all Mother could do to hold on.

The wreckage of the first Lynx tumbled down the side of the tower – flaming, smoking.

It landed on a grassy strip at the base of the tower with a massive metal-crushing *whump!*

Mother looked over at the second Lynx helicopter, the one that had shot its buddy out of the sky . . . and saw its pilot.

Book II.

His voice came over her earpiece. '*Hey there. I picked this baby up on the roof. Unfortunately, the pilot was a reluctant seller. I was wondering where you'd got to.*'

'Ha-de-fucking-ha, Book,' Mother said, hauling herself up into the fifth elevator. 'How about getting me off this damn tower.'

'*Be happy to. But can you get something for me first?*'

Mother charged through a corridor on the 39th floor, leading with her Colt.

The place was a mess. Bullet holes lined the walls. Anything made of glass had been shattered.

If the IG-88 team was still here, they weren't showing themselves.

'*It's back near that internal staircase,*' Book's voice said in her ear. '*The room where we found Rosenthal. It must be some kind of interrogation facility.*'

'Got it,' Mother said.

She could see the doorway near the top of the curving stairs, hurried into it.

She was confronted by a two-way mirror that looked into an adjacent interrogation room. Two video cameras peered through the mirror. Thick manila folders and two digital video tapes lay on a table nearby.

'It's an interrogation centre, all right,' Mother said. 'I got files. I got DV tapes. What do you want?'

'*All of it. Everything you can carry. Plus anything with Majestic-12 or CincLock-VII on it. And grab the tapes, including any that are still in the cameras.*'

Mother grabbed a silver Samsonite suitcase lying on the floor and stuffed it with the files and digital video tapes. The two cameras also had tapes in them, so she grabbed them, too.

And then she was out.

Out the door and up the fire stairs to the roof.

She hit the roof running, dashed out into the rain, just as Book landed his Lynx on it. She climbed inside and the chopper lifted off, leaving the smoking ruins of the King's Tower smouldering in its wake.

OFFICES OF THE DEFENSE INTELLIGENCE AGENCY, SUB-LEVEL 3, THE PENTAGON
26 OCTOBER, 0700 HOURS LOCAL TIME
(1200 HOURS IN LONDON)

Dave Fairfax's boss caught him as he was leaving his office to go to St John's Hospital and find Dr Thompson Oliphant.

'And just where do you think you're going, Fairfax?' His name was Wendel Hogg and he was an asshole. A big guy, Hogg was ex-Army, a two-time veteran of war in Iraq, a fact which he never failed to tell people about.

The thing was, Hogg was stupid. And in the tradition of stupid managers worldwide, he (a) clung rigidly and inflexibly to rules, and (b) despised talented people like David Fairfax.

'I'm going out for coffee,' Fairfax said.

'What's wrong with the coffee here?'

'I've tasted hydrofluoric acid that was better than the coffee here.'

Just then, a small waif-like young woman entered the office. She was the mail clerk, a quiet mousy girl named Audrey. Fairfax's eyes lit up at the sight of her – unfortunately, so did Hogg's.

'Hey, Audrey,' Fairfax said, smiling.

'Hi, Dave,' Audrey replied shyly. Others might have said she was plain, but Fairfax thought she was beautiful.

Then Hogg said loudly, 'Thought you said you were leaving, Fairfax. Hey, while you're doing a Starbucks run, why don't you get us a couple of grande frappacinos. And make it snappy, will ya.'

A million witty retorts passed through Fairfax's brain, but instead he just sighed. 'Whatever you say, Wendel.'

'*Hey*,' Hogg barked. 'You will address me as Sergeant Hogg or Sergeant, young man. I didn't take a bullet in Eye-raq to be called *Wendel* by some spineless little keyboard-tapper like you, Fairfax. 'Cause when the time comes, boy, to stand up and stare into the enemy's eyeballs,' – he threw a cocksure grin at Audrey – 'who would you want holding the gun, you or me?'

Fairfax's face reddened. 'I'd have to say you, Wendel.'

'Damn straight.'

And with an embarrassed nod to Audrey, Fairfax left the office.

EMERGENCY WARD, ST JOHN'S HOSPITAL, ARLINGTON, USA
26 OCTOBER, 0715 HOURS

Fairfax entered the ER of St John's, went over to the reception counter.

It was quiet at this time of the morning. Five people sat slumped like zombies in the waiting area.

'Hi, my name is David Fairfax. I'm here to see Dr Thompson Oliphant.'

The desk nurse chewed bubble gum lazily. 'Just a second. *Dr Oliphant!* Someone here to see you!'

A second nurse appeared from one of the curtained-off bed-bays. 'Glenda, shhh. He's out back catching some shut-eye. I'll go get him.'

The second nurse disappeared down a back hallway.

As she did so, an exceedingly tall black man stepped up to the reception counter beside Fairfax.

He had deep dark skin and the high sloping forehead common to the inhabitants of southern Africa. He wore big fat Elvis sunglasses and a tan trenchcoat.

The Zulu.

'Good morning,' the Zulu said stiffly. 'I would like to see Dr Thompson Jeffrey Oliphant, please.'

Fairfax tried not to look at the bounty hunter – tried not to betray the fact that his heart was now beating very very fast.

Tall and lanky, the Zulu was gigantic – the size of a professional basketball player. The top of Fairfax's head was level with his chest.

The desk nurse popped a bubble-gum bubble. 'Geez, old Tommy's popular this morning. He's out back, sleeping. Someone's just gone to get him.'

At that moment, a bleary-eyed doctor appeared at the end of the long 'Authorised Personnel Only' corridor.

He was an older guy: grey-haired, wrinkled face. He wore a white labcoat and he rubbed his eyes as he emerged from a side room putting on his glasses.

'Dr Oliphant?' the Zulu called.

'Yes?' the old doctor said as he came closer.

Fairfax was the first to see the weapon appear from under the Zulu's tan trenchcoat.

It was a Cz-25, one of the crudest submachine-guns in the world. It looked like an Uzi only meaner – the ugly twin brother – with a long forty-round magazine jutting out of its pistol grip.

The Zulu whipped up the gun, levelled it at Oliphant, and oblivious to the presence of at least seven witnesses, pulled the trigger.

Standing right next to the big assassin, Fairfax did the only thing he could think to do.

He lashed out with his right hand, punching the gun sideways, causing its initial burst to strafe a line of bullet holes along the wall next to Oliphant's head.

People ducked.

Nurses screamed.

Oliphant dived to the floor.

The Zulu backhanded Fairfax, sending him crashing into a nearby janitor's trolley.

Then the Zulu walked – just walked – around the reception desk and into the staff-only corridor, toward Oliphant, his Cz-25 extended.

He fired ruthlessly.

The nurses scattered out of the way.

Oliphant scrambled on his hands and knees into a supply room that branched off the corridor, bullet-sparks raking the ground at his toes.

Fairfax lay among the shattered janitorial supplies from the trolley he'd slammed into. He saw a bag of white powder that had been on the trolley: 'ZEOLITE-CHLORINE – INDUSTRIAL-STRENGTH CLEANING AGENT – AVOID SKIN CONTACT'. He grabbed it.

Then he leapt to his feet and ran forward – while everyone else ran *away* from the action – and peered down into the staff-only corridor where he saw the Zulu stop in front of an open doorway and raise his Cz-25.

Fairfax hurled the bag of powdered chlorine through the air. It hit the Zulu square in the side of the head and exploded in a puff of white dust.

The Zulu screamed, staggering away from the doorway, swatting at his powder-covered head, trying desperately to remove the burning zeolite on his skin. His Elvis sunglasses now bore a layer of white powder on their lenses. His flesh had started bubbling.

Fairfax dashed forward, slid on the floor underneath the Zulu, peered in through the doorway – and saw Dr Thompson Oliphant cowering underneath some supply shelves, covering his face.

'Dr Oliphant! Listen to me! My name is David Fairfax. I'm with the Defense Intelligence Agency. I'm not much of a hero, but I'm all you've got right now! If you want to get through this, you'd better come with me!'

Oliphant extended his hand and Fairfax grasped it, lifting the doctor to his feet. Then they ducked under the swatting Zulu and raced out past the reception counter into the early morning air.

The automatic sliding doors opened for them – just as the doors themselves shattered under Cz-25 bullet-fire.

The Zulu was moving again and coming after them with a vengeance.

An ambulance was parked right outside the Emergency Ward's entrance.

'Get in!' Fairfax yelled, throwing open the driver's side door. Oliphant jumped in the passenger side.

Fairfax fired her up and hit the gas. The ambulance peeled off the mark, but not before the two of them heard an ominous *whump!* from somewhere at the back of the vehicle.

'Uh-oh . . .' Fairfax said.

In his side mirror he saw the tall dark figure of the Zulu standing on the rear bumper, his hands clinging to the ambulance's roof rails.

The Zulu was on the ambulance!

The ambulance's tyres squealed as Fairfax gunned it out of the undercover turning bay and into the parking lot proper.

He bounced the white van over a gutter and a nature strip hoping to dislodge the Zulu from its bumper. The ambulance rocked wildly as it jounced down another gutter and Fairfax was certain that no one could have held on after all that.

But then the rear doors of the ambulance were hurled

open from the outside and the Zulu stepped into the rear compartment!

'Shit!' Fairfax yelled.

The Zulu no longer had his Cz-25, having discarded it in favour of holding onto the ambulance with both hands.

But now, safely inside the speeding ambulance, he withdrew a long-bladed machete from his trenchcoat and stared at Fairfax and Oliphant with blazing fury in his bloodshot eyes.

Fairfax eyed the machete. 'Oh, man . . .'

The Zulu swept forward through the rear compartment, clambering quickly over a locked-down wheeled gurney.

Fairfax had to do something fast.

He saw the road up ahead divide – one lane heading left for the exit, the other sweeping to the right, up a curving concrete ramp that gave access to the hospital's multi-storey parking lot.

He chose right, and yanked the steering wheel hard over, hitting the gas as they charged up the spiralling ramp – the centrifugal force of their high-speed turn causing the Zulu in the back to lose his balance and slam against the outer wall, his forward progress momentarily halted.

But they could only go up for so long, Fairfax thought. The parking structure was only six storeys high.

He had five floors to think of something else.

At the same time, someone else was watching the ambulance's wild rise up the tightly curving ramp from across the street.

A strikingly beautiful woman with long legs, muscular shoulders and cool Japanese eyes.

Her real name was Alyssa Idei, but in the bounty hunting world she was known simply as the Ice Queen. She'd already collected the bounty on Damien Polanski and now she was after Oliphant.

She wore only black leather – tight hipster pants, biker jacket and killer boots. Her long black hair was tied back. Under her jacket, tucked into a pair of shoulder holsters, were two high-tech Steyr SPP machine pistols.

She started up her Honda NSX and pulled out from the kerb, and headed for the multi-storey parking lot.

Tyres squealing, Fairfax's ambulance wound its way up the curving ramp, its open rear doors flailing wildly.

They hit Level 3.

Three floors to go before they reached the roof – before the Zulu in the back would be able to move freely again.

But now Fairfax knew what he was going to do.

He was going to drive the ambulance off the top level of the parking structure – leaping out of it at the last moment with Oliphant, leaving the Zulu inside.

'Dr Oliphant!' he yelled, glancing back at the Zulu. 'Listen up and listen fast because I don't know if we'll get another chance to talk about this! You're a target in an international bounty hunt!'

'What!'

'You have an eighteen-million-dollar price on your head! I think it has something to do with a NATO study that you did back in 1996 with a guy named Nicholson at USAMRMC! The MNRR Study. What was that study about?'

Oliphant frowned. He was still in shock, and trying to assimilate this line of questioning with the ongoing attempt on his life was hard.

'MNRR? Well, it was . . . it was . . .'

The ambulance continued its dizzying ascent.

Level 4 and rising.

'It was . . . it was like the Soviet Cobra tests, a test of—'

As Oliphant spoke, Fairfax stole a glance back at the Zulu – and suddenly saw that the demonic figure of the bounty hunter was far closer than he had expected him to be and was now *swinging his machete right at Fairfax's head!*

No defence.

No escape.

The machete whistled forward.

And slammed into the headrest of Fairfax's seat, its steel blade stopping – dead – a millimetre from Fairfax's right ear.

Jesus!

But now the Zulu was on them. Somehow, he had managed to manoeuvre his way forward, despite the powerful inertia of the turning-and-rising ambulance.

Level 5 . . .

And now Fairfax's eyes narrowed, focused.

He slammed his foot down on the gas pedal.

The ambulance responded, increased its speed.

They hit the top of the curving ramp doing 40, the ambulance almost tipping over sideways, all-but travelling on two wheels.

Then they raced out onto the rooftop – at this hour, it was completely empty – and Fairfax straightened the steering wheel and the ambulance, coming out of its hard turn, bounced back down onto all four wheels, the abrupt change of direction causing the Zulu to fly to the *other* side of the rear compartment and bang into the wall . . . leaving his machete wedged in Fairfax's head-rest.

Fairfax gunned the ambulance, aimed it directly at the edge of the deserted rooftop parking area.

'Dr Oliphant! Get ready to jump!' he yelled.

They rocketed toward the edge of the roof, toward the pathetic little fence erected there.

Fairfax shifted in his seat. 'Get ready . . . on three. One . . . two . . . thr—'

The Zulu lunged into the driver's seat from behind and grabbed both Fairfax *and* Oliphant!

Fairfax was stunned.

Now none of them could get out!

He saw the edge of the rooftop rushing at him at phenomenal unavoidable speed, so in desperation he yanked the steering wheel hard over and for what it was worth, slammed on the brakes.

The ambulance fishtailed, skidded wildly.

And so rather than hitting the fence head-on as Fairfax had intended it to, it did a screeching four-wheel skid, spinning a full 180 degrees so that instead, it slammed into the rooftop's fence *rear-end first*.

The ass end of the ambulance blasted through the fence and with Fairfax, Oliphant and the Zulu inside it, the whole ambulance went shooting off the edge of the roof, six storeys above the world, and fell—

—only about ten feet.

As the backward-travelling ambulance passed over the edge of the roof and blasted through the little fence, its front bumper bar caught hold of a surviving fence post and anchored the ambulance to the roof.

As such, the ambulance's fall was cut dramatically

short. No sooner was most of its bulk over the edge than the whole vehicle jolted to a sudden halt.

And so now it hung vertically from the top floor of the parking structure, hanging by its nose, its rear doors flailing open beneath it.

Inside the ambulance, everything that should have been horizontal was now vertical.

Oliphant still sat in the passenger seat, only now facing upwards, his back pressing into his seat.

Fairfax hadn't been so lucky.

As they had hit the fence, he had been yanked from his seat by the Zulu and hurled into the rear section of the ambulance.

But then the ambulance had gone vertical, sending both of them tumbling ass over head.

And with its rear doors swinging open beneath them – revealing the six-storey drop – Fairfax and the Zulu had clutched at anything they could find.

The big Zulu had grabbed the locked-down gurney. Fairfax had clutched a shelf on the wall.

And so they hung there, inside the vertical ambulance, with a clear drop through the vehicle's rear doors yawning beneath them.

But the Zulu wasn't finished.

He *still* wanted to get to Oliphant.

He stretched upward, reaching for his machete, still wedged in the headrest of the driver's seat.

'No!' Fairfax yelled, lunging forward.

But he was too late.

Hanging onto the wheeled gurney with one hand, the Zulu lashed his fingers around the machete's grip and yanked it free.

He turned his bloodshot eyes on Fairfax, and his mouth widened into a sinister yellow-toothed grin.

'Bye-bye!' he said, drawing the machete back for the final blow.

'Whatever you say, asshole,' Fairfax said, seeing it.

The Zulu swung.

The blade whistled towards Fairfax's head.

Just as Fairfax lashed out with his foot and kicked open the locks that held the gurney in place.

The response was instantaneous.

The wheeled gurney dropped like a stone, out through the open doors at the bottom of the vertical ambulance . . .

. . . with the Zulu on it!

Fairfax watched as the big man fell with the gurney, his wide eyes receding to specks as he fell and fell and fell.

The gurney flipped on the way down, causing the Zulu to hit the ground first. He impacted against the concrete with a sickening thud, his internal organs shattering. But he was still alive.

Not for long. A second later, the leading edge of the gurney came slamming down against his head, crushing it like a nut.

It took a few minutes for Fairfax and Oliphant to negotiate their way out of the vertical ambulance, but they made it by climbing out through the front windshield and hauling themselves up over the bonnet.

The two of them slumped on the roof of the parking structure, breathless.

Fairfax peered down at the ambulance still hanging from the edge of the rooftop.

For his part, Oliphant was jabbering, overwhelmed with shock:

'It stood for . . . Motor Neuron . . . Motor Neuron Rapidity of Response . . . we were testing American and British soldiers for response times, response times to certain stimuli . . . all kinds of stimuli: visual, aural, touch . . . *reflexes* . . . it was all about reflexes.

'Christ, we must have tested over three hundred soldiers, and they all had different response times . . . some were super fast, others clumsy and slow.

'But our superiors never told us what the study was for . . . of course, we all had a theory. Most of us thought it was for commando-team selection, but some of the techs said it was for a new security system, some *amazing* new security system for ballistic missiles called CincLock . . . and then all of a sudden, the study was cancelled, the official reason being that the Department of Defense had canned the primary project, but we all thought it was because they'd got the information they needed—'

Shwat!

Still looking down at the ambulance, Fairfax heard the noise behind him.

He turned.

To see the now-headless body of Dr Oliphant kneeling beside him, swaying in position before – *whump* – it dropped to the concrete floor.

Standing over the corpse, holding a glistening short-bladed samurai sword in one tight fist, was a young leather-clad Japanese woman.

Alyssa Idei.

Bounty hunter.

She grabbed Oliphant's head by the hair and held it casually by her side. Then in one fluid movement, she sheathed her sword and drew one of her Steyr machine pistols and pointed it at Fairfax.

She gazed at him over the gun. Eyes unblinking. Ice cold.

But then, strangely, a confused frown creased her perfect features, and she jerked her chin at Fairfax.

When it came her voice was as smooth as honey. 'You are not a bounty hunter, are you?'

'No . . .' Fairfax said tentatively. 'No, I'm not.'

'And yet you battle with the Zulu. Why?'

'I . . . I've a friend on your bounty list. I want to help him.'

Alyssa Idei seemed to have trouble grasping this. 'This man was your friend?'

'Well, not this guy. One of the other guys on the list.'

'And you do battle with the Zulu to help your friend?'

'Yes,' Fairfax said. 'I do.'

Her frown vanished, replaced by genuine curiosity. 'What is your name, friend-helper?'

'Er, David Fairfax.'

'Fair Fax. David Fair Fax,' she said slowly, rolling his name around in her mouth. 'I do not see such displays of loyalty often, Mr Fair Fax.'

'No?' Fairfax said.

She eyed him sexily. 'No. Your friend must be quite a man to inspire this bravery in you. Such bravery, Mr Fair Fax, is rare. It is also alluring. Intoxicating.'

Fairfax gulped. 'Oh.'

Alyssa said, 'And so I shall let you live. So that you may further help your friend – and so that we might meet again in fairer circumstances. But understand this, David Fair Fax, if we find ourselves together again, in a situation where you are protecting your friend, you will receive no such favour again.'

Then she holstered her gun and spun on the spot, sliding her lithe body into her low-slung sports car.

And she was gone.

Fairfax just watched the high-speed Honda whiz out of sight, shooting down the ramp, the headless body of Thompson Oliphant lying on the concrete beside him, the sun rising in the distance, and the sound of police sirens cutting through the dawn.

FOURTH ATTACK

FRANCE–ENGLAND

26 OCTOBER, 1400 HOURS (FRANCE)

E.S.T. (NEW YORK, USA) 0800 HOURS

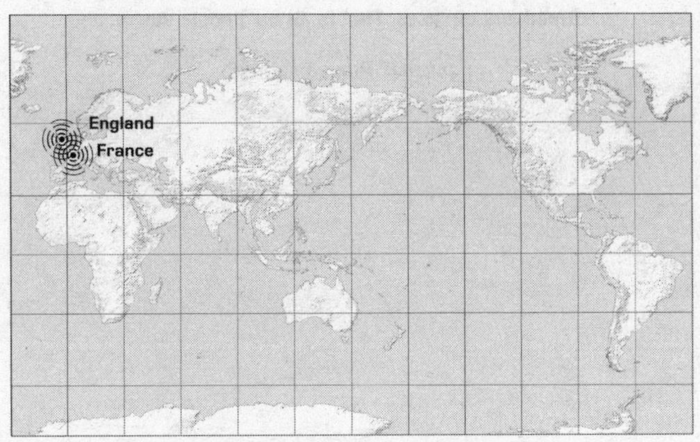

We live in a double world: carnival on the surface, consolidation underneath, where it counts.

From: *No Logo* by Naomi Klein

(HARPER COLLINS, LONDON, 2000)

Bread and circuses. That is all the people desire.

Juvenal, Roman satirist

FORTERESSE DE VALOIS, BRITTANY, FRANCE
26 OCTOBER, 1400 HOURS LOCAL TIME
(0800 HOURS E.S.T. USA)

The three tiny figures crossed the mighty stone bridge that connected the Forteresse de Valois to mainland France.

Shane Schofield.

Libby Gant.

Aloysius Knight.

They each carried a white medical transport box.

Three boxes. Three heads.

Owing to the fact that Schofield was one of the most wanted men in the world – and the fact that they were about to enter the inner sanctum of this bounty hunt – Schofield and Gant were partially disguised.

They now wore the charcoal battle uniforms and helmets of IG-88, taken from the men on the Hercules. In addition to their own weapons – now cleaned of chaff – they also carried MetalStorm rifles. For extra effect, Schofield wore several bloodstained bandages across his jaw and normal sunglasses over his eyes, just enough to cover his features.

In his thigh pocket, however, he also carried one of Knight's chunky modified Palm Pilots.

Knight pressed the doorbell to the castle. 'Okay, since I'm the only one of us who's done this before, I'll take the heads in to the assessor. You'll be asked to wait behind, in a secure area of some sort.'

'A secure area?'

'Assessors don't take kindly to bounty hunters who try to storm their offices and steal their money. It's happened before. As such, assessors usually have rather nasty protective systems. And if this assessor is who I think he is, then he's not a very nice person.

'In any case, just keep your eye on your Pilot. I'm not sure how much information I'll be able to syphon out of his computer, but hopefully I can pull enough so that we can find out who's paying for this hunt.'

Knight had an identical Palm Pilot in his own pocket. Like many such devices, it came with an infra-red data transfer feature, so you could send documents from your computer to your Palm Pilot wirelessly.

Knight's modifications to his Pilot, however, included a search program that allowed his device to access – wirelessly – *any* computer that he could get within ten feet of.

Which meant he could do something very special indeed: he could hack into standalone computers. If he could get close enough.

The castle's gates opened.

Monsieur Delacroix appeared, dapper as always.

'Captain Knight,' he said formally. 'I was wondering if I might be seeing you.'

'Monsieur Delacroix,' Knight said. 'I had a feeling you'd be the assessor. I was just saying to my associates here what a charming fellow you were.'

'But of course you were,' Delacroix said drily. He eyed Schofield and Gant in their IG-88 gear. 'New helpers. I did not know you had been recruiting from Monsieur Larkham's fold.'

'Good help is hard to find,' Knight said.

'Isn't it just,' Delacroix said. 'Why don't you come inside.'

They passed through the castle's showroom-like garage, filled with its collection of expensive cars: the Porsche GT-2, the Aston Martin, the Lamborghini, the turbo-charged Subaru WRX rally cars.

Delacroix walked in the lead, pushing a handcart with the three head boxes stacked on it.

'Nice castle,' Knight said.

'It is rather impressive,' Delacroix said.

'So who owns it?'

'A very wealthy individual.'

'Whose name is—'

'—something I am not authorised to divulge. I have instructions on this matter.'

'You always do,' Knight said. 'Guns?'

'You may keep your weapons,' Delacroix said, uninterested. 'They won't be of any use to you here.'

They descended some stairs at the rear of the garage, entered a round stone-walled anteroom that preceded a long narrow tunnel.

Delacroix stopped. 'Your associates will have to wait here, Captain Knight.'

Knight nodded to Schofield and Gant. 'It's okay. Just don't be shocked when the doors lock.'

Schofield and Gant took a seat on a leather couch by the wall.

Delacroix led Knight down the narrow torch-lit tunnel.

They came to the end of the forbidding passageway, to a well-appointed office. Delacroix entered the office ahead of Knight, then turned, holding a remote in his hand.

Wham! Wham! Wham!

The three steel doors in the tunnel whomped down into place, sealing Schofield and Gant in the ante-room and Knight in the tunnel.

Knight didn't even blink.

Delacroix set about examining the heads – heads that were originally captured by Demon Larkham in the caves of Afghanistan: the heads of Zawahiri, Khalif and Kingsgate.

Laser scans, dental exams, DNA . . .

Knight stood inside the long stone tunnel, trapped, waiting.

He noticed the boiling oil gutters set into its walls. 'Hmmm,' he said aloud. 'Nasty.'

Through a small perspex window set into the steel door, he could see into Delacroix's office.

He saw Delacroix at work, saw the immense panoramic window behind the Swiss banker's desk revealing the glorious Atlantic Ocean.

It was then, however, that Knight noticed the ships outside.

On the distant horizon he saw a cluster of naval vessels: destroyers and frigates, all gathered around a mighty aircraft carrier that he instantly recognised as a brand-new, nuclear-powered Charles de Gaulle-class carrier.

It was a Carrier Battle Group.

A French Carrier Battle Group.

Schofield and Gant waited in the ante-room.

A whirring sound from up near the ceiling caught Schofield's attention.

He looked up – and saw six strange-looking antennas arrayed around the ceiling of the round ante-room, embedded in the stone walls. They looked like stereo speakers, but he recognised them as deadly microwave emitters.

He also saw the source of the whirring sound: a security camera.

'We're being watched,' he said.

In another room somewhere in the castle, someone was indeed watching Schofield and Gant on a black-and-white monitor.

The watcher was gazing intently at Schofield, as if he was peering right through Schofield's bandages and sunglasses.

Monsieur Delacroix finished his tests.

He turned to Knight, still captive in the tunnel.

'Captain Knight,' Delacroix said over the intercom. 'Congratulations. Each of your heads has carded a perfect score. You are now $55.8 million richer.'

The Swiss banker pressed his remote and the three steel doors whizzed up into their slots.

Knight stepped into Delacroix's office just as the banker sat down behind his enormous desk and started tapping the keys on his standalone laptop computer.

'So,' Delacroix said, hands poised over the keyboard. 'To which account would you like me to wire the bounty? Am I to assume you are still banking with Alan Gemes in Geneva?'

Knight's eyes were glued to Delacroix's computer.

'Yes,' he said as he hit the 'TRANSMIT' button on the Palm Pilot in his pocket.

Instantly, the Pilot and Delacroix's computer began communicating.

In the stone-walled ante-room, Schofield saw his Palm Pilot spring to life.

Data whizzed up the screen at dizzying speed. Documents filled with names, numbers, diagrams:

Source	Delivery Sys.	W-H	Origin	Target	Time
Talbot	Shahab-5	TN76	35702.90	00001.65	1145
			5001.00	5239.10	
	Shahab-5	TN76	35702.90	00420.02	1145
			5001.00	4900.25	
	Shahab-5	TN76	35702.90	01312.15	1145
			5001.00	5358.75	

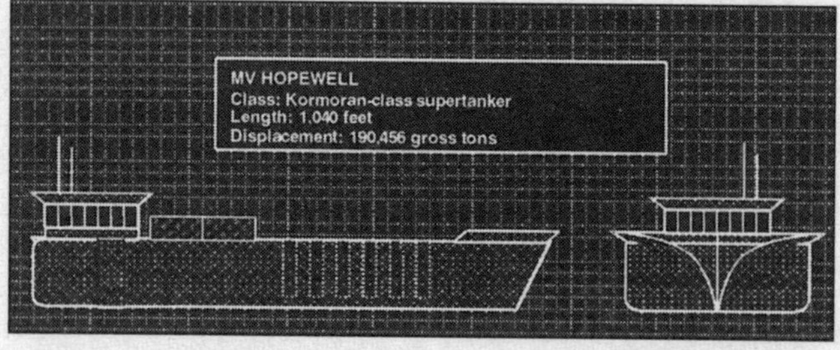

SUBJECT: PAYMENT OF ASSESSOR'S COMMISSION

PAYMENT OF THE ASSESSOR'S COMMISSION WILL BE MADE BY INTERNAL ELECTRONIC FUNDS TRANSFER WITHIN AGM-SUISSE FROM ASTRAL-66 PTY LTD'S PRIVATE ACCOUNT (NO. 437-666-21) IN THE AMOUNT OF US$3.2 MILLION (THREE POINT TWO MILLION US DOLLARS) PER ASSESSMENT.

Executive Itinerary

The proposed order of travel is as follows: Asmara (01/08), Luanda (01/08), Abuja (05/08), N'djamena (07/08) and Tobruk (09/08).

01/08 – Asmara (embassy)
03/08 – Luanda (stay with M. Loch, R's nephew)

	Name	Nat.	Org.
1.	ASHCROFT, William H.	UK	SAS
2.	CHRISTIE, Alec P.	UK	MI-6
3.	FARRELL, Gregory C.	USA	Delta
4.	KHALIF, Iman	AFGH	Al-Qaeda
5.	KINGSGATE, Nigel E.	UK	SAS
6.	McCABE, Dean P.	USA	Delta

Schofield saw the last document, recognised it.

The bounty list.

The Pilot continued to download other documents. Careful to keep it concealed, Schofield clicked on the list, opening it.

This list was slightly different to the one he had taken from the leader of Executive Solutions, Cedric

Wexley, in Siberia. Some of the names on it had been shaded in. The full document read:

ASSESSOR'S MASTER LIST

VERIFIED REPORTS. INFORMATION CORRECT AS AT:
26 OCTOBER, 1412 HOURS

	Name	Nat.	Org.
1.	ASHCROFT, William H.	UK	SAS
2.	CHRISTIE, Alec P.	UK	MI-6
3.	FARRELL, Gregory C.	USA	Delta
4.	KHALIF, Iman	AFGH	Al-Qaeda
5.	KINGSGATE, Nigel E.	UK	SAS
6.	McCABE, Dean P.	USA	Delta
7.	NAZZAR, Yousef M.	LEBN	HAMAS
8.	NICHOLSON, Francis X.	USA	USAMRMC
9.	OLIPHANT, Thompson J.	USA	USAMRMC
10.	POLANSKI, Damien G.	USA	ISS
11.	ROSENTHAL, Benjamin Y.	ISR	Mossad
12.	SCHOFIELD, Shane M.	USA	USMC
13.	WEITZMAN, Ronson H.	USA	USMC
14.	ZAWAHIRI, Hassan M.	SAUDI	Al-Qaeda
15.	ZEMIR, Simon B.	ISR	IAF

The dead, Schofield thought with a chill. *It's a list of the targets who have already been eliminated.*

And verified as dead.

Schofield could have added Ashcroft and Weitzman to that list – Ashcroft had been beheaded in Afghanistan by the Spetsnaz bounty hunters, the Skorpions, and Weitzman had been killed on the cargo plane.

Which meant that, at the very best, only five of the original fifteen names remained alive: Christie, Oliphant, Rosenthal, Zemir and Schofield himself.

Schofield frowned.

Something bothered him about this list, something he couldn't quite put his finger on . . .

Then he glimpsed the word 'ASSESSOR' on one of the other documents.

He retrieved it.

It was an email:

SUBJECT: PAYMENT OF ASSESSOR'S COMMISSION

PAYMENT OF THE ASSESSOR'S COMMISSION WILL BE MADE BY INTERNAL ELECTRONIC FUNDS TRANSFER WITHIN AGM-SUISSE FROM ASTRAL-66 PTY LTD'S PRIVATE ACCOUNT (NO. 437-666-21) IN THE AMOUNT OF US$3.2 MILLION (THREE POINT TWO MILLION US DOLLARS) PER ASSESSMENT.

THE ASSESSOR IS TO BE **M. JEAN-PIERRE DELACROIX** OF AGM-SUISSE.

Schofield gazed at the words.

'ASTRAL-66 PTY LTD.'

That was where the money was coming from. Whatever it was, Astral-66 was paying for this bounty hunt—

'Good afternoon,' a pleasant voice said.

Schofield and Gant looked up.

A very handsome young man stood at the base of the stone stairs that led up to the garage. He was in his late thirties and clad in designer jeans and a Ralph Lauren shirt which he wore open over a T-shirt in the manner of the very wealthy. Schofield immediately noticed his eyes: one blue, one brown.

'Welcome to my castle.' The handsome young man smiled. His smile seemed somehow dangerous. 'And who might you be?'

'Colton. Tom Colton,' Schofield lied. 'This is Jane

Watson. We're with Aloysius Knight, seeing Monsieur Delacroix.'

'Oh, I see . . .' the handsome man said.

He extended his hand.

'Killian. Jonathan Killian. You both look like you've seen a fair amount of action today. May I get you a drink, or something to eat? Or perhaps my personal physician could give you some clean bandages for your wounds.'

Schofield shot a glance down the tunnel, searching for Knight.

'Please . . .' Killian guided them up the stairs. Not wanting to attract unnecessary attention, they followed him.

'I've seen you before,' Schofield said as they walked up the stone stairway. 'On TV . . .'

'I do make the odd appearance from time to time.'

'Africa,' Schofield said. 'You were in Africa. Last year. Opening factories. Food factories. In Nigeria . . .'

This was all true. Schofield recalled the images from the news – footage of this Killian fellow shaking hands with smiling African leaders amid crowds of happy workers.

They came up into the classic car garage.

'You've a good memory,' Killian said. 'I also went to Eritrea, Chad, Angola and Libya, opening new food processing plants. Although many don't know it yet, the future of the world lies in Africa.'

'I like your car collection,' Gant said.

'Toys,' Killian replied. 'Mere toys.'

He guided them into a corridor branching off the garage. It had dark polished floorboards and pristine white walls.

'But then I enjoy playing with toys,' Killian said.

'Much as I enjoy playing with *people*. I like to see their reactions to stressful situations.'

He stopped in front of a large wooden door. Schofield heard laughter coming from behind it. Raucous male laughter. It sounded like a party was going on in there.

'Stressful situations?' Schofield said. 'What do you mean by that?'

'Well,' Killian said, 'take for instance the average Westerner's inability to comprehend the Islamic suicide bomber. Westerners are taught since birth to fight "fair": the French duel at ten paces, English knights jousting, American gunslingers facing off on a Wild West street. In the Western world, fighting is fair because it is presumed that both parties actually *want* to win a given battle.'

'But the suicide bomber doesn't think that way,' Schofield said.

'That's right,' Killian said. 'He doesn't want to win the *battle*, because the battle to a suicide bomber is meaningless. He wants to win a far grander war, a psychological war in which the man who dies *against his will* – in a state of distress and terror and fear – loses, while he who dies when he is spiritually and emotionally ready, wins.

'As such, a Westerner faced with a suicide bomber goes to pieces. Believe me, I have seen this. Just as I have seen people's reactions to other stressful situations: criminals in the electric chair, a person in water confronted by sharks. Oh, to be sure, I love to observe the look of pure horror that crosses a man's face when he realises that he is, without doubt, going to die.'

With that, Killian pushed open the door—

—at the same moment that something dawned on Schofield:

His problem with the master list.

On the master bounty list, McCabe and Farrell's names had been shaded in.

McCabe and Farrell, who had died in Siberia that morning, had been officially listed as dead.

And paid for.

Which meant . . .

The great door swung open—

—and Schofield and Gant were met with the sight of a dining room filled with the members of Executive Solutions, twenty of them, eating and drinking and smoking. At the head of the table, his broken nose wrapped in a fresh dressing, sat Cedric Wexley.

Schofield's face fell.

'And *that*,' Killian said, 'is the look I'm talking about.' The billionaire offered Schofield a thin, joyless smile. 'Welcome to my castle . . . Captain Schofield.'

Schofield and Gant ran.

Ran for all they were worth.

They bolted away from the dining room, dashed down the splendid corridor, Jonathan Killian's scornful laughter chasing them all the way.

The ExSol men were out of their seats in seconds, grabbing their weapons, the sight of another $18.6 million too good to resist.

Killian let them hustle past him, enjoying the show.

Schofield and Gant burst into the classic car garage.

'Damn. So many choices,' Schofield said, ripping off his bandages and gazing at the multi-million-dollar selection of cars before him.

Gant looked over her shoulder, saw the Executive Solutions mercenaries thundering down the hallway in pursuit. 'You've got about ten seconds to choose the fastest one, buster.'

Schofield eyed the Porsche GT-2. Silver and low, with an open targa top, it was an absolute beast of a car.

'Nah, it just isn't me,' he said, leaping instead toward the equally-fast rally car beside it – an electric blue turbo-charged Subaru WRX.

*

Nine seconds later, the men of ExSol burst into the garage.

They got there just in time to see the WRX blasting down the length of the showroom, already doing sixty.

At the far end of the showroom, the garage's external door was opening – thanks to Libby Gant standing at the controls.

The ExSol men opened fire.

Schofield stopped the rally car on a dime, right next to Gant.

'Get in!'

'What about Knight?'

'I'm sure he'll understand!'

Gant dived in through the Subaru's passenger window, just as the garage door opened fully to reveal the castle's sundrenched internal courtyard . . .

. . . and the surprised face of Major Dmitri Zamanov.

Accompanied by six of his Skorpions, and holding a medical transport box in his hands.

A pair of Russian Mi-34 high-manoeuvre helicopters stood in the gravel courtyard behind the Spetsnaz commandos, their rotor blades still turning.

'Oh, man,' Schofield breathed. 'Could this get any worse?'

Down in Monsieur Delacroix's office, Aloysius Knight spun at the sound of gunfire up in the garage.

He looked for Schofield in the ante-room at the other end of the tunnel.

Not there.

'Damn it,' he growled, 'can't this guy stay out of trouble for more than five minutes?'

He bolted out of the office.

Monsieur Delacroix didn't even bother to look up.

Schofield's turbo-charged WRX stood before Zamanov in the entry to the garage.

The two men locked eyes.

The look of surprise on Zamanov's face quickly transformed into one of sheer hatred.

'Floor it!' Gant yelled, breaking the spell.

Bam. Schofield hit the gas pedal.

The rally car shot off the mark, exploding through the doorway, scattering the Skorpions as they dived out of the way.

The WRX zoomed across the castle's courtyard, kicking up gravel, before it shot like a rocket out through the giant portcullis and sped across the drawbridge, heading for the mainland.

Dmitri Zamanov clambered to his feet just as *shoom!-shoom!-shoom!-shoom!-shoom!* five more cars whipped past him, blasting out of the garage after the WRX. There was a red Ferrari, a silver Porsche GT-2, and three yellow Peugeot rally cars with 'AXON' sponsorship logos on their sides.

ExSol.

In hot pursuit.

'Fuck!' Zamanov yelled. 'It's him! It's Schofield! *Go!* Go, go, go! Catch him and bring him to me! Before Delacroix gets his head, I am going to skin him alive!'

Four of the Skorpions immediately leapt to their feet and dashed for their two choppers, leaving Zamanov and two others at the castle with their head.

The chase was on.

WHITMORE AIRFIELD (ABANDONED)
40 MILES WEST OF LONDON
1230 HOURS LOCAL TIME
(1330 HOURS IN FRANCE*)

Thirty minutes *earlier* – at the time Schofield, Gant and Knight had been arriving at the Forteresse de Valois – Book II and Mother had been landing their stolen Lynx helicopter at the abandoned airfield where Rufus had dropped them off.

They didn't expect to find Rufus still there. He'd said that after unloading them, he would head to France to catch up with Knight.

But when they landed, they saw the *Black Raven* parked inside an old hangar, surrounded by undercover police cars with strobe lights on their roofs.

Rufus stood sadly by his plane, helpless, covered by six trenchcoat-wearing undercover types and a platoon of heavily-armed Royal Marines.

Mother and Book were grabbed as soon as they landed.

* Even though some areas in France, including Brittany, are significantly west of London, the whole of France adheres to a single time zone, one hour ahead of England.

One of the trenchcoat-wearing men approached them. He was young, clean-cut, and he held a cellphone in his hand as if he was halfway through a call.

When he spoke his accent was American.

'Sergeants Newman and Riley? My name is Scott Moseley, US State Department, London Office. We understand you're helping Captain Shane M. Schofield of the United States Marine Corps in his efforts to avoid liquidation in an international bounty hunt. Is that correct?'

Book and Mother blanched.

'Uh, yeah . . . that's right,' Book II said.

'The United States Government has become aware of the existence of this bounty hunt. From the information available to us at this time, we have assessed the presumed reason for it and have come to the conclusion that the issue of keeping Captain Schofield alive is one of supreme national importance. Do you know where he is?'

'We might,' Mother said.

'So what's this all about then?' Book II asked. 'Tell us the grand conspiracy.'

Scott Moseley's face reddened. 'I don't personally know the details,' he said.

'Oh, *come on*,' Book II groaned, 'you've gotta give us more than that.'

'Please,' Moseley said. 'I'm just the messenger here. I don't have the clearance to know the full story. But believe me, I'm *not* here to hinder your efforts. All I have been told is this: the person or persons behind this bounty hunt have the capacity and perhaps the desire to destroy the United States of America. That is all I've been told. Beyond that, I know nothing.

'What I do know is this: I am here at the direct orders

of the President of the United States and my orders are these: to help you. In any way I can. Anywhere you want to go. Anything you need to help Captain Schofield stay alive, I am authorised to give you. If you want weapons, they're yours. If you need money, I have it. Hell, if you want Air Force One to take you anywhere in the world, it is at your disposal.'

'Cool . . .' Mother breathed.

'How do we know we can trust you?' Book II said.

Scott Moseley handed Book his cellphone.

'Who's there?' Book said into it.

'Sergeant Riley?' a firm voice at the other end said. Book II recognised it instantly – and froze.

He'd met the owner of that voice before, during the mayhem at Area 7.

It was the voice of the President of the United States.

This was real.

'Sergeant Riley,' the President said. 'The full resources of the United States Government are entirely at your command. Anything you need, just tell Undersecretary Moseley. *You have to keep Shane Schofield alive*. Now I have to go.'

Then he hung up.

'*Right*.' Book II whistled.

'So,' Scott Moseley said. 'What do you need?'

Mother and Book exchanged a look.

'You go,' Book said. 'Save the Scarecrow. I'm going to find out what this is all about.'

'Ten-four,' Mother said.

She turned quickly, pointing at Rufus, but addressing Moseley. 'I need him. And his plane, fully fuelled. Plus free passage out of England. We know where the Scarecrow is and we have to get to him fast.'

'I can arrange the fastest possible—' Moseley said.

'Yeah, but I don't trust you yet,' Mother growled. 'Rufus, I trust. And he's just as fast as anyone else.'

'Okay. Done.' Scott Moseley nodded to one of his men. 'Fuel the plane. Clear the skies.'

Moseley turned to Book. 'What about you?'

But Book wasn't finished with Mother. 'Hey, Mother. Good luck. Save him.'

'I'll do my best,' Mother said. Then she dashed off to join Rufus at the Sukhoi. After a few minutes, its tanks replenished, the *Raven* rose into the sky and blasted off into the distance, afterburners blazing.

Only when it was gone did Book II turn to face Scott Moseley. 'I need a video player,' he said.

Schofield's rally car boomed along the coast of north-western France.

The road leading away from the Forteresse de Valois was known as La Grande Rue de la Mer – the Great Ocean Road.

Carved into the cliffs overlooking the Atlantic Ocean, it was a spectacular coastal highway, a twisting turning blacktop that featured low concrete guard-fences perched over sheer 400-foot drops, treacherous blind corners and the occasional tunnel that carved through rocky outcroppings.

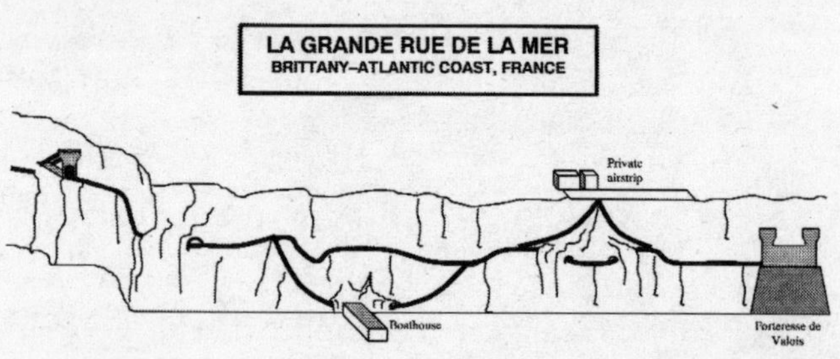

In truth, since the fifteen miles of land surrounding the Forteresse de Valois belonged to Jonathan Killian, it was actually a private road. At two points along its length, side-roads branched off it – one headed upward, to Killian's private airstrip, while a second by-road plunged steeply downward, plummeting to the water's edge, providing access to an enormous boatshed.

Schofield's electric blue WRX ripped along the spectacular ocean road at 180 kilometres per hour. Its engine didn't so much roar as *whizz*, its turbocharger engaged. With its powerful all-wheel-drive system, the rally car was perfect for the Great Ocean Road's short tight bends.

Behind it, moving equally fast, were the five supercars of ExSol – the Porsche, the Ferrari and the three Peugeots – all in hot pursuit.

'Knight!' Schofield called into his throat-mike. 'You out there? We're . . . ah . . . in a little trouble here.'

'*I'm on my way*,' came the calm reply.

At that same moment, a mile behind Schofield's WRX – and a long way behind the chase – one final car came shooting out of the Forteresse de Valois and whipped across its drawbridge.

It was a Lamborghini Diablo.

V-12. Rear spoiler. Super low. Supercool. Superfast.

And painted black, of course.

Schofield keyed his satellite radio system.

'Book! Mother! Do you read me?'

Mother's voice answered him immediately. '*I'm here, Scarecrow.*'

'We're no longer at the castle,' Schofield said. 'We're on the road leading away from it. Heading north.'

'*What happened?*'

'Started out okay, but then just about every bad guy in the world arrived.'

'Have you destroyed everything yet?'

'Not yet, but I'm thinking about it. Are you on the way?'

'Almost there. I'm with Rufus in the Raven. *Book stayed in London to find out more about this hunt. I'm about thirty minutes away from you.'*

'Thirty minutes,' Schofield said grimly. 'I'm not sure we're gonna last that long.'

'You have to, Scarecrow, because I've got a lot to tell you.'

'Executive summary. Twenty-five words or less,' Schofield said.

'The US Government knows about the bounty hunt and they're throwing everything behind keeping you alive. You just became an endangered species. So get your ass to US soil. An embassy, a consulate. Anything.'

Schofield threw the WRX round a tight bend – and was suddenly presented with a vista of the road ahead of him.

The Great Ocean Road stretched away into the distance, twisting and turning like a flat black ribbon, hugging the coastal cliffs for miles.

'The US Government wants to *help* me?' Schofield said. 'In my experience, the US Government only looks after the US Government.'

'Uh, Scarecrow . . .' Gant said, interrupting. 'We have a problem.'

'What?' Schofield snapped to look forward. 'Damn. ExSol must have called ahead . . .'

Half a mile in front of them the Ocean Road forked, with a side-road branching off it to the right, heading up the cliff-face. It was the side-road that led up to the airstrip, and right now two big semi-trailer rigs – minus their long trailers – were rushing down its steep slope at considerable speed, rumbling toward Schofield and Gant's fleeing car.

Hovering in the air above the two rigs was a sleek Bell Jet Ranger helicopter with 'AXON CORP' written on its flanks, also coming from the direction of the airfield.

ExSol has radioed ahead, Schofield thought, *and sent everyone they could from the airfield.*

'Those rigs are coming straight for us!' Gant said.

'No,' Schofield said. 'They're not going to ram us. They're going to block the road.'

Sure enough, the two semi-trailer rigs arrived at the junction of the airstrip road and the Great Ocean Road and promptly turned sideways, skidding to simultaneous halts, splaying their combined bulk across the road.

Blocking it completely.

'Mother,' Schofield said into his radio. 'We have to go. Please get here as soon as you can.'

The WRX whipped along the winding cliff-side road, rapidly approaching the two semi-trailer rigs.

Then, 200 yards short of the road block, Schofield hit the brakes and the WRX squealed to a stop in the middle of the road.

A stand-off.

Two rigs. One rally car.

Schofield checked his rear-view mirror – the gang of five ExSol supercars was shooting along the Ocean Road behind him.

Beyond the ExSol cars loomed the giant stone castle, dark and sombre, before suddenly two helicopters dropped in front of the fortress, blasting through the air in pursuit as well.

Zamanov's two Skorpion Mi-34 choppers.

'Between a rock and a hard place,' Schofield said.

'A very hard place,' Gant said.

Schofield whirled back to face the road in front of him.

His eyes swept the scene – two rigs, the Axon helicopter, sheer rock wall to the right, 400-foot drop to the left, protected by a low concrete fence.

The fence, he thought.

'Pursuit cars are almost on us . . .' Gant warned.

But Schofield was still gazing at the concrete guard-rail fence. The Axon chopper hovered just out from it, almost at road level.

'We can do that,' he said aloud, his eyes narrowing.

'Do *what*?' Gant turned, alarmed.

'Hang on.'

Schofield slammed his foot down on the gas pedal.

The WRX roared off the mark, racing toward the rigs.

The rally car picked up speed fast, all four of its wheels giving power, its turbocharger screaming – *tzzzzzzzzz!*

60 kilometres an hour became 80 . . .

100 . . .

120 . . .

The WRX rushed toward the road block.

The two drivers of the rigs – ExSol men who had been waiting up at the airfield – swapped looks. *What was this guy doing?*

And then, very suddenly, Schofield cut left . . . bringing the rally car close to the concrete guard-rail fence.

Screeeeeeech!

The WRX hit the fence, its left-side wheels scraping against the concrete barrier, pressing against it, pinching against it, causing the whole left-hand side of the car to lift a little off the road . . .

. . . before abruptly – *ka-whump!* – the WRX mounted the fence!

Its left-hand wheels lifted clear off the asphalt, now riding *along the top of the fence*, so that the car was travelling at a 45-degree angle.

Schofield and Gant's world tilted sideways.

'There's still not enough room!' Gant yelled, pointing at the rig parked closest to the fence.

She was right.

'I'm not done yet!' Schofield yelled.

And with that he yanked the steering wheel hard to the *right*.

The response was instantaneous.

The WRX lurched sideways, its front half going right, its tail section going left – swinging dangerously out toward the ocean until finally its tail section slid . . .

. . . *off the edge of the concrete guard-rail.*

The WRX's rear wheels now hung 400 feet above the ocean!

But the rally car was still moving fast, still skidding wildly forward, its underside *sliding* along the top of the guard-rail fence – its front tyres hanging over the landward side of the fence, its rear wheels hanging above the ocean – so that now *none* of its wheels was touching the ground.

'*Ahhhhhhh!*' Gant yelled.

The WRX slid laterally along the guard-rail, its weight almost perfectly balanced, its underside scraping and shrieking and kicking up a firestorm of sparks until, to the amazement of the rig drivers, *it slid right past their road block*, squeezing through the gap between the outermost rig and the fence, a gap that until now had been too narrow for a car to pass through.

But then the inevitable happened.

With a fraction more of its weight hanging over the ocean side of the fence, the car – despite its forward momentum – began to tilt backwards.

'We're going to drop!' Gant shouted.

'No we're not,' Schofield said calmly.

He was right.

For just at that moment, the tail of the sliding car smacked at tremendous speed *against the nose of the Axon chopper* hovering just out from the fence.

The rear section of the car bounced off the chopper's nose at speed – ricocheting off it like a pinball – the impact powerful enough to punch the sliding WRX *back* over the fence and back onto the road . . . on the other side of the road block.

Just as Schofield had planned.

The WRX's tyres caught bitumen again, regained their traction, and the rally car shot off down the road once more.

Not a moment too soon.

Because a second later, the two rigs backed up, allowing the five ExSol pursuit cars to shoot between them like bullets out of a gun and catch up to Schofield's car.

The ExSol cars were all over them.

The two European sportscars that ExSol had 'borrowed' from Jonathan Killian – the red Ferrari and the silver Porsche, both low and sleek and brutally fast – were right on Schofield's tail.

The two mercenaries inside the Porsche made full use of its open-air targa roof – it allowed one man to stand up and fire at Schofield's WRX. The gunman in the Ferrari had to lean out of its passenger window.

As the rear window of the WRX shattered under a hail of gunfire, Gant turned to Schofield.

'Can I ask you a question!' she yelled.

'Sure!'

'Is there, like, some secret *school* where they teach you stuff like that? Death-defying driving school?'

'Actually, they call it "Offensive Driving",' Schofield said, glancing over his shoulder. 'It was a special course at Quantico given by a retired Gunnery Sergeant named Kris Hankison. Hank left the Marines in '91 and became a stunt driver in Hollywood. Makes a bundle. But every second year, as a kind of payback to the Corps, he offers the course to Marines assigned to Marine Security Guard Battalion. I got invited last year. You think that was good, you wouldn't believe what Hank can do on four wheels—'

Brrrrrrrrrrr!

A line of bullets razed the road beside Schofield's WRX, chewing up the bitumen, smacking against his driver's door. A split-second later one of the nimble Skorpion Mi-34 choppers roared by overhead.

But then the road bent right, hugging the cliff-face – and the chopper continued straight while the WRX whipped out of its line of fire just as—

SLAM!

—a colossal gout of earth exploded out from the rock wall on the right-hand side of the road, sending a starburst of dirt spraying out spectacularly behind the speeding rally car.

'What the—?' Schofield spun, searching for the source of the massive explosion.

And he found it.

'Oh, this cannot be happening . . .' he breathed.

He saw a *warship* powering in toward the coast, separating itself from a larger group of naval vessels on the horizon.

It was a French Tourville-class destroyer and its powerful 3.9-inch forward-mounted guns were firing, each shot accompanied by a belch of smoke and a noise so loud that it reverberated right through one's chest: *Boom! Boom! Boom!*

Then a second later . . .

SLAM!

SLAM!

SLAM!

The shells *rammed* into the cliff-side roadway, raining dirt all around Schofield's speeding car. Explosions of asphalt and dirt flew high into the air, leaving lethal craters in their wake – craters that took up nearly half the roadway.

After the first shellburst hit, Schofield's WRX screamed over the edge of its crater, blasting through the dustcloud above it and, looking down, Schofield saw that the shell had gouged a semi-circular hole in the Ocean Road that led all the way down to the sea.

The other shells rained down on the Great Ocean Road, striking it left and right. Schofield responded by flinging the rally car right and left, avoiding the newly-created craters by centimetres.

The Axon helicopter behind him banked and swayed, also trying to avoid the destroyer's deadly rain.

But the two more nimble Skorpion Mi-34 choppers didn't care, they just continued to pursue Schofield with a vengeance, their side-mounted cannons shredding the road.

And then Schofield's WRX rounded a bend and zoomed into a cliff-side tunnel and the two Russian choppers rose quickly, swooping over the jagged cliffs, and suddenly Schofield and Gant were enveloped by silence.

Not for long.

Into the tunnel behind them rushed the two ExSol sportscars – the Ferrari and the Porsche – their engines roaring, each car's gunner firing at the fleeing WRX.

Schofield swung left, toward the ocean side of the tunnel and abruptly discovered that this tunnel wasn't technically a tunnel – precisely because its entire seaward wall wasn't a wall at all. It was a series of thin columns that rushed by in a fluttering blur, allowing drivers to take in the view as they passed through the tunnel.

Schofield caught this information just as he saw a Skorpion chopper appear outside the blurring line of pillars and start firing *into* the exposed tunnel!

Bullets slammed into the road, his car, and against the far wall.

Schofield weaved right, away from the barrage, pressed his WRX up against the right-hand wall of the curving tunnel, losing speed . . .

. . . and in a second the pursuit cars were on him, the Porsche ramming into his rear bumper, the Ferrari boxing him in on the left, their two ExSol shooter-passengers letting fly.

Automatic gunfire ripped into the WRX.

Schofield's side window shattered—

—just as a deadly shape appeared at the end of the tunnel.

The second Skorpion Mi-34 chopper, rising above the roadway, its side-mounted missile pods poised and ready to fire.

'We're dead,' Schofield said matter-of-factly.

A flare of yellow backblast issued out from the back of one of the chopper's missile pods just as without warning the chopper itself exploded in mid-air – hit by a shell from the French destroyer off the coast. The Mi-34's missile exploded too, having never cleared its pod.

The massive naval shell hit the Skorpion helicopter so hard that the chopper was hurled against the edge of the roadway, where it crumpled like an aluminium can before falling 400 feet straight down. It hadn't been a deliberate strike, Schofield felt. The chopper had just got in the way.

'Close,' Gant said.

'Just a little,' he said as their car blasted out of the tunnel, racing past the spot where the Mi-34 had fallen, still boxed in against the rock wall by the two ExSol cars.

The three cars whipped along a short stretch of road. But then Schofield saw another tunnel yawning before them, 200 yards awa –

Bang!

The Ferrari rammed into the WRX's left side, forcing it closer to the rock wall.

Schofield grappled with his steering wheel.

The Porsche, meanwhile, pushed up against his rear bumper.

At first Schofield didn't know why they had done this, then he looked forward and saw that the arched entrance to the upcoming tunnel was *not* flush against the rock wall – it jutted out about six feet.

And so long as the Ferrari and the Porsche kept Schofield and Gant's car pressed up against the rock wall and travelling forward, the WRX would slam right into the protruding archway.

Schofield guessed they had about five seconds.

'This is very bad . . .' Gant said.

'I know, I know,' Schofield said.

Four seconds . . .

The three cars raced in formation along the narrow cliff-side roadway.

Three seconds . . .

The Ferrari pushed them up against the rocky wall on their right. The WRX's right wheels lifted slightly, rubbing against the hard stone wall. But the Porsche behind it kept pushing it forward fast.

'Please do something,' Gant said.

Two seconds . . .

The stone archway of the tunnel rushed toward them.

'Okay . . .' Schofield said. 'You want to play nasty? Let's play nasty.'

One . . .

Then, just as the WRX was about to slam at tremendous speed into the arched entrance of the tunnel, Schofield allowed the Ferrari to push him *closer* to the wall, driving him further up it, making the WRX rise up to about 60 degrees, its right-hand wheels riding clear up onto the wall itself.

And then time slowed and Schofield did the impossible.

He let the WRX ride so high up the rocky wall that, five metres short of the tunnel's archway, the electric blue rally car went too high . . . and *rolled* . . . to the left, turning completely upside down . . . so that it landed, on its roof . . . *on the roof of the low-slung Ferrari travelling beside it.*

And so, for a brief instant in time, the WRX and the Ferrari were travelling rooftop-to-rooftop, the WRX's wheels pointing skyward, its roof resting momentarily on the roof of the lower red Ferrari!

And then time sped up again and the WRX rolled off the Ferrari, bouncing back down to earth, now safely on the ocean side of the scarlet red supercar, and blasted into the tunnel with the Ferrari on its right.

The Porsche, unfortunately, had no options.

Travelling right behind Schofield it had intended to pull away at the last moment. Its driver, however, had never imagined that Schofield might *roll over the top of* the Ferrari. When Schofield did so, the Porsche driver stared at his feat for a split second too long.

As such, it was the Porsche that hit the archway at colossal speed. Instant fireball.

The Ferrari was only slightly more fortunate.

Having rolled over the top of it, Schofield now started ramming *it* into the wall of the tunnel. He did a better job than they had, cutting across the bow of the Ferrari, causing it to jackknife against the tunnel's right-hand wall and flip and tumble – spinning over and over like a toy flung by a child – bouncing down the confined space of the tunnel, skimming off its walls, before it stopped on its roof, wrecked and crumpled, its occupants deader than disco.

Schofield and Gant blasted out of the tunnel, just as the second Skorpion Mi-34 attack chopper swooped in alongside them, flying parallel to the cliff-side roadway with a sniper in its right-side doorway firing viciously.

One thing was clear – while Schofield was driving as fast as he could, the nimble chopper was merely cruising.

'Fox!' Schofield called. 'We have to get rid of that chopper! Nail that sniper!'

'Gladly,' Gant said. 'Lean back!'

Schofield did so as Gant raised her Desert Eagle pistol and fired it across his body, out through his window at the chopper.

Two shots. Both hit their mark.

And the sniper dropped . . . out of the chopper's door.

But he was buckled to a safety rope, so after about forty feet of falling, his rope snapped taut and his fall abruptly stopped.

'Thanks, honey babe!' Schofield called, watching the suspended figure when suddenly Gant shouted, 'Scare-crow! Look out! Another fork!'

He snapped forward and saw a new fork in the road, this one with a side-road branching left and downward, while the Ocean Road continued flat to the right.

Left or right, he thought. *Pick a side.*

A shellburst from the incoming French destroyer hit the right-hand road.

Left it is.

He swung the car left, tyres squealing, and careered down the steeply sloping side-road.

The chopper followed.

Half a mile behind Schofield, Aloysius Knight was shooting along the Great Ocean Road in his shiny black Lamborghini Diablo.

The two semi-trailer rigs that had formed the road block before now rumbled along directly in front of him, while beyond them, he saw the three yellow Axon-sponsored Peugeots that ExSol had taken from the castle.

And about fifty yards beyond the Peugeots, he saw Schofield's blue WRX reach a fork in the road, hounded by the remaining Skorpion Mi-34 helicopter.

Knight stole a glance left at the destroyer out on the ocean, just as two bird-like shadows shot through the air over the warship, heading directly for the coastal road.

They looked decidedly like *fighter jets*, originating from the French aircraft carrier on the horizon.

Uh-oh, Knight thought.

He faced forward again just in time to see Schofield's car cut left at the fork in the road, disappearing down a side-road set into the cliff-face.

At which point, he saw Schofield's pursuers do a strange thing.

They split up.

Only one of the Axon Peugeots followed Schofield down the side-road. The other two went right, following the Ocean Road, skirting a newly-formed crater in the roadway.

Then the two trailer rigs came to the fork and went left, charging *down* the hill after Schofield.

Co-ordinated movement, Knight thought. *They've got a plan.*

And then Knight himself reached the fork and without any hesitation, he gunned the Lamborghini down the left-hand roadway, shooting down the hill after Schofield.

Schofield's WRX whizzed down the steep boathouse road, burning around blind corners, skidding around tight bends.

As it sped along, a storm of bullets hammered its flanks and the rock walls all around it – it was still under heavy fire from the Mi-34 chopper flying low through the air behind it, firing at the WRX with its side-mounted machine-guns.

The chopper's dead sniper still hung limply from its open side door, his body swaying wildly, occasionally bouncing on the road, leaving blood on the asphalt.

More fire came from the yellow Peugeot rally car that had followed Schofield down the boathouse road, from the shooter poking out of its passenger-side window with a Steyr.

Two hundred yards behind this speeding gun battle, Knight was also driving hard.

His Lamborghini easily hauled in the two semi-trailer rigs, and he whizzed past them in a fluid S-shaped move before they even knew he was there.

Knight came up behind the yellow Peugeot, tried to get around it on the right, but the Peugeot blocked him. Tried left and gunned it hard – very hard – and in a daring move, overtook the Peugeot on the ocean side of the road.

The Lamborghini shot past the yellow rally car, the driver of the Peugeot looking left just in time to see the Diablo rocket by in a blur of black – at the same time as an M-67 grenade came lobbing in through his open driver's window.

The Lamborghini shot down the road as the Peugeot erupted in a ball of flames. The flaming Peugeot promptly missed the next curve and blasted right through the guard-rail fence there and fell – a long, slow drop that ended in the Atlantic Ocean far, far below.

Knight's Lamborghini was now twenty yards behind Schofield's WRX and the Mi-34 chopper above it.

Knight saw that Schofield was now racing down a long straight stretch of road that ended at a tunnel at the very base of this side-road – a tunnel that gave access to an enormous boatshed.

'Schofield!' Knight called into his radio. 'Don't shoot behind you, okay! The Lamborghini is me!'

'*The Lamborghini. Why doesn't that surprise me,*' said Schofield's voice. '*Nice of you to join us. Anything you can do about this damn helicopter?*'

Knight took in the scene: saw Schofield's blue WRX up ahead, rapidly approaching the tunnel – saw the underbelly of the Mi-34 directly above and behind the WRX, saw the swaying Russian sniper dangling from it, banging and bouncing on the road right in front of his speeding Diablo.

Chopper – sniper – tunnel, he thought.

All he needed was an escape vehicle.

Knight glanced at his rear-view mirror: it was filled by the grille of the first rig – it was a Mack rig, with a distinctive long-nosed bonnet – rumbling down the road behind him.

Thank you very much.

'Hang on, Schofield. I've got this sucker.'

He powered forward, bringing the Lamborghini under the Mi-34 chopper, out of its sight. Then with a rather morbid bang, he charged his car right *into* the dangling sniper's corpse, so that the body bounced up onto his bonnet and then dropped in through the Diablo's open targa roof.

Knight whipped out a pair of handcuffs – the bounty hunter's most valuable tool – and cuffed the dead sniper's safety harness to the steering wheel of his Lamborghini.

He then hit the cruise control and jumped out of his seat, climbing up and out through the targa roof.

At that moment, the big Mack rig caught up with him and rammed into the back of the Lamborghini.

But Knight was ready for the impact, and as the two vehicles touched, he made his move – dashing across the flat rear section of the Lamborghini, firing his pistol into the windshield of the Mack as he did so, killing its driver, and then leaping from the rear of the Lamborghini onto the long nose of the Mack!

Within seconds, he was through the rig's shattered windscreen and in its driver's seat, in control of the big rig – and with a front row seat for what was about to happen.

Schofield's WRX shot into the tunnel at the base of the hill.

The Skorpion chopper – knowing it had to go over the tunnel and recapture Schofield on the other side – lifted, or rather, tried to lift.

But the lightweight Mi-34 chopper *couldn't* rise, owing to the weight of the Lamborghini now anchored to it.

The Skorpion pilot realised the implications of this a second too late.

The driverless Lamborghini rushed into the tunnel's arched entrance, while the chopper rushed *over* it, and to the pilot's horror, the vertical rope connecting the two vehicles went taut and . . . folded . . . as it hit the archway.

The Skorpion chopper and the Lamborghini came together like a pair of scissor blades.

The Diablo was lifted completely off the ground, flying upwards, crunching into the ceiling of the tunnel, crumpling in an instant, bringing down a rain of tiles as it did so.

For its part, the Mi-34 was yanked *downward* by the rope, and it slammed down into the rocks above the tunnel and exploded in a shower of fire and rubble.

Knight shot under it all – at the wheel of the Mack rig – roaring into the tunnel, shooting past the fiery remains of his discarded Lamborghini.

Up ahead, Schofield blasted out the other end of the same tunnel, started zooming up the hill.

He rounded a corner, saw the upwardly-sloping road ahead – lots of sweeping bends and blind corners, and at the top of the road, the two other yellow Peugeots that had taken the high road.

They'd gone ahead, taking the shorter route, and doubled back, so that now they were shooting *down* this road, on a collision course with him and Gant.

Schofield's WRX powered up the hill, now trailed by only two vehicles, the two rigs: Knight's long-nosed Mack and the second rig, a snub-nosed Kenworth.

But then the WRX swept around a blind corner and was abruptly confronted by another unexpected sight:

A fighter jet had swung into a hover just out from the bend, its nose pointed menacingly downward, an arsenal of missiles hanging from its wings.

Schofield recognised it instantly as a Dassault Mirage 2000N-II, the French equivalent of the Harrier jump-jet. Converted from the regular Mirage 2000N, the 'II' was a hover-capable fighter stationed only on France's newest and biggest aircraft carriers. It looked a lot like a Harrier, stocky and hunchbacked, with semi-circular air intakes on either side of a two-man cockpit.

The Mirage's guns erupted and a swarm of laser-like tracer bullets tore into the rock walls above Schofield's car.

Schofield floored it, whipping past the hovering plane as it wheeled around heavily in the air, its bullet-storm chasing him, but he shot around another bend just as some of its tracers sheared off his rear bumper.

'Here, quickly, take the wheel,' Schofield said to Gant.

She slipped over into the driver's seat while he dipped into a pocket on his combat webbing and removed some bullets – Knight's orange-banded rounds. Bull-stoppers.

'People, no. Fighter planes, yes,' he said as he loaded the orange bullets into his Desert Eagle's magazine, finishing at the same time as a second Mirage swooped down over the road right in front of the WRX, its guns blazing.

But now, Schofield was ready to respond.

He lifted himself out the passenger window, sat on its sill, and pointed his Desert Eagle dead ahead.

The Mirage's bullets tore up the road in front of the WRX just as Schofield started firing repeatedly at the hovering plane – *blam!-blam!-blam!-blam!-blam!blam!-blam!-blam!-blam!* – hitting it in both of its air intakes at the same time as some of the fighter's tracers sizzled in through the windscreen of his WRX.

Schofield's gas-expanding bullets did their job.

As the first bullets hit the Mirage's intake fans, their internal gases blasted outward, tearing the fans' blades to pieces, warping them, causing them to jam and the plane to stall and also to allow the following bullets to race fully *into* the jet engines themselves and detonate within the plane's highly volatile fuel injection chambers.

Two small bullets was all it took to destroy a $600 million warplane.

Its engines failing, the Mirage wheeled wildly around in the sky, spraying tracer bullets everywhere, before – *boom!* – the French fighter blasted out into a thousand pieces, showering liquid fire, before it just dropped out of the sky, landing in a crumpled smoking heap on the road 50 yards in front of the speeding WRX.

Schofield dropped back inside the passenger window . . .

. . . to see Gant slumped against her door, blood gushing from a giant wound to her left shoulder. A two-inch-wide hole could be seen in the driver's seat behind her, matching the location of her wound.

She'd been hit by one of the Mirage's tracer bullets.

'Oh, no . . .' Schofield breathed. He dived across the seat, hit the brakes.

The WRX squealed to a halt, just short of the wreckage of the Mirage.

'Fox!' Schofield yelled. 'Libby!'

Her eyes opened, heavy-lidded. 'Ow, that hurts . . .' she groaned.

'Come on.' Schofield kicked open the door and lifted her out, carrying her in his arms. Then, into his radio: 'Knight! Where are you!'

'*I'm in the first rig. With another one close behind me. Where are – hang on, I see you.*'

'Fox has been hit. We need a ride.'

'*When I pull up, get in fast, 'cause that other rig is going to be right on my ass.*'

And then Schofield saw Knight: saw the long-nosed Mack rig rumbling up the slope, moving quickly.

With a loud shriek of its brakes, the Mack shuddered to a stop beside the WRX.

Knight threw open the door, and Schofield lifted Gant and himself in. Knight jammed the truck back into gear and hit the gas a bare moment before the snub-nosed Kenworth rig appeared around the bend behind them, coming at full speed, its engine roaring.

The Mack jounced and bounced over the wreckage of the Mirage fighter strewn across the road, picking up speed. The second rig just barged right through the Mirage's remains before ramming hard into the back of Knight's still-accelerating rig.

Knight, Schofield and Gant were all thrown forward by the impact.

Knight and Schofield turned to each other and said at exactly the same time: 'There are two rally cars coming at us from in front!'

They both paused. Mirror images.

'What happened to her!' Knight said.

'She got shot by a fighter plane,' Schofield said.

'Oh.'

The two trucks charged up the hill, their exhaust stacks belching black smoke.

Then suddenly the two yellow rally cars that had gone ahead came into view, rounding a wide bend *right in front of* Knight and Schofield's rig, roaring *down* the same slope – both cars featuring men leaning out their passenger windows, holding AK-47 machine-guns.

They might as well have been firing pea-shooters.

The giant Mack rig blasted right through the left-hand Peugeot, blowing it to smithereens, while the second Axon rally car just fishtailed out of the way, side-swiping the rock wall on the landward side of the roadway before skidding to a jarring halt, the two rigs rumbling past it.

The Mack reached the top of the hill and rejoined the flatter main road at a fork junction.

The snub-nosed Kenworth was right behind it, closely followed by the last-remaining Peugeot. Rejoining the chase, the rally car leapt up onto the main road a split second before – *SLAM!* – the entire fork junction erupted in a cloud of dirt, hit by a shell from the ever-present French destroyer.

The two big rigs flew around a bend, the ocean dropping away to their left, when suddenly they were confronted by the yawning entrance to another cliff-side tunnel. This tunnel bent away in a long curve to the right, hugging the cliff-face, and was clearly longer than any of the previous tunnels.

The Mack thundered into the tunnel doing ninety, just as behind it, the Peugeot pulled alongside the Kenworth and the gunman in the rally car's window unleashed a volley of fire at the Mack's rear-most tyres.

The Mack's tyres were blasted apart, started slapping against the roadway, and the big rig's rear-end started fishtailing wildly.

Which was when the Kenworth rig made its move, and powered forward.

'They're coming alongside us!' Schofield yelled.

In the confines of the tunnel, the snub-nosed rig pulled up next to the Mack's right-hand flank.

'I'll take care of it,' Knight said. 'Here, take the wheel.'

With that, Knight jumped out of the driver's seat and charged aft into the Mack's sleeping compartment where he quickly fired two shots into its rear window, a window which opened onto the rig's flat trailer-connection section. Within seconds he had disappeared out through the window, into the roaring wind.

The two rigs rushed through the curving tunnel side-by-side, whipping past its ocean-side columns.

Schofield drove, glancing at the wounded Gant beside him. She was hit badly this time.

There came a loud aerial boom from somewhere nearby, and Schofield snapped round to see the second Mirage fighter whip past the blurring columns on his left, shooting ahead of the chase.

Not a good sign, he thought.

And then the snub-nosed rig came fully alongside his own on the right. He saw two ExSol men inside its cabin, and as it drew level with the Mack, he saw the gunner climb quickly across the driver and throw open the door closest to the Mack.

He was going to come across.

Schofield raised his Desert Eagle pistol in response – *click*.

No ammo left.

'Crap!'

The Executive Solutions man leapt across the gap between the two speeding semi-trailer rigs, landing on the passenger step of Schofield's Mack. He raised his machine-gun, pointing it in through the window, an unmissable shot—

—at the same time as Schofield drew his Maghook from his thigh holster, aimed it at the thug and pulled the trigger—

Ppp-fzzz . . .

The Maghook didn't fire. It just emitted a weak fizzing sound. It was out of propulsion gas.

'Goddamn it!' Schofield yelled. 'That never happens!'

But now he was out of options: he and Gant were sitting ducks.

The ExSol man in the window saw this, and he leered, his finger squeezing on his trigger.

At which moment he was squashed like a pancake as the Kenworth rig – his rig – rammed viciously into the Mack, hitting it so hard that both trucks were lifted momentarily off the road!

The hapless mercenary simply exploded, his body popping in a burst of red, his eyes bugging before he dropped out of Schofield's view and fell to the rushing roadway beneath the two rigs.

And as the man dropped from sight, he revealed the new driver of the snub-nosed Kenworth rig – Aloysius Knight.

For when the ExSol mercenary had jumped over from the doorway of the Kenworth to the doorway of the Mack, another figure had crossed over *in the other direction*, from the rear section of the Mack to the rear section of the Kenworth rig.

Knight.

Now the two rigs raced side-by-side through the long curving tunnel, pursued only by the last yellow Peugeot.

But with its blown-open rear tyres, Schofield's Mack was dangerously unstable. It slipped and slid wildly, trying to get traction.

Schofield keyed his radio. 'Knight! I can't hold this truck! We have to come over to you!'

'*All right, I'll come in closer. Send your lady over.*'

The Kenworth swung in next to the Mack, rubbing up against its side.

Schofield quickly secured the Mack's steering wheel in place with his seatbelt. Then he shuffled over, kicked open the passenger door, and started to help Gant move.

At the same time, Knight opened his driver's side door and extended his spare hand.

Abruptly, gunfire.

Smacking into both trucks' frames. But it was just wild fire from the trailing Peugeot.

Schofield made the transfer, handed Gant over to Knight – who pulled her across the gap into the Kenworth's cab, before laying her gently on the passenger seat.

With Gant safely across, Schofield started to step across the gap—

—just as a shocking burst of a zillion tracer bullets ripped horizontally through the air in front of him, creating a lethal laser-like barrier, cutting him off from Knight and Gant's rig.

Schofield snapped to look forward and saw the source of this new wave of gunfire.

He saw the end of the curving tunnel, saw the road bend away to the right beyond it, and saw, rising ominously into the air just out from the turn, the second Mirage 2000N-II fighter, its six-barrelled mini-gun blazing away.

And then, to Schofield's horror, the line of sizzling tracer rounds swung in toward his rig and – *bam!-bam!-bam!-bam!-bam!-bam!-bam!-bam!-bam!-bam!-bam!* – an unimaginable barrage of bullets slammed into the metal grille of the Mack, hammering it with a million pock-marks.

The Mack's engine caught fire, hydraulic fluid sprayed everywhere, and suddenly Schofield could see nothing through his windshield. He pumped the brakes – no good; they were history. Tried the steering wheel – it worked only slightly, enough for him to say to the fighter plane:

'If I'm going down, you're going down with me.'

The Mack careered down the length of the tunnel, together with the Kenworth.

And still the Mirage's withering fire didn't stop.

The two rigs hit the end of the tunnel – separated now – and Aloysius Knight had no choice but to take the bend to the right, while Schofield's Mack – its bonnet blazing, its rear tyres sliding – could do nothing but rush *straight ahead*, ignoring the corner.

Schofield saw it all before it happened.

And he knew he could do nothing.

'Good God . . .' he breathed.

A second later, the speeding Mack truck missed the corner completely and blasted *right through* the guard-rail fence and shot out into the clear afternoon sky, heading straight for the hovering Mirage fighter.

The Mack truck soared through the air in a glorious arc, nose high, wheels spinning, its path through the sky traced by the line of black smoke issuing out from its flaming bonnet.

But its arc stopped abruptly as the massive trailer rig slammed at tremendous speed into the Mirage fighter hovering just out from the cliff-side roadway.

The truck and the plane collided with astonishing force, the Mirage lurching backwards in mid-air under the weight of the mighty impact.

Already on fire, the Mack completely blew up now, its flaming bonnet driving into the nose of the hovering French fighter. For its part, the Mirage just rocked – then swayed – and then *exploded*, blasting out in a brilliant blinding fireball.

Then it dropped out of the sky, falling 400 feet straight down the cliff-face with the remains of the Mack truck buried in its nose, before it smashed into the waves below with a single gigantic splash.

And in the middle of it all, in the middle of the tangled mechanical mess, without a rope or a Maghook to call on, was Shane M. Schofield.

Knight and Gant saw it all from their rig as they sped away along the winding cliff-side road.

They saw Schofield's Mack blast through the guard-rail and crash into the hovering Mirage after which came the fiery explosion and the long drop to the ocean below.

No one could have survived such an impact.

Despite her wounds, Gant's eyes widened in horror. 'Oh God, no. Shane . . .' she whispered.

'Son of a bitch,' Knight breathed.

A flurry of thoughts rushed through his mind: Schofield was dead – a man worth millions to Knight *if* he could have kept him alive – what did he do now – and what did he do with this wounded woman who was worth absolutely nothing to him?

The first thing you do is get out of here alive, a voice said inside him.

And then suddenly – *shoom!* – the last-remaining Peugeot rally car whizzed past his rig, heading quickly down the road.

Surprised, Knight looked ahead and saw the road before him.

It contained a strange but impressive feature: at the next curve, a small castle-like structure arched over the roadway.

Made of stone and topped with tooth-like battle-ments, it was a two-storey gatehouse which must have been as old as the Forteresse de Valois itself. Presumably, it marked the outer boundary of the Forteresse's land.

On the far side of this gatehouse, however, was a compact drawbridge, spanning a twenty-foot section of empty space in the roadway. You only got over the gap if the drawbridge was lowered, and at the moment, it was.

But then the Peugeot arrived at the gatehouse and disgorged one of its occupants who ran inside – and suddenly, before Knight's eyes, the drawbridge slowly began to rise.

'No . . .' he said aloud. 'No!'

He floored it.

The Kenworth rig roared toward the medieval gatehouse, picking up speed.

The drawbridge rose slowly on its iron chains.

It was going to be close.

The big rig rushed forward.

The bridge rose slowly: *one foot, two feet, three feet . . .*

The men in the Peugeot opened fire as Knight's rig thundered over the last fifty yards.

Knight ducked. His windshield shattered.

The drawbridge kept rising . . .

. . . and then the rig roared in through the gatehouse's archway, whipping past the Executive Solutions men . . .

. . . and raced up the ramp-like drawbridge, easily doing a hundred, before – *voom!* – it launched itself off the leading edge of the bridge, shooting high into the sky, soaring over the vertiginous gap in the road beneath it and . . .

Whump!

. . . the big rig hit solid ground again, banging down on the roadway, bouncing once, twice, three times, before Knight regained control.

'Phwoar,' he sighed, relieved. 'That was—'

SLAM!

The road in front of the rig erupted in a mushroom cloud of dirt.

A shellburst from the destroyer.

Knight hit the brakes and his rig skidded sharply, lurching to a halt inches away from a newly created hole in the road.

Knight groaned.

The *entire* road in front of him had simply vanished – the whole width of it vaporised – the distance across the chasm to the other side at least thirty feet.

He and Gant were trapped – perfectly – on the vertical cliff-face, bounded both in front and behind by sheer voids in the roadway.

And at that moment, as if right on cue, the Axon corporate helicopter – which had watched the entire chase from a safe distance high above the road – hovered into view beside them, its pilot speaking into his helmet radio.

'Fuck,' Knight said.

FIFTH ATTACK

ENGLAND–FRANCE–USA

26 OCTOBER, 1400 HOURS (ENGLAND)

E.S.T. (NEW YORK, USA) 0900 HOURS

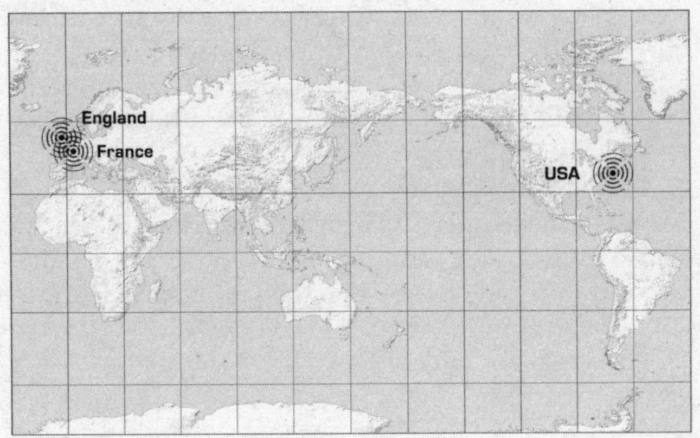

We must guard against the acquisition of unwarranted influence, whether sought or unsought, by the military–industrial complex.

President Dwight D. Eisenhower,

Farewell address to the nation, JANUARY, 1961

UNITED STATES EMBASSY, LONDON, ENGLAND
1400 HOURS LOCAL TIME
(0900 HOURS E.S.T. USA)

'*In their opinion, the war on terror isn't going far enough. While the members of Majestic-12 didn't plan the September 11 attacks, make no mistake, they are taking full advantage of them . . .*'

The man talking on the television screen was Benjamin Y. Rosenthal, the Mossad agent who had been killed on the roof of the King's Tower an hour ago.

Book II watched the TV intently. Behind him stood the State Department guy, Scott Moseley.

Arrayed on the desks around them were documents – hundreds of documents. Everything Benjamin Rosenthal knew about Majestic-12 and this world-wide bounty hunt.

Book scanned the pile of documents again:

Surveillance photos of men in limousines arriving at economic summits.

Secretly taped phone transcripts.

Stolen US Department of Defense files.

Even two documents taken from the French central intelligence agency – the notorious DGSE. One was a DGSE dossier on several of the world's leading businessmen who had been invited to a private dinner with the French President six months ago.

The second document was far more explosive. It outlined the recent capture by the DGSE of 24 members of the terrorist organisation Global Jihad, who had been planning to fly a tanker plane into the Eiffel Tower. Like Al-Qaeda, Global Jihad was a truly world-wide terrorist group, made up of fanatical Islamists who wanted to take the concept of holy war to a whole new global level.

The document that Book now saw was especially notable because one of Global Jihad's leading figures, Shoab Riis, had been among those caught. Normally the capture of such a high-profile terrorist would have been publicised worldwide. But the French had kept Riis's arrest to themselves.

Rosenthal had added a comment in the margin: ***'All were taken to DGSE headquarters in Brest. No trial. No newspaper reports. None of the 24 was ever seen again. Possible connection to Kormoran/Chameleon. Is France working with M-12? Check further.'***

But the most revealing evidence of all was in the Mossad videotapes of Rosenthal's interrogation.

Put simply, Rosenthal had been sitting on dynamite.

First, he had known the composition of Majestic-12:

The Chairman: Randolph Loch, military industrialist, seventy years old, head of Loch-Mann Industries, the defence contractor. L-M Industries manufactured spare parts for military aircraft like the Huey and Black Hawk helicopters. It had made a fortune out of Vietnam and Desert Storm.

The Vice-Chair: Cornelius Kopassus, the legendary Greek container-shipping magnate.

Arthur Quandt, patriarch of the Quandt family steel empire.

Warren Shusett, the world's most successful investor.

J. D. Cairnton, chairman of the colossal Astronox Pharmaceutical Company.

Jonathan Killian, chairman and CEO of Axon Corp, the vast missile and warship-building conglomerate.

The list went on.

Apart from the absence of a few retail fortunes – like the Walton family in America, the Albrechts in Germany or the Mattencourts in France – it could have been a list of the Top Ten Richest People on earth.

And as Major Benjamin Rosenthal had discovered, they were all men whose fortunes would be considerably enlarged by one thing.

Rosenthal on the screen: '*Their fortunes are based on military action. War. World War II was the foundation of the Quandt steel empire. In the '60s, Randolph Loch was one of the most vocal supporters of the US going to Vietnam. Warfare consumes oil. Warfare consumes steel. Warfare calls for the construction of thousands of new ships, helicopters, guns, bombs, pharmaceutical kits. In a world of big business, global warfare is the biggest business of them all.*'

And at another time:

'*Look at the "War on Terror". The United States dropped over four thousand bombs on the mountains of Afghanistan, and for what result? They didn't destroy bridges or supply routes, or military nerve centres. But when four thousand bombs are used, four thousand bombs must be replenished. And that means buying them. And what happened after Afghanistan? Surprise, surprise: another fight was found, this time with Iraq.'*

Another cut:

'*Do not underestimate the influence these men wield. They make Presidents, and they break them. From Bill Clinton's impeachment to the rise of a former KGB agent named Vladimir Putin to the Presidency of Russia, Majestic-12 always has a say in who sits in the seats of world power and for how long. Even if it doesn't directly bankroll a given President's campaign, it always maintains the ability to bring him down at any given moment.*

'*To this end Majestic-12 has forged strong links with leading figures in the world's major intelligence agencies. The Director of the CIA: a former business partner of Randolph Loch. The head of MI-6: Cornelius Kopassus's brother-in-law. That Killian fellow has been a regular visitor to the Paris home of the Director of the DGSE.*

'*After all,*' the Mossad agent smiled, '*who knows more about a country's leaders than that country's own intelligence service?*'

On the TV screen, Rosenthal became serious:

'*More than anything else, though, the war that M-12 loved the most, the war that garnered them more wealth than they ever dreamed of, was the one war that was never actually fought: the US–Soviet Cold War.*

'*Desert Storm. Bosnia. Somalia. Afghanistan. Iraqi Freedom. They pale in comparison to the absolute goldmine that was the Cold War. For as the US–Soviet arms race continued apace and indirect Cold War clashes occurred in Korea and Vietnam, the members of M-12 amassed fortunes of monstrous proportions.*

'*But then in 1991 the impossible happened: the Soviet Union collapsed and it all disappeared.*

'The Berlin Wall fell and like a dam breaking, American consumerism flooded the globe. And the biggest winners in the globalised world were no longer American military manufacturers. They were American consumer goods retailers: Nike, Coca-Cola, Microsoft. Or European companies like BMW and L'Oreal. I mean, honestly, make-up retailers!

'And so ever since, the members of Majestic-12 have been looking for the one thing that will, without question, restore them to their former glory . . .'

At that moment, with a flourish, Rosenthal extracted another document from one of his files and held it to the camera.

'. . . *a new Cold War.*'

Book II now held that very same document in his hands.

The TV screen in front of him was paused, the image of Rosenthal frozen.

Book scanned the document. It read:

Source	Delivery Sys.	W-H	Origin	Target	Time
Talbot	Shahab-5	TN76	35702.90	00001.65	1145
			5001.00	5239.10	
	Shahab-5	TN76	35702.90	00420.02	1145
			5001.00	4900.25	
	Shahab-5	TN76	35702.90	01312.15	1145
			5001.00	5358.75	
Ambrose	Shahab-5	TN76	28743.05	28743.98	1200
			4104.55	4104.64	
	Shahab-5	TN76	28743.05	28231.05	1200
			4104.55	3835.70	
Jewel	Taep'o-Dong-2	N-8	23222.62	23222.70	1215
			3745.75	3745.80	
	Taep'o-Dong-2	N-8	23222.62	24230.50	1215
			3745.75	3533.02	
	Taep'o-Dong-2	N-8	23222.62	23157.05	1215
			3745.75	4930.52	
Hopewell	Taep'o-Dong-2	N-8	11900.00	11622.50	1230
			2327.00	4000.00	
	Taep'o-Dong-2	N-8	11900.00	11445.80	1230
			2327.00	2243.25	
Whale	Shahab-5	TN76	07040.45	07725.05	1245
			2327.00	2958.65	
	Shahab-5	TN76	07040.45	07332.60	1245
			2327.00	3230.55	

Names and numbers leapt out at Book, and at first he couldn't make head or tail of it.

But then, slowly, parts of it began to make sense. He recognised the two most repeated names.

Shahab-5 and Taep'o-Dong-2.

The *Shahab-5* and the *Taep'o-Dong-2* were missiles.

Long-range intercontinental ballistic missiles.

The Shahab-5 was built by Iran. The Taep'o-Dong-2 by North Korea.

If international terrorist organisations like Al-Qaeda or Global Jihad were to ever get their hands on missiles that could deliver nuclear strikes against the West, it would be the Shahab and the Taep'o-Dong.

And each of the missiles was nuclear-tipped, as evidenced by the notations: TN-76 and N-8. The TN-76 was a French-made nuclear warhead; the N-8 was North Korean.

But this list didn't belong to any terrorist organisation.

It belonged to Majestic-12.

And then it hit Book.

Could this be Majestic-12 impersonating a terrorist organisation?

He turned quickly, unpaused the image of Rosenthal on the screen.

The Israeli agent spoke again: '*This new Cold War is an enhanced War against Terrorism. A fifty-year War on Terror.*

'*Majestic-12 are utilising two US projects to execute their plan: one is called "Kormoran", the other "Chameleon". Kormoran encompasses the launch vessels: missile-launching warships disguised as container ships or supertankers. These supertanker shells are built by the Kopassus Shipping Group, while the missile-launch systems are inserted into those shells at Axon plants in Norfolk, Virginia and Guam. These ships – ordinary-looking supertankers and container ships – can sit in harbours and ports around the world and yet never be noticed. That is Kormoran.*

'The "Chameleon" project, however, is far more sinister. Indeed, it is perhaps the most sinister programme ever devised by the United States. It centres on the missiles themselves. You see, the missiles mentioned in the document are not pure Shahabs or Taep'o-Dongs.

'Rather, they are US-built clones of those missiles. What you have to understand is that every major missile in the world has its own personal characteristics: flight signature, contrail wake, even the blast signature left after an impact. Chameleon is designed to exploit these differences. It is a deep-black US project under which America is building intercontinental ballistic missiles that mimic the characteristics of ICBMs built by other countries.

'Clone missiles.

'But Chameleon isn't limited to Iranian Shahabs and North Korean Taep'o-Dongs. Other missiles that have been cloned include the Indian Agni-II, the Pakistani Ghauri-II, the Taiwanese Sky Horse, the UK Trident-II D-5, the French M-5, the Israeli Jericho 2B, and of course the Russian SS-18.

'They are designed to start wars, but to make it look like someone else fired the first shot. If ever the US needs an excuse to wage war, it simply fires a clone of whichever country it seeks to blame.

'The thing is, just as the Chameleon Project has been contracted to the Axon Corporation, the Kormoran supertanker shells are built by Kopassus Shipping. And that is the key. Both projects are contracted to companies owned by M-12 members.'

*

'At 11.45 on October 26 we are going to see a rain of nuclear missiles. A rain such as the world has never seen. Co-ordinated. Precise. Missiles falling in fifteen-minute intervals, to accommodate the global news media. One missile hit is reported just as another lands, then another – striking major cities around the world. London, New York, Paris, Berlin. The world is plunged into chaos, wondering which major city will be next.

'And when it is over, the investigation begins, and the missiles – by their flight characteristics and blast signatures – are determined to be Iranian and North Korean.

'Terrorist weapons.

'The world is aghast. Then, naturally, horror turns to anger. The War on Terror must be expanded. It has already been going for two years. Now it runs for another fifty. A new Cold War has begun and the military–industrial complex is mobilised like never before. And Majestic-12 makes billions.'

Book's mind raced.

Disguised supertankers. Cloned missiles. And all of it created by his own government. He couldn't believe it. He knew the US Government could do terrible things, but setting up other nations with false missiles?

And now these cloned missiles were to be fired – not by the US Government, but by the missiles' builders, the men of Majestic-12 – on major cities around the world: New York, London, Paris and Berlin . . .

New York, London, Paris . . .

And now Book saw the decimalised numbers on the list in a new light.

They were co-ordinates.

GPS co-ordinates of both the launch boats and the targeted cities.

It was then that he noticed the names of the Kormoran supertankers – *Ambrose, Talbot, Jewel Hopewell, Whale*. Cute joke. They were all named after ships from the *Mayflower* fleet, the ships that had seeded the New World. Just as Majestic-12 was now attempting to create a new world.

But what did all this have to do with Shane Schofield and a bounty hunt requiring his death by 12 noon today? Book thought.

And then he recalled Rosenthal himself, shouting in the rain on the roof of the King's Tower in London:

'It's all about reflexes. Superfast reflexes. The reflexes of the men on that list are the best in the world. *They passed the Cobra tests*, and only someone who passed the Cobra tests can disarm the CincLock-VII missile security system, and CincLock-VII is at the core of Majestic-12's plan.'

CincLock-VII . . . Book thought.

He flicked through the many folders in front of him, searching for those words.

It didn't take him long to find them.

There was a whole file marked 'AXON CORP – PATENTED CINCLOCK SECURITY SYSTEM'.

It was filled with documents belonging to Axon Corp and the US Department of Defense. The first document's cover sheet was marked:

PROJECT: CHAMELEON-042
(VARIANT INCORPORATING
CINCLOCK-VII LAUNCH SECURITY SYSTEM)

US DEPARTMENT OF DEFENSE
SECURITY LEVEL: 009

TOP SECRET

Contractor: Axon Corporation LLC
Progress Report: May, 2002

Book flicked to the section marked 'SECURITY', read the lead paragraph:

DISARM SYSTEM – CINCLOCK VII

In keeping with the high level of security necessary for such a weapon, the *Chameleon* series of missiles has been equipped with Axon's patented CincLock-VII disarm system. The most secure anti-tamper mechanism in the world today, CincLock-VII employs three unique defensive protocols. Unless all three protocols are applied in the prescribed sequence, system activation (or de-activation) is impossible.

The key to the system is the second protocol. It is based on the well-established principles of pattern-recognition (Haynes & Simpson, MIT 1994, 1997, 2001), whereby only a person who is familiar with, and well-practised in, an established sequential pattern can enter it on demand. A stranger to the system, unless he or she is possessed of abnormally quick motor-neural reflexes, cannot hope to overcome such a system (op. cit. Oliphant & Nicholson, USAMRMC, 1996, NATO MNRR study).

Employing these principles, field tests have shown the CincLock VII system to be 99.94% secure against unauthorised use. No other security system in the military can boast such a success rate.

PROTOCOLS

The three protocols of the CincLock VII unit are as follows:

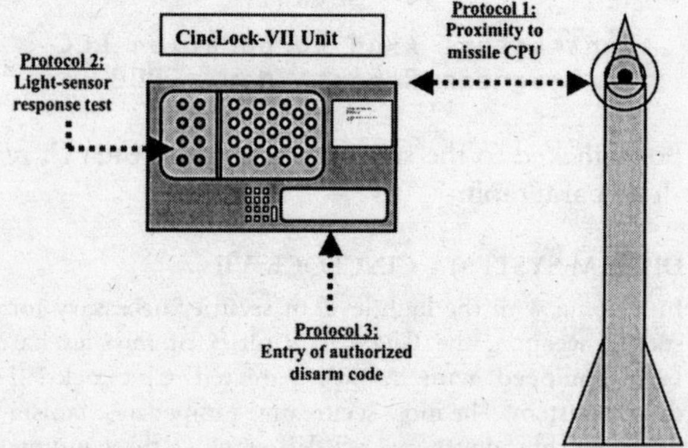

1. *Proximity*. To ensure against unauthorised arming/disarming, the CincLock unit is *not* attached to the delivery system. It is a portable disarming unit. The first protocol, then, is proximity to the delivery system. CincLock will only operate within sixty (60) feet of a Chameleon missile's central processing unit.
2. *Light-sensor response unit*. Once inside the proximity perimeter, the user must establish a wireless modem connection with the disarm system. This is effected by satisfying Axon's patented light-sensor interface. It is here that the principles of pattern recognition play their crucial part. (See NATO MNRR Research Program results, USAMRMC, 1996.)
3. *Security code*. Entry of the relevant disarm or override code.

To this last line Rosenthal had added: ***'Universal Disarm Code insertion was supervised by subject Weitzman. Latest intelligence suggests use of a yet-to-be-determined Mersenne Prime.'***

Another page, however, was clipped to this protocol section. It was a Mossad telephone intercept transcript:

Trans log: **B2-3-001-889**
Date: **25 April, 1515 hours E.S.T.**
Rec from: **Axon Corp, Norfolk, VA, USA**
Katsa: **ROSENTHAL, Benjamin Y (452-7621)**

VOICE 1 (DALTON, P.J. AXON CHIEF OF ENGINEERING): Sir, the D.O.D. inspection report is in. It's good. They're very pleased with our progress. And they particularly loved CincLock. Couldn't get enough of it. Christ, they were like kids with a new toy, trying to crack it.

VOICE 2 (KILLIAN, J.J. AXON CHAIR AND CEO): Excellent, Peter. Excellent. Anything else?

VOICE 1: (DALTON) The next oversight inspection. D.O.D asked if we had a preferred date.

VOICE 2: (KILLIAN) Why don't we make it October 26. I believe that date would suit some of our partners on this project very nicely.

Book II leaned back in his chair.

So there was the significance of the date.

October 26.

Killian had set it as the date for a Department of Defense oversight team to examine his installation plants.

But then Book saw the next document, and suddenly the meaning of the bounty hunt became clear.

Ironically, it was the most innocuous of all the documents he had seen so far. An internal email from Axon Corp:

From: Peter Dalton
To: All Engineering Staff, Project 'C-042'
Date: 26 April, 2003, 7:58 p.m.
Subject: NEXT D.O.D. INSPECTION

Ladies and gentlemen, I am pleased to announce that last week's six-monthly inspection by the Department of Defense Oversight Committee went spectacularly well. I thank you all for your hard work, especially over the past few months.

They were impressed with our progress and amazed by our technological gains.

The next six-monthly inspection is slated for 26 October at the Norfolk installation plant, to commence at 12 noon, department heads only. As usual, strict security clearance provisions will apply for the week preceding the inspection.

Regards,

PD

And that was it.

At 12 noon today, October 26, the Department of Defense would be sending an inspection team into Axon's missile construction facility in Norfolk, Virginia.

And presumably at that time, they were going to discover that something was amiss at the plant, that the missiles had been tampered with in some way, or perhaps even gone – stolen – at which point . . .

. . . the US Government would go searching for the only men in the world who were able to disarm the Cinc-Lock system.

Men with abnormally quick reflexes.

The men on the list.

And then it dawned on Book – for some reason, Jonathan Killian and Majestic-12 *wanted* the US Government to carry out that inspection today. Although he didn't know why yet, somehow today's inspection was an integral part of their plan.

Which made him understand something else more clearly. It had always bothered Book that this bounty hunt might only serve to *warn* the very men who could foil M-12's plans.

But now this explained it.

At 12 noon today, the US Government was going to

discover *something* at Axon's Norfolk plant, something about the state of the Chameleon missiles and the Kormoran launch ships. Something which was crucial to Majestic-12's plan to start a new Cold War.

'We have to get to that plant,' Book said aloud.

He turned to Scott Moseley. 'Mr Moseley. Call the Department of Defense. Tell them to send their Kormoran–Chameleon inspection team in early. And get on the horn to our people in Guam. Get someone to check out Axon's plant there as well.'

'Got it,' Moseley said.

Book then turned his attention to the stream of decimalised numbers on the launch list: the GPS coordinates of the launch sites and the targets. 'Better find out where these missiles are going to be fired from and what they're aiming at.'

As he booted up a GPS plotting program on his computer, he keyed his satellite radio. 'Scarecrow! It's Book! Come in! I've got some big news for you . . .'

NEAR THE FORTERESSE DE VALOIS
BRITTANY, FRANCE
26 OCTOBER, 1500 HOURS LOCAL TIME
(0900 HOURS E.S.T. USA)

The Axon chopper that had swung to a halt in front of Aloysius Knight and Libby Gant could be seen zooming away along the coastline, getting smaller and smaller, heading back toward the Forteresse de Valois – with Knight and Gant now inside it.

A lone figure treading water in the ocean waves at the base of the cliffs watched it fly away.

Schofield.

Naturally, when his blazing Mack had launched itself off the roadway and smashed into the hovering Mirage fighter jet, Schofield hadn't been in it.

As soon as his truck's tyres had left the road, he had bailed out the driver's side door, dropping into the air beneath the flying rig.

The truck hit the fighter.

Gigantic explosion. Colossal noise. Metal flying everywhere.

But Schofield had been *under* the blast when it had

happened – well below the fireball, but also out of Gant or Knight's sight – and he fell like a bullet through the air.

His first thought had been: *Maghook.*

Not this time. Out of propellant.

Damn.

He kept falling – not vertically, but at a slanting angle thanks to the inertia of the truck – the cliff-face streaking past him at phenomenal speed. He saw the ocean waves below him, rushing upwards. If he hit the water from this height, his body would explode against the surface and burst like a tomato.

Do something! his mind screamed.

Like what!

And then he remembered—

—and quickly yanked the ripcord on his chest webbing. The ripcord that was attached to the attack parachute still on his back. He'd been wearing it ever since the battle on board the Hercules. It had been so compact that he'd almost forgotten it was there.

The attack parachute blossomed above him, a bare eighty feet above the water.

It didn't slow his fall completely, but it did enough.

He lurched in the air about twenty feet above the waves, his downward speed significantly reduced, before – *shoom* – he entered the water feet-first and disengaged the parachute, allowing himself to shoot into the ocean trailing a finger of bubbles above him.

And not a second too soon.

For a moment later, the Mack rig and the Mirage fighter crashed down in a flaming metal heap into the waves nearby.

*

Schofield surfaced a short distance out from the cliffs, amid some of the burning remains of the fighter jet.

Careful to stay out of sight, he trod water amid the floating debris and sure enough, a minute later, he saw the Axon chopper swing around a nearby cliff-bend and zoom back toward the castle.

Had Gant and Knight got away? Or were they in that chopper?

'Fox! Fox! Come in! This is Scarecrow,' he whispered into his throat-mike. 'For what it's worth, I'm still alive. Are you okay?'

A single laboured cough answered him. It was an old technique – she was up there but she obviously couldn't talk. They'd caught her.

'One for yes, two for no. Are you in that Axon chopper I just saw?'

Single cough.

'Are you wounded badly?'

Single cough.

'Really badly?'

Single cough.

Shit, Schofield thought.

'Is Knight with you?'

Single cough.

'Are they taking you back to the castle?'

Single cough.

'Hang in there, Libby. I'm coming for you.'

Schofield looked around himself and was about to start swimming for the shore when abruptly he saw the French destroyer surging to a halt 200 yards away from him off the coast.

On the side of the great ship, he saw a small patrol boat being lowered into the water, with at least a dozen men on board it.

The patrol boat dropped into the ocean and immediately zipped away from the destroyer, heading directly for him.

Schofield could do nothing except watch the French patrol boat approach him.

'I'm sure the French have forgotten about that thing in Antarctica,' he muttered to himself.

Then his earpiece burst to life.

'*Scarecrow! It's Book! Come in! I've got some big news for you.*'

'Hey, Book, I'm here.'

'*Can you talk?*'

Schofield rose and fell with the waves of the Atlantic. 'Yeah, sure, why not.' He eyed the patrol boat, now only 150 yards away. 'Although I have to warn you, I think I'm about to die.'

'*Yes, but I know why*,' Book II said.

'Book, patch Gant and Knight in on this transmission,' Schofield said. 'They can't talk, but I want them to hear this, too.'

Book did so.

Then he told them all about the Kormoran 'supertankers' and the Chameleon clone missiles, and Majestic-12's plan to start a new Cold War – on Terror – by firing those missiles on the major cities of the world. He also told them about the CincLock VII security system which only Schofield and those on the list could disarm, and the incorporation by Ronson Weitzman of the US Universal Disarm Code into it, a code which Rosenthal had described as 'a yet-to-be-determined Mersenne Prime'.

Schofield frowned.

'A Mersenne Prime . . .' he said. 'A Mersenne prime number. It's a *number* . . .'

The image of General Ronson Weitzman in the Hercules flashed across his mind, babbling incoherently under the influence of the British truth drug: 'It wasn't just Kormoran. It was Chameleon, too . . . oh God, Kormoran and Chameleon together. Boats and missiles. All disguised. *Christ* . . . But the Universal Disarm Code, it changes every week. At the moment, it's . . . the sixth . . . oh my God, the sixth m . . . m . . . mercen . . . mercen—'

Mercen . . .

Mersenne.

At the time, Schofield had thought Weitzman was just mixing up his sentences, trying to say the word 'mercenary'.

But he wasn't.

Under the influence of the drug, Weitzman had been telling the truth. He had been naming the code.

The Universal Disarm Code was the sixth Mersenne prime number.

As Book relayed his tale to Schofield and the others, behind him Scott Moseley was busy inserting the GPS co-ordinates from the launch list into the plotting program.

'I've got the first three boats,' Moseley said. 'The first co-ordinate must be the location of the Kormoran launch boat, the second is the target.'

He handed Book the document: now with place names added to it and highlighted:

Source	Delivery Sys.	W-H	Origin	Target	Time
Talbot	Shahab-5	TN76	35702.90	00001.65	1145
			5001.00	5239.10	
			(E. Channel)	(London)	
	Shahab-5	TN76	35702.90	00420.02	1145
			5001.00	4900.25	
			(E. Channel)	(Paris)	
	Shahab-5	TN76	35702.90	01312.15	1145
			5001.00	5358.75	
			(E. Channel)	(Berlin)	
Ambrose	Shahab-5	TN76	28743.05	28743.98	1200
			4104.55	4104.64	
			(New York)	(New York)	
	Shahab-5	TN76	28743.05	28231.05	1200
			4104.55	3835.70	
			(New York)	(Washington, D.C.)	
Jewel	Taep'o-Dong-2	N-8	23222.62	23222.70	1215
			3745.75	3745.80	
			(San Fran)	(San Fran)	
	Taep'o-Dong-2	N-8	23222.62	24230.50	1215
			3745.75	3533.02	
			(San Fran)	(Los Angeles)	
	Taep'o-Dong-2	N-8	23222.62	23157.05	1215
			3745.75	4930.52	
			(San Fran)	(Seattle)	

Moseley plotted the points on a map. 'The first boat is in the English Channel – off Cherbourg, France, up near the Normandy beaches.'

Book relayed this to Schofield, 'The first boat is in the

English Channel, near Cherbourg, off the Normandy beaches. It'll fire on London, Paris and Berlin. The next two boats are in New York and San Francisco, each set to take out multiple cities.'

'Christ,' Schofield said as he hovered in the water.

The patrol boat was fifty yards away, almost on him now.

'Okay, Book. Listen,' he said, just as a low wave smacked him in the face. He spat out a mouthful of salt water. 'Submarine interdiction. Those missile boats can't launch if they're on the bottom of the ocean. Decode the GPS locations of all the Kormoran supertankers and contact any attack subs we have nearby. 688Is, boomers, I don't care. Anything with a torpedo on board. Then send them to take out those Kormoran launch boats.'

'That might work for some of the tankers, Scarecrow, but it won't work for all of them.'

'I know,' Schofield said. 'I know. If we can't destroy a launch vessel, then we'll have to board it and disarm the missiles in their silos.

'The thing is, a light-signal response unit would require the disarmer – me – to be reacting to a disarm program on the unit's screen. Which means I'd have to be sitting within sixty feet of *each missile's control console* to disarm them, but I can't be everywhere around the world at the same time. Which means I'll need people on each launch boat connecting me via satellite to that boat's missiles.'

'You need people on each boat?'

'That's right, Book. If there are no subs in the area, someone's going to have get on board each Kormoran boat, get within sixty feet of its missile console, attach a satellite uplink to that console and then patch me in via satellite. Only then can I use a CincLock unit to personally stop *all* the missile launches.'

'Holy shit,' Book said. 'So what do you want me to do?'

Another wave splashed over Schofield's head. 'Let's tackle the first three boats first. Get yourself to New York, Book. And call David Fairfax. Send him to San Francisco. I want people I know on those tankers. If I get out of this alive, I'll try for the tanker in the English Channel. Oh, and ask Fairfax what the sixth Mersenne prime number is. If he doesn't know, tell him to find out.

'And last, send that Department of Defense inspection team in early – the one that was going to visit Axon's missile-construction plant in Norfolk, Virginia, at 12 noon. I want to know what's happened at that plant.'

'Already done that,' Book II said.

'Nice work.'

'What about you?' Book said.

At that exact moment, the French patrol boat swung to a halt above Schofield. Angry-looking sailors on its deck eyed him down the barrels of FAMAS assault rifles.

'They haven't killed me yet,' Schofield said. 'Which means someone wants to talk with me. It also means I'm still in the game. Scarecrow, out.'

And with that Schofield was hauled out of the water at gunpoint.

THE WHITE HOUSE, WASHINGTON, USA
26 OCTOBER, 0915 HOURS LOCAL TIME
(1515 HOURS IN FRANCE)

The White House Situation Room buzzed with activity.

Aides hustled left and right. Generals and Admirals spoke into secure phones. The words on everyone's lips were 'Kormoran', 'Chameleon' and 'Shane Schofield'.

The President strode into the room just as one of the Navy men, an Admiral named Gaines, pressed his phone to his shoulder.

'Mr President,' Gaines said, 'I've got Moseley in London on the line. He's saying that this Schofield character wants me to deploy attack submarines against various surface targets around the world. Sir, please, I'm not seriously supposed to let a thirty-year-old Marine *captain* control the entire United States Navy, am I?'

'You'll do exactly as Captain Schofield says, Admiral,' the President said. 'Whatever he wants, he gets. If he says deploy our subs, you deploy the subs. If he says blockade North Korea, you blockade North Korea. People! I thought I was clear about this! I don't want you coming to me to check on everything Schofield asks for. The fate of the world could be resting on that man's shoulders. I know him and I trust him. Hell, I'd trust him with my life. Anything short of a nuclear strike, you do it and advise me later. Now do as the man says and dispatch those subs!'

OFFICES OF THE DEFENSE INTELLIGENCE AGENCY, SUB-LEVEL 3, THE PENTAGON 26 OCTOBER, 0930 HOURS LOCAL TIME (1530 HOURS IN FRANCE)

A battered and bruised David Fairfax trudged back into his office on the bottom floor of the Pentagon, flanked by a pair of policemen.

Wendel Hogg was waiting for him, with Audrey by his side.

'Fairfax!' Hogg roared. 'Where in all hell and damnation have you been!'

'I'm going home for the day,' Fairfax said wearily.

'Bull*shit* you are,' Hogg said. 'You are going on report! Then you are going upstairs to face a disciplinary hearing under Pentagon Security Regulations 402 and 403 . . .'

Too tired to care, Fairfax could only stand there and take it.

'. . . and then, *then*, you're going to be outta here for good, you little wise-ass. And you're finally gonna learn that you ain't special, that you ain't untouchable, and—' Hogg shot a look at Audrey – 'that this country's security is best left to men like me, men who can fight, men who are prepared to hold a weapon and put their lives on the—'

He never finished his sentence.

For at that moment a squad of twelve Force Reconnaissance Marines stomped into the doorway behind Fairfax. They wore full battle dress uniforms and were *heavily* armed – Colt Commando assault rifles, MP-7s, deadly eyes.

Fairfax's eyes widened in surprise.

The Marine leader stepped forward. 'Gentlemen. My name is Captain Andrew Trent, United States Marine Corps. I'm looking for Mr David Fairfax.'

Fairfax swallowed.

Audrey gasped.

Hogg just went bug-eyed. 'What in cotton-pickin' hell is going on here?'

The Marine named Trent stepped forward. He was a big guy, all muscle, and in his full battle dress uniform, a seriously imposing figure.

'You must be Hogg,' Trent said. 'Mr Hogg, my orders come direct from the President of the United States. There is a serious international incident afoot and at this critical time, Mr Fairfax is perhaps the fourth most important person in the country. My orders state that I am to escort him on a mission of the highest importance and guard him with my life. So if you don't mind, Mr Hogg, *get out of the man's way*.'

Hogg just stood there, stunned.

Audrey just gazed at Fairfax, amazed.

Fairfax himself hesitated. After this morning's events, he didn't know who to trust.

'Mr Fairfax,' Trent said. 'I've been sent by Shane Schofield. He says he needs your help again. If you still don't believe me, here . . .'

Trent held out his radio. Fairfax took it.

At the other end was Book II.

Within twenty-two minutes, Dave Fairfax was sitting on board a chartered Concorde jet, heading west across the country at supersonic speed, his destination: San Francisco.

On the way to the airport, Book had briefed him on what Schofield needed him to do. Book had also asked him a maths question: what was the sixth Mersenne prime number.

'The sixth Mersenne?' Fairfax had said. 'I'm going to need a pen, some paper and a scientific calculator.'

And so now he sat in the passenger cabin of the Concorde – head bent over a pad, writing furiously, concentrating intensely – shooting across the country all alone.

Alone, that is, except for the team of twelve United States Marines protecting him.

AXON CORPORATION SHIPBUILDING AND MISSILE ATTACHMENT PLANT, NORFOLK, VIRGINIA, USA
26 OCTOBER, 0935 HOURS LOCAL TIME
(1535 HOURS IN FRANCE)

Surrounded by two teams of United States Marines, the Department of Defense inspection team in charge of the Kormoran–Chameleon Joint Project approached the missile installation facility in Norfolk, Virginia.

The Axon plant loomed above them – a giant industrial landscape comprising a dozen interconnected buildings, eight enormous dry-docks and innumerable cranes lancing into the sky.

This was where Axon Corp installed its cutting-edge missile systems onto US naval vessels. Sometimes Axon even built the vessels here as well.

At the moment, a lone mammoth supertanker sat in one of the plant's dry-docks, covered by gantry cranes, towering above the industrial shoreline.

But strangely, at 9.30 in the morning, there was not a sign of life anywhere.

*

The Marines stormed the plant.

There was no firefight.

No battle.

Within minutes, the area was declared secure, the Marine commander declaring over the radio:

'*You can let those D.O.D. boys in now. But let me warn you, it ain't pretty in here.*'

The smell was overwhelming.

The stench of rotting human flesh.

The main office area was bathed in blood. It was smeared on the walls, caked on benchtops, some of it had even dried as it had dripped down steel staircases, forming gruesome maroon stalactites.

Fortunately for Axon's legions of construction workers, the plant had been in security lockdown for the week preceding the official inspection, so they had been spared.

The company's senior engineers and department heads, however, hadn't been so lucky. They lay slumped in a neat row in the main lab side-by-side, having been executed on their knees, one after the other. Foul starbursts of blood stained the wall behind their fallen bodies.

Over the past week, rats had feasted on their remains.

Five bodies, however, stood out amid the carnage – they had quite obviously not been Axon employees.

The men of Axon, it seemed, had not gone down without a fight. Their small security force had nailed some of the intruders.

The five suspicious bodies lay at several locations around the plant, variously shot in the head or in the body, AK-47 machine-guns lying on the ground beside their corpses.

All were dressed in black military gear, but all also wore black Arab howlis, or headcloths, to cover their faces.

And despite the sorry state of their vermin-ravaged bodies, one other thing about them was clear: they all bore on their shoulders the distinctive double-scimitar tattoo of the terrorist organisation, Global Jihad.

The Department of Defense inspection team assessed the damage quickly, aided by agents from the ISS and FBI.

They also took a call from a secondary team checking out Axon's Pacific plant in Guam. A similar massacre, it seemed, had happened there as well.

When this news came in, one of the D.O.D. men got on the phone, dialling a secure line at the White House.

'It's bad,' he said. 'In Norfolk: we have fifteen dead – nine engineers, six security staff. Enemy casualties: five terrorists, all dead. Forensics indicate that the bodies have been decomposing for about eight days. Actual time of death is impossible to tell. Same story in Guam, except only one terrorist was killed there.

'All the terrorists here have been identified by the FBI as known members of Global Jihad – including one pretty big fish, a guy named Shoab Riis. But sir, the worst thing is this: there must have been more terrorists involved. Three of the Kormoran supertankers are missing from the Norfolk plant, and two more from the Guam facility . . . and all of them are armed with Chameleon missiles.'

AIRSPACE ABOVE THE FRENCH COAST
26 OCTOBER, 1540 HOURS LOCAL TIME
(0940 HOURS E.S.T. USA)

The *Black Raven* rocketed down the French coastline heading toward the Forteresse de Valois.

'So, Rufus,' Mother said, 'there's something I've got to know. What's the story with your boss? I mean, what's an honest grunt like you doing with a murderous bastard like this Knight guy?'

In the front seat of the Sukhoi, Rufus tilted his head.

'Captain Knight ain't a bad man,' he said in his drawling Southern accent. 'And definitely not as bad as everyone says he is. Sure, he can kill a man cold – and believe me, I seen him do it – but he weren't born that way. He was *made* that way. He ain't no saint, for sure, but he isn't an evil man. And he's always looked after me.'

'Right . . .' Mother said. She was worried about this bounty hunter who was supposedly protecting Schofield.

'So what about all that stuff in his file then? How he betrayed his Delta unit in the Sudan, warned Al-Qaeda of the attack and let his own guys walk into a trap. Thirteen men, wasn't it? All killed because of him.'

Rufus nodded sadly.

'Yeah, I seen that file, too,' he said, 'and let me tell you, all that stuff about Sudan, it's horseshit. I know because I was there. Captain Knight never betrayed no one. And he sure as hell never left thirteen men to die.'

'He never left them there?' Mother asked.

'No, ma'am,' Rufus said, 'Knight killed those cock-suckers himself.'

'I was a chopper pilot back then,' Rufus said, 'with the NightStalkers, flying D-boys like Knight in on black ops. We were doing night raids into Sudan, taking out terrorist training camps after the embassy bombings in Kenya and Tanzania in '98. We were flying out of Yemen, skimming into Sudan from across the Red Sea.

'I got to know Knight at the base in Aden. He was kinda quiet, kept to himself most of the time. He read books, you know, thick ones, with no pictures. And he was always writing letters to his young wife back home.

'He was different to most of the guys in my unit, the chopper pilots. They weren't so nice to me. See, I'm kinda smart, but in my own way – I can do maths and physics easy as pie, and because of that I can fly a plane or a helicopter better than any man alive. Thing is, I ain't so good in social environments. Sometimes I just don't get the humour in jokes, especially dirty ones. That kinda thing.

'And the other NightStalker pilots, well, they liked to joke with me – like sending one of the hospital nurses over to my table in the mess hall to talk all sexy with me. Or putting me down for briefings that I wasn't meant to attend. Stuff like that. Instead of calling me Rufus, they called me "Doofus".

'Then some of the Rangers at the base started calling

me that, too. I hated it. But Captain Knight, he never called me that. Never once. He always called me by my name.

'Anyway, one time, he was walking past my dorm just after some of them pilot bastards had taken all my bedside books while I was sleeping and switched 'em with some dirty magazines. They was all laughing at me when Captain Knight asked what was going on.

'A pilot named Harry Hartley told him to fuck off, mind his own business. Knight just stood there in the doorway, dead still. Again Hartley told him to beat it. Knight didn't move. So Hartley approached him angrily and took a swing at him. Knight dropped the asshole using only his legs, then he pressed a knee to Hartley's throat and said that my pilot skills were very much his business and that I was to be left alone . . . or else he'd come back.

'No one ever played a joke on me again.'

Mother said, 'So what happened with the thirteen soldiers who died in Sudan then?'

'When he went out on a mission,' Rufus said, 'Knight often worked alone. Delta guys are allowed to do that, run solo. One man acting alone can often do more damage than an entire platoon.

'Anyway, one night, he's in Port Sudan, staking out an old warehouse. Place is a ghost town, deserted, run-down to all hell. Which is why Al-Qaeda had a training camp there, inside a big old warehouse.

'So Knight gets inside the warehouse and waits. That night, there's a big meeting there but this ain't your usual backstreets-of-Sudan meeting between Al-Qaeda buyers and Russian arms dealers. No, it's fucking Bin Laden himself and three CIA spooks, and they're talking about the Embassy bombings.

'Knight sends a silent digital signal out, giving his location, calling for back-up, and indicating that OBL himself is there. He offers to liquidate OBL, but command tells him to stand down. They're sending a Delta hit team in on his signal.

'The Delta team is sent from Aden, sixteen men in a Black Hawk, flown by me. Of course, by the time we get to the warehouse in Port Sudan, Bin Laden is gone.

'We meet Knight at the rendezvous point on the coast – an abandoned lighthouse. He's pissed as hell. The leader of the Delta hit squad is a punk named Brandeis, Captain Wade Brandeis. He tells Knight that something bigger is at stake here. Something way over Knight's head.

'Knight turns on his heel, heads for the chopper in disgust. Then, behind him, that fucker Brandeis just nods to two of his guys and says, "The chopper pilot, too. He can't go back after seeing this." And so these Delta assholes raise their MP-5s at Knight's back *and* at me in my chopper.

'There was no time for me to shout, but I didn't have to. Knight had heard 'em move. He told me later that he heard the sound of their sleeves brushing against their body armour – the sound of someone raising a gun.

'A second before they fired, Knight dashed forward and tackled me into my own helicopter's hold. The Delta guys rushed us, silenced guns blazin' away, hammering the chopper. But Knight is moving too fast. He pushes me out the other side of the chopper, yanks me across a patch of open ground and into the lighthouse.

'You wouldn't believe what happened inside that lighthouse after that. The Delta team came in after us, the *whole* Delta hit team. Sixteen men. Only three came out.

'Knight killed nine Delta commandos inside that lighthouse before Brandeis and two other guys cut their losses and headed outside. Then, knowing that Knight was still inside fighting with four of his own men, Brandeis planted a Thermite-Amatol demolition charge at the front door.

'Don't know if you've ever seen a Thermite charge go off before, but they are mighty big blasters. Well, that charge went off and that old lighthouse fell like a big old California redwood. The whole area shook like an earthquake when it hit the ground.

'When the dust settled, there was nothing left – *nothing* – just a pile of rubble. Nobody inside could have survived. Not us. Not the four Delta guys Brandeis had left in there.

'So Brandeis and the other two took off in my chopper and headed back to Aden.

'As it turned out, the building's collapse did kill the last four D-boys. Squashed 'em like flapjacks. But not Knight and me. Knight had seen Brandeis leave the lighthouse, and guessed that he'd blow the building. So Knight zip-lined us down the hollow well-shaft of the lighthouse – past the four Delta guys on the stairs – and bundled us both into a storm cellar at the base of the building.

'The lighthouse fell, but that storm cellar held. It was strong, concrete-walled. Took the pair of us two whole days to dig ourselves out of the rubble.'

'Man . . .' Mother said.

'Turned out Brandeis was working for some group inside the US military called the Intelligence Convergence Group, or ICG. Heard of them?'

'Yeah. Once or twice,' Mother said grimly.

'Don't hear about the ICG much any more,' Rufus

said. 'They say it was a bad-ass government agency that infiltrated military units, big companies and universities with its agents and then reported back to the government. But there was a purge a couple of years back that wiped it out. But some members like Brandeis survived. Turned out the ICG had been behind the attacks on the US embassies in Africa – they were liquidating some spies in those offices and had got Al-Qaeda to do their dirty work.

'To cover itself for the lighthouse bloodbath, though, the ICG blamed the whole thing on Knight. Said that he'd been taking millions from Al-Qaeda. Attributed all thirteen Delta deaths to Knight by saying that he pre-warned Al-Qaeda of their arrival. Knight was placed at the top of the Department of Defense's Most Wanted Persons List. His file was marked Classification Zebra: shoot on sight. And the US Government put a price on his head: two million dollars, dead or alive.'

'A bounty hunter with a price on his head. Nice,' Mother said.

Rufus said, 'But then the ICG did the worst thing of all. Remember I told you that Knight had a young wife. He also had a baby. ICG had them killed. Set it up as a home invasion gone wrong. Killed the woman and the baby.

'And now, now the ICG is dead and Knight's family is dead, but the price on Knight's head remains. The US Government occasionally sends a hit squad after him, like they did in Brazil a few years ago. And, of course, Wade Brandeis is still on active duty with Delta. I think he's a major now, still based in Yemen.'

'And so Knight became a bounty hunter,' Mother said.

'That's right. And I went with him. He saved my life,

and he's always been good to me, always respected me. And he ain't never forgot Brandeis. Got a tattoo on his arm just to remind himself. Boy, is he waiting for the chance to meet that cat again.'

Mother took this all in.

She found herself reliving the mission she'd endured with Schofield and Gant at that remote ice station in Antarctica a few years back, an adventure which had involved their own battle with the ICG.

Fortunately for them, they had won. But at around the same time, Aloysius Knight had also been doing battle with the ICG – and he'd lost. Badly.

'He sounds like a Shane Schofield gone wrong,' she whispered.

'What?'

'Nothing.'

Mother gazed out at the horizon, a peculiar thought entering her mind. She found herself wondering: what would happen to Shane Schofield if he ever *lost* such a contest?

A few minutes later, the *Black Raven* hit the coast of Brittany.

Rufus and Mother saw the cliff-side roadway winding away from the Forteresse de Valois – saw the exploded-open craters in the road, the shell impacts on the cliffs, saw the crashed and smoking remains of trailer rigs, rally cars and helicopters strewn all over the place.

'What the hell happened here?' Rufus gaped.

'The Scarecrow happened here,' Mother said. 'The big question is, where is he now?'

THE FRENCH AIRCRAFT CARRIER, *RICHELIEU*, ATLANTIC OCEAN, OFF THE FRENCH COAST 26 OCTOBER, 1545 HOURS LOCAL TIME (0945 HOURS E.S.T. USA)

The giant French Super Puma naval helicopter landed on the flight deck of the aircraft carrier – with Shane Schofield in it, handcuffed and disarmed and covered by no fewer than six armed sailors.

After the patrol boat had picked him up near the cliffs, Schofield had been taken to the French destroyer. From there he had been whisked by helicopter to the colossal Charles de Gaulle-class carrier, *Richelieu,* hovering on the ocean farther out.

No sooner had the helicopter landed on the flight deck than the ground beneath it moved – downward. The Super Puma had landed on one of the carrier's gigantic side-mounted elevators, and now that elevator was descending.

The elevator lurched to a halt in front of a massive internal hangar bay situated directly underneath the flight deck. It was filled with Mirage fighters, anti-submarine planes, fuel trucks and jeeps.

And standing in the middle of it all, awaiting the

arrival of the elevator containing the chopper, was a small group of four very senior French officials:

One Navy Admiral.

One Army General.

One Air Force Commodore.

And one man in a plain grey suit.

Schofield was shoved out of the Super Puma, his hands cuffed in front of him.

He was brought before the four French officials.

Apart from Schofield's half-dozen guards, the maintenance hangar had been cleared of personnel. It made for an odd sight: this cluster of tiny figures standing among the aeroplanes inside the cavernous but deserted hangar bay.

'So this is the Scarecrow,' the Army General snorted. 'The man who took out a team of my best paratroopers in Antarctica.'

The Admiral said, 'I also lost an entire submarine during that incident. To this day, it has not been accounted for.'

So much for forgetting about Antarctica, Schofield thought.

The man in the suit stepped forward. He seemed smoother than the others, more precise, more articulate. Which made him seem more dangerous. 'Monsieur Schofield, my name is Pierre Lefevre, I am from the Direction Générale de la Sécurité Extérieure.'

The DGSE, Schofield thought. *The French version of the CIA. And aside from the Mossad, the most ruthless intelligence agency in the world.*

Great.

'So, Pierre,' he said, 'what's the story? Is France in league with Majestic-12? Or just Jonathan Killian?'

'I do not know what you are talking about,' Lefevre said airily. 'All we know is what Monsieur Killian has told us, and the Republic of France sees a tactical advantage in allowing his organisation's plan to run its course.'

'So what do you want with me?'

The Army General said, 'I would like to rip your heart out.'

The Navy Admiral said, 'And I would like to show it to you.'

'*My* objective is somewhat more practical,' Lefevre said calmly. 'The Generals will get their wish, of course. But not before you answer some of my questions, or before we see for ourselves whether Monsieur Killian's plan is truly foolproof.'

Lefevre laid his briefcase on a nearby bench and opened it . . . to reveal a small metallic unit the size of a hardback book.

It looked like a mini-computer, but with two screens:

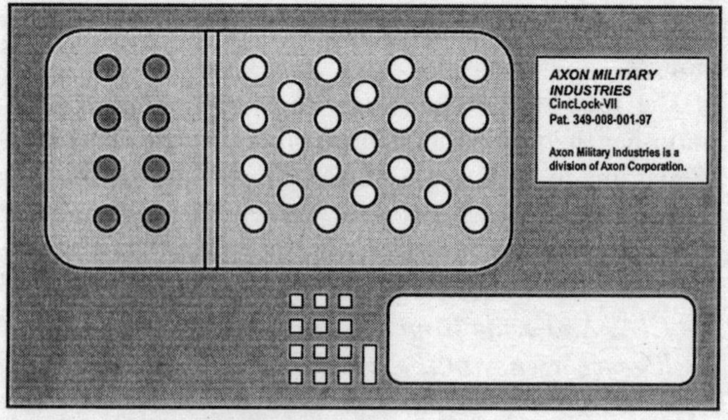

one large touch-screen on the upper half, and a smaller elongated screen on the bottom right. The top screen glowed with a series of red and white circles. Next to the smaller screen was a ten-digit keypad, like on a telephone.

'Captain Schofield,' Lefevre said, 'allow me to introduce to you the CincLock-VII security system. We would like to see you disarm it.'

FORTERESSE DE VALOIS, BRITTANY, FRANCE
26 OCTOBER, 1600 HOURS LOCAL TIME
(1000 HOURS E.S.T. USA)

They dragged Libby Gant into the dark underground pit.

Bloodied and wounded and teetering on the edge of consciousness, she noticed its circular stone walls, the pool of tidal seawater that filled most of its floor area. Seawater which contained two prowling sharks.

Thunk.

The upper half of the guillotine's wooden stocks came down over Gant's neck, pinning her head firmly in place.

The armed man covering her shot home the lock. Gant had never seen him before: he had carrot-red hair, vacant black eyes, and an exceedingly ugly rat-like face.

The imposing frame of the guillotine loomed above her – her head now fastened twelve feet beneath its suspended blade.

Gant grimaced. She could barely even kneel. The tracer wound to her chest burned with pain.

Next to Rat Face stood one of the bounty hunters – Cedric Wexley's No. 2, a psychotic ex-Royal Marine named Drake. He covered Gant with a Steyr-AUG assault rifle.

Gant noticed that Drake was wearing a strange-looking flak vest – a black utility vest equipped with all manner of odd-looking devices, like a Pony Bottle and some mountaineering pitons.

It was Knight's vest.

That made her look up.

And she saw him.

There, fifteen feet in front of her – standing on a stone platform which was itself two inches under the water-line, his eyes squeezed painfully shut since his amber glasses had been removed, his back pressed against the curved stone wall of the pit, his wrists manacled and his holsters glaringly empty – was Aloysius Knight.

A voice echoed across the watery dungeon.

'"Turning and turning in the widening gyre, the falcon cannot hear the falconer. Things fall apart, the centre cannot hold. Mere anarchy is loosed upon the world." Yeats, I believe.'

Jonathan Killian appeared in the viewing balcony – with the bounty hunter Cedric Wexley at his side.

Killian gazed out over the Shark Pit like an emperor at the Colosseum, his eyes falling on Gant, fifty yards away, on the other side of the pit.

'Anarchy is loosed upon the world, Lieutenant Gant,' he said pleasantly. 'I must say I like the sound of that. Don't you?'

'No,' Gant groaned with pain.

They didn't have to raise their voices; their words echoed across the dungeon.

Killian said, 'And Captain Knight. I find your actions most disturbing. A bounty hunter of your fame *hindering* a hunt. There can be only one conclusion: you are being paid to do so.'

Knight just stared back at the young billionaire, said nothing.

'It concerns me to think that someone wishes to foil the plans of the Council. Who is paying you to save Schofield, Captain Knight?'

Knight said nothing.

'Noble silence. How predictable,' Killian said. 'Perhaps when I have your tongue wrenched from your mouth, you will wish you had spoken sooner.'

'We know your plan, Killian,' Gant said through clenched teeth. 'Start a new Cold War to make *money*. It won't work. We'll blow the lid on it, inform the US Government.'

Killian snorted.

'My dear Lieutenant Gant. Do you honestly think I fear *governments*? The modern Western government is but a gathering of overweight middle-aged men trying to gloss over their own mediocrity with the attainment of high office. Presidential planes, Prime Ministerial offices, they are but the *illusion* of power.

'As for a new Cold War,' Killian mused, 'well, that is more the Council's plan than my own. My plan would embody somewhat more *vision*.

'Consider that poem by Yeats. I particularly love the notion of the falconer no longer being able to command his falcon. It suggests a nation that is no longer capable of controlling its most deadly weapon. The weapon has developed a mind of its own, realised its own deadly potential. It has outgrown its owner and attained dangerous independence.

'Now place that in the context of the US defence industry. What happens when the missile builders no longer choose to obey their masters? What happens when the military–industrial complex decides it no longer needs the United States Government?'

'The Scarecrow will stop you,' Gant said defiantly.

'Yes. Yes. The Scarecrow,' Killian said. 'Our mutual friend. He is a special one, isn't he? Did you know that the Council was so concerned about his presence on the list that they went to the trouble of arranging a sham mission to Siberia just to trap him? Needless to say, it didn't work.'

'No shit.'

'But if he is still alive,' Killian said, 'then, yes, it is something of a problem.'

Killian locked eyes with Gant . . .

. . . and she felt her spine turn completely to ice. There was something in his glare that she had never seen before, something truly terrifying.

Aloysius Knight saw it, too, and he immediately became concerned. This was happening too fast. He shifted in his stance, strained against his manacles.

'Now,' Killian said, 'in any standard story, a villain like me would seek to draw out the troublesome Schofield by holding his beloved Lieutenant Gant hostage. I believe this was exactly Demon Larkham's thinking earlier today.'

'Yes,' Gant said warily. 'It was.'

'But it didn't work, did it?' Killian said.

'No.'

'Which is why, Lieutenant Gant, I must do something *more* to flush Shane Schofield out. Something that will make *finding me* far more important to him than disrupting the Council's plan. Mr Noonan.'

At that moment Rat Face – Noonan – grasped the release lever on the guillotine and Gant swallowed in horror.

Then she looked over at Knight, locking eyes with him.

'Knight,' she said. 'When you get out of here, tell Schofield something for me. Tell him I would have said yes.'

Then, without pause or patience, Rat Face pulled the lever and the guillotine's terrible blade dropped from its perch and rushed down its guide-rails toward Gant's exposed neck.

Chunk.

Libby Gant's headless body dropped to the ground at the base of the guillotine.

A hideous waterfall of blood gushed out from its open neck, spilling across the stone stage before flowing off it into the seawater at the platform's edge.

The blood in the water quickly attracted the sharks. Two pointed grey shadows appeared at the edge of the guillotine's stage, searching for the source of the blood.

'Jesus, *no*!' Aloysius Knight yelled, straining at his chains, staring at the gruesome sight in total apoplectic shock.

It had happened so fast.

So quickly.

Without any hesitation.

Libby Gant was dead.

Despite the pain of the light hitting them, Knight's eyes were wide, his face white. 'Oh God, no . . .' he gasped again.

He snapped to glare up at Jonathan Killian – but Killian's face was a mask. His cool hard stare had not changed at all.

And then suddenly one of the men in the pit was coming towards Knight.

It was Drake, the ExSol mercenary, carrying one of Knight's Remington shotguns and wearing his utility vest. The other man, Rat Face, was leaving the pit via a steel door over by the guillotine.

'What about this one?' Drake asked Killian.

Killian waved a hand. 'No guillotines for the Black Knight. No games that might permit him to escape. Shoot him in the head and then feed him to the sharks.'

'Yes, sir,' Drake said.

The giant mercenary strode across a narrow stone bridge between the guillotine's stage and Knight's wall-platform, each step kicking up a shallow splash.

As Drake approached him, the squinting Knight assessed his options.

There weren't many.

He could barely see.

His hands were manacled.

Drake was coming closer.

Thinking furiously, Knight bit his lip so hard that he drew blood. He spat the gob of bloody saliva away in disgust.

Drake halted about six feet from him, out of range from anything Knight could do – like strangle him with his legs, or kick him in the crotch.

Drake raised Knight's silver Remington, aimed it at Knight's head. 'Heard you were better than this, Knight.'

At which point, Knight nodded down at Drake's feet and said, 'I am.'

Drake frowned.

And looked down – to see one of the tiger sharks in the water *right next to his boots*, drawn to the edge of the platform by Knight's blood-laced saliva.

Just as Knight had hoped.

'Ah—' Drake took an involuntary step back from the big ten-foot shark at his feet . . .

. . . and walked into the strike zone of a far more dangerous predator.

What Knight did next, he did very *very* fast.

First, he whip-snapped his body upwards, lashing out with his legs, and grabbed Drake hard around the ribs from behind. Knight squeezed and there came a hideous *snap-snap-snap*, the sound of Drake's ribs breaking.

Drake roared with pain.

Then Knight yanked the mercenary closer so that he could reach something hanging from the utility vest – *his* utility vest – that Drake was wearing.

Knight pulled a mountaineering piton from the vest and one-handed, jammed the piton into his left-hand manacle and pressed its release.

With a powerful spring-loaded *thwack*, the piton expanded in an instant—

—and the old iron manacle around Knight's wrist cracked open and suddenly his left hand was free.

Up on the viewing balcony, Cedric Wexley saw what was happening and immediately whipped up his gun, but Knight was holding Drake in the way with his legs.

And he wasn't finished with Drake either.

He used his now-free left hand to grab a second item from the vest: the miniature blowtorch.

Knight yanked the blowtorch from its pouch and immediately pulled the trigger, firing it at point-blank range *into Drake's back*.

The mini-blowtorch burst to life, emitting a superheated blue flame.

Drake roared.

The spike-like blue flame lanced right through his body, emerging from the other side – the front side – like the blade of a luminescent sword.

Drake's face, shocked and dying, fell back against Knight's chest.

'You got off lightly,' Knight growled, applying more power, blasting the insides of Drake's body to nothing.

Then the body went limp, and fell, and as it did so, Knight unclasped his utility vest from it, at the same time using his piton to break open his other manacle.

As Drake fell, however, Knight became exposed to Cedric Wexley up in the viewing balcony, who started firing.

But now Knight was completely free.

He dived behind Drake's corpse, let bullet after bullet hit it before, without warning, he rolled Drake's body into the blood-stained water, right in front of the nearest tiger shark, and then, to everyone's surprise . . .

. . . leapt into the water after it himself!

The shark lunged at Drake's corpse, bit into it with an almighty crunch, started tearing it to shreds. The second shark came over quickly and joined in the frenzy.

A churning bloody foam spilled out across the pool. Waves sloshed every which way.

After a few minutes, however, the frenzy died down and the water was calm once more.

But there was no sign of Knight.

Indeed, Aloysius Knight never surfaced again inside the deadly pool.

He did surface, however, *outside* the Forteresse de Valois, amid the waves of the Atlantic Ocean.

Exactly six minutes after he'd dived underneath the sharks feeding on Drake's body, he breached the surface of the ocean, still holding his Pony Bottle to his lips.

The mini-scuba bottle had only just had enough air in it to get him through the long underwater passage that connected the Shark Pit to the open sea.

Knight didn't bob in the water for long. A homing transponder on his vest took care of that.

In a matter of minutes, the hawk-shaped shadow of his Sukhoi S-37 swung into place above him, blasting the water around him with its thrusters.

Then a harness fell out of the plane's bomb bay and slapped into the water beside him, and within moments, Aloysius Knight was sitting inside the *Black Raven*, back with Mother and Rufus.

'You all right, Boss?' Rufus said, throwing him a new pair of yellow-lensed glasses.

Knight caught them as he slumped to the floor of the *Raven*'s rear holding cell, put them on. He didn't answer Rufus's question. Just nodded. He was still shell-shocked by the horrific execution he had just witnessed in the Shark Pit.

Mother said, 'What about the Scarecrow? And my little Chickadee?'

Knight looked up at her sharply.

Behind his yellow glasses, his eyes were the picture of horror. He gazed at Mother, wondering what to say.

Then abruptly he stood. 'Rufus. Do you have a fix on Schofield? Those MicroDots I put on his Palm Pilot should have rubbed off on his hand.'

'I've got him, Boss. And he's still moving. Looks like someone took him to that French carrier off the coast.'

Knight turned to Mother, took a deep, deep breath. 'Schofield's alive, but' – he swallowed – 'there could be a problem with the girl.'

'Oh dear God, no . . .' Mother said.

'I can't talk about it now,' Knight said. 'We have to rescue Schofield.'

THE FRENCH AIRCRAFT CARRIER, *RICHELIEU*, ATLANTIC OCEAN, OFF THE FRENCH COAST

Shane Schofield was thrown into a small steel-walled room adjoining the below-decks hangar. The door slammed shut behind him.

There was nothing in the room but a table and a chair.

On the table sat Lefevre's CincLock-VII disarming unit. Next to the unit, with a little red pilot light burning brightly on its top, was:

A phosphorus grenade.

High in the corner of the room, hidden behind a dark glass plate, Schofield heard a camera whirring.

'*Captain Schofield.*' The DGSE agent's voice came over some speakers. '*A simple test. The phosphorus grenade you see before you is connected by shortwave radio to the CincLock unit on the table. The only way to disarm the grenade is through the CincLock unit. For the purposes of this exercise, the final disarm code is 123. The grenade will go off in one minute. Your time starts . . . now.*'

'Holy shit,' Schofield said, sitting down quickly.

He examined the CincLock unit up close.

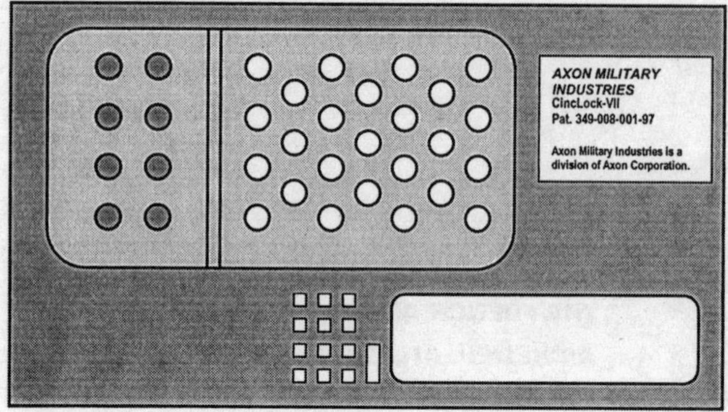

White and red circles filled the main screen – red on the left, white on the right.

Bing.

A message appeared on the lower screen:

FIRST PROTOCOL (PROXIMITY): SATISFIED.
INITIATE SECOND PROTOCOL.

Immediately, the white circles on the main screen began to flash – each one blinking for a brief instant, one at a time, in a slow random sequence.

The screen squealed in protest.

SECOND PROTOCOL (RESPONSE PATTERN): FAILED
DISARM ATTEMPT RECORDED.
THREE FAILED DISARM ATTEMPTS WILL RESULT IN
DEFAULT DETONATION.
SECOND PROTOCOL (RESPONSE PATTERN):
RE-ACTIVATED.

'What?' Schofield said to the screen.

'*Fifty seconds, Captain,*' Lefevre's voice said. '*You have to touch the illuminated circles in the prescribed order.*'

'Oh. Right.'

The white circles began to flash again, one after the other.

And now Schofield began pressing them – just after they flashed.

'*Forty seconds . . .*'

The white circles' sequence became faster. Schofield's hands began to move faster with them, touching the circles on the screen.

Then, abruptly, one of the red circles on the *left* side of the display illuminated.

Schofield wasn't ready for it. But hit it anyway, and got it in time. The white circles resumed their sequence, now blinking very quickly. Schofield's fingers increased their pace, too.

'*Thirty seconds . . . you're doing well . . .*'

Then another red circle flashed.

And this time Schofield was too slow.

The screen beeped angrily.

SECOND PROTOCOL (RESPONSE PATTERN): FAILED
DISARM ATTEMPT RECORDED.
THREE FAILED DISARM ATTEMPTS WILL RESULT IN
DEFAULT DETONATION.
SECOND PROTOCOL (RESPONSE PATTERN):
RE-ACTIVATED.

'Damn it!' Schofield yelled, eyeing the grenade on the table beside him.

And the white circles began their blinking sequence for a third and final time.

'*Twenty-five seconds left . . .*'

But this time Schofield was prepared, knowing what he had to do. His hands now moved fluidly across the screen, punching the white circles as they blinked, breaking left every so often as a red circle flashed.

'*Ten seconds, nine . . .*'

The sequence became faster. The darting moves to the reds became more frequent – to the point, Schofield thought, where it became a test of his reflexes.

'*Eight, seven . . .*'

His eyes stayed focused on the display. His fingers kept dancing. Sweat trickled into his eyes.

'*Six, five . . .*'

The lights kept blinking: white-white-red-white-red-white.

'*Four, three . . .*'

Bing – a message sprang up on the screen:

SECOND PROTOCOL (RESPONSE PATTERN): SATISFIED.
THIRD PROTOCOL (CODE ENTRY): ACTIVE.
PLEASE ENTER AUTHORISED DISARM CODE.

'*Two . . .*'

Schofield typed '1-2-3-ENTER' on the keypad. The numbers appeared on the smaller screen.

'*One . . .*'

Bing.

THIRD PROTOCOL (CODE ENTRY): SATISFIED.
DEVICE DISARMED.

Schofield exhaled, slumped back in his chair.

The door to the room opened. Lefevre entered, dove-clapping.

'*Oh, très bien! Très bien!*' he said. 'Very good, Captain.'

Two burly French naval commandos covered Schofield on either side.

Lefevre smiled. 'That was most impressive. *Most* impressive. Thank you, Captain. You've just reassured us of the verity of Majestic-12's claims. Not to mention the merit of this disarm system. I'm sure the Republic of France will find many uses for it. It really is such a shame that we have to kill you now. Gentlemen, take Captain Schofield back up to the hangar and string him up with the other one.'

Schofield rose into the air, his legs and arms spread wide, star-like.

He stood on the forward lifting prongs of a forklift, one foot on each horizontal prong, while his wrists were handcuffed to the vehicle's vertical steel runners.

The forklift was parked in a corner of the *Richelieu*'s deserted main hangar bay, behind the exhausts of several Rafale fighter jets. Seated in a semi-circle in front of it were the three French military officers and the DGSE agent, Lefevre.

'Bring in the British spy,' Lefevre said to one of Schofield's guards.

The guard hit a button on the wall nearby and the steel wall beside Schofield suddenly began to rise – it was in fact a door, a great fighter-sized steel door – revealing darkness beyond it.

Out from the darkness came a second forklift, on which stood another captured individual, crucified in the same manner as Schofield.

There was only one difference.

The man on this second forklift had been thoroughly tortured. His face, his shirt, his arms – they were all covered with blood. His head hung limply over his chest.

Lefevre said, 'Captain Schofield, I'm not sure if you have met Agent Alec Christie of British Intelligence.'

Christie. From MI-6. And the bounty list.

So this was where Christie had got to.

'Over the last two days, Mr Christie has been a fountain of information for us regarding Majestic-12,' Lefevre said. 'It seems that for the last eighteen months, he has been well placed in Loch-Mann Industries as a personal bodyguard to Mr Randolph Loch, the Chairman of M-12. But while Mr Christie was watching Loch, we were watching Christie.

'However, in one of his more lucid moments last night, Mr Christie told us something of concern. He stated that Randolph Loch has been most displeased of late with one of the younger members of M-12, our friend Jonathan Killian.

'According to Mr Christie, Randolph Loch commented several times that Killian was quote, "pestering him with this follow-up idea". It appears that Mr Killian does not think Majestic-12's plan goes far enough. In light of your own investigations, Captain Schofield, do you know anything about this "follow-up idea"?'

Schofield said, 'Killian's *your* friend. Why don't you ask him?'

'The Republic of France does not have friends.'

'I can see why.'

'We have useful acquaintances,' Lefevre said. 'But sometimes, one must watch one's acquaintances as closely as one's enemies.'

'You don't trust him,' Schofield said.

'Not an inch.'

'But you give him protection, sanctuary.'

'For as long as it suits us. It may no longer suit us.'

Schofield said, 'But now you're worried he's playing you.'

'Yes.'

Schofield thought about that for a moment.

Then he said, 'One of M-12's Chameleon missiles is aimed at Paris.'

'Oh, please. We know that. We are *prepared* for that. That is the very idea behind my country's involvement with Majestic-12. That was why we provided them with the bodies of the Global Jihad terrorists. For while America, Germany and Britain suffer catastrophic losses, France will be seen as the only Western nation to have defeated this threat.

'Where New York, Berlin and London will be lost, Paris will stand tall. France will be the only nation to have successfully shot down one of these terrible terrorist missiles.

'It took America three whole months to retaliate for September 11. Imagine how shell-shocked they will be when they lose *five entire cities*. But France, France will be the nation who beat off these heinous attacks. The only Western nation who moved fast enough. It will make us – strong and capable and completely unhurt – the world's leader in this new Cold War period.

'Captain Schofield, our friends in Majestic-12 want money out of all of this, because for them money is power. The Republic of France does not want that kind of power – wc want something far more important than that. We want a global power shift. We want to lead the world.

'The twentieth century was the American century. A sad bankrupt time in the history of this planet. The twenty-first century will be the French century.'

Schofield just stared at Lefevre and the generals.

'You guys are really messed up, you know that,' he said.

*

Lefevre pulled some photos out of his briefcase, showed them to the elevated Schofield.

'Back to Killian. These are photos of Monsieur Killian during his tour of Africa last year.'

Schofield saw standard newspaper pics: Killian standing with African leaders, opening factories, waving to crowds.

'A goodwill tour to promote his charitable activities,' Lefevre said. 'During that tour, however, Killian attended meetings with the leaders and defence ministers of several strategically significant African nations: notably Nigeria, Eritrea, Chad, Angola and Libya.'

'Yes . . .' Schofield said expectantly.

Lefevre paused, delivered the punch. 'Over the last eleven hours, the Air Forces of Nigeria, Eritrea, Chad and Angola have all scrambled, with over two hundred fighter planes converging on airfields in eastern Libya. Now, taken individually, these air forces are relatively small. Taken together, however, they make up a veritable aerial armada. My final question for you, Captain, is *what are they doing*?'

Schofield's mind raced.

'Captain Schofield?'

But Schofield wasn't listening. He could only hear Jonathan Killian's voice in his head, saying: 'Although many don't know it, the future of the world lies in Africa.'

Africa . . .

'Captain Schofield?' Lefevre said.

Schofield blinked. Came back.

'I don't know,' he answered honestly. 'I wish I did, but I honestly don't.'

'Hmmm,' Lefevre said. 'That is exactly what Mr Christie said, too. Which might mean you are both speaking the truth. Of course, it might also mean that you need some more persuasion.'

Lefevre nodded to the driver of Christie's forklift.

The driver fired up the engine and drove the vehicle a few yards to the left, so that Christie – raised up on the forklift's prongs – was positioned right behind the thrusters of a nearby Rafale fighter jet. The driver then quickly jumped out of his seat and ran away.

A moment later, Schofield saw why.

ROOOOAAAARRRRR!

The fighter's engines rumbled to life. Schofield saw another French soldier standing in its cockpit.

The battered and ragged Alec Christie looked up at the sound of the colossal noise, and found himself staring into the yawning rear thruster of the Rafale fighter. He didn't seem to care. He was too beaten, too weary to bother straining at his bonds.

Lefevre nodded to the man in the cockpit.

The man hit the plane's thrust controls.

Instantly, a shocking tongue of white-hot fire blasted out from the rear thruster of the Rafale, engulfing the immobile Christie.

The heat-blast battered the British agent's body like a wind-fan – the piping-hot air blasted his hair backwards, ripped the skin off his face, burned his clothes in a nanosecond – until ultimately it tore his body to pieces.

Then, abruptly, the burst stopped and the hangar was silent again.

All that remained of Alec Christie were four grisly quarters, charred and disgusting, dangling from the forklift's prongs.

'This is very bad,' Schofield swallowed.

Lefevre turned to him. 'Does that refresh your memory at all?'

'I'm telling you, I don't know,' Schofield said. 'I don't know about Killian or the African countries, or if they have anything in common. This is the first I've heard of them.'

'Then I am afraid we have no further need for you,' Lefevre said. 'It is now time for the Admiral and the General to have their wish and watch you die.'

And with that, Lefevre nodded to Schofield's forklift driver. Schofield's vehicle moved forward, stopping alongside Christie's charred forklift, in front of the Rafale's second rear thruster.

Schofield gazed into the dark depths of the thruster.

'General?' Lefevre said to the old Army officer, the man who had lost an entire paratrooper unit to Schofield in Antarctica. 'Would you like to do the honours?'

'With pleasure.'

The General stood up from his chair, and climbed up into the Rafale's cockpit, glaring at Schofield all the way.

He leaned into the cockpit, reached for the flight stick, his thumb hovering over the 'AFTERBURN' switch.

'Good-bye, Captain Schofield,' Lefevre said matter-of-factly. 'World history will have to continue without you. *Au revoir*.'

The General's thumb came down on the 'BURN' switch.

Just as a gigantic explosion boomed out from somewhere above the main hangar.

Klaxons sounded.

Warning lights flashed to life.

And the entire aircraft carrier was suddenly awash with the red lighting of an emergency.

The General's thumb had frozen a millimetre above the burn switch.

An ensign ran up to the Navy Admiral. 'Sir! We're under attack!'

'*What?*' the Admiral yelled. 'By whom!'

'It looks like a Russian fighter, sir.'

'A Russian fighter? *One* Russian fighter! This is an aircraft carrier, for God's sake! Who in their right mind would attack an aircraft carrier with a single plane?'

The *Black Raven* hovered level with the flight deck of the *Richelieu*, raining gunfire and missiles down on the fighter planes parked there.

Four missile smoke-trails extended out from the Sukhoi's wings and then separated to pursue different targets.

One Rafale fighter on the deck was instantly blasted to pieces, while two anti-aircraft missile stations were obliterated. The fourth missile whizzed into the main hangar bay and rammed into an AWACS plane, destroying it in a billowing explosion.

Inside the *Raven*, Rufus flew brilliantly.

In the gunner's seat behind him sat Knight, swivelling around in the plane's 360-degree revolving rear chair, lining up targets and then blazing away with the *Raven*'s guns.

'Mother! You ready?' Knight called.

Mother stood in the converted bomb bay behind the cockpit – armed to the teeth: MP-7, M-16, Desert Eagle pistols; she even had one of Knight's rocket launcher packs strapped to her back.

'Fuckin'-A.'

'Then go!' Knight hit a button.

Whack!

The floor of the bomb bay/holding cell snapped open and Mother dropped down through it, whizzing down on her Maghook's rope.

Inside the French aircraft carrier's control tower, chaos reigned.

Comm-techs were shouting into their radio-mikes, relaying information to the captain.

'— damn thing got under our radars! Must have some sort of stealth mechanism—'

'— They've hit the anti-aircraft stations on the flight deck—'

'— Get those fighters to the catapults *now*!'

'Sir! The *Triomphe* says it has a clear shot . . .'

'Tell it to fire!'

*

In response to the order, an anti-aircraft missile streaked out from one of the destroyers in the carrier group – heading straight for the *Black Raven*.

'Rufus! I hope you fixed our electronic counter-measures when we were in Archangel!'

'Taken care of, Boss.'

The missile zoomed towards them at phenomenal speed.

But at the last possible moment, it hit the *Raven*'s electronic jamming shield and veered wildly away . . .

. . . and slammed into the outer hull of the aircraft carrier!

'Escorts! Cease fire! Cease fire!' the captain yelled. 'That plane is too close to us! You're hitting us! Electronics Department – find out what its jamming frequency is and neutralise it! We'll have to destroy it with fighters.'

Inside the main hangar bay of the carrier, Schofield was still quasi-crucified in front of the thrusters of the parked Rafale fighter.

Abruptly, the deck around him banked steeply as the immense carrier wheeled around in the face of the *Black Raven*'s surprise assault.

Lefevre and the French generals were now all on radios, looking for answers.

All, that is, except for the Army General in the cock-pit of the Rafale.

After the initial distraction, he now glared back at Schofield. He wasn't going to miss this opportunity.

He reached for the 'AFTERBURN' switch again, gripped the control stick just as – *sprack!* – a bullet entered his ear and the cockpit around him was sprayed with his brains.

In all the confusion, no one had noticed the shadowy figure that had landed on the open-air starboard elevator adjoining the main hangar, a figure that had whizzed to the bottom of a vertical rope like a spider on a thread, a figure bearing arms.

Mother.

Carrying an MP-7 in one hand and an M-16 in the other, Mother stormed through the hangar bay towards Schofield.

She was like an unstoppable force of nature.

The squad of French paratroopers that had been guarding Schofield came at her from all sides – from behind vehicles, from around parked fighter jets.

But Mother just strode forward, nailing them left, right and centre, never once losing her stride.

She loosed two shots to the left – hit two paratroopers in their faces. Swung right – firing her M-16 pistol-style – and another three bad guys went down.

A paratrooper rose from the wing of a Rafale above her and Mother just somersaulted, firing as she rolled, peppering him with bloody holes.

She threw two smoke grenades next, and in the haze that followed, she moved and hunted like a vengeful ghost.

Four French paratroopers went down, sucked into the smoke-haze – so, too, the French Admiral. Not even the spy, Lefevre, could escape her. A four-bladed shuriken throwing knife whistled out of the smoke near him and entered his Adam's apple. He would die slowly.

Then suddenly, Mother burst out of the cloud haze right next to Schofield on his forklift.

'Hey, Scarecrow. How's it hanging?' she said.

'Feeling much better now that you're here,' Schofield said.

Two of Knight's pitons made short work of his handcuffs. In seconds he was on solid ground again, free.

But before Mother could hand him some guns, Schofield dashed over to Lefevre's body lying on the ground nearby.

He picked up something from the ground beside the dying Frenchman, returned to Mother's side. She handed him an MP-7 and a Desert Eagle.

'Ready to do some damage?' she asked.

Schofield turned to her, his eyes catching the RPG pack on her back.

'I'm ready to do some serious damage,' he said.

They ran towards a jeep parked nearby.

In rapid two-by-two catapult launches, four state-of-the-art Rafale fighters shot down the runway of the *Richelieu* and took off.

They wheeled around in the sky above the carrier, turning back in deadly formation, heading for the hovering *Black Raven*.

'They're coming!' Rufus yelled.

'I see them!' Knight called.

He whirled around in his revolving seat, hammering on his triggers like a kid playing a video game.

Two Rafales shot toward them, cannons blazing.

A phalanx of orange tracer bullets sizzled through the air all around the *Raven*. The *Raven* banked and rolled in the sky, dodging the tracers, at the same time returning fire from its own revolving belly-mounted gun.

Then the first two planes overshot them – twin sonic booms. But that was only the first act, a distraction to hide the main show.

For the *other* two French fighters had swung around low, skimming over the ocean waves from the other direction, coming at the Sukhoi from below and behind.

Still hovering above the carrier's starboard elevator, the Sukhoi swivelled in mid-air, faced these two new planes head-on.

'Damn it,' Rufus said, eyeing his countermeasures screen. 'The bastards are screwing with our jamming frequency . . . it's flicking on and off. We're losing missile jam.'

The two new Rafales fired two missiles each.

Knight blasted away with his cannons at the missiles, hit two of them, but the other two missiles ducked and rose and swerved too well.

'Rufus . . . !'

The missiles roared toward them.

Rufus saw them coming, and a moment before it was too late, saw the answer.

The missiles rushed forward, zooming in for the kill . . .

. . . just as Rufus swung the *Black Raven* inside the massive doorway that opened off the aircraft carrier's starboard elevator, manoeuvring his airborne fighter *inside the ship's main hangar*!

The missiles – unlike the shots from the destroyer, *Le Triomphe* – were fitted with electronic detection systems that didn't allow them to strike their own carrier. As such, they ditched into the ocean, detonating in twin hundred-foot geysers.

Inside the carrier's tower, radar operators stared at their screens in confusion, shouted into their radio-mikes:

'—Where the fuck did it go?—'

'—*What?* Say again—'

'What happened?' the captain asked. 'Where are they?'

'Sir. They're inside us!'

The *Black Raven* now hovered *inside* the cavernous hangar of the French aircraft carrier.

'I like your style, Rufus,' Knight said as he started firing indiscriminately at the array of parked planes, helicopters and trucks.

Like a giant bird trapped inside a living room, the *Black Raven* powered over the interior of the hangar, overturning entire planes with its backwash, flinging fuel trucks into the walls.

It shoomed across the hangar causing untold mayhem and destruction, its two high tail fins even scraping against the ceiling once.

Knight called into his radio: 'Mother! Where are you?'

A lone jeep shot towards the aft end of the elongated hangar bay, driving at full speed, zooming under tilting planes and bouncing fuel trucks, with Mother at the wheel and Schofield crouched in the back.

Mother yelled, 'I'm at the other end of the hangar bay, trying to avoid your mess!'

'*Do you have Schofield?*'

'I've got him.'

'*Want us to pick you up while we're in here?*'

Mother turned to Schofield, bent over in the back with her – or rather, Knight's – RPG pack. 'You wanna be picked up in here?'

'No! Not yet!' he yelled. 'Tell Knight to get outside. He doesn't want to be in here in the next two minutes! In fact, he doesn't want to be anywhere near this ship! Tell him we'll meet him outside!'

'Copy that,' Knight said, moments later.

He turned. 'Rufus! Time to bail!'

'You got it, Boss!' Rufus said. 'Now, where is that other . . . ah,' Rufus said, spotting a second open-air elevator on the opposite side of the hangar bay.

He powered up the Sukhoi, brought her swooping across the interior of the hangar bay, the roar of her engines drowning out all other sound, before – *shoom* – the *Raven* blasted out through the port-side elevator and into blazing sunlight.

Meanwhile, in the back of his speeding jeep, Schofield rummaged through the RPG pack that Mother had brought.

It was indeed Knight's Russian-made RPG pack – which meant it contained a disposable rocket launcher and various explosive-tipped rocket charges.

He found the one he was looking for.

The notorious Soviet P-61 Palladium charge.

A Palladium charge – comprising a palladium outer shell around a liquid core of enhanced hydrofluoric acid – has only one purpose: to take out civilian nuclear power plants in a terrible, terrible way.

Nuclear *weapons* require a core consistency of 90% enhanced uranium. The nuclear *reactors* in civilian power plants, on the other hand, have a core consistency of around 5%; while reactors on nuclear-powered aircraft carriers hover at around 50% – as such, neither of these reactors can *ever* create a nuclear explosion. They can leak radiation – as happened at Chernobyl – but they will never create a mushroom cloud.

What they do release every single second, however, are massive quantities of hydrogen – highly flammable hydrogen – an action which is nullified by the use of 'recombiners' which turn the dangerous hydrogen (H) into very safe water (H_20).

Mixing *palladium* with hydrogen, however, has the opposite effect. It multiplies the deadly hydrogen, producing *vast* quantities of the flammable gas which can then be triggered by the addition of a catalyst like hydrofluoric acid.

As such, the P-61 charge operates as a two-stage detonator.

The first stage – the initial blast – mixes Palladium with hydrogen, multiplying the gas at a phenomenal rate. The second stage of the weapon ignites that gas with the acid.

The result is a colossal explosion – not quite as big as a nuclear blast, but perhaps the only explosion in the world big enough to crack the reinforced hull of an aircraft carrier.

'There!' Schofield yelled, pointing at two gigantic cylindrical vents at the aft end of the hangar bay, fan-covered vents which expelled excess hydrogen out the rear port flank of the carrier. 'The reactor's exhaust vents!'

The jeep whipped through the hangar bay, weaving past flaming fighter jets.

Schofield stood up in the rear section of the jeep, hoisted the RPG launcher onto his shoulder, aimed it at a gigantic fan set into the side of the exhaust stacks.

'As soon as I fire, Mother, hit the gas and head for the ascending ramp! We're gonna have about thirty seconds between the first stage and the second stage. That means thirty seconds to get off this boat!'

'Okay!'

Schofield peered down the sights of the launcher. '*Au revoir* to you, assholes.'

Then he jammed his finger down on the trigger.

The launcher fired, sending its Palladium-tipped RPG rocketing into the upper reaches of the hangar, a dead-straight smoke-trail extending through the air behind it.

The Palladium charge smashed through the fan in the right-hand exhaust vent and disappeared inside it, heading downward, searching for heat.

No sooner was it away than Mother floored the jeep, wheeling it around in a tight circle before disappearing into the tunnel-like ascension ramp that allowed vehicle access from the hangar to the upper flight deck.

Round and round the jeep went, rising upwards.

As it circled higher, tyres squealing, there came an awesome muffled *boom* from deep within the bowels of the aircraft carrier.

The Palladium charge had hit its target.

Schofield hit his stopwatch: 00:01 . . . 00:02 . . .

In the air above the *Richelieu*, the *Black Raven* was still engaged in the dogfight of its life with the four French Rafale fighters.

It banked hard, screaming through the air, and took one of the Rafales out with its last remaining missile.

But then Rufus heard a shrill *beeeeeeeeep* from his console.

'They've fully hacked our countermeasure frequency!' he called. 'We just lost missile shield completely!'

At that moment, another of the Rafales got on their

tail and the two planes roared over the ocean together, the Rafale trailing the Sukhoi, blazing away at it with orange tracers.

As the *Raven* rushed forward, Knight swung around in his revolving gunner's chair and opened fire on the trailing plane with the Raven's underslung revolving gun, raking the French fighter's cockpit with a withering rain of fire, shattering its canopy, ripping the pilot to bits, causing his plane to plough into the sea with a jarring explosive splash.

'Boss!' Rufus called suddenly. 'I need guns forward! Now!'

Knight spun. What he hadn't seen was that this trailing Rafale had been driving the *Raven* toward . . . the other two French fighters!

The two waiting Rafales launched one missile each—

—twin fingers of smoke lanced into the air, arcing in towards the *Black Raven*'s nose –

—but Rufus rolled the sleek black plane, flying it on its side just as he engaged his custom-fitted – and very rare – *secondary* countermeasures: a system known as 'Plasma Stealth' that enveloped the entire aircraft in a cloud of ionised gas particles.

The two missiles went berserk, splitting in a V-shape to avoid the ion cloud around the Sukhoi, and the *Raven* bisected them at blinding speed – leaving one missile to ditch wildly into the sea and the other to wheel around in the sky.

But the *Raven* was still on a collision course with the two incoming Rafales.

Knight swung forward, opened fire – and destroyed the left-hand wing of one Rafale a moment before the *Raven* overshot the two French fighters with a deafening roar.

There was only one Rafale left now, but not for long. A moment after it passed Knight's plane, the last French Rafale was hit by its own missile – the one that had gone rogue after being assailed by the Sukhoi's Plasma Stealth mechanism.

Knight and Rufus turned to see the final explosion, but as they did so, there came another noise from across the waves – a deep ominous *boom* from within the aircraft carrier.

'Faster, Mother. Faster,' Schofield eyed his stopwatch:

00:09 . . .

00:10 . . .

The jeep shot up the circular ramp, kicking up sparks against the ramp's close steel walls.

Abruptly, the entire carrier banked sharply, turning to port, tilting the whole world thirty degrees.

'Keep going!' Schofield yelled.

The first-stage blast of the Palladium charge had knocked out the *Richelieu*'s hydrogen recombiners: that was the ominous boom.

Which meant that uncontrolled hydrogen was now building inside the carrier's cooling towers at an exponential rate. In exactly thirty seconds the second stage of the palladium charge would detonate, igniting the hydrogen and bringing about aircraft carrier Armageddon.

00:11

00:12

The jeep burst out from the ascension ramp into sunlight, bounced to a halt.

There was pandemonium on the flight deck.

Smoking planes, charred anti-aircraft guns, dead

sailors. One Rafale fighter – nose down, its front wheels destroyed – blocked the *Richelieu*'s No. 2 take-off runway. The fighter must have been just about to take off when the *Black Raven* had hit it with a missile.

Schofield saw it instantly.

'Mother! Head for that broken fighter!'

'That thing ain't gonna fly, Scarecrow! Not even for you!' Mother yelled.

00:15

00:16

Amid the chaos, the jeep skidded to a halt beside the destroyed Rafale fighter. Mother was right. With its nose down and its front wheels crumpled, it wasn't going anywhere.

00:17

00:18

'I don't want the plane,' Schofield said. 'I want this.'

He jumped out of the jeep, reached down and grabbed the catapult hook that lay on the runway in front of the destroyed plane. The small, trapezoidal catapult hook had formerly been attached to the front wheels of the plane. Normally you would attach it to the steam-driven catapult mechanism that ran for the length of the flight deck in order to get your plane to take-off speed in the space of ninety metres.

Schofield, however, wedged the catapult hook crudely under the front axle of his jeep and then clipped the other end of the hook to the deck catapult.

00:19

00:20

'Oh, you cannot be serious . . .' Mother said, eyeing the empty runway in front of their jeep – a runway that simply stopped at the bow horizon of the ship. The catapult's rails stretched away for the length of the flight deck like a pair of railway tracks heading toward a cliff edge.

00:21

00:22

Schofield jumped back into the jeep beside Mother.

'Put her into neutral and buckle up!' he said.

00:23

00:24

Mother snatched up her seatbelt, clicked it on. Schofield did the same.

00:25

Then he drew his MP-7 and levelled it at the nearby catapult controls, long since abandoned during the *Black Raven*'s attack . . .

00:26

. . . and fired.

00:27

Ping!

The bullet slammed into the launch lever, triggering the catapult.

And the jeep shot off the mark at a speed that no humble jeep had ever gone before.

Ninety metres in 2.2 seconds.

Schofield and Mother were thrust into their seats, felt their eyeballs ram into the backs of their sockets.

The jeep shot down the runway at *unbelievable* speed.

The deck blurred with motion.

The jeep's front tyres blew out after fifty metres.

But it still kept rocketing forward – like a cannonball out of a cannon – propelled by the tremendous force of the catapult.

Truth be told, they weren't travelling as fast as a fighter jet on take-off, since a fighter is also propelled by its own thrusters.

But Schofield didn't want to fly.

He just wanted to get off this aircraft carrier before she –

Blew.

The jeep hit the edge of the runway . . . and shoomed straight off it . . . blasting out into the sky . . . nose up, wheels spinning . . . *just as the entire aircraft carrier behind it shattered spontaneously.*

There was no fire.

No billowing clouds.

There was just a mighty, mighty BANG! as every

exterior steel wall of the aircraft carrier *instantaneously* expanded outward – pushed out by the tremendous pressure of ignited hydrogen – bursting at the seams like the Incredible Hulk busting out of his clothes.

A starburst of a billion rivets was thrown high into the sky.

The rivets were thrown for miles, and rained down for the next whole minute. A helicopter that had just taken off from the rear of the carrier was shredded by the sudden rivet-wave, destroyed in mid-flight.

Dislodged pieces of the carrier – including entire plates of steel – flew out into the air and slammed down into the surrounding French destroyers, denting their sides, smashing their bridge windows.

The greatest damage to the *Richelieu* occurred at the aft end of the carrier, around the epicentre of the blast: the cooling vents.

The exterior walls there were simply ripped apart at the seams – at the vertical rivet joints – opening up wide gashes on both sides of the carrier, gashes into which the Atlantic Ocean flowed without mercy.

And the *Richelieu* – the largest and greatest aircraft carrier ever built by France – began to sink unceremoniously into the ocean.

Schofield and Mother's jeep, however, flew off the bow of the massive carrier.

As it soared through the air in front of the ship, they unclipped their seatbelts and pushed themselves up and out of the jeep, allowing themselves to sail through the sky above it.

The drop from the flight deck to the water level was about twenty-five metres.

The jeep hit the water first. A large foamy explosion of spray.

Schofield and Mother hit it next. Twin splashes.

It hurt, but they angled their bodies as they entered the water – so that they entered it boots-first and knifed under the surface not a moment before the carrier erupted and its storm of rivets blasted across the surface of the ocean like a rain of deadly shrapnel.

The mighty aircraft carrier was sinking fast, ass-end first.

It was a truly spectacular sight.

And then, as its hapless crew hurried for the lifeboats or simply leapt for their lives into the ocean, the great warship went vertical – its bow rising high, its aft section completely submerged.

The rest of the French carrier group was frozen in shock.

Outside full-scale war, this sort of thing was unthinkable. No country had lost an aircraft carrier since World War II.

Which was probably why they were slow to react when, a minute after the explosion, the *Black Raven* swung into a hovering position ten feet above the waves of the Atlantic and plucked two tiny figures from the chop, raising them up on a cable-harness into its rear bomb bay.

Once the two figures were safely inside it, the sleek Sukhoi rose into the air and blasted off into the sky, away from the shattered remains of the *Richelieu* carrier group.

*

Aloysius Knight strode back into the holding cell of the *Black Raven*, saw Schofield and Mother lying there looking like a pair of drowned rats.

Schofield glanced up at Knight as he entered. 'Set a course for the English Channel, off Cherbourg. That's where the first Kormoran ship is. We have to find it before it launches its missiles on Europe.'

Knight nodded. 'I've already told Rufus to take us there.'

Schofield paused.

Knight appeared unusually sombre, almost . . . sensitive. What was going on?

Schofield looked around the tight confines of the holding cell, and it hit him.

'Where's Gant?' he asked.

It was then that, behind his amber-tinted glasses, Knight's eyes wavered – just slightly. Schofield saw it and at that moment, he felt something inside him that he had never felt before.

Absolute, total dread.

Aloysius Knight swallowed.

'Captain,' he said, 'we have to talk.'

SIXTH ATTACK

ENGLISH CHANNEL–USA

26 OCTOBER, 1700 HOURS (E. CHANNEL)

E.S.T. (NEW YORK, USA) 1100 HOURS

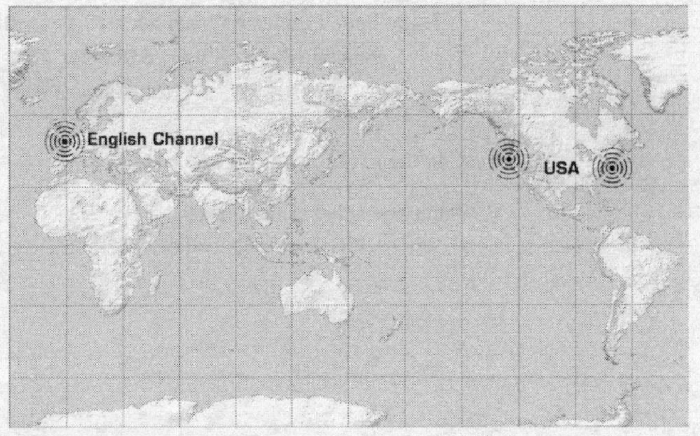

40 (a) (ii) In the event of a conflict involving the major global powers, it is highly likely that the poverty-stricken populations of Africa, the Middle East and Central America – some of which outnumber the populations of their Western neighbours by a ratio of 100-to-1 – will flood over Western borders and overwhelm Western city centres.

From: United States National Security Council
Planning Paper Q-309, 28 October, 2000
(UN PRESS, NEW YORK)

'Who must do the hard things? He who can.'

Quote attributed to Confucius

ENGLISH CHANNEL COASTLINE,
NORTHERN FRANCE
26 OCTOBER, 1700 HOURS LOCAL TIME
(1100 HOURS E.S.T. USA)

With a burst from its thrusters, the *Black Raven* landed on a cliff-top overlooking the English Channel, lashed by driving rain.

Out of its cockpit stepped Shane Schofield. He dropped to the muddy ground and staggered away from the fighter, oblivious to the storm around him.

After Knight had finished telling him about what had happened in the Shark Pit with Gant and Jonathan Killian and the guillotine, Schofield had said only three words.

'Rufus. Land now.'

Schofield stopped at the edge of the cliff, jammed his eyes shut.

Tears mixed with the rain hammering against his face.

Gant was dead.

Dead.

And he hadn't been there. Hadn't been there to save

her. In the past, no matter what happened, he'd *always* been able to save her.

But not this time.

He opened his eyes. Stared into space.

Then his legs gave way beneath him and he dropped to his knees in the mud, his shoulders heaving violently with every desperate sob.

Mother, Knight and Rufus watched him from the open cockpit of the *Raven*, twenty yards away.

'Fuck me . . .' Mother breathed. 'What the hell is he going to do now?'

Schofield's mind was a kaleidoscope of images.

He saw Gant – smiling at him, laughing, holding his hand as they strolled along the beach at Pearl, rolling up close against him in bed. God, he could almost feel the warmth of her body in his mind.

He saw her fighting in Antarctica and in Utah. Saving his life with a one-in-a-million Maghook shot inside Area 7.

And then – shocking himself – he saw Killian at the castle saying, 'I love to observe the look of pure horror that appears on a person's face when they realise that they are, without doubt, going to die.'

And he saw the world from now on . . .

Without her.

Empty.

Meaningless.

And with that, he looked down at the Desert Eagle pistol in his holster . . . and he drew it.

*

'Hey there, champ,' a voice said from behind him. 'Whatcha planning on doing with that gun?'

It was Mother.

Standing right behind him.

Schofield didn't turn around when he spoke. 'Nobody cares, Mother. We could save the world and nobody would give a shit. People would go on living their lives, completely unaware of soldiers like us. Like Gant.'

Mother's eyes were locked on the gun in his hand. Rain dripped off it.

'Scarecrow. Put the gun away.'

Schofield looked down at the Desert Eagle, seemed to notice it for the first time.

'Hey,' Mother said. Solely to distract him, she asked a question that she already knew the answer to. 'What did she mean when she said, "Tell him, I would have said yes"?'

Schofield looked away into the distance, spoke like an automaton.

'She could read me like a book. I could never keep anything secret from her. She knew I was going to propose in Tuscany. That's what she was gonna say yes to.'

He shifted his grip on the gun. Bit his lip. Another tear streaked down his face. 'Jesus, Mother. She's dead. She's fucking dead. There's nothing left for me now. Screw it. The world can fight its own battles.'

With a quick move, he placed the gun under his chin and pulled the –

But Mother moved faster.

She tackled him just as the gun went off and the two of them went rolling in the mud by the cliff edge.

And they fought – Mother trying to pin his gun-hand, Schofield trying to push her clear.

Taller, stronger and far bulkier, at first Mother had the jump on him. She pinned him underneath her great weight and punched his gun-wrist. The Desert Eagle dropped out of his hand. Then she smacked him hard in the face—

The blow had a strange effect on Schofield.

It seemed to focus him.

With almost disturbing ease, he grabbed Mother's left wrist with two fingers and twisted it. Mother roared with pain and Schofield – with perfect centre-of-gravity manipulation – threw her clear off him.

And they both stood.

Facing each other on the wind-lashed cliff, squaring off in the driving rain.

'I won't let you do it, Scarecrow!' Mother yelled.

'I'm sorry, Mother. It's too late.'

Mother moved.

She advanced quickly, unleashing a bone-crushing right, but Schofield ducked it, hit her back, square on the nose. Mother swung again, but Schofield – perfectly balanced in the mud – avoided that blow too, and hit her again.

Mother staggered back to a standing position. 'You're gonna have do more than that to get rid of me!'

She lunged at him again, driving into him with her shoulders, tackling him linebacker-style, lifting him off his feet and sending them both crashing to the earth.

Over by the *Black Raven*, Aloysius Knight and Rufus just stood there in the rain, watching the fight like stunned spectators.

Rufus took a step forward, making to intervene – but

Knight stopped him with a light hand to the chest, never taking his eyes off the battle.

'No,' he said. 'This is for the two of them to sort out.'

Schofield and Mother rolled in the mud, struggling.

Mother seemed to have him pinned when suddenly Schofield landed a short sharp elbow to her jaw and – again with surprising strength – rolled her clear.

He stood.

She stood.

Both were dripping with mud.

Mother staggered slightly, tiring, but she re-engaged anyway, swinging blindly.

Schofield parried every blow easily now, martial-arts-style. Mother roared in frustration just as he spun on one knee and swept her legs out from under her, and Mother fell unceremoniously onto her butt in the mud.

Having won for himself the distance he needed, Schofield walked back over to his gun, picked it up.

'Scarecrow, no!' Mother called, tears welling in her eyes. 'Please, Shane, don't . . .'

And for some reason, that stopped him.

Schofield paused.

Then he realised what it was.

For as long as he could remember, Mother had never called him by his first name. Not even in situations outside the Marine Corps.

He lowered the gun an inch, gazed at her.

She looked pathetic: on her knees on the ground, covered in mud, tears streaking down her face.

'Shane,' she called, 'the world may not care. The world may not know that it needs people like you and Gant. But I care! And I know that I need you! Shane, I have a husband and some beautiful nieces – they're thirteen years old and they all dress like Britney fucking Spears – and I have a mother-in-law who hates my guts.

'But I love them all, love 'em to death, and I don't want to see them living in a world of suffering and death that is run by a bunch of billionaire motherfuckers. *But I can't stop that from happening*. I can't. No matter what I do, no matter how hard I try, in the end I'm just not smart enough, not quick enough, not good enough. But you are. You can beat them. And do you know why? I do. I've always known it. And my little Chickadee knew it, too, and that was why she loved you. *It's because you can do things that other people can't.*'

Mother was on her knees in the mud, eyes filled with tears.

'Shane, I ain't the smartest kid in the class, but I know this: people are people. They're selfish and they're self-centred, they do stupid things and they have absolutely no idea that there are heroes like you out there looking after them every day.'

Schofield didn't say a word.

The rain smacked against his cheeks.

But Mother had broken the spell.

Life was coming back into his eyes.

'I don't call you Shane,' she said. 'You probably know that. But do you know why?'

Schofield was rooted to the spot. Frozen.

'No. Why?'

'Cause you ain't a regular fucking fella. You ain't a "Brad" or a "Chad" or a "Warren". You're the Scarecrow. *The fucking Scarecrow*.

'You're more than just an ordinary guy. Which is why I've never treated you like an ordinary guy. You're better than all of them. But if you off yourself now, if you take the easy way out, then you're taking the path that Brad or Chad or Warren would take. That ain't you. That ain't the Scarecrow. The Scarecrow is made of tougher stuff than that. Now, I ain't saying living is going to be easy – I don't know if any normal person could bounce back after hearing what you just heard – but if anyone can, it's you.'

Schofield was silent for a long time.

Then at last he spoke.

'I'm going to kill them all, Mother,' he said. 'The bounty hunters who caught her. All the bounty hunters involved in this hunt. Plus everyone on Majestic-12 who made this happen. And when it's all over – however it turns out, whether the world survives this crisis intact or whether it goes to hell on a handcart – I'm going to find Jonathan Killian and I'm going to blow his fucking brains out.'

Mother smiled through her tears. 'Sounds good to me.'

'But Mother,' he added somewhat ominously, 'I won't guarantee what I'll do *after* that.'

'Then I guess I'll just have to fight you again,' Mother said.

And at that, Schofield blinked.

Life had fully returned.

Mother nodded. 'Scarecrow. Nobody else may ever say this, so I'll just say it for me . . . and for Ralph, and for the six Britney clones and my bitch from hell mother-in-law. Thank you.'

Schofield came over to her, extended his hand. Mother clasped it and let him haul her up.

Before he could move off, however, she embraced him in a mighty hug, engulfing his body in her massive frame. Then she kissed him on the forehead and guided him back to the *Raven* with one arm around his shoulders.

'I miss her already,' she said as they walked.

'Me, too,' Schofield said. 'Me, too.'

They walked together.

'Mother, I'm sorry I hit you.'

'Hey, it's okay. I hit you first.'

'Thanks for fighting me. Thanks for not letting me go.'

UPPER NEW YORK BAY, USA
26 OCTOBER, 1125 HOURS LOCAL TIME

Exactly eleven minutes after his Concorde had touched down on the tarmac at JFK, Book II was sitting in the back of a Marine Corps CH-53E Super Stallion helicopter, blasting over the Statue of Liberty and Upper New York Bay, the mighty steel-and-glass mountain range of New York City spread out behind him.

Seated in the hold with him were twelve fully-armed Force Reconnaissance Marines.

'You found *terrorists* at the plant?' Book shouted into his mike, puzzled. He was talking to the leader of the Department of Defense team that had checked the Axon plant earlier, a man named Dodds.

'*Yes. All from Global Jihad, including – wait for it – Shoab Riis. Looks like it was a hell of a fight there,*' Dodds said.

'Global Jihad,' Book said. 'But that just doesn't make—' He cut himself off.

Suddenly he understood.

Majestic-12 needed someone to blame for all this. And who better than a terrorist organisation?

For, really, how could Axon Corp help it if Global Jihad terrorists stole their missiles and ships. But where could Majestic-12 find a team of genuine Global Jihad terrorists?

'France,' Book II said aloud. 'It's always fucking France.'

Dodds said, 'Book, what the hell is going on? Everyone here is scared shitless. This could be the biggest terrorist attack in history and they're going to use our own missiles against us.'

'This isn't a terrorist thing, Dodds,' Book said. 'It's a business thing. Trust me, the terrorists were already dead when they got to that plant. I'm starting to think that the French Secret Service has been giving Majestic-12 some quiet assistance. I gotta go. Book, out.'

Book turned his gaze back toward the container ships and supertankers resting at anchor off Staten Island – a pack of leviathans awaiting permission to enter the Hudson and East Rivers.

Thanks to the Kormoran project, each one of them was a potential missile launch vessel.

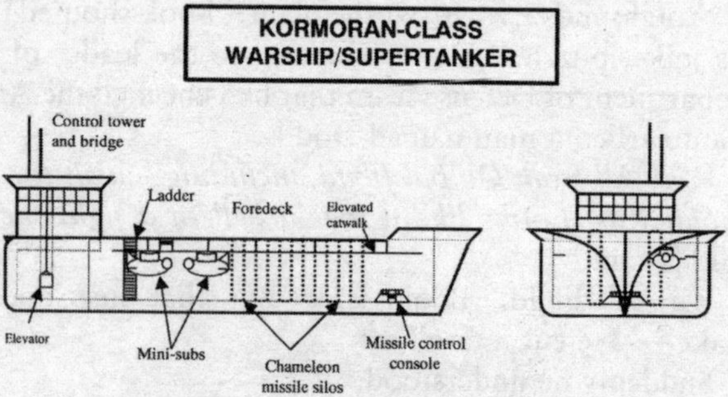

KORMORAN-CLASS WARSHIP/SUPERTANKER

'So which one is it?' the pilot asked.

'Just go to GPS co-ordinates 28743.05 – 4104.55,' Book said. 'That's where it'll be.'

The pilot adjusted his dials, flew by his GPS locator.

Book checked the launch list on his hand-held computer for the hundredth time. After he had spoken with Schofield earlier, he and Scott Moseley had calculated the GPS locations of the last two Kormoran tanker-launchers:

Hopewell	Taep'o-Dong-2	N-8	11900.00	11622.50	1230
			2327.00	4000.00	
			(Taiwan Sts)	(Beijing)	
	Taep'o-Dong-2	N-8	11900.00	11445.80	1230
			2327.00	2243.25	
			(Taiwan Sts)	(Hong K)	
Whale	Shahab-5	TN76	07040.45	07725.05	1245
			2327.00	2958.65	
			(Arab n Sea)	(New Dehli)	
	Shahab-5	TN76	07040.45	07332.60	1245
			2327.00	3230.55	
			(Arab n Sea)	(Islamabad)	

After that, he and Moseley had then plotted *all* the boats on a map of the world:

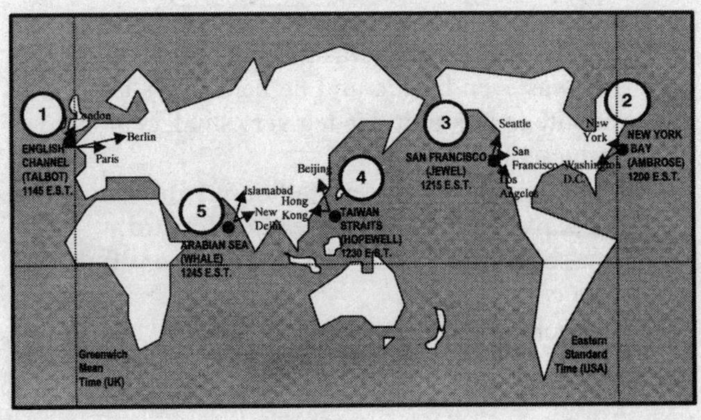

The sum of it all?

In addition to the three tankers set to fire their nuclear-tipped missiles on America, England, France and Germany, there were two extra Kormoran ships out there: one in the Arabian Sea, ready to fire on both India and Pakistan, and another in the Taiwan Straits, aiming cloned Taep'o-Dong ICBMs at Beijing and Hong Kong.

'Jesus H. Christ . . .' Book whispered.

He shook himself out of it, hit his satellite mike.

'Fairfax? You there? How you doing out West?'

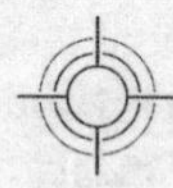

PACIFIC OCEAN,
TWO MILES OFF SAN FRANCISCO BAY
0825 HOURS LOCAL TIME
(1125 HOURS E.S.T. USA)

Dave Fairfax sat in a Super Stallion of his own, flanked by his own Marine Recon team, his right foot shaking incessantly – a nervous gesture that betrayed his rather extreme fear.

He wore a helmet that was too big and a bulletproof vest that was even bigger, and he held in his lap a real-time satellite uplink unit. He felt very small compared to the Marines all around him.

At the moment, his Super Stallion was powering low over the waves of the Pacific, heading toward –

A lone supertanker lying silently at anchor off the San Francisco coast.

'Hi, Book,' Fairfax yelled into his newly-acquired throat-mike. 'We have our tanker, and she's a big one, all right. She's exactly where she should be; her position matches the GPS co-ordinates you gave me. Tanker identified as the MV *Jewel,* registered in Norfolk, Virginia, to the Atlantic Shipping Company, a deep subsidiary of Axon Corporation.'

Fairfax's foot kept shaking. He wished it would stop.

'Oh, and I got that Mersenne prime for you,' he said. 'God, man, Mersennes are very cool mathematics. There are only thirty-nine that we know of, but some of those are, like, two million digits long. They're a very rare kind of prime number. You get them by applying a strict formula: Mersenne Prime = $2^p - 1$, where "p" is a prime number, but where the answer is also prime. Three is the first Mersenne Prime because $2^2 - 1 = 3$, and both 2 and 3 are prime. So they start small, but end up very big. The sixth Mersenne is 131071. It's based on the prime number, 17. That is, $2^{17} - 1 = 131071$, which is also prime—'

'*So the answer is 131071,*' Book said.

'Uh, yes,' Fairfax said.

'*I'll pass that on to the Scarecrow,*' Book said. '*Thanks, David. Out.*'

The signal went dead.

Fairfax scowled at his treacherous foot.

'Goes with the job, Mr Fairfax,' the Marine leader, Trent, said, nodding at Fairfax's foot. 'But if the Scarecrow trusts you to do this, then you must be up to the challenge.'

'I'm glad *he* thinks I'm up for it,' Fairfax muttered.

The Super Stallion roared toward the tanker.

ENGLISH CHANNEL,
NORTH OF CHERBOURG, FRANCE
26 OCTOBER, 1725 HOURS LOCAL TIME
(1125 HOURS E.S.T. USA)

The *Black Raven* shot like a bullet through the rain-driven sky, searchlights blazing, zooming high over a constellation of supertanker lights on the English Channel.

While Rufus, Mother and Knight searched the sea for their target, Schofield was talking on the radio with Book II.

'*Okay, I'm sending it all through now*,' Book's voice said.

Schofield's Palm Pilot pinged: it now had Book's plots of all the Kormoran ships on it. Schofield's eyes widened at the location names: the Arabian Sea, the Taiwan Straits . . .

'*And Fairfax figured out the sixth Mersenne for you*,' Book said. '*It's 131071*.'

'131071 . . .' Schofield wrote it down on his hand. 'Thanks, Book. Tell David I'll be in touch with him shortly. Scarecrow, out.'

He switched channels, patched in to the US Embassy in London. 'Mr Moseley. What's the word on our submarines?'

'I've got good news and bad news,' Scott Moseley's voice said.

'Give me the good news.'

'The good news is we have Los Angeles-class attack subs in both the Arabian Sea and the Taiwan Straits –

close enough to take out the launch boats at those locations.'

'And the bad news.'

Moseley said, 'The bad news is the other three launch boats: the ones in New York, San Francisco and the English Channel. They're going to fire too soon. We don't have any 688s close enough to get to any of those launch vessels in time. Book and Fairfax are going to have to go in and disarm them *in situ*, on board.'

'Okay,' Schofield said.

'Found it!' Rufus pointed to a supertanker rolling at anchor in the raging sea, its deck illuminated by powerful floodlights – just another gigantic supertanker nestled in amongst all the others waiting off the French coast. 'Transponder signal identifies it as the MV *Talbot* and its location matches the GPS location perfectly.'

'Good work, Rufus,' Schofield said. 'Mr Moseley, thanks for your help. Now I have to get to work.'

Schofield turned to Knight and Mother. 'We take the launch tankers in the order that they'll fire. This one first. Then we hightail it out of here and disarm the others by remote from a safe location. Good for you?'

'Good for me,' Knight said.

'Fuckin' dandy,' Mother said.

'Hold on, people,' Schofield said, his face deadly. 'We're going in.'

ENGLISH CHANNEL
1730 HOURS LOCAL TIME
(1130 HOURS IN NEW YORK)

The *Black Raven* swooped in low over the supertanker's main deck, cutting across the beams of the ship's flood-lights.

Rain fell all around it – slanting, stinging rain.

Forks of lightning slashed the sky.

Then the bomb bay on the *Raven* opened and three figures rappelled down from it: Schofield, Knight and Mother.

They were all fully armed – MP-7s, Glock pistols, Remington shotguns – thanks to the *Raven*'s onboard arsenal. Schofield and Mother even wore two spare utility vests that Knight kept for himself aboard the *Raven*.

The three of them landed on the superlong foredeck of the *Talbot*, in front of its control tower, while above them the *Black Raven* peeled away into the rainy sky.

And not a moment too soon.

For no sooner were Schofield and the others on the deck than the entire area around them exploded with bullet sparks from a pair of snipers firing from the control tower.

NEW YORK BAY
EAST COAST, USA

At the exact same time on the other side of the Atlantic, Book II and his team of Marines were storming their supertanker – the *Ambrose* – in New York Bay.

Like Schofield, they rode ziplines from their chopper down to the tanker's elongated foredeck.

Like Schofield, they entered under fire.

Unlike Schofield, however, they didn't have the advantage of darkness and pouring rain. It was 11:30 a.m. on this side of the world. Broad daylight.

The two snipers waiting for them inside the bridge of the *Ambrose* opened fire before Book's men had reached the bottom of their ropes.

Two Marines fell immediately. Dead.

Book hit the deck hard, landing with a heavy thump, returned fire.

SAN FRANCISCO
WEST COAST, USA

It was the same on the West Coast.

Fairfax's team stormed their supertanker – the *Jewel* – under heavy sniper fire from its control tower.

But Trent's men saw it coming.

Their own crack shooter nailed both of the enemy snipers with two shots from the open door of their Super Stallion.

The Marines stormed the ship, landing on the roof of the supertanker's control tower – with Dave Fairfax running in their midst.

They found the snipers' nest on the bridge: two snipers had been firing out through the supertanker's high-visibility bridge windows.

The two snipers had deep black skin, and wore khaki African military fatigues.

'What the hell?' Andrew Trent said when he saw their shoulder insignia.

Both snipers wore the badge of the Eritrean Army.

THE ENGLISH CHANNEL

Lightning lit up the sky – waves crashed against the side of the supertanker – thunder roared – bullets banged down against the foredeck.

Knight and Mother nailed the two snipers up on the bridge of the *Talbot* with a blitzkrieg of fire.

'I should have known!' Schofield shouted as they charged across the foredeck toward a door at the base of the control tower. 'Killian wouldn't leave the ships unguarded!'

'So who are they? Who did he get to do the guarding?' Mother yelled.

On the way to the tower, they found a large access hatch sunk into the deck. Knight and Schofield opened it . . .

. . . to be met by the deafening *brack-a-brack!* of automatic gunfire and the sight of a long vertical ladder disappearing down into the ship's vast missile hold.

Of more immediate interest to Schofield and Knight, however, was what they saw at the base of the ladder.

The source of the gunfire.

To their utter amazement, they saw a team of black-clad commandos – brandishing Uzis and M-16s with clinical precision, and firing them ferociously at an unseen enemy.

Schofield jammed the hatch shut again.

'I think we interrupted someone's battle,' he said.

Mother yelled, 'What did you see down there?'

'We're not the first people to arrive at this tanker,' Schofield said.

'What! Who's down there?'

Schofield exchanged a look with Knight.

'Not many elite units use Uzis these days,' Knight said. 'Zemir. I'd say it's the Sayaret Tzanchanim.'

'I agree,' Schofield said.

'Would someone *please* tell me what's going on!' Mother yelled in the rain.

'My guess,' Schofield called, 'is that we've been beaten to this ship by the only other man in the world who can disarm the CincLock security system. It's that Israeli Air Force guy from the list – Zemir – with a crack team of Israel's best troops, the Sayaret Tzanchanim, protecting him.'

'Hey, this day has been so weird, I'd believe fucking anything,' Mother said. 'So where now?'

Schofield checked his watch.

1735 hours.

1135 in New York.

Ten minutes to launch.

He said, 'We let the Israelis do the dirty work downstairs. Hell, I'm happy to let Zemir be the hero and disarm those missiles. As for us: into the tower. I want to check those snipers. See who we're up against before we go running into that mess downstairs to help Zemir.'

They came to the door at the base of the tower, flung it open just as—

Bam!

—they were assaulted by the blinding white beam of a helicopter searchlight.

Schofield spun in the doorway, rain in his face.

'Oh, you have got to be joking . . .' he said.

There, landing on the long flat foredeck of the supertanker – a hundred yards away, its searchlight panning the area – was an obviously stolen Alouette helicopter.

It touched down on the deck.

And out of it stepped three men in Russian battledress uniforms and carrying Skorpion machine pistols . . .

Dmitri Zamanov and the last two remaining members of the Skorpions.

'Damn. I forgot,' Knight said, 'you've still got a price on your head. It's Zamanov. Run.'

Into the control tower. Up some ladder-stairs. Emerging onto the bridge.

1736.

Fairfax's voice in Schofield's ear: '*Scarecrow. We've taken the bridge of the San Francisco tanker. Found enemy snipers wearing the uniforms of the Eritrean Army . . .*'

Schofield went straight over to the bodies of his snipers.

African soldiers.

Commandos. Khaki fatigues. Black helmets.

And on their shoulders, a crest – but *not* the crest of Eritrea.

Rather, it was the badge of the Nigerian Army's elite commando unit: the Presidential Guard.

As veterans of Africa's many civil wars, the Nigerian Presidential Guard were CIA-trained killers who in the past had been used against their own citizens as much as against their nation's enemies. In the streets of Lagos and Abuja, the Presidential Guards were known by another name: the Death Squads.

Killian's protection team.

Two snipers up here. And more men downstairs, guarding the missile silos – the unseen enemy that the Israelis were fighting right now in the hold.

'Mr Fairfax. Did you say yours were Eritrean?'

'*That's right.*'

'Not Nigerian?'

'*Nope. My Marines confirm it. Definitely Eritrean insignia.*'

Eritrea? Schofield thought –

'Scarecrow,' Mother said, opening a storeroom door wide. Four body bags lay on the floor of the storeroom. Mother quickly unzipped one – to reveal the stinking corpse of a Global Jihad terrorist.

'Ah, now I get it,' Schofield said. 'The whipping boys.'

He keyed his sat-mike: 'Mr Fairfax. Tell your Marines to stay sharp. There'll be more African troops down in the main hold, guarding the silos. Sorry, David. It's not over for you yet. You have to get past those troops and get your satellite uplink unit within sixty feet of the missiles' control console for me to disarm them.'

'*Ten-four,*' Fairfax's voice signed off. '*We're on the case.*'

Mother joined Knight at the windows of the bridge, searching the area outside for Zamanov.

'Do you see him?' Mother said.

'No, the little Russian ratbastard's disappeared,' Knight said. 'Probably gone after Zemir.'

Suddenly Rufus's voice exploded in their earpieces: '*Boss. Scarecrow. I got a new contact closing in on your tanker. A large cutter of some kind. Looks like the French Coast Guard.*'

'Christ,' Schofield said, moving to the windows, seeing a large white boat approaching them on their starboard side.

Schofield couldn't believe it.

In addition to the Nigerian Death Squad, the Israeli

shock troops and the Russian bounty hunters already on this supertanker, they now had a group of French maritime police on the way!

'That ain't the Coast Guard,' Knight said, peering through some night-vision binoculars.

Through them he could see a big white cutter, charging through the chop – could see its knife-like bow, its big foredeck gun, its glassed-in wheelhouse, and blood-bursts all over the wheelhouse's windows.

Armed men stood at its wheel.

'It's Demon Larkham and IG-88,' Knight said.

1738.

Seven minutes to launch.

'Damn it, more bounty hunters,' Schofield said. 'Rufus! Can you take them out?'

'*Sorry, Captain, I'm outta missiles. Used them all against that French carrier.*'

'Okay, okay . . .' Schofield said, thinking. 'All right, Rufus, you keep to your instructions, okay. If we can't disarm those missiles in time, we'll be needing your special help later.'

'*Got it.*'

Schofield spun, still thinking, thinking, thinking.

Everything was happening too fast. The situation was spiralling out of control. Missiles to disarm, the Israelis already on board, Nigerian troops, more bounty hunters . . .

'Focus!' he shouted aloud. 'Think, Scarecrow. What do you ultimately have to achieve?'

Disarm the missiles. I have to disarm the missiles by 1745 hours. Everything else is secondary.

His eyes flashed to an elevator at the back of the bridge.

'We're going down to the hold,' he said.

1739 hours.

NEW YORK BAY
1139 HOURS

On the foredeck of their supertanker, in bright morning sunshine, Book's team of Marines dived for cover.

Book scrambled into a deck hatch, slid down a very long ladder into darkness, followed by his Marine escorts.

He hit the floor, looked around.

He stood in a cavernous hold, easily 300 yards long. A dozen cylindrical missile silos stretched away into darkness, like colossal pillars holding up the ceiling.

And bunkered down in front of the farthest missile silo, taking cover behind a heavily fortified barricade of steel crates and forklifts, was a team of heavily-armed African commandos.

THE ENGLISH CHANNEL
1739 HOURS

The elevator doors opened to reveal the aft section of the supertanker's main hold.

Schofield, Knight and Mother emerged, leading with their guns.

The missile hold was absolutely enormous – a massive interior space the size of three football fields stretched end-on-end. And in its forward half, the Chameleon missile silos: high reinforced titanium cylinders stretching all the way up to the underside of the supertanker's foredeck. Inside them: the most devastating weapons known to man.

And in that forward section of the ship, a *brutal* battle was underway.

A dozen Nigerian commandos were bunkered down beneath the farthest pair of missile silos, covering the missile control console – an elevated platform mounted ten feet off the ground on steel struts, and the place Schofield needed to be within sixty feet of in order to disarm the missiles.

The Nigerians were positioned behind a very well-prepared barricade, and they fired machine guns and hurled grenades at their Israeli attackers.

Bullets and grenades hit the silos, but did no damage – the walls of the silos were far too strong.

In between Schofield and this battle were all sorts of supply materials: shipping containers, missile spare parts; he even saw two yellow mini-submarines with hemispherical glass cockpits suspended from chains high up near the ceiling catwalks.

Schofield recognised the subs as heavily-modified ASDSs – Advanced SEAL Delivery Systems. With their glass domes, these shallow-water mini-submarines were often used by the US Navy to visually inspect the exterior hull of an aircraft carrier or ballistic missile submarine for sabotage devices. It was a given that a project as important as Kormoran–Chameleon would be equipped with them.

1740.

Schofield, Knight and Mother dashed forward, ducking low, winding their way between the supply materials, observing the battle.

Just as the Israelis launched a ruthless offensive.

They sent a few men to the right to draw the Nigerian fire, then they hit the Nigerian barricade with three rocket-propelled grenades from the left.

The grenades shot down the length of the missile hold . . . three white smoke-trails, flying together . . . and hit the Nigerian barricade.

It was like a dam bursting.

The Nigerians flew into the air. Some screamed. Others burned.

And the Israelis stormed forward, killing the Nigerians where they fell, shooting them in the heads, at the same moment as . . .

. . . a gigantic steel loading door set into the starboard wall of the hold rumbled open, rising into the air on its runners.

The massive door opened fully and – *whump!* – a wide steel boarding plank clanged to the floor from *outside* the aperture and like a crew of sixteenth-century pirates boarding a galleon, the men of IG-88 flooded into the missile hold, charging into it from their stolen Coast Guard boat, their devastating MetalStorm guns blazing.

Schofield watched as – now under fire from at least twenty IG-88 men – the Israeli commandos, the crack Sayaret Tzanchanim, seized the area around the missile control console.

They formed a tight semi-circle around the elevated console platform, all facing aft, firing their Uzis and M-16s at IG-88.

Under their protection, the Israelis' leader – a man who could only be Simon Zemir – climbed up onto the steel platform and went straight over to the console, flipped open a briefcase and extracted a CincLock-VII disarm unit.

'Sneaky bastard Israelis,' Mother said. 'Is there any US technology that they haven't stolen?'

'Probably not,' Schofield said, 'but today they're our bestest buddies. We watch over them while they watch over Zemir.'

1741.

From behind his missile silo, Schofield watched as Zemir's CincLock unit illuminated like a laptop and Zemir stared at its touchscreen, flexing his fingers in anticipation of the disarm sequence he was about to face.

He's going to disarm the missile system, Schofield thought.

Excellent. We might get out of here without much hassle after all.

But then, to his absolute horror, Schofield saw three shadowy figures descending by rope from the rafters of the missile hold *above and behind* Zemir's console platform.

None of the Sayaret Tzanchanim saw them. They were too busy firing at Demon Larkham and his IG-88 bounty hunters.

'No,' Schofield whispered. '*No, no, no . . .*'

The three shadowy figures whizzed down their ropes at lightning speed.

Zamanov and his Skorpions.

Ziplining down from the ship's foredeck, from a hatch near the bow.

Schofield broke cover, yelled uselessly above the gunfire: '*Behind* you!'

Of course, the Israelis responded immediately.

By firing at him. Even Zemir himself looked up, about to start the disarm sequence.

Schofield dived back behind his silo, rolled to the ground, peered back out—

—just in time to see the three Skorpions land lightly on the elevated platform a few yards *behind* the preoccupied Zemir.

And Schofield could only watch, powerless, as in the strobe-like glare of the Israelis' muzzle-flashes, Zamanov crept silently forward, drew his Cossack fighting sword and swung the blade at Zemir's neck from behind in a brutal horizontal slashing motion.

And in that instant, Shane Schofield became the last person on the bounty list still alive.

And the only man on earth capable of disarming the CincLock-VII missile security system.

Zemir's head dropped off his shoulders. He had not even been able to start the disarm sequence.

Schofield's mouth fell open. 'This cannot be happening.'

One of the Sayaret Tzanchanim glanced over his shoulder – in time to see Zemir's headless corpse drop off the console platform and down to the floor, spilling blood; to see Zamanov stuff Zemir's ragged head into his rucksack and whiz back up his retractable zipline –

Blam!

Covering the fleeing Zamanov, the other two Skorpions shot the Israeli trooper in the face – just as two more Sayaret Tzanchanim soldiers were blasted by IG-88 fire from the *other* direction.

Fire from both directions – twin forces of professional bounty hunters – assailed the Israeli commando team.

And as the remaining Sayaret Tzanchanim noticed Zemir's fallen body and the fleeing Skorpions above it, they became confused and in the face of IG-88's superior firepower, lost formation.

They were decimated.

IG-88 overwhelmed them. Within moments, the entire Israeli force was dead.

1742.

IG-88 took control of the barricade. Demon Larkham strode like a conquering general into the enemy blockade. He pointed up at the ceiling, at Zamanov and his Skorpions fleeing on their retractable ziplines with Zemir's head in their possession.

The three Skorpions hit the ceiling next to a wide cargo hatch.

Zamanov's two companions climbed up through the hatch first, stepping up into the pouring rain on the foredeck, reached back down as Zamanov handed them the severed head of Simon Zemir.

Supermachine-gun fire riddled their bodies.

The two Skorpions on the foredeck convulsed violently, their chests exploding in bloody fountains.

A six-man subteam of IG-88 troopers stood in the rain waiting for them. Demon Larkham had anticipated this, and so had already dispatched a second team to the foredeck.

The rucksack containing Zemir's head dropped to the deck, and the IG-88 subteam ran forward, grabbed it.

Outnumbered and outgunned, Zamanov ducked below the floorline, swung over to a catwalk high above the missile hold and disappeared into the shadows.

Down in the missile hold itself, Schofield was speechless.

This was unbelievable.

With three minutes to go till the nuclear missiles fired, Zemir was dead and IG-88 held the control console. Twenty of them, with MetalStorm guns!

He needed some kind of distraction, a *really big* distraction.

'Call Rufus,' he said to Knight.

'You sure?'

'It's the only way.'

'Right,' Knight said. 'You're a truly crazy man, Captain Schofield.' Then Knight spoke into his throat-mike. 'Rufus. How is Plan B coming along?'

Rufus's voice came in. '*I got the nearest one for you! And she's one big momma! I'm a hundred yards out, engines running, and pointed straight at you!*'

One hundred yards away from the *Talbot*, a second supertanker was powering through the storm with Rufus at the helm.

Waiting its turn to unload its cargo at Cherbourg, the giant 110,000-ton container ship, the MV *Eindhoven*, had been sitting at rest in the Channel, its engines idling, when Rufus had landed the *Black Raven* on its foredeck.

Now, but for Rufus, it was empty, its sailing crew of six having wisely decided to depart on a lifeboat after Rufus had strafed their bridge windows with two M-16s.

'What do you want me to do!' Rufus shouted into his radio.

On the *Talbot*, Schofield assessed the situation.

The Rufus Plan was always meant to be a last resort – a means by which Schofield could *sink* the false supertanker if he failed to disarm its missiles.

He stole a glance at the control console and its barricade and suddenly his blood froze.

Demon Larkham was looking directly back at him. He'd spotted them.

The Demon smiled.

'Rufus,' Schofield said. 'Ram us.'

17:42:10.

Demon Larkham's men charged out from behind their barricade, winding their way between the missile silos, their MetalStorm rifles blazing.

Coming after Schofield.

Schofield led Mother and Knight over to a lifeboat positioned beside the open cargo door on the starboard side of the hold.

'Quickly,' he yelled. 'Get in!'

They all dived into the lifeboat, then snapped up to return fire.

The IG-88 men closed in.

Schofield fired hard. So did Mother and Knight, trying to hold them off until Rufus arrived.

But the IG-88 troopers kept advancing.

'Come on, Rufus,' Schofield said aloud. 'Where are you . . . ?'

And then – magnificently – Rufus arrived.

It sounded like the end of the world.

The shriek of rending metal, of steel striking steel.

The collision of the two supertankers on the surface of the English Channel, veiled in sleeting rain, was an awesome, *awesome* sight.

Two of the largest moving objects on the planet – each nearly a 1,000 feet long and each weighing more than 100,000 tons – collided at ramming speed.

Rufus's stolen tanker, the *Eindhoven*, ploughed bow-first right into the port flank of the *Talbot*, hitting it perfectly perpendicularly.

The sharpened bow of the *Eindhoven* drove like a knife into the side of the *Talbot*, smashing into it like a battering ram.

The port flank of the *Talbot* just crumpled inward. Seawater gushed in through the gigantic gash the *Eindhoven* created in its side.

And like a boxer recoiling from a blow, the entire supertanker rocked wildly in response to the impact.

At first, it rolled to starboard, so great was the force of Rufus's ramming strike. But then as seawater began to enter the *Talbot* en masse, the missile-firing supertanker tilted dramatically – and fatally – back to port.

At which point it rolled over onto its left-hand side and began to sink.

Fast.

*

The scene inside the missile hold of the *Talbot* would have made Noah gulp.

In here, the impact had been a thunderous experience.

Not even Schofield had been prepared for the sheer power of the blow, or the sudden appearance of the *Eindhoven*'s pointed bow thrusting unexpectedly *right through* the port-side wall of the missile hold.

In response, the entire hold had swayed to starboard, throwing everyone off their feet.

Then seawater began to enter the hold through the gigantic gash – in monumental proportions.

A tidal wave of water, ten feet high and utterly immense in its force, rushed into the hold, swallowing several members of IG-88 in an instant, lifting forklifts and cargo containers and missile parts clear into the air.

The water rushed underneath Schofield's lifeboat, lifting it off its mounts. Schofield immediately released the craft from its davits and gunned the engine.

Within seconds, the hold's floor was completely under water, the water level rising fast.

And as it filled, the *Talbot* rolled dramatically to port – toward the fatal gash, tilting at least 30 degrees – and Schofield, blasting forward in the motorised lifeboat on the level surface of the water, saw the whole hold all around him start to roll.

17:42:30

From outside, it all made for a very unusual sight.

The *Eindhoven* was still embedded in the side of the *Talbot* – while the *Talbot*, taking on water in incredible quantities, lay foundering half-tilted on its left-hand side, literally hanging off the bow of the *Eindhoven*.

But so great was the weight of the water rushing into

its belly, the *Talbot* was actually driving the bow of the *Eindhoven* under the surface as well – as such, the *Talbot*'s long foredeck and bridge tower remained above the waterline, slanted at a steep 30-degree sideways angle, while its left-hand flank drove the *Eindhoven*'s bow relentlessly downward, toward the waves.

On board the *Eindhoven*, Rufus didn't need to be told what to do.

He raced for the *Raven*, still parked on the foredeck of his tanker, climbed into the cockpit and lifted off into the rain-swept sky.

17:43:30.

Inside the rapidly-filling *Talbot*, Schofield was moving fast.

In fact, very very fast.

His motorised lifeboat whipped across the surface, slicing in between the now-slanted missile silos with Mother and Knight positioned on its flanks, shooting at their enemies floating in the water. It was like speed-boating through a forest of half-fallen trees.

After the impact, Demon Larkham and most of his men had all made for the starboard side of the hold – the high side – the only part of the hold still above water.

Schofield, however, cut a beeline for the control console at the forward end of the missile hold.

17:43:48

17:43:49

17:43:50

His lifeboat carved through the chop, his two loyal shooters blazing away, killing IG-88 men as they whistled by.

The lifeboat came alongside the elevated control

console. The wire-frame control console was also tilted at a dramatic angle, barely a foot above the rising waterline.

'Cover me!' Schofield yelled. From where he stood in his lifeboat, he could see the console's illuminated display screen, saw stark red numerals on it ticking downward in hundredths of a second – the countdown to missile launch.

00:01:10.88
00:01:09.88
00:01:08.88

The digitised hundredths of a second whizzed by in such a blur that they looked like 8s.

Schofield pulled his CincLock-VII unit – the one he'd taken from the French – from a waterproof pouch on his vest and once again saw the unit's display.

White and red circles hovered on the touchscreen.

Bing.

A message appeared:

MISSILE LAUNCH SEQUENCE IN PROGRESS.
PRESS 'ENTER' TO INITIATE DISARM SEQUENCE.
FIRST PROTOCOL (PROXIMITY): SATISFIED.
INITIATE SECOND PROTOCOL.

Like before, the white circles on the screen began to blink slowly on and off.

Schofield punched them as they did so.

The countdown ticked ever-downward.

00:01:01
00:01:00
00:00:59

Then abruptly the *Talbot* lurched sharply. The entire supertanker, still hanging off the bow of the *Eindhoven*, was now slowly slipping off it!

With the unexpected jolt, Schofield missed one of the white circles.

The display beeped:

SECOND PROTOCOL (RESPONSE PATTERN):
FAILED DISARM ATTEMPT RECORDED.
THREE FAILED DISARM ATTEMPTS WILL RESULT
IN DEFAULT DETONATION.
SECOND PROTOCOL (RESPONSE PATTERN):
REACTIVATED.

'Shit,' Schofield said.

He started all over again.

The supertanker was still sinking.

He felt water lapping against his boots.

While Schofield punched at the touchscreen, Aloysius Knight fired at the IG-88 force on the high starboard side of the hold.

He loosed a new burst, before suddenly he saw it.

'Oh, no . . .' he breathed.

'What?' Mother called.

'The starboard-side cargo door,' Knight said. 'It's about to go under.'

He was right. Owing to the leftward tilt of the ship, the massive starboard-side cargo doorway had until now been well above the waterline.

But now the rising water was about to hit it. And that was very bad – because once it did, seawater would start entering the *Talbot* from *both* sides of the ship.

After that, the *Talbot* would go down with frightening speed—

'Knight!' Mother yelled. 'Check right!'

'Oh, crap,' Knight said.

Over to their right, six of Demon Larkham's men were climbing out of the water into two motorised lifeboats.

They were coming for them.

'Captain Schofield!' Knight called. 'Are you done yet?'

'Almost . . . !' Schofield yelled, his eyes locked on the screen.

00:00:51
00:00:50
00:00:49

The two IG-88 lifeboats swung over to the starboard side of the water-filled hold, picked up the Demon and the remaining IG-88 force – sixteen men in total.

Then they charged toward Schofield and the missile control console.

Knight and Mother fired.

The two IG-88 boats blasted across the water, skimming through the forest of slanted missile silos, firing as they sped.

In the meantime, Schofield was still in his own world, punching red and white circles.

00:00:41
00:00:40
00:00:39

Then he hit the final white circle and the screen changed to:

SECOND PROTOCOL (RESPONSE PATTERN): SATISFIED.
THIRD PROTOCOL (CODE ENTRY): ACTIVE.
PLEASE ENTER AUTHORISED DISARM CODE.

'All *right*,' Schofield said. The Universal Disarm

Code. The sixth Mersenne prime was still written on his hand: 131071.

He started punching the numerical keypad on the CincLock unit when without warning the lifeboat beneath him moved and –

Beep!

The screen squealed in protest.

FIRST PROTOCOL (PROXIMITY): FAILED.
ALL PROTOCOLS REACTIVATED.

'What!' Schofield snapped his eyes up to find Knight gunning their lifeboat *away* from the missile console, while Mother fired off their stern at two pursuing IG-88 boats.

They weaved in between the missile silos.

'Sorry, Captain!' Knight yelled. 'But we had to go! We were dead if we stayed there!'

'Yeah, well we have to get back within range of that console in about ten seconds! Because I need at least twenty-five seconds to complete the response pattern!'

Bullet geysers raked the water all around their speeding lifeboat.

00:00:35
00:00:34
00:00:33

Knight brought the lifeboat round. 'How close do you have to be!'

'Sixty feet!'

'All right!'

Bullets whizzed past their ears, pinged off the missile silos.

Knight swung their boat around and brought it into a wide circular path around the steel island that was the control console, a circle that included the occasional weaving run in amongst the forest of silos.

00:00:27

00:00:26

00:00:25

Schofield's screen beeped to life.

FIRST PROTOCOL (PROXIMITY): SATISFIED.

INITIATE SECOND PROTOCOL.

The light-response display began – which meant so did Schofield's screen-tapping.

Mother kept firing at the IG-88 boats behind them.

Knight drove with one hand, fired with the other, careful to keep their boat within sixty feet of the control console.

00:00:16

00:00:15

00:00:14

But then the IG-88 boats, now aware of the circular path Knight was taking, split up.

One of them pivoted in the water, and took off in the opposite circular direction: the effect being that the first IG-88 boat was now driving Schofield's boat toward the second one.

Oblivious to the chase, Schofield's hands moved more quickly now.

Red-white-white . . .

Tap-tap-tap . . .

00:00:11

00:00:10

00:00:09

Knight saw IG-88's plan. He fired at the oncoming boat's driver.

Blam!-blam!-blam! . . .
Miss-miss-miss . . .

00:00:08
00:00:07
00:00:06

Schofield's hands were a blur now, tapping smoothly left and right.

Mother hit one of their pursuers. But then roared as she took a sizzling-hot round to her shoulder.

00:00:05
00:00:04
00:00:03

They came on collision course with the second IG-88 boat, Knight still firing at its driver.

Blam!-blam!-blam! . . .
Miss-miss . . .
Hit.

00:00:02

The driver flopped and fell, dead. The IG-88 boat peeled away, and Knight kept his boat within the sixty-foot zone of the console.

00:00:01

And Schofield's hand movements changed slightly. Instead of tapping circles, it looked as if he was entering a—

00:00:00

Too late.

None of the Chameleon missiles, however, fired.

The countdown timer on the console was frozen at:

00:00:00.05

The seconds may have hit zero, but the very last second – calculated in blurring digital hundredths – had yet to fully expire when Schofield had punched in the Universal Disarm Code and hit 'ENTER'.

The screen now read:

THIRD PROTOCOL (CODE ENTRY): SATISFIED.

AUTHORISED DISARM CODE ENTERED.

MISSILE LAUNCH ABORTED.

Schofield breathed a sigh of relief.

No missiles had launched.

London, Paris and Berlin were safe.

It was then, however, that the open starboard side door of the MV *Talbot* went slowly under the waterline.

SHOOOOOOM!!!

The roar was absolutely deafening.

It was, literally, like the opening of the floodgates.

Like an invading army overwhelming its enemy's lines, an unimaginable quantity of seawater came gushing in over the threshold of the *Talbot*'s wide starboard-side doorway.

A *wall* of water – a super tidal wave of unstoppable, ravenous liquid.

The result was instantaneous.

The entire supertanker rolled dramatically, *righting itself* as the inrushing water from the starboard side began to balance off against the inflow from port.

This righting of the *Talbot*, however, had one very important side-effect: it served to disengage the *Talbot* from the bow of the *Eindhoven*. And with the loss of its grip on the other supertanker, the *Talbot* lost its only means of staying afloat.

And so it began to sink – at speed – into the depths of the English Channel.

For Schofield, Knight and Mother, in their lifeboat on the water's surface inside the missile hold, the noise was all-consuming.

The roar of the waterfall flooding into the hold echoed throughout the ship. Waves crashed against steel walls. Whirlpools formed.

And the water level rose at frightening speed.

Indeed, to Schofield, it seemed as if the ceiling was lowering itself toward them. Quickly.

Within moments, they found themselves speeding along the surface *halfway up* the gigantic missile silos, twenty feet below the steel catwalks suspended from the roof.

In addition to this, with the breaching of the starboard-side door, Demon Larkham and his IG-88 men broke away from their chase, heading instead for the various ladders that led to the hold's ceiling.

'Damn, he's good,' Knight said. 'The Demon's heading topside, for the foredeck. He's going to cover all the hatches. Then he just waits for us to come up – which we'll have to do eventually.'

'Then we have to find another way out,' Schofield said. 'All I need now is to get away from this ship and find a safe place to hole up while I disarm the missiles aimed at America.'

Schofield pulled out his Palm Pilot to see which was the next Kormoran ship to launch.

He called up the bundle of documents that he had seen on the Pilot before:

Source	Delivery Sys.	W-H	Origin	Target	Time
Talbot	Shahab-5	TN76	35702.90	00001.65	1145
			5001.00	5239.10	
	Shahab-5	TN76	35702.90	00420.02	1145
			5001.00	4900.25	
	Shahab-5	TN76	35702.90	01312.15	1145
			5001.00	5358.75	

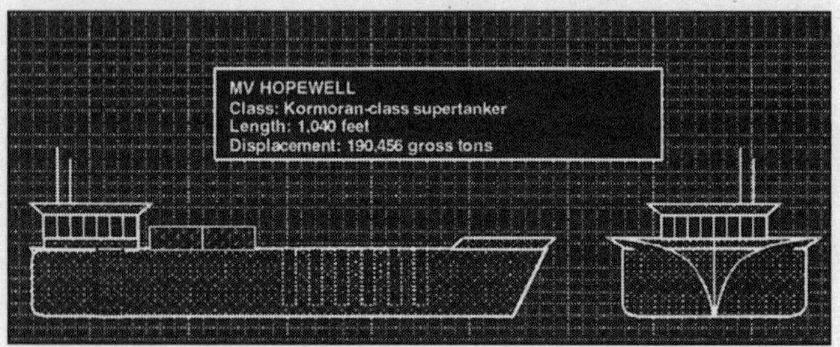

SUBJECT: PAYMENT OF ASSESSOR'S COMMISSION

PAYMENT OF THE ASSESSOR'S COMMISSION WILL BE MADE BY INTERNAL ELECTRONIC FUNDS TRANSFER WITHIN AGM-SUISSE FROM ASTRAL-66 PTY LTD'S PRIVATE ACCOUNT (NO. 437-666-21) IN THE AMOUNT OF US$3.2 MILLION (THREE POINT TWO MILLION US DOLLARS) PER ASSESSMENT.

Executive Itinerary

The proposed order of travel is as follows: Asmara (01/08), Luanda (01/08), Abuja (05/08), N'djamena (07/08) and Tobruk (09/08).

01/08 – Asmara (embassy)
03/08 – Luanda (stay with M. Loch, R's nephew)

	Name	Nat.	Org.
1.	ASHCROFT, William H.	UK	SAS
2.	CHRISTIE, Alec P.	UK	MI-6
3.	FARRELL, Gregory C.	USA	Delta
4.	KHALIF, Iman	AFGH	Al-Qaeda
5.	KINGSGATE, Nigel E.	UK	SAS
6.	McCABE, Dean P.	USA	Delta

He clicked on the abbreviated launch list. The full list came up:

Source	Delivery Sys.	W-H	Origin	Target	Time
Talbot	Shahab-5	TN76	35702.90	00001.65	1145
			5001.00	5239.10	
	Shahab-5	TN76	35702.90	00420.02	1145
			5001.00	4900.25	
	Shahab-5	TN76	35702.90	01312.15	1145
			5001.00	5358.75	
Ambrose	Shahab-5	TN76	28743.05	28743.98	1200
			4104.55	4104.64	
	Shahab-5	TN76	28743.05	28231.05	1200
			4104.55	3835.70	

Jewel	Taep'o-Dong-2	N-8	23222.62	23222.70	1215
			3745.75	3745.80	
	Taep'o-Dong-2	N-8	23222.62	24230.50	1215
			3745.75	3533.02	
	Taep'o-Dong-2	N-8	23222.62	23157.05	1215
			3745.75	4930.52	
Hopewell	Taep'o-Dong-2	N-8	11900.00	11622.50	1230
			2327.00	4000.00	
	Taep'o-Dong-2	N-8	11900.00	11445.80	1230
			2327.00	2243.25	
Whale	Shahab-5	TN76	07040.45	07725.05	1245
			2327.00	2958.65	
	Shahab-5	TN76	07040.45	07332.60	1245
			2327.00	3230.55	

He saw the familiar list.

It was the same as the one Book II had decrypted before. He saw the GPS locations of the first three boats: *Talbot*, *Ambrose* and *Jewel*.

The *Ambrose* was next: set to fire at 12 noon from GPS co-ordinates 28743.05,4104.55.

That's right, he remembered. *New York*.

Wait a second. His mind stopped short.

This list was different to Book's list.

He looked at it more closely.

Some of the missiles on the lower half of the list had been altered.

Book's list had featured only two varieties of missile: the Shahab and the Taep'o-Dong.

Yet this one featured several others in their place: the Sky Horse (from Taiwan), the Ghauri-II (Pakistan), the Agni-II (India) and the Jericho-2B (Israel).

It also, Schofield saw, had an *extra* launch vessel on

it – the last entry, the *Arbella* – set to fire more than two hours after the first group of missiles.

This wasn't even mentioning another disturbing fact: the Taiwanese and Israeli missiles on this list were armed with *American* nuclear warheads, the powerful W-88—

A withering volley of bullets smacked the water next to Schofield. He hardly noticed.

When he looked up, he saw that Knight had brought their lifeboat alongside a ladder leading up to a ceiling catwalk. Once upon a time that catwalk had been suspended eighty feet above the floor of the hold. Now it was barely *eighteen* feet above the fast-rising water level.

On it, however, sixty yards away in *both* directions and closing fast, were two four-man teams of IG-88 troops. They had just burst down through hatches in the ceiling and were now charging down the length of the catwalk from either end, firing hard, their bullets hitting the girders all around Schofield's boat.

Ping!-ping!-ping!-ping!-ping!

'Bastard!' Knight yelled. 'He's not waiting for us to come up. He's forcing us up!'

Mother lifted Schofield up by the collar. 'Come on, handsome, you can get back to your computer later.' She hauled him out of the lifeboat and up the ladder, covering him with her body.

They climbed the ladder quickly, shooting as they did so, reached the catwalk, where they were met by a million impact sparks.

Mother took up a covering position while Knight led Schofield aft.

Ping!-ping!-ping!-ping!-ping!

Bullets were spraying everywhere.

Knight and Schofield fired at the IG-88 men coming from the stern-end of the catwalk. Schofield went dry.

'Are we actually going anywhere in particular!' he yelled.

'Yes! To a safe place!' Knight called, still firing. 'A place where you can do your disarming thing, and where, at the same time, we can all get out of this sinking death-trap! Here!'

Knight cut sharply right, running past a small maintenance shack erected at a T-junction of this catwalk and another, emerging behind the shack to behold—

—the two yellow mini-submarines suspended on chains from the ceiling of the missile hold.

Like the catwalks, the subs weren't very high up anymore. Seventeen feet above the water level. A wide hood-like awning covered both the two subs and the catwalk between them. It now partially covered Schofield and Knight from the IG-88 teams.

Ping!-ping!-ping!-ping!-ping!

Trailing a dozen yards behind Knight and Schofield, Mother came to the maintenance shack at the T-junction, still returning fire at the IG-88 troops, now only twenty yards away from her on either side.

Schofield watched as she tried to make a break for the mini-subs, but the IG-88 troops blocked her way with a storm of bullets.

Mother ducked inside the shelter of the maintenance shack.

She was cut off.

'Mother!' Schofield yelled.

'*Get out of here, Scarecrow!*' she said over the radio.

The IG-88 men assaulted her shack with the most violent fusillade of MetalStorm rounds Schofield had seen yet.

The shack erupted in bullet impacts.

Mother ducked out of view – and Schofield feared that she'd been hit – but then she popped up again, firing and yelling, and took out two of the IG-88 men.

'*Scarecrow! I said, get out of here!*'

'I'm not leaving without you!'

'*Go!*' She loosed two more shots.

'I won't lose you and Gant in one day!'

Mother's voice became serious. '*Scarecrow. Go. You're more valuable than an old grunt like me.*' Mother looked over at him from the shack. '*You always were. My value comes in keeping you alive. At least let me do that. Now, go, you sexy little thing! Go! Go! Go!*'

And with that, Schofield saw Mother do something both courageous and suicidal.

She stood fully upright in the windows of the shack and, issuing a primal yell of 'Yaaaahhhhhhh!', started firing with two guns at *both* of the IG-88 forces.

Her sudden move stopped the two IG-88 teams in their tracks – each of them lost their front man in a gruesome fountain of blood – but crucially, it gave Schofield and Knight the opening they needed to escape.

'Get in!' Knight yelled, hitting the 'HATCH' button on one of the yellow submarines. With a quick iris-like motion, the circular hatch on top of the sub opened. 'Don't let her sacrifice count for nothing!'

Schofield took a half-step into the hatch, looked back at Mother – just as the two IG-88 forces overwhelmed her with their fire.

'Damn it, no . . .' he breathed.

A volley of MetalStorm bullets hit Mother, slamming into her chest armour . . .

Mother snapped upright, swaying, not firing anymore, her mouth open, her eyes suddenly blank—

—and then she fell and in the haze of smoke and flying glass, Schofield lost sight of her as she dropped out of sight below the maintenance shack's window frames.

A moment later the two IG-88 forces put the issue beyond doubt.

At the exact same time, both IG-88 teams fired rocket launchers at the maintenance shack.

Two fingers of smoke lanced toward Mother's little shack from both fore and aft.

They hit it together and – *boom!* – the shed's four walls blasted outward, the whole structure exploding in an instant, its flat floor section just dropping through the air to the water sixteen feet below.

Schofield made to step out of the sub but Knight pushed him back in.

'No! We go! Now!' Knight yelled above the gunfire.

He shoved Schofield into the mini-sub, and Schofield landed inside it—

—only to discover that someone else was already there.

Schofield's feet hit the floor of the mini-sub, and he looked up to see a sword blade rushing directly at his face.

Reflex action.

He whipped up his empty H&K pistol and – *clang!* – the blade rushing at his throat hit the pistol's trigger-guard and stopped: one inch from Schofield's neck.

Dmitri Zamanov stood before him.

He held a short-bladed Cossack sword in his hands, and his eyes blazed with hatred.

'You chose the wrong hiding place,' the Russian bounty hunter growled.

Then before Schofield could move, he punched two buttons.

First, the internal 'HATCH' button.

The hatch whizzed shut, its steel door irising closed.

And second, the 'ASDS RELEASE' button, and suddenly Schofield felt his stomach turn as the entire mini-submarine dropped from its chains and fell sixteen feet straight down, landing with a massive splash in the rising body of seawater.

'Goddamn it!' Aloysius Knight couldn't believe it. 'What is this shit!'

One moment, he'd been shoving Schofield into the

yellow ASDS and was about to climb in after him – the next, the sub's hatch closed right in front of him and then the whole fucking thing dropped down into the water below!

Hypercharged bullets hit the girders all around him as the IG-88 teams rushed past the destroyed maintenance shack and onto the submarine catwalk.

So Knight did the only thing he could do. He dived into the second mini-submarine, bullet-marks sizzling across the soles of his boots as he did so.

Schofield and Zamanov fought.

No style here. No graceful technique.

It was pure street-fight.

In the tight confines of the mini-sub, they rolled and punched – and punched and punched.

Schofield's empty gun was useless, but Zamanov's Cossack sword was the key.

Which was why the first thing Schofield had done after their sub had bounced with a splash into the water was hit Zamanov's wrist, causing him to drop the sword.

And then they wrestled – ferociously – Schofield because he was fuelled by Mother's recent sacrifice, Zamanov because he was a psychopath.

They hurled each other into the sub's walls, fighting with venom, drawing blood with every blow.

Schofield broke Zamanov's cheekbone.

Zamanov broke Schofield's nose, while another of his blows dislodged Schofield's earpiece.

Then Zamanov tackled Schofield, throwing him against the sub's control panel, and all of a sudden – *shoosh* – the mini-sub began to . . .

. . . submerge.

Schofield peeled himself off the instrument panel, saw that he'd knocked the 'BALLAST' switch. The ASDS was going under.

And suddenly they were underwater. Out through the sub's two hemispherical domes, Schofield saw the now-submerged world of the missile hold.

Everything was silent, tinged with blue – the floor, the missile silos, the dead bodies – an amazing man-made underwater seascape.

The *Talbot* was now leaning slightly to starboard, the hold's floor tilted at least 20 degrees to that side.

Zamanov scooped up his sword.

The yellow mini-sub continued its slow-motion freefall through the watery hold.

And Zamanov and Schofield engaged – Zamanov swinging lustily, Schofield grabbing the bounty hunter's sword-hand as it came down.

But then, with a muffled crash, their ASDS hit the floor of the missile hold . . .

. . . and started to slide on its side *toward the open starboard cargo door*!

Schofield's world tilted crazily.

Both men were thrown sideways.

The sub slid down the sloping floor before, to Schofield's utter horror, it tipped off the edge of the doorway and fell out through it, into the open sea.

The little yellow sub fell quickly through the darkened water of the English Channel – beneath the gigantic hull of the MV *Talbot*.

The sheer size of the foundering supertanker above it

dwarfed the ASDS. The mini-sub looked like an insect underneath a sinking blue whale.

But while the supertanker was sinking slowly and gradually, the mini-sub – its ballast tanks full – was descending at speed.

More than that.

It shot vertically down through the water, free-falling like an express elevator.

The average depth of the English Channel is about 120 metres. Here, off Cherbourg, it was 100 metres deep, and the ASDS was covering that depth quickly.

Inside it, Schofield and Zamanov fought in near darkness, struggling in the ghostly blue glow of the mini-sub's instrument lights.

'After I *kill* you, I am going to cut your *fucking* American heart out!' Zamanov roared as he struggled to extract his sword-hand from Schofield's grasp.

Up until then, the fight had used more or less standard moves. But then Zamanov went for what Marines call 'the Lecter move' – a very uncivilised tactic.

He bared his teeth and tried to bite Schofield's face.

Schofield recoiled instantly, stretched his face out of range, and Zamanov got what he really wanted – his sword-hand back.

He made to swing, just as with a jarring thud, their sub hit the bottom of the Channel and both men fell to the floor.

They rose together, moving like lightning.

Zamanov leapt up and swung – just as Schofield lunged forward, ducking inside Zamanov's swing arc, at the same time whipping something metallic from his borrowed utility vest and *jamming it into the Russian's mouth!*

Zamanov didn't have time for shock, because Schofield didn't hesitate.

He activated the mountaineering piton – and turned his head away, not wanting to see this.

With a powerful *snap!* the piton's pincer-like arms expanded, shooting instantaneously outward, searching for something to wedge themselves against.

What they found were Zamanov's upper and lower jaws.

Schofield never saw the actual event, but he heard it.

Heard the foul *crack* of Zamanov's lower jaw being stretched far further than it ever was designed to go.

Schofield turned back to see the Russian's jaw hanging grotesquely from his face, dislocated and broken. The upper arm of the piton, however, had done more damage: it had bruised Zamanov's brain, leaving Zamanov frozen bolt upright in mid-stance, the shock having shut down his entire body.

The Russian fell to his knees.

Schofield seized his sword, stood over the fallen bounty hunter.

Zamanov's eyes blinked reflexively. The only sign that he was still conscious.

Schofield wanted to run him through, or even cut his head off, to do to Zamanov what he had done to others . . .

But he didn't.

He *couldn't*.

And so he just let the Russian waver where he knelt, and then he watched as a moment later Zamanov fell flat on his face with a final bloody splat.

*

The fight over, Schofield grabbed his dislodged earpiece, put it back in his ear –

'*Schofield! Schofield! Come in!*' Knight's voice blared in his ear. '*Are you alive out there!*'

'I'm here,' Schofield said. 'I'm on the bottom. Where are you?'

'*I'm in the other sub. Put your exterior lights on so I can see where you are.*'

Schofield did so.

At which moment Knight's voice said, '*Oh, fuck me . . .*'

'What?'

'*Do you have power?*' Knight said quickly.

Schofield tried his instrument panel. No response. 'I have air, but no propulsion. Why? What is it? Can't you just come and get me?'

'*There's no way I can make it in time.*'

'In time? In time for what? What's the problem?'

'*It's a . . . uh . . . very big one . . .*'

'What?'

'*Look up, Captain.*'

Schofield peered up through the top dome of his mini-submarine.

And saw the hull of the supertanker – impossibly huge – gliding steadily down through the water above him, freefalling through the Channel waters like the moon falling out of the sky . . . its colossal mass heading straight for him.

Schofield swallowed at the awesome sight: 100,000 tons of pure supertanker was about to land right on top of his tiny submarine.

Its bulk was so vast, so immense, that it generated a deep vibrating *rrmmmmmm* as it moved down through the water.

'Now you don't see that every day,' Schofield said to himself. 'Knight!'

'*I can't make it in time!*' Knight yelled in frustration.

'Shit,' Schofield said, looking left and right.

Options! his mind screamed. He couldn't swim away from the tanker. At 1,000 feet long and 200 feet wide, it was just too big. He'd never get out from under it in time.

The only other alternative was to stay here and be crushed to death.

Some choice. Certain death or certain death.

But if that was all there was, then at least he might be able to achieve something before death came.

And so on the bottom of the English Channel, Shane Schofield keyed his satellite mike.

'Book! How are you doing over there in New York?'

'*We own the* Ambrose, *Scarecrow. All enemy troops are down. We're at the control console now, and I've plugged the satellite uplink into it. I have the time as 1152. You've got eight whole minutes to disarm this thing.*'

Schofield saw the supertanker falling through the water above him – a silent freefalling giant. At its current speed, it would hit the bottom in less than a minute.

'You might have eight minutes, Book, but I don't. I have to disarm those missiles now.'

And so he pulled his CincLock-VII unit from its waterproof pouch and hit its satellite uplink.

The unit came to life:

SAT-LINK: CONNECT 'AMBROSE-049'–UPLINK
  CONNECTION MADE.
ACTIVATE REMOTE SYSTEM.
MISSILE LAUNCH SEQUENCE IN PROGRESS.
PRESS 'ENTER' TO INITIATE DISARM SEQUENCE.
FIRST PROTOCOL (PROXIMITY): SATISFIED.
INITIATE SECOND PROTOCOL.

The red and white circles from the New York launch ship's missile control console appeared on Schofield's screen.

And with the mighty hull of the *Talbot* thundering down through the great blue void above him, Schofield started the disarm sequence.

The supertanker was gathering speed.

Falling, falling . . .

Schofield's moves became faster.

The supertanker was eighty feet above him.

A red circle blinked, Schofield punched it.

Sixty feet . . .

Fifty feet . . .

The noise of the falling supertanker grew louder – *rrmmmmmm.*

Forty feet . . .

Thirty feet . . .

Schofield hit the last red circle. The display blinked:

SECOND PROTOCOL (RESPONSE PATTERN): SATISFIED.
THIRD PROTOCOL (CODE ENTRY): ACTIVE.
PLEASE ENTER AUTHORISED DISARM CODE.

Twenty feet . . .

The water all around his little submarine darkened dramatically, consumed by the shadow of the supertanker.

Schofield entered the Universal Disarm Code: 131071.

Fifteen feet . . .

The screen beeped:

THIRD PROTOCOL (CODE ENTRY): SATISFIED.
AUTHORISED DISARM CODE ENTERED.
MISSILE LAUNCH ABORTED.

And as he waited for the end – the true end; the end that he physically could not escape – Schofield closed his eyes and thought about his life and people who had been in it:

He saw Libby Gant smiling that 1,000-watt smile, saw her kissing him tenderly – saw Mother Newman shooting hoops on her garage basketball court, saw her big wide grin on her big wide face – and tears welled in his eyes.

That there were still missiles to disarm somehow didn't bother Schofield. Someone else would have to solve that this time.

When it came, the end came swiftly.

Ten seconds later, the supertanker MV *Talbot* hit the bottom of the English Channel with an earth-shaking, earth-shuddering *boom*.

It landed right on top of Schofield's stricken ASDS and crushed it in a single pulverising instant.

The thing was, Schofield wasn't in the sub when it happened.

Seconds before the *Talbot* hit the bottom – when it was barely twelve feet off the seabed, its shadow looming over the mini-sub, and Schofield was lost in his thoughts – a dull metallic *clunk* was heard hitting the outside of his ASDS.

Schofield snapped to look out the windows and saw a *Maghook* attached to the metal exterior of his little submarine, its rope stretching away across the ocean floor, disappearing into the darkness to the side of the falling supertanker.

Knight's voice exploded in his ear: '*Schofield! Come on! Move! Move! Move!*'

Schofield was electrified into action.

He took a breath and hit the 'HATCH' button.

The hatch irised open and water *gushed* into the sunken mini-submarine. It took barely two seconds for it to completely fill the sub, and suddenly Schofield was outside, moving fast, grabbing the Maghook attached to the sub's flank.

No sooner had he clutched it than Knight – at the other end of the rope – hit the hook's demagnetise switch and the Maghook's rope began to reel itself in quickly.

Schofield was yanked across the ocean floor at phenomenal speed – the falling supertanker looming above him, its great endless hull hovering over his body like the underside of a planet, while a foot below him, the sandy ocean floor zoomed by at dizzying speed.

And then abruptly Schofield emerged from beneath the supertanker, his feet sliding out from under it just as the gigantic vessel hit the bottom of the English Channel with a singular reverberating *boom* that sent sand and silt billowing out in every direction, consuming Schofield in a dense underwater cloud.

And waiting for him in that cloud – sitting atop the second ASDS, breathing from a new Pony Bottle and holding Gant's Maghook in his hands – was Aloysius Knight.

He handed Schofield the Pony Bottle and Schofield breathed its air in deeply.

Within a minute, the two of them were inside Knight's mini-sub. Knight repressurised the sub, expunged it of seawater.

And then the two warriors rose through the depths of the English Channel, a short silent journey that ended with their little yellow sub breaching the storm-riddled surface – where it was assaulted by crashing waves and the blinding glare of brilliant halogen spotlights: spotlights that belonged to the *Black Raven* hovering low over the water, waiting for them.

AIRSPACE ABOVE THE ENGLISH CHANNEL
1805 HOURS LOCAL TIME
(1205 HOURS E.S.T. USA)

The *Black Raven* shot through the sky, heading south over the English Channel.

A dripping-wet Aloysius Knight dropped into his gunner's chair. The equally-soaked Schofield, however, never stopped moving.

Inside the *Raven*'s rear holding cell, he pulled out his modified Palm Pilot. There was unfinished business to attend to.

He pulled up the missile-firing list – the one that was different to Book's earlier list. He compared the two lists.

Okay, he thought, *the first three entries are the same as on Book's list.*

But not the last three: the missiles are different. And there's that extra entry at the end.

To those last three entries, he added the GPS locations that he'd got from Book. The first two of them read:

```
Hopewell  Sky Horse-3    W-88  11900.00     11622.50   1230
                                2327.00      4000.00
                                (Taiwan Sts) (Beijing)
```

	Sky Horse-3	W-88	11900.00	11445.80	1230
			2327.00	2243.25	
			(Taiwan Sts)	(Hong K)	
Whale	Ghauri-II	R-5	07040.45	07725.05	1245
			2327.00	2958.65	
			(Arab n Sea)	(New Delhi)	
	Agni-II	I-22	07040.45	07332.60	1245
			2327.00	3230.55	
			(Arab n Sea)	(Islamabad)	

And suddenly this list took on a whole new dimension.

The cloned missiles being fired on Beijing and Hong Kong from the MV *Hopewell* were clones of the Taiwanese Sky Horse ICBM. They were also armed with *American* warheads.

While the missiles firing from the MV *Whale* on New Delhi were clones of the Pakistani Ghauri-II – and the ones being fired on Islamabad were replicas of the Indian Agni-II.

'Hot damn . . .' Schofield breathed.

How would China react to Taiwanese nuclear strikes?

Badly.

And how would Pakistan and India react to mutual nuclear bombardment?

Very badly.

Schofield frowned.

He couldn't understand why his list differed from Book's.

Okay, think. Where did Book get his original list from?

From the Mossad agent, Rosenthal, who had acquired it during his many months shadowing Majestic-12.

So where did I get mine from?

Schofield thought back.

'Oh, Jesus . . .' he said, remembering.

He'd received it on his Palm Pilot when he and Gant had been sitting in the stone ante-room in the Forteresse de Valois, waiting while Aloysius Knight had been in Monsieur Delacroix's office, hacking wirelessly into Delacroix's standalone computer.

Schofield turned to Knight. 'When you were with Delacroix at the castle, did he say anything about whose office you were in?'

Knight shrugged. 'Yeah. He said something about it not being his office. Said it belonged to the man who owned the castle.'

'Killian,' Schofield said.

'Why?'

But now Schofield understood.

'There must have been another computer in that office. In a drawer or on a side table,' he said. 'You said it yourself. Your Pilot would retrieve documents from *any computer* in the room. When you initiated the wireless hack, you picked up documents from *another* computer in that office. Killian's computer.'

'Yeah, so?'

Schofield held up the new list. 'This isn't Majestic-12's plan. *Their* plan involves starting a global Cold War on Terror. M-12 wants *terrorist* missiles striking major centres – Shahabs and Taep'o-Dongs. Which was why they left the bodies of the Global Jihad guys at the Axon plant and on the supertankers: to make the world think that terrorists stole the Kormoran ships.

'But this list shows something else entirely. It shows that Killian's company installed *different* Chameleon missiles on the Kormoran ships – not the ones Majestic-

12 was expecting. Killian is planning something much worse than a global war on terrorism. He's set it up so that each of the world's major powers is *seemingly* hit by its most-hated enemy.

'The West is hit by terrorist strikes. India and Pakistan are hit by each other. China is hit by what appear to be Taiwanese missiles.'

Schofield's eyes widened at the realisation.

'It's Killian's extra step. This isn't M-12's plan at all. This is Killian's own plan. And it won't produce any kind of Cold War at all. It'll produce something much much worse. It'll produce total global warfare. It'll produce *total global anarchy*.'

Rufus said, 'You're saying that Killian has been deceiving his rich buddies on Majestic-12?'

'Exactly,' Schofield said.

But then, again, he remembered Killian's words from the Forteresse de Valois: 'Although many don't know it yet, the future of the world lies in Africa.'

'The future of the world lies in Africa,' Schofield said. 'There were African guard squads on each of the boats. Eritreans. Nigerians. Oh, shit. *Shit!* Why didn't I see it before . . .'

Schofield brought up one of the other documents on his Palm Pilot:

Executive Itinerary

The proposed order of travel is as follows: Asmara (01/08), Luanda (01/08), Abuja (05/08), N'djamena (07/08) and Tobruk (09/08).

01/08 – Asmara (embassy)
03/08 – Luanda (stay with M. Loch, R's nephew)

This was the itinerary of Killian's tour of Africa the previous year.

Asmara: the capital of Eritrea.

Luanda: the capital of Angola.

Abuja: Nigeria.

N'djamena: Chad.

And Tobruk: the site of Libya's largest Air Force base.

Killian hadn't been opening factories – he had been forging alliances with five key African nations.

But why?

Schofield spoke: 'What would happen if the major powers of the world descended into anarchic warfare? What would happen elsewhere in the world?'

'You'd see some old scores settled, that's for sure,' Knight said. 'Ethnic wars would reignite. The Serbs would go after the Croats, the Russians would wipe out the Chechens, and that's not even mentioning everybody who wants to nail the Kurds. Then there'd be the opportunists, like the Japanese in WWII. Countries seizing the opportunity to grab resources or territory: Indonesia would snatch East Timor back . . .'

'What about Africa?' Schofield said. 'I'm thinking of National Security Council Planning Paper Q-309.'

'*Whoa*,' Knight said.

Schofield remembered the policy word for word. 'In the event of a conflict involving the major global powers, it is highly likely that the poverty-stricken populations of Africa, the Middle East and Central America – some of which outnumber the populations of their Western neighbours by a ratio of 100-to-1 – will flood over Western borders and overwhelm Western city centres.'

Q-309 was a policy based on history – the long history of wealthy self-indulgent elites falling to impoverished but numerically overwhelming underclasses: the fall of Rome to the barbarians, the French Revolution, and now the wealthy Western world succumbing to the sheer numbers of the Third World.

Jesus, Schofield thought.

Anarchic global warfare would provide just such an opportunity for the Third World to rise up.

And if Killian had given forewarning to a few key African nations, then . . .

No, it's not possible, Schofield's mind protested. *For the simple reason that Killian's plan just didn't seem big enough.*

It didn't guarantee *total* global anarchy.

And then Schofield saw the final entry on the missile list – the entry that had not been on Book II's list at all, an entry describing a missile to be fired nearly two hours after all the others.

He brought it up on his screen:

```
Arbella   Jericho-2B     W-88  04402.25      04145.10    1400
                               1650.50       2130.00
```

A Jericho-2B clone, Schofield thought. *The Jericho was a long-range ballistic missile belonging to Israel; and this one was armed with an American W-88 warhead.*

And the target?

Using Book II's map, Schofield plotted the GPS coordinates of the target.

His finger came down on the map . . . and as it did so, Schofield felt a bolt of ice-cold blood shoot through his entire body.

'God save us all,' he breathed as he saw the target.

The last clone missile – ostensibly Israeli in origin, with an American nuclear warhead on it – was aimed at a target in Saudi Arabia.

It was aimed at the holy city of Mecca.

The cockpit fell silent.

The sheer idea of it was just too great, too *shocking*, to contemplate. An Israeli missile armed with an American warhead striking the most sacred Muslim site on the planet on one of the most holy Muslim days of the year.

In the post-September 11 world, there could be no more provocative act.

It would ignite global chaos – no American citizen or embassy or business would be safe. In every city in every country, enraged Muslims would seek vengeance.

It would create a worldwide Muslim–American war. The first truly global conflict between a religion and a nation. Which would itself become the precursor for total global revolution – the rise of the Third World.

'God, October 26, it's been staring me in the face all day,' Schofield said. 'The first day of Ramadan. I hadn't even thought about the significance of the date. Killian even chose the most provocative day.'

'So where's it going to fire from?' Knight asked.

Schofield quickly plotted the GPS co-ordinates of the last Chameleon missile's launch location . . . and he frowned.

'It's not coming from a boat,' he said. 'The launch location is *on land*. Somewhere inside Yemen.'

'Yemen?' Rufus said.

'It borders Saudi Arabia to the south. Very close to Mecca,' Knight said.

'Yemen . . .' Schofield said, thinking fast. 'Yemen . . .'

At some time today, he had been told about Yemen, had heard of something *inside* Yemen –

He remembered.

'There's a Krask-8 clone in Yemen,' he said.

He'd heard it right at the start of all this, during his briefing on Krask-8. During the Cold War, the Soviets had constructed land-based ICBM facilities identical to Krask-8 in their client states – states like Syria, the Sudan, and Yemen.

Schofield's mind raced.

Krask-8 had been owned by the Atlantic Shipping Company. David Fairfax had discovered that earlier today.

And the Atlantic Shipping Company – he now knew – *was a subsidiary of Axon Corp.*

'Goddamn,' Schofield breathed. 'Rufus: set a course heading due south-east and give it everything you've got. Afterburners all the way.'

Rufus looked doubtful. 'Captain, I don't mean to be rude, but even flying at full speed, there's no way we can get from here to Yemen inside of two hours. That's a 6,000-kilometre trip, which is at least four hours travel time. Besides, on full burn, we'll chew up all our gas before we even reach the French Alps.'

'Don't worry about that,' Schofield said. 'I can arrange for fuel to be delivered in flight. And we're not going all the way to Yemen in *this* bird.'

'Whatever you say,' Rufus said. He banked the *Raven*, directed her south-east, and hit the afterburners.

While this was happening, Schofield keyed his satellite mike. 'Mr Moseley. You still with us?'

'*Sure am,*' came the reply from London.

'I need you to do an asset search on a company for me. It's called the Atlantic Shipping Company. Search for any land holdings that it has in Yemen, especially old Soviet sites.

'I also need two more things. First, I need express passage across Europe, including several mid-air refuellings. I'll send you our transponder signal.'

'*Okay. And the second thing?*'

'I need you to fuel up a couple of very special American planes for me. Planes that are currently at the Aerostadia Italia Airshow in Milan, Italy.'

The next thirty minutes went by in a blur.

Around the world, an array of forces sprang into action.

THE ARABIAN SEA, OFF THE COAST OF INDIA
26 OCTOBER, 2105 HOURS LOCAL TIME
(1205 HOURS E.S.T. USA)

The supertanker MV *Whale* hovered off the coast of India on a languid sea, the giant vessel seemingly gazing at the shared coastline of India and Pakistan, its missiles ready to fire.

It never saw the Los Angeles-class attack submarine approach it from behind, two miles away.

Likewise, the African commandos in its control tower never saw the sub's torpedoes on their scopes until it was too late.

The two Mark 48 torpedoes hit the *Whale* together, blasting open its flanks with simultaneous explosions, sinking it.

THE TAIWAN STRAITS, INTERNATIONAL WATERS BETWEEN CHINA AND TAIWAN
0110 HOURS (27 OCT) LOCAL TIME
(1210 HOURS E.S.T. USA, 26 OCT)

The MV *Hopewell* suffered a similar fate.

Parked inconspicuously in a sealane in the middle of the Taiwan Straits, not far from a long line of supertankers and cargo freighters, it was hit by a pair of wire-guided American Mark 48 torpedoes.

Some night-watchmen on other ships claimed to see the explosion on the horizon.

Radio calls to the *Hopewell* went unanswered and by the time anyone got to its last known location, there was nothing there.

The *Hopewell* was gone.

No one ever laid eyes on the submarine that sank it. Indeed, the US Government would later deny that it had any 688Is in the area at the time.

WEST COAST, USA, NEAR SAN FRANCISCO
26 OCTOBER, 0912 HOURS LOCAL TIME
(1212 HOURS IN NEW YORK)

Inside the vast missile hold of the Kormoran-class supertanker *Jewel*, covered by twelve United States Marines and standing over the bodies of a dozen dead African commandos, David Fairfax plugged his satellite uplink into the vessel's missile control console.

The satellite signal shot up into the sky and bounced over to Schofield in the *Black Raven*, flying over France, heading for Italy.

And while Schofield disarmed the CincLock system from afar, Fairfax held the console – at times protecting the uplink with his body, shielding it from two Eritrean commandos who had survived his Marine-enhanced entry.

He was scared out of his mind, but in the midst of bullets and gunfire and exploding grenades, he held that console.

Within a couple of minutes, the last two Eritrean soldiers were dead – nailed by the Marines – and the MV *Jewel*'s launch system was neutralised by Schofield in the *Raven* and David Fairfax fell to the floor with a deep sigh of relief.

AEROSTADIA AIRFIELD, MILAN, ITALY
26 OCTOBER, 1900 HOURS LOCAL TIME
(1300 HOURS IN NEW YORK)

With a blast from its retros, the *Black Raven* landed vertically on the tarmac of the Aerostadia Airfield in Milan.

It was evening already in northern Italy, but the US Air Force contingent at the airshow had been working overtime for the last forty-five minutes, fuelling two very special aeroplanes at the express orders of the State Department.

The *Raven* landed a hundred yards from a spectacular-looking B-52 bomber, parked on the runway.

Two small black bullet-shaped planes hung from the big bomber's wings, looking like a pair of oversized missiles.

But these weren't missiles.

They were X-15s.

Many people believe that with a top speed of Mach 3, the SR-71 'Blackbird' is the fastest plane in the world.

This is not entirely true. The SR-71 is the fastest *operational* plane in the world.

One plane, however, has gone faster than it has – a

lot faster, in fact – attaining speeds of over 7,000 km/h, more than Mach 6. That plane, though, never made operational status.

That plane was the NASA-built X-15.

Most aeroplanes use jet engines to propel them through the sky, but jet power has a limit and the SR-71 has found that limit: Mach 3.

The X-15, however, is *rocket*-powered. It has few moving parts. Instead of shooting ignited compressed air out behind it, an X-15 ignites solid hydrogen fuel. Which makes it less like a jet plane, and more like a missile. Indeed, the X-15 has been described by some observers as a missile with a pilot strapped to it.

Only five X-15s were ever built, and two of those – as Schofield knew – were making an appearance at the Aerostadia Italia Airshow, scheduled to start in a few days.

Schofield leapt out of the *Raven*, crossed the tarmac with Knight and Rufus by his side.

He gazed at the two X-15s slung from the wings of the B-52.

They weren't big planes. And not exactly pretty either. Just functional – designed to cut through the air at astronomical velocity.

Speed-slanted letters on their tailfins read: *NASA*. Along the side of each black plane were the words US AIR FORCE.

Two colonels met Schofield: one American, one Italian.

'Captain Schofield,' the American colonel said, 'the X-15s are ready, fully fuelled and ready to fly. But we have a problem. One of our pilots broke his ribs in a training accident yesterday. There's no way he can handle the G-forces of these things in his condition.'

'I was hoping I could use my own pilot anyway,' Schofield said. He turned to Rufus. 'Think you can handle Mach 6, Big Man?'

A grin cracked Rufus's hairy face. 'Does the Pope shit in the woods?'

The Air Force colonel guided them to the planes. 'We've also received some satellite radar scans from the National Reconnaissance Office. Could be a problem.'

He held up a portable viewscreen the size of a clipboard.

On it were two infra-red snapshots of the south-eastern Mediterranean, the Suez Canal and the Red Sea. One wider shot, the other zoomed in.

On the first image, Schofield saw a large cloud of red dots that seemed to be hovering over the Suez Canal area:

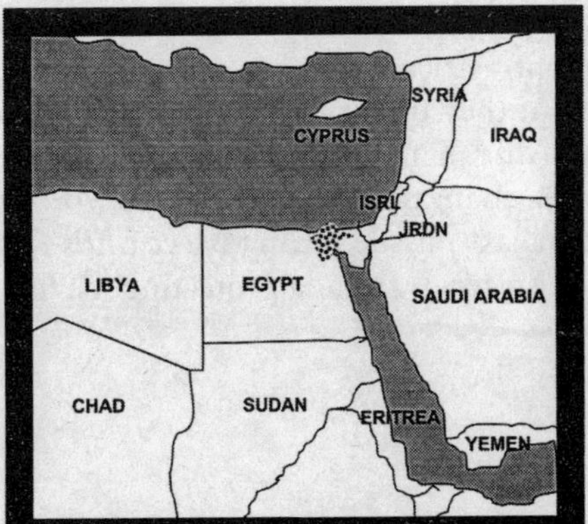

On the second satellite photo, the image became clearer.

There were about *one hundred and fifty* dots in the 'cloud'.

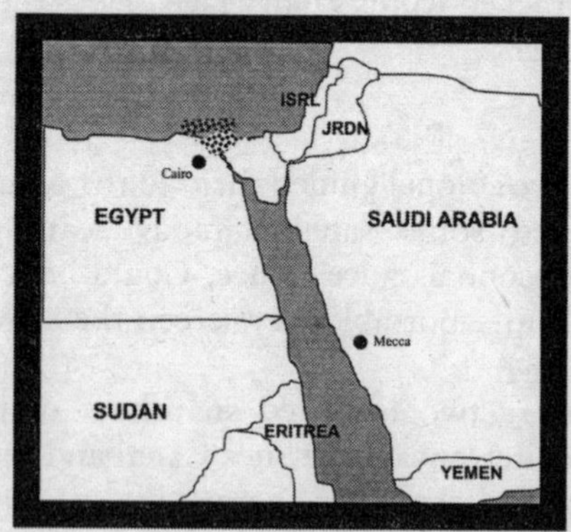

'What the hell are those dots?' Rufus said slowly.

The colonel didn't have to answer him, because Schofield already knew.

'They're planes,' he said. 'Fighter jets from at least five different African nations. The French saw them scramble but they didn't know why. Now I do. They're from five African nations that would like to see the world order changed. Nations that do *not* want to see us stop that last missile hitting Mecca. It's Killian's last safeguard. An aerial armada protecting the final missile.'

The B-52 bomber thundered down the runway with the two X-15s hanging from its outstretched wings.

It soared into the sky, rising steadily to its release height.

Schofield sat with Rufus inside the two-man cockpit of the right-hand X-15. It was a tight fit for Rufus, but he managed. Knight was in the other plane, with a NASA pilot.

Schofield had his CincLock-VII disarm unit strapped to his utility vest, next to the array of other weapons in its pouches. The plan was a long shot – since no one else in the world could disarm the Chameleon missile aimed at Mecca, he would have to go into the Krask-8 clone in Yemen with only Knight by his side.

They expected resistance to be waiting for them – probably in the form of an African commando unit – so Schofield had requested a Marine team be dispatched from Aden to meet them there. But whether it would arrive in time was another question.

Scott Moseley called in from London.

'*Captain, I think I've found what you're looking for,*' he said. '*The Atlantic Shipping Company owns two thousand acres of desert in Yemen, about two hundred miles south-west of Aden, right on the mouth of the Red Sea. On that land are the remains of an old Soviet submarine repair facility. Our satellite pics are from the*

'80s, but it looks like a big warehouse surrounded by some support buildings—'

'That's it,' Schofield said. 'Send me the co-ordinates.'

Moseley did so.

Schofield punched them into his plane's trip computer.

Flight distance to southern Yemen: **5,602 KILOMETRES.**

Flight time in an X-15 travelling at 7,000 km/h: **48 MINUTES.**

Time till the Mecca ICBM launched: **ONE HOUR.**

It was going to be close.

'You ready, Rufus?' he said.

'Yeah, baby,' Rufus replied.

When the B-52 reached release height, its pilot came over the comms: '*X-15s, we just got word from the USS* Nimitz *in the Med. She's the only carrier within range of your attack route. She's sending every plane she has to escort you: F-14s, F/A-18s, even five Prowlers have volunteered to ride shotgun for you. You must be one important man, Captain Schofield. Prepare for flight systems check. Release in one minute—*'

As the pilot signed off, Knight's voice came over Schofield and Rufus's earpieces. His voice was low, even.

'Hey, Ruf. Good luck, buddy. Remember, you're the best. The *best.* Stay low. Stay focused. Trust your instincts.'

'Will do, Boss,' Rufus said. 'Thanks.'

'And Schofield,' Knight said.

'Yes?'

'Bring my friend back alive.'

'I'll try,' Schofield said softly.

The B-52 pilot spoke again. '*Flight systems check is complete. We are go for launch. Gentlemen, prepare for release. On my mark, in five, four . . .*'

Schofield stared forward, took a deep, deep breath.

'*Three . . .*'

Rufus gripped his control stick firmly.

'*Two . . .*'

Over in his plane, Knight looked over at Schofield and Rufus on the other wing.

'*One . . . mark.*'

CLUNK-CLUNK!

The two X-15s dropped from the wings of the B-52 bomber, swooping briefly before –

'Engaging rocket thrusters . . . *now!*' Rufus said.

He hit the thrust controls.

The X-15's tail cone ignited, hurling its afterburner flame a full 100 feet into the air behind it.

Schofield was thrown back into his seat with a force he had never even *imagined*.

His X-15 shot off into the sky – *cracking* the air with sonic booms, literally ripping the fabric of the sky – its flight signature just one continuous roar that would be heard all the way across the Mediterranean Sea.

And so the two X-15s rocketed to the south-east, toward the Suez Canal and the Red Sea and a small decrepit base in Yemen from which a Chameleon missile would soon be launched, a missile that would shatter the existing world order.

In their way: the greatest aerial armada ever assembled by man.

After only twenty minutes of flying, Rufus caught sight of it.

'Oh my *Lord* . . .' he breathed.

They hung in the orange evening sky like a swarm of insects: the squadron of African fighters.

It was an incredible sight – a veritable *wall* of moving pinpoints spread out across the Egyptian coastline, guarding the airspace over the Suez Canal.

One hundred and fifty warplanes.

All manner of fighter planes made up the aerial armada.

Old planes, new planes, red planes, blue planes – anything that could carry a missile – a motley collection of once-great fighters purchased from First World nations after their First World use-by dates had expired.

The Sukhoi Su-17 – built in 1966 and long since discarded by the Russians.

The MiG-25 Foxbat – superseded in the 1980s by more modern variants, but which could still hold its own against all but the best American planes.

The French-made Mirage V/50 – one of France's biggest military exports, which they sell to anyone: Libya, Zaire, Iraq.

There were even a few feisty Czech L-59 Albatrosses, a favourite among African nations.

Performance-wise, all these fighters lost ground to more modern planes like the F-22 Raptor and the F-15E. But when they came equipped with top-of-the-line air-to-air missiles – Sidewinders, Phoenixes, Russian R-60Ts and R-27s, missiles that were easily obtainable at the arms bazaars of Romania and the Ukraine – this older force of fighters could match it with the best of them. Fighters may be expensive and hard to get, but good-quality missiles can be bought by the dozen.

And if nothing else, Schofield thought, *these guys have the advantage of sheer numbers*.

The best-equipped F-22 in the world could not hold off a force of this size forever. Ultimately, sheer force of numbers would overwhelm even the best technology.

'What do you think, Rufus?'

'This baby wasn't built to fight, Captain,' Rufus said. 'She was built for speed. So that's what we're gonna do with her – we're gonna fly her low and fast and we're gonna do what no pilot has ever done before: we're gonna *outrun* any missiles those bastards throw at us.'

'Missiles chasing us,' Schofield said. 'Nice.'

Rufus said, 'For what it's worth, Captain, we've got exactly one piddly little single-barrel gun pointing out from our nose. I think it's there for decoration.'

Just then, a new voice came over their headsets: '*American X-15s, this is Captain Harold Marshall of the USS* Nimitz. *We have you on our scopes. The Jolly Rogers are en route. They will intercept you as you reach the enemy force. Five Prowlers have been sent ahead at hundred-mile intervals to provide electronic jamming for you. It's going to get hot in there, gentlemen, but hopefully we can punch a hole big enough for you guys to shoot through.*' There was a pause. '*Oh, and Captain Schofield, I've been informed of the situation. Good luck. We're all right behind you.*'

'Thank you, Captain,' Schofield said softly. 'Okay, Rufus. Let's rock.'

*

Speed.

Pure, unadulterated speed. 7,000 km/h is about 2,000 metres per second. Seven times supersonic is super super fast.

The two X-15s ripped through the sky toward the swarm of enemy aircraft.

As they came within twenty miles of the African planes, a phalanx of missiles issued out from the armada – forty tail-like smoketrails streaming toward them.

But no sooner had the first missile been loosed, than its firer – a Russian MiG-25 Foxbat – erupted in a burst of orange flames.

Six other African planes exploded, hit by AIM-120 AMRAAM air-to-air missiles, while twenty of the missiles loosed by the African armada exploded harmlessly in mid-air, hitting chaff-deploying dummy missiles that had been fired from—

—an incoming force of American F-14 fighters bearing ominous skull-and-crossbones symbols on their tailfins.

The famous 'Jolly Rogers' from the *Nimitz*. About a dozen F-14 Tomcats, flanked by nimble F/A-18 Hornets.

And suddenly a gigantic aerial battle, unheard of in modern warfare, was underway.

The two X-15s banked and swerved as they shot through the ranks of the African armada, avoiding mid-air explosions, dive-bombing fighters, waves of tracer bullets and superfast missile smoketrails.

All manner of fighter planes whipped through the twilight sky – MiGs, Mirages, Tomcats and Hornets, rolling, diving, engaging, exploding.

At one point, Schofield's X-15 swooped upside-down to avoid one African fighter, only to come on a head-on collision course with another African bogey – a Mirage – but just as the two planes were about to slam nose-to-nose into each other, the African plane exploded – hit from underneath by a brilliant AMRAAM shot – and Schofield's X-15 just blasted *right through* its flaming remains, sheets of burning metal scraping against the X-15's flanks, the severed hand of the enemy plane's dead pilot smearing a streak of blood across the X-15's canopy right next to Rufus's eyes.

And yet the African missiles never hit the NASA rocket planes.

They would get close, and then the missiles would just swerve wildly around the X-15s as if the two NASA planes were protected by some kind of invisible bubble.

In actual fact, they were.

Care of the five US Navy EA-6B Prowlers – with their directional AN/ALQ-99F electronic jamming pods – that were flying parallel to the X-15s, ten miles away.

Nuggetty and tough, the Prowlers knew that they could never keep up with the superfast X-15s, so they had cleverly placed themselves parallel to Schofield's flight-path but spaced out, each Prowler protecting the rocket planes with its jamming signal before passing the X-15s onto the next Prowler, like relay runners passing a baton.

'*American X-15s, this is Prowler Leader*,' a voice said in Schofield's headset. '*We can cover you up to the Canal, but we just ain't fast enough to keep up. You'll be on your own from there.*'

'You've done more than enough already,' Schofield said.

'Christ! Look out!' Rufus yelled.

For right then, in the face of the Prowlers' long-range

electronic protection, the African planes embarked on a new strategy.

They started doing kamikaze dives at the X-15s.

Suicide runs.

Electronic countermeasures may be able to disrupt the homing systems of a missile, but no matter how good they are, they cannot stop a man wilfully flying his plane into another.

A half-dozen fighter jets rained down on the two X-15s, screaming through the sky, loosing withering waves of tracer bullets as they did so.

The two X-15s split up.

Rufus rolled his plane right and down, while the other X-15 banked left, avoiding its dive-bomber by a bare foot, but not before a lone tracer bullet from one of the kamikazes entered its canopy from the side and exited out the other side: a flight path that also entailed a short trip through the head of Knight's pilot.

Blood and brains splattered the interior of the X-15.

The plane peeled away into the sky, out of control, heading eastward, away from the battle.

Knight scrambled into the front seat – where he quickly unbuckled the dead pilot and hurled his body into the back. Then Knight himself took the controls, trying desperately to bring the plane up before she ploughed into the Mediterranean Sea.

The sea rushed up before him – faster, faster, faster…

Boom.

*

For their part, Schofield and Rufus had swung their plane low over the sea – so low in fact that they were now rushing barely twenty feet above the waves, kicking up a continuous whitewater geyser behind them at the same time as criss-crossing missiles blasted into the water all around them.

'I see the Canal!' Rufus yelled above the din.

It lay about twenty miles ahead of them, the mouth of the Suez Canal – a modern-day marvel of engineering; two colossal concrete pillars flanking the entry to the mighty sealane that gave access to the Red Sea.

And above it, more planes from the African armada.

'Rufus! Bank left!' Schofield yelled, peering up through their canopy.

Rufus did so – rolling them on their side just as two Czech L-59s went screaming past them on either side and buried themselves in the sea.

And then all of a sudden they hit the confines of the Canal—

—and lost the electronic protection of the Prowlers.

Schofield's X-15 blasted down the length of the Suez Canal, flying low, banking around anchored ships, turning the mighty concrete-walled canal into little more than an obstacle-filled trench – but effectively flying *under* the main body of the aerial armada.

They had run the blockade.

But then into the Canal behind them shot two American-made Phoenix missiles that had somehow found their way onto the wing-mounts of an African fighter jet.

The X-15 rushed down the water-filled trench.

The two Phoenix missiles gained on it.

Two suicide fighters rained down – coming at the X-15 from either side in a scissor formation – but Rufus rolled the rocket plane and the two fighters missed it by inches – blasting instead into the sandy banks of the Canal, exploding in twin geysers of sand and fire.

And then the two Phoenix missiles came *alongside* the X-15's tail and Schofield saw an amazing thing: he could *read* the stencilled lettering on their sides: 'XAIM-54A – HUGHES MISSILE SYSTEMS.'

'Rufus . . . !' he yelled.

'I know!' Rufus called back.

'Please do something!'

'Was just about to!'

And suddenly Rufus swung them to the right, up over the bank of the Canal, swinging them around in a wide wide circle, heading *back* towards the Mediterranean.

The two missiles followed, swooping around in identical semi-circles, unaffected by the incredible G-forces.

Since the bulk of the African armada had been protecting the Egyptian coastline, only about six African fighter planes remained back here.

These planes saw the X-15 swoop around in its wide circle, coming back toward them, and thought that this was their lucky day.

Wrong.

The X-15 – circling, circling – shot through their midst like a bullet through a stand of trees, blasting between two African MiGs with barely 10 feet to spare on either side . . .

. . . but leaving the MiGs in the path of the two Phoenix missiles.

Boom-boom!

The MiGs exploded and the X-15 continued its wide circle until it was back in the trench of the Canal, back on its south-easterly course.

However, its wide circle – easily 200 kilometres wide

– had allowed one of the African planes to loose a last-ditch missile, its finest: a single stolen American AIM-120 AMRAAM, the best air-to-air missile in the world.

The AMRAAM shot through the air behind the speeding X-15, closing in on it like a hungry hawk.

'I can't shake it!' Rufus yelled.

'How long will it stay on our tail?' Schofield asked. 'Doesn't it have a cut-out switch if the chase goes too long?'

'No! That's the thing about AMRAAMs! They just chase you all day and all night! Wear you down and then kill you.'

'Well, no AMRAAM has ever chased one of these planes before! Keep going! Full throttle! Maybe we can outrun it—'

A voice in his earpiece cut him off.

It was Scott Moseley, and his voice sounded dead, shocked.

'*Uh, Captain Schofield. I have some really bad news.*'

'What?'

'*Our early warning satellites just picked up an ICBM launch signature from south-central Yemen. Flight characteristics indicate that it is a Jericho-2B intercontinental ballistic missile, heading north toward Mecca. Captain, Killian knows you're coming. He's fired the missile early.*'

'Oh, no way!' Schofield yelled, staring off into the sky. 'You have got to be kidding. That is not fair. That is not fucking fair!'

He looked at the weapons strapped to his chest, guns that he had planned to use to storm the missile base in Yemen. All useless now.

He held up the CincLock-VII disarm unit and just shook his head . . .

Then he froze.

Staring at the CincLock unit.

'Mr Moseley. Do you have telemetry on that missile signal?'

'*Sure.*'

'Send it through.'

'*You got it.*'

A moment later, Schofield's trip computer beeped and a map similar to the one he had seen earlier appeared on its screen. An arrow-like icon representing the Chameleon missile approaching Mecca tracked northwards up the screen.

Schofield punched in his own transponder signal into the computer and a second icon appeared on the screen, tracking southward:

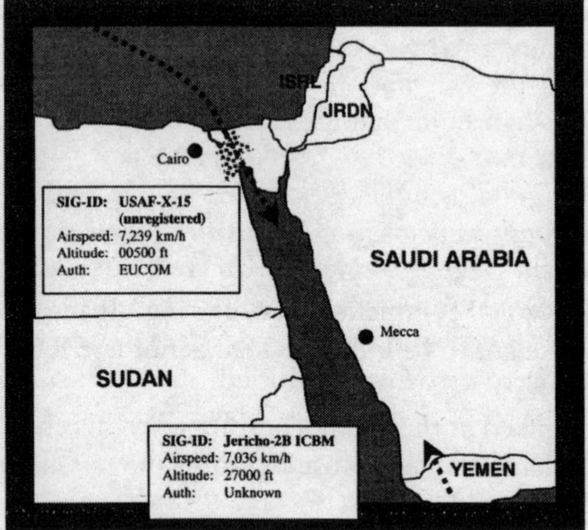

Schofield saw the flight data on the screen: signal IDs, airspeeds, altitudes.

He almost didn't need to do the math.

The picture said it all.

Two aircraft were converging on Mecca: his X-15 and the Chameleon missile, labelled by the satellite's automated recognition system as a Jericho-2B intercontinental ballistic missile.

Both aircraft were travelling at practically the same speed and were roughly equidistant from Mecca.

'Rufus,' Schofield said flatly.

'Yeah?'

'We're not going to Yemen any more.'

'I kinda figured that,' Rufus said, defeat in his voice. 'What are we going to do now?'

But Schofield was hitting buttons on his computer, doing rapid calculations. It would be absolutely incredible if this worked.

He and Rufus were still about 1,000 kilometres from Mecca. Time to target: **8:30.**

He did the calculations for the Chameleon missile. It was slightly further away. Its countdown read:

TIME TO TARGET: 9:01 . . . 9:00 . . . 8:59 . . .

That's good, Schofield thought. *We'll need the extra thirty seconds to overshoot Mecca and swing around . . .*

Schofield's eyes gleamed at the very idea of it. He looked down at the CincLock unit strapped to his chest, gripped it in his hands.

'Sixty feet,' he whispered aloud.

Then he said, 'Hey Rufus. Have you ever chased a missile?'

TIME TO TARGET: 6:00 . . . 5:59 . . . 5:58 . . .

Schofield's X-15 shot through the darkening sky at bullet speed – still pursued by the AMRAAM missile.

'You want me to fly *alongside* it?' Rufus said, dumbstruck.

'That's exactly what I want you to do. We can still disarm that ICBM, we just have to be within sixty feet of it,' Schofield said.

'Yeah, but *in flight*? Nobody can keep a plane side-by-side with a missile at Mach 6.'

'I think you can,' Schofield said.

From where he was sitting, Schofield didn't see the grin cross Rufus's broad bearded face.

'What do you need me to do?' the big pilot said.

Schofield said, 'ICBMs fly high and then come down vertically on their targets. This Chameleon is currently at 27,000 feet. She should stay at that altitude until she's practically over Mecca, and then she'll start her dive. At Mach 6, it'll take her about five seconds to make that vertical run. But I need at least twenty-five seconds to disarm her. Which means we have to get alongside her while she's flying level at 27,000 feet. Once she goes vertical, it's all over. We're screwed. Think you can bring us around so that we're travelling beside her?'

'You know, Captain,' Rufus said softly, 'you're a lot

like Aloysius. When you talk to me, you make me feel like I could do anything. Consider it *done*.'

TIME TO TARGET: 2:01 . . . 2:00 . . . 1:59 . . .

The X-15 blasted into the sky, chased by the AMRAAM, shooting down the length of the Red Sea while at the same time rising – rising, rising – to an altitude of 27,000 feet.

'We just passed Mecca!' Rufus yelled. 'I'm going to start our turn now. Keep an eye out, we should be able to see that Chameleon any minute now . . .'

Rufus banked the speeding rocket plane, bringing it round in a *wiiiide* 180-degree arc that would hopefully end with the X-15 coming alongside the nuclear missile, joining it on its flight path toward Mecca.

The X-15 rolled onto its side, shot through the air, banking left in its gigantic turn.

The sudden course-change allowed the AMRAAM missile behind it – ever-closing, ever-ravenous – to reel them in even more. It was only a hundred yards behind the X-15 now, and still closing.

TIME TO TARGET: 1:20 . . . 1:19 . . . 1:18 . . .

'There it is!' Rufus yelled. 'Dead ahead!'

Schofield strained against the G-forces to peer out over Rufus's shoulder, out at the twilight Arabian sky.

And he saw it.

The mere sight of the intercontinental ballistic missile took his breath away.

It was incredible.

The Jericho-2B clone ICBM looked like a spaceship from a science fiction movie – something that was far too big, far too sleek, and moving far too fast to exist on Earth.

The seventy-foot-long cylinder shot like a spear through the sky, a white-hot tailflame blazing from its base like a magnesium flare, leaving an impossibly long smoketrail in its wake. The smoketrail extended, snakelike, a God-sized python, *over* the distant horizon, streaking away toward the missile's source, Yemen.

And the sound it made.

A single, continuous *BOOOOOOOOOOOOOM!*

If Schofield's X-15 was ripping the fabric of the sky, then this baby was shredding it to pieces.

The banking X-15 roared round in a giant semicircle, careering in toward the moving ICBM, while itself trailed by the dogged AMRAAM.

TIME TO TARGET: 1:00 . . . 0:59 . . . 0:58 . . .

One minute.

And then, like the arms of a flattened Y converging to meet at the stem, the X-15 rocket plane and the Chameleon missile came alongside each other.

But they weren't level yet.

The X-15 was just behind and to the left of the ICBM – parallelling the horizontal column of smoke shooting out of the ICBM's base.

TIME TO TARGET: 0:50 . . . 0:49 . . . 0:48 . . .

But the rocket plane was moving slightly faster than the missile, so it was gradually hauling the ICBM in.

Noise was everywhere. The roar of supersonic speed.

BOOOOOOOOOOOOOOOOOOOOOOOOM!

TIME TO TARGET: 0:40 . . . 0:39 . . . 0:38 . . .

'Get me closer, Rufus!' Schofield called.

Rufus did so – and the nose-cone of the X-15 came alongside the tail of the roaring ICBM.

The CincLock VII unit didn't respond. They still weren't close enough to the missile's CPU.

The X-15 crept forward, edging up the length of the Chameleon missile.

'Closer!'

TIME TO TARGET: 0:33 . . . 0:32 . . . 0:31 . . .

Out through the cockpit canopy, Schofield saw the lights of a city down in the evening darkness below.

The holy city of Mecca.

TIME TO TARGET: 0:28 . . . 0:27 . . . 0:26 . . .

And the X-15 came level with the mid-point of the missile and Schofield's disarm unit beeped:

FIRST PROTOCOL (PROXIMITY): SATISFIED.
INITIATE SECOND PROTOCOL.

'I'm gonna get you,' Schofield said to the ICBM.

The reflex response pattern on his unit began its sequence, and Schofield began hitting its touchscreen.

The two rocket-propelled aircraft carved a sonic tear through the sky, travelling side-by-side at astronomical speed.

And then the AMRAAM behind the X-15 made its move.

Rufus saw it on his scopes. 'Come *on,* Captain . . . !'

'I just . . . have . . . to do . . . this first . . .' Schofield grimaced, concentrating on the reflex-response test.

TIME TO TARGET: 0:19 . . . 0:18 . . . 0:17 . . .

The AMRAAM powered forward, closing in on the tailflame of the X-15.

'It's approaching lethal range!' Rufus yelled. Lethal range for an AMRAAM was twenty yards. It didn't have to actually hit you, only explode close to you. 'You've got maybe five seconds!'

'We don't have five seconds!' Schofield shouted, not taking his eyes off the screen, his fingers moving quickly over it.

TIME TO TARGET: 0:16 . . . 0:15 . . . 0:14 . . .

'I can't take evasive action!' Rufus yelled desperately. 'I'll move us out of proximity! Jesus Christ! We can't come this far to lose now! Two seconds!'

Schofield kept hitting the touchscreen.

TIME TO TARGET: 0:13 . . . 0:12 . . .

'One second!'

And the AMRAAM entered lethal range – twenty yards from the X-15's tailpipe.

'No!' Rufus yelled. 'Too late – !'

'*Not if I can help it,*' a voice said suddenly in their earpieces.

Then, in a supersonic blur, something black and fast shot sideways *across the wake of the X-15* – cutting in between the AMRAAM and Schofield's X-15, so that the AMRAAM hit it and not Schofield's plane.

An explosion rocked the sky and Rufus whirled around in his seat to see the front half of *another* X-15 rocket plane go tumbling through the air, its rear-end vaporised, destroyed by the AMRAAM.

Knight's X-15.

He must have survived the death of his pilot and then stayed on their trail, catching up with them while they'd made their two time-consuming circling manoeuvres. And now he had flown himself into the path of the AMRAAM missile that had been about to take them out!

The shattered front half of Knight's X-15 fell through the sky, nose-first, before abruptly, its canopy jettisoned and a flight seat blasted out from the falling wreckage, a parachute blossoming above it a moment later.

TIME TO TARGET: 0:11 . . . 0:10 . . .

Schofield hardly even noticed the explosion. He was consumed with the reflex pattern on his touchscreen: white, red, white, white, red . . .

TIME TO TARGET: 0:09 . . .

'Whoa, shit! It's going vertical!' Rufus yelled.

With a sickening roll, the Chameleon missile abruptly changed course, banking *downward*, pointing its nose directly down at Mother Earth.

Rufus manoeuvred his control stick and the X-15 copied the move – and went vertical with the ICBM – and suddenly the two rocketcraft were travelling supersonically, side-by-side, heading *straight down!*

'Aaaaaaaaahhh!' Rufus yelled.

Schofield's eyes remained fixed to the touchscreen, focused, his fingers moving quickly.

TIME TO TARGET: 0:08 . . .

The X-15 and the ICBM raced toward the Earth like two vertical bullets.

TIME TO TARGET: 0:07 . . .

The lights of Mecca rushed up toward Rufus's eyes.

TIME TO TARGET: 0:06 . . .

Schofield's fingers danced.

And the CincLock disarm unit beeped.

SECOND PROTOCOL (RESPONSE PATTERN): SATISFIED.

THIRD PROTOCOL (CODE ENTRY): ACTIVE. PLEASE ENTER AUTHORISED DISARM CODE.

TIME TO TARGET: 0:05 . . .

Schofield punched in the Universal Disarm Code and the screen beeped again:

THIRD PROTOCOL (CODE ENTRY): SATISFIED.

AUTHORISED DISARM CODE ENTERED.

At which point the crucial line appeared:

MISSILE FLIGHT ABORTED.

*

What happened next happened in a blur.

High above the minarets of Mecca, the supersonically-travelling Chameleon missile self-destructed in a spectacular explosion. It looked like a gigantic firecracker – a spectacular starburst of sparks spraying out in every direction.

It was moving so amazingly fast, however, that its blasted-apart pieces were just stripped away by the onslaught of uprushing wind. The charred remains of the cloned Jericho-2B would later be found over an area 100 miles in diameter.

Schofield's X-15, on the other hand, suffered a far different fate.

The shock wave from the Chameleon's blast sent it spiralling away from the explosion, completely out of control, rocketing toward the Earth.

Rufus fought heroically with his stick and by doing so managed one single thing: to avoid crashing into any of the inhabited parts of Mecca.

But that was all he achieved. For a bare second later, the X-15 slammed into the desert like a meteor from outer space, smashing vertically into the sandy landscape in a thumping, slamming, earth-shuddering impact that could be heard more than fifty miles away.

And for a moment its fiery explosion lit up the dark desert sky as if it were midday.

The X-15 hit the desert floor doing Mach 3.

It hit the ground hard and in a single flashing, blinding instant, the rocket plane transformed into a ball of fire.

Nothing could have survived the crash.

A split second before the impact, however, two ejection seats could be seen catapulting clear of the crashing plane's cockpit, shooting diagonally out into the sky – seats that contained Schofield and Rufus.

The two flight seats floated back down to earth on their parachutes, landing a mile away from the flaming crater that marked the final resting place of the X-15.

The two seats hit the dusty ground, rocked onto their sides.

There was no movement in them.

For there, lying slumped against their seatbacks, sat Shane Schofield and Rufus, both unconscious, both knocked out by the colossal G-forces of their supersonic ejection.

After a time, Schofield awoke – to the sound of voices.

His vision was blurry, blood seeped down his face, and his head throbbed with a terrible ache. Bruises were forming around his eyes – the natural by-product of ejecting.

He saw shadows surrounding his flight seat. Some men were trying to unbuckle his seatbelts.

He heard their voices again.

'Crazy sons of bitches, ejecting at that speed.'

'Come on, man, hurry up, before the fucking boy scouts from the Marines arrive.'

At the edge of his consciousness, Schofield noted that they were speaking English.

With American accents.

He sighed with relief. It was over.

Then, with the whistling cut of a knife, his seatbelt came free and Schofield tumbled out of his seat onto the sand.

A man appeared at the rim of his vision. A Westerner, wearing military gear. Through the haze of his mind, Schofield recognised the man's uniform: the customised battle outfit of the US Special Forces' Delta Detachment.

'Captain Schofield . . .' the man said gently, his voice blurry to Schofield's slow mind. 'Captain Schofield. It's okay. You're safe now. We're from Delta. We're on your side. We've also picked up your friend, Captain Knight, a few miles from here.'

'Who—' Schofield stammered. 'Who are you?'

The Delta man smiled, but it wasn't a friendly smile. 'My name is Wade Brandeis. From Delta. We've come from Aden. Don't worry, Captain Schofield. You're perfectly safe with me.'

SEVENTH ATTACK

FRANCE

27 OCTOBER, 0700 HOURS (FRANCE)

E.S.T. (NEW YORK, USA) 0100 HOURS

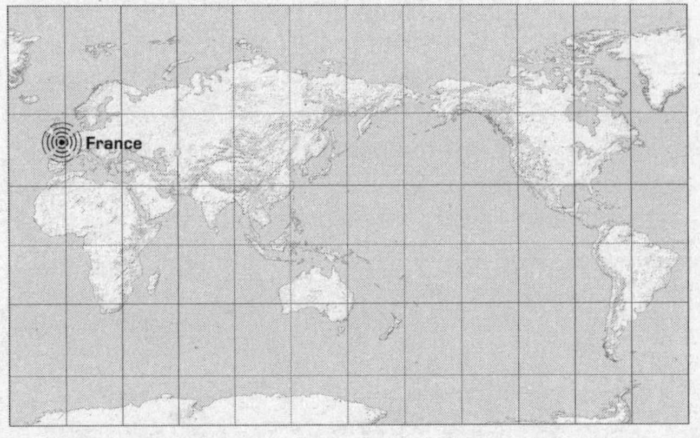

Beware the fury of a patient man.

John Dryden

Schofield dreamed.

Dreamed of being lifted out of his crashed flight seat . . . and flex-cuffed . . . then being loaded into the back of a private Lear jet . . . and the jet taking off . . .

Voices in the haze.

Brandeis saying, 'I heard it first from a couple of guys in the 'Stan. They said he turned up at a cave-hunting site and bolted inside. Said it had something to do with a bounty hunt.

'Then I get a call a few hours ago from a guy I know in ISS – he's one of those background guys, real old-school CIA, knows everything about everyone, so he's fucking *untouchable*. He's also ex-ICG. Good man. Ugly fuck, though. Looks like a goddamned rat. Name's Noonan, Cal Noonan, but everyone I know just calls him the Rat.

'As always, the Rat knows everything. For instance, he knows I'm working out of Aden. He confirms that there's a price on Schofield's head: eighteen million bucks. He also says that Schofield is on his way to Yemen. If I'm interested, he says, he can arrange leave for me and a few trusted men.

'He also says, wait for it, that *Aloysius Knight* is with Schofield, and that there's a price on Knight's head, too:

two million dollars. Hell, I'd bring Knight in for fucking free. But if someone wants to give me two million bucks to do it, that's even better.'

The plane flew on. Schofield slept.

He woke briefly, uncomfortable. He was still wearing his utility flak vest, but all the weapons on it had been removed. The only thing they hadn't taken was the tightly-rolled Soviet chemical body bag. Not much of a weapon.

He shifted – and caught a glimpse of Knight and Rufus, also flex-cuffed, sitting a few rows back, covered by armed Delta operators. Rufus was asleep, but Knight was wide awake. He seemed to see Schofield rouse, but Schofield couldn't keep his eyes open.

He dropped back to sleep.

Another waking moment.

The sky outside the window next to him had changed from black to pale blue.

Dawn.

And then the voices came again.

'So where are we taking them?'

'Some castle,' Brandeis said. 'Some castle in France.'

FORTERESSE DE VALOIS, BRITTANY, FRANCE
27 OCTOBER, 0700 HOURS

It was raining heavily when Schofield's jet landed at Jonathan Killian's private airstrip on the coast of Brittany.

A quick transfer to a covered truck and soon – under the watchful eye of Brandeis and his five-man Delta team – Schofield, Knight and Rufus were taken down a steep cliff-side road, heading toward the familiar castle built on its rocky mount just off the coastal cliffs.

The mighty Forteresse de Valois.

The lone truck crossed the massive drawbridge connecting the castle to the mainland, shrouded by rain and lightning.

During the short trip, Knight told Schofield about his history with Wade Brandeis: about that night in Sudan and Brandeis's treacherous ICG links.

'Believe me, I know about the ICG,' Schofield said.

'I've been meaning to catch up with Brandeis for a long time,' Knight said.

As he spoke, Schofield saw the two tattoos on Knight's arm again: 'SLEEP WITH ONE EYE OPEN' and

'BRANDEIS' and suddenly realised that they were in truth a single tattoo: 'SLEEP WITH ONE EYE OPEN BRANDEIS'.

'The thing is,' Knight said, 'Brandeis isn't a bounty hunter, and it shows.'

'How?'

'He's just broken the first rule of bounty hunting.'

'Which is?'

'If you have a choice between bringing someone in dead or alive,' Knight said, 'dead is better.'

At that moment, the truck entered the gravel courtyard inside the castle and crunched to a halt.

Schofield, Knight and Rufus were all shoved out of it, covered by Brandeis and his Delta men.

Monsieur Delacroix was waiting for them.

The Swiss banker stood at the entrance to the classic-car garage, prim and proper as ever.

He was flanked by Cedric Wexley and ten mercenaries from Executive Solutions, Jonathan Killian's private security force.

'Major Brandeis,' Delacroix said. 'Welcome to the Forteresse de Valois. We've been expecting you. Come this way, please.'

Delacroix guided them into the garage and then down some stone stairs to the ante-room that Schofield had seen before – but instead of turning *left* toward the long forbidding tunnel that took you to the verification office, he turned *right*, through a small stone doorway that opened onto a tight medieval stairwell that spiralled downwards.

Lit by flaming torches, the stairwell went down and down, round and round, descending deep into the bowels of the castle.

It ended at a thick steel door set into a solid stone frame.

Delacroix hit a switch and with an ominous rumble the steel door rose into the ceiling. Then the dapper Swiss banker stood aside, allowing Brandeis and his prisoners to enter first.

They passed through the doorway—

—and emerged inside a wide circular pit, a dungeon in which sloshing seawater wended its way between an irregular series of elevated stone platforms. In the laneways of water, Schofield saw two sharks, prowling. And on the nearest elevated stage he saw . . .

. . . a twelve-foot-tall guillotine.

He froze, caught his breath.

This was the dungeon that Knight had told him about before. The terrible dungeon in which Libby Gant had met her end.

This was the Shark Pit.

Once they had all stepped out into the Shark Pit, the steel door behind them slid back into place, sealing them all inside.

Monsieur Delacroix, wisely, had remained outside.

Someone else, however, was waiting for them inside the Pit.

A man with carrot-red hair and a sinister rat-like face.

'Hey, Noonan,' Brandeis said, stepping forward, taking the man's hand.

Schofield remembered Knight's horrifying description of Gant's death, and how a man with red hair and a rat face had pulled the lever that had ended her life.

Schofield glared at the murderer.

For his part, Rat Face turned and glared insolently back at him.

'So this is the Scarecrow,' Rat Face said. 'Resilient little fucker, aren't you. I went to a lot of trouble to arrange that little mission in Siberia yesterday. Set the scene. Sent ExSol to wait for you. Then made sure that it was McCabe and Farrell and you who were sent into the trap. Then I cut your comms from Alaska. McCabe and Farrell weren't good enough. But not you. You survived.

'But not now. Now, there's no escape. In fact, you're gonna buy it the same way your girlfriend did.' Rat Face turned to the Delta men holding Schofield. 'Put him in the guillotine.'

Schofield was shoved over to the guillotine by two of Brandeis's D-boys. His head was thrust into the stocks, while his hands stayed out, flex-cuffed behind his back.

'No!' a voice called from across the Pit.

Everyone turned.

Jonathan Killian appeared on a balcony overlooking the Pit, flanked by Cedric Wexley and the ten men from Executive Solutions, plus the just-arrived Monsieur Delacroix.

'Put him in face up,' Killian said. 'I want Captain Schofield to see the blade coming.'

The Delta men did as they were told, and rolled Schofield over so that his face was pointed upwards. The 12-foot guide rails of the wooden guillotine stretched away from him to the stone ceiling. At their peak he saw the glistening blade, suspended high above him.

'Captain,' Killian said. 'Through courage and audacity, you have saved the existing world order. Spared the lives of millions of people who will never even know your name. You are, in the true sense of the word, a hero. But your victory is at best temporary. Because I will continue to live – continue to rule – and ultimately my time will come. You, on the other hand, are about to discover what really happens to heroes. Mr Noonan. Drop the blade, and then shoot Captain Schofield's protectors in the head—"

'Killian!' Schofield called.

Everyone froze.

Schofield's voice was even, cold. 'I'll be coming for you.'

Killian smiled. 'Not in this life, Captain. Drop the blade.'

Rat Face strode to the side of the guillotine, and looking down at Schofield, gripped the lever.

At the same time, Wade Brandeis raised his Colt .45 to Knight's head.

'I'll see you in Hell, Scarecrow,' Rat Face said.

Then he yanked the lever, releasing the blade.

The guillotine's blade thundered down its guide rails.

And Schofield could do nothing but watch it rush down toward his face.

He shut his eyes and waited for the end.

Chunk!

But the end didn't come.

Schofield felt nothing.

He opened his eyes—

—to see that the guillotine's diagonal blade had been stopped a foot above his neck, its deadly downward rush halted by a five-bladed shuriken throwing knife that had lodged itself with a loud *chunk* in the vertical wooden guide rail of the guillotine.

So recently had it been thrown, the shuriken was still quivering.

Aloysius Knight was also saved as – a split-second after the shuriken had hit the guillotine – a bullet slammed into Wade Brandeis's gun-hand, sending his pistol splashing into the water, blood gushing from his hand.

Schofield turned . . . to see an unexpected but very welcome apparition emerge from the waters of the Shark Pit.

It was a fearsome image – a warrior in grey battle uniform, scuba gear and bearing shuriken throwing knives and guns. Lots and lots of guns.

If Death exists, he's afraid of one person.

Mother.

*

Mother exploded from the water, now with an MP-7 in each hand, firing them hard. Two of the five Delta men dropped immediately, hit in their chests.

Then things started happening everywhere.

For Knight and Rufus, Mother's entry had been distraction enough to allow them to king-hit their captors and, together, leap over their bound hands jump-rope style – bringing their wrists in front of their bodies – and hold up their plastic flex-cuffs.

Mother didn't need instructions.

Two shots – and the flex-cuffs were history. Knight and Rufus were free.

Over on the viewing balcony, Cedric Wexley quickly threw his ten-man team into action – he sent four over the balcony into the Pit, while he ordered the other six out through the back door of the balcony, into a corridor.

Then he himself whipped up his M-16 and hustled Jonathan Killian out of the dungeon.

Down in the Pit, Knight snatched up a Colt Commando rifle from one of the fallen D-boys and started firing at the four ExSol men leaping down into the Pit from the balcony.

Beside him, Rufus – still unarmed – whirled and killed a third Delta man with a driving flat-palmed blow to the nose.

'Rufus!' Knight yelled. 'Get Schofield out of those stocks!'

Rufus scrambled for the guillotine.

*

Over by the guillotine, the rat-faced man named Noonan was ducking ricochets, a short distance from the still-pinned Schofield.

When he spotted a brief gap in the gunfire, he reached up for the shuriken throwing knife holding the guillotine blade suspended above Schofield's head. If he could remove it, the blade would fall, decapitating Schofield.

Noonan's hand gripped the shuriken knife—

—just as a diving backhand punch from Rufus sent him flying.

Noonan landed on his stomach near the edge of the stone platform, and found himself eye-to-eye with one of the tiger sharks in the water. He recoiled instantly, clambered to his feet.

Rufus, however, landed next to Schofield, and now covered by the rifle-firing Knight, yanked up the guillotine's stocks and pulled Schofield free.

One shot from Knight severed Schofield's flex-cuffs, but then suddenly, inexplicably, Rufus hurled Schofield around and covered him with his own body.

An instant later, the big man was assailed in the back by several rapid-fire bullets.

'Ah!' he roared, his body jolting with three hits.

The volley had come from Wade Brandeis – standing nearby on one of the stone islands, nursing his bloodied right hand while firing a Colt Commando wildly with his unnatural left.

'No!' Aloysius Knight yelled.

He turned his own gun on Brandeis – but the rifle went dry, so instead he just hurled himself across the slick platform, sliding on his chest, and slammed into Brandeis's legs, tackling the Delta man and sending both of them tumbling into the shark-infested pool.

*

Free from the guillotine, Schofield turned to see Noonan staggering toward the steel door that led out from the Shark Pit.

As he ran, Noonan pulled a remote from his jacket and hit a button.

The thick steel door rose, opening. Noonan bolted for it.

'Damn it, shit!' Schofield yelled, taking off after him. 'Mother!'

Mother was on a nearby stage, taking cover behind one of the random stone objects in the Pit and firing at the two remaining D-boys with a pistol when she heard Schofield's shout.

She turned fast and loosed a volley at the fleeing Noonan. She didn't hit him, but her burst did cut him off from the exit, forcing him to stop and take cover behind a stone block.

She didn't get to see if this actually helped Schofield, though, because the momentary distraction had given her two Delta opponents the opening they needed.

One of them nailed her in the chest with a dozen rapid-fire shots from his Colt. Of course, her borrowed flak vest was bulletproof, so the shots just jolted her backwards, shot after shot after shot.

Under the weight of heavy fire, Mother staggered backwards, and just as the D-boy firing at her raised his aim for the kill-shot to her head—

—she dropped abruptly—

—into the water, and the kill-shot went high.

*

Mother sank underwater.

Brief merciful silence.

Then she came up – knowing what would be waiting – breaching the surface with her pistol extended, and nailed the two D-boys just as they themselves fired at her.

The two Delta men dropped, their faces bloody messes.

Mother sighed with relief.

It was then that she felt an odd swell in the water around her.

She turned . . .

. . . and saw a large bow-wave *surging* through the water toward her, the high dorsal fin of a tiger shark scything through the waves, charging at her.

'Oh, no way!' she yelled. 'No fucking way! I've survived far too much today to end up as fish food!'

She fired her pistol at the inrushing shark – *blam!-blam!-blam!-blam!-blam!-blam!*

The shark didn't slow down.

Mother's shots hit it, but the big shark just powered through the waves.

Blam!-blam!-blam!

The shark *still* didn't slow down.

It rose out of the frothing water, jaws wide—

—just as Mother, still firing, raised one of her legs instinctively and—

—*chomp!*

The shark clamped down on her left leg.

And Mother didn't react at all.

Her left leg was her artificial leg, made of titanium. A replacement for an injury from a previous adventure.

Two of the shark's teeth broke. Shattered into fragments.

'Try eating this, motherfucker,' Mother said, levelling her pistol at the tiger shark's brain.

Blam.

The shark bucked violently in the water, but when it came down, it was stilled, dead, its jaws clamped around Mother's left leg, as if even in its last moment of life, it had been unwilling to let go of its prize.

For her part, Mother just kicked the 10-foot shark away from her and leapt out of the pool to get back into the action.

While Mother had been firing at the shark, on the other side of the Pit, Schofield had chased after Noonan and caught him – tackling him – just as he had arrived at the open doorway to the dungeon.

The ISS man tried to kick Schofield clear, but Schofield just flung Noonan back into the dungeon and started hitting him – with venom.

One punch, and Noonan staggered backwards.

'I know you pulled the lever . . .' Schofield said grimly.

Second punch, and Noonan's nose broke, spraying blood.

'I know she died in pain . . .'

The third punch, and Noonan's jaw broke. He slipped, lost his footing.

'You killed a beautiful thing . . .'

Schofield grabbed Noonan two-handed and hurled him head-first *into* the guillotine. Noonan's head slid into the stocks underneath the razor-sharp blade, which itself was still held up by the shuriken.

'So now you're gonna die in pain . . .' Schofield said.

And with that Schofield yanked the shuriken out of the guillotine's wooden guide rails – causing the blade to drop the final two feet.

'No!' Noonan screamed. 'Noooo—!'

Chunk.

Noonan's rat-like head hit the stone floor like a bouncing ball, his eyelids blinking rapidly in those first moments after decapitation before they settled into a blank stare, forever frozen in a final look of absolute utter horror.

Ten yards away from the guillotine, floating in the shark-infested water, Aloysius Knight was engaged in the fight of his life with Wade Brandeis.

With their equal Delta training, they were perfectly matched, and as such, they traded punches and tactics, splashing and ducking under the surface in a fight that could only be to the death.

Then suddenly both men rose above the surface, nose-to-nose. Only now Brandeis had a small gun pressed up against Knight's chin. He had him.

'I always had the wood on you, Knight!'

Knight spoke through clenched teeth:

'You know, Brandeis, ever since that night in Sudan, I've thought of a thousand ways to kill you. But until right now, I'd never thought of this one.'

'Huh?' Brandeis grunted.

And with that, Knight yanked Brandeis around in the water and brought him right into the path of the inrushing second tiger shark.

The big ten-foot shark *rammed* into Brandeis at full speed, taking him in its mouth, its gnashing chomping teeth inches away from Knight's own body. But the

shark only had eyes for Brandeis, drawn by his bleeding right hand.

'Sleep with one eye open, you fuck,' Knight said.

Caught in the grip of the massive shark, Brandeis could only stare back at him – and scream as he was eaten alive.

Knight clambered out of the water, out of the bloody froth that had once been Wade Brandeis, and headed back to join Schofield.

Knight rejoined Schofield behind the guillotine – at the spot where Schofield had just pulled the wounded Rufus out of the line of fire of the four ExSol men now traversing across the Pit's stone islands.

Schofield had also collected some weapons – two Colt Commando assault rifles, one MP-7, one of Knight's H&K 9mm pistols, plus Knight's own fully-loaded utility vest, taken from one of the dead Delta men.

Mother joined them.

'Hey, Mother,' Knight said. 'Last time I saw you, you were inside that maintenance shack in the *Talbot*, just before it was RPG'd by the Demon's boys. What'd you do, hide in the floor?'

'Screw the floor,' Mother said. 'That damn shack was hanging from the roof of the hold. It had a hatch in the ceiling. That was where I went. But then, of course, the whole fucking boat sank . . .'

Knight said, 'So how did you know we were here?'

Mother pulled out a Palm Pilot from a waterproof pouch in her vest. 'You've got a lot of nice toys, Mr Knight. And *you*,' Mother turned to Schofield, 'have got MicroDots all over your hands, young man.'

'Nice to see you, Mother,' Schofield said. 'It's good to have you back.'

A volley of bullets from the ExSol men hit the guillotine.

Schofield turned quickly, eyeing the open doorway ten yards away.

'I'm going upstairs now,' he said abruptly, 'to get Killian. Mother, stay with Rufus, and take care of these assholes. Knight, you can come or you can stay. It's your choice.'

Knight held his gaze. 'I'm coming.'

Schofield – still wearing his stripped utility vest – gave Knight one of the rifles, the 9 mm pistol and the full utility vest he had picked up. 'Here. You can use these things better than I can. Let's move. Mother, cover fire, please.'

Mother whipped up her gun, sprayed covering fire at the ExSol mercenaries.

Schofield dashed for the door. Knight took off after him . . . but not before quickly grabbing something from Mother.

'What are you taking that for?' Mother shouted after him.

'I've got a feeling I'm gonna be needing it,' was all Knight said before he disappeared through the stone doorway after Schofield.

The Knight and the Scarecrow.

Storming up the spiralling stone stairwell – illuminated by firelight, rising from the depths of the dungeon – two warriors of equal awesome skill, covering each other, moving in tandem, their Colt Commando machine-guns blazing.

Like the six ExSol men guarding the stairwell had a chance.

As Schofield had suspected, Cedric Wexley had dispatched his six remaining mercenaries to this side of the Pit, to cut off their escape.

The ExSol mercs had divided themselves into three pairs stationed at regular intervals up the stairwell, firing from alcoves in the walls.

The first two mercenaries were ripped to shreds by fire from the uprushing warriors.

The second pair never even heard it coming as two shuriken throwing knives whipped *around* the corner of the curving stairwell – banking through the air like boomerangs – and lodged in their skulls.

The third pair were cleverer.

They'd set a trap.

They had waited at the top of the stairwell, inside the long stone tunnel beyond the ante-room – the tunnel with the boiling-oil gutters – the same tunnel that led to the verification office, where Wexley himself now stood with Killian and Delacroix.

Schofield and Knight arrived at the top of the stairwell, saw the two mercenaries in the tunnel, and the others beyond them.

But this time when Schofield moved, Knight didn't.

Schofield dashed through the ante-room, firing at the two mercenaries in the tunnel, taking them down just as they tried to do the same to him.

Knight leapt up after him shouting, 'No, wait! It's a tra—"

Too late.

The three large steel doors came thundering down from the ceilings of the tunnel and the ante-room. A fourth sealed off the stairwell leading down from the ante-room.

Wham! Wham! Wham! Wham!

And Schofield and Knight were separated.

Schofield: trapped in the tunnel with the two fallen ExSol mercenaries.

Knight: caught in the ante-room.

Schofield froze in the sealed-off tunnel.

He'd hit both of the mercenaries in here – they now lay sprawled on the floor, one dead, the other whimpering.

Killian's voice came over the speakers: '*Captain Schofield. Captain Knight. It was a pleasure to know you both*—"

Knight spun in the ante-room, saw the six microwave emitters arrayed in a circle around the ceiling, embedded in the rock.

'Deep shit . . .' he breathed.

Killian's voice boomed: '*—but the game ends now. It seems only fitting that your deaths be hard-won.*'

Inside the office, Killian peered through the small perspex window that allowed him to see into the boiling-oil tunnel. He saw Schofield there, trapped like a rat.

'Good-bye, gentlemen.'

And Killian hit the two buttons on his remote that triggered each chamber's booby trap: the microwave emitters in Knight's ante-room, and the boiling-oil gutters in Schofield's tunnel.

First, Killian heard the humming vibrations from the ante-room, quickly followed by the sound of repeated gunshots.

This had happened before.

People had sometimes tried to shoot their way out through the ante-room's steel doors. It had never worked. On a couple of occasions, some had attempted to shoot the microwave emitters themselves, but bullets weren't powerful enough to penetrate the emitters in their reinforced stone emplacements.

Then with an explosive spurt, steaming yellow oil sprayed across the tiny perspex window separating Killian from the tunnel holding Schofield, blotting out his view of Shane Schofield.

But he didn't need to see Schofield to know what was happening.

As the superheated boiling oil sprayed its way down the length of the tunnel, Killian could hear Schofield's screams.

A minute later, after both the screaming and the gunshots had ceased, Killian opened the steel doors—

—to be confronted by a surprising sight.

He saw the bodies of the two ExSol men lying in the tunnel, blistered and scorched by the boiling oil. One of them had his arms frozen in a defensive cowering posture – he had died screaming in agony, trying to fend off the oil.

Schofield, however, was nowhere to be seen.

In his place, standing at the ante-room end of the tunnel was a dark man-sized shape.

A body bag, standing upright.

It was a black polymer-plastic body bag. A Markov Type-III, to be precise. The best the Soviets had ever built – and the only item that Wade Brandeis had *not* taken from Schofield's vest. Capable of keeping *in* any kind of chemical contamination, now it seemed that it had successfully kept boiling oil *out*.

In a flash the zipper on the body bag whizzed open from the inside and Schofield emerged from it, leading with his MP-7.

His first shot hit Killian's hand – sending the remote flying from his grip – thus keeping the tunnel's doors open.

His second shot blew off Killian's left earlobe. Seeing the gun in Schofield's hand, Killian had ducked reflexively behind the doorframe. A nanosecond slower and the shot would have taken off his head.

Schofield stormed down the narrow tunnel toward the office, his MP-7 blazing.

Cedric Wexley returned fire from the cover of the office doorway.

Bullets flew every which way.

Chunks of stone fell off the wall-columns that lined the tunnel.

The floor-to-ceiling panoramic window in the office behind Wexley shattered completely.

But the key question in a stand-off like this was simple: who would run out of ammunition first? Schofield or Wexley?

Schofield did.

Ten feet short of the office doorway.

'Shit!' he yelled, ducking behind a stone column that barely concealed him.

Wexley smiled. He had him.

But then, strangely, *another* source of gunfire assailed Wexley's position – gunfire that came from behind Schofield, from the ante-room end of the tunnel.

Schofield was also perplexed by this and he turned . . .

. . . to see Aloysius Knight charging down the length of the tunnel, his Colt Commando raised and firing.

Schofield caught a fleeting glimpse of the ante-room in the distance behind Knight.

On its stone floor were 9 mm shell casings – a dozen of them – relics of Knight's shooting spree during the activation of the microwave emitters.

But they weren't regular shell casings.

These shell casings had orange bands around them.

The emplacements of the six microwave emitters in the ante-room may have been able to withstand regular bullets. But they'd been no match for Knight's gas-expanding bull-stoppers.

Knight's fire was all that Schofield needed.

Wexley was forced to return fire and within moments he was dry too. Unfortunately, so was Knight.

Schofield sprang.

He flew into the office at speed, striking Wexley in his already broken nose, breaking it again.

Wexley roared with pain.

And Wexley and Schofield engaged. Brutal hand-to-hand combat. South African Reccondo vs United States Marine.

But as they came together in a flurry of moves and parries, Monsieur Delacroix stepped forward, a glistening knife appearing from his right sleeve-cuff and he lunged at Schofield with it.

The blade got within an inch of Schofield's back before Delacroix's wrist was clutched from the side by an exceedingly strong grip and suddenly Delacroix found himself staring into the eyes of Aloysius Knight.

'Now that just isn't fair,' Knight said, a moment before he was stabbed deep in the thigh by a second knife that had appeared from Delacroix's other cuff.

Delacroix's knife-wielding hands moved like lightning, forcing the now-limping Knight to step back across the floor.

The blades were the sharpest things Knight had ever seen. Or felt. One of them slashed across his face, carving a line of blood across his cheek.

What had previously been all dapper-Swiss-banker

was now a perfectly-balanced bladesman exhibiting the exquisite knife skills only associated with the –

'Swiss Guards, hey, Delacroix?' Knight said as he moved. 'You never told me that. Nice. Very nice.'

'In my trade,' Delacroix sneered, 'a man must know how to handle himself.'

Schofield and Wexley traded blows by the doorway.

Wexley was bigger and stronger than Schofield, skilful, too.

Schofield, however, was quicker, his now-famous reflexes allowing him to evade Wexley's more lethal blows.

But after the exertions of the previous twenty-four hours and the crash of the X-15 and the trip as a captive to France, his energy levels were low.

As such, he over-extended with one punch.

Wexley nailed him for the error – a withering blow to the nose that would have killed any other man – and Schofield staggered, but as he fell, he managed to unleash a ruthless blow of his own to Wexley's Adam's apple.

Both men fell, dropping to the floor together – Wexley went sprawling across the open doorway, gasping, while Schofield slumped against the doorframe beside him.

Wexley groaned, and rising to his knees, drew a Warlock hunting knife from his boot.

'Too late, asshole,' Schofield said.

The strange thing was, he had no weapon in his hands. He had something better. He had Killian's remote.

'This is for McCabe and Farrell,' he said, hitting a button on the remote.

Immediately, the steel door above Wexley came thundering down out of its recess, slamming into Wexley's head like a pile-driver, driving it down into the stone floor where – *sprack!* – it cracked Wexley's head in an instant, flattening it.

With Wexley dead, Schofield turned to find the man he really wanted.

He saw him standing behind the desk.

Jonathan Killian.

Knight was still fighting Delacroix when he saw Schofield approach Killian over by the desk.

It wasn't that Knight was worried about Killian. Far from it. He was worried about what Schofield was going to do.

But he couldn't get away from Delacroix . . .

Schofield stopped in front of Killian.

The contrast couldn't have been more marked. Schofield was covered in dirt and grime, bloodied and beaten and worn. Apart from his bullet-nicked ear and wounded hand Killian was relatively neat and tidy, his clothes perfectly pressed.

The shattered floor-to-ceiling panoramic window overlooking the Atlantic yawned beside them.

The thunderstorm outside raged. Lightning forks tore the sky. Rain lanced in through the broken window.

Schofield gazed at Killian without emotion.

When he didn't speak, Killian just smirked.

'So, Captain Schofield. What are your intentions now? To kill me? I am a defenceless civilian. I have no military skills. I am unarmed.' Killian's eyes narrowed. 'But then, I don't think you could kill me. Because if you killed me now in rank cold blood, it would be my final victory, and perhaps my greatest achievement. For it would only prove one thing: *that I broke you.* I turned the last good man in the world into a cold-hearted murderer. And all I did was kill your girl.'

Schofield's eyes never wavered.

His whole appearance was unnaturally still.

When he finally spoke, his voice was low, dangerous.

'You once told me that Westerners don't understand suicide bombers,' he said slowly. 'Because suicide bombers don't fight fair. That the battle is meaningless to a suicide bomber, because he wants to win a far more important war: a psychological war in which the man who dies in a state of terror or fear – the man who dies *against his will* – loses.' Schofield paused. 'While the man who dies when he is emotionally ready, wins.'

Killian frowned.

Schofield never flinched, not even when a totally fatalistic, nihilistic smile washed across his face.

Then he grabbed Killian roughly by the throat and brought the billionaire right up close to his face and growled, 'You're not emotionally ready to die, Killian. But I am. Which means I win.'

'Jesus Christ, no . . .' Killian stammered, realising what was about to happen. 'No!!!'

And with those words, hauling the screaming Jonathan Killian with him, Shane Schofield stepped out through the shattered panoramic window beside them, out into the storm, and the two of them – hero and villain – fell together through 400 feet of sky down to the jagged rocks below.

At the very same moment that Schofield pulled Killian right up close to his face, Aloysius Knight had got the jump on Delacroix.

A quick sidestep to the left had caused Delacroix to stab one of his knives deep into the wood-panelled wall of the office – and allowed Knight to whip his blowtorch out from his utility vest and jam it into Delacroix's mouth and pull the trigger.

The blue flame from the blowtorch blasted out the back of Delacroix's head, spiking right through his skull, sending burnt brains flying across the room. The Swiss banker slumped instantly, dead, a char-rimmed hole driven right through his head.

Knight emerged from behind the fallen Delacroix just in time to see Shane Schofield step out into the storm, taking the screaming Killian with him.

Schofield fell through the rain with Jonathan Killian at his side.

The rocky mount rushed past them, while directly below them, Schofield saw the rocks, assaulted by the waves of the Atlantic, that would end his life.

And as he fell, a strange peace came over him. This was the end, and he was ready for it.

Then suddenly, from out of nowhere, something

struck him hard in the back and he jolted sickeningly and without warning . . .

. . . stopped falling.

Jonathan Killian shrank away from him – falling, falling, falling – disappearing with the rain, before slamming into the rocks at the base of the mount where he bent at an obscene angle and then vanished in a foul explosion of his own blood. He screamed all the way down.

And yet Schofield did not fall.

He just hung from the panoramic window at the end of a Maghook rope – from the Maghook that had just been fired by Aloysius Knight, the Maghook he had taken from Mother before – a desperate last-gasp shot that he had fired as he leaned out the window a second after Schofield had jumped – the bulbous magnetic head of the Maghook having attached itself to the metal plate inside the back section of Schofield's borrowed flak vest.

Schofield allowed himself to be reeled back up to the office like a fish on a line. When he got there, Knight hauled him back inside.

'I'm sorry, buddy,' Knight said. 'But I just couldn't let you go like that. That said, I still think you made your point to Killian.'

Ten minutes later, as the sun appeared on the horizon, a lone Aston Martin sped away from the Forteresse de Valois with Aloysius Knight at the wheel and Shane Schofield, Mother and Rufus inside it.

The car took the side-road leading up to the castle's airfield. There, after a very one-sided gunbattle, its occupants stole an Axon helicopter and flew off toward the rising sun.

Over the next few months, a strange variety of incidents took place around the world.

Just a week later, in Milan, Italy, it was claimed that there had been a break-in at the Aerostadia Italia Airshow, and that an aircraft had been stolen from one of the airshow's outlying hangars.

After the disappointing non-appearance of the fabled US X-15 rocket planes already, this was not the kind of publicity that the airshow needed.

Witnesses claimed that the aircraft taken was a sleek, black fighter which – so they said – took off vertically. While this description matched the description of the experimental Russian Sukhoi S-37, airshow and Italian Air Force officials were quick to point out that no such plane had been slated to appear at the show.

In the lead-up to Christmas, there was also a spate of unfortunate deaths among some of the world's richest families.

Randolph Loch disappeared while on safari in southern Africa. His entire private hunting party was never found.

In March, the Greek shipping magnate Cornelius Kopassus suffered a fatal heart attack in his sleep.

Arthur Quandt was found dead with his mistress in the spa of his Aspen lodge.

Warren Shusett was murdered in his isolated country mansion.

J. D. Cairnton, the pharmaceutical tycoon, was hit and killed by a speeding truck outside his company's New York headquarters. The driver of the truck was never found.

Heirs took over their empires.

The world kept turning.

The only connection made to their deaths was in a confidential memo to the President of the United States.

It read simply: 'SIR, IT IS OVER. MAJESTIC-12 IS NO MORE.'

MAJORCA, SPAIN
9 NOVEMBER, 1100 HOURS

The hired Volkswagen circled the charming cobble-stoned piazza on the Spanish island of Majorca, the famed luxury hideaway for the rich and reclusive.

'So where are we going again?' Rufus asked.

'We're going to meet our employer,' Knight said. 'The person who engaged us to keep Captain Schofield alive.'

Knight parked the car outside a streetside café.

Their employer was already there.

She sat at one of the sidewalk tables, smoking a cigarette, her eyes hidden behind a pair of opaque Dior sunglasses.

She was a very distinguished-looking woman – late forties, dark hair, high cheekbones, porcelain skin, her posture all at once refined and cultured and confident.

Her name was Lillian Mattencourt.

Billionaire owner of the Mattencourt cosmetics empire.

The richest woman in the world.

'Why if it isn't my knight in shining armour,' she said as they approached her table. 'Aloysius, my dear. Do sit down.'

*

Over tea, Mattencourt smiled warmly.

'Oh, Aloysius, you have done well. And you shall be rewarded handsomely.'

'Why?' Knight said. 'Why didn't you want him killed?'

'Oh, my dashing young knight,' Lillian Mattencourt said. 'Is it not obvious?'

Knight had thought about this. 'Majestic-12 wanted to start a new Cold War. And Jonathan Killian wanted global anarchy. But your fortune is based on the opposite of that. You want people to feel safe, secure, to be happy little consumers. Your fortune rests on the maintenance of global peace and prosperity. And nobody buys make-up during wartime. Warfare would ruin you.'

Mattencourt waved his answer away. 'My dear boy, are you always so cynical? Of course, what you say is absolutely true. But it was only one small part of my reasoning.'

'What was it then?'

Mattencourt smiled. Then her tone became deadly. 'Aloysius. Despite the fact that I have a greater net wealth than all but a few of them, and despite the fact that my father was once a member of their little club, for many years now, for the sole and single reason that I am a woman, Randolph Loch and his friends have consistently refused to let me join their Council.

'Put simply, after years of suffering their various innuendos and sexual taunts, I decided that I'd had enough. So when I learned of their bounty hunt through sources of my own within the French government, I decided that the time was right to teach them a lesson. I decided, Aloysius, *to hurt them*.

'And the best way to achieve that was to take from

them that which they desired most – their precious plan. If they wanted certain people dead, then I wanted them alive. If they wanted to destroy the existing global order, then I did not.

'I had heard of Captain Schofield. His reputation is well known. Like yourself, he is a rather resilient young man. If anyone could defeat Majestic-12 it was him, with you by his side. As such, he became the man you would protect.'

Lillian Mattencourt raised her nose and inhaled the fresh Mediterranean air, a sign that this meeting was over.

'Now, run along, my brave little foot soldier. Run along. You have done your job and done it well. By tonight, your money will be in your account. All $130.2 million of it, the equivalent I believe of seven heads.'

And with that she stood, donned her hat, and left the café, making for her 500 Series Mercedes Benz on the far side of the piazza.

She was inside the car and about to start it when Knight saw the shadowy figure standing in an alleyway not far from it.

'Oh, you cunning bastard,' Knight said a split second before Lillian Mattencourt keyed the ignition.

The explosion rocked the piazza.

Potted plants were thrown across the cobblestones. Table umbrellas were blown inside-out. Bystanders started running toward the flaming ruins of Lillian Mattencourt's Mercedes.

And the man who had been standing in the alleyway walked casually over to Knight's table and sat down beside him.

His flame-scarred face and bald head were covered by sunglasses and a cap.

'Well, if it isn't the Demon,' Knight said flatly.

'Hello, Captain Knight,' Demon Larkham said. 'Two weeks ago, you stole something from me. From a cargo plane travelling between Afghanistan and France. Three heads, if I recall. $55.8 million worth of bounty.'

Knight saw three other members of IG-88 standing nearby, guns under their jackets, flanking him and Rufus.

No escape.

'Oh yeah, that.'

Demon Larkham's voice was low. 'Others would kill you for what you did, but I'm not like that. The way I see it, things like this happen in our profession. It is the nature of the game and I enjoy that game. Ultimately, however, I believe that what happens on the field, stays on the field. That said, considering this unfortunate incident' – Demon waved at the smoking remains of Lillian Mattencourt's car – 'and the amount of money that you have just seen go up in smoke, what do you say we consider the debt settled.'

'I'd say that would be a good idea,' Knight said evenly, his lips tight.

'Until we meet again then, Captain,' the Demon said, standing. 'See you on the next safari.'

And with that, Demon Larkham and his men were gone, and all Aloysius Knight could do was gaze after them ruefully and shake his head.

MOTHER'S HOUSE, RICHMOND, VIRGINIA, USA 1 MARCH, 1200 NOON FOUR MONTHS LATER

The sun shone brightly over the BBQ underway in Mother's backyard.

It was a Sunday and a small but very close crowd had gathered for a casual get-together.

Mother's trucker husband Ralph was there – tending to the sausages with an oversized spatula. Their nieces were inside, miming to Britney Spears's latest hit.

David Fairfax sat in a deck chair under the clothes-line, nursing a beer, swapping stories with Book II and Mother about their adventures the previous October: tales of chases in parking lots near the Pentagon, office towers in London, Zulu bounty hunters, British bounty hunters, and their mirror-image assaults on supertankers on either side of the United States.

They also talked about Aloysius Knight.

'I heard the government cleared his record, cancelled the bounty and took him off the Most Wanted List,' Fairfax said. 'They even said he could come back to Special Forces if he wanted to.'

'So has he?' Book II asked.

'I don't even think he's come back to the States,' Fairfax said. 'Mother? What do you know about Knight?'

'He phones every now and then,' she said, 'but no, he hasn't come back to the States. If I were him, I don't know if I would either. As far as Special Forces is concerned, I don't think Knight is a soldier any more. I think he's a bounty hunter now.'

Thinking about Knight made Mother look over her shoulder.

Over in a corner of the yard, by himself, sat Schofield – clean-shaven and wearing jeans and a T-shirt and a pair of reflective Oakleys. He sipped on a Coke, staring up into the sky.

He had hardly spoken to anyone since he had arrived, which was not unusual these days. Gant's death in France had hit him hard. He'd been on indefinite leave ever since, and didn't look like coming back to active duty any time soon.

Everyone gave him a bit of space.

But just then, as Ralph was sizzling the onions, the doorbell rang.

Courier delivery. For the attention of Shane Schofield. Care of Mother's address.

A large cardboard envelope.

Mother took it to Schofield in the yard. He opened it. Inside the envelope was a lone gift-shop card with a cheesy cartoon of a cowboy that read: 'YOUR NEW LIFE BEGINS TODAY, BUCKAROO!'

Inside it was a handwritten message:

SCARECROW,

I'M SORRY I COULDN'T MAKE IT TODAY, BUT A NEW JOB CAME UP.

HAVING SPOKEN WITH MOTHER RECENTLY, I REALISED THAT THERE IS SOMETHING I SHOULD HAVE TOLD YOU FOUR MONTHS AGO.

DID YOU KNOW THAT, STRICTLY SPEAKING, MY CONTRACTUAL COMMITMENT TO MY EMPLOYER TO KEEP YOU ALIVE EXPIRED WHEN YOU DISARMED THAT MISSILE OVER MECCA. MY TASK WAS TO KEEP YOU ALIVE 'UNTIL 12 NOON, 26 OCTOBER OR UNTIL SUCH TIME AS CAPTAIN SCHOFIELD'S REASON FOR ELIMINATION HAS BEEN UTILISED TO ITS FULLEST POTENTIAL.'

I HAVE NEVER GONE BEYOND THE LETTER OF A CONTRACT BEFORE. TO BE HONEST, I ACTUALLY THOUGHT ABOUT LEAVING YOU IN THAT DUNGEON – AFTER ALL, BY THEN, YOUR REASON FOR ELIMINATION HAD INDEED BEEN UTILISED TO THE FULLEST.

BUT AFTER WATCHING THE WAY YOUR MEN – AND YOUR WOMEN – STOOD BY YOU OVER THE COURSE OF THAT AWFUL DAY, AFTER OBSERVING THE LOYALTY THEY HAD TO YOU, I CHOSE TO STAY AND FIGHT BY YOUR SIDE.

LOYALTY IS NOT SOMETHING THAT SIMPLY HAPPENS, CAPTAIN. IT IS ALWAYS PREDICATED BY AN INDEPENDENT SELFLESS ACT: A SUPPORTIVE WORD, A KINDLY GESTURE, AN UNPROVOKED ACT OF GOODNESS. YOUR MEN ARE LOYAL TO YOU, CAPTAIN, BECAUSE YOU ARE THAT RAREST OF MEN: A GOOD MAN.

PLEASE LIVE AGAIN. IT WILL TAKE TIME. BELIEVE ME, I KNOW. BUT DO NOT ABANDON THE WORLD JUST YET – IT CAN BE A TERRIBLE PLACE, BUT IT CAN ALSO BE A BEAUTIFUL PLACE, AND NOW MORE THAN EVER IT NEEDS MEN LIKE YOU.

AND KNOW THIS, SHANE 'SCARECROW' SCHOFIELD. YOU HAVE WON MY LOYALTY, A FEAT WHICH NO MAN HAS ACHIEVED FOR A VERY LONG TIME.

ANYTIME, ANYWHERE, IF YOU NEED HELP, JUST MAKE THE CALL AND I'LL BE THERE.

YOUR FRIEND,

THE BLACK KNIGHT

P.S. I AM SURE SHE IS WATCHING OVER YOU RIGHT NOW.

Schofield folded up the card.

And stood up.

And started walking out of the yard and down the driveway, heading for his car out on the street.

'Hey!' Mother called, concerned. 'Where are you going, champ?'

Schofield turned to her and smiled – a sad but genuine smile. 'Thank you, Mother. Thank you for worrying about me. I promise, you won't have to do it for too much longer.'

'What are you doing?'

'What am I doing?' he said. 'I'm going to try and start living again.'

The next morning he appeared at the personnel offices of Marine Headquarters in the Navy Annex building in Arlington.

'Good morning, sir,' he said to the Colonel in charge. 'My name is Captain Shane Schofield. The Scarecrow. I'm ready to get back to work.'

AN INTERVIEW WITH MATTHEW REILLY

THE WRITING OF *SCARECROW*

WARNING – Some of the later questions in this interview address plot points in *Scarecrow*. Be careful if you are reading them before you read the book!

What were you trying to achieve with this new novel?

From the very beginning, I was aware that *Scarecrow* would be closely compared to my other books. This is natural – hey, as soon as you write *two* books, people automatically compare them and decide which is their favourite. With that in mind, what I really wanted was for *Scarecrow* to be seen as a new *kind* of Matthew Reilly novel, a faster book, a book that was more densely packed with plot: a book that was a stylistic leap forward from my previous efforts. I'm hoping people will see *Contest, Ice Station, Temple* and *Area 7* as 'Matthew Reilly Version 1.0' and *Scarecrow* as the beginning of 'Matthew Reilly Version 2.0'.

It's funny, in the interview at the back of *Area 7*, I mentioned that I wanted to create a new level of speed and pace in my next book – and then I'd meet people at book signings and they'd say 'How are you possibly going to make it *faster*?' I like to think that *Scarecrow* has lived up to the promise of being faster and completely out-of-control!

How have you tried to achieve this?

Mainly by combining action and exposition – I wanted my characters to be running away from the bad guys *while* they were figuring stuff out. A lot of thrillers have rest breaks between the action scenes during which the author spells out the plot. I wanted to fuse the action and the plot advancement together. The result is that *Scarecrow* is about the same length as *Area 7*, but has a lot more happening in it.

What was the inspiration for the bounty hunters in *Scarecrow*?

It's odd, you know, but for me bounty hunters have only ever appeared in two storytelling spheres: westerns and the original *Star Wars* trilogy (I haven't read any of Janet Evanovich's books, but I believe her lead character is a bounty hunter).

The idea of international bounty hunters, with their own planes and units and even submarines, was something I adapted from the (real-life) concept of mercenary forces: private armies that sell themselves and their hardware to the highest bidder. In Australia, such forces got a lot of press when Papua New Guinea engaged a mercenary army a few years ago; I also read about them operating in Sierra Leone, helping the government stay in power in exchange for diamonds.

In addition to this, I have always been intrigued by the concept of the Wild West freelance bounty hunter, a concept which was adapted to a sci-fi environment in the *Star Wars* trilogy, in particular *The Empire Strikes Back*. Indeed, this is why Demon Larkham's gang – the InterContinental Guards, Unit 88, or 'IG-88' – is proudly named after the obscure bounty hunter of the same name in *The Empire Strikes Back*. (For those who don't know, IG-88 was the very tall robot bounty hunter who stands in the background as Darth Vader offers a reward for the bounty hunter who finds the *Millennium Falcon*. IG-88 utters no dialogue, nor does he actually move, but he became one of those cult *Star Wars* action figures – probably because he was always the one left on the shelf!)

In any case, the idea of these elite hunters-of-men really appealed to me, and I wanted to fashion a story whereby my hero, Shane Schofield – an able warrior himself – was being pursued by the best manhunters on the planet. And thus *Scarecrow* was born.

Speaking of bounty hunters, you introduce in *Scarecrow* a character named Aloysius Knight, a.k.a. the Black Knight. What lay behind his creation?

I had a lot of fun creating Aloysius Knight. From the start, he was designed to be Schofield's darker shadow, his amoral twin (he even has an eye dysfunction to match Schofield's). I wanted him to be the equal of Schofield in battle skills, but darker, more ruthless – as shown, for example, when we first meet him at Krask-8, when he kills the pleading mercenary in cold blood.

But most of all, I wanted Knight to be a guy whose reputation preceded him. The men of ExSol are worried that he's coming to Siberia. David Fairfax discovers that he's the second-best bounty hunter in the world – at a time when Knight is standing right in front of Schofield.

As a writer, it's very liberating to create characters such as Knight – it's the same with Mother – because you can do all sorts of things with him. For the simple reason that there are no boundaries. Characters like Knight and Mother are not governed by socially acceptable norms, and so are fun to write about. They swear, they kill bad people, they do crazy things. But having said that, there is one special thing common to both Mother and Knight: their loyalty to their friends – Mother to Schofield, and Knight to his pilot, Rufus. However wild and crazy they may be, they stand by their friends.

As an interesting aside, Knight is named after St Aloysius (pronounced *allo-wishus*) Gonzaga, a Jesuit saint and the namesake of my old high school, St Aloysius' College, in Sydney.

[THIS QUESTION CONTAINS PLOT SPOILERS]
Okay. To the big question: how could you kill Gant! Seriously, *Scarecrow* sees some of the biggest 'character moments' you've written. What made you make those choices?

You cannot believe how hard that scene was for me to write. Unlike other characters who have met their end in my previous books, Gant had been with me for two-and-a-half books, and I virtually considered her a member of the family. I've never considered myself to be an emotional, fall-in-love-with-my-characters kind of writer, but I remember vividly the day I wrote that terrible scene – I recall physically standing up from my computer and saying (aloud, to my empty office) 'Can I really do this?'

And so I thought about it. A lot. But then I said to myself 'No. This is what makes my novels different to other kinds of books. No character is safe. I've got to hold my nerve.'

It took me another day before I could sit down and actually type the scene, but I did. In the end, though, this is the essential feature of the action-thriller novel – the reader must believe that the hero and his friends *might not make it*.

Ultimately, however, it was a 'character motivation' thing that made me go through with killing Libby Gant. I decided that I wanted to see what would happen to the hero, Schofield, if such a terrible thing happened. What that led to was one of my favourite scenes in all of my books: the fistfight between Schofield and Mother (I don't know about you, but ever since I created them, I have wondered who would win a fight between Schofield and Mother: in the end, the answer is Schofield).

How do you interact with your military advisors?

This is a good question. My two military guys, Paul Woods and Kris Hankison, are two of the most knowledgable men I've ever known. And their input into my books has been beyond value, for the simple reason that no matter how much research you do on a given topic, someone 'in the industry' will always be able to give you that little bit of nuance, that little bit extra. That is what Paul and Kris do for me on military matters.

That said, sometimes the dictates of my story mean that I have to say to them, 'Sorry, guys, but I'll have to invoke poetic licence on this point.' A good example is the big MOAB bomb in *Scarecrow*. MOABs are actually satellite-guided, but my story required Gant to place a laser inside the Karpalov Coal Mine. So, despite the protests of the guys, I made the MOAB laser-guided.

The best thing about my military advisors is that they have a keen sense of the tone of my books – they know that my novels are outrageous and over-the-top. So they accept that I sometimes have to bend the truth (and, hell, the laws of physics!) for the sake of a roller-coaster story.

Matthew. The French. They were the bad guys in *Ice Station*. And now *Scarecrow*. What have you got against the French?

Ha! Er, yes, the French do cop a bit of a pasting in *Scarecrow*. You have to understand, though, that I don't dislike France. Not at all!

What it boils down to is this: I write fiction. And I'm always looking for new dastardly villains. Back in the days of the Cold

War, authors could just make the Soviet Union the evil bad guy. But that doesn't apply any more. The world has changed. The way I see it – and as I suggested in *Ice Station* – international alliances are more fickle than we imagine. And France, more than any other major Western nation, has been a vocal and active opponent of United States hegemony. Since Shane Schofield is American, France is often at cross-purposes with him.

Add to that France's chequered geopolitical history – the sinking of the *Rainbow Warrior*, her nuclear testing in the Pacific Ocean, and her outspoken opposition to the US invasion of Iraq – and you have a nation that could, in the world of fiction, have nefarious anti-US plans.

But I stress: it's fiction!

So what else have you been doing?

Since finishing *Scarecrow*, I have completed two screenplays. I enjoy writing scripts in between my books – a novel takes me a year to write, whereas a screenplay takes me about two months. I adapted my own short story, *Altitude Rush*, into a full-length screenplay, and have finished the first part of an epic science fiction trilogy that I think will rock the world one day!

Any more books on the way?

Yes indeed. Earlier this year I signed a new two-book deal with my publishers, Pan Macmillan, so there will be at least two more books from me. I have now moved to producing one book every two years – I would love to be able to produce a book every year, but I fear the quality would suffer and I just don't want to end up churning out books simply to keep to a timetable.

Not sure what they'll be about at this stage. One will probably be a Schofield book, although maybe Aloysius Knight could get a novel of his own. And I keep getting asked at book signings if I will be writing a sequel to *Temple*!

Any final words?

As always, I just hope you enjoyed the book. Keep reading and take care.

Matthew Reilly
Sydney, Australia
November 2003

SEVEN ANCIENT WONDERS

FOR NATALIE

In ancient times, at the peak of the Great Pyramid at Giza, there stood a magnificent Capstone made of gold.

It disappeared in antiquity.

A COLLECTION OF WONDERS FROM AROUND THE WORLD

Title of a collection of documents written by Callimachus of Cyrene, Chief Librarian of the Alexandria Museion, lost when the famous Library was destroyed in 48 BC.

COWER IN FEAR, CRY IN DESPAIR,
YOU WRETCHED MORTALS
FOR THAT WHICH GIVETH GREAT POWER
ALSO TAKES IT AWAY.
FOR LEST THE BENBEN BE PLACED AT SACRED SITE
ON SACRED GROUND, AT SACRED HEIGHT,
WITHIN SEVEN SUNSETS OF THE ARRIVAL OF RA'S PROPHET,
AT THE HIGH-POINT OF THE SEVENTH DAY,
THE FIRES OF RA'S IMPLACABLE DESTROYER WILL DEVOUR US ALL.

4,500-year-old hieroglyphic inscription found on the summit of the Great Pyramid at Giza in the place where the Capstone once stood.

I HAVE BOTH HELD AND BEHELD UNLIMITED POWER AND OF IT I KNOW BUT ONE THING. IT DRIVES MEN MAD.

Alexander the Great

FIRST MISSION
THE COLOSSUS

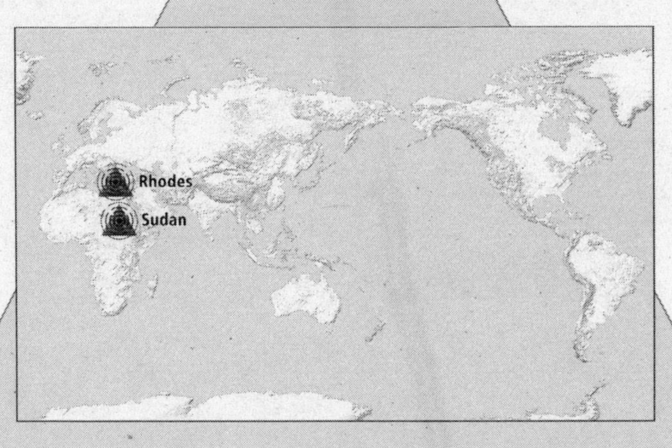

SUDAN
14 MARCH, 2006
6 DAYS BEFORE TARTARUS

THE GREATEST STATUE IN HISTORY

It towered like a god above the mouth of Mandraki harbour, the main port of the island state of Rhodes, much like the Statue of Liberty does today in New York.

Finished in 282 BC after twelve years of construction, it was the tallest bronze statue ever built. At a stupendous 110 feet, it loomed above even the biggest ship that passed by.

It was crafted in the shape of the Greek Sun-god, Helios—muscled and strong, wearing a crown of olive leaves and a necklace of massive golden pendants, and holding a flaming torch aloft in his right hand.

Experts continue to argue whether the great statue stood astride the entrance to the harbour or at the end of the long breakwater that formed one of its shores. Either way, in its time, the Colossus would have been an awesome sight.

Curiously, while the Rhodians built it in celebration of their victory over the Antigonids (who had laid siege to the island of Rhodes for an entire year), the statue's construction was paid for by Egypt—by two Egyptian Pharaohs in fact: Ptolemy I and his son, Ptolemy II.

But while it took Man twelve years to build the Colossus of Rhodes, it took Nature 56 years to ruin it.

When the great statue was badly damaged in an earthquake in 226 BC, it was again Egypt who offered to repair it: this time the new Pharaoh, Ptolemy III. It was as if the Colossus meant more to the Egyptians than it did to the Rhodians.

Fearing the gods who had felled it, the people of Rhodes declined Ptolemy III's offer to rebuild the Colossus and the remainder of the statue was left to lie in ruins for nearly 900 years—until 654 AD when the invading Arabs broke it up and sold it off in pieces.

One mysterious footnote remains.

A week after the Rhodians declined Ptolemy III's offer to re-erect the Colossus, the *head* of the mammoth fallen statue—all sixteen feet of it—went missing.

The Rhodians always suspected that it was taken away on an Egyptian freighter-barge that had left Rhodes earlier that week.

The head of the Colossus of Rhodes was never seen again.

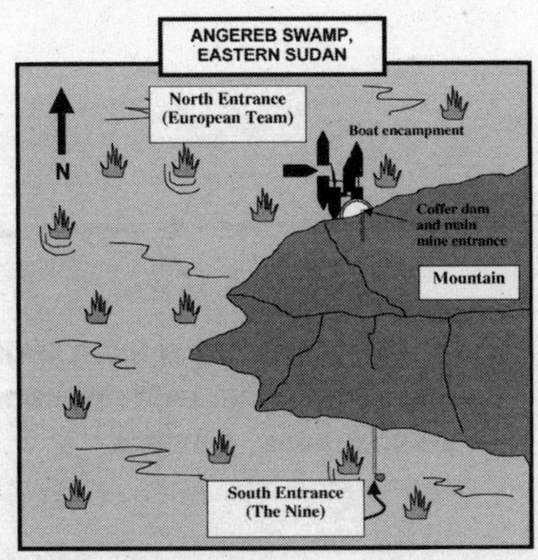

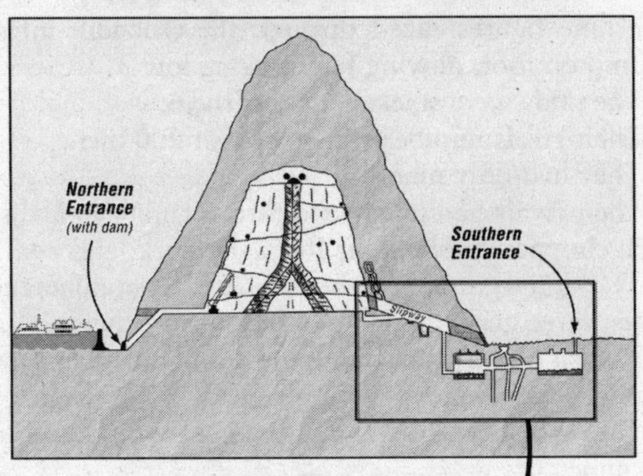

THE SOUTHERN ENTRANCE

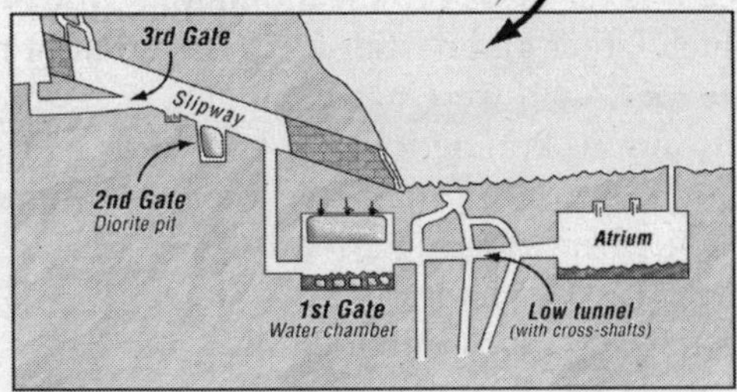

ANGEREB SWAMP
BASE OF THE ETHIOPIAN HIGHLANDS
KASSALA PROVINCE, EASTERN SUDAN

14 MARCH, 2006, 4:55 P.M.
6 DAYS BEFORE THE ARRIVAL OF TARTARUS

The nine figures raced through the crocodile-infested swamp on foot, moving fast, staying low.

The odds were stacked against them.

Their rivals numbered in excess of 200 men.

They had only nine.

Their rivals had massive logistical and technical support: choppers, floodlights for night work, and boats of every kind—gunboats, houseboats, communications boats, three giant dredging barges for the digging—and that wasn't even mentioning the temporary dam they'd managed to build.

The Nine were only carrying what they'd need inside the mine.

And now—the Nine had just discovered—a *third* force was on its way to the mountain, close behind them, a much larger and nastier force than that of their immediate foes, who were nasty enough.

By any reckoning it was a hopelessly lost cause, with enemies in front of them and enemies behind them, but the Nine kept running anyway.

Because they had to.

They were a last-ditch effort.

The last throw of the dice.

They were the very last hope of the small group of nations they represented.

Their immediate rivals—a coalition of European nations—had found the northern entrance to the mine two days ago and were now well advanced in its tunnel system.

A radio transmission that had been intercepted an hour before revealed that this pan-European force—French troops, German engineers and an Italian project leader—had just arrived at the final entry trap on their side of the mine. Once they breached that, they would be inside the Grand Cavern itself.

They were progressing quickly.

Which meant they were also well versed in the difficulties found inside the mine.

Fatal difficulties.

Traps.

But the Europeans' progress hadn't been entirely without loss: three members of their point team had died gruesome deaths in a snare on the first day. But the leader of the European expedition—a Vatican-based Jesuit priest named Francisco del Piero—had not let their deaths slow him down.

Single-minded, unstoppable and completely devoid of sympathy, del Piero urged his people onward. Considering what was at stake, the deaths were an acceptable loss.

The Nine kept charging through the swamp on the south side of the mountain, heads bent into the rain, feet pounding through the mud.

They ran like soldiers—low and fast, with balance and purpose, ducking under branches, hurdling bogs, always staying in single file.

In their hands, they held guns: MP-7s, M-16s, Steyr-AUGs. In their thigh holsters were pistols of every kind.

On their backs: packs of various sizes, all bristling with ropes, climbing gear and odd-looking steel struts.

And above them, soaring gracefully over the treetops, was a small shape, a bird of some sort.

Seven of the Nine were indeed soldiers.

Crack troops. Special forces. All from different countries.

The remaining two members were civilians, the elder of whom was a long-bearded 65-year-old professor named Maximilian T. Epper, call-sign: *Wizard*.

The seven military members of the team had somewhat fiercer nicknames: *Huntsman, Witch Doctor, Archer, Bloody Mary, Saladin, Matador* and *Gunman*.

Oddly, however, on this mission they had all acquired new call-signs: *Woodsman, Fuzzy, Stretch, Princess Zoe, Pooh Bear, Noddy* and *Big Ears*.

These revised call-signs were the result of the ninth member of the team:

A little girl of ten.

The mountain they were approaching was the last in a long spur of peaks that ended near the Sudanese–Ethiopian border.

Down through these mountains, flowing out of Ethiopia and into the Sudan, poured the Angereb River. Its waters paused briefly in this swamp before continuing on into the Sudan where they would ultimately join the Nile.

The chief resident of the swamp was *Crocodylus niloticus*, the notorious Nile crocodile. Reaching sizes of up to 6 metres, the Nile crocodile is known for its great size, its brazen cunning, and its ferocity of attack. It is the most man-eating crocodilian in the world, killing upwards of 300 people every year.

While the Nine were approaching the mountain from the south, their EU rivals had set up a base of operations on the northern side, a base that looked like a veritable floating city.

Command boats, mess boats, barracks-boats and gunboats, the small fleet was connected by a network of floating bridges and all were facing toward the focal point of their operation: the massive coffer dam that they had built against the northern flank of the mountain.

It was, one had to admit, an engineering masterpiece: a 100-metre-long, 40-foot-high curved retaining dam that held back the waters of the swamp to reveal a square stone doorway carved into the base of the mountain 40 feet *below* the waterline.

The artistry on the stone doorway was extraordinary.

Egyptian hieroglyphs covered every square inch of its frame—but taking pride of place in the very centre of the lintel stone that surmounted the doorway was a glyph often found in pharaonic tombs in Egypt:

Two figures, bound to a staff bearing the jackal head of Anubis, the Egyptian god of the Underworld.

This was what the afterlife had in store for grave-robbers—eternal bondage to Anubis. Not a nice way to spend eternity.

The message was clear: do not enter.

The structure inside the mountain was an ancient mine delved during the reign of Ptolemy I, around the year 300 BC.

During the great age of Egypt, the Sudan was known as 'Nubia', a word derived from the Egyptian word for gold: *nub*.

Nubia: the Land of Gold.

And indeed it was. It was from Nubia that the ancient Egyptians sourced the gold for their many temples and treasures.

Records unearthed in Alexandria revealed that this mine had run out of gold 70 years after its founding, after which it gained a second life as a quarry for the rare hardstone, diorite. Once it was exhausted of diorite—around the year 226 BC—Pharaoh Ptolemy III decided to use the mine for a very special purpose.

To this end, he dispatched his best architect—Imhotep V—and a force of 2,000 men.

They would work on the project in absolute secrecy for three whole years.

The northern entrance to the mine had been the main entrance.

Originally, it had been level with the waterline of the swamp, and through its doors a wide canal bored horizontally into the mountain. Bargeloads of gold and diorite would be brought out of the mine via this canal.

But then Imhotep V had come and reconfigured it.

Using a temporary dam not unlike the one the European force was using today, his men had held back the waters of the swamp while his engineers had lowered the level of the doorway, dropping it *40 feet*. The original door was bricked in and covered over with soil.

Imhotep had then disassembled the dam and allowed the swampwaters to flood back over the new doorway, concealing it for over 2,000 years.

Until today.

But there was a *second* entrance to the mine, a lesser-known one, on the south side of the mountain.

It was a back door, the endpoint of a slipway that had been used to dispose of waste during the original digging of the mine. It too had been reconfigured.

It was this entrance that the Nine were seeking.

Guided by the tall white-bearded Wizard—who held in one hand a very ancient papyrus scroll, and in the other a very modern sonic-resonance imager—they stopped abruptly on a mud-mound about 80 metres from the base of the mountain. It was shaded by four bending lotus trees.

'Here!' the old fellow called, seeing something on the mound. 'Oh dear. The village boys *did* find it.'

In the middle of the muddy dome, sunken into it, was a tiny square hole, barely wide enough for a man to fit into. Stinking brown mud lined its edges.

You'd never see it if you weren't looking for it, but it just so happened that this hole was exactly what Professor Max T. Epper was searching for.

He read quickly from his papyrus scroll:

'In the Nubian swamp to the south of Soter's mine,
Among Sobek's minions,
Find the four symbols of the Lower Kingdom.
Therein lies the portal to the harder route.'

Epper looked up at his companions. 'Four lotus trees: the lotus was the symbol of the Lower Kingdom. Sobek's minions are crocodiles, since Sobek was the Egyptian crocodile god. In a swamp to the south of Soter's mine—Soter being the other name for Ptolemy I. This is it.'

A small wicker basket lay askew next to the muddy hole—the kind of basket used by rural Sudanese.

'Those stupid, stupid boys.' Wizard kicked the basket away.

On their way here, the Nine had passed through a small village. The villagers claimed that only a few days ago, lured by the Europeans' interest in the mountain, four of their young men had gone exploring in the swamp. One of them had returned to the village saying the other three had disappeared down a hole in the ground and not come out again.

At this point, the leader of the Nine stepped forward, peered down into the hole.

The rest of the team waited for him to speak.

Not a lot was known about the leader of this group. Indeed, his past was veiled in mystery. What *was* known was this:

His name was West—Jack West Jr.

Call-sign: *Huntsman.*

At 37, he had the rare distinction of being both militarily *and* university trained—he had once been a member of the most elite special forces unit in the world, while at another time, he had studied ancient history at Trinity College in Dublin under Max Epper.

Indeed, in the 1990s, when the Pentagon had ranked the best soldiers in the world, only one soldier in the top ten had *not* been an American: Jack West. He'd come in at No. 4.

But then, around 1995, West disappeared off the international radar. Just like that. He was not seen at international exercises or on missions again—not even the allied invasion of Iraq in 2003, despite his experience there during Desert Storm in '91. It was assumed he had quit the military, cashed in his points and retired. Nothing was seen or heard of him for over 10 years . . .

. . . until now.

Now, he had re-emerged.

Supremely fit, he had dark hair and laser-sharp blue eyes that seemed perpetually narrowed. Apparently, he had a winning smile, but that was something rarely seen.

Today, like the rest of his team, he wore a decidedly non-military uniform: a rugged caramel-coloured canvas jacket, tattered cargo pants and steel-soled Salomon hiking boots that bore the scars of many previous adventures.

His hands were gloved, but if you looked closely at the left cuff of his jacket, you might catch a glimpse of silver steel. Hidden under the sleeve, his entire left forearm and hand were artificial, mechanical. How they came to be that way not many people knew; although one of those who did was Max Epper.

Expertly trained in the art of war, classically trained in the lore of history, and fiercely protective of the little girl in his care, one thing about Jack West Jr was clear: if anyone could pull off this impossible mission, it was him.

Just then, with a squawk, a small brown peregrine falcon swooped in from above the treeline and landed lightly on West's shoulder—the high-flying bird from before. It eyed the area around West imperiously, protectively. Its name, Horus.

West didn't even notice the bird. He just stared down into the dark square hole in the mud, lost in thought.

He brushed back some mud from the edge, revealing a hieroglyph cut into the rim:

'We meet again,' he said softly to the carving.

He turned. 'Glowstick.'

He was handed a glowstick which he cracked and tossed down the hole.

It fell for 20 feet, illuminating a pipe-like stone shaft on its way down, before—*splonk!*—it landed in water and revealed—

Lots of crocodiles. Nile crocodiles.

Snapping, snarling and grunting. Sliding over each other.

'More of Sobek's minions,' West said. 'Nice. Very nice.'

Just then the team's radioman, a tall Jamaican with bleached dreadlocks, a heavily pockmarked face and tree-trunk-sized arms, touched his earpiece in alarm. His real name was V.J. Weatherly, his original call-sign *Witch Doctor,* but everyone here just called him *Fuzzy*.

'Huntsman,' he said, 'the Europeans just breached the Third Gate. They're inside the Grand Cavern. Now they're bringing in some kind of crane to overshoot the lower levels.'

'Shit . . .'

'It gets worse. The Americans just crossed the border. They're coming in fast behind us. Big force: 400 men, choppers, armour, with carrier-launched fighter support on the way. And the ground force is being led by the CIEF.'

That really got West's attention.

The CIEF—the Commander-in-Chief's In Extremis Force, pronounced 'seef'—was America's very best special operations unit, a unit that answered only to the President and possessed the real-life equivalent of a licence to kill. As West knew from hard experience, you didn't want to be around when the CIEF arrived.

He stood up. 'Who's in command?'

Fuzzy said ominously, 'Judah.'

'I didn't think he'd come himself. Damn. Now we'd really better hurry.'

West turned to his team.

'All right. Noddy—you've got sentry duty. Everybody else . . .'

He pulled an odd-looking helmet from his belt, put it on.

'. . . it's time to rock and roll.'

And so into the subterranean dark they went.

Fast.

A steel tripod was erected above the pipe-like shaft and, led by West, one after the other, eight of the Nine abseiled down it on a rope strung from the tripod.

One lone man, a dark-haired Spanish commando—once known as *Matador*, now *Noddy*—remained up top to guard the entrance.

The Entry Shaft

West sizzled down the drop-rope, shooting past three steeply slanted cross-shafts that intersected with the main shaft.

His falcon sat snugly in a pouch on his chest, while on his head he wore a weathered and worn *fireman*'s helmet, bearing the badge 'FDNY Precinct 17'. The battered helmet was fitted with a wraparound protective eye visor and on the left side, a powerful pen-sized flashlight. The rest of his team wore similar helmets, variously modified with flashlights, visors and cameras.

West eyed the cross-shafts as he slid down the rope. He knew what perils lay within them. 'Everyone. Stay sharp. Do not, I repeat, do not make any contact with the walls of this shaft.'

He didn't and they didn't.

Safely, he came to the bottom of the rope.

The Atrium

West emerged from the ceiling at one end of a long stone-walled room, hanging from his drop-rope.

He did not lower himself all the way to the floor, just kept hanging about 8 feet above it.

By the eerie yellow light of his original glowstick, he beheld a rectangular room about thirty metres long. The room's floor was covered by a shallow layer of swamp-water, water that was absolutely *crawling* with Nile crocodiles—not an inch of floorspace was crocodile-free.

And directly beneath West, protruding half out of the water, were the waterlogged, half-eaten bodies of two twentysomething Sudanese men. The bodies lolled lifelessly as three big crocs took great crunching bites out of them.

'Big Ears,' West said into his throat microphone, 'there's a sight down here that's not PG-13. Tell Lily not to look down when you two reach the bottom of the rope.'

'*Righto to that, boss*,' came an Irish-accented reply over his earpiece.

West fired a luminescent amber flare down the length of the atrium.

It was as if the chamber came alive.

Deeply cut lines of hieroglyphs covered the walls, *thousands* of them.

And at the far end of the chamber, West saw his goal: a squat trapezoidal doorway, raised several feet off the watery floor.

The eerie yellow glow of the flare also revealed one other important feature of the atrium—its ceiling.

Embedded in the ceiling was a line of handrungs, leading to the far raised doorway. Each rung, however, was lodged in a dark square hole that disappeared up into the ceiling itself.

'Wizard,' West said, 'I've got handrungs.'

'*According to the inscription in Imhotep's tomb, we have to avoid the third and the eighth rungs*,' Wizard's voice said. '*Drop-cages above them. The rest are okay.*'

'Gotcha.'

The Eight traversed the atrium quickly, swinging hand-over-hand down the length of the chamber, avoiding the two suspect handrungs, their feet dangling just a few feet above the crocs.

The little girl—Lily—moved in the middle of the group, clinging to the biggest trooper of the Nine, her hands clasped around his neck, while he swung from rung to rung.

The Low Tunnel

A long low tunnel led away from the atrium, heading into the mountain.

West and his team ran down it, all bent forward. Horus had been set free and she flew out in front of West, gliding down the passageway. Lily ran fully upright.

Water dripped from the low stone ceiling, but it hit their firemen's helmets and rolled off their curved backs, away from their eyes.

The tunnel was perfectly square—1.3 metres wide, 1.3 metres high. Curiously, these were exactly the same dimensions as the passageways inside the Great Pyramid at Giza.

Like the entry shaft earlier, this horizontal tunnel was intersected by three cross-shafts: only these were vertical and they spanned the entire width of the tunnel, cutting across it via matching holes in the ceiling and floor.

At one point, Lily's guardian, the large trooper named Big Ears, mis-stepped—landing on a trigger stone just before he leapt across one of the cross-shafts.

He knew his mistake immediately and stopped abruptly at the edge of the shaft—

—just as a gushing waterfall of swampwater came blasting out of the upper hole, forming a curtain of water in front of him, before disappearing into the matching hole in the floor.

Had he jumped, the rush of water would have taken him and Lily down into the unknown depths of the lower hole.

'Careful, brother dearest,' the team member in front of him said after the water had passed. She was the only woman in the group and a member of the crack Irish commando unit, the Sciathan Fhianoglach an Airm. Old call-sign: *Bloody Mary*. New one: *Princess Zoe*. Her brother, Big Ears, was also a member of the SFA.

She reached out and caught his hand and with her help he leapt over the cross-shaft and, with Lily between them, they took off after the others.

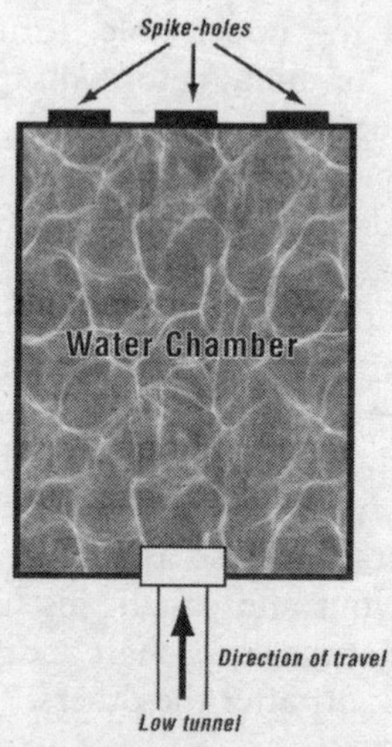

THE WATER CHAMBER

The Water Chamber (The First Gate)

The low tunnel opened onto a chamber the size of a small chapel. Incongruously, the floor of this chamber seemed to be made up of a lush carpet of green grass.

Only it wasn't grass.

It was algae. And beneath the algae, water—a rectangular pool of perfectly flat, undisturbed water.

And no crocs. Not a single one.

At the far end of the chamber—beyond the long placid pool, just above the waterline—were three low rectangular holes, burrowing into the far wall, each roughly the size of a coffin.

An object floated in the pool near the entrance. West recognised it instantly.

A human body. Dead.

The third and last Sudanese man.

Breathless, Wizard came up alongside West. 'Ah-ha, the First Gate. Ooh my, how clever. It's a false-floor chamber, just like we saw beneath the volcano in Uganda. Ah, Imhotep V. He always respected the classic traps . . .'

'Max . . .' West said.

'Ooh, and it's connected to a Solomon's Choice of spike holes: three holes, but only one is safe. This is some gate. I bet the ceiling is on rollers—'

'*Max*. You can write a book about it later. The state of the water?'

'Yes, sorry, ahem . . .' Wizard pulled a dipstick from a water testing kit on his belt and dipped it into the algae-covered pool. Its tip quickly turned a vivid red.

Wizard frowned. 'Extremely high levels of the bloodworm *Schistosoma mansoni*. Be careful, my friend, this water is beyond septic. It's teeming with *S. mansoni*.'

'What's that?' Big Ears asked from behind them.

'It's a microscopic bloodworm that penetrates the body through the skin or any exposed orifice, and then lays eggs in the bloodstream,' West answered.

Wizard added, 'Infection leads to spinal cord inflammation, lower-body paralysis and, ultimately, a cerebral aneurism and death. Ancient grave robbers went mad after entering places like this. They blamed angry gods and mystical curses, but in all likelihood it was the *S. mansoni*. But at these levels, gosh, this water will kill you in minutes. Whatever you do, Jack, don't fall in.'

'Okay then,' West said, 'the jump-stone configuration.'

'Right, right . . .' The older man hurriedly pulled a notebook from his jacket pocket, started flipping pages.

A 'false-floor chamber' was a fairly common booby trap in the ancient Egyptian world—mainly because it was very simple to build and exceedingly effective. It worked by concealing a safe pathway of stepping-stones beneath a false layer of liquid—which could be anything really: quicksand, boiling mud, tar, or, most commonly, bacteria-infected water.

You defeated a false-floor chamber by knowing the location of the stepping-stones in it.

Wizard found the page he was after. 'Okay. Here it is. Soter's Mine. Nubia. First Gate. Water chamber. Ah-ha.

Five by five grid: the sequence of the jump-stones is 1-3-4-1-3.'

'1-3-4-1-3,' West repeated. 'And which spike hole? I'm going to have to choose quickly.'

'Key of life,' Wizard said, consulting his notebook.

'Thanks. Horus, chest.' On command, the falcon immediately whizzed to West's chest and nestled in a pouch there.

West then turned to the assembled group behind him: 'Okay, folks, listen up. Everyone is to follow me closely. If our friend Imhotep V follows his usual modus operandi, as soon as I step on the first stepping-stone, things are gonna get frantic. Stay close because we won't have much time.'

West turned and contemplated the placid pool of algae-covered water. He bit his lip for a second. Then he took a deep breath.

Then *he jumped out into the chamber*, out over the surface of the pool, angling his leap way out to the left.

It was a long jump—he couldn't have just *stepped* that far.

Watching, Wizard gasped.

But rather than plunging into the deadly water, West landed lightly on the surface of the flat green pool—looking like he was walking on water.

His thick-soled boots stood an inch deep. He was standing on some kind of stepping-stone hidden underneath the algae-covered surface.

Wizard exhaled the breath he'd been holding.

Less obviously, West did, too.

But their relief was shortlived, for at that moment the trap mechanism of the water chamber came loudly and spectacularly to life.

The ceiling started lowering!

The *entire* ceiling of the chamber—a single great block of stone—began rumbling downwards, descending toward the flat green pool!

The intention was clear: in about 20 seconds it would reach the waterline and block all access to the three low rectangular holes at the far end of the room.

Which left only one option: leap across the concealed stepping-stones and get to the correct rectangular hole before the lowering ceiling hit the waterline.

'Everyone! Move! Follow me step for step!' West called.

And so, with the ceiling lowering loudly above him, he danced across the chamber with big all-or-nothing jumps, kicking up splashes with every landing. If he misjudged even one stepping-stone, he'd land in the water and it'd be game over.

His path was dictated by the grid-reference Wizard had given him: 1-3-4-1-3, on a five-by-five grid. It looked like this:

EXIT

1	2	3	4	5
1	2	3	4	5
1	2	3	4	5
1	2	3	4	5
1	2	3	4	5

ENTRY

Direction of travel

West came to the far wall of the chamber, while his team crossed it behind him. The wide ceiling of the water chamber kept lowering above them all.

He eyed the three rectangular holes cut into the end-wall. He'd seen these kinds of holes before: they were spike-holes.

But only one hole was safe, it led to the next level of the labyrinth. The other two would be fitted with sharp spikes that lanced down from the upper sides of the rectangular holes as soon as someone entered them.

Each of the spike-holes before him had a symbol carved above it:

Pick the right hole. While the ceiling lowered behind him, about to push his team into the water.

'No pressure, Jack,' he said to himself. 'Okay. Key of life, key of life . . .'

He saw the symbol above the left-hand hole:

Close, but no. It was the hieroglyph for magic. Imhotep V was trying to confuse the flustered, panicking explorer who found himself in this pressure-filled situation and didn't look closely enough.

'How's it coming, Jack?' Big Ears and the girl appeared beside him, joining him on the last stepping-stone.

The ceiling was low now, past halfway and still descending. There was no going back now. He had to pick the right hole.

'West . . .' someone urged from behind him.

Keeping his cool, West saw the symbol above the centre hole . . .

. . . and recognised it as the hieroglyph for *ankh*, or long life, otherwise known to the ancient Egyptians as 'the key of life'.

'It's this one!' he called.

But there was only one way to prove it.

He pulled his falcon from his pouch and handed it to the little girl. 'Hey, kiddo. Take care of Horus for me, just in case I'm wrong.'

Then he turned and crouch-dived forward, rolling *into* the centre hole, shutting his eyes momentarily, waiting for a half-dozen rusty spikes to spring down from its upper side and punch through his body—

—nothing happened.

He'd picked the right hole. Indeed, a tight cylindrical passage opened up in the darkness beyond this hole, bending vertically upward.

'It's this one!' He called back as he started ferrying his team into it, pulling them through.

Big Ears and Lily went first, then Wizard—

The ceiling was four feet off the water's surface.

Fuzzy and Zoe clambered up next.

The final two troopers in West's team rolled into the hole and last of all went West himself, disappearing into the rectangular hole just as the lowering stone ceiling rumbled past him and hit the surface of the water chamber with a resounding *boom*.

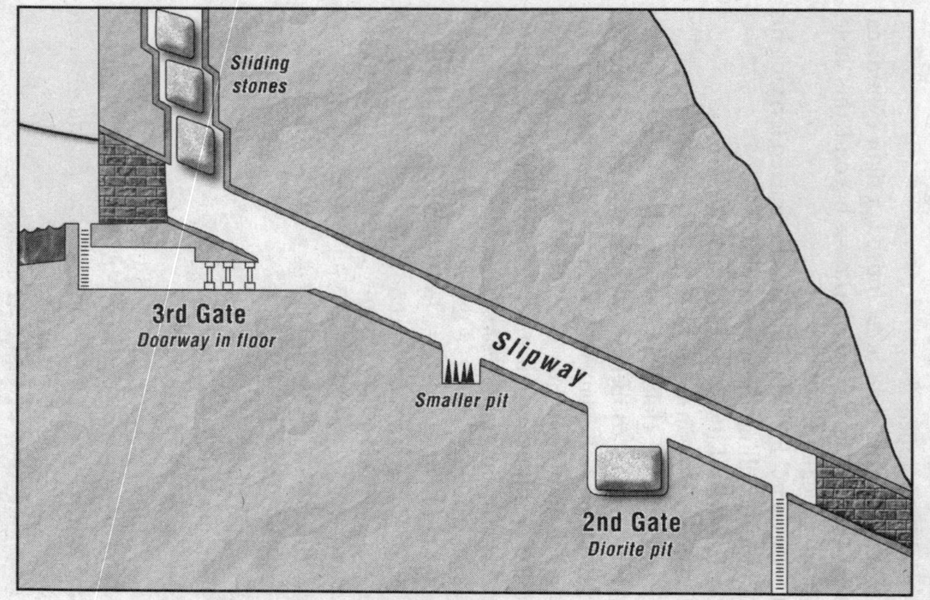
Sliding stones
3rd Gate
Doorway in floor
Slipway
Smaller pit
2nd Gate
Diorite pit

THE SLIPWAY

The Slipway and the Second Gate

The tight vertical passage from the spike-hole rose for about 50 feet before opening onto a long tunnel that sloped upward at a steep angle, boring up into the heart of the mountain.

West fired a new amber flare up into the tunnel.

It was the ancient slipway.

About the width of a car, the slipway was effectively a long straight stairway flanked by two flat stone trackways that abutted the walls of the tunnel. These trackways had once acted like primitive railway tracks: the ancient miners had slid giant containers filled with waste up and down them, aided by the hundreds of stone steps that lay in between them.

'Fuzz,' West said, peering up the tunnel. 'Distance?'

Fuzzy aimed a PAQ-40 laser rangefinder up into the darkness.

As he did so, West keyed his radio: 'Noddy, report.'

'*The Americans aren't here yet, Huntsman,*' Noddy's voice replied, '*but they're closing fast. Satellite image puts their advance choppers 50 klicks out. Hurry.*'

'Doing the best we can,' West said.

Wizard interrupted: 'Don't forget to tell Noddy that we'll be out of radio contact for the time the Warblers are initiated.'

'You hear that?'

'*I heard. Noddy, out.*'

Fuzzy's rangefinder beeped. 'I got empty space for . . . 150 metres.'

West grimaced. 'Why do I get the feeling it isn't empty at all.'

He was right.

The ascending slipway featured several traps: blasting waterfall-shafts and some ankle-breaking trap-holes.

But the Eight just kept running, avoiding the traps, until halfway up the inclined tunnel they came to the Second Gate.

The Second Gate was simple: a ten-foot-deep diorite pit that just fell away in front of them, with the ascending slipway continuing beyond it five yards away.

The lower reaches of the pit, however, had no *side* walls: it just had two wide yawning 8-foot-high passageways that hit the pit at right angles to the slipway. And who knew what came out of them . . .

'Diorite pit,' West said. 'Nothing cuts diorite except an even harder stone called *diolite*. Can't use a pick-axe to get yourself out.'

'Be careful,' Wizard said. 'The Callimachus Text says this Gate is connected to the next one. By crossing this one, we trigger the Third Gate's trap-mechanism. We're going to have to move fast.'

'That's okay,' West said. 'We're really quite good at *that*.'

They ended up crossing the pit by drilling steel rock-screws into the stone ceiling with pneumatic pressure-guns. Each rock-screw had a handgrip on it.

But as West landed on the ledge on the other side of

the pit, he discovered that the first step on that side was one large trigger stone. As soon as he touched it, the wide step immediately sunk a few inches *into* the floor—

—and *boom!* Suddenly the ground shook and everyone spun. Something large had dropped into the darkened tunnel up ahead of them. Then an ominous *rumbling* sound came from somewhere up there.

'*Shit!* The next Gate!' West called.

'Swear jar . . .' Lily said.

'Later,' West said. 'Now we *run*! Big Ears, grab her and follow me!'

The Third Gate

Up the steep slipway they ran, keeping to the stairs inside the rails.

The ominous rumbling continued to echo out from the darkness above them.

They kept running, straining up the slope, pausing only once to cross a five-foot-long spiked pit that blocked their way. But strangely, the stone railway tracks of the slipway still flanked this pit, so they all crossed it rather easily by taking a light dancing step on one of the side rails.

As he ran, West fired a flare into the darkness ahead of them—

—and thus revealed their menace.

'It's a sliding stone!' Wizard called. 'Guarding the Third Gate!'

A giant square-shaped block of granite—its shape filling the slipway perfectly and its leading face covered in vicious spikes—was sliding down the slipway, coming directly towards them!

Its method of death was clear: if it didn't push you into the spiked pit, it would slide over that pit on the stone runners and push you into the lower diorite pit . . . where it would fall in after you, crushing you, before whatever came out of the side passages made its big entrance.

Jesus.

Halfway between the sliding stone and the Eight, sunken into the angled floor of the slipway, was a doorway that opened onto a horizontal passage.

The Third and last Gate.

The Eight bolted up the slope.

The block gained speed—heading down the slope, propelled only by gravity and its immense bulk.

It was a race to the Gate.

West and Big Ears and the girl came to the doorway cut into the sloping floor, ducked inside it.

Wizard came next, followed by Fuzzy and Princess Zoe.

The sliding granite block slid across the top of the doorway just as the last two members of the team were approaching it.

'Stretch! Pooh! Hurry!' West called.

The first man—a tall thin fellow known as Stretch—dived, slithering in under the sliding stone a nanosecond before it completely covered the doorway.

The last man was too late.

He was easily the pudgiest and heaviest in the group. He had the olive skin and deep lush beard of a well-fed Arab sheik. His call-sign in his own country was the rather mighty *Saladin*, but here it was—

'Pooh Bear! No! *Nooo!*' the little girl screamed.

The stone slid over the doorway, and despite a final desperate lunge, Pooh Bear was cut off, left in the slipway, at the mercy of the great block.

'No . . . !' West called, hitting the underside of the sliding stone as it went by, sweeping the helpless Pooh away with it.

'Oh dear, poor Aziz . . .' Wizard said.

For a moment, no-one spoke.

The seven remaining members of the group stood in stunned silence. Lily started to sob quietly.

Then West blinked—something inside him clicking into action.

'Come on, everyone. We've got a job to do and to do it we have to keep moving. We knew this wasn't going to be a cakewalk. Hell, this is only the beginning—'

He turned then, gazing at the horizontal corridor awaiting them. At its far end was a ladder cut into the end-wall, a ladder that led up to a circular manhole cut into the ceiling.

White light washed down through the manhole.

Electric light.

Man-made light.

'—and it's about to get a lot worse. 'Cause we just caught up with the Europeans.'

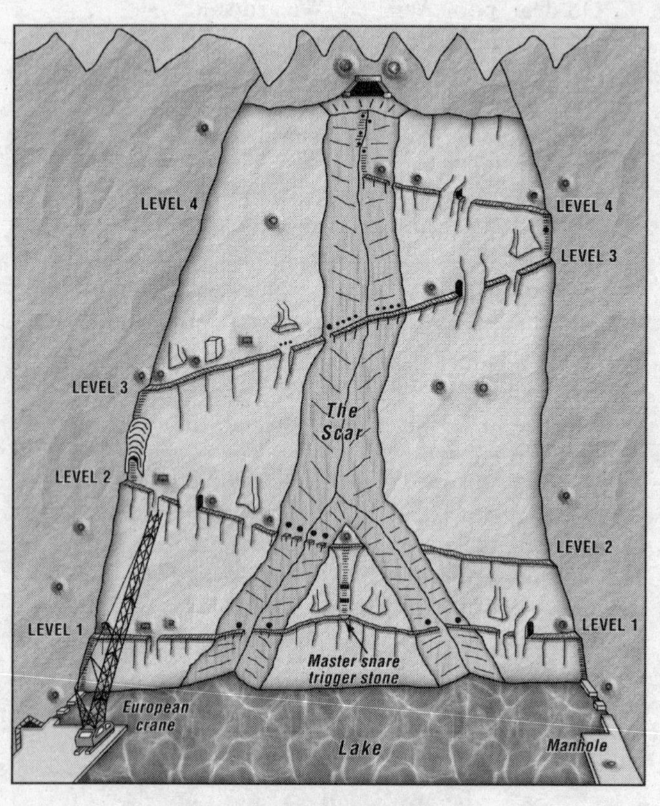

THE GRAND CAVERN

The Grand Cavern

West poked his head up through the manhole to behold an absolutely *awesome* sight.

He was at the base of a gargantuan cavern situated right in the belly of the mountain, a cavern easily 400 feet high.

A former rock quarry, it was roughly triangular in shape, wide at the base, tapering to a point at the top.

West was at the extreme south end of the cavern, while opposite him at the northern end, one hundred yards away, were the Europeans: with their floodlights, their troops . . . and a half-built crane.

Without doubt, however, the most striking feature of the cavern was its charcoal-coloured diorite rockface.

The rockface rose for the full height of the cavern, soaring into darkness beyond the reach of the Europeans' floodlights: a giant black wall.

As a quarry, the ancient Egyptians had mined this diorite seam systematically—cutting four narrow ledges out of the great wall, so that now the rockface looked like a 30-storey office building that had been divided into four step-like tiers. Each ledge ran for the entire width of the rockface, but they were perilously narrow: barely wide enough for two men to stand on side-by-side.

If that wasn't dangerous enough, Imhotep V had adapted this already-unusual structure into a masterpiece of protective engineering.

In short, he'd laid hundreds of traps all over it.

The four narrow ledges swung back and forth, each rising steadily before ending at a cut-into-the-rock ladder that led to the next level.

The only exception was the wall-ladder between the first and second levels: its ladder was situated in the exact centre of the cavern, equidistant from the northern and southern entrances, as if Imhotep V was encouraging a race between rival parties who arrived at the same time.

Since each narrow ledge was cut from pure diorite, a grappling hook would be useless—it could never get a purchase on the hard black stone. To get to the top, one had to traverse *every level* and defeat the traps on them.

And how many traps there were!

Small arched forts dotted the great wall at irregular intervals, spanning each of the ledges, concealing traps.

Hundreds of basketball-sized wall-holes littered the rockface, containing God-only-knew what kinds of lethal liquids. And where holes were not possible, long stone chutes slid snake-like down the rockface—looking a bit like upside-down chimneys that ended with open spouts ready to spew foul liquids over the unwary intruder.

Seeing the holes, West detected the distinctive odour of oil in the air—giving him a clue as to what might come out of some of them.

And there was the final feature.

The Scar.

This was a great uneven crevice that ran all the way down the rockwall, cutting across the ledges and the

rockface with indifference. It looked like a dry riverbed, only it ran vertically not horizontally.

At the top of the cavern, it was a single thick crevice, but it widened toward the base, where it forked into two smaller scars.

A trickling waterfall dribbled down its length, from some unknown source high up inside the mountain.

To cross the Scar on any of the four ledges meant either tip-toeing across a foot-wide mini-ledge or leaping a small void . . . in both cases in front of wall-holes or other shadowy recesses.

The trickling waterfall that rolled down the Scar fed a wide lake at the base of the rockface—a lake that now separated West and his team from the European force, a lake that was home to about sixty Nile crocodiles, all variously sleeping, sloshing or crawling over each other.

And at the very top of the colossal structure: a small stone doorway that led to this mine's fabled treasure:

The head of an ancient wonder.

Peering over the rim of the manhole, West gazed at the Europeans and their half-finished crane.

As he watched, dozens of men hauled more pieces of the giant crane into the cavern, handing them to engineers who then supervised the attachment of the pieces to the growing machine.

In the midst of this activity, West spied the leader of the European expedition, the Jesuit, del Piero, standing perfectly erect, his hands clasped behind his back. At 68, del Piero had thinning slicked-down black hair, ghost-like grey eyes, deep creases on his face, and the severe expression of a man who had spent his life frowning at people.

But it was the tiny figure standing next to del Piero who seized West's attention.

A small boy.

With black hair and even blacker eyes.

West's eyes widened. He had seen this boy before. Ten years ago . . .

The boy stood at del Piero's side with his hands clasped behind his back, mimicking the imperious stance of the old Jesuit.

He seemed to be about Lily's age.

No, West corrected himself, *he was exactly Lily's age*.

West's gaze shifted back to the crane.

It was a clever plan.

Once finished, the crane would lift the Europeans up over the first ledge and land them on the second.

Not only did this allow them to avoid about ten traps, it also enabled them to avoid the most dangerous trap of all in this cavern:

The Master Snare.

West knew about it from the Callimachus Text—which he suspected del Piero and the Europeans could have had a Vatican copy of. That said, they could have become aware of it from other ancient texts written about Imhotep V.

While the other Imhoteps had their own signature traps, Imhotep V had invented the Master Snare, a trap that was triggered in advance of the system's innermost vault—thus making the final leg of the journey a matrix of trap-beating versus time. Or as Wizard liked to say, 'Beating booby traps is one thing; beating them against the clock is another.'

That said, the Master Snare was not so crude as to

destroy the entire trap system. Like most of Imhotep's traps, it would reset itself to be used again.

No, in most cases the Master Snare left you in a do-or-die predicament: if you were good enough, you could take the treasure. If you weren't, you would die.

The Callimachus Text stated that the trigger stone for the Master Snare of this system lay in the very centre of the first level, at the base of the ladder there.

Wizard appeared at West's side, peered out from the manhole. 'Mmm, a crane. With that, del Piero and his men will avoid triggering the Master Snare. It'll give them more time up in the Holy of Holies. Very clever.'

'No, it's not clever,' West said flatly. 'It's against *the rules*.'

'The rules?'

'Yes, the rules. This is all part of a contest that has been held for the last 4,000 years, between Egyptian architects and grave-robbers. And this contest has an honour code—we attack, Imhotep V defends. But by skipping a major trigger stone, del Piero is cheating. He's also showing his weakness.'

'Which is?'

'He doesn't believe he can beat the Master Snare.' West smiled. 'But we can.'

West dropped back down to the base of the ladder, turned to his team of six.

'Okay, kids. This is what we've trained for. Leapfrog formation, remember your places. Lily, you're with me in the middle. Fuzzy, you're the point for the first disable. Then Big Ears, Zoe and Stretch. Wizard, you'll have to cover for Pooh Bear, who was going to cover the fifth. I'll trigger the Master Snare.'

Everyone nodded, game faces on.

West turned to Wizard. 'Okay, Professor. You got those Warblers ready? Because as soon as we break cover, those Europeans are going to open fire.'

'Ready to go, Huntsman,' Wizard said, holding up a large gun-like object that looked like an M-203 grenade launcher. 'I'll need maybe four seconds before you can make a break for it.'

'I'll give you three.'

Then they all put their hands into the middle, team-style, and called '*Kamaté!*', after which they broke, with Wizard leading the way up the ladder, venturing into the fray . . .

Wizard popped up out of the manhole, his grenade launcher raised. He fired it three times, each shot emitting a loud puncture-like phump.

Phump!-Phump!-Phump!

The rounds that burst out of the grenade launcher *looked* like grenades, but they weren't grenades—fat and round and silver, they fanned out to three corners of the giant cavern, little red pilot lights on them blinking.

The Europeans heard the first shot and by the third had located Wizard.

A French sniper on the cabin of the crane swung his rifle round, drew a bead on Wizard's forehead, and fired.

His bullet went haywire.

It peeled downwards almost as soon as it left the barrel of the Frenchman's rifle—where it struck an unfortunate croc square in the head, killing it.

The 'Warblers' at work.

The three odd-looking silver rounds that Wizard had fired were more formally known as Closed Atmospheric Field Destabilisers (Electromagnetic), but everyone just called them 'Warblers'.

One of Wizard's rare *military* inventions, the Warblers created a magnetic field that disrupted the flight of high-subsonic metal objects—specifically bullets—creating a gunfire-free zone.

Wizard, one of the leading experts in electromagnetic applications, had sold the revolutionary technology to Raytheon in 1988 for $25 million, most of which went to the New York venture capital company that had bankrolled his research. Walking away with only $2 million, Wizard had sworn to never work again with venture capitalists.

Ironically, the US Army—as always, thinking it knew better—ordered Raytheon to rework the Warbler system, creating *huge* problems that had stalled the program for over fifteen years. It had yet to enter active service.

Naturally, Wizard—a Canadian, not an American—had kept a few working prototypes for himself, three of which he was now using.

The Six burst out from their manhole, one after the other, moving fast, heading for the nearest embedded ladder that led up to the first level.

As he ran in the middle of the group, West set Horus free and the little peregrine falcon soared above the forward-moving group.

The Jamaican, Fuzzy, led the way—dancing along a narrow stone walkway that lay flush against the right-hand wall of the cavern. Pushed up against the walkway's low edge was a crush of crocodiles.

Fuzzy held in his hands a lightweight titanium bar welded in the shape of an X.

Halfway along its length, the walkway ended briefly at a small void. In the centre of this void was a raised square stepping-stone that also stood flush against the wall and an inch above the croc-filled water.

Cut into the stone wall immediately *above* this stepping-stone was a dark hole about a metre in diameter.

Fuzzy didn't miss a beat.

He leapt from the walkway onto the stepping-stone—

—and immediately heard a rush of water from up inside the wall-hole, accompanied by a low crocodilian growl—

—at which point he jammed his titanium X-bar into the wall-hole and hit a switch on the bar.

Thwack!

The X-shaped bar expanded with a powerful springloaded motion, so that suddenly it was wedged tightly in the mouth of the circular wall-hole.

Not a second too soon.

An instant later, a burst of water gushed out of the wall-hole, immediately followed by the jaws of a massive crocodile that slammed at tremendous speed *into* the X-bar!

The croc roared angrily but its jaws were caught against the X-bar, unable to get past. The rush of water sprayed all around Fuzzy, but didn't knock him over.

'Trap One! Clear!' he called.

The others were already there with him, moving fast, and as Fuzzy kept watch over the writhing croc trapped in the wall-hole, they danced safely by.

Now Big Ears went ahead, racing forward to disable the next trap, while the rest of them followed, step-jumping past Fuzzy, heading for the ladder at the base of the giant rockface.

The Europeans could only watch in helpless amazement as the Seven raced along the opposite wall to the base of the rockface.

Alone among them, Francisco del Piero eyed West—eyed him with an ice-cold gaze—watched him running with Lily at his side, gripping her hand.

'Well, well, well,' del Piero said. 'Who have you got there, Captain West . . .?'

The Seven hit the base of the rockface.

The building-sized wall towered above them, black as the night.

Big Ears had already done his work, disabling two hand-chopping traps halfway up the rock-cut ladder.

Now Princess Zoe leapfrogged ahead. She moved with great athleticism, easily the match of the men. About 30, she had shoulder-length blonde hair, freckles, and the luminous blue eyes that only Irish girls possess.

Onto the First Level she flew, raising two aerosol cans as she did so, filling two wall-holes with a dense expanding foam. Whatever evils had been in those wall-holes were caught by the foam and neutralised.

No sooner had she done this than she was leapfrogged by the seventh member of the group, the tall, thin trooper named Stretch. Once known as Archer, he had a long, sanguine, bony face. He hailed from the deadly Israeli sniper unit, the Sayaret Matkal.

Stretch arrived at the right-side arm of the Scar, where he triggered a huge trap from a safe distance: a bronze cage that fell out of a dark recess in the Scar and clattered down to the lake.

Had any of the team been walking on the foot-wide mini-ledge in front of the recess, the cage would have caught them and taken them down to the lake, to be either eaten by the crocs or drowned under the weight of the cage itself.

★

Now West and Lily took the lead, crossing the mini-ledge across the Scar, stepping out onto the centre section of the First Level.

Here they found the trigger stone for the Master Snare at the base of the wall-ladder leading up to Level 2. West made to step on it—

'Captain West!'

West froze in mid-stride, turned.

Del Piero and his troops were staring up at him from the base of their half-finished crane, holding their useless guns stupidly in their hands.

'Now, Captain West, please think about this before you do it!' del Piero called. 'Is it *really* necessary? Even if you trigger the Master Snare, you are only postponing the inevitable. If you do somehow get the Piece, we'll kill you when you try to leave this mountain. And if you don't, my men will just return after the Snare has run its course and we will find the head of the Colossus and the piece of the Capstone it contains. Either way, Captain, we get the Piece.'

West's eyes narrowed.

Still he didn't speak.

Del Piero tried Wizard. 'Max. Max. My old colleague, my old friend. Please. Reason with your rash young protégé.'

Wizard just shook his head. 'You and I chose different paths a long time ago, Francisco. You do it your way. We'll do it ours. Jack. Hit the trigger.'

West just stared evenly down at del Piero.

'With pleasure,' he said.

And with that he *stomped* on the trigger stone set into the floor at his feet, activating the Master Snare.

★

The spectacle of Imhotep's Master Snare going off was sensational.

Blasting streams of black crude oil shot out from the hundreds of holes that dotted the cavern: holes in the rockface and its sidewalls.

Dozens of oil waterfalls flowed down the rockface, cascading over its four levels. Black fluid flooded out from the sidewalls, falling a clear 200 feet down them into the croc lake.

The crocs went nuts, scrambling over each other to get away from it—disappearing into some little holes in the walls or massing on the far side of the lake.

In some places on the great tiered rockface, oil came *spurting* out of the wall, forced out of small openings by enormous internal pressure.

Worst of all, a *river* of the thick black stuff came pouring down the main course of the Scar, a vertical cascade that tumbled down the vertical riverbed, overwhelming the trickle of water that had been running down it.

And then the clicking started.

The clicking of many stone-striking mechanisms mounted above the wall-holes.

Striking mechanisms made of flint.

Striking mechanisms that were designed to create sparks and . . .

Just then, a spark from one of the flints high up on the left sidewall touched the crude oil flowing out from the wall-hole an inch beneath it.

The result was stunning.

The superthin waterfall of oil became a superthin waterfall of *fire* . . .

. . . then this flaming waterfall hit the oil-stained lake at the base of the cavern and set it alight.

The lake blazed with flames.

The entire cavern was illuminated bright yellow.

The crocs screamed, clawing over each other to get to safety.

Then more oilfalls caught alight—some on the sidewalls, others on the rockface, and finally, the great sludge waterfall coming down the Scar—until the entire Great Cavern looked like Hell itself, lit by a multitude of blazing waterfalls.

Thick black smoke billowed everywhere—smoke which had no escape.

This was Imhotep's final masterstroke.

If the fire and the traps didn't kill you, smoke inhalation would, especially in the highly prized upper regions of the cavern.

'Fools!' del Piero raged. Then to his men: 'What are you standing there for! Finish the crane! You have until they get back to the Second Level to do so!'

West's team was now moving faster than ever, leapfrogging each other beautifully amid the subterranean inferno.

Up the rockface they went, first to the left along the Second Level, crossing the left arm of the Scar before the thick fire-waterfall got there, dodging wall-holes, jumping gaps in the ledge, nullifying the traps inside the arched forts that straddled the narrow walkway.

Droplets of fire were now raining down all around them—spray from the oilfalls—but the fiery orange drops just hit their firemen's helmets and rolled off their backs.

Then suddenly West's team ran past the unfinished

arm of the Europeans' crane and, for the first time that day, they were in front.

In the lead in this race.

Up the wall-ladder at the end of Level 2, on to Level 3, where they ran to the right, avoiding some chute traps on the way and coming to the fiery body of the Scar. Here West fired an extendable aluminium awning into the Scar's flame-covered surface with his pressure-gun.

The awning opened lengthways like a fan, causing the fire-waterfall to flow *over* it, sheltering the mini-ledge. The team bolted across the superthin ledge.

Then it was up another ladder to the Fourth Level—the second-highest level—and suddenly six 10-ton *block boulders* started raining down on them from way up in the darkness above the giant rockface.

The great blocks boomed as they landed on the diorite ledge of Level 4 and tumbled down the rest of the massive tiered wall.

'Get off the ladder!' West yelled to the others. 'You can't dodge the boulders if you're on it—'

Too late.

As West called his warning, a boulder smacked horribly into the last man on the ladder, Fuzzy. The big Jamaican was hurled back down the rockface.

He landed heavily on the Third Level—setting off a trap of spraying flaming oil (it looked like a flamethrower) but he snap-rolled away from the tongue of fire—in the same motion avoiding a second boulder as it slammed down on the ledge an inch away from his eyes!

His roll took him off the ledge, but Fuzzy managed to clasp onto the edge with his fingertips, avoiding the 30-foot drop down to Level 2.

★

The final wall-ladder was embedded in the centre of the Scar itself, flanked by two fiery waterfalls.

Wizard erected another awning over the mini-ledge leading to the ladder, then allowed West and Lily to rush past him.

'Remember,' Wizard said, 'if you can't get the Piece itself, you must at least note the inscription carved into it. Okay?'

'Got it.' West turned to Lily. 'It's just us from here.'

They crossed the mini-ledge, came to the rough stone-carved ladder.

Drops of fire rained down it, bouncing off their firemen's helmets.

Every second or third rung of the ladder featured a dark gaping wall-hole of some kind, which West nullified with 'expand-and-harden' foam.

'Jack! Look out! More drop-stones!' Wizard called.

West looked up. 'Whoa shit . . . !'

A giant drop-boulder slicked with oil and blazing with flames came roaring out of a recess in the ceiling directly above the ladder and came free-falling towards him and Lily.

'Swear jar . . .' Lily said.

'I'll have to owe you.'

West quickly yanked an odd-looking pistol from his belt—it looked like a flare gun, with a grossly oversized barrel. An M-225 handheld grenade launcher.

Without panic, he fired it up at the giant boulder freefalling towards them.

The grenade shot upwards.

The boulder fell downwards.

Then they hit and—*BOOM!*—the falling boulder exploded in a star-shaped shower of shards and stones, spraying outward like a firecracker, its pieces sailing *out and around* West and Lily on the ladder!

West and Lily scaled the rest of the ladder, flanked by flames, until finally they were standing at the top of the Scar, at the top of the giant rockface, past all the traps.

They stood before the trapezoidal door at the peak of the fire-filled cavern.

'Okay, kiddo,' he said. 'You remember everything we practised?'

She loved it when he called her kiddo.

'I remember, sir,' she said.

And so with a final nod to each other, they entered the holy inner sanctum of Imhotep V's deadly labyrinth.

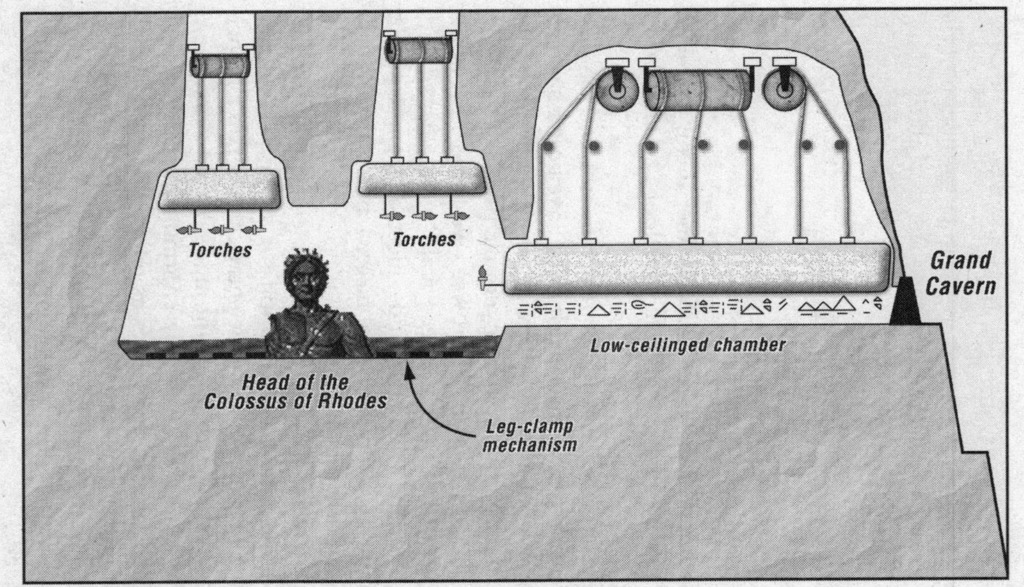

THE INNERMOST CAVE

The Innermost Cave

And still the traps didn't stop.

A wide low-ceilinged chamber met them: its ceiling was maybe two metres off the floor . . . *and getting lower.*

The chamber was about thirty metres wide and its entire ceiling was lowering! It must have been one single piece of stone and right now it was descending on the dark chamber like a giant hydraulic press.

If they'd had time to browse, West and Lily would have seen that the chamber's walls were *covered* with images of the Great Pyramid—most of them depicting the famous pyramid being pierced by a ray of light shooting down from the Sun.

But it was what lay beyond the entry chamber that seized West and Lily's attention.

At the far end of the wide entry chamber, in a higher-ceilinged space, stood a giant mud-covered *head.*

The head was absolutely enormous, at least sixteen feet high, almost three times as tall as West.

Despite the layer of mud all over it, its features were stunning: the handsome Greek face, the imperious eyes, and the glorious golden crown fitted above the forehead.

It was the head of a colossal bronze statue.

The most famous bronze statue in history.
It was the head of the Colossus of Rhodes.

Right in front of it, however, separating the great bronze head from the low-ceilinged entry hall, was a moat of perfectly calm crude oil that completely surrounded the Colossus' head.

The great god-sized head rose up from this oil pool like a creature arising from primordial slime. It sat on no holy pedestal, no ceremonial island, no nothing.

Suspended *above* the pool was an extra problem: several flaming torches now blazed above it, lit by ancient flint-striking mechanisms. They hung from brackets attached to the end of the entry hall's lowering ceiling—meaning that very soon they would touch the oil pool . . . and ignite it . . . cutting off all access to the Colossus' head.

'Time to run,' West said.

'You bet, sir,' Lily replied.

They ran.

Down the length of the entry hall, beneath its wide lowering ceiling.

Smoke now began to enter the chamber from outside, creating a choking haze.

They came to the oil moat.

'If Callimachus is correct, it won't be too deep,' West said.

Without missing a step, he strode into the pool—plunging to his waist in the thick goopy oil.

'Jump,' he said to Lily, who obliged by leaping into his arms.

They waded across the moat of oil—West striding with Lily on his shoulders—while above them the fiery torches continued their descent toward the pool, the entry hall's ceiling coming ever lower.

With his exit fast diminishing, Jack West Jr stopped a few yards short of the head of the Colossus of Rhodes.

It towered over him, impassive, covered in centuries of mud.

Each of its eyes was as big as Lily was.

Its nose was as big as he was.

Its golden crown glimmered despite its mud coating, while three golden pendants hung from a chain around its neck.

The pendants.

They were each about the size of a fat encyclopaedia and trapezoidal in shape. Embedded in the exact centre of each pendant's upper surface was a round diamond-like crystal.

On the front slanting side of each pendant was a series of intricately carved symbols: an unknown language that looked kind of like cuneiform.

It was an ancient language, a dangerous language, a language known only to a chosen few.

West gazed at the three golden pendants.

One of them was the Second Piece of the Golden Capstone, the mini-pyramid that had once sat atop the Great Pyramid at Giza.

Comprised of seven horizontal pieces, the Golden Capstone was perhaps the greatest archaeological artefact in history—and in the last month, it had become the subject of the greatest worldwide treasure hunt of all time. This piece, the Second, was the segment of the Golden Capstone that sat one place below the fabled First Piece, the small pyramid-shaped pinnacle of the Capstone.

Three pendants.

But only one was the correct one.

And choosing the correct one, West knew, was a do-or-die proposition that all depended on Lily.

He had to take one more step forward to reach them and that meant triggering the final trap.

'Okay, kiddo. You ready to do your thing? For my sake, I hope you are.'

'I'm ready,' Lily said grimly.

And with that, West stepped forward and—

—*chunk!*—

—an unseen mechanism *beneath* the surface of the oil pool clamped tightly around his legs, pinning them in an ancient pair of submerged stone stocks.

West was now immobile . . . within easy reach of the three pendants.

'Okay, Lily,' he said. 'Go. Make your choice. And stay off me, just in case you're wrong.'

She leapt from his arms, onto the half-submerged collarbone of the great statue just as—

Whoosh!

A huge 10-ton drop-stone *directly above* West came alight with flames and . . . lurched on its chains!

Imhotep V's final trap in the quarry mine was what is known as a 'reward trap'. It allowed the rightful claimant to the Second Piece to have it, *if* they could identify the correct one.

Choose the right 'pendant' and the flaming drop-stone remained in place and the submerged leg-clamps opened. Choose the wrong one, and the drop-stone fell, crushing you *and* igniting the oil pool.

Lily stared at the strange text on each pendant. It looked extremely odd, this little girl evaluating the incredibly ancient symbols.

West watched her, tense, expectant . . . and suddenly worried.

'Can you read it?' he asked.

'It's different to the other inscriptions I've read . . .' she said distractedly.

'*What*—?' West blanched.

Abruptly Lily's eyes lit up in understanding. 'Ahh, I get it. Some of the words are written *vertically* . . .'

Then her eyes narrowed . . . and focused. They blazed in the firelight, scanning the ancient symbols closely now.

To West, it seemed as if she had just entered a trance-like state.

Then the flaming drop-stone above him creaked again. He snapped to look up.

The torch-riddled ceiling above the moat kept lowering.

Smoke was now billowing into this area from the main cavern.

West swivelled to see the entry chamber behind him getting smaller and smaller . . .

Lily was still in her trance, reading the runes intently.

'*Lily* . . .'

'Just a second . . .'

'We don't have a second, honey.' He eyed the hazy smoke-filled chamber closing behind them. The smoke was getting denser.

Then, abruptly, one of the flaming torches attached to the descending ceiling dislodged from its bracket . . .

. . . and fell.

Down toward the oil moat where West stood helpless!

'Oh, God no—' was all he had time to breathe.

The flaming torch dropped through the air, into the oil moat—

—before, six inches off the surface, it was plucked from the air by the swooping shape of Horus, his falcon.

The little bird gripped the flaming torch in its talons, before dropping it safely in the closing entry hall.

'Why don't you leave it to the last second next time, bird,' West said.

Sitting now, Horus just returned his gaze, as if to say: *Why don't you stop getting into stupid predicaments like this, human.*

In the meantime, Lily's eyes glinted, staring now at the symbols on the rightmost of the three pendants:

She read in a low voice:

'*Beware. Atone.*
Ra's implacable Destroyer cometh,
And all will cry out in despair,
Unless sacred words be uttered.'

Rama
Rath

Then Lily blinked and returned to the present.

'It's this one!' she said, reaching down for the pendant she had just read.

West said, 'Wait, are you sure—'

But she moved too quickly and lifted the golden pendant from its shallow recess on the Colossus' neck.

The flaming drop-stone lurched.

West snapped up and winced, waiting for the end.

But the drop-stone didn't fall and—*chunk!*—suddenly his legs were released from their submerged bonds.

Lily had picked the right one.

She jumped happily back into his arms, holding the heavy golden trapezoid like a newborn baby. She threw him a winning smile:

'That felt really weird.'

'It looked really weird,' West said. 'Well done, kiddo. Now, let's blow this joint.'

The Outward Charge

Back they ran.

West charged through the waist-deep oil pool, pushing hard with every stride, the torch-edged ceiling descending above him.

They hit the floor of the entry hall as the lowering ceiling hit 70 centimetres in height.

The smoke coming in from outside was now choking, dense.

Lily crouch-ran across the wide low-ceilinged space, while Horus swooped through the haze.

West was the slowest, scrambling on all fours, slipping every which way in his oil-slicked boots, until at the very end of the chamber, as the ceiling became unbearably low, he dived onto his belly, sliding headfirst for the entire last 4 metres, emerging just as the ceiling hit the floor with a resounding *boom* and closed off the Colossus' chamber.

Wizard was waiting for them outside on Level 4.

'Hurry! Del Piero's men have almost finished their crane—they'll be on Level 2 any second now!'

Level 4

The other members of the team—Big Ears, Stretch and Princess Zoe—were also waiting on Level 4, covering the first three traps on the way back down.

When he reached them, West handed Big Ears the priceless golden trapezoid, which the big man placed inside a sturdy backpack.

Down the giant rockwall they went, again in leapfrog formation, sliding down ladders, dancing across booby-trapped ledges, all the while dodging flaming waterfalls and fire-rain. Giant drop-stones now fell constantly from the upper regions of the cave, tumbling dangerously down the rockface, blasting through the smoke.

Level 3

West scooped up Fuzzy as they came to Level 3. 'Come on, old friend,' he said, hoisting the big Jamaican onto his shoulder.

They ran down the sloping ledgeway, across the face of Level 3, covering their mouths to avoid inhaling the smoke.

The Europeans had almost finished their crane by now. It was lined with armed men, all waiting for the last piece of the crane to be screwed into place, thus giving them access to Level 2—where they would cut off West and his team.

The last piece of the crane fell into place.

The Europeans moved.

Level 2

West led the way now, leaping down onto Level 2 ahead of Fuzzy, where he landed like a cat—

—and was confronted by a crossbow-wielding French paratrooper, the first member of the European force to step off the now-finished crane.

Quick as a gunslinger, West drew a Glock pistol from one of his thigh holsters, raised it and fired it at the French trooper at point-blank range.

And for some reason *his* bullet defied Wizard's Warblers and slammed into the Frenchman's chest, dropping him where he stood.

No blood sprayed.

In fact, the man didn't die.

Rubber bullet.

West fired another rubber round—similar to those used by police in riot situations—at the next French paratrooper on the nearby crane, just as the Frenchman pulled the trigger on his crossbow.

West ducked and the arrow-bolt missed high, while his own shot hit its mark, sending the French commando sailing off the crane and into the lake below, still crowded with panicking crocodiles.

Screams. Splashing. Crunching. Blood.

'Move!' West called to his crew. 'Before they switch to rubber rounds, too.'

Now everyone in his team had their guns drawn and as they passed the crane's arm, they traded shots with the two dozen French paratroopers on it.

But they got past the crane just as fifteen French paratroopers came streaming off it, and headed down to Level 1—

Level 1

—where they saw the Europeans' *second* effort to cut them off.

Down on the ground level, a team of German Army engineers had almost finished building a temporary floating bridge across the croc lake—in an attempt to get to West's manhole entrance on the southern side of the cavern before West and his team did.

They had two segments of the bridge to put in place, segments that were being brought across the half-finished bridge right now.

'Go! Go! Go!' West called.

The flaming cavern—already alive with smoke and flames and falling boulders—was now zinging with crossbow bolts and rubber bullets.

The aluminium crossbow bolts were only mildly affected by the Warblers—they flew wildly, but their first few metres of flight were still deadly.

West's team was running across Level 1, racing the bridge-builders on the ground level.

Big Ears carried Lily. West helped Fuzzy. Princess Zoe and Stretch fired at the paratroopers behind them, while Wizard—coughing against the smoke—led the way, nullifying the traps ahead of them. Above them, Horus soared through the hazy black air.

They had just reached the ladder at the far right-hand end of Level 1 when suddenly a stray French crossbow bolt hit Big Ears in the shoulderblade, knocking him off his feet—causing him to stumble forward onto his face and . . .

. . . fall off the edge of the ledge, dropping Lily over it!

Lily fell.

Thirty feet.

Into the oily water near the base of the ladder, not far from the walkway that hugged the right-hand wall of the cavern.

By chance she landed in both a croc-free and a fire-free space.

But not for long. The crocs weren't far away, and no sooner had her splash subsided than a large one saw her and charged straight for her.

Big Ears was dangling over the edge of Level 1 directly above her, helpless. 'I can't get to her!'

'I can!' another voice called.

West.

He never missed a step.

Running full tilt, he just leapt off the edge of Level 1 and sailed in a high curving arc through the air toward the croc-lake below.

The big bull croc that was charging at Lily never saw him coming. West landed square on its back, a mere foot away from Lily, and the two of them—man and croc—went under the black water's surface with a great splash.

They surfaced a second later, with the frenzied croc bucking like a bronco and West on its back, gripping it in a fierce headlock.

The croc growled and roared, before—*crrrrack*—West brutally twisted its neck, breaking it. The croc went limp. West jumped clear, whisking Lily out of the water and onto the walkway flanking the lake not a moment before six more crocs attacked the carcass of the dead one.

'Th . . . thanks,' Lily gasped, wiping oil from her face and still shaking.

'Anytime, kiddo. Anytime.'

Ground Level

The rest of the team joined them on the walkway.

Now Fuzzy *and* Big Ears were injured. But they were still mobile, helped along by Zoe and Wizard, while West and Lily were covered by Stretch.

They all hopscotched over the stepping-stone and its wall-hole—inside which the trapped croc still writhed behind Fuzzy's X-bar—and dashed for their manhole, just as the German engineers brought the final piece of their temporary bridge into place.

Forty armed German troops waited for the bridge to be completed. Some fired wayward crossbow shots at the Seven, while others jammed newly found rubber-bullet magazines into their MP-7 sub-machine guns and started firing.

West and Lily came to the manhole. In they went. The others followed, while Stretch covered them all. Big Ears went in . . . then Fuzzy . . . Wizard . . . Zoe and . . .

. . . the final piece of the bridge fell into place . . .

. . . as Stretch jumped into the manhole and the army of Germans charged over the bridge and the chase through the slipway system began.

The Ante-Chamber (Outward Bound)

Being the last person in a retreating formation sucks. You're covering the rear, the bad guys are right on your ass, and no matter how loyal your team is, there's always the risk of being left behind.

By the time the tall and lanky Stretch had landed in the long ante-chamber beneath the manhole, the others were already entering the slipway at the far end.

'Stretch! Move it!' West called from the slanted doorway. 'Zoe's gone ahead to trigger another sliding stone to run interference for us!'

As if to confirm that, a familiar *whump* echoed out from the upper regions of the slipway, followed by the rumble of a new sliding stone grinding down the slope.

Stretch bolted toward the slipway—as a dozen wraith-like figures rained down the manhole behind him, entering the ante-chamber.

Gunfire.

Rapid-fire.

Freed from the effects of the Warblers, the Europeans were now gladly employing live ammunition.

Stretch was done for.

He was still five steps away from the safety of the slipway when the first few Germans behind him went down in a hail of withering fire.

For just as they had fired, so too had someone else, someone standing guard in the doorway to the slipway.

Pooh Bear.

Holding a Steyr-AUG assault rifle.

The heavy-bearded Arab—who had last been seen getting cut off behind the previous sliding stone—waved Stretch on.

'Come on, Israeli!' Pooh Bear growled. 'Or I'll gladly leave you behind!'

Stretch staggered the last few steps into the slipway and past Pooh Bear just as a dozen bullet-sparks exploded out all around the stone doorway.

'I thought you were dead,' Stretch said, panting.

'Please! It'll take more than a *rock* to kill Aziz al Anzar al Abbas,' Pooh Bear said in his deep gruff voice. 'My legs may be stout, but they can still run with some speed. I simply outran the rock and took cover in that spiked pit, and let it pass over me. Now move!'

The Slipway

Down the slipway the Eight ran, dancing around the edge of the small spiked pit—the air filled with the rumble of the new sliding stone—then over the diorite pit that was the Second Gate. The cracked and broken remains of the first sliding stone from before lay strewn about its base.

The Eight swung over the diorite pit, hanging from the steel handholds they'd drilled into the rock ceiling earlier.

'Noddy!' West called into his radio mike when he landed safely on the other side. 'Do you copy?'

There was no answer from Noddy, their man guarding the swamp entrance.

'It's not the Warblers!' Wizard called. 'There must be someone jamming us—'

He was cut off by six Germans who raced into the slipway and opened fire—

—not a moment before the large spike-riddled sliding stone loomed up behind them, rumbling over the doorway to the ante-chamber!

The six Germans ran down the slipway, chased by the sliding stone.

When they came to the spiked pit, one panicked and lost his balance and fell in, chest-first—impaling himself on the vicious spikes sticking up from the stone pit.

The others got to the larger diorite pit of the Second Gate too late.

Two managed to grip West's steel handholds for a couple of swings before all five of the remaining German troops were either impaled on the spikes on the leading edge of the sliding stone or jumped into the diorite pit to avoid those spikes just as—*whoosh!*—a blast of churning white water shot across the pit, sweeping them away, screaming.

West's team raced ahead now. The sliding stone had given them the lead they needed.

Having been blocked off momentarily behind it, and not having experienced the slipway before, the remainder of the German troops were more cautious.

West's team increased their lead.

They swept down the tight vertical shaft to the spike-hole where West had correctly chosen the key of life, the ceiling of the water chamber having reset itself . . .

Still no radio contact with Noddy.

Across the water chamber, its stepping-stones still submerged beneath the algae-covered pool . . .

Still no radio contact.

Crouch-running down the length of the low tunnel, leaping over its cross-shafts . . .

And finally they came to the croc-filled atrium with its hand-rungs in the ceiling and the vertical entry shaft at its far end.

'Noddy! Are you out there?' West called into his radio. 'I repeat, Noddy, can you hear me—'

Finally he got a reply.

'*Huntsman! Hurry!*' Noddy's Spanish-accented voice replied suddenly in his earpiece, loud and hard. '*Get out! Get out now! The Americans are here!*'

Two minutes later, West emerged from the vertical entry shaft and found himself once again standing in the mud of the mountain swamp.

Noddy was waiting for him, visibly agitated, looking anxiously westward. 'Hurry, hurry!' he said. 'They're coming—'

Shlat!

Noddy's head exploded, bursting like a smashed pumpkin, hit by a high-speed .50 calibre sniper round. His body froze for a brief moment before it dropped to the ground with a dull smack.

West snapped to look westward.

And he saw them.

Saw two-dozen high-speed swampboats sweeping out of the reeds some three hundred metres away, covered by two Apache helicopters. Each swampboat held maybe ten special forces troops, members of the CIEF.

Then suddenly on one of them the muzzle of a Barrett sniper rifle flashed—

—West ducked—

—and a split second later the bullet sizzled past his ears.

'Get Stretch up here!' he yelled as his team emerged from the hole in the mud.

Stretch was pushed up.

'Give me some sniping, Stretch,' West said. 'Enough to get us out of here.'

Stretch pulled a vicious-looking Barrett M82A1A sniper rifle off his back, took a crouching pose and fired back at the American hovercrafts.

Crack. Sizzle.

And two hundred metres away, the American sniper was hurled clear off his speeding swampboat, his head snapping backwards in a puff of red.

Everybody was now up and out of the hole.

'Right,' West said. 'We make for our swamprunners. Triple time.'

The Eight raced across the swamp, once again running on foot through the world of mud.

They came to their swampboats, hidden in a small glade, covered by camouflage netting.

Their two boats were known as 'swamprunners', shallow-draft flat-bottomed steel-hulled boats with giant fans at their sterns, capable of swift speeds across swamps of unpredictable depth.

West led the way.

He jumped onto the first swamprunner, and helped the others on after him.

When everyone was on board the two boats, he turned to grab the engine cord—

'Hold it *right there*, partner,' an ice-cold voice commanded.

West froze.

They came out of the reeds like silent shadows, guns up.

Eighteen mud-camouflaged CIEF specialists, all with

Colt Commando assault rifles—the lighter, more compact version of the M-16—and dark-painted faces.

West scowled inwardly.

Of course the Americans had sent in a *second* squad from the south, just in case—hell, they'd probably found his boats by doing a satellite scan of the swamp, then sent this squad who'd just come out and waited.

'Damn it . . .' he breathed.

The leader of the CIEF team stepped forward.

'Well, would you look at that. If it isn't *Jack West . . .*' he said. 'I haven't seen you since Iraq in '91. You know, West, my superiors still don't know how you got away from that SCUD base outside Basra. There musta been three hundred Republican Guards at that facility and yet you got away—*and* managed to destroy all those mobile launchers.'

'I'm just lucky, I guess, Cal,' West said evenly.

The CIEF leader's name was Sergeant Cal Kallis and he was the worst kind of CIEF operative: an assassin who liked his job. Formerly from Delta, Kallis was a grade-A psycho. Still, he wasn't Judah, which meant West still held out a hope of getting out of here alive.

At first Kallis completely ignored West's comment. He just whispered into a throat-mike: 'CIEF Command. This is Sweeper 2-6. We're a klick due south of the mountain. We got 'em. Sending you our position now.'

Then he turned to West, and spoke as if their conversation had never been interrupted:

'You ain't lucky anymore,' he said slowly. Kallis had cold black eyes—eyes that were devoid of pity or emotion. 'I got orders that amount to a hunting licence, West. Leave no bodies. Leave no witnesses. Something about a piece of gold, a very valuable piece of gold. Hand it over.'

'You know, Cal, when we worked together, I always thought you were a reasonable guy—'

Kallis cocked his gun next to Princess Zoe's head. 'No you didn't and no I wasn't. You thought I was "a cold-blooded psychopath"—they showed me the report you wrote. The Piece, West, or her brains learn how to fly.'

'Big Ears,' West said. 'Give it to him.'

Big Ears unslung his backpack, threw it into the mud at Kallis's feet.

The CIEF assassin opened it with his foot, saw the glistening golden trapezoid inside.

And he smiled.

Into his throat-mike, he said: 'Command. This is Sweeper 2-6. We have the prize. Repeat, we have the prize.'

As if on cue, at that moment two US Apache helicopters boomed into identical hovers in the air above West and his team.

The air shook. The surrounding reeds were blown flat.

One chopper lowered a harness, while the other stood guard, facing outwards.

Kallis attached the pack holding the Piece to the harness. It was winched up and that helicopter quickly zoomed off.

Once it was gone, Kallis touched his earpiece, getting some new instructions. He turned to West . . . and grinned an evil grin.

'Colonel Judah sends his regards, West. Seems he'd like to have a word with you. I've been instructed to bring you in. Sadly, everybody else dies.'

Quick as a rattlesnake, Kallis then re-asserted his aim at Princess Zoe and squeezed the trigger—just as the remaining Apache helicopter above him exploded in a fireball and dropped out of the sky, hit by a Hellfire missile from . . .

. . . the Europeans' Tiger attack helicopter.

The charred remains of the Apache smashed to the ground right behind the ring of CIEF troops—crashing in a heap, creating a giant splash of swampwater—in the process scattering the CIEF men as they dived out of the way.

The Tiger didn't hang around—it shot off after the other Apache, the one with the Piece of the Capstone in it.

But its missile shot had done enough for West.

Principally, it allowed Princess Zoe to leap clear of Kallis and dive to the floor of her swamprunner just as West started it up and yelled: 'Everybody out! Now!'

His team didn't need to be told twice.

While the Delta men around them clambered back to their feet and fired vainly after them, West's two swamprunners burst off the mark and disappeared at speed into the high reeds of the swamp.

Kallis and his men jumped into their nearby swamp-boats—four of them—and gunned the engines.

Kallis keyed his radio, reported what had happened to his bosses, finishing with: 'What about West?'

The voice at the other end was cold and hard, and the instructions it gave were exceedingly odd: 'You may do whatever you want with the others, sergeant, but Jack West and the girl must be allowed to escape.'

'Escape?' Kallis frowned.

'Yes, sergeant. Escape. Is that clear?'

'Crystal clear, sir. Whatever you say,' Kallis replied.

His boats roared into action.

★

West's two swamprunners skimmed across the swamp at phenomenal speed, banking and weaving, propelled by their huge turbofans.

West drove the lead one; Stretch drove the second one.

Behind them raced Kallis's four swampboats, bigger and heavier, but tougher—the men on their bows firing hard.

West was making for the far southern end of the swamp, 20 kilometres away, where a crumbling old road had been built along the shore of the vast waterfield.

It wasn't a big road, just two lanes, but it was made of asphalt, which was crucial.

'Sky Monster!' West shouted into his radio mike. 'Where are you!'

'*Still in a holding pattern behind the mountains, Huntsman. What can I do for you?*' came the reply.

'We need exfil, Sky Monster! Now!'

'*Hot?*'

'As always. You know that paved road we pinpointed earlier as a possible extraction point?'

'*The really tiny potholed piece-of-shit road? Big enough to fit two Mini Coopers side-by-side?*'

'Yeah, that one. We're also going to need the pick-up hook. What do you say, Sky Monster?'

'*Give me something hard next time, Huntsman. How long till you get there?*'

'Give us ten minutes.'

'*Done. The* Halicarnassus *is on its way.*'

The two swamprunners blasted across the waterfield, ducking the constant fire from the four pursuing CIEF swampboats.

Then suddenly, geyser-explosions of water began erupting all around West's boats.

Kallis and his team had started using mortars.

Bending and banking, West's swamprunners weaved away from the explosions—which actually all fell a fraction short—until suddenly the road came into view.

It ran in an east-to-west direction across the southern edge of the swamp, an old blacktop that led inland to Khartoum. Like many of the roads in eastern Sudan, it actually wasn't that bad, having been built by the Saudi terrorists who had once called these mountains home, among them a civil engineer named Bin Laden.

West saw the road, and risked a smile. They were going to make it . . .

At which moment, three more American Apache helicopters arrived, roaring across his path, shredding the water all around his boats with blazing minigun fire.

The Apaches rained hell on West's two boats.

Bullets ripped up the water all round them as the boats sped through the swamp.

'Keep going! Keep going!' West yelled to his people. 'Sky Monster is on the way!'

But then fire from one of the Apaches hit Stretch's turbofan. Smoke billowed, the fan clattered, and the second swamprunner slowed.

West saw it instantly—and knew what he had to do.

He pulled in alongside Stretch's boat and called: 'Jump over!'

A quick transfer took place, with Stretch, Pooh Bear, Fuzzy and Wizard all leaping over onto West's swamprunner—the last of them, Wizard, leaping across a split second before one of the Apaches let fly with a Hellfire missile and the second swamprunner was blown out of the water, disappearing in a towering geyser of spray.

Amid all this mayhem, West kept scanning the sky above the mountains—and suddenly he saw it.

Saw the black dot descending toward the little road.

A black dot that morphed into a bird-like shape, then a plane-like shape, then finally it came into focus and was revealed to be a huge black plane.

It was a Boeing 747, but the most bizarre 747 you would ever see.

Once upon a time, it had been a cargo plane of some sort, with a rear loading ramp and no side windows.

Now, it was painted entirely in black, dull black, and it bristled with irregular protrusions that had been added to it: radar domes, missile pods, and most irregularly of all: revolving gun turrets.

There were four of them—one on its domed roof, one on its underbelly, and two nestled on its flanks, where the plane's wings met its fuselage—each turret armed with a fearsome six-barrelled Gatling minigun.

It was the *Halicarnassus*. West's very own plane.

With a colossal roar, the great black jumbo jet swooped downwards, angling for the tiny road that bordered the swamp.

Now with all seven of his people on one swamprunner, West needed help and the *Halicarnassus* was about to provide it.

Two missiles lanced out from its belly-pods, missing one Apache by inches, but hitting the one behind it.

Boom. Fireball.

Then the great plane's underside minigun blazed to life, sending a thousand tracer rounds sizzling through the air all around the third Apache, giving it the choice of either bugging out or dying. It bugged out.

West's lone swamprunner swept alongside the straight roadway, raced parallel to it. The road was elevated a couple of feet above the water, up a low gently-sloping bank.

At the same moment, above and behind West's boat, the big 747 *landed* on the little country road!

Its wheels hit the road, squealing briefly before rolling forward with its outer tyres half off the road's edges. The big jet then taxied down the roadway—*coming alongside* West's skimming swamprunner, its wings stretching out over the waters of the swamp.

The *Halicarnassus* was coasting, rolling.

West's boat was speeding as fast as it could to keep up.

Then with a bang, the loading ramp at the back of the 747 dropped open, slammed down against the roadway behind the speeding plane.

A second later, a long cable bearing a large hook at its end came snaking out of the now-open cargo hold. It was a retrieval cable, normally used to snag weather balloons.

'What are you going to do now, my friend!' Pooh Bear yelled to West above the wind.

'This!'

As West spoke, he jammed his steering levers hard left, and the swamprunner swept leftward, bouncing up the riverbank *and out of the water*, dry-sliding on its flat-bottomed hull onto the bitumen road close behind the rolling 747!

It was an incredible sight: a big black 747 rolling along a country road, with a *boat* skidding and sliding along the road right behind it.

West saw the loading ramp of the plane, very close now, just a few yards in front of his sliding boat. He also saw the slithering retrieval cable bumping and bouncing on the road right in front of him.

'Stretch! The cable! Snag it!'

At the bow of the dry-sliding swamprunner, Stretch used a long snagging pole to reach out and snag the retrieval cable's hook. He got it.

'Hook us up!' West yelled.

Stretch did so, latching the cable's hook around the boat's bow.

And suddenly—*whap!*—the swamprunner was yanked forward, pulled along by the giant 747!

Dragged now by the *Halicarnassus*, the swamprunner looked like a waterskier being pulled by a speedboat.

West yelled into his radio, 'Sky Monster! Reel us in!'

Sky Monster initiated the plane's internal cable spooler, and now the swamprunner began to move gradually forward, hauled in by the cable, pulled closer and closer to the loading ramp.

While this was going on, the 747's belly-mounted gun turret continued to swing left and right, raining hell on Kallis's pursuing swampboats and the two remaining Apaches, keeping them at bay.

At last, West's swamprunner came to the loading ramp. West and Pooh Bear grabbed the ramp's struts, held the boat steady.

'Okay, everyone! All aboard!' West yelled.

One after the other, his team leapt from the swamprunner onto the lowered loading ramp—Wizard with Lily, then Zoe helping Fuzzy, Stretch helping Big Ears, and finally Pooh Bear and West himself.

Once West had landed on the loading ramp, he unhooked the swamprunner and the boat fell away behind the speeding 747, tumbling end over end down the little black road.

Then the loading ramp lifted and closed, and the 747 powered up and pulled away from the American Apaches and swampboats. It hit take-off speed and rose smoothly into the air.

Safe.

Clear.

Away.

The *Halicarnassus* flew south over the vast Ethiopian highlands.

While the others collapsed in the plane's large main cabin, West went straight up to the cockpit where he found the plane's pilot: a great big hairy-bearded New Zealand Air Force pilot known as *Sky Monster*. Unlike the others in the group, this had actually been his call-sign *before* he'd joined the team.

West gazed out at the landscape receding into the distance behind them—the swamp, the mountain, the vast plains beyond it—and thought about del Piero's Europeans engaging the superior American force. Del Piero would have little luck.

The Americans, as always the last to arrive but the greatest in brute force, had allowed West and the Europeans to squabble over the Piece, to lose men finding it, and then, like opportunistic lions, they'd muscled in on the hyenas and taken the prize.

And as the *Halicarnassus* soared into the sky away from the danger, West gazed at the large American force now gathered at the western edge of the swamp.

A disquieting thought lingered in his mind.

How had the Americans even known about this place?

The Europeans very probably had a copy of the Callimachus Text and, of course, they had the boy. But the Americans, so far as West knew, had neither.

Which meant there was no way they could have known that this was the resting place of the Colossus of Rhodes.

West frowned.

Was his team's cover blown? Had the Americans discovered their base and followed them here? Or worse: was there a traitor in his team who had given their position away with a tracing beacon?

In any case, Judah now knew that West was involved in this treasure hunt. He might not know exactly who West was working for, but he knew West was involved.

Which meant that things were about to get very intense.

Safe at last, but without their prize, West's plane sped away to the south, disappearing over the mountains.

Exhausted and dirty, West trudged back down into the main cabin. Head down in thought, he almost walked straight past Lily, curled up in the darkness under the stairs, sobbing quietly.

West crouched down beside her and with a gentleness that defied his battered state, brushed away her tears. 'Hey, kiddo.'

'They . . . they just *killed* him,' she swallowed. 'Killed Noddy.'

'I know.'

'Why'd they have to do that? He never hurt any of them.'

'No, he didn't,' West said. 'But what we're doing here has made some big countries very angry—because they're afraid of losing their power. That's why they killed Noddy.' He tousled her hair as he stood to go. 'Hey. I'll miss him, too.'

Tired, sore and himself saddened by the loss of Noddy, West retired to his small bunkroom in the aft section of the plane.

He collapsed into his bunk and no sooner had his head hit the pillow than he was asleep.

He slept deeply, his dreams filled with vivid visions—of booby-trapped chambers, stone altars, chants and screams, waterfalls of lava, and of himself running frantically through it all.

The interesting thing was, these dreams weren't the product of West's imagination.

They had actually happened, ten years previously . . .

A PREVIOUS MISSION

THE VOLCANO

NORTH-EASTERN UGANDA

20 MARCH, 1996

10 YEARS EARLIER

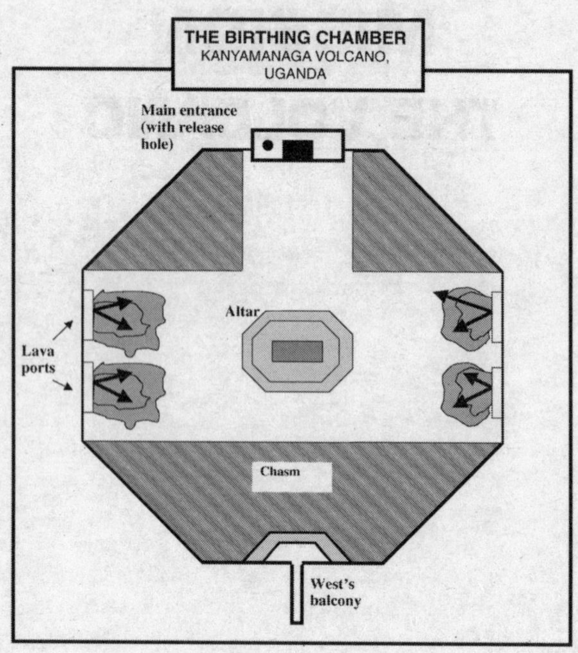
THE BIRTHING CHAMBER
KANYAMANAGA VOLCANO, UGANDA
Main entrance (with release hole)
Altar
Lava ports
Chasm
West's balcony

INSIDE THE KANYAMANAGA VOLCANO
UGANDA, AFRICA
20 MARCH, 1996, 11:47 A.M.

The images of West's dreams:

West running desperately down an ancient stone passageway with Wizard at his side, toward the sounds of booming drums, chanting and a woman's terrified screams.

It's hot.

Hot as Hell.

And since it's inside a volcano, it even *looks like* Hell.

It is just the two of them—plus Horus, of course. The team does not even exist at this time.

Their clothes are covered in mud and tar—they've survived a long and arduous path to get here. West wears his fireman's helmet and thick-soled army boots. Ten years younger, at age 27 he is more idealistic but no less intense. His eyes are narrow, focused. And his left arm is his own.

Boom-boom-boom! go the drums.

The chanting increases.

The woman's screams cut the air.

'We must hurry!' Wizard urges. 'They've started the ritual!'

They pass through several booby-trapped passageways—each of which West neutralises.

Ten disease-carrying molossid bats burst forth from a dark ceiling recess, fangs bared—only to have Horus launch herself off West's shoulder and plunge into their midst, talons raised. A thudding mid-air collision. Squeals and shrieks. Two bats smack down against the floor, brought down by the little falcon.

That splits the bats and the two men dash through them, Horus catching up moments later.

West is confronted by a long downward-sloping shaft. It's like a 100-metre-long stone pipe, steeply slanted, big enough for him to fit if he sits down.

Boom go the drums.

The evil chanting is close now.

The woman's frenzied screams are like nothing he has ever heard: pained, desperate, primal.

West shoots a look to Wizard.

The older man waves him on. 'Go! Jack! Go! Get to her! I'll catch up!'

West leaps feet-first into the pipe-shaft and slides fast.

Five traps later, he emerges from the bottom of the long stone pipe on . . .

. . . a balcony of some kind.

A balcony which overlooks a large ceremonial cavern.

He peers out from the balcony's railing and beholds the horrifying sight.

The woman lies spreadeagled on a rough stone altar, tied down, legs spread wide, writhing and struggling, *terrified*.

She is surrounded by about twenty priest-like figures

all wearing hooded black robes and fearsome jackal masks of the Egyptian god Anubis.

Six of the priests pound on huge lion-skin drums.

The rest chant in a strange language.

Incongruously, surrounding the circle of robed priests, all facing outward, are sixteen paratroopers in full battle-dress uniforms. They are French, all brandishing ugly FN-MAG assault rifles, and their eyes are deadly.

Beyond all this, the chamber itself catches West's attention.

Cut into the very flesh of the volcano, it branches off the volcano's glowing-red core and is octagonal in shape.

It is also ancient—very ancient.

Every surface is flat. The stone walls are so perfectly cut they look almost alien. Sharp-edged rectangular pipe-holes protrude from the sidewalls.

Hieroglyphics cover the walls. In giant letters above the main door, the biggest carving reads:

'Enter the embrace of Anubis willingly, and you shall live beyond the coming of Ra. Enter against your will, and your people shall rule for but one eon, but you shall live no more. Enter not at all, and the world shall be no more.'

Interestingly, the raised pattern on the high ceiling exactly matches the indentations on the floor fifty feet below.

The ceiling also features a tiny vertical shaft bored into it—in the exact centre, directly above the altar.

This ultra-narrow vertical shaft must reach all the way to the surface because right now, a beam of noonday sunlight—perfectly vertical, laser-thin and dazzlingly bright—shines down through the tiny hole, hitting . . .

. . . the altar on which the woman lies.

And one other thing:

The woman is pregnant.

More than that.

She is in the process of giving birth . . .

It is obviously painful, but it's not the only reason for her screams.

'*Don't take my child!*' she cries. 'Don't . . . you . . . take . . . my . . . baby!'

The priests ignore her pleas, keep chanting, keep drumming.

Separated from the ceremonial chamber by a chasm fifty feet wide and God-only-knows how deep, West can only stare helplessly at the scene.

And then, suddenly, a new cry joins the wild cacophony of sounds.

The cry of a baby.

The woman *has given birth* . . .

The priests cheer.

And then the chief priest—he alone is dressed in red robes and wears no mask—pulls the child from the woman's body and holds it aloft, illuminated by the vertical laser beam of sunlight.

'A boy!' he cries.

The priests cheer again.

And in that moment, as the chief priest holds the child high, West sees his face.

'Del Piero . . .' he breathes.

The woman wails, 'Please God, no! Don't take him! No! *Noooo!*'

But take him they do.

The priests sweep out the main entrance on the far side of the chamber, crossing a short bridge, their cloaks billowing, the boy held tightly in their midst, flanked by the armed paratroopers.

As they do, the noonday Sun moves on and the dazzling vertical laser beam of light vanishes.

The chief priest—Francisco del Piero—is the last to leave. With a final look, he stomps on a trigger stone in the main doorway and then disappears.

The response is instantaneous.

Spectacular streams of lava come blurting out of the rectangular holes in the walls of the cavern. The lava oozes across the floor of the chamber, heading toward the central stone altar.

At the same time, the ceiling of the chamber starts *lowering*—its irregular form moving towards the matching configuration on the floor. It even has a special indentation in it to accommodate the altar.

The woman on the altar doesn't notice.

Either from emotional torment or loss of blood, she just slumps back onto the altar and goes still, silent.

Wizard arrives at West's side, beholds the terrible scene.

'Oh my God, we're too late,' he breathes.

West stands quickly.

'It was del Piero,' he says. 'With French paratroopers.'

'The Vatican and the French have joined forces . . .' Wizard gasps.

But West has already raised a pressure-gun and fires it into the lowering ceiling of the chamber. The piton drives into the stone. A rope hangs from it.

'What on Earth are you doing?' Wizard asks, alarmed.

'I'm going over there,' West says. 'I said I'd be there

for her and I failed. But I'm not going to let her get crushed to nothing.'

And with that, he swings across the gaping chasm.

The ceiling keeps lowering.

The lava keeps spreading across the floor from either side, approaching the altar.

But with his quick swing, West beats it, and he rushes to the middle of the chamber, where he stands over the body of the woman.

A quick pulse-check reveals that she is dead.

West squeezes his eyes shut.

'I'm so sorry, Malena . . .' he whispers, '. . . so sorry.'

'Jack! Hurry!' Wizard calls from the balcony. 'The lava!'

The lava is eight metres away . . . and closing on him from both sides.

Over at the main entrance, a waterfall of oozing lava pours out of a rectangular hole *above* the doorway, forming a curtain across the exit.

West places his hand on the woman's face, closes her eyes. She is still warm. His gaze sweeps down her body, over the sagging skin of her abdomen, the skin over her pregnant belly now rumpled with the removal of the child formerly there.

Then for some reason, West touches her belly.

And feels a tiny little kick.

He leaps back, startled.

'Max!' he calls. 'Get over here! *Now!*'

★

A gruesome yet urgent image: flanked by the encroaching lava and the steadily lowering ceiling, the two men perform a Caesarean delivery on the dead woman's body using West's Leatherman knife.

Thirty seconds later, Wizard lifts a *second* child from the woman's slit-open womb.

It is a girl.

Her hair is pressed against her scalp, her body covered in blood and uterine fluid, her eyes squeezed shut.

West and Wizard, battered and dirty, two adventurers at the end of a long journey, gaze at her like two proud fathers.

West in particular gazes at the little infant, entranced.

'Jack!' Wizard says. 'Come on! We have to get out of here.'

He turns to grab their loosely hanging rope—just as the spreading lava reaches it and ignites it with a *whoosh!*

No escape that way.

Holding the baby, West spins to face the main entrance.

Fifteen metres of inch-deep lava blocks the way.

And then there's the curtain of falling lava blocking the doorway itself.

But then he sees it, cut into the left side of the stone doorframe: *a small round hole* maybe a handspan wide, veiled by the same waterfall of superheated lava.

West says, 'How thick are your soles?'

'Thick enough for a few seconds,' Wizard replies. 'But there's no way to switch off that lavafall.'

'Yes, there is,' West nods over at the small hole. 'See that hole. There's a stone dial inside it, hidden behind that curtain of lava. A cease mechanism that switches off the lavafall.'

'But, Jack, anyone who reaches in there will lose their—'

Wizard sees that West isn't listening. The younger man is just staring intently at the wall-hole.

West bites his lip, thinking the unthinkable.

He swallows, then turns to Wizard: 'Can you build me a new arm, Max?'

Wizard freezes.

He knows it's the only way out of this place.

'Jack. If you get us out of here, I promise you I'll build you a better arm than the one you were born with.'

'Then you carry her and let's go.' West hands the baby to Wizard.

And so they run, West in the lead, Wizard and the baby behind him, across the inch-deep pool of slowly spreading lava, crouching beneath the descending ceiling, the thick soles of their boots melting slightly with every stride.

Then they arrive at the lava-veiled doorway, and with no time to waste, West goes straight to the small hole next to the doorframe, takes a deep breath and—

—thrusts his left arm into the hole, up to the elbow, *through* the waterfall of lava!

'*Ahhhh!*'

The pain is like nothing he has ever known. It is excruciating.

He can see the lava *eating* through his own arm like a blowtorch burning through metal. Soon it will eat all the way through, but for a short time he still has feeling in his fingers and that's what he needs, because suddenly he touches something.

A stone dial inside the wall-hole.

He grips the dial, and a moment before his entire lower arm is severed from his body, Jack West Jr turns it and abruptly all the lavafalls flowing into the chamber stop.

The ceiling freezes in mid-descent.

The lavafall barring the doorway dries up.

And West staggers away from the wall-hole . . .

. . . to reveal that his left arm has indeed been severed at the elbow. It ends at a foul stump of melted bone, flesh and skin.

West sways unsteadily.

But Wizard catches him and the two of them—plus the child—stumble out through the doorway where they fall to the floor of a stone tunnel.

West collapses, gripping his half-arm, going into shock.

Wizard puts the baby down and hurriedly removes West's melting shoes—before also removing his own a bare second before their soles melt all the way through.

Then he dresses West's arm with his shirt. The red-hot lava has seared the wound, which helps.

Then it is over.

And the final image of West's dream is of Wizard and himself, sitting in that dark stone tunnel, spent and exhausted, with a little baby girl between them, in the belly of an African volcano.

And Wizard speaks:

'This . . . this is unprecedented. Totally unheard of in all recorded history. Two oracles. *Twin* oracles. And del Piero doesn't know . . .'

He turns to West. 'My young friend. My *brave* young friend. This complicates matters in a whole new way. And it might just give us a chance in the epic struggle to come. We must alert the member states and call a meeting, perhaps the most important meeting of the modern age.'

A MEETING OF NATIONS

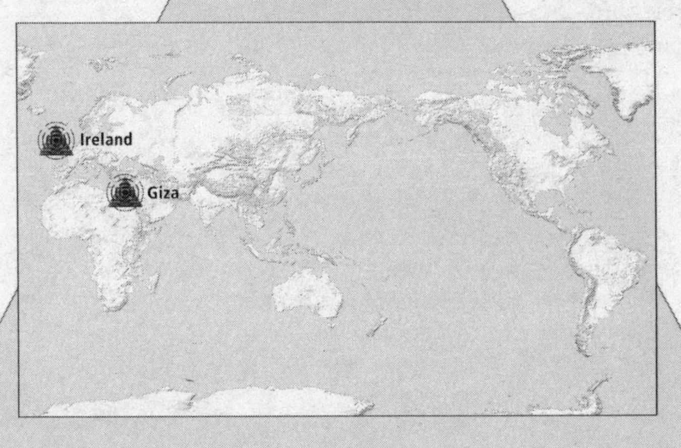

COUNTY KERRY, IRELAND
28 OCTOBER, 1996
7 MONTHS LATER

O'SHEA FARM
COUNTY KERRY, IRELAND
28 OCTOBER, 1996, 5:30 P.M.

To the untrained eye, it seemed like just another lonely old farmhouse on a hilltop overlooking the Atlantic. To the trained eye, however, it was something else entirely. The experienced professional would have noticed no less than twenty heavily-armed Irish commandos standing guard around the estate, scanning the horizon.

To be sure, this was an unusual setting for an international meeting, but this was not a meeting that the participants wanted widely known.

The state of the world at that time was grim. Iraq had been chased out of Kuwait, but now it played cat-and-mouse games with UN weapons inspectors. Europe was furious with the United States over steel tariffs. India and Pakistan, already engaged in a phony war, were both on the verge of entering the Nuclear Weapons Club.

But all these were *big* ticket issues, and the small group of nations gathered together today were not big ticket players in world affairs. They were small countries—mice, not lions—relative minnows of world affairs.

Not for long.

The mice were about to roar.

Six of the seven delegations now sat in the main sitting room of the farmhouse, waiting. Each national delegation consisted of two or three people—one senior diplomat, and one or two military personnel.

The view out through the windows was breathtaking—a splendid vista of the wild waves of the Atlantic smashing against the coast—but no-one at this gathering cared much for the view.

The Arabs checked their watches impatiently, frowning. Their leader, a wily old sheik from the United Arab Emirates named Anzar al Abbas, said: 'There's been no word from Professor Epper for over six months. What makes you think he'll even come?'

The Canadians, typically, sat there calmly and patiently, their leader simply saying, 'He'll be here.'

Abbas scowled.

While he waited, he flipped through his briefing kit and started re-reading the mysterious book extract that had been provided for all the participants at the meeting.

It was headed 'The Golden Capstone' . . .

THE GOLDEN CAPSTONE

From: ***When Men Built Mountains: The Pyramids***
by Chris M. Cameron
(Macmillan, London, 1989)

Perhaps the greatest mystery of the pyramids is the most obvious one: the Great Pyramid at Giza stands nine feet shorter than it should.

For once upon a time at its peak sat the most revered object in all of history.

The Golden Capstone.

Or, as the Egyptians called it, the *Benben*.

Shaped like a small pyramid, the Capstone stood nine feet tall and was made almost entirely of gold. It was inscribed with hieroglyphics and other more mysterious carvings in an unknown language, and on one side—the south side—it featured the Eye of Horus.

Every morning it shone like a jewel as it received the first rays of the rising sun—the first earthly object in Egypt to receive those sacred rays.

The Great Capstone was actually made up of seven pieces, its pyramidal form cut into horizontal strips, creating six pieces that were trapezoidal in shape and one, the topmost piece, that was itself pyramidal (small pyramids such as this were called *pyramidions*).

We say that the Capstone was made *almost* entirely of gold, because while its body was indeed crafted from solid gold, it featured a thin bore-hole that ran vertically down through its core, in the exact centre of the Capstone.

This hollow was about two inches wide and it cut downward through each of the seven pieces, punching holes in all of them. Embedded in each of those circular holes could be found a crystal, not unlike the lens of a magnifying glass. When placed in sequence those seven crystals served to concentrate the Sun's rays on those days when it passed directly overhead.

This is a crucial point.

Many scholars have noted that the construction of the Great Pyramid by the pharaoh Khufu curiously coincides with the solar event known as the Tartarus Rotation. This phenomenon involves the rotation of the Sun and the subsequent appearance of a powerful sunspot that comes into alignment with the Earth.

Accomplished Sunwatchers that they were, the Egyptians certainly knew of the Sun's rotation, sunspots, and indeed of the sunspot that we call 'Tartarus'. Aware of its intense heat, they called it 'Ra's Destroyer'. (They also knew of the smaller sunspot that precedes Tartarus by seven days, and so labelled it 'The Destroyer's Prophet'.)

The last Tartarus Rotation occurred in 2570 BC, just a few years after the Great Pyramid was completed. Interestingly, the next Rotation will occur in 2006, on March 20, the day of the vernal equinox, the time when the Sun is perfectly perpendicular to the Earth.

Those theorists who link the construction of the pyramid to Tartarus also claim that the Capstone's unique 'crystal array' has the ability to capture and harness solar energy, while the more outrageous authors claim it possesses fabulous paranormal powers.

Having said this, however, it should be noted that the Golden Capstone only sat atop the Great Pyramid for a very short time.

The day after the Tartarus Rotation of 2570 BC, the Capstone was removed, and taken to a secret location where it rested for over 2,000 years.

It has since disappeared from history altogether, so that now all that remains of it is an ominous inscription found on the empty summit of the Great Pyramid at Giza itself:

Cower in fear, cry in despair,
You wretched mortals
For that which giveth great power
Also takes it away.
For lest the Benben be placed at sacred site

On sacred ground, at sacred height,
Within seven sunsets of the arrival of Ra's prophet,
At the high-point of the seventh day,
The fires of Ra's implacable Destroyer will devour us all.

A door slammed somewhere. Abbas looked up from his reading.

Footsteps.

Then the sitting room door opened, and through it stepped—

—Professor Max T. Epper and Captain Jack West Jr.

Epper wore a classic academic's tweed coat. His beard back then was just as white and long as it would be 10 years later.

West wore his miner's jacket and some brand-new steel-soled boots. His ice-blue eyes scanned the room, sharp as lasers, ever watchful.

And his left arm ended at the elbow.

Everyone noticed it.

Whispers rippled across the room.

'The ones who found the Scrolls of the Museion . . .' one of the Arabs whispered.

'Epper is Professor of Archaeology at Trinity College in Dublin, a brilliant fellow, but he also has doctorates in physics and electromagnetics . . .'

'And Huntsman?'

'He *was* military, but not anymore. Worked alongside the Americans in Iraq in '91. But after what the Americans did to him there, well—'

'What on earth has happened to his arm?'

Abbas stood up. 'Where is the girl, Maximilian? I thought you were bringing her.'

'We left her at a secure location,' Epper said. 'Her safety at this juncture is of paramount importance. Her actual presence at this meeting, my old friend Anzar, is not.'

Epper and West sat down at the table, joining the six delegations.

Epper sat with the Canadians.

West sat alone, attaching himself to none of the seven countries at the table. *He* was the seventh delegation. His home nation had sent no other representative, having decided that his presence at this meeting was sufficient.

That nation: Australia.

The host, the leader of the Irish delegation, General Colin O'Hara, formally opened the meeting.

'My friends, welcome to Ireland, and to a meeting of tremendous significance. I will get directly to the point. Seven months ago, members of a European military-archaeological team found the pregnant wife of the Oracle of Siwa in her hideaway in Uganda. It is not known how they found her, but we do know that the leader of the European expedition was the eminent Vatican historian Father Francisco del Piero. Del Piero's specialty is ancient Egyptian religious practices, particularly Sun worship.

'In accordance with the dictates of an ancient Egyptian Sun cult, del Piero and his team took the pregnant woman to a remote volcano in Uganda on the day of the vernal equinox, March 20.

'At noon on the day of the equinox, by the so-called

"pure" light of the Sun, in a chamber cut into the flank of the volcano, the Oracle's wife gave birth to a son, whom del Piero immediately abducted.

'Del Piero and his military escorts then left, leaving the mother to die inside the chamber.

'But then something most unexpected occurred.

'After del Piero's team had departed, the Oracle's wife gave birth to *another* child, a girl. Through the extraordinary efforts of Professor Epper and Captain West, this baby girl was recovered, alive and well . . .'

There was, of course, more to it than that, West thought as he listened.

He and Epper had actually found the Oracle's wife a day *before* the Europeans. Her name was Malena Okombo and she had been living in hiding, in fear of her abusive husband, the present-day Oracle of Siwa. Pregnant with the Oracle's heir (or heirs), she had fled from his fists and rages, the petulant rages of a spoilt man. West had sympathised with Malena immediately, promised to look after her. But then the Europeans had arrived the following day in great numbers and abducted her—leading to the incident at the volcano.

O'Hara was still talking: 'It is this extremely fortunate occurrence—the birth of a second Oracle—that brings us together today. Professor Epper, if you will . . .'

Epper stood up. 'Thank you, Colin.' He addressed the assembled delegates. 'Ms Kissane, gentlemen. Our eight small nations come together today at a pivotal moment in history.

'The actions of Father del Piero and his men in Uganda can mean only one thing, a most dangerous thing. The Europeans are making their move. After 2,000 years of searching, they have just secured the key to discovering the greatest, most sought-after treasure in human history: the Golden Capstone of the Great Pyramid.'

'Allow me to elaborate,' Epper said.

'As you will have read in your briefing materials, there was once a magnificent Golden Capstone that sat atop the Great Pyramid. It, however, was removed from the apex of the structure soon after the Great Pyramid was completed, staying there for only a few short years.

'It is not mentioned in any Egyptian records after that time nor is its final resting place known.

'Over the ages since then, the Golden Capstone has been the subject of countless myths and legends. The Persian King, Cambyses, tried to find it at the Siwa Oasis in the Western Desert, only to lose 50,000 men in the attempt, consumed in a sandstorm of unusual ferocity.

'Julius Caesar tried to locate it, but failed. Napoleon took an entire army to Egypt to find it, and failed. The tale of Jason and the Argonauts and their attempt to acquire a mystical, all-powerful "Golden Fleece"—written by Appollonius of Rhodes—is widely believed to be a thinly-veiled allegory for the search for the Golden Capstone.

'But all the legends have one thing in common. In all of them the Capstone is said to possess unusual properties. It is said to be a source of immense power; it is said to contain the secret to perpetual motion; it is said to be a solar polariser, capable of absorbing the rays of the Sun.

'And then, of course, there are the occult myths: that the Capstone is a talisman of evil, forged in a bloody ceremony by occultist priests; that the nation that claims it as their own and keeps it in their lands will be unconquerable in battle; that it is a piece of alien technology brought to Earth thousands of years ago as a gift from a higher civilisation.'

The representative of New Zealand said: 'And now the European Union wants it—'

'Ahem,' O'Hara said. 'These nations do *not* represent the European Union. Ireland and Spain are members of the EU, and Father del Piero does not act in our name. While it calls itself an EU mission, it is really a coalition of four "Old European" states: France, Germany, Italy and the Vatican.'

At the mention of France the New Zealander visibly stiffened. Relations between New Zealand and France had been tense ever since the bombing by French agents of the Greenpeace boat, the *Rainbow Warrior,* in Auckland Harbour in 1985. 'Old Europe then. My point is if Old Europe wants the Capstone, you can be assured that her enemies are aware of this—'

'They are,' Abbas said firmly. 'The Americans are already putting together a rival expedition.'

'Wait a second,' the head of the Jamaican delegation said. 'America and Europe are *enemies*?'

'As only ex-friends can be,' Epper said. 'Through the vehicle of the EU, Old Europe has been waging economic warfare on the United States for the last five years. It began when America started unfairly subsidising its steel industry, shutting more efficient European producers out of its market.'

Spain said, 'The US pressures other nations to *open* their markets, but then it closes off its own home market to them, protecting its own weak industries with tariffs like the steel one.'

Canada nodded. 'And ex-friends, like ex-wives and

ex-husbands, make for the bitterest of foes. Europe and America despise each other. And their enmity will only get worse over time.'

Epper said, 'Which is why we are all here today. Our eight small nations are not the enemies of the United States or Old Europe. Indeed, we have fought by their side on many previous occasions. But on this matter, we have decided that we cannot sit idly by while these so-called "Great Powers" engage in a battle for the most powerful artefact known to humankind.

'No. We are gathered here today because we believe that the Capstone should not belong to *any* one superpower. Its power is simply too great. In short, we are here to save the world.'

'So what about the baby girl—' Abbas asked.

Epper held up his hand. 'In a moment, Anzar, in a moment. Just a little more background first. Throughout history, the Capstone has been sought by many powerful individuals: Julius Caesar, Augustus Caesar, Richard the Lionheart, Napoleon, Lord Kitchener and, most recently, by Adolf Hitler and the Nazis. It is worshipped by organisations such as the Templars and the Freemasons, and, this will surprise some, the Catholic Church. All of them believe the same thing: whosoever finds the Capstone and performs an ancient ritual with it will rule the Earth for a thousand years.'

The room was silent.

Epper went on.

'Only one man in history is believed to have actually held the Capstone in his possession and harnessed its awesome power. He is also the one who, according to legend, broke the Capstone down into its seven individual Pieces—so that no one man could ever have it whole again. He then had those Pieces spread to the distant corners of the world, to be buried within seven colossal monuments, the seven greatest structures of his age.'

'Who?' Abbas said, leaning forward.

'The only man ever to rule the entire world of his era,' Epper said. 'Alexander the Great.'

'Seven colossal monuments?' Abbas said suspiciously. 'You're talking about the Seven Wonders of the Ancient World? Alexander had the seven Pieces of the Capstone buried within the Seven Wonders?'

'Yes,' Epper said, 'although in his lifetime, they weren't *known* as the Seven Ancient Wonders. That label was coined later, in the year 250 BC, by Callimachus of Cyrene, the Chief Librarian of the Library at Alexandria. Why, at the time of Alexander's death in 323 BC, only five of the Seven Wonders had actually been built.'

'My ancient history is a little rusty,' Abbas said. 'Can you remind me of the Seven Wonders, please?'

It was the young Irish woman who answered him, quickly and expertly: 'In order of construction, they are: the Great Pyramid at Giza. The Hanging Gardens of Babylon. The Temple of Artemis at Ephesus. The Statue of Zeus at Olympia. The Mausoleum at Halicarnassus. The Lighthouse at Alexandria. And the Colossus of Rhodes.'

'Thank you, Zoe,' Epper said.

'I thought the Hanging Gardens were a myth,' Abbas said.

Epper said, 'Just because something has not been *found* yet does not make it a myth, Anzar. But we digress. In his lifetime, Alexander visited all five of the existing Wonders. The last two Wonders—the Lighthouse and the Colossus—would be built by his closest friend and general, Ptolemy I, who would himself later become Pharaoh of Egypt.

'This creates a curious coincidence: taken together, these two titans of their age visited *all seven* of the sites that would subsequently be called the Seven Ancient Wonders of the World.

'Sure enough, soon after their deaths, the concept of seven "great" structures came into being.

'But don't be fooled. This was no coincidence at all. As I've said, the idea of *the* Seven Wonders of the World was first espoused by Callimachus of Cyrene in 250 BC. He did this in a text called "A Collection of Wonders around the World" now known simply as the Callimachus Text.

'Callimachus, however, was not publishing some idle list. He was a man who knew everything about Alexander, Ptolemy *and* the Golden Capstone.

'By pinpointing these seven structures—and let's be honest, there were other just-as-impressive monuments in existence at the time that were not included—Callimachus was drawing a map, a clear and specific map to the location of the Pieces of the Golden Capstone.'

'According to the Callimachus Text, the Capstone was cut into Pieces like so.' Epper drew a pyramid on the whiteboard and cut across it horizontally, dividing it into seven bands.

'Seven Pieces: one pyramidal tip, six trapezoidal base Pieces, all of varying sizes, which we number from the top down, one through seven. Then they were hidden in each of the Seven Wonders.'

'Wait,' Abbas said, 'the Seven Wonders of the Ancient World have long since fallen, been disassembled, or simply disappeared. How can we find these Pieces in structures that no longer exist?'

Epper nodded. 'This is a good point. Apart from the Great Pyramid, *none* of the Seven Wonders has survived to the present day. The Callimachus Text, however, has.

'And let me make something else clear: while it bears his name, Callimachus was not the only person to write it. His Text is a compendium of writings from many writers, all of them members of a secret cult who updated it and revised it over the course of 1,500 years. They *did* keep track of every Wonder, even after they fell, and by extension they kept track of every Piece of the Capstone. Allow me to explain.'

'There is a well-known story about Alexander the Great. Before he embarked on his campaign in Persia, Alexander visited an Oracle at the desert oasis of Siwa in Egypt. During this visit the Oracle confirmed Alexander's belief that he was a god, no less than the son of Zeus.

'Less well known, however, is the *gift* that the Oracle is said to have given Alexander when he departed Siwa. It was never seen, but according to the historian Callisthenes, it occupied "a whole covered wagon that required eight donkeys to draw it".

'Whatever this gift was, it was heavy. Very heavy. Alexander would take it in its shrouded wagon with him on his all-conquering campaign across Persia.'

'You believe the Oracle gave the Capstone to Alexander?' Abbas said.

'I do. I further believe that during that campaign, Alexander systematically hid those Pieces at the five then-existing Wonders. He then left the last two Pieces with his trusted friend, Ptolemy I, who as we know would go on to build the last two Ancient Wonders.

'For, you see, this "Oracle at Siwa" was more than just a seer. The Oracle was—and is to this day—the High Priest of an ancient Sun-cult known as the Cult of Amun-Ra. Interestingly, Egyptian records knew this cult by another name: the Priests of the Capstone. That's right. They are the ones who placed the Golden Capstone on the apex of the Great Pyramid. They are also the ones who took it down.

'This Cult of Amun-Ra has endured to the present day, under many guises. For instance, the Knights of St John of Malta, and some sections of the Catholic Church.

'The Freemasons, too, have long attached great significance to the Great Pyramid—and are often accused of being a thinly-veiled reincarnation of the Cult of Amun-Ra. Indeed, one very famous Freemason, Napoleon Bonaparte, was initiated into the order's highest ranks *inside* the King's Chamber of the Great Pyramid.

'Other famous individuals who have been associated with the Cult of Amun-Ra include Thomas Jefferson, Frederic-Auguste Bartholdi, the designer of the Statue of Liberty, Dr Hans Koenig, the famous Nazi archaeologist, and the American Vice-President Henry Wallace, the man behind the now infamous inclusion of a capstone-bearing pyramid on the US one-dollar bill.

'For our purposes, it should be noted that *all* of the Chief Librarians of the Library at Alexandria were key members of the Cult—among them Apollonius of Rhodes and Callimachus of Cyrene.'

★

Epper continued. 'As time passed and each Wonder fell, Callimachus's successors in the Cult of Amun-Ra kept careful watch over the Pieces of the Capstone, recording their resting places in the Callimachus Text.

'For example, when the Colossus of Rhodes was toppled by an earthquake, Egyptian cultists spirited away its head, rescuing the Capstone Piece on its neckpiece. The Colossus' new resting place was then noted in the Callimachus Text—but in a secret language.

'And here, Anzar, lies the importance of the little girl.

'You see, Callimachus and his successors wrote all of their entries in an ancient language, a language unlike any other in the history of man, a language that has defied translation for over 4,500 years, even by modern supercomputers.

'It is a mysterious language known as the Word of Thoth.

'Now, we believe that Father del Piero possesses a Vatican copy of the Callimachus Text—copied in secret by a Vatican spy in the 13th century. But he cannot translate it. And so he went in search of the one person in the world capable of reading the Word of Thoth: the Oracle of Siwa.

'For while Alexander has come and gone, the Oracle of Siwa lives to this very day, albeit in hiding somewhere in Africa.

'In a single unbroken line spanning more than 4,500 years, the Oracle—male or female, the Oracle can be either—has always spawned one child. And the Oracles' offspring have inherited the preternatural "sight" associated with the Oracle, thus becoming the next one.

'The extent of this "sight" has been debated over the years, but one talent peculiar to the Oracle has been documented by Egyptian, Greek and Roman writers alike:

the Oracle of Siwa is the only person alive who is *born* with the ability to read the Word of Thoth.

'Since Callimachus's followers died out sometime in the 14th century, the Oracle is now the only person on Earth who can decode the Callimachus Text and thus reveal the locations of the Seven Ancient Wonders.'

'As we have just heard, led by Francisco del Piero, the European coalition did not locate the Oracle himself, but they did find his pregnant wife, which is just as well: the Oracle, a foul, distasteful man by all accounts, was killed two months later in a drunken accident. Had he been located sooner, this mission would have been significantly easier and could have started immediately.

'In any case, now the Europeans have a new-born Oracle—a boy—which means that when he reaches sufficient age, he will be able to decode the Text. According to ancient sources, a new Oracle begins to command his or her abilities around the age of ten.

'Once del Piero has the ability to decode the Callimachus Text, his European force will commence upon the greatest treasure hunt in history: a search for the seven Pieces of the Golden Capstone.'

The Irish woman, Zoe Kissane, leaned forward: 'Only on this occasion, by some fluke, the Oracle's wife gave birth to twins. And we have the other child: a girl.'

'Correct,' Epper said. 'And now it becomes a race. A race based solely on the maturation of two children. As they grow, they will learn to command their abilities, and when they are able to read the Word of Thoth, they will be able to decipher the Callimachus Text.'

★

'Which means the girl's wellbeing is of the utmost importance,' O'Hara said. 'She is to be guarded around the clock, nurtured and brought to maturity, so that when the time comes, she can translate the Text and guide us to the Wonders before the Europeans or the Americans can get them.'

Epper nodded in agreement. 'Make no mistake, people. The odds are against us. Our rivals from America and Old Europe are already employing hundreds of scientists in pursuit of this goal. When the time comes, they will send entire armies after those seven Pieces.

'We do not have their resources, or their numbers. But having said that, we are not entirely without advantages.

'First. Aiding our quest is the fact that the two superpowers do not know we are embarking on it. They don't know we have the girl.

'And second: we are not after the entire Capstone. We only need to get one Piece. If we do that, we deprive our adversaries of the power of the entire Capstone. Granted, getting just one Piece will be a titanic task.'

Epper scanned the room.

'This is a weighty responsibility, too weighty for one nation alone to bear. Which is why we have all come together today, a group of small nations who are prepared to join forces to combat the great powers of our time. And so the following course of action is proposed: each member of this group of nations will provide one soldier to share in the guardianship of the girl—both in her growth and in our ultimate quest to find one Piece of the Capstone.

'But I warn you. This will be a long mission, a mission of years, not months. It will also be one of constant vigilance, self-sacrifice and discipline. The group of chosen soldiers will accompany Captain West and myself to the safehouse where the girl is now being kept. There we shall guard her and raise her, in absolute secrecy, until she is ready to fulfil her destiny.'

The six delegations formed into huddles, whispered among themselves. Since he was his own delegation, West didn't need to discuss anything with anyone.

At length, they reconvened, each nation presenting its selected guardian.

Canada already had Max Epper.

Sheik Abbas said, 'On behalf of the United Arab Emirates, I offer the services of my second son, Captain Aziz al Anzar al Abbas.'

The trooper who had been sitting beside Abbas for the duration of the meeting stood. He was a rotund fellow, short and round—some would say chubby—with a bushy black beard and turban.

'Captain Aziz al Anzar al Abbas, heavy arms, explosives, 1st Commando Squadron, at your command. Call-sign: *Saladin*.'

Then the Spaniards' representative stood: tall, handsome and athletic, he looked like Ricky Martin, only tougher. 'Lieutenant Enrique Velacruz. Unidad de Operaciones Especiales, Spanish Marines. Underwater destruction and demolition. Call-sign: *Matador*.'

The Jamaicans introduced a tall dreadlocked fellow named Sergeant V.J. Weatherly, call-sign: *Witch Doctor*.

The New Zealanders offered a big hairy-faced NZAF pilot nicknamed *Sky Monster*.

Last of all, the Irish proffered two representatives: one of which was the only woman to join this special multinational unit.

They sent Zoe Kissane and the giant fellow who sat

at her side, her brother, Liam. Both hailed from the famed Irish commando unit, the Sciathan Fhianoglach an Airm.

She introduced herself: 'Sergeant Zoe Kissane, hostage rescue, advanced medical. Call-sign: *Bloody Mary*.'

He did too: 'Corporal Liam Kissane, also hostage rescue, bomb disposal, heavy arms. Call-sign: *Gunman*.'

And there they stood, around the wide table, the eight chosen representatives of eight small nations who were about to embark on the mission of their lives.

They would acquire a ninth member soon—Stretch, from Israel—but he would not be a member of their choosing.

They prepared to leave. A plane was waiting to take them out of Ireland and to the secret safehouse.

At the door, Abbas spoke to his son, Saladin, in Arabic. One word kept arising: '*bint*'.

The short fat trooper nodded.

As he did so, West stepped past them, walking out the door.

'If you're going to talk about her,' he said, 'please stop calling her "the girl". She has a name, you know.'

'You named her?' Saladin said, surprised.

'Yes,' West said. 'I named her Lily.'

They commenced their journey to the safehouse.

It was in Africa, in Kenya, but for secrecy's sake they took a long circuitous route to get there, taking several flights over several days.

On one of these flights, Saladin said to Epper, 'At the meeting we were given an extract from a book. It told of the Capstone and the Tartarus Sunspot. What is this Tartarus Sunspot and what relationship does it bear with the Great Pyramid and its Capstone?'

Epper nodded. 'Good question. It is a most curious relationship, but one that takes on a new level of importance at this time.'

'Why?'

'Because in ten years' time, in March 2006, we will see the second great turning of the Sun in modern times, a solar event that has not occurred in over 4,500 years.'

The big-bearded Arab frowned. 'The second great turning of the Sun? What is that?'

'Although you can't see it, our Sun actually spins on its own axis, much like the Earth does. Only it doesn't turn in a flat, even rotation as we do. Rather, it rocks slowly up and down as it spins. As such, every 4,000–4,500 years, a certain section of the Sun—a sunspot known as the Tartarus Sunspot—comes into direct alignment with our planet. This is a bad thing.'

'Why?'

'Because the Tartarus Sunspot is the single hottest point on the surface of the Sun,' Zoe Kissane said, coming over and sitting down. 'The ancient Greeks named it after one of the two realms of their Underworld. The nicer realm was the Elysian Fields: it was a place of eternal happiness. The nasty one, a cursed land of screaming, flames and punishment, was known as the Tartarus Plains.'

'Global temperatures have been rising steadily for twenty years now,' Epper said, 'because the Tartarus Sunspot is approaching. When it shines directly upon the Earth, as it has done before, for about two weeks, temperatures will rise to unbearably high levels, around 110° Celsius.

'Rainforests will shrivel. Rivers will boil. Humankind will have to move indoors for that time. It will be a literal scorching of the Earth, but it is survivable.

'The problem is: the polar ice caps will melt, causing massive global floods. The oceans will rise by perhaps 15 metres. Many coastal cities worldwide will be severely damaged. But as I say, this is survivable, given due warning.'

'Okay . . .' Saladin said.

Epper wasn't finished. 'Now, we have geological records of similar mass global water-risings in the past—specifically in the years 15,000 BC, 10,500 BC and 6,500 BC.

'The flood of 15,000 BC is believed to have been the giant oceanic movement that flooded the Persian Gulf; while the flood of 10,500 BC is widely acknowledged as the "Great Flood" mentioned in religious texts worldwide: Noah's flood in the Bible, the floods mentioned in ancient Sumerian texts; even the Australian Aborigines refer to a Great Flood in their Dreamtime folklore.

'The most recent global flood, that of 6,500 BC, broadly correlates with the worldwide episode of water-rise known as the Flandrian transgression, where entire coastlines were submerged by about twenty metres.'

Epper leaned forward to make his point: 'All three of these major global floods occurred during a Tartarus Rotation.

'The thing is,' he raised a finger, 'in 2,570 BC, during the most recent Tartarus Rotation, *no such mass global flooding took place*.'

Saladin frowned. 'You're saying that something stopped the cataclysm? Something to do with the pyramids?'

'Yes,' Epper said. 'It's complicated but, you see, prior to King Djoser in 2,660 BC the Egyptians *never* built pyramids. And after Menkaure in 2,503 BC they stopped building giant ones. The fact is: for a period of 160 years, the Egyptians went on an absolute frenzy of pyramid-building, the high-point of which was the Great Pyramid. *And then they never did it again.*

'They just stopped . . . immediately after the Tartarus Rotation of 2,570 BC. Later Egyptian architecture was certainly impressive and colossal—*but it didn't involve pyramids*.'

'So you think the Egyptians knew something about the coming of this Tartarus Sunspot?' Saladin said. 'What, were they visited by aliens or something and told to build the Great Pyramid and put this special Capstone on it?'

Epper just raised his bushy eyebrows theatrically. 'I don't know why the Egyptians started building pyramids. But they did. In a rush and on a scale never seen before then and not seen since. And for some reason, the Tartarus Sunspot had no effect on planet Earth in the year 2,570 BC. The Great Pyramid was built, the sunspot passed—harmlessly—and the Egyptians took down the Golden Capstone, hid it, and stopped building pyramids.'

'So how do you explain it?' Saladin asked.

'Putting aside for the moment all the occultist literature, I believe the crystals in the Capstone are the key. I think the Capstone is a polariser, a crystal array that absorbs the superhot rays of the Tartarus Sunspot, rendering them harmless.'

'And the occultist literature? These tales about obtaining global power for a thousand years?'

Epper's face became grave. 'The scientist in me scoffs at them. But something else gives me pause before discarding them completely. I've seen enough in my life to know that some things defy scientific explanation.

'The inscription on the summit of the Great Pyramid tells of placing the "Benben"—that's another word for the Capstone—*at sacred site, on sacred ground, at sacred height* within seven days of the arrival of the minor sunspot, Ra's Prophet.

'This is a reference to an ancient ritual, a ritual passed down through the Cult of Amun-Ra, a ritual to be performed at the arrival of the Tartarus Sunspot. This ritual involves the intoning of a sacred incantation—the words of which are carved *into* the very Pieces of the Capstone.

'But this ritual can be performed in *two* ways: one for good, the other for ill. With the Capstone in place atop the Great Pyramid, if you utter the noble incantation—known as the ritual of peace—the world will be spared the wrath of Tartarus and life will go on. This is also to our advantage: if we fail in our quest to obtain a Piece of the Capstone, we could yet be able to utter the good incantation over the replaced Capstone.'

'And the evil spell?' Saladin asked hesitantly.

Epper's face went grim.

'The evil incantation—the ritual of *power*—will also spare the world from the blaze of Tartarus by capturing the Sun's rays in the Capstone's crystal array, but at a terrible price.

'For, according to the ancient texts, when the entire Capstone is placed on the summit of the Great Pyramid at noon on the seventh day and a designated amount of pure soil from one nation is placed in a crucible inside it *and* the ritual of power is uttered, "all earthly power" will be invested in that nation for 1,000 years.'

Epper stared at Saladin. 'The Capstone is the ultimate test of mankind's mettle. In the face of cataclysm, it can be used selflessly for the universal good, or it can be used selfishly, to attain absolute power.'

'Or there is the third option,' Saladin said. 'Our option. If we obtain a single Piece of this Capstone and withhold it, we condemn the world to two weeks of catastrophic weather and floods, but not 1,000 years of slavery. A lesser-of-two-evils argument, Dr Epper?'

'Something like that,' Epper said quietly. 'Either way, my Arab friend, the fate of the world now depends on our efforts.'

A GIRL NAMED LILY

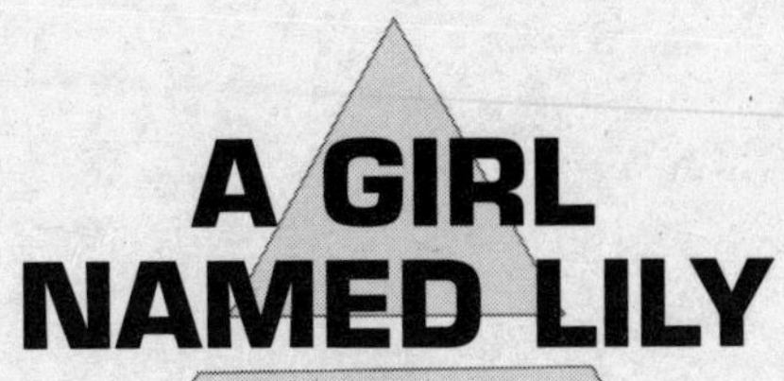

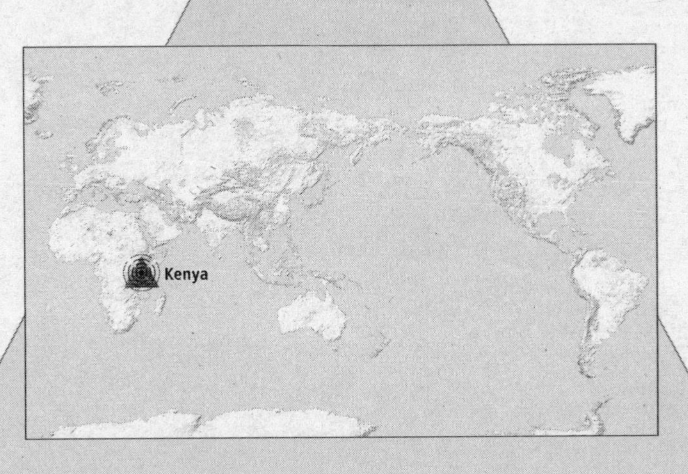

VICTORIA STATION, KENYA
1996–2006

VICTORIA STATION
SOUTHERN KENYA
1996–2006

Within days of the historic meeting, the team was in Kenya—living and working and training—at a remote farm-station near the Tanzanian border. On a clear day, to the south they could see the mighty cone of Kilimanjaro peeking above the horizon.

Far from the Western world.

Far from their enemies.

The farm—very deliberately—had wide flat treeless pastures stretching for two miles in every direction from the central farmhouse.

There would be no unexpected visitors to this place.

The team raised few eyebrows among the locals.

To the Kenyans, Victoria Station was just another working farm, populated by a few foreigners, all working for the old man, Epper, and his lovely wife, Doris. Grey-haired, patient and kind, she had come from Canada to join her husband on this mission and provide a much-needed grandmotherly figure on the farm.

Of course, the locals soon became aware of a baby

girl on the property—every now and then, Doris or a worker from the farm would come into town to buy baby food, formula milk, diapers and sometimes toys.

But the Kenyans simply assumed that the olive-skinned girl was the daughter of the young blonde woman at the farm, who in turn was presumably the wife of one of the men.

The locals, however, never noticed that every single night, there were always two members of the team patrolling the perimeter of the property.

Lily grew up quickly.

Indeed, she transformed rapidly from a happy gurgling baby into an inquisitive toddler who on taking her first steps became an absolute security nightmare.

It was not uncommon to see seven crack commandos frantically upturning chairs, couches or hay bales trying to find a giggling little girl who could disappear seemingly almost at will.

Then she began to talk and to read.

Inevitably, she was the product of many influences.

When she saw Saladin kneeling towards Mecca, she asked him what he was doing. It was he who taught her about Islam—only growing tongue-tied once when, as a four-year-old, she asked him why some Islamic women wore head-covering burqas.

'If they do not wear the burqa, some men will not . . . er . . . respect them,' Saladin said, clearing his throat.

'Zoe doesn't wear a burqa,' Lily said.

Several members of the team were eating nearby at

the time: Zoe, Epper and West. Smiling, Zoe looked expectantly at Saladin, waiting for his answer.

'Well, no, she doesn't, because she is not a Muslim.'

'But you can see her head, right?' Lily asked.

'Yes . . .'

'Which means, according to Islam, you mustn't respect her.'

Saladin blushed bright pink. 'Well, no . . . I do respect Miss Zoe. Very much.'

'Then why do Muslim women wear these burqa things?'

Saladin was helpless.

It was Zoe who saved him. 'Not all men are as gentlemanly as Aziz, Lily. They can't control their urges as well as he can.'

'Urges?' Lily asked, zeroing in on the new word.

Zoe said, 'And *that* is a topic we will address when you're a little older.'

All this time, a sheet of paper hung in the kitchen, attached by a magnet to the refrigerator—on it were seven boxes, filled with a strange kind of writing, reproductions of the seven main verses in the Callimachus Text.

It was positioned so that Lily saw it every day when she went to get her morning juice. When she asked what it said, Doris Epper answered: 'We don't know. We're hoping that one day you'll be able to tell us.'

It looked like this:

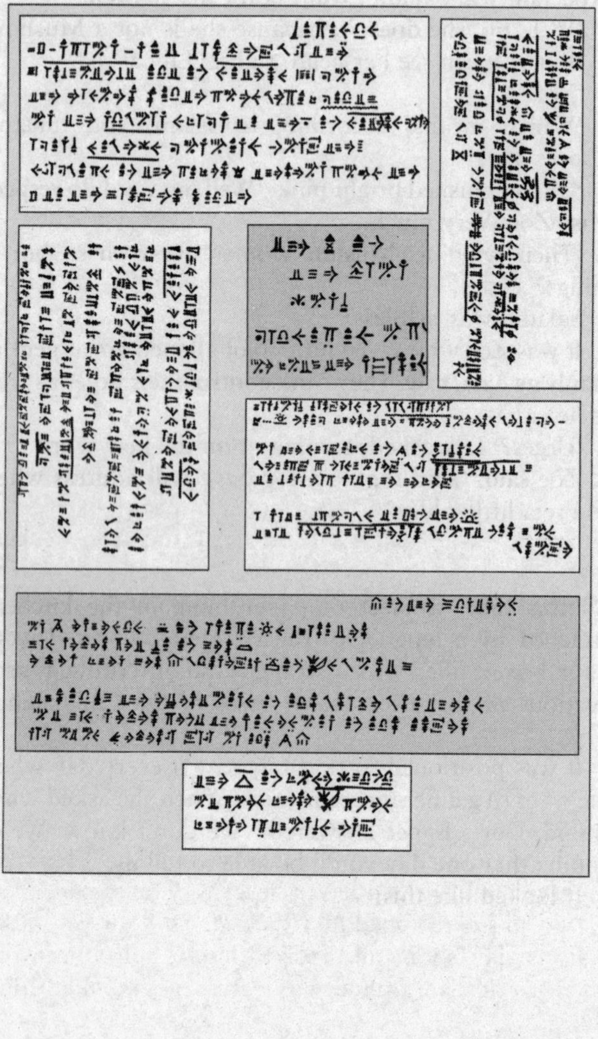

When she hit five years of age, Max Epper took charge of her schooling, teaching her maths, science, ancient history and languages—with an emphasis on Latin, Greek and cuneiform.

It turned out she had a singular aptitude for languages, learning them quickly and fluidly—with almost unnatural ease.

By age 7, she had mastered Latin and Greek.

By 8, she was deciphering Egyptian hieroglyphics.

By 9, she had outstripped Epper in his knowledge of cuneiform—translating all three of the ancient languages from the Bisitun Monument.

Not to mention the modern languages she was learning just by speaking with her multinational guardians. She particularly loved the difficult Gaelic tongue spoken by her Irish protectors, Zoe and Liam Kissane.

Epper was a wonderful teacher.

Lily just adored him—loved his wise old face, his kind blue eyes, and the gentle yet clever way he taught.

And so she renamed him *Wizard*.

Every day, she would race to his schoolroom in the east wing of the farmhouse to learn new and interesting things.

Poems like 'The Charge of the Light Brigade' were acted out with verve and energy.

Simple arithmetic was illustrated with farming examples.

And science was a blast—literally. For Wizard had all manner of crazy home-made inventions in his workshop at the farm. Gadgets and tools that emerged from his dabblings in electromagnetism and foam epoxies.

He once told Lily that a long time ago he had worked at a laboratory called Sandia in the United States, and that it was a secret place where they made secret things.

She liked that. Secret things.

She got along with the team members in different ways.

Although she wasn't a very girly girl, Zoe taught Lily some necessary girly things—like brushing her hair, filing her nails and how to make boys do her bidding.

Matador, the Spanish trooper, spent a lot of time in the gym they'd set up in the smaller barn. At first he let Lily watch him work out. Then, as she grew bigger, he let her sit on one end of a plank of wood while he bench-pressed it, balancing her mass with lead weights at the other end, lifting her high into the air. She loved that.

Witch Doctor, the Jamaican commando, taught her how to tread in silence—they would terrorise Doris Epper, sneaking up on her when she dozed on the veranda in the afternoon sun.

But the soldier she bonded with most was Zoe's brother, Liam, call-sign Gunman.

Gunman was a big guy, broad and tall, easily six-foot-three—with a wide honest face, a fully-shaven head, and large jug ears.

He wasn't all that smart, but he was a great commando.

With Lily, though, he just clicked—perhaps because they were of an equal intelligence level, even though he was 24 and she was just a kid.

They watched movies and read books together.

They played the video game Splinter Cell endlessly in dual-player mode—killing baddies left, right and centre, co-ordinating their moves with loud shouts and commands. They actually made a good team, winning the inaugural 'Victoria Station Dual-Player Splinter Cell Competition', defeating Wizard and Zoe in a hard-fought final.

They went on adventures around the station—including one visit to a giant hangar concealed in the western hills of the property, inside which they found the towering *Halicarnassus*.

Lily gazed in awe at the great 747, and felt a thrill of excitement when she walked up to it, touched it and read a peculiar inscription on its underbelly: 'PRESIDENT ONE—AIR FORCE OF IRAQ'.

But most of all, no-one would ever forget the famous tea party held on the front lawn one summer, with Mister Bear, Little Dog, Big Dog, Barbie, Lily and Gunman—huge Gunman, all six feet of him, hunched over on a tiny plastic chair, sipping from a plastic teacup, allowing Lily to pour him another cup of imaginary tea.

Everyone in the team saw it—watching from inside the farmhouse, alerted by a whisper from Doris. The thing was, no-one ever—*ever*—teased Gunman about the incident.

This was unusual.

They were soldiers. They could and did make fun of

each other on a regular basis, but for some reason, Gunman's relationship with Lily was off-limits.

Well, except for the time he and Lily broke into Aziz's workshop in the big barn, took a plasticine-like substance from his lock-box and used it to blow up Barbie's campervan.

Both Gunman and Lily copped hell for that.

And so, gradually, the team became a family—a family centred around the protection and nurturing of one little girl.

Of course, Lily loved the attention—like when she discovered ballet and put on a one-girl show to a cheering audience of seven commandos and two grandparent-like figures.

And still every day, when she appeared in the kitchen for breakfast, whoever happened to be there at the time would turn to see if she noticed the sheet of paper magnetised to the fridge.

But then one day, when she was seven, there was a commotion.

As the team was eating breakfast, a radio squawked: '*All units. This is Sentry One, I have an intruder coming in through the main gate.*'

Everyone leapt up, alarmed at the presence of an outsider, worried that other nations might know of their mission.

The intruder turned out to be a lone man—tall and thin, with a sanguine face—walking casually down the dirt road from the main gate.

Three hidden guns were trained on him as he rang the doorbell.

Wizard answered the door. 'Can I help you, young man?'

'Indeed you can, Professor Epper,' the thin man said. He had a dry pale face, with high cheekbones and deep hollow eye sockets.

Wizard blanched, did a double-take.

The intruder's grey eyes never blinked. He knew that he had just chilled Wizard to the very bone.

'Professor Max T. Epper,' he said, 'Professor of Archaeology at Trinity College, Dublin, and the representative of Canada on a secret eight-nation task force protecting the daughter of the Oracle of Siwa, with a view to obtaining the lost Capstone of the Great Pyramid. My name is Lieutenant Benjamin Cohen, call-sign *Archer*, formerly of the Sayaret Matkal, now of the Israeli Mossad. I've been sent by my government to join your task force.'

West stepped out from behind Wizard.

'Why hello, Jack,' Archer said familiarly. 'Haven't seen you since Desert Storm. Heard about what you did at that SCUD base outside Basra. Very nice. And Israel appreciated your efforts; although we still don't know how you got out. My bosses said you were involved in this, which was why they sent me. They thought you would accept me more than you would a total stranger.'

'They were right, Ben,' West said. 'It's the only thing keeping you alive right now.'

'Don't shoot the messenger.'

'Why not?' West said and for the briefest of moments, Archer's confident air fell.

West said, 'I don't like having my hand forced, Ben, and you've got us over a barrel here.'

Archer said seriously, 'This is big, Jack. Affairs of state. Fate of the world and all that. This confrontation between Europe and the US has been coming for a long time. Let's just say, Israel always likes to be involved. If it makes you feel better, I have orders to place myself under your direct command.'

West pondered this a moment.

Then he said, 'No contact with home. No reporting back to Mossad until the mission is achieved.'

'I *have* to report back sometime—'

'No reporting back to Mossad until the mission is achieved or I blow your brains out right now, Ben.'

Archer held up his hands, smiled. 'Can't argue with that. You've got a deal.'

★

The team was stunned—but they knew they didn't have any choice in the matter.

Either they allowed Archer to join their team or the Israelis would just advise the Americans of their mission.

How the Israelis had discovered them, they didn't know—but then the Mossad *is* the most ruthless and efficient intelligence service in the world. It knows everything.

What was also apparent, however, was that Israel did *not* want to see the Capstone fall into the hands of either America or Europe—which meant Israel had an interest in the mission succeeding. That was good.

The big question, however, was what Israel planned to do at the end of the mission. Could Archer and Israel be trusted then?

At first, hardly anyone even spoke to Archer—which the ever-cool Israeli didn't seem to mind at all.

But no man is an island, and one day he joined West as he carried out some repairs on the station . . . and so began the process of becoming part of the team.

And slowly, over the course of many months, by working and sweating and training with the others, he became accepted as one of them.

One member of their little community, however, always regarded Archer with great suspicion.

Saladin.

As an Arab and a Muslim, he distrusted the Israeli intensely, but he also knew that Archer's presence in Kenya was now a given.

He would often say that while he had to accept Archer's presence, he didn't have to like it.

As all this was happening, Lily's development was proceeding apace.

She was always inquisitive, always watching.

Watching Saladin go off into the big barn and disappear inside his explosives workshop. He was so sweet and cuddly, she renamed him Pooh Bear.

Watching the new man, Archer, go out to the western paddock and practise firing his ultralong Barrett sniper rifle at far-off targets—and hitting the target *every single time*. She watched him closely, even when he disassembled his rifle. He was so tall and thin, she started calling him Stretch. (She also noticed that Pooh Bear and Stretch hardly ever even spoke. She did not know why.)

Watching Witch Doctor do chin-ups. From an early age, she had loved his wild dreadlocked hair. He became Fuzzy.

Watching the two youngest troopers, Matador and Gunman, jog together, train together and drink together. This earned them their new callsigns: Noddy and Big Ears.

And, of course, watching Zoe.

Idolising Zoe.

Being the only twenty-something female Lily knew, it wasn't unexpected that Zoe would become her feminine role model.

And Zoe Kissane was a good role model. She could

outlast the men in fitness tests, outwit most of them at dinner-table discussions, and she could often be found studying history books deep into the night.

It was not uncommon to find Lily sitting in an armchair late at night beside Zoe, fast asleep with a book open, trying to imitate the pretty Irish woman.

Naturally, Lily called her Princess Zoe.

But above all, the one person Lily enjoyed watching most was Jack West Jr.

She would never forget the day in 2000 when Wizard had presented West with a shiny new silver arm.

With Zoe assisting, Wizard spent the whole day attaching the high-tech arm to West's left elbow, pausing every now and then to frown and say something like, 'The arm's CPU is experiencing interference from somewhere. Aziz, would you turn off the television set, please.' Eventually, he changed some frequencies on the arm's central processing unit and it worked to his satisfaction.

The four-year-old Lily had watched them keenly as they worked.

She was aware that West had lost his arm on the day she was born, in the process of saving her life, so she really wanted his new arm to work.

At the end of the day, the arm was on, and West flexed his new metal fingers. His new hand could actually grip things far more tightly and firmly than his natural right hand could.

True to his word, Wizard had built West an arm that was better than the one he'd been born with.

★

Other things about West intrigued Lily.

For one thing, of all the team at the farm, he hung out with her the least.

He didn't play with her.

He didn't teach her any special subject.

He would spend most days in his study, poring over old books—*really* old books with titles like *Ancient Egyptian Building Methods*, *Imhotep and the Architects of Amun-Ra* and one *really* old scroll titled in Greek: *A Collection of Wonders from around the World*.

Lily loved his study.

It had lots of cool stuff arrayed around its walls: sandstone tablets, a crocodile skull, the skeleton of some ape-like creature Lily couldn't recognise, and hidden in one corner, a glass jar filled with a very strange kind of rusty-red sand. On a secret mission of her own late one night, she discovered that the jar's lid was sealed tight, too tightly for her to open. It remained a mystery.

There was also a medium-sized whiteboard attached to the far wall, on which West had scribbled all sorts of notes and pictures. Things like:

> *HOWARD CARTER (1874-1939):*
> *Found **Tutankhamen**'s tomb; also discovered **Queen Hatshepsut**'s unused tomb (KV20) in **Valley of the Kings** in 1903. Empty tomb, never used. Unfinished carving on tomb's east wall is only known picture of Capstone atop Great Pyramid **receiving vertical shaft of sunlight**:*

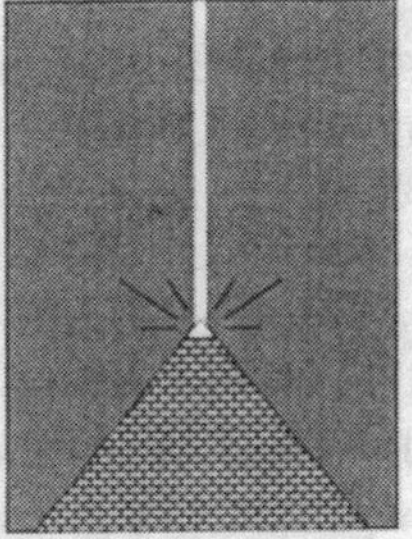

After this West had noted: '***Queen Hatshepsut**: only female pharaoh, prolific obelisk builder*'.

One note on the board, however, caught Lily's eye.

It was at the very bottom corner of the whiteboard, under all the others, almost *deliberately* out of the way. It read simply: '**4 MISSING DAYS OF MY LIFE—CORONADO?**'

Once, late at night, she had seen West staring at those words, tapping his pencil against his teeth, lost in thought.

Whenever West worked in his study, his falcon always sat loyally on his shoulder—alerting him with a squawk when anyone approached.

Lily was intrigued by Horus.

She was an absolutely stunning bird, proud in her bearing and laserlike in her intensity. She didn't play with Lily—despite Lily's continued efforts to coax her.

Bouncing balls, fake mice, nothing Lily used could draw the falcon out into play. No, whatever silly thing Lily did to get her attention, Horus would just stare back at her with total disdain.

Horus, it seemed, cared for only one person.

Jack West.

This was a fact Lily would confirm through experimentation. One day, when once again Horus would not be drawn from West's shoulder, Lily threw her rubber mouse *at West*.

The falcon moved with striking speed.

She intercepted the tossed mouse easily—in mid-air halfway between Lily and West—her talons clutching the toy rodent in twin vice-like grips.

Dead mouse.

Lesson learned.

But research was not the only thing West did.

It didn't escape Lily's notice that while she was busy studying in her classroom, Huntsman would often disappear into the old abandoned mine in the hills beyond the western paddock, not far from the aeroplane hangar. Strangely, he would wear an odd uniform: a fireman's helmet and his canvas jacket. And Horus always went with him.

Lily was strictly forbidden from going into those caves.

Apparently, Wizard had built a series of traps in the mine tunnels—traps based on those in the ancient books that he and West studied—and Huntsman would go in there to test himself against the traps.

Lily found Jack West Jr to be a bit of a mystery.

And she wondered at times, as children do, if he even liked her at all.

But one thing Lily *didn't* know was just how closely she herself was being observed.

Her progress with languages was being carefully monitored.

'She continues to excel,' Wizard reported, just after she turned nine. 'Her transliteration skills are like nothing I have ever seen. And she doesn't even know how good she is. She plays with languages the way Serena Williams plays with spin on a tennis ball—she can do things with it, twist it this way and that, in ways you or I can't even begin to imagine.'

Big Ears reported, 'She's physically fit, good endurance. If it ever becomes necessary, she can run six miles without breaking a sweat.'

'And she knows every inch of my study,' West said. 'She sneaks in there once a week.'

Zoe said, 'I know it isn't mission-related, but she's actually becoming quite good at something else: ballet. Watches it on cable. Now I know lots of little girls *dream* of becoming prima ballerinas, but Lily is actually very good at it, especially considering she's self-taught. She can hold a toe-pose unaided for close to twenty seconds—which is exceptional. The kid just loves ballet, can't get enough of it. It's a girl thing. Think you can get some ballet DVDs the next time you go to Nairobi, Wizard?'

'Certainly.'

'Ballet, you say . . .' West said.

It came as a surprise to Lily when she arrived at breakfast one day—again ignoring the sheet on the fridge—and found West waiting for her in the kitchen, alone, dressed and ready to go somewhere.

'Hey, kiddo. Want to go out for a surprise?'

'Sure.'

The surprise was a private plane trip to Cape Town and a visit to a performance of *The Nutcracker Suite* by the South African Royal Ballet.

Lily sat through the entire performance with her mouth agape, her eyes wide with wonder, entranced.

West just looked at her the whole time—and maybe once, just once, he even smiled.

In 2001, she saw the first *Lord of the Rings* movie. That Christmas, Sky Monster, proud of the New Zealand–born team behind the film, gave her the three books by Tolkien and read them with her.

By the time the third film had come and gone in 2003, Lily and Sky Monster had re-read the books to within an inch of their lives.

And from those readings of *The Lord of the Rings*, Lily got her own callsign.

Sky Monster bestowed it on her, naming her after her favourite character in the epic.

Eowyn.

The feisty shieldmaiden from Rohan who kills the Witch-King of Angmar, the Ringwraith whom no *man* can kill.

Lily loved her callsign.

And still, every day, she would enter the kitchen and get her juice—and see the sheet of paper with the strange writing on it stuck to the fridge door.

Then one morning, a few days before her tenth birthday, she looked at the uppermost box on it and said, 'Huh. I get it now. I know what that says.'

Everyone in the kitchen at the time—Doris, Wizard, Zoe and Pooh Bear—whirled around instantly.

'What does it say, Lily?' Wizard said, gulping, trying not to show his excitement.

'It's a funny language, uses letters and pictures to create sounds. It says,

Colossus.
Two entrances, one plain, one not,
Carved by the fifth Great Architect,
Out of Great Soter's tenth mine.
The easier route lies below the old mouth. Yet
In the Nubian swamp to the south of Soter's mine,
Among Sobek's minions,
Find the four symbols of the Lower Kingdom.
Therein lies the portal to the harder route.'

The next day, the entire team left Victoria Station on board the *Halicarnassus*, bound for the Sudan.

That same day the Sun rotated on its axis and the small sunspot that the Egyptians called Ra's Prophet appeared on its surface.

In seven days, on March 20, the Tartarus Rotation would occur.

SECOND MISSION
THE LIGHTHOUSE

TUNISIA
15 MARCH, 2006
5 DAYS BEFORE TARTARUS

THE PHAROS

As a Wonder of the World, the Lighthouse at Alexandria has always been, terribly unfairly, the perennial runner-up.

It is second in height to the Great Pyramid at Giza—by a mere 29 metres.

It stood, intact and functioning, for 1,600 years, until it was hit by a pair of devastating earthquakes in 1300 AD. Only the Great Pyramid survived for longer.

But ultimately it would defeat the Pyramid on one important count: it was useful.

And because it survived for so long, we have many descriptions of it: Greek, Roman, Islamic.

By today's standards, it was a skyscraper.

Built on three colossal levels, it stood 117 metres high, the equivalent of a 40-storey building.

The first level was square—broad, solid and powerful. The foundation level.

The second level was octagonal and hollow.

The third and uppermost level was cylindrical and also hollow—to allow for the raising of fuel to the peak.

At the summit of the tower stood its crowning glory, Sostratus's masterpiece: the mirror.

Ten feet high and shaped like a modern satellite dish, the mirror was mounted on a sturdy base and could rotate 360 degrees. Its concave bronze shape reflected the rays of the Sun to warn approaching ships of the dangerous shoals and submerged rocks just off Alexandria.

By night, a huge bonfire was lit in front of the mirror, allowing the great lighthouse to send its beam twenty kilometres out into the darkened sea.

Interestingly, like the Colossus of Rhodes a few years later, it was built at the request of Ptolemy I of Egypt—Alexander the Great's close friend and general.

AIRSPACE OVER AFRICA

15 MARCH, 2006, 0200 HOURS

5 DAYS BEFORE THE ARRIVAL OF TARTARUS

The *Halicarnassus* roared toward Kenya.

The huge black 747, with its bristling array of missiles and gun turrets, cut a mean figure in the sky. It looked like a gigantic bird of prey—death on wings.

Inside it, West's multinational team was still recovering from their disastrous mission in the Sudan.

In the main cabin of the jumbo, West, Wizard, Lily and Pooh Bear all sat in contemplative silence. The cabin was fitted with couches, some tables, and wall-consoles for radio and communications gear.

Wizard stood. 'I'd better call the Spanish Army attaché. Tell them about Noddy . . .'

He went to a nearby wall-console, grabbed the secure sat-phone there, started dialling.

West just stared into space, replaying in his mind everything that had gone wrong in the Sudan.

Lily sat with Pooh Bear, gazing at the team's original copy of the Callimachus Text.

As for the others, Fuzzy and Big Ears were in the infirmary in the rear of the plane, being treated by Zoe; and Sky Monster was up in the cockpit, flying the plane, with Stretch keeping him company.

In the main cabin, Lily scanned another entry of the Callimachus Text. The symbols on the page were ancient, alien.

Then suddenly she squealed, 'Hey!'

West snapped up. Wizard also spun.

'This entry here. I couldn't understand it before, but for some reason, I can now. It's more complex than the last one. Uses new symbols. But I can read it now.'

'What's it say?' West leapt to her side.

Lily read it alound:

'The Pharos.
Look for the base that was once the peak of the Great Tower
In the deepest crypt of Iskender's Highest Temple,
Soter's illustrious House to the Muses,
Among the works of Eratosthenes the measurer, Hipparchus the stargazer,
And Archimedes and Heron the machine makers,
There you will find ~~it~~ EUCLID'S INSTRUCTIONS
Surrounded by Death.'

Lily frowned. 'The word "it" has been crossed out and replaced with "Euclid's instructions". I don't know what they are.'

'I do,' Wizard said, reaching for a high-tech stainless-steel trunk behind him. It opened with a vacuum-sealed *hiss*. The trunk was fitted with many pigeonholes, each pigeonhole containing an ancient scroll. Wizard's collection was huge—there were at least 200 tightly rolled scrolls.

'Now where is that index? Ah, here it is.' Wizard pulled a computer printout from a sleeve in the trunk's lid. On it was a very long typewritten list. 'Now, Euclid's Instructions . . . Euclid's Instructions. I'm sure I saw that title once before. Ah, good, there we are. Just a moment.'

Wizard proceeded to rummage through his scrolls. As he did so, West typed out Lily's translation of the Text.

Stretch entered the main cabin, noticed the activity immediately. 'What's going on?'

'We may have had a development,' West said. He read one line from the translation. '"Soter's illustrious House to the Muses". A House to the Muses is a "museion" or "museum". Soter was Ptolemy I. *Soter's House to the Muses* is the Library at Alexandria, otherwise known as the Museion.'

'So,' Pooh Bear said, 'in the deepest crypt of the Alexandria Library, among those works mentioned, we'll find "the base that was once the peak of the Lighthouse", whatever that is. I thought the Library was destroyed in antiquity.'

'It was,' Zoe said, coming into the main cabin. 'By the Romans in 48 BC. The Biblioteca Alexandrina was the centre of all learning in the ancient world, possessed of over 700,000 scrolls and the writings of some of the greatest thinkers in human history, and the Romans *razed it to the ground*.'

She saw West's translation. 'God. Look at those names. It's like a Who's Who of history's greatest minds. Eratosthenes: he calculated the circumference of the Earth. Hipparchus mapped the constellations. Archimedes figured out volume and was a prolific inventor. And Heron. Well. Heron invented geared cogwheels and a primitive steam engine *2,000 years* before James Watt was even born.'

Pooh Bear asked, 'And now?'

Zoe sighed. 'The Library is gone. Long since buried underneath modern-day Alexandria. They know where it stood—and the Egyptian Government recently built a new library not far from the old site—but the Romans did their work well. Just as they had done with Carthage a hundred years previously, the Library was removed from existence. Not a single brick, text or crypt remains.'

'So all its scrolls were destroyed, then?'

'Many were, but a large portion of them was spirited away from the Library in the days before the Roman invasion. The scrolls were reputedly taken to a secret location, deep in the Atlas Mountains—and to date, have never been officially found.'

When Zoe said this last sentence, she threw West and Wizard a sideways look.

'Not everyone announces it to the world when they find something important,' West said.

'*What*—?' Pooh Bear said, whirling to face the scrolls Wizard was rummaging through. 'Are you telling me that those scrolls are—'

'Ah-ha! Here it is!' Wizard exclaimed.

He extracted an ancient scroll from a pigeonhole. It was beautifully made, with ornate rollers at each end and thick cream-coloured parchment.

Wizard unrolled it, read it.

'Hmmm. Greek text. Handwriting matches that of other known Euclidian texts. One of the greatest mathematicians in history, Euclid. He created plane geometry, you know, a grid with an x and y axis, which we now call Euclidian Geometry. This scroll is undoubtedly written by him, and its title is simply "Instructions". Which makes it Euclid's Instructions, I suppose.'

'What does it say?' Pooh Bear asked.

Wizard scanned the scroll. 'It just seems to restate some

of Euclid's more mundane discoveries. No reference to any ancient wonder or Golden Capstone.'

'Damn,' West said.

'Bugger,' Zoe said.

'Wait a second . . .' Wizard held up his hand. 'Look at this.'

He had unfurled the scroll to its edges, revealing a small handwritten notation at the extreme bottom of the parchment, right where it met the lower roller.

Written across the bottom of the scroll were a few lines of text, not in classical Greek, but in another language: the cuneiform-like strokes of the Word of Thoth. It read:

'Lily?' Wizard said.

Lily scanned the ancient document for a moment, then read it aloud:

'Base removed before the Roman invasion,
Taken to Hamilcar's Forgotten Refuge.
Follow the Deadly Coast of the Phoenicians
To the inlet of the two tridents,
Where you will behold the easier entrance to

The sixth Great Architect's masterwork.
The Seventh has lain there ever since.'

'There's that word again,' Pooh Bear said, 'base. Why do they call it a base?'

But West wasn't listening. He turned to Wizard, his face alive with excitement. 'The Callimachus Text doesn't give the location of the Pharos Piece . . .'

'No,' Wizard said. 'This scroll does. And this is the only copy. Which means—'

'—neither the Europeans nor the Americans can possibly know where this Piece rests. Max, we've got a clear run at this one.'

They stared at each other in amazement.

'Holy shit,' West said, smiling. 'We might just have a chance in this race.'

The *Halicarnassus* zoomed through the dawn, arriving at the northern coast of Libya, soaring over the frothy white line where the waters of the Mediterranean met the shores of the North African desert.

Inside it, West, Wizard and Zoe were making swift progress on Euclid's Instructions.

'"The Phoenicians" was another name for the people of Carthage—the trading state annihilated by Rome in the Third and last Punic War. The state of Carthage approximated modern-day Tunisia, directly south of Italy, across the Mediterranean,' Wizard said.

'And Hamilcar is Hamilcar Barca,' West said, 'father of Hannibal and commander of the Carthaginian forces in the First Punic War. I didn't know he had a refuge, let alone a forgotten one.'

Zoe commented, 'Hamilcar died in Spain in 228 BC, between the First and Second Punic Wars. He must have ordered the construction of a faraway fortress and never lived to see it.'

Wizard was on his computer: 'I'm checking my database for any references to "Hamilcar's Refuge". But I've already found this: the "Deadly Coast" was a name used by Alexandrian sailors to describe the coast of modern-day Tunisia. For 100 miles the shore is all cliffs—400 feet high and plunging vertically into the sea. Major shipwreck area even in the 20th century. Oh dear. If your ship goes down close to the shore, you can't climb out of the water because of the cliffs. People have been known to die within an arm's length of dry land. No wonder the ancient sailors feared it.'

West added, 'And the sixth Great Architect is Imhotep VI. He lived about 100 years after Imhotep V. Clever trap-builder—fortified the island-temple of Philae near Aswan. Known for his predilection for concealed underwater entrances. There are *six* at Philae alone.'

Stretch said, 'Wait a moment. I thought the Egyptian civilisation was finished by the time of the Punic Wars.'

'A common misconception,' Wizard said. 'People tend to think that the ancient Greek, Roman and Egyptian civilisations existed separately, one after the other, but that's not true, not at all. They *co-existed*. While Rome was fighting Carthage in the Punic Wars, Egypt was still flourishing under the Ptolemies. In fact, an independent Egypt would continue to exist right up until Cleopatra VII, the famous one, was defeated by the Romans in 30 BC.'

'So what are these two tridents?' Pooh Bear asked.

'My guess is they are rock formations just out from the coastal cliffs,' Wizard said. 'Markers. Triple-pointed rock formations that look like tridents, marking the location of the Refuge.'

'One hundred miles of sheer-cliffed coast,' Pooh Bear groaned. 'It could take *days* to patrol that kind of terrain by boat. And we don't have days.'

'No,' West said. 'We don't. But I'm not planning on using a *boat* to scan that coastline.'

An hour later, the *Halicarnassus* was soaring high above

the Tunisian coast, travelling parallel to it, heading westward, when suddenly its rear loading ramp opened and a tiny winged figure leapt out of the plane and plummeted down through the sky.

It was a man.

West.

Shooming head-first down through the air, his face covered by a wickedly aerodynamic oxygen-supplying full-face helmet.

But it was the object on his back that demanded attention.

A pair of lightweight carbon composite *wings*.

They had a span of 2.6 metres, upturned wingtips, and in their bulky centre (which covered a parachute), they possessed six compressed-air thrusters that could be used to sustain a gliding pattern when natural glide failed.

West rocketed down through the sky at a 45-degree angle, his bullet-shaped winged body slicing through the air.

The Deadly Coast came into view.

Towering yellow cliffs fronted onto the flat blue sea. Giant, immovable. Waves crashed against them relentlessly, exploding in gigantic showers of spray.

West zoomed lower, hitting 180 km/h, before at around 800 feet . . .

. . . he swooped upwards and entered a slower, more serene glide pattern.

Now he soared, three hundred feet above the waves of the Mediterranean, parallel to the massive coastal cliffs.

He was flying near the Tunisian–Libyan border, a particularly desolate stretch of the North African coastline. Broad flat sandplains stretched away from the sheer cliffs of the coast. About a klick inland, those plains rammed up against a mountain range made up of a few extinct volcanoes that ran parallel to the shore.

It was a land devoid of life. Desolate. Depressing. A place where nothing grows.

As he flew, West scanned the cliffs, searching for any rock formations on them that resembled a pair of tridents.

After ten minutes of gliding, he lost his natural glide pattern, so he ignited a compressed-air thruster. With a sharp *hiss-wapp*, it lifted him to a higher altitude, allowing him to glide for longer.

Then after about forty minutes—and three more compressed-air assists—he saw them.

Two rock-islands positioned about fifty metres out from the coastal cliff-face, their rocky shapes each resembling a three-fingered human hand pointing toward the sky.

Or a trident.

Two tridents.

The section of cliff immediately behind the two tridents looked particularly forbidding—vertical and rough, with the upper section of the great cliff partially overhanging its base. Very difficult to scale.

'Wizard! Come in!' West called into his radio mike. 'I've found them!'

An hour later, the *Halicarnassus* had landed on the flat sandy plain, dropped off a Land Rover four-wheel drive from its belly, and then lifted off to take up a holding pattern a hundred miles to the south.

Bouncing along in the Land Rover, the team joined West—now standing on the windswept cliff overlooking the two tridents. The team numbered seven, since the injured Fuzzy had stayed in the *Halicarnassus* with Sky Monster, along with Horus. Big Ears, however, was there and still mobile, thanks to a cocktail of painkillers.

Technically, they were in Tunisia. The landscape was empty and dry. There wasn't a village or human settlement for fifty miles in any direction.

In fact, the landscape could better be described as a moonscape: the flat sandplain, the occasional meteorite crater, and of course the chain of mountains guarding the landward approach about a kilometre inland.

'You know,' Big Ears said, 'they filmed *Star Wars* in Tunisia. The Tatooine scenes.'

'I can see why,' West said, not turning from the view of the sea. 'It's totally alien.'

Wizard came alongside West, handed him a printout. 'This is the only reference my database has for Hamilcar's Refuge. It's a hand-drawn sketch on papyrus found in a worker's hut in Alexandria, an Egyptian worker who must have worked on Imhotep VI's reconfiguration of Hamilcar's Refuge.'

The papyrus sheet bore a carefully-crafted diagram on it:

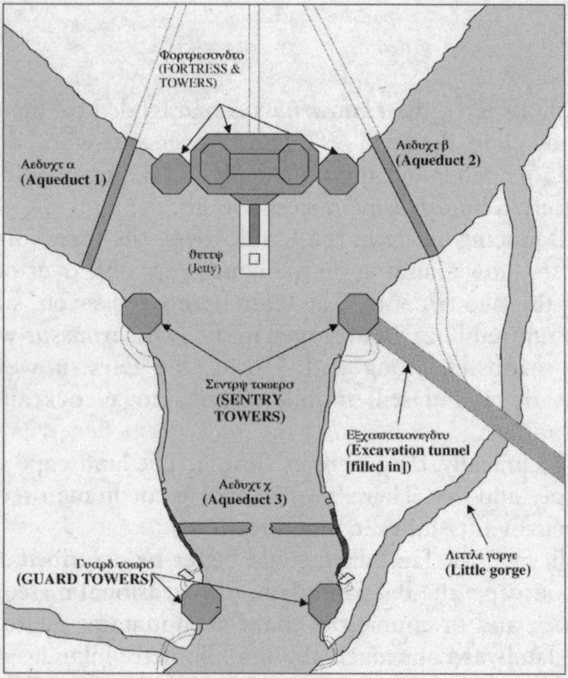

It was hard to tell exactly what the image depicted. Cut off at the top and bottom, it didn't seem to show the entire structure.

'Aqueducts and guard towers,' West said, 'and a filled-in excavation tunnel. Jesus, this place must be huge.' He scanned the landscape all around him, but saw nothing but barren desert and the harsh coast. 'But if it's so huge, where the hell is it?'

He checked his printout of the Euclidian clue:

Follow the Deadly Coast of the Phoenicians
To the inlet of the two tridents,
Where you will behold the easier entrance to
The sixth Great Architect's masterwork.
The Seventh has lain there ever since.

'"The inlet of the two tridents",' he read aloud. 'We've found the two tridents, so there's supposed to be an inlet here. But I don't see one. It's all just one seamless coastline.'

It was true.

There was no bay or inlet in the coast anywhere nearby.

'Just hold on a moment . . .' Epper said.

He dug into his rucksack and extracted a tripod-mounted device.

'Sonic-resonance imager,' he said, erecting the tripod on the sand. He then aimed it *downward* and hit a switch. 'It'll show us the density of the earth beneath our feet.'

The sonic-resonance imager pinged slowly.

Piiiing-piiiing-piiiing.

'Solid sandstone. All the way to the imager's depth limit,' Wizard said. 'As you'd expect.'

Then he swivelled the imager on its tripod and aimed it at the ground a few yards to the west, the section of coastline directly in line with the two tridents—

Ping-ping-ping-ping-ping-ping . . .

The imager's pinging went bananas.

West turned to Wizard. 'Explain?'

The old man looked at his display. It read:

TOTAL DEPTH: 8.0 M.
SUBSTANCE ANALYSIS: SILICON OVERLAY 5.5 M;
GRANITE UNDERLAY 2.5 M.

Wizard said, 'Depth here is eight metres. Mix of hard-packed sand and granite.'

'*Eight* metres?' Pooh Bear said. 'How can that be? We're *130* metres above sea level. That would mean there's 92 metres of empty air beneath that section of ground—'

'Oh, no way . . .' West said, understanding.

'Yes way . . .' Wizard said, also seeing it.

West looked back inland at the sandplain stretching to the nearest mountain a kilometre away. The sand *appeared* to be seamless. 'Amazing the things you can do with a workforce of 10,000 men,' he said.

'What? *What?*' Pooh Bear said, exasperated. 'Would you two mind telling the rest of us mere mortals what in the blazes you're talking about?'

West smiled. 'Pooh. There *was* once an inlet here. I imagine it was a narrow crevice in the coastal cliffs that cut inland.'

'But it's not here now,' Pooh said. 'How does *an entire inlet* disappear?'

'Simple,' West said. 'It doesn't. It's still here. It's just been hidden. Concealed by the labour of 10,000 workers. The keepers of the Capstone put a roof over the inlet, bricked in the entrance and then covered it all over with sand.'

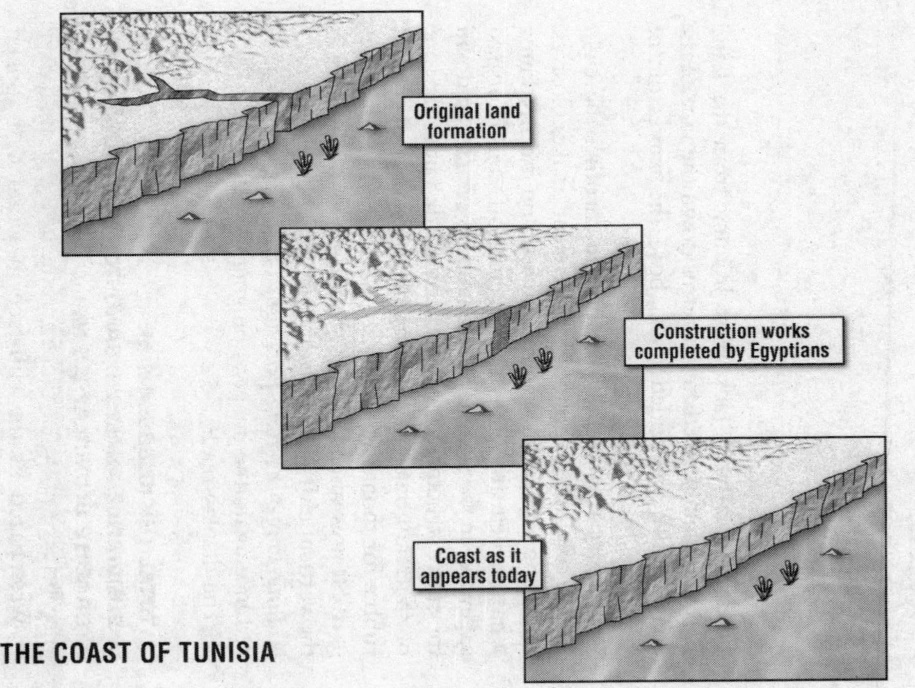

THE COAST OF TUNISIA

Five minutes later, Jack West Jr hung from the Land Rover's winch cable fifteen metres down the face of the coastal cliff, suspended high above the waves of the Mediterranean Sea.

He probably could have blasted through the eight metres of sand and granite with conventional explosives, but using explosives was risky when you did not know what lay beneath you—it could close off tunnels or passageways in the system below; it could even bring down the entire structure, and West's team didn't have the time or the manpower to sift through thousands of tons of rubble for months.

West now aimed Wizard's sonic-resonance imager at the vertical cliff-face in front of him.

Ping-ping-ping-ping-ping-ping . . .

Once again the imager's pinging went wild.

The display read:

TOTAL THICKNESS: 4.1 M.
SUBSTANCE ANALYSIS: SANDSTONE OVERLAY 1.6 M; GRANITE UNDERLAY 2.5 M.

West gazed at the cliff-face in wonder. It looked exactly like the rest of the coastline: same colour, same texture; rough and weatherworn.

But it was a hoax, a ruse, an entirely *artificial* cliff.

A false wall.

West smiled, called up. 'It's a false wall! Only four metres thick. Granite, with a sandstone outer layer.'

'*So where is the entrance?*' Zoe asked over his radio.

West gazed straight down the sheer cliff-face—at the waves crashing at its base.

'Imhotep VI reconfigured this one. Remember what I said before: he was known for his concealed underwater entrances. Haul me up and prep the scuba gear.'

Minutes later, West again hung suspended from the Land Rover's superlong winch cable, only now he had been lowered all the way down the false cliff-face. He dangled just a few metres above the waves crashing at its base.

He was wearing a wetsuit, full face-mask, and a lightweight scuba tank on his back. His caving gear—fireman's helmet, X-bars, flares, ropes, rockscrew drill and guns—hung from his belt.

'Okay! Lower me in, and do it fast!' he called into his throat-mike.

The others obeyed and released the cable's spooler, lowering West *into* the churning sea at the base of the cliff.

West plunged underwater—

—and he saw it immediately.

The vertical cliff continued under the surface, but about 6 metres below the surface it stopped at a distinctly man-made opening: an enormous square doorway. It was huge. With its bricked frame, the doorway looked like a great aeroplane hangar door carved into the submerged rockface.

And engraved in its upper lintel was a familiar symbol:

West spoke into his face-mask's radio. 'Folks. I've found an opening. I'm going in to see what's on the other side.'

Guided by his Princeton-Tec underwater flashlight, West swam through the doorway and into an underwater passage that was bounded by walls of granite bricks.

It was a short swim.

About ten metres in, he emerged into a much wider area—and instantly felt the tug of unusually strong tidal motion.

He surfaced in darkness.

While he couldn't see beyond the range of his flashlight, he sensed that he was at one end of a vast internal space.

He swam to the left, across the swirling tide, to a small stone ledge. Once he was out of the water and on the ledge, he fired a flare into the air.

The dazzling incandescent flare shot high into the air, higher and higher and higher, until it hovered nearly 250 feet above him and illuminated the great space.

'Mother of God . . .' he breathed.

At that very same moment, the others were peering down the cliff-face outside, waiting for word from West.

Suddenly, his crackly voice came in over their radios: '*Guys. I'm in. Come on down and prepare to be amazed.*'

'Copy that, Huntsman,' Zoe said. 'We're on our way.'

Lily stood a short distance from the group, staring inland, out across the plain.

As the others started shouldering into their scuba gear, she said, 'What's that?'

They all turned—

—in time to see a C-130 Hercules cargo plane bank lazily around in the sky high above them, and release about a dozen small objects from its rear.

The objects sailed down through the air in co-ordinated spiralling motions.

Parachutes. Soldiers on parachutes.

Heading straight for their position on the cliff-top!

The Hercules continued on, touching down on the plain several klicks to the east, stopping near one of the larger meteorite craters.

Wizard whipped a pair of high-powered binoculars to his eyes—zoomed in on the plane.

'American markings. Oh, Christ! It's Judah!'

Then he tilted his binoculars upward to see the incoming strike team directly above him.

He didn't need much zoom to see the Colt Commando assault rifles held across their chests, and the black hockey helmets they wore on their heads.

'It's Kallis and his CIEF team! I can't imagine how, but the Americans have found us! Everybody, move! Down the cable! Into the cave! Now!'

Exactly six minutes later, a pair of American combat boots stomped onto the spot where Wizard had just been standing.

Cal Kallis.

In front of him stood the abandoned Land Rover with its winch cable stretched out over the edge of the cliff-face and down to the waves 400 feet below.

Kallis looked out over the edge just in time to see the last two members of West's team vanish under the waves with scuba gear on.

He keyed his radio mike. 'Colonel Judah, this is Kallis. We've just missed them at the sea entrance. Immediate pursuit is a viable option. Repeat, immediate pursuit is viable. Instructions?'

'*Engage in pursuit*,' the cold voice at the other end said. '*Instructions are as before: you may kill any of the others, but not West or the girl. Go. We'll enter via the second entrance.*'

West's team surfaced inside the dark cave behind the false cliff.

As soon as his head broke the surface, Wizard called, 'Jack! We've got trouble! The Americans are right behind us!'

One by one, West hauled the others out of the water and onto the small stone ledge to the left.

'*How?*' he said to Wizard.

'I don't know. I just don't know.'

West scowled. 'We'll figure it out later. Come on. I *hate* having to rush through uncharted trap systems and now we've got to. Get a look at this place.'

Wizard looked up at the cavern around them.

'Oh my . . .' he gasped.

HAMILCAR'S REFUGE (LONG VIEW)

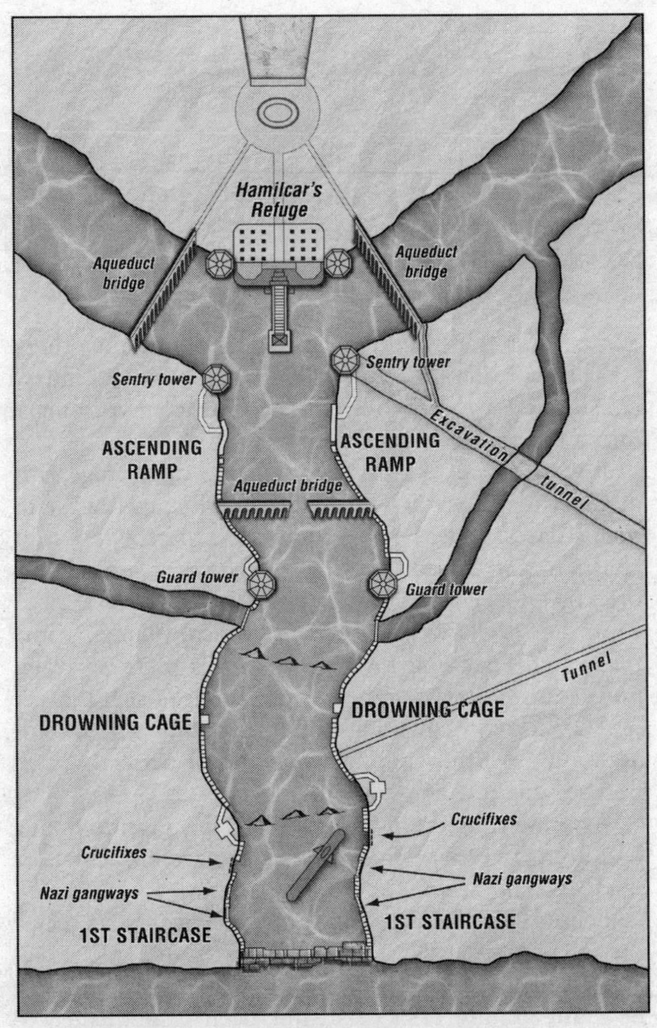

HAMILCAR'S REFUGE (OVERHEAD VIEW)

Wizard stared in wonder at the sight. So did the others.

Through sheer force of will, Imhotep VI had indeed constructed a *ceiling* over the natural inlet—turning it into a most unique cavern.

It wasn't wide, maybe twenty metres on average, fifty at the widest. But it was long, superlong. Now lit by many flares, it was revealed to be a narrow twisting chasm that stretched away into darkness for several hundred metres.

Its side walls were sheer and vertical, plunging into the water. Spanning the upper heights of these walls, however, were massive beams of granite—each the size of a California Redwood—laid horizontally side-by-side across the width of the inlet, resting in perfectly fitted notches dug just below ground level.

At some time in the distant past, this granite ceiling had been covered over with sand, concealing the entire inlet.

Behind West's team stood the great wall that sealed the inlet off from the sea. Four hundred feet tall, it was a colossal structure, strong and proud, and on this side its giant granite bricks had not been camouflaged to match the coastline. It looked like a massive brick wall.

Of immediate importance to West and his team, however, was what lay behind this wall.

The roofed chasm.

Cut into the sheer cliffs on either side of the chasm's central waterway were a pair of narrow ledge-like paths.

The two paths ran in identical manner on either side of the twisting, bending chasm—perfect mirror images of each other. They variously rose to dizzying heights as long bending stairways or descended below the waterline; they even delved momentarily into the walls themselves before emerging again further on. At many points along the way, the paths and staircases had crumbled, leaving voids to be jumped.

The waterway itself was also deadly. Fed by the surging tide outside, small whirlpools dotted its length, ready to suck down the unwary adventurer who fell in, while two lines of tooth-like boulders blocked the way for any kind of boat.

Spanning the watercourse was a beautiful multi-arched aqueduct bridge built in the Carthaginian style, but sadly it was horribly broken in the middle.

As a final touch, vents in the walls spewed forth plumes of steam, casting an ominous haze over the entire scene.

Wizard raised a pair of night-vision binoculars to his eyes and peered down the length of the great chasm.

The world went luminescent green.

In deep shadow at the far end of the cavern, only partially visible beyond its twists and turns, he saw a structure. It was clearly huge, a fortress of some kind, with two high-spired towers and a great arched entrance, but because of the bends in the chasm and the haze, he couldn't see it in its entirety.

'Hamilcar's Refuge,' he breathed. 'Untouched for over 2,000 years.'

'Maybe not,' West said. 'Look over there.'

Wizard did, and his jaw dropped.

'My goodness . . .'

There, wrecked against some rocks in the middle of the waterway, lying half-in half-out of the water, was the great rusted hulk of a World War II–era submarine.

Emblazoned on its conning tower, corroded by time and salt, were the Nazi swastika and the gigantic number: '*U-342*'.

'It's a Nazi U-boat . . .' Big Ears breathed.

Zoe said, 'Hessler and Koenig . . .'

'Probably,' Wizard agreed.

'Who?' Big Ears asked.

'The famous Nazi archaeological team: Herman Hessler and Hans Koenig. They were experts on the Capstone, and also founding members of the Nazi Party, so they were buddies of Hitler himself. In fact, with Hitler's blessing, they commanded a top secret scientific expedition to North Africa in 1941, accompanied by Rommel's Afrika Korps.'

Big Ears said, 'Let me guess, they were after the Capstone, they disappeared and were never heard from again?'

'Yes and no,' Zoe answered. 'Yes, they were after the Capstone, and yes, Hessler never returned, but Koenig did, only to be caught by the British when he arrived, on foot, in Tobruk, staggering out of the desert, starving and almost dead from thirst. I believe he was ultimately handed over to the Americans, who asked to interrogate him. Koenig would ultimately be taken back to the States with a bunch of other German scientists, where I believe he still lives.'

West turned to Wizard. 'How far behind us is Kallis?'

'Five minutes at the most,' Wizard said. 'Probably less.'

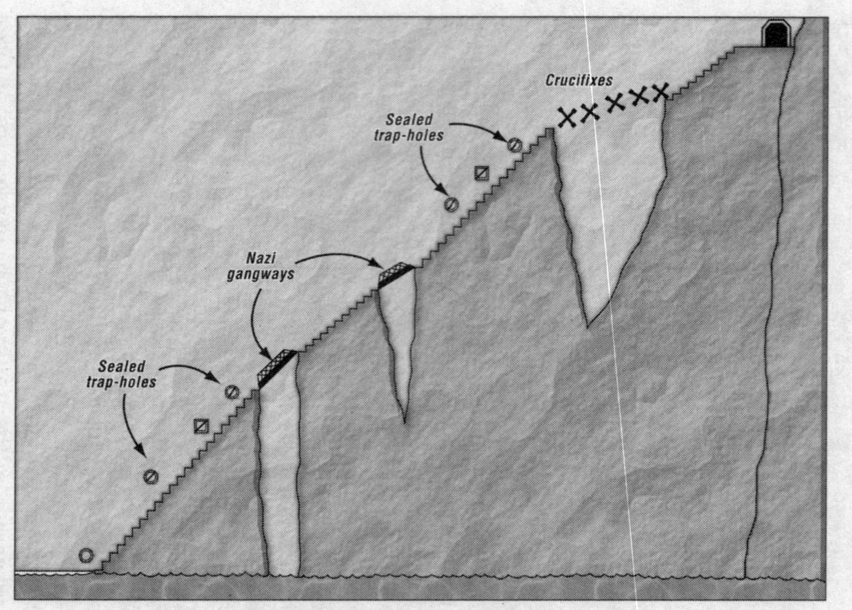

THE FIRST STAIRCASE and THE CRUCIFIXES

'Then we have to get cracking. Sorry, Zoe, but you'll have to continue the history lesson on the way. Come on, people. Dump your bigger scuba tanks, but keep your pony bottles and your masks—we might need them.' A pony bottle was a small handheld scuba tank with a mouthpiece. 'Wizard, fire up a Warbler or two.'

The First Staircase (Ascending)

West and his team took the left-hand cliff-path.

It quickly became a staircase that rose and twisted up the left-hand wall like a slithering snake. After a minute of climbing, West was 80 feet above the swirling waterway below.

At two points along the ascending stone staircase there were four-foot gaps that preceded stepping-stone-like ledges.

And facing onto those ledges were wall-holes just like the one that Fuzzy had neutralised at the base of the quarry in Sudan.

West didn't know what deadly fluid these wall-holes spewed forth, for the Nazis had—very conveniently—neutralised them long ago, riveting sheets of plate steel over the holes, then laying steel catwalk-gangways over the gaps in the stairs.

West danced across the first catwalk-bridge and past the sealed wall-hole.

Whump!

A great weight of some unseen liquid banged against the other side of the steel plate, trying to burst its way through. But the plate held and West and his team ran by it.

No sooner were they past the second plugged-up wall-hole than—

Zing-smack!

A bullet sizzled past their heads and ricocheted off the wall above them.

Everyone spun.

To see a member of Kallis's CIEF team hovering in the water at the base of the great wall, his Colt rifle raised and aimed.

The CIEF man let fly with a spray on full auto.

But Wizard had initiated a Warbler in Big Ears's backpack and the bullets fanned outward, away from the fleeing group.

More CIEF men surfaced at the base of the false wall—until there were three, six, ten, twelve of them gathered there.

West saw them.

And once all his people were past the two gaps in the rising staircase, he jimmied the two Nazi gangways free, sending them free-falling into the water 80 feet below. Then he used his X-bar like a crowbar to prise off the Nazi plate covering the second wall-hole. The plate came free, exposing the hole.

Then West took off after the others.

The Crucifixes

Up they ran, following the narrow winding staircase that hugged the left-hand cliff.

About 150 feet up, they came to a wider void in the stairs, about twenty feet across.

Some handholds had been gouged out of the cliff-face, allowing one to climb sideways across the void, resting one's feet on a two-inch-wide mini-ledge.

Strange X-shaped hollows—each the size of a man—

lined the wall of the void, curiously in sync with the handholds.

'Crucifixes,' Wizard said as West caught up. 'Nasty. Another of Imhotep VI's favourites.'

'No choice then. I'll go up and over,' West said.

Within seconds, he was free-climbing up the cliff-face, gripping cracks in its surface with only his finger-tips, crossing it sideways above the trap-laden void.

As he climbed, Wizard peered anxiously at the pursuing CIEF force. They were themselves trying to negotiate the two stepping-stone ledges fifty yards below.

West landed on the other side, and quickly strung a rope—with a flying fox attached to it—across the void.

The CIEF team got past the first stepping-stone ledge.

West pulled the others across the void on the flying fox. First Lily, then Zoe, Big Ears and Wizard.

One of the Delta men leapt onto the second stepping-stone ledge—and a gush of superheated *mud* came blasting out of the now-exposed wall-hole there and enveloped him.

The mud was a deep dark brown, thick, viscous and heavy. It was volcanic mud. It seared the skin from the man's body in an instant before its immense weight hurled him down to the water 80 feet below.

Wizard's eyes boggled. 'Oh my . . .'

The remaining CIEF men were more cautious, and they skirted the wall-hole carefully.

In the meantime, Stretch and—last of all—Pooh Bear were hauled across the wider void on the flying fox.

No sooner had Pooh Bear's feet touched solid ground than the first member of the pursuing CIEF team arrived at the other side of the void, only twenty feet away!

West immediately cut his team's rope, letting it fall into the abyss, and took off around the next bend.

The first CIEF man, energised by how close he was to his enemy, immediately set about using the handholds gouged into the wall of the void.

It happened when his hands hit the second and third handholds.

Like slithering tentacles, two bronze manacles came springing out of the wall and clasped tightly around his wrists.

Then, a great man-sized bronze cross *fell out* of the X-shaped recess in the wall, *right in front of* the hapless CIEF man.

And the operation of the crucifix trap suddenly became apparent to the CIEF trooper: the manacles were attached to the big heavy cross and he was now held tight by them.

He shrieked as the cross tipped out of its recess and fell 150 feet straight down the sheer cliff-face, plunging into the water at the bottom with a gigantic splash . . .

. . . where it sank, taking the CIEF man with it.

He screamed the whole time, right up to the point where the weight of the cross took him under.

West and his team ran.

The Sinkhole Cave

It was probably the first time in history someone could claim to have been *helped* by Adolf Hitler's Nazi regime, but it was largely the Nazis' bridge-building efforts from 60 years previously that kept West and his team ahead of Kallis's men.

At the next bend in the chasm, halfway up the high vertical wall, the ledge-path bored *into* the cliff-face, cutting the corner.

The short tunnel there took them to a square diorite-walled sinkhole cave, 20 feet across and 30 feet deep. Steaming, bubbling volcanic mud—heated by a subterranean thermal source—filled the entire base of the sinkhole. The tunnel continued on the opposite side of the cave.

But the Nazis had once again bridged this gap—so West's crew ran across the bridge, then promptly kicked it into the sinkhole behind them.

The Second Staircase (Descending)

They emerged on the other side of the bend—where they fired some new flares—and beheld a steep staircase that plunged down the curving wall of the chasm before them, hugging it all the way down to the water at its base.

Indeed, the staircase seemed to continue *into* the water . . . right into the mouth of a swirling whirlpool.

But yet again, the Nazis had bridged this peril with a gangway.

West flew down the stairs—running beneath a large and rather ominous wall-hole mounted above the tunnel's doorway.

'Jack!' Wizard called. 'Trigger stones! Find them and point them out for the rest of us, will you!'

West did so, avoiding any step that was askew or suspicious, and identifying it for the next person in their line.

Their progress was slowed at two places along the staircase—where the stairs had decayed and fallen away, meaning they had to make precarious jumps over the voids.

It was just as the last man in their line—Pooh Bear—was leaping over the second void that another CIEF trooper appeared at the top of the staircase!

Pooh Bear jumped.

The CIEF man charged.

And in his hurry, Pooh Bear landed awkwardly . . . and slipped . . . and fell, dropping clumsily onto his butt, and landing squarely on a trigger stone.

'Blast!' Pooh Bear swore.

Everyone froze, and turned.

'You stupid, stupid Arab . . .' Stretch muttered.

'Stretch . . . not now,' West snapped.

An ominous rumbling came from the wall-hole at the top of the long curving staircase.

'Let me guess,' Stretch said. 'A big round boulder is going to roll out of that hole and chase us down the stairs, just like in *Raiders of the Lost Ark*.'

Not exactly.

Three wooden boulders, all a metre in diameter and clearly heavy, came rushing out of the hole in quick succession—and each was fitted with hundreds of outward-pointing bronze *nails*.

They must have weighed 100 kilograms each and they bounded down the stairway, booming with every impact, bearing down on the team.

West scooped up Lily. 'Go! *Go! Go!*'

The team bolted down the stairs, chased by the nail-ridden boulders.

So did the lone CIEF trooper.

West came to the base of the stairs, to the Nazi gangway balanced across the whirlpool there at an odd angle.

He sprang across it, leading Lily by the hand, followed by Zoe and Big Ears, then Wizard and Stretch.

But the CIEF man was also fleet-footed and, chased

by the nail-boulders, he hurdled the two voids easily and almost caught up with Pooh Bear, running last of all, red-faced and breathless.

But at the final moment, Pooh dived forward, leaping full-stretch onto the gangway. The CIEF man did the same, but in the instant he leapt into the air, the first of the nail-boulders *slammed* into him, piercing his body with at least twenty jagged nails, and swept him into the whirlpool at the base of the stairs, closely followed by the other two boulders, which bounced off the gangway's handrails and away into the water.

'Ouch . . .' said Pooh Bear, lying on the gangway.

'Come on, Pooh!' West called. 'No time for resting now.'

'Resting? Resting! Pity those of us who don't have your energy, Captain West.' And so with a groan, Pooh Bear hauled himself up and took off after the others.

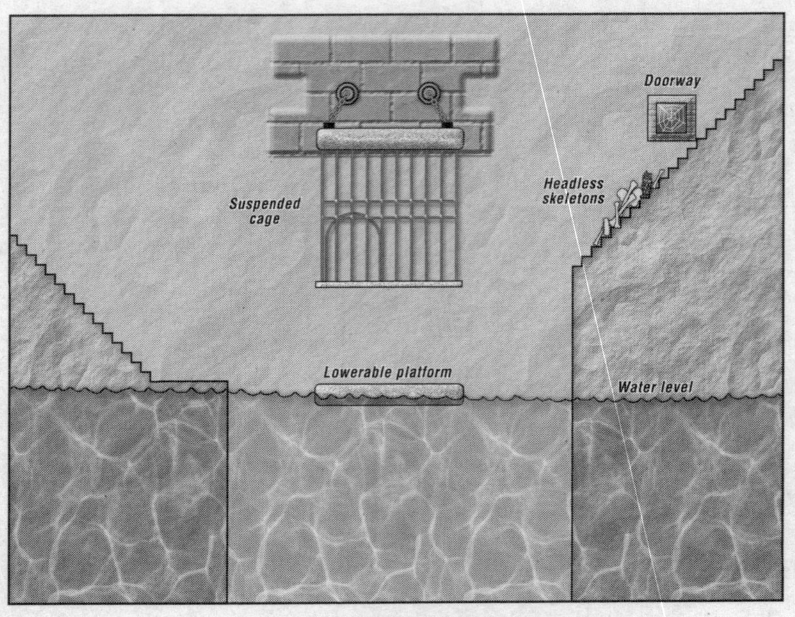

THE DROWNING CAGE

The Drowning Cage

Crossing the Nazi gangway, they arrived at a sizeable stone platform separated from the next large stepping-stone by a five-foot-wide gap of water.

A further five feet beyond that stepping-stone was another staircase, going upwards. However, this staircase was difficult to access—its first step lay seven feet *above* the swirling water, an impossible leap.

The biggest problem, however, lay above the stepping-stone itself.

A great cube-shaped cage was suspended above it, ready to drop the moment someone landed on it.

'It's a drowning cage,' Wizard said. 'We jump onto the stepping-stone and the cage traps us. Then *the whole platform* lowers into the water, cage and all, drowning us.'

'But it's the only way across . . .' Zoe said.

Stretch was covering the rear. 'Figure something out, people. Because Kallis is here!'

West spun—

—to see Kallis emerge from the sinkhole cave at the top of the staircase behind them.

'What do you think, Jack?' Wizard asked.

West bit his lip. 'Hmmm. Can't swim around it because of the whirlpools. And we can't climb up and around it: the wall here is polished smooth. There just doesn't seem to be any way to avoid it . . .'

Then West looked over at the ascending staircase *beyond* the drowning cage's stepping-stone.

Three Nazi skeletons lay on it—all headless. But beyond them, he saw something else:

A square doorway sunk into the wall, covered in cobwebs.

'There *is* no way to avoid it,' he said aloud, 'so don't avoid it. Wizard. The Templar Pit in Malta. Where we found the Museion scrolls. It's just like that. You have to enter the trap in order to pass it.'

Stretch urged, 'Some action, people. Kallis is halfway down the stairs . . .'

Zoe said to West: 'Enter the trap in order to pass it? What do you mean?'

'Hurry *up*, people . . .' Stretch said. 'Warblers don't work at point-blank range.'

West spun to see Kallis gaining on them, still with nine more men, only thirty yards away and closing.

'Okay, everyone,' he said, 'you have to trust me on this one. No time to go in groups, we have to do this together.'

'A bit all or nothing, isn't it, Jack?' Zoe said.

'No other choice. People, get your pony bottles ready. Then we all jump onto that stepping-stone. Ready . . . go!'

And they all jumped together.

The seven of them landed as one on the wide stepping-stone—

—and immediately, the great cage above it dropped, clanging down around them like a giant mousetrap, trapping them under its immense weight—

—and the entire ten-foot-wide stepping-stone began *to sink* into the swirling depths of the waterway!

'I hope you're right, Jack!' Zoe yelled. She grabbed her pony bottle from her belt, put its mouthpiece to her mouth. You breathe from a pony bottle just like you do from a regular scuba tank, but it only has enough air for about three minutes.

The cage went knee-deep in water.

West didn't answer her, just waded over to the wall-side of the cage and checked its great bronze bars.

And there he found it—a small archway cut into the cage's wall-side bars, maybe three feet high, large enough for a man to crawl through.

But the stone wall abutting that side of the cage was solid rock. The little arch led nowhere . . .

The cage sank further into the swirling water and the little arch went under.

Waist-deep.

Big Ears lifted Lily into his arms, above the swirling waterline.

On the stairway behind them, Cal Kallis paused, grinned at their predicament.

'*Jack . . .*' Zoe called, concerned.

'*Jack . . .*' Wizard called, concerned.

'It has to come,' West whispered to himself. 'It has to—'

The cage went two-thirds under, and as it did so, West cracked a glowstick, put his pony bottle to his mouth, and ducked under the choppy surface.

Underwater.

By the light of his glowstick, West watched the cage's bars slide past the stone wall . . .

Solid rock.

Nothing but solid rock flanked the cage on that side.

It can't be, his mind screamed. *There has to be something down here!*

But there wasn't.

There wasn't anything down there.

West's heart began to beat faster. He had just made the biggest mistake of his life, a mistake that would kill them all.

He resurfaced inside the swirling cage.

The water was chest-deep now, the cage three-quarters under.

'Anything down there!' Zoe called.

West frowned, stumped. 'No . . . but there should be.'

Stretch shouted, 'You've killed us all!'

Neck-deep.

'Just grab your pony bottles,' West said grimly. He looked to Lily, held high in Big Ears's arms. 'Hey, kiddo. You still with me?'

She nodded vigorously—scared out of her wits. 'Uh-huh.'

'Just breathe through your pony bottle like we practised at home,' he said gently, 'and you'll be all right.'

'Did you mess up?' she whispered.

'I might have,' he said.

As he did so, he locked eyes with Wizard. The old man just nodded: 'Hold your nerve, Jack. I trust you.'

'Good, because right now I don't,' West said.

And with that, the great bronze cage, with its seven trapped occupants, went completely under.

With a muffled *clunk*, the cage came to a halt, its barred ceiling stopping exactly three feet below the surface.

The underwater currents were extremely strong. On the cage's outermost side, the silhouette of a whirlpool could be seen: a huge inverted cone of downward-spiralling liquid.

Pony bottle to his mouth, West swam down to check the little arch one final time . . .

. . . where he found something startling.

The little arch had stopped perfectly in line with a small dark opening in the stone wall.

Shape for shape, the arch matched the opening exactly, so that if you crawled through the arch, you escaped *into* the submerged wall.

West's eyes came alive.

He spun to face the others, all trapped in the submerged cage with pony bottles held to their mouths, even Lily.

He signalled with his hands:

Wizard would go first.

Then Big Ears with Lily. Zoe, Stretch, Pooh Bear, and West last of all.

Wizard swam through the arch, holding a glowstick in front of him, and disappeared into the dark opening in the wall.

West signalled for Big Ears to wait—wait for Wizard to give them the all-clear.

A moment later, Wizard reappeared and gave an enthusiastic 'OK' sign.

So through the little arch they went, out of the cage and into the wall, until finally only Jack West Jr remained in the cage.

No-one saw the relief on his face. He'd made the call, and almost killed them all. But he'd been right.

Kicking hard, he swam out of the cage, his boots disappearing into the tiny opening.

The opening in the wall quickly turned upwards, becoming a vertical shaft, complete with ladder handholds. This shaft rose up and out of the sloshing water before opening onto a horizontal passage that led *back* to the main chasm, emerging—unsurprisingly—at the cobweb-covered doorway a few steps up the ascending staircase, the same doorway West had observed earlier.

As they stepped out from the passage, West saw Kallis and his men arriving at the base of the previous staircase, stopped there by the now-resetting cage.

Lying on the steps in front of West were the three headless Nazi skeletons he had spied before.

Wizard said, 'Headless bodies at the *bottom* of a stairway mean only one thing: blades at the top somewhere. Be careful.'

Retaking the lead, West gazed up this new stairway. 'Whoa. Would you look at that . . .'

At the top of the stairs was a truly impressive structure: a great fortified guard tower, leaning out from the vertical cliff 200 feet above the watery chasm.

The ancient guard tower was strategically positioned

on the main bend of the chasm. Directly opposite it, on the other side of the roofed chasm, was its identical twin, another guard tower, also jutting out from its wall, and also possessing a stairway rising up from a drowning cage down at water-level.

West had taken one step up this stairway when—

'Is that you, Jack!' a voice called.

West spun.

It hadn't come from Kallis.

It had come from further away.

From the other side of the chasm.

West snapped round.

And saw a *second* American special forces team standing on the path on the other side of the chasm, on the platform preceding the drowning cage on that side.

They had emerged from a side doorway in the rock-wall over there, *twenty-four men* in total.

At their head stood a man of about 50, with steely black eyes and, gruesomely, *no nose*. It had been cut off sometime in the distant past, leaving this fellow with a grotesque misshapen stump where his nose should have been.

Yet even with this glaring facial disfigurement, it was the man's clothing that was his most striking feature right now.

He wore steel-soled boots just like West did.

He wore a canvas jacket just like West did.

He wore a belt equipped with pony bottles, pitons and X-bars, just like West did.

The only difference was his helmet—he wore a light-weight caver's helmet, as opposed to West's fireman's helmet.

He was also older than West, calmer, more confident. His small black eyes radiated experience.

He was the one man West feared more than any other on Earth. The man who had been West's last field commander in the military. The man who had once left West for dead on the plains outside Basra in Iraq.

He was a former commander of Delta Team Six, the best within Delta, but was now the commanding officer of the CIEF, the very best special forces unit in the world.

He was Colonel Marshall Judah.

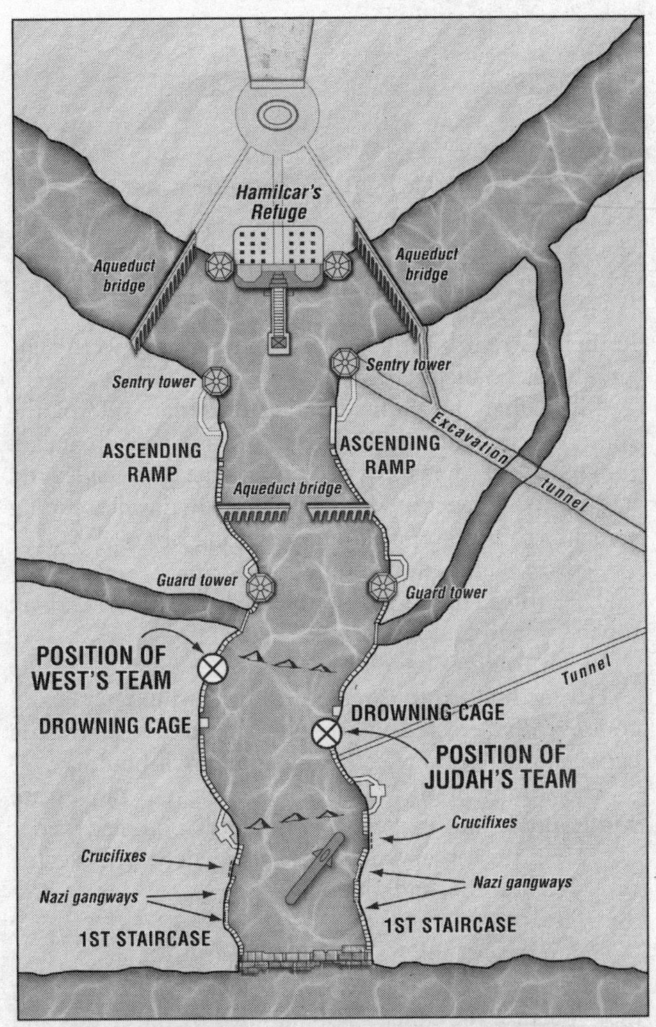

HAMILCAR'S REFUGE (COMPARATIVE POSITIONS)

In their current positions, West and his team were marginally ahead of Judah.

Given that the paths running on either side of the chasm were identical, West's team was one trap ahead. Judah had yet to pass the drowning cage on his side, and had just stepped out onto the base of the descending stairway over there, in doing so setting off—

—three nail-studded boulders.

The three boulders tumbled down the stairway toward Judah and his men.

Judah couldn't have cared less.

He just nodded to three of his men, who quickly and competently erected a sturdy tripod-like barricade between their team and the oncoming nail-boulders.

The titanium-alloy barricade blocked the entire width of the stairway and the boulders slammed into it one after the other, each one being deflected by the sturdy barricade and bouncing harmlessly away into the water.

Judah never took his eyes off West.

'How are those dreams going, Jack? Still trapped in that volcano?' he called. 'Still haunted by the chants and the drums?'

On his side of the chasm, West was stunned. *How could Judah know that . . . ?*

It was exactly the response Judah had wanted. He

smiled a thin, cold smile. 'I know even more than that, Jack! More than you can possibly suspect.'

West was rattled—but he tried not to show it.

It didn't work.

Judah nodded at the fireman's helmet now back on West's head. 'Still using that fireman's hat, Jack? You know I never agreed with that. Too cumbersome in tight places. It always pains a teacher to see a talented student employing foolish methods.'

West couldn't help himself—he glanced up at his helmet.

Judah followed through, driving home his edge. 'Looks like we've got something of a race on our hands here, Jack. Think you can outrun me? Do you seriously think *you* can outrun *me*?'

'Everybody,' West said quietly to his people, not taking his eyes off Judah. 'We have to run. Fast. Now. Go!'

West's team bolted up the stairs, heading for the guard tower at their peak.

Judah just nodded calmly to his men, who immediately began erecting a long gangway to bypass their drowning cage and reach the ascending stairway on their side of the chasm.

The race was on.

The Guard Tower and the Gorge

West and his team ran up their stairway.

Just before the guard tower, a narrow gorge cut across their path. It was maybe fifteen feet across, with sheer vertical sides. This little gorge actually sliced all the way across the *main* chasm, and as such, had a twin over on the other side.

And once again, the Nazis had been helpful. It seemed that the ancient Carthaginians had built a complex chain-lowered *drawbridge* to span this gorge—a draw-bridge that the Nazis had managed to lower into place, spanning the void.

Taking any luck they could get, West and his team sprinted across the ancient drawbridge, and arrived at the guard tower high up on the next bend in the chasm.

There was a ladder hewn into the guard tower's curved flank, a ladder that wound *around* the outside of the structure, meaning they had to free-climb 200 feet above nothing but the swirling waters below.

Two head-chopping blades sprang out from slits in the wall-ladder, but West neutralised them with sticky foam and his team, roped together, successfully climbed around the gravity-defying guard tower.

★

On the other side of the chasm, Judah's long lightweight bridge fell into place and his men ran across it, completely avoiding their drowning cage, reaching the base of their ascending staircase.

The wall-ladder on the outside of West's guard tower brought his team up onto its balcony.

A tight tunnel in the back of the balcony delved into the chasm-wall itself and emerged on the other side of the bend, where West fired off three self-hovering flares . . .

. . . to gloriously reveal the far end of the chasm and their goal.

'*Holy* shit . . .' Big Ears gasped.

'Swear jar,' Lily said instantly.

Standing there before them in all its splendour, towering above the waterway, lording over it, easily fifteen storeys tall and jutting out from the far facing rockwall, was a gigantic ancient fortress.

The steaming vents of the chasm gave the fortress a grim haunting look.

A super-solid square-shaped keep formed the core of the structure, with a giant gaping archway in its exact centre. This central section was flanked by two soaring defensive towers, high-spired pinnacles in the darkness. The style of these towers matched that of the guard tower that West had just passed through—only these were taller, stretching all the way up from the water.

Stretching downward from the Great Arch in the centre of the keep was a wide guttered rampway that lanced all the way down to the waterway, ending at a flat stone jetty. At least forty metres in length, with stairs nestled in its centre, the rampway resembled the step-ramps on Hatshepsut's mortuary temple near the Valley of the Kings.

Never finished and never used for its intended purpose—and long since concealed by an ingenious Egyptian architect—this was Hamilcar's Refuge.

West snatched his printout from his pouch, examined it:

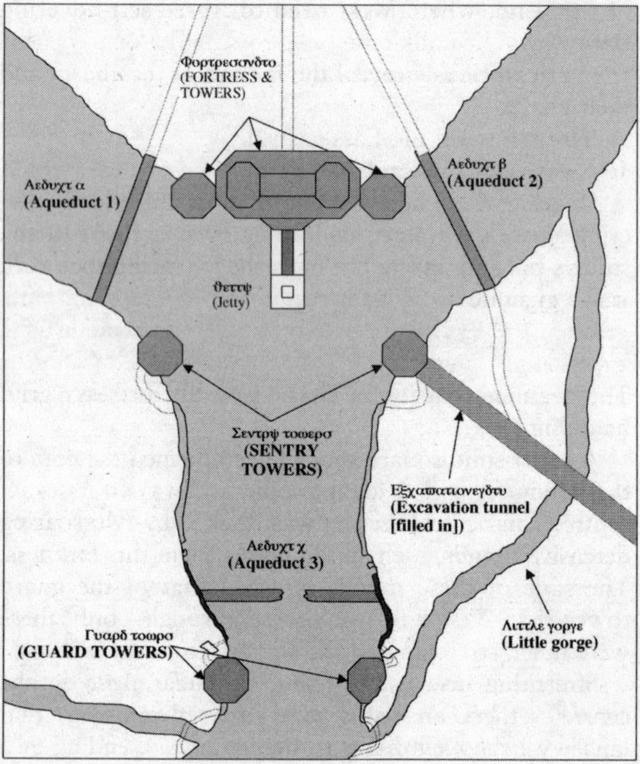

Just like on the ancient drawing, the chasm before him ended at a Y-junction, splitting into two diverging channels. The Refuge sat nestled in the V at the top of the Y, facing the long upright 'stem'.

Two more spire-like 'sentry towers' sat on either side of the stem, facing the two towers of the Refuge itself.

As if all this weren't colossal enough, the Refuge featured two more soaring aqueduct bridges to add to the broken one in the main chasm—200 feet high and made of many bricked arches.

These two new bridges spanned the Y-channels of the waterway, but unlike the one crossing the main chasm, they were whole and intact.

It was Zoe who noticed the rockwall behind the Refuge.

'It slopes *backward*,' she said. 'Like the cone of a—'

'Come on, we don't have time,' West urged them on.

The final stretch of the chasm featured a descending stairway followed by an *ascending* ramp. The ramp slithered up the left-hand wall of the chasm, bending with every curve. Curiously, it bore a low upraised gutter on its outer edge, the purpose of which was not readily apparent.

Of course, this stairway–ramp combination was mirrored on Judah's side of the chasm.

West and his team charged down their descending stairway, avoiding a couple of blasting steam vents on the way.

In the meantime, Judah's team had just crossed their little gorge and arrived at their guard tower.

They started climbing around it.

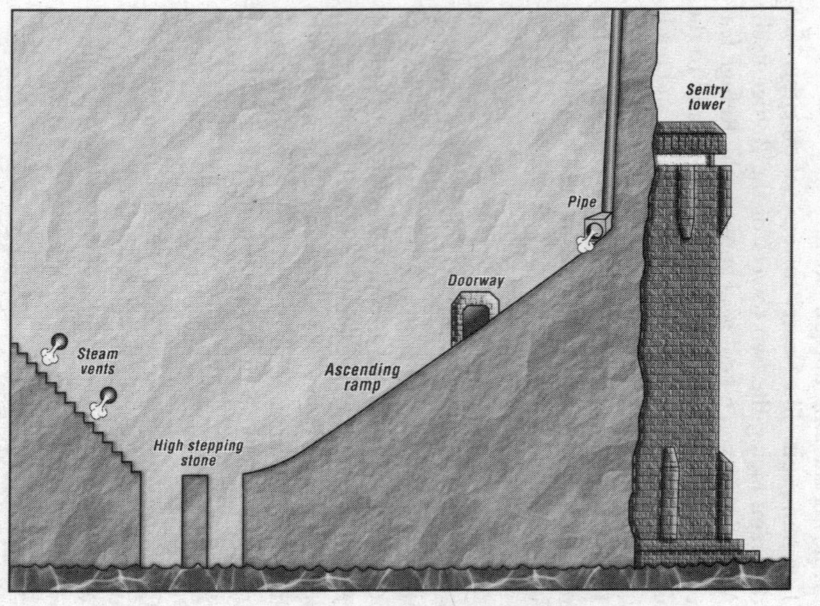

THE ASCENDING RAMP

The Ascending Ramp

An unusually high stepping-stone separated the base of the descending stairway from the base of the ascending ramp. It jutted out from the wall about thirty feet above the waterway.

The guttered ascending ramp rose above West and his team, stretching upward for maybe 100 metres, ending at the left-hand sentry tower. It was maybe four feet wide, enough for single-file only, and a sheer drop to the right of it fell away to the swirling waters below.

The ramp featured two openings along its length: one two-thirds of the way up that looked like a doorway; the second all the way at the very top of the ramp, that looked more like a *pipe*.

Ominously, a wispy thread of steam issued out from the pipe, dissipating as it spread into the chasm.

Wizard was enthralled. 'Ooh, it's a single-exit convergence trap . . .'

'A what?' Pooh Bear said.

West said, 'He means it's a race between us and whatever liquid comes out of that pipe. We have to get to the doorway before the liquid does. I assume the high stepping-stone triggers the contest.'

'What kind of liquid?' Big Ears asked.

Wizard said, 'I've seen crude-oil versions. Heated quicksand. Liquid tar . . .'

As Wizard spoke, West stole a glance back at Judah's men.

They were climbing around the outside of their guard tower, high above the waterway, moving in a highly co-ordinated way—far faster than his team had.

The first CIEF man climbed over the balcony and disappeared inside the tower.

'No time to ponder the issue,' he said. 'Let's take the challenge.'

And with that he jumped onto the stepping-stone and bounced over onto the ascending ramp.

No sooner had his foot hit the stepping-stone than a blast of superhot volcanic mud vomited out from the pipe at the top of the ramp. Black and thick, the mud was so hot it bore thin streaks of golden-red magma in its oozing mass.

The ramp's gutter instantly came into effect.

It funnelled the fast-oozing body of superheated mud down the ramp, towards West's team!

'This is why we train every day,' West said. 'Run!'

Up the ramp the seven of them ran.

Down the ramp the red-hot mud flowed.

It was going to be close—the ramp was obviously constructed in favour of the mud.

But West and his team were fit, prepared. They bounded up the slope, heaving with every stride, and they came to the doorway set into the wall just as the mud did and they charged in through it one after the other, West shepherding them through, diving in himself just as the volcanic mud slid by him, pouring down the ramp, where it ultimately tipped into the waterway at the bottom, sending up a great hissing plume of steam.

Judah's team, close behind West's, handled their ramp in a different way.

They sent only one man up it: a specialist wearing a large silver canister on his back and holding a device that looked like a big-barrelled leafblower.

The specialist raced up the ramp and beat the flowing mud to his doorway, where, instead of disappearing inside, he fired his big 'leafblower' *at the ramp*.

Only instead of hot air, the device he held spewed forth a billowing cloud of supercooled liquid nitrogen, which instantly turned the leading edge of the mudflow into a solid crust that acted like a dam of sorts, funnelling the rest of the oncoming mud off and over the outer edge of the ramp!

This allowed Judah and his team to just stride up their ramp in complete safety, heading for the sentry tower on their side—moving ever forward.

In stark contrast, West and his team arrived in their sentry tower breathless and on the run.

'Even if we get this Piece of the Capstone,' Stretch said, 'how can we possibly get it out? How can we get it past the Americans? And if it's a large Piece, it'll be nine feet square of near-solid gold—'

Pooh Bear scowled. 'Always argue the negative, don't you, Israeli. Sometimes I wonder why you even bothered to come on this mission.'

'I came to keep an eye on all of you,' Stretch retorted.

Wizard said, 'If we can't *get* the Piece, we at least need to *see* the Piece. Lily has to see the positive incantation carved into its upper side.'

West ignored them all.

He just peered out from the balcony of the sentry tower, down at the Great Arch of the Refuge.

He eyed the jetty at the bottom end of the guttered rampway stretching down from the Great Arch. The jetty stood at a point exactly halfway between the two sentry towers and it was covered by a small four-pillared marble gazebo. The vertical distance from West's balcony to the little gazebo: maybe 50 metres.

'Big Ears. I need a flying fox to that gazebo.'

'Got it.'

Big Ears whipped out his M-16, loaded a grappling

hook into its underslung grenade launcher, aimed and fired.

The hook whizzed out across the chasm, arcing high through the air, its rope wobbling behind it. Then it shot downward, toward the marble gazebo on the jetty, until—*thwack!*—the hook whiplashed around one of the gazebo's pillars and took hold.

'Nice shot, brother,' Zoe said, genuinely impressed.

Big Ears looped his end of the hook's rope around a pillar in the sentry tower's window and the rope went taut—creating a long steep zipline that stretched down and across the chasm, from the high sentry tower down to the low jetty.

'Lily,' West said, 'you're with me from here. Grab on. We go first.'

Lily leapt into West's arms, wrapped her hands around his neck. West then slung a compact handlebar-like flying fox over the rope and pushed off—

—and the two of them sailed out over the immense chasm, across the face of Hamilcar's Refuge, tiny dots against the great ancient fortress—

—before they slid to a perfect halt on the surface of the little jetty that lay before the dark looming structure.

'Okay, Zoe, come on down,' West said into his radio.

Zoe whizzed down the rope on her own flying fox, landing deftly next to West and Lily.

'Wizard, you're nex—' West said.

Bam!

Gunshot.

It echoed loudly across the great chasm.

West spun, saw one of Judah's snipers aiming a long-barrelled Barrett rifle out from their sentry tower's balcony . . . and suddenly realised that he was no longer within the protective range of the Warbler.

But strangely no bullet-impact hit near him, Zoe or Lily.

And then the realisation hit West.

The sniper wasn't aiming for them.

He was aiming at the—

'Damn it, no . . .'

Bam!

Another shot.

Ping! Shwack!

The flying fox's *rope* was severed right in its middle and went instantly slack, cut clean in two. It dropped, limp, into the water.

And suddenly West, Zoe and Lily were out on the jetty, all on their own, completely separated from the rest of their team.

'No choice now,' West said grimly. Then, into his radio: 'Big Ears, Pooh Bear, Stretch. Give us some cover fire. Because in four seconds we're gonna need it!'

Exactly four seconds later, right on cue, a withering barrage of gunfire blazed out from Judah's sentry tower.

A wave of bullets hammered the marble gazebo where West, Zoe and Lily were taking cover.

Impact-sparks exploded all around them.

But then the reply came from West's team, on their tower: roaring fire, aimed at the opposite sentry tower.

Bullets zinged back and forth across the main chasm, between the two towers.

The cover fire had its intended effect: it forced Judah's men to cease firing briefly and thus gave West the opening he needed.

'Okay, now!' he yelled to Zoe and Lily.

Out of the gazebo they ran, up the wide guttered rampway that gave access to the fortress, tiny figures before the enormous ancient citadel.

They flew up the stairs and, to the sound of gunfire outside, disappeared inside the dark yawning entrance to Hamilcar Barca's long-abandoned Refuge.

They entered a high-ceilinged many-pillared hall. The pillars ran in long sideways lines, so that the hall was exceedingly wide but not very deep.

It was absolutely beautiful—every column was ornately decorated, every ghost-like statue perfectly cut. It was also curiously Roman in its styling—the heavy-trading Carthaginians had been incredibly similar to their Roman rivals. Perhaps that was why they had been such bitter enemies over three bloody Punic Wars.

But this hall was long-deserted. Its floor lay bare, covered in a layer of grey ash.

It had also been modified by the Ptolemaic Egyptian engineers.

A wide ascending tunnel bored into the earth behind the fortress, continuing in a straight line from the Great Arch's entry rampway. Indeed, this tunnel and the rampway were connected by a flat path that crossed the pillared hall and also featured raised gutters on its edges.

Zoe said, 'Looks like these gutters are designed to funnel some kind of liquid that flows out from the tunnel's core, through this hall, and down the front ramp.'

'No time to stop and stare,' West said. 'Keep moving.'

They ran across the stupendous hall, dwarfed by its immense pillars, and entered the gently-sloping tunnel sunk into its innermost wall.

★

At the same time, outside in the chasm, Big Ears, Stretch, Wizard and Pooh Bear were engaged in their fierce gun-battle with the CIEF force over in the other sentry tower.

'Keep firing!' Wizard yelled above the din. 'Every moment we keep Judah pinned down is another moment Huntsman has inside the Refuge—'

He was abruptly cut off as, all of a sudden, the entire chasm shook and shuddered.

For a moment, he and the others stopped firing.

So did Judah's men—in fact, they suddenly started to abandon their position on their sentry tower.

'What is this . . . ?' Big Ears eyed the cavern around him.

'It feels like an earthquake . . .' Pooh Bear said.

'It's not an earthquake,' Wizard said, realising.

The next instant, the source of the great rumbling burst out of the wall at the base of Judah's sentry tower, just above the waterline of the main chasm itself.

It was an M-113 TBV-MV (Tunnel-Boring Vehicle, Medium Volume). The military equivalent of a commercial tunnel-boring engine, it was in truth an M-113A2 bridge-laying vehicle that had been adapted for tunnel-making.

The size of a tank, it had a huge pointed nose that whizzed around and around, screw-like, obliterating everything in its path. Chewed-up rock and dirt were 'digested' through the centre of the vehicle and disposed out the rear. It also bore on its roof a foldable mechanical bridge.

The tunnel-boring vehicle poked out through the wall at the base of the sentry tower and stopped, its drill-bit still spinning, only twenty horizontal metres from the jetty that West had ziplined down to.

'They drilled through the filled-in excavation tunnel

. . .' Wizard breathed in awe. 'How clever. It wouldn't have given a modern tunnel-borer much resistance.'

'It helps if you have the logistics,' Stretch said.

'Which they do,' Pooh Bear said.

At that moment, the tunnel-boring vehicle engaged its internal engines to fold forward the steel bridge on its roof. The mechanical bridge unfolded slowly, stretching out in front of the tunnel-borer until it was fully flat and extended. At which point, it touched down lightly against the jetty twenty metres away.

The American tunnel and the jetty were now connected.

'Man, they're good . . .' Big Ears said.

A second later, Judah's team rushed across the bridge, guns up, having raced down the internal stairs of their sentry tower.

They fired up at Wizard's men as they crossed the metal bridge.

Big Ears and the others tried to halt them with more cover fire, but it was no use.

Judah's men were across the waterway and racing up the rampway into Hamilcar's Refuge.

They were going in, only a minute behind West, Zoe and Lily.

West, Zoe and Lily raced up the ascending tunnel behind the fortress, guided by glowsticks.

As he ran, West noticed large clumps of dried solidified mud clinging to the edges of the rampway. He frowned inwardly. *Dried mud? How had it come to be here?*

'*Jack! Zoe!*' Wizard's voice called in their earpieces. '*Judah's crossed over the waterway! I repeat, Judah has crossed the waterway! He's right behind you!*'

After about a hundred metres of dead-straight, steadily-rising tunnel, they emerged in a high dome-ceilinged chamber—

—and froze.

'What the—' Zoe breathed. 'There are *two* of them . . .'

The chamber was perfectly circular and it reeked of gaseous sulphur, the smell of volcanoes. It was also distinctly holy, reverential, a shrine.

Alcoves lined its curved walls—housing broken and decayed Carthaginian statues—while on the chamber's far side rose a wide granite dam, behind which simmered a wide pool of bubbling volcanic mud, the source of the foul sulphurous odour.

And lying on the floor before West, Lily and Zoe were six skeletons of long-dead Nazi soldiers. All were hideously deformed: the bottom half of each man was missing, their legs simply gone. Indeed, the lower ends of their spinal columns seemed to have *melted* . . .

Beyond the grisly skeletons, however, was the main feature of the holy chamber.

Rising up in the chamber's exact centre, 10 feet above the floor of the perfectly round room, was an elevated platform, fitted with a single flight of wide rising steps, and on it—to West's surprise—lay not one but *two* Ancient Wonders.

Mounted atop the island-like platform, aimed upwards like a satellite dish, stood the fabled Mirror of the Lighthouse of Alexandria.

It was completely covered in grey volcanic ash, but its outline was unmistakable. With its wide 15-foot dish, it was simply *astonishing* in its beauty.

West's eyes, however, fell immediately to its base.

Its solid trapezoidal base, also covered in a layer of grey ash.

Suddenly something made sense: the continual use of the word 'base' in the texts he had followed to get here. He recalled the original clue to the location of the Pharos Piece:

Look for the base that was once the peak of the Great Tower

And Euclid's Instructions:

Base removed before the Roman invasion,
Taken to Hamilcar's Forgotten Refuge.

The Mirror of the Lighthouse was a wonder unto

itself, but its base—its plain trapezoidal base—was of immensely greater value.

Its base was the Seventh Piece of the Golden Capstone.

But there was a second monument standing proudly atop the platform—next to the Mirror, on the right-hand side.

It was a huge octagonal marble pillar, standing upright, perhaps eight feet in height and seven feet in circumference. Its upper portions had long since been hacked away, but its lower section was perfectly intact.

And just like the Mirror, its base was trapezoidal.

It was *another* Piece of the Capstone.

'Oversized octagonal pillar . . .' Zoe said, her mind racing. 'Only one ancient structure was known to possess oversized octagonal pillars—'

'The Mausoleum at Halicarnassus,' West said. 'Lily hasn't been able to read its entry yet, but I bet when she does, the Callimachus Text will say that its Piece is with the Pharos Piece. When you find one, you find the other. Zoe, we just hit the jackpot. We just found two Pieces of the Capstone.'

'We have to do something!' Pooh Bear growled.

'What *can* we do?' Stretch sighed. 'They're done for. This mission is over. I say we save ourselves.'

They were still in their sentry tower, having watched Judah's force enter the Refuge.

'Typical of you, Israeli,' Pooh said. 'Your first instinct is always self-preservation. I don't give up so easily, or give up on my friends so easi—'

'Then what do you suggest, you stupid stubborn Arab?'

But Pooh Bear had gone silent.

He was staring out to the left of the fortress, out towards the high multi-arched aqueduct that spanned the channel on that side of the Y-junction.

'We cross that,' he said determinedly.

In the holy chamber, West approached the central island.

In addition to the two priceless treasures standing on it, one other thing was visible atop the raised island: a seventh Nazi skeleton, lying all on its own, curled in the foetal position on the topmost step.

Unlike the others, this skeleton was not deformed in any way. It was whole and intact, still wearing its black SS uniform. Indeed, its bones were still covered in decaying flesh.

West approached the island and its flight of steps cautiously—the whole flight was probably just one great big trigger stone.

He scanned the skeleton.

Saw a pair of spindly wire-framed glasses still sitting on its nose, saw the red swastika armband, saw the purple amethyst ring on its bony right hand, the ring of a Nazi Party founding member.

'Hessler . . .' he gasped in recognition. It was Hermann Hessler, the Nazi archaeologist, one-half of the famed Hessler–Koenig team.

Oddly, the skeleton's right hand was outstretched, seemingly *reaching* down the steps, as if it had been Hessler's last earthly movement, grasping for . . .'

. . . a battered leatherbound notebook that lay on the bottom step.

West grabbed the notebook, flipped it open.

Pages of diagrams, lists, and drawings of each of the Ancient Wonders stared back at him, interspersed with German notes written in Hermann Hessler's neat handwriting.

Suddenly, his earpiece roared to life:

'*Jack! Zoe!*' Wizard's voice called. '*You have to hide! Judah's going to be there any moment now—*'

West spun, just as a bullet sizzled out of the entry tunnel behind him and whizzed over his head, missing his scalp by centimetres.

'You two, that way!' he ordered Zoe and Lily to the left side of the doorway, while he himself scampered to the right of the stone doorframe, peered back, and saw dark shadows rising up the tunnel, approaching fast.

Decision time.

There was no way he could get to the podium containing the Lighthouse's Mirror and the Mausoleum's

Pillar before Judah's force arrived. No way to allow Lily to glimpse their carved incantations.

His eyes scanned the chamber for an escape.

There was some open space on the far side of the island, but it offered no escape: only the wide granite dam that held back the pool of superhot mud lay over there—presumably waiting to be set off by the trigger-stone steps.

And in an instant, it all made sense: the rising tunnel with the clumps of dried mud at its edges, the guttered path in the hall below and the similarly gutter-lined stairs down at the Great Arch: this molten mud, when released from its dam, would flow *around* the raised island containing the Mirror and Pillar and then down through the Refuge, all the way to the water in the chasm, killing any crypt-raiders in the process and protecting the two Pieces.

The half-bodied Nazi skeletons, melted at the waist, now also made sense: they'd been killed trying to outrun the mud. Hessler himself must have been trapped atop the podium as it had been surrounded by the stuff. He had then died in perhaps the worst way of all—of starvation, in the dark, alone. His buddy, Koenig, must have escaped somehow and trekked across the desert to Tobruk.

Among the many statue alcoves that lined the circular wall of the chamber, West also saw two smaller openings on either side of the main entry doorway.

They were low arched tunnels, maybe a metre high—and elevated slightly above the floor of the chamber by about 2 feet.

West didn't know what they were, and right now he didn't care.

'Zoe! That little tunnel! Get Lily out of here!'

Zoe swept Lily into the low arched tunnel on their side of the doorway, while West himself charged over to the right-hand one and peered down it.

The low tunnel disappeared downwards in a long dead-straight line.

'No choice,' he said aloud.

He ducked inside the little arched tunnel—just as Zoe and Lily did the same on the other side of the chamber—a bare second before Judah's force swept into the holy chamber.

At that exact same moment, four tiny figures were hustling across the superhigh aqueduct bridge that spanned the left arm of the Y-junction.

Led by the frumpy but determined Pooh Bear they looked like a team of tightrope walkers. But they made it across and disappeared into the small metre-high arched tunnel on the far side.

Marshall Judah stepped into the domed chamber and gazed up at the Mirror and the Pillar.

He grinned, satisfied.

His eyes searched the area for West—scanning the many alcoves, nooks and crannies.

No sign of him. Yet.

He called: 'I know you're in here, Jack! My, my, twice in two days. Looks like you've failed again . . .'

His men fanned out, searching the chamber, guns up.

West backed down his little arched tunnel, praying that the darkness concealed him.

As he moved, he drew his H&K pistol from his thigh holster and aimed it up the tunnel—when with startling suddenness, a CIEF trooper appeared at the top of the tunnel, gun up!

West's finger balanced on his trigger—firing might save him momentarily, but it would also give away his position . . .

But the trooper didn't fire.

He just peered down the tunnel, squinting, searching.

He couldn't see West . . .

But then the CIEF trooper reached for the pair of night-vision goggles hanging from his belt.

★

At the same time, in the domed chamber itself, Marshall Judah was evaluating the podium-island in the middle of the room with a portable X-ray scanner.

The staircase giving access to the island was indeed one great big trigger stone. And the domed roof was solid diorite—offering no purchase for drilled handholds.

The situation was clear, and typical of Imhotep VI: to get onto the raised island, you had to trigger the trap.

Which meant Judah and his men would have to be quick.

'Gentlemen,' he said. 'It is an Imhotep VI, Type 4 trap. Time will be short. Prepare the rollers. I want an eight-man lifting team for the Mirror Piece, and a four-man team for the Pillar Piece.'

'Do you want us to take the Mirror and the Pillar themselves?' one lieutenant asked.

'I don't give a shit about the Mirror and the Pillar. All I want are the Pieces,' Judah snapped.

The CIEF men got into position.

They brought forward two six-wheeled 'roller units'—to convey the heavy Pieces out.

'Okay, here we go,' Judah said.

And with those words, he trod on the first step of the staircase, setting off the deadly trap mechanism.

At that moment, several things happened.

The trooper who had been peering down West's tunnel placed his night-vision goggles to his eyes—and immediately saw West, crouched in the tunnel like a trapped animal.

The trooper whipped up his Colt Commando—

Bam!

Gunshot.

From West.

The trooper dropped dead, hit right between the eyes.

In the chamber, three other CIEF men saw their comrade go down and they charged for the right-hand arched tunnel, leading with their guns.

But at the exact moment the CIEF trooper fell, Judah had stepped on the stairway, setting off its trap mechanism.

And the mighty nature of that trap meant he didn't see the CIEF trooper behind him fall.

For as Judah stepped onto the trigger stone, the great granite dam at the far end of the chamber instantly began to lower, *releasing the pool of boiling volcanic mud behind it into the chamber!*

With a titanic whoosh, the foul stinking body of mud oozed over the lowering dam and began to fan out slowly into the round chamber.

Judah's men rushed forward, clambering up onto the central island, where they pushed the Mirror and Pillar from their bases.

The spreading body of mud split into two fat fingers that oozed around both sides of the island . . .

A quick wipe to each base revealed its glittering golden surface beneath the layer of ash.

Then the CIEF teams grabbed the two bases, moving fast.

The fingers of mud were two-thirds of the way around the island now and moving quickly, ready to devour anything that lay in their paths . . .

Leaving the Pharos's Mirror and the Mausoleum's Pillar lying pathetically on their sides on the island, Judah's team bounded off the raised platform, returning to the chamber's main doorway just as the two creeping fingers of molten mud enveloped the base of the island and touched, surrounding the island completely, sealing it off.

But the mud continued to flow, spreading ever *outward* . . .

Judah's eight-man A-team loaded the Mirror's base onto one of the six-wheeled rollers—a couple of them noting that unlike the other Piece, the Pharos Piece had a human-shaped indentation carved into its underside. Curious. But they didn't have time to examine it now.

The B-team loaded the Mausoleum Piece onto their roller.

And then they were off, led by Judah, racing back down the entry tunnel with the two large golden trapezoids in their midst.

By this time, the three CIEF men who had seen West's victim fall arrived at the right-hand arched tunnel—but with the spreading mud closing in behind them.

Guns up, they peered down the tunnel and saw West, trapped, dead to rights . . .

. . . a moment before they were all assailed by a withering volley of gunfire from somewhere behind them.

The three CIEF men convulsed in grotesque spasms, erupting in a thousand blood-spurts, peppered by automatic gunfire.

This volley of gunfire had come from the *left*-hand arched tunnel, on the other side of the main entrance, where Pooh Bear and Big Ears now stood, their Steyr-AUG and MP-7 sub-machine guns still smoking!

Guided only by Wizard's incomplete sketch of the Refuge, they had guessed—correctly—that their aqueduct's tunnel led to the same place as the fortress's main ascending tunnel.

West ran to the top of his tunnel, peered out, saw his lifesaving team-mates on the other side of the lava-filled chamber—saw Lily and Zoe safely in their midst.

He would have yelled his thanks, but he arrived there just in time to see the spreading body of mud reach his tunnel's raised entrance and *swallow* the corpses of the four CIEF men as it went by.

The molten mud just seared right through their bodies, liquefying them in an instant, before oozing over them, *absorbing them* into its mass.

It was the same on the other side of the chamber—the creeping body of mud had just flowed across the entrance to Pooh Bear's little tunnel and was now heading quickly towards the main doorway of the domed chamber.

The effect was simple.

West was now cut off from both his comrades on the far side of the chamber *and* from the main entrance.

And the level of the flowing mud river was *rising*.

Any second now, it would rise up over the lips of the two arched aqueduct tunnels . . . and flow down them!

From the look on his face, Pooh Bear had seen this, too.

'Pooh Bear! Get out of here!' West called.

'What about you!' Pooh yelled back.

West nodded back down his aqueduct tunnel. 'No other option! I have to go this way!'

'Jack!' Wizard called.

'What!'

'Judah used a tunnel-boring vehicle to drill *through* the old filled-in excavation tunnel! They must be planning to take the Pieces out that way! Check your sketch!

You may still be able to get a look at the Pieces! All may not be lost!'

'I'll do my best!' West nodded at the expanding mud pool. 'Now get out of here! Call Sky Monster! Get to the *Halicarnassus*! I'll catch up somehow!'

And with that, West's team split, went their separate ways, disappearing into the two arched tunnels on either side of the domed chamber—the chamber whose perfectly round floor was now little more than a lake of stinking dark mud, a lake that surrounded a raised island containing the only existing remains of two Ancient Wonders, now lying discarded and broken on their sides.

West bolted down his aqueduct tunnel as fast as his legs could carry him. It was long and tight and dead-straight.

In the main tunnel of the fortress, Marshall Judah and his two teams were also hustling, pushing their six-wheeled rollers—bearing the two Pieces of the Capstone—down the slope.

They rushed through the many-pillared hall of the fortress before they emerged in the chasm and raced down the guttered rampway that stretched down from the front of the Refuge.

While in the left-hand aqueduct tunnel, Pooh Bear, Big Ears, Stretch, Wizard, Zoe and Lily also rushed headlong through their own tight dark passageway.

All three groups ran for good reason—for in the domed chamber high behind them, the radially-expanding mud lake finally reached the edge of the round room and began to rise up and over the lips of the three tunnels . . .

. . . at which point it flooded rapidly down each of them!

Three surging fingers of mud roared down the three sloping tunnels.

Since they were tight and small, the two rivers of mud flowing down the aqueduct tunnels moved faster than the one flowing down the wider main tunnel.

As he ran, West turned to see the boiling hot liquid pouring down the tunnel behind him. It moved powerfully, relentlessly, as if it had a will of its own, a will bent on destroying any living thing in its path.

Then, abruptly, West burst out into open space—and found himself standing on the high aqueduct bridge that spanned the right-hand arm of the Y-junction.

The bridge was very high—at least 200 feet—long, and very narrow, barely wide enough for one person to stand on. For it was not made for human crossing. Its surface wasn't even flat; rather, it contained a sunken 2-foot-wide channel for mud to flow across.

'Oh man . . .' he breathed.

He stepped out onto the high aqueduct bridge, and suddenly saw Judah's men appear on the jetty far below him, pushing their pair of six-wheeled rollers across their fold-out metal bridge. In the recently-bored tunnel on the other side of their bridge, the big tunnel-boring vehicle's front screw was now folded open, waiting to be loaded. Judah was going to use the tunnel-boring vehicle to carry the Pieces out of here.

West remembered Wizard's newsflash from before.

'Check the sketch . . .' he'd said.

With a glance back at the oncoming mud, he snatched his printout of the ancient sketch:

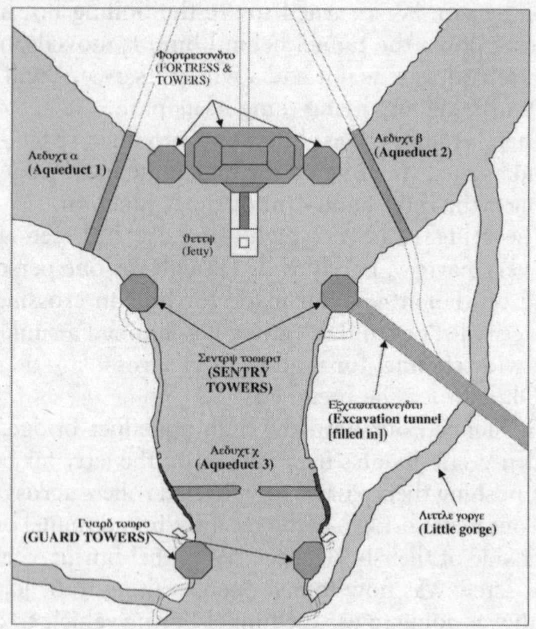

Okay, I'm here, he saw the right-hand aqueduct, labelled *Aqueduct* 2.

Max was right. This aqueduct bridge linked up with the excavation tunnel—the same tunnel that Judah had reopened with his tunnel-borer and which he was now using to get the Pieces out.

West looked up.

If he hurried, he might be able to . . .

He bolted, raced out across the high aqueduct bridge—while far below him, Judah's CIEF team loaded their tunnel-boring vehicle with the two golden trapezoids.

★

On the other side of the Y-junction, Pooh Bear emerged from his aqueduct tunnel—just in time to see the aqueduct bridge in front of him get hit, spectacularly, by a rocket-propelled grenade . . . right in the middle!

One of Judah's men had been waiting for them, keeping an eye on the bridge through the crosshairs of an RPG launcher.

The RPG hit the multi-arched bridge in the exact centre. A huge explosion billowed outwards, hurling bricks and blasted rock in every direction. When the cloud dissipated it revealed that the aqueduct bridge was now in two pieces, with a gaping void in its middle.

Pooh Bear spun—saw the long finger of dark mud stretching down the tunnel behind him, coming inexorably closer.

And now he and his team had nowhere to go, no bridge to escape across!

'This is terrible,' he breathed.

West dashed across his aqueduct bridge unseen, but still pursued by the elongated finger of mud behind him.

He reached the little tunnel on the other side of the chasm and disappeared into it at speed—just as Judah's people clamped shut the folding front section of their M-113 tunnel-borer and withdrew the temporary bridge.

Judah shouted, 'CIEF units, fall in! We're leaving!'

The tunnel-boring vehicle was like a tank, with great tracked wheels and a box-shaped armoured body. The main hold of this body was hollow and it usually held troops. When used as a tunnel-borer, however, it conveyed crushed rock through its body and disposed of it out the rear, laying it against the walls of the tunnel as hard-packed dirt.

Now that the tunnel had been bored, the hold of the M-113 was being used to house the two Pieces of the Capstone.

Four armed CIEF men sat in there with them, guarding them.

The rest of Judah's force leapt into four cage-framed Light Strike Vehicles—dune buggies essentially—to escort their prize out of the excavation tunnel.

By this time, Cal Kallis and his team, who had been on West's side of the main chasm, had crossed the main chasm via the broken aqueduct and joined Judah.

'Mr Kallis,' Judah said, pointing up at Pooh Bear's team, trapped up on the partially-destroyed left-hand aqueduct. 'West's people do not leave this place alive. I want snipers taking them down one at a time if necessary. Join us when you're done.'

Then Judah turned and jumped into one of the chase cars.

The CIEF convoy fired up their engines and moved off into the tunnel—two of the small LSVs in front, followed by the big M-113 tunnel-borer, then the other two LSVs behind.

They left Cal Kallis and his men at the mouth of the tunnel, standing at the waterline—eyeing Pooh Bear's trapped team.

Pooh Bear spun to check the mud behind him. It was close now—only ten metres away and approaching fast.

The aqueduct bridge before him now offered no escape.

But about twenty metres across the cliff-face from him was one of the Refuge's high-spired towers—and it was connected to Pooh Bear's bridge by an inch-thin ledge.

'This way!' he ordered the others.

And so they edged out across the ledge, standing on their tip-toes, Wizard, Zoe and Lily, Stretch and Big Ears, and finally Pooh Bear, who stepped off the remains of the aqueduct bridge a bare second before the stream of mud shot past him, flowed out over the bridge, and fell—gloriously, as a waterfall of thick dark mud—off the newly-formed void in its middle, down to the waterway 200 feet below.

Moments later, an even larger body of mud came roaring out of the main entry of Hamilcar's Refuge. It moved fast, pouring down the rampway and out over the jetty, before it tipped out into the waterway, kicking up a hissing geyser of steam.

The huge geyser shot up into the air, its cloudy haze positioned directly *in between* Pooh Bear and Kallis, giving Pooh Bear several valuable seconds of movement.

But then the haze from the geyser began to dissipate and Kallis's snipers opened fire with a vengeance.

West ran through darkness. Alone.

Guided only by the light of a single glowstick.

His little tunnel was tight, only big enough for him to run through bent-over.

After about a hundred metres, however, he heard engine noises up ahead and suddenly—

—he burst out into a wider tunnel, with hard-packed walls of dirt and wide enough for a tank to pass through. Low mounds of dirt lay at regular intervals along the centre of the roadway—mounds left behind by the tunnel-borer. A long line of fading American glowsticks had been left along its length to illuminate the way back.

It was the excavation tunnel.

The engine noises came from his right, from over a crest in the sloping roadway—the sound of light car engines and the deep-throated diesel roar of the tunnel-boring vehicle.

Judah and his CIEF team.

Approaching fast.

West chucked his glowstick and, thinking fast, quickly rolled out *onto the roadway*.

He rolled into the middle of the tunnel, lying length-ways in a dark shadowy spot, pressing himself close to one of the dirt-mounds in the centre of the road, half-burying himself in the dirt.

Judah's convoy rose above the crest, headlights blazing.

The lead light strike cars whizzed by West on either side, avoiding the dirt-mound by inches, before . . .

. . . the great M-113 tunnel-boring vehicle thundered

over the crest and rumbled right over the top of West, its huge tracked wheels clanking by on either side of his body!

No sooner was it over him than West quickly whipped out his MP-7 sub-machine gun and, using its grip as a hook, latched it over a pipe on the underbody of the TBV—and suddenly he was swept along with it, hanging from the huge vehicle's underbelly!

He had to work fast.

He guessed that he had about thirty seconds till they came to the gorge—the narrow gorge that cut across the excavation tunnel: his escape route.

Vastly outnumbered and outgunned, he could never hope to beat all of Judah's CIEF force and take the Pieces. Working alone, there was no way he could carry the two huge Pieces anyway.

The thing was, he didn't want to *carry* them—he just needed to *see* them and take a couple of quick photos of the carvings on their upper sides.

West clambered forward along the underside of the moving tunnel-borer, pulling himself forward hand-over-hand, until he came to the front of the great lumbering vehicle—where he climbed up and over its bow and commenced his one-man war against the CIEF.

Marshall Judah sat in the passenger seat of one of the rear LSVs, keeping an eye on his tunnel-borer up ahead.

He never saw West disappear under it—nor did he see West climb forward along its underbelly to its front bumper—nor did he see West shoot its driver right between the eyes and leap inside the driver's hatch.

No, all Judah saw was several sudden lightning-flashes of gunfire flaring within the big tunnel-borer—before he saw it veer out of control to the left and grind horribly against the left-hand wall of the tunnel!

The big vehicle crunched against the wall, still moving forward but losing speed, and as it did so, more flashes could be seen flaring within it—only these weren't muzzle flashes from guns, they were different, almost like . . . *camera* flashes.

Then the big tunnel-borer regained its alignment and pulled away from the wall, continuing on down the tunnel, where it rumbled across a sturdy ancient stone bridge that spanned a thirty-foot-wide cross-gorge. The drop to the watery floor of the gorge was about eighty feet.

Judah couldn't be sure, but as he watched the tunnel-borer race across the bridge, he could have sworn he saw a figure leap off its roof and drop into the narrow black gorge, splashing into the water below.

Either way, as soon as it was across the ancient bridge, the tunnel-borer again lurched leftward, crunching against the wall, before grinding to a slow laboured halt about 80 metres down the tunnel.

The escort cars converged on it, unloaded their men, guns up—

—and found the two golden Pieces still in it, safe and sound.

The driver of the M-113 and the four CIEF guards in it were all dead, shot to bits. Their blood covered the walls of the hold. All had got their guns out—but not a single one of them had got a round off.

Judah just gazed at the human wreckage inside the tunnel-boring vehicle, the work of Jack West Jr.

'West, West, West . . .' he said to the air. 'You always were good. Perhaps the best pupil I ever had.'

Then he reorganised his men and the convoy shot off down the tunnel again, safe and away.

Sniper rounds slammed into the cliff all around Pooh Bear's team as they tip-toed across the cliff-face to the fortress's left-hand tower.

The Warbler in Big Ears's backpack was working admirably—bending the bullets away—and one by one, Pooh's team made it to the high-spired tower attached to the fortress.

Far below them, mud continued to flow out of the mouth of the great citadel, while above them, the dark ceiling of the chasm was close now, barely twenty feet above the peak of their tower.

Then abruptly Kallis's men stopped firing.

Pooh Bear exchanged a worried look with Wizard.

Change of tactics.

A brutal change of tactics.

Frustrated by the electromagnetic field of the Warbler, Kallis and his team started firing RPGs at the tower.

It looked like a fireworks display: long hyper-extending fingers of smoke lanced upward from their tunnel, streaking up toward the mighty ancient citadel.

'Oh my Lord,' Wizard breathed. 'The Warbler won't work against RPGs! RPGs are too heavy to divert magnetically! Somebody do something—'

It was Stretch who came up with the answer.

Quick as a flash, he unslung his sniper rifle, aimed and fired it *at the first oncoming RPG!*

The bullet hit the RPG a bare thirty feet from the tower and the RPG detonated in mid-flight, exploding just out of reach of the tower.

It was an incredible shot. A single shot, fired under pressure, hitting a high-velocity target in *mid-flight*!

Even Pooh Bear was impressed. 'Nice shot, Israeli. How many times can you do that?'

'As long as it takes for you to figure out a way out of here, Arab,' Stretch said, eyeing a second incoming RPG through his sights.

Pooh Bear evaluated their position. Their aqueduct was shattered, uncrossable. The main entrance to the fortress was filled with flowing mud. No dice there. And the main chasm, with its traps and deadly whirlpools, was guarded by Kallis's CIEF team.

'Trapped,' he said, grimacing in thought.

'Isn't there *any* way out of here?' Big Ears asked.

'This place was sealed long ago,' Wizard said.

They all stood in silence.

'Why not go up?' a small voice suggested.

Everyone turned.

It was Lily.

She shrugged, pointed at the 'planked' granite ceiling not far above the pinnacle of their tower. 'Can't we go out that way? Maybe with one of Pooh Bear's demolition charges?'

Pooh Bear's frown became a grin. 'Young lady, I like your style.'

A minute later, as Stretch kept the incoming RPGs at bay, Pooh Bear fired a grappling hook up at the high ceiling of the chasm, almost directly above his tower.

The hook he fired was a rock-penetrating climbing hook—but instead of rope, attached to it was a Semtex-IV demolition charge.

The climbing hook slammed into the granite ceiling, embedded itself in it.

One, one-thousand.

Two, one-thousand.

Three—

The Semtex charge went off.

Fireball. Explosion. Dustcloud.

And then, with an almighty *craaaack!* one of the granite planks that formed the chasm's ceiling broke in two, and fell from its place, tumbling out of the ceiling formation. It was easily as big as a California Redwood tree, and the great granite plank created a huge splash as it hit the waterway far below.

A cascade of sand streamed in through the newly-formed rectangular opening in the ceiling, followed by a blazing beam of sunlight that illuminated the tower and lit up the chasm in an entirely new way.

Pooh Bear and the others had completely lost track of time, of how long they'd been in the chasm system. It was actually just after noon.

Kallis's men were still firing RPGs. And Stretch was still picking them off, shot for shot.

Once the Semtex charge had created its opening in the ceiling, Big Ears fired a second grappling hook—only this one *did* have a rope attached to it.

The hook flew up through the big rectangular hole in the ceiling, disappearing up into the daylight, where it landed and caught hold of something.

'Up we go!' Pooh Bear called. 'Big Ears. You first. Stretch, you're last.'

'As always . . .' Stretch muttered.

'Wizard, call the *Halicarnassus*, send them a pick-up signal.'

'What about Huntsman?' Lily asked.

'*I'll catch up with you all later,*' a voice said in their earpieces.

West's voice.

'*I've got pictures of the Pieces,*' he said. '*But I can't get back to you guys at the fortress. I'll have to get out another way. I'll call you later.*'

And so up the rope they went, climbing up into the blinding daylight, all the while protected by Stretch's incredible sniping skills.

When at last Stretch himself had to go, he bolted for the rope, latched onto it and started climbing.

Almost immediately, an RPG slammed into the tower beneath him and with an awesome *booooom*, the left-hand tower of Hamilcar's Refuge burst outward in a star-shaped spray of giant bricks and shattered rock—bricks and rock that sailed way out into the chasm before plunging down into the waterway below.

And when the smoke cleared, the tower stood deprived of its pinnacle, its upper reaches charred and broken, its high-spired balcony simply gone. The great tower had been decapitated.

All that remained in its place was a rectangular hole in the ceiling, through which glorious sunshine now streamed.

Pooh Bear and his team had escaped.

The *Halicarnassus* would pick them up ten minutes later, swooping down to the desert plain for a rapid extraction.

There was, however, no further word from West.

Indeed, as the *Halicarnassus* soared away from the American forces massed around a crater two miles west of the covered Refuge, all contact with West appeared lost.

For the remainder of that day, no-one would hear a word from Jack West Jr.

At 2:55 a.m. the next morning, West finally sent a pick-up signal—from a position *one hundred kilometres north* of the concealed inlet that housed Hamilcar's Refuge, a position that put him out in the middle of the Mediterranean Sea!

It was a small Italian resort island, conveniently possessing its own airstrip.

The staff at the resort would long recall the night a dark 747 jumbo jet touched down unannounced on their airstrip and performed a brilliant short-runway landing procedure.

They didn't know what the plane was, or why it had landed briefly on their island.

Two days later, one of their diving expeditions would find a sixty-year-old World War II–era Nazi U-boat lying aground on a rocky reef just off the southern tip of the island, a submarine that had not been there two days previously.

Its conning tower blazed with the number '*U-342*'.

It would become one of the resort's favourite dive spots from then on.

His face dark and grim, West strode into the *Halicarnassus*'s main cabin and without stopping or speaking to any of the assembled team—including Lily—he grabbed Wizard by the arm and hauled him into the back office of the plane with the words: 'You. Me. Office. *Now.*'

West slammed the door and whirled around.

'Wizard. We've got a mole in our team.'

'What?'

'Fool me once, shame on you. Fool me twice, shame on me,' West said. '*Twice* now Judah and his Americans have arrived at our location only hours after we got there. The Sudan wasn't conclusive, since they could have tracked the Europeans there. But Tunisia was different. First, the Europeans weren't in Tunisia. Second, even if Judah has a copy of the Callimachus Text, he couldn't have found Hamilcar's Refuge. He needed Euclid's Instructions to find it and *we* have the only copy in existence. They followed us there. Someone on our team *led them there*. Sent up a tracing signal, or somehow got a message out to Judah.'

Wizard's face fell. The thought of a rat in their ranks actually pained him—he felt like they had all become something of a family. 'Jack, we've been working with these people for *ten years*. How could any of them undermine our mission now?'

'Stretch hasn't been with us for ten years. He's only been with us for three. And he wasn't a part of the original team. He crashed the party, remember. And he represents Israel, not the coalition of the minnows.'

Wizard said, 'But he's really become a part of the team. I know he and Pooh Bear have Arab–Israeli issues, but I'd say he's blended in rather well.'

'And if he hasn't been making secret reports to the Mossad, I'll eat my own helmet,' West said.

'Hmmm, true.'

West threw out another option: 'Pooh Bear? The Arab world is five hundred years behind the West. They'd love to get their hands on the Capstone, and Pooh's father, the Sheik, was unusually keen for the United Arab Emirates to be involved in this mission.'

'Come on, Jack, Pooh Bear would step in front of a runaway bus to save Lily. Next theory.'

'Big Ears trained with Judah at Coronado in the States a few months before our mission began—'

'Freight train,' Wizard said simply.

'What does that mean?'

'If Pooh Bear would step in front of a bus to protect Lily, then Big Ears would step in front of a freight train to save her. And as I recall, you yourself also once went to a US-sponsored training course at Coronado Naval Base in the States, a course conducted by Marshall Judah and the CIEF. That's not even mentioning your mysterious work with him in Desert Storm.'

West slumped back in his chair, thought about it all.

The problem with a multinational team like this was the motivations of its members—you just never knew if they had the team's interests at heart or their own.

'Max. This is not what we need. We're going up against the two biggest fish in the world and getting our asses kicked. We're hanging on by our fingertips.'

He took a deep breath.

'I can't believe I'm going to do this: conduct surveillance on my own team. Max, set up a microwave communications net around this plane. A net that will catch all incoming and outgoing signals. If someone's communicating with the outside world, I want to know about it when it happens. We gotta plug this leak. Can you do that?'

'I will.'

'We keep this to ourselves for the time being, and we watch everyone.'

Wizard nodded. 'I've got another issue for you.'

West rubbed his brow. 'Yes?'

'While you were getting away from Tunisia on that U-boat, I set Lily to work on the Callimachus Text again. It's odd, she says that the language of the Text gets more and more difficult. But at the same time she herself is progressing in skill: sections that she couldn't read yesterday, she can suddenly comprehend today. It's as if the very language of the Text is determining the order in which we can find the Pieces.'

'Uh-huh. And . . .'

'She's read the next three entries—the Mausoleum one came next and it just said, "I lie with the Pharos". The next two entries concern the Statue of Zeus at Olympia and the Temple of Artemis at Ephesus.

'Following on from the ones we've already translated, these new entries confirm a curious pattern: the Text is guiding us through the Seven Wonders of the Ancient World from the youngest Wonder to the oldest. The Colossus, the most recently built, came first, then

the Pharos, then the Mausoleum. The next two, those of the Statue of Zeus and the Temple of Artemis, are the next oldest Wonders in the progression.'

'The Middle Wonders,' West said, nodding. 'And you say Lily has now read the entries for them?'

'Yes. And in doing so, she has revealed some very serious problems.'

Wizard told West the situation.

After he'd done so, West sat back in his chair and frowned, deep in thought.

'Damn . . .' he said. Then he looked up. 'Assemble everyone in the main cabin. It's time to make a tough decision.'

The entire team gathered in the main cabin of the *Halicarnassus*.

They sat in a wide circle, variously sitting on couches or at the desk-like consoles that lined the walls. Even Sky Monster was there, leaving the plane to fly on autopilot for a while.

West spoke.

'Okay, here's the state of play. We're 0-for-2 after two efforts at the plate. In those two missions, three Pieces of the Capstone have been unearthed and we have none of them.

'But we're not completely dead yet. We may not have got any of the Pieces, but so long as we keep seeing the Pieces and accumulating the lines of the positive incantation carved into them, we still have a chance, albeit a very slim one.'

'Very, *very* slim,' Stretch said.

West threw Stretch a look that would've frozen water. Stretch retreated immediately. 'Sorry. Go on.'

West did. 'So far the Callimachus Text has been an excellent guide. It has led us accurately to the Colossus and to the Pharos Pieces, and the Mausoleum Piece.

'But now,' West said seriously, 'now Lily has managed to translate the next two entries, and we have a problem.'

He flicked a switch, projecting Lily's translations of

the next two entries of the Callimachus Text onto a pull-down screen. They read:

The Statue of cuckolded Zeus,
Cronos's Son, the false deity.
While his statue was immense, his power was illusory.
No thunderbolts did he wield, no wrath did he bear,
No victory did he achieve.
Indeed, it was only the Victory in his right hand that made him great,
Oh winged woman, whither didst thou fly?

The Temple of the Huntress,
In heavenly Ephesus.
The sister of Apollo, Ra's charioteer,
Has never let go of her Piece,
Even when her Temple burned on the night of Iskender's birth.
Through the exertions of our brave brothers,
It has never left the possession of our Order.
Nay, it is worshipped every day in our highest temple.

Zoe saw the first problem immediately. 'There are no *clues* in these verses . . .' she said with dismay.

'There's nothing for us to go on,' Fuzzy said.

'More than that,' Stretch said, 'the writers of the first verse didn't even know where the Statue of Zeus *went*. This is a total dead-end.'

'You do always argue the negative, don't you, Israeli?' Pooh Bear scowled. 'After all they've done, have you no faith in Wizard and Huntsman?'

'I believe in what is achievable,' Stretch shot back.

'Gentlemen. Please,' Wizard cut in. He turned to Stretch. 'It's not a *total* dead-end, Benjamin. Close, but not total. The Zeus verse is indeed disappointing, as it offers no clues at all to the location of its Piece.

'But the verse about the Temple of Artemis—the goddess of the hunt and, in Greek lore, Apollo's sister—is actually quite clear about the location of its Piece of the Capstone.

'It states that, through the efforts of its priests over the ages, the Artemis Piece has never left the possession of the Cult of Amun-Ra. It even gives us an exact location: the highest temple of the Cult of Amun-Ra. Unfortunately, this means that the Piece is almost certainly already in the hands of our European competitors.'

'What do you mean?' Sky Monster asked. 'I didn't realise that the Cult of Amun-Ra was still around. I thought it died out. What is it and where is its "highest temple"?'

'Why, Sky Monster,' Wizard said, 'the Cult of Amun-Ra is most certainly alive and well. Indeed, it is one of the most widespread religions in the world today.'

'A religion?' Big Ears asked. 'Which one?'

Wizard said simply: 'The Cult of Amun-Ra, my friend, is the Roman Catholic Church.'

'Are you saying that the Catholic Church—*my* Catholic Church, the church I have attended all my life—is *a Sun-cult*?' Big Ears asked in disbelief.

Very Irish and hence very Catholic, he spun to face West—who just nodded silently, as if it was the most obvious thing in the world.

'Come on,' Big Ears said. 'I read *The Da Vinci Code*, too. It was a fun book and it had a great conspiracy theory, but this is something else.'

Wizard shrugged. 'Although its everyday followers don't know it, the Catholic Church is indeed a thinly veiled reincarnation of a very ancient Sun-cult.'

Wizard counted the points off his fingers:

'The virgin birth of the Christ character is a direct retelling of the Egyptian legend of Horus—only the names have been changed. Look at the vestments Catholic priests wear: emblazoned with the Coptic Cross. But 2,000 years before that symbol was the Coptic Cross, it was the Egyptian symbol, *ankh*, meaning life. Look at the Eucharistic chamber on any altar: it is in the shape of a dazzling golden *Sun*. And what is a halo? A Sun-disc.

'Go to Rome and look around. Look at all the obelisks—the ultimate symbols of Sun worship, pointing up at their deity. They are all genuine Egyptian obelisks, transported from Egypt to Rome by Pope

Sixtus V and erected in front of *every major church* in the city, including St Peter's Basilica. There are more obelisks in Rome than any other city in the world, including any Egyptian city! Why, Liam, you tell me, what word do you say at the end of every single Catholic prayer you utter?'

'Amen,' Big Ears said.

'The Ancient Egyptians had no vowels in their writing. *Amen* is simply another way of spelling *Amun*. Every time you pray, Liam, you intone the most powerful god of ancient Egypt: Amun.'

Big Ears's eyes went wide. 'No way . . .'

Zoe brought the conversation back to the point: 'But the Artemis verse says that its Piece is *worshipped every day* in the Cult of Amun-Ra's *highest temple*. If what you say is true, then the highest temple of the Roman Catholic Church would be St Peter's Basilica in the Vatican in Rome.'

'That is my conclusion too,' Wizard said.

'Welcome to Problem No. 1,' West said. 'If the Artemis Piece is in St Peter's Basilica, it could be *anywhere* in there. The cathedral itself is a behemoth, the size of about seven football fields, and beneath it is a labyrinth of tombs, crypts, chambers and tunnels. For all we know, it could be on display in a crypt, worshipped every day by only the most senior cardinals, or it could be embedded in the floor of the main cathedral, twenty feet underground. Searching for a golden trapezoid in there would be like searching for a needle in a mountain of haystacks. It could take years, and we don't have years.'

'And Problem No. 2?' Zoe asked.

Wizard said, 'The Zeus piece. As you said before, this verse gives us absolutely nothing. Beyond the usual legends *we have no way of knowing where it is*.'

A silence fell on the room. This situation had not been anticipated. The Callimachus Text had served them so well so far, none of them had thought that it would completely fail them on the later Pieces.

'So what do we do?' Zoe asked.

'There is one option,' West said solemnly. 'But it's not one that I'd take lightly.'

'And that is . . . ?'

'We get outside help,' West said. 'Help from an expert on the Capstone, perhaps the greatest living expert on it. A man who has devoted his life to pursuing it. A man who knows more about the Seven Ancient Wonders than anyone else alive.'

'Sounds like a guy we should have consulted 10 years ago,' Fuzzy said.

'We would have if we could have,' Wizard said, 'but this man is . . . *elusive*. He is also psychotic, clinically insane, in fact.'

'Who is he?' Sky Monster asked.

'His name is Mullah Mustapha Zaeed . . .' West said.

'Oh no, this is outrageous—' Stretch sat upright.

'The Black Priest of Kabul—' Pooh Bear breathed.

West explained for the others.

'Zaeed is Saudi by birth, but he's been linked to dozens of Islamic fundamentalist terrorist groups as far afield as Pakistan, Sudan, and Afghanistan, where he was sheltered by the Taliban until September 11, 2001. A qualified mullah, he's a teacher of fundamentalist Islam—'

'He's an assassin,' Stretch spat, 'responsible for the deaths of at least twelve Mossad agents. Zaeed's been on the Red List for fifteen years.' The Mossad Red List was a list of terrorists whom any Mossad agent was permitted to shoot *on sight* anywhere around the world.

'If the Mossad can't find him, how on Earth are we going to find him at such short notice?' Zoe asked.

West looked to Stretch as he spoke: 'Oh, the Mossad knows where he is, they just can't get to him.'

The tight-lipped expression on Stretch's face said this was true.

'So where is he then?' Pooh Bear asked.

West turned to Stretch.

Stretch practically growled as he spoke. 'Mustapha Zaeed was picked up by US forces during Operation Enduring Freedom, the invasion of Afghanistan after 9/11, the one that toppled the Taliban regime. In early 2002, Mustapha Zaeed was taken to Camp X-Ray, the temporary terrorist prison at Guantanamo Bay, Cuba. He's been there ever since.'

'Guantanamo Bay,' Zoe repeated. 'Cuba. The most heavily guarded, most secure military compound *in the world*. And what—we're just going to stroll in there and walk out with a known terrorist?'

West said, 'Naval Station Guantanamo Bay is designed for two things: to keep the Cubans from retaking it, and to keep prisoners *in*. Its guns are pointed landward and inward. That leaves us one open flank—the sea side.'

Zoe said, 'I'm sorry, but are you seriously thinking of sneaking into Guantanamo Bay and busting out one of its inmates?'

'No,' West said, standing. 'I'm not planning on *sneaking* in at all. No, I suggest we do the one thing the Americans least expect. I suggest we launch a frontal assault on Guantanamo Bay.'

THIRD MISSION
THE BATTLE OF GUANTANAMO BAY

GUANTANAMO BAY, CUBA
17 MARCH, 2006
3 DAYS BEFORE TARTARUS

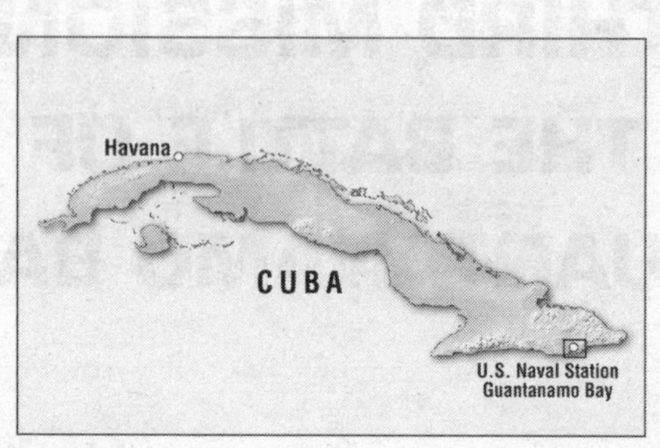
Havana
CUBA
U.S. Naval Station
Guantanamo Bay

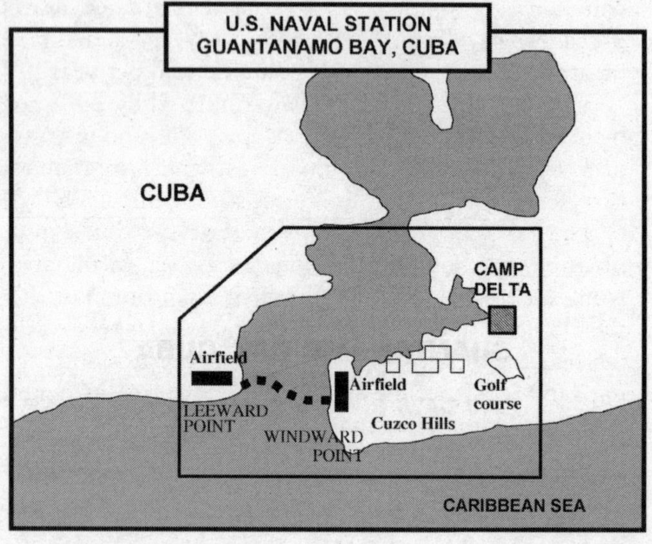
U.S. NAVAL STATION
GUANTANAMO BAY, CUBA
CUBA
CAMP
DELTA
Airfield
Airfield
Golf
course
LEEWARD
POINT
Cuzco Hills
WINDWARD
POINT
CARIBBEAN SEA

NAVAL STATION GUANTANAMO BAY
SOUTH-EASTERN CUBA
17 MARCH, 2006, 3:35 A.M.
3 DAYS BEFORE THE ARRIVAL OF TARTARUS

Naval Station Guantanamo Bay is a true historical oddity.

Born out of two treaties between the United States and Cuba made in the early 20th century—when the US had Cuba over a barrel—Cuba essentially leases a small chunk of its south-eastern coast to America at the obscenely low rent of US$4,085 a year (the actual price mentioned in the treaty is '$2,000 in gold per year').

Since the treaty can only be terminated by the agreement of *both* parties—and since the US has no intention of agreeing to such a termination—what it amounts to is a permanent US military outpost on Cuban soil.

The Bay itself is situated at the extreme southern tip of Cuba, opening onto the Caribbean Sea, facing away from America. Occupying both of its promontories is the US base, and it is very very small—maybe six kilometres deep by ten kilometres long, its twisting and turning landside fenceline barely 25 kilometres in length.

After all that, its most well-known feature (apart from appearing in the Tom Cruise movie *A Few Good Men*) is its status in International Law: for as far as International Law is concerned, Guantanamo Bay does not exist. It floats in a kind of legal limbo, free of the constraints of the Geneva Conventions and other troublesome treaties.

Which was exactly why the United States chose it as a prison for the 700 'stateless combatants' that it captured in Afghanistan during Operation Enduring Freedom.

The Bay itself bends northward like a fat slithering snake, bounded by dozens of inlets and marshy coves. Its western side is known as *Leeward*, and it contains little of interest except for the base's airstrip, Leeward Point Field.

It is on the eastern side of the Bay—*Windward*—where all the real activity takes place. This is where the various Marine barracks and prison complexes are situated. An inactive airfield, McCalla Field, occupies the eastern side of the harbour entrance. Further inland, there are administrative buildings, a school, shops and a housing estate for the Marines who live on base.

Further inland still, at Radio Range, in the dead heart of Naval Station Guantanamo Bay, you will find Camp Delta. (Camp X-Ray, with its notorious open-air chain-link cages, was always intended to be temporary. In April 2002, all of its detainees were shipped to the newly constructed Camp Delta, a more permanent complex.)

Camp Delta is made up of six detention camps: Camps 1, 2, 3, 4, Echo and Iguana. Camp 3 is the 'SuperMax' facility. Only the most dangerous prisoners live in Camp 3.

Prisoners like Mullah Mustapha Zaeed.

In short, Camp Delta, nestled in the centre of the world's most heavily fortified base, is a maze of cinder-block buildings and chain-link fences, all topped with razor-wire and guarded by stony-faced US Army Military Police.

It is a forbidding installation, one of the bleakest places on Earth.

And yet after all that, only 500 metres from the Camp's outermost razor-wire fence is something you would find only in an American military base: a golf course.

With two heavily defended airfields to choose from, naturally West aimed for the golf course.

'I know Gitmo . . .' he said, standing in the cockpit of the *Halicarnassus* as it roared down through the night sky, descending on Guantanamo Bay.

After a quick refuelling in friendly Spain, they had soared off over the Atlantic, commencing the five-hour flight to Cuba.

'. . . I went there once, after some wargames my country did with the CIEF. Believe it or not, I actually played on the golf course—Christ, a golf course in a military base. Thing is, there aren't many trees and the last few holes—the 16th, 17th and 18th—run end-on-end, separated by only low bushes. They're wide and straight and long, about 450 metres each. About runway length. What do you say, Sky Monster? Think you can do it?'

'Can I?' Sky Monster scoffed. 'My friend, give me something harder next time!'

'Great.' West made to leave the cockpit. 'See you down on the ground.'

Ten minutes later, West strode into the lower hold of the

Halicarnassus, dressed entirely in black and wearing his back-mounted carbon-fibre wings.

Zoe was waiting for him, also dressed in black, also wearing a wing-set. The tight form-fitting bodysuit brought out the best in her slender figure. Lean and shapely, Zoe Kissane was beautiful and *fit*.

'I hope you're right about this,' she said.

'Surprise is the key. Their guns are pointed at the Cubans and at their 700 prisoners. The Americans don't think anyone is stupid enough to take Guantanamo Bay head-on.'

'Nope. Only us,' Zoe said.

'Have you checked out Stretch's satellite image of Camp Delta?'

'Three times,' Zoe said. 'The intel from Mossad says that Zaeed is in hut C-12 of Camp 3, solitary confinement. Hope we can spot it in the dark. Is there anything Mossad doesn't know?'

'Mossad knows what my Aunt Judy eats for breakfast.' West checked his watch. 'We're eight minutes out. Time to fly.'

Moments later, the rear ramp of the 747 rumbled open and they leapt out of it together, disappearing into the night sky.

Inside the *Halicarnassus* itself, every battle station was manned.

Big Ears, Fuzzy, Pooh Bear and Stretch all sat in the great black plane's four gun turrets—Big Ears and Pooh Bear on the wing-mounted turrets, Fuzzy on the underbelly, and Stretch up on the 747's domed roof.

Their six-barrelled miniguns were currently loaded with superlethal 7.62 mm armour-piercing tracer rounds—but they had special instructions from West as to what to use later, when the battle got really hot.

Wizard, Lily and Horus had been dropped off at a safe island location nearby—it was far too dangerous to bring Lily on this mission.

The *Halicarnassus* thundered through the night sky.

It flew without lights, so it was little more than a dark shadow against the clouds; and it had long ago been stripped of its transponder—so it gave off no electronic signature.

And its black radar-absorbent paint, the same as that used on the B-2 Stealth Bomber, deflected any radar scans the Americans projected from Gitmo.

It was a ghost.

A ghost the American forces at Guantanamo Bay would not know existed until it was right on top of them.

In the end, it was a pair of night sentries who saw it—or, rather, *heard* it—first. They were posted on one of the most far-flung sentry towers on the base, on a remote headland overlooking the ocean about two klicks east of Windward Point, near the Cuzco Hills.

They saw the huge black shadow come roaring in low over their heads, zooming in from the south, from over the Caribbean Sea.

They called it in immediately.

And so the alert went out, and the 3,000-strong American force at Guantanamo Bay declared war on Jack West Jr and his team.

The *Halicarnassus* shot low over the Cuzco Hills, bearing down on the rumpled moonlit landscape of Guantanamo Bay. It was 3:45 in the morning.

Then the big 747 banked sharply to the left and disappeared below the treeline . . .

. . . landing right on the fairway of the 16th hole of the Guantanamo Bay Golf Course, its winglights blazing to life as it did so!

The plane's massive tyres ripped up the pristine fairway, churning up great ragged chunks of grass, its glaring winglights lighting the way. It romped down the 16th hole, rumbled onto the 17th.

The stand of bushes separating the 17th from the 18th hole loomed in front of it and Sky Monster just smashed straight through them, crunching over them in an instant, and the rampaging *Halicarnassus* rumbled down the 18th fairway.

Klaxons and alarms wailed all over Guantanamo Bay. Flashing lights erupted everywhere.

Marines leapt out of their beds.

Guard-tower sentries scanned the perimeter down the barrels of their M-16s.

Spotlights searched the sky for more aircraft.

The word went out: they were being attacked . . . *from the golf course!*

Two crack teams of Recon Marines were dispatched to the golf course, while Black Hawk helicopters and a much larger force were assembled to follow up behind them.

And every single jail on the base was instantly placed into lockdown—every gate was double-locked via computer, every guard-post sentry team was doubled.

It was chaos.

Pandemonium.

And in all the chaos and confusion that had followed the *Halicarnassus*'s spectacular landing on the golf course, no-one noticed the two black-winged figures that descended over Gitmo with graceful silent swoops, landing lightly and silently on the flat concrete roof of hut C-12 in Camp 3 of Camp Delta.

West detonated a Semtex charge on the roof of the cinder-block cabin, blasting a hole in it big enough for him to fit through.

He jumped down through the hole—

—and landed in darkness on the roof of a cube-shaped wire-mesh cage. A blowtorch made short work of the cage's roof and West leapt down into it—

—to see a skeletal wraith-like figure come rushing out of the darkness at him, arms outstretched!

West pivoted quickly and sent Zaeed thudding into the wall, where he pinioned the terrorist and shone his barrel-mounted flashlight right into the man's eyes.

By the light of the flashlight, Zaeed looked positively *scary*.

The terrorist's beard and hair had been shaved off, leaving him with a crude stubble on both his angular chin and his scalp. He was thin, malnourished. And his eyes—those eyes—they were hollow, sunken into his skull, accentuating his overall appearance of a living skeleton. They blazed with madness.

'Mustapha Zaeed?'

'Ye-yes . . .'

'My name is West. Jack West Jr. I'm here to offer you a one-time deal. We get you out of here, and you help us find the Seven Wonders of the Ancient World and from them, the Golden Capstone of the Great Pyramid. What do you say?'

Any resistance Zaeed still harboured disappeared in an instant at the mention of the Wonders. In his wild eyes, West saw several things at once: recognition, comprehension and naked ravenous ambition.

'I will go with you,' Zaeed said.

'Then let's move—'

'Wait!' Zaeed shouted. 'They implanted a microchip in my neck! A locater! You have to extract it, or they'll know where you've taken me!'

'We'll do it on the plane! Come on, we've got to run!' West called above the sirens. 'Zoe! Rope!'

A rope was hurled into the hut from the hole in the roof, and together West and Mustapha Zaeed scrambled up it, out of the cell.

Over at the golf course, the two teams of Recon Marines arrived to behold the *Halicarnassus* standing on the ruins of the shed that had once been their clubhouse, illuminating the area for a full 500 yards with a dozen outward-pointed floodlights.

Blinded by the dazzling lights, the Marines spread out around the big black 747, raised their guns—

—just as a withering volley of gunfire erupted from the *Halicarnassus*'s four revolving gun turrets.

The volley of bullets slammed into the Recon Marines, sent them flying backwards through the air, slamming them into trees and vehicles.

But they weren't dead.

The bullets were rubber bullets, like those West and his team had used in the quarry in Sudan.

West's instructions to his team had been simple: *you only kill someone who wants to kill you. You never ever kill men who are just doing their job.*

And as far as West was concerned, he had no quarrel with the Marine guards at Guantanamo Bay—only with their government and its backers.

The rubber bullets, however, had another effect on the Recon Marines—it made them think this was an *exercise*, an elaborate surprise in the dead of night designed by their superiors to test their response.

And so they actually became *less* lethal. They concentrated on surrounding and containing the plane, rather than destroying it.

But then, to their surprise, the big black 747 started moving again, rolling around in a tight circle until it was pointed back up the 18th fairway of the golf course.

Then with its guns still blazing, the big plane's engines fired up. The roar they made was absolutely deafening in the night.

Then the great plane started rumbling *back up* the fairway, having unloaded not a single trooper, having done—seemingly—absolutely nothing.

But then came the most amazing sight.

Two *winged* figures came shooting over the treetops from behind the Recon Marines—black-clad figures wearing carbon-fibre wing-sets—chasing after the fleeing 747, firing compressed air thrusters on their backs. They flew in a series of long swoops, like hang-gliders powered by the odd thrust of compressed air.

And as the Marines saw the winged figures more closely, their hearts sank for they now understood that this hadn't been an exercise at all.

For one of the low-flying winged intruders carried a *man* harnessed to his chest: a shaven-headed man still dressed in the bright orange coveralls of a Camp 3 detainee.

This was a jailbreak . . .

The two winged figures swooped in low over the right-hand wing of the rolling *Halicarnassus*, where they landed deftly and ran inside an emergency door which swung shut behind them.

Then the *Halicarnassus* picked up speed and thundered down the two fairways and just before it hit the woods at the far end, it lifted off, taking to the air.

Three Black Hawk choppers followed for a short while, firing after it in vain, but they could never hope to keep up with the fleeing 747.

A couple of F-15 strike fighters would be dispatched 10 minutes later, but by the time they were in the air and on the right heading, the ghostly 747—defying their radar scans and transponder searches—was gone.

It was last seen heading south, disappearing somewhere over Cuba's nearest neighbour in that direction.

Jamaica.

An hour later, in another part of the world, a digital teleprinter printed out an intercepted radio transmission:

TRANS INTERCEPT:
SAT BT-1009/03.17.06-1399
A40-TEXT TRANSMISSION
FROM: USAF SECURE FREQUENCY, ASWAN MILITARY AIRFIELD (EGYPT)
TO: UNSPECIFIED DESTINATION, MARYLAND (USA)

VOICE 1 (USA): The President is becoming increasingly anxious, Colonel. And his mood was not lifted by a report that just came in from Gitmo: someone broke a terrorist out of Camp Delta, a Saudi named Zaeed who we've discovered has connections with the Capstone project.

VOICE 2 (EGYPT): It was West. He's bold, I'll give him that. He must have hit a snag and decided he needed Zaeed.

VOICE 1 (USA): Does he? Do we need this Zaeed?

VOICE 2 (EGYPT): No. We got all we needed from Mustapha Zaeed while he was under.

[LONG PAUSE]

VOICE 1 (USA): Colonel Judah, should we be nervous? The President has ordered that a draft 'Address to the Nation' be written, concerning the evacuation of the coastal cities, just in case you don't succeed.

VOICE 2 (EGYPT): Tell him we will succeed. To date, everything has gone according to plan. West is containable at any time we choose, but it's also very useful to have him running around. And the Europeans have acted just as we anticipated. Tell the President to go ahead and write his speech, but he'll never have to use it. Judah, out.

A GIRL NAMED LILY

PART II

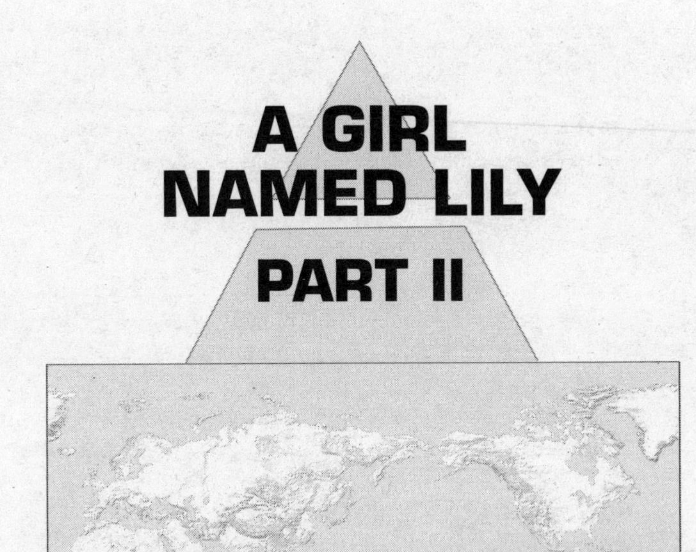

VICTORIA STATION, KENYA

2003–2006

VICTORIA STATION
SOUTHERN KENYA
2003–2006

Throughout the team's time in Kenya, a large glass jar sat on top of the kitchen bench.

It was the 'Swear Jar'. Every time a member of the team was caught swearing or cursing in front of Lily, they had to put a dollar in it.

And since they were soldiers, it was nearly always full. The proceeds of the Swear Jar went toward toys or books or ballet clothes for Lily.

Naturally, since it was she who would ultimately benefit from their indiscretion, Lily loved catching team-members swearing. It became commonplace for any curse heard around the station to be followed by her voice chiming: 'Swear Jar!'

She was also given pocket money in return for doing chores around the farm.

It was West and Wizard's idea. They wanted her upbringing—already highly unusual—to appear, at least to her, as normal as possible. Doing chores with the other team-members—gathering wood with Big Ears; helping Pooh Bear clean his tools; and on a very momentous occasion, feeding Horus for West—made her feel like she was contributing; made her feel like she was part of a family. It also just made her a nice kid.

As she grew older, however, she grew increasingly curious, and she began to learn more about the team around her.

She learned, for example, that Pooh Bear was the second son of the most powerful sheik in the United Arab Emirates.

And that Wizard had once studied to be a Catholic priest but never went through with it.

She also discovered that Zoe had once been reassigned from the armed forces to study archaeology under Wizard at Trinity College, Dublin.

Apparently, Jack West had studied there with her—having also been sent by his home country to learn from the Canadian professor.

West's home country.

Lily was ever curious about Australia. It was indeed a curiosity, full of contradictions. Eighty per cent of its enormous landmass was made up of desert, yet it also possessed supermodern cities like Sydney, famous beaches like Bells and Bondi, and superb natural formations like Uluru and the Great Barrier Reef, which—she discovered—had been named as one of the Seven *Natural* Wonders of the World.

Over time, Lily developed more sophisticated questions about Australia, including its place in international relations. Australia only had a population of 20 million people, so despite its physical size, globally speaking it was a small country.

And yet while its military was equally small, one particular aspect of it was world-renowned: Australia was the home of what was widely acknowledged to be the best special forces unit in the world, the SAS—West's former regiment.

Another thing piqued her interest: during the 20th century, Australia had been one of America's closest and most loyal allies. In World War II, Korea, Vietnam, Kuwait, Australia had always been the first country to stand beside the United States.

And yet not now.

This perplexed Lily, so she decided to ask West about it.

One rainy day, she went into his study, and found him working in darkness and silence (with Horus perched on his chair-back) staring at his computer screen, chewing on a pen, deep in thought.

Lily strolled around his office, idly touching the books on the shelves. She saw his whiteboard with the words '4 MISSING DAYS OF MY LIFE—CORONADO?' still written on it. She also noticed that the sealed glass jar with the rusty-red dirt in it had been removed.

He didn't acknowledge her presence, kept staring at his computer monitor.

She came round behind him, saw the image on his screen. It was a digital photo of some giant hieroglyphics carved into a wall somewhere. Lily translated them quickly in her head:

ENTER THE EMBRACE OF ANUBIS WILLINGLY, AND YOU SHALL LIVE BEYOND THE COMING OF RA.

ENTER AGAINST YOUR WILL, AND YOUR PEOPLE SHALL RULE FOR BUT ONE EON, BUT YOU SHALL LIVE NO MORE.

ENTER NOT AT ALL, AND THE WORLD SHALL BE NO MORE.

'What do you reckon?' West asked suddenly, not turning to face her.

Lily froze, put on the spot. 'I . . . I don't know . . .'

West swivelled. 'I'm thinking it's about death and the afterlife, in the form of an address from Amun to the Jesus-like character, Horus. "The embrace of Anubis" is death. If Horus accepts his death willingly, he will rise again and confer a benefit on his people. A bit like Christ dying on the cross. But enough of that. What brings you here today, kiddo?'

A vigorous discussion followed about Australian–American relations, about the rise of America as a sole superpower, and the concerns of Australia that its friend was becoming something of a global bully. 'Sometimes a good friend,' West said, 'has to show tough love. It's also much better to get taught a difficult lesson from your friend than from your enemy.'

West then abruptly changed the subject. 'Lily, there's something I have to tell you. When all this comes to a head, if it turns out as I hope it will, I'm probably going to have to go away for a while—'

'Go away?' Lily said, alarmed.

'Yes. Lie low. Go someplace where no-one can find me. Disappear.'

'Disappear . . .' Lily gulped.

'But I want *you* to be able to find me, Lily,' West said, smiling. 'Now, I can't tell you where I'm going, but I can point you in the right direction. If you can solve this riddle, you'll find me.'

He handed her a slip of paper, on which was written:

> *My new home is home to both tigers and crocodiles.*

> *To find it, pay the boatman, take your chances and journey*
> *Into the jaws of Death,*
> *Into the mouth of Hell.*
> *There you will find me, protected by a great villain.*

'And that, kiddo, is all I'll say. Now scram.'

Lily scampered out of the study, gripping the slip of paper.

She would pore over West's riddle for months—even going so far as to punch every word of it into Google—trying to figure it out.

She had other questions, however, which *were* answered.

Such as where West had acquired Horus.

'Horus's former owner was once Huntsman's teacher,' Wizard said, as the two of them sat outside in the brilliant African sunshine.

'He was a nasty man named Marshall Judah. Judah was an American colonel who taught Jack how to be a better soldier at a place called Coronado.

'Judah would walk around the Coronado base with Horus on his shoulder, yelling at the troops. And as an example to them, he would beat Horus if she didn't perform as she had been trained. He would say, "The only way to get obedience is through discipline and brute force!"

'Huntsman didn't like this. Didn't like seeing Judah being so cruel to the falcon. So when West left Coronado, he stole the bird from her cage in Judah's office. Ever since, Jack has treated Horus with kindness and love, and she returns his affection tenfold.

'Lily, as you grow up, you'll find that some people in this world are not very nice at all. They favour cruelty over kindness, power over sharing, anger over understanding.

'These people think only of themselves. They seek to rule over others, not for others' sakes, but for their own desire for power. Lily, one day you are going to be very powerful—*very* powerful—and I hope that if you learn nothing else from us here, you learn that the truly great people think of others first and themselves last.

'For an example of this, look no further than Huntsman and Horus. A beaten bird will obey a cruel master out of fear. But a kind master it will die for.'

One day, Lily was helping Wizard organise some of his ancient scrolls.

She loved all his old stuff—the parchments, the tablets. To her, they held within them all the mysteries of ancient faraway times.

On that particular day Wizard was collating everything he had on a series of Egyptian architects all named *Imhotep.*

Lily noticed some design plans for a quarry-mine in a place called Nubia, with four rising levels and lots of water-driven booby traps. Marked on the plans were descriptions of all the traps, and in the case of a set of concealed stepping-stones, five numbers written in Egyptian hieroglyphics: ***1-3-4-1-4***. Wizard placed those plans in a file marked 'Imhotep V'.

She also saw a really old drawing that looked like an ancient game of Snakes and Ladders. It was titled: '*Waterfall Entrance—Refortification by Imhotep III in the time of Ptolemy Soter*' and it looked like this:

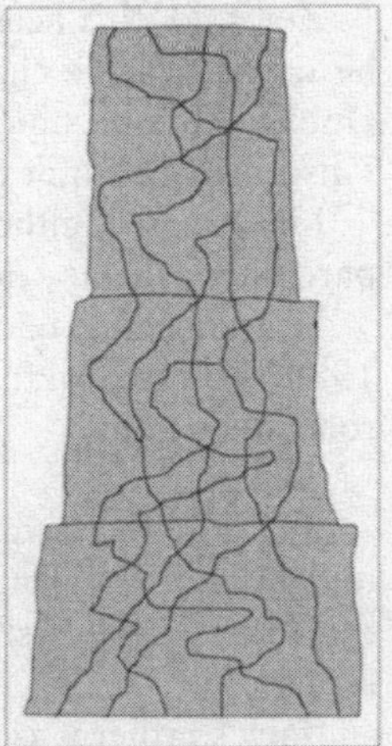

Wizard noticed Lily's interest and so he taught her things about the various Imhoteps.

Imhotep III, for instance, lived during the time of Alexander the Great and his friend, Ptolemy I, and he was called 'the Master Moat Builder'—he had been known to divert entire rivers in order to provide his structures with uncrossable moats.

'This waterfall entrance,' Wizard said, 'must have been a beautiful decorative cascade at a palace in ancient Babylon, near modern-day Baghdad in Iraq. The lines dictate the course of the flowing water. Sadly, in all the excavations of Babylon over the years, it has never been found. Such a shame.'

Lily spent the rest of that day curled up behind some boxes in the corner of Wizard's study, reading all manner of parchments, absolutely rapt.

She hardly even noticed when Zoe came in and started chatting with Wizard. It was only when West's name came up that she started listening more closely.

Zoe said, 'It's been good to see him again. Although he seems to have changed since we studied together in Dublin. He's become even quieter than he already was. I also hear he's quit the Army.'

Lily listened, although she never looked up from the parchment she appeared to be reading.

Wizard leaned back. 'Gosh, Dublin. When was that—1989? You two were so young. Jack's been down a long road since then.'

'Tell me.'

'He quit the Army soon after Desert Storm. But to understand why, you have to understand why he joined the Army in the first place: to both please and spite his father.

'Jack's father was a great soldier in his time, but Jack

was better. His father had wanted him to join the military straight after high school, but Jack wanted to study, to go to university. But he acquiesced to his father's wishes . . . and quickly became a much more formidable soldier than his father had ever been.

'Jack rose through the ranks, was fast-tracked to the SAS Regiment. He particularly excelled at desert missions; he even set a new record on the desert survival course, lasting 44 days without being captured.

'But unlike his father, Jack didn't like what they were turning him into: a killing machine, an *exceptionally good* killing machine. His superiors knew this, and they were worried that he'd quit—that was when they sent him to study with me in Dublin. They hoped it would satisfy his intellectual needs for the time being, and then he'd stay on with the Regiment. And I suppose it did satisfy him, for a time.'

'Hold on a minute,' Zoe said. 'I need to backtrack for a moment. Jack told me once that his father was American. But he joined the *Australian* Army?'

'That's right,' Wizard said. 'Thing is, Jack's *mother* is not American. To please his father, he joined the military, but to spite his father, he joined the military of his mother's birth-nation: Australia.'

'Ah . . .' Zoe said. 'Go on.'

Wizard said, 'Anyway, as you know, Jack's always had a sharp mind, and he started to look at Army life critically. Personally, I believe he just enjoyed studying ancient history and archaeology more.

'In any case, things started to go downhill when Jack's superiors sent him to a series of multinational special forces exercises at Coronado in 1990—exercises hosted by the Americans at their SEAL base, where they invited crack teams from all their allies to partake in high-end wargames. It's a huge opportunity for smaller nations, so the Australians sent West. In 1990, the exercises were hosted by none other than Marshall Judah, who instantly saw Jack's potential.

'But something happened at Coronado that I don't know about fully. Jack was injured in a helicopter accident and lay unconscious in the base hospital for four days. The four missing days of Jack West's life. When he woke up, he was sent back home, no serious damage done, and after a few months, he was back on active duty—just in time for Desert Storm in 1991.

'Jack West was one of the first men on the ground in Iraq in 1991, blowing up communications towers. After two weeks, however, he found himself serving under Judah. Seems Judah had personally asked the Pentagon to request that Jack be reassigned to him. Australia—ever loyal to the Americans—complied.

'And so Jack West Jr made his name in Desert Storm. Did some incredible things deep behind enemy lines, including that miraculous escape from the SCUD base in Basra—where, it should be said, Judah and the Americans had left him for dead.

'But when it was all over and he was back home, he walked into the office of his commanding officer, Lieutenant General Peter Cosgrove, and informed him that he would not be renewing his contract with the Regiment.

'Now Cosgrove and I have known each other for a long time. He's a very clever fellow and, through me, he was aware of *this* upcoming mission and he thought fast, and came up with a way of keeping West happy but also keeping him in the fold: he assigned West to me, as part of a long-term open-ended mission, to take part in archaeological research connected to the discovery of the Capstone.

'That was how West and I came to work together again. That was how we came to be the ones who found the scrolls from the Alexandria Library and, ultimately, Lily and her ill-fated mother. And that's why West is here on this mission.'

After discussing a few more unrelated topics, Zoe left.

Wizard returned to his work . . . at which moment, he seemed to remember that Lily was still in the corner, behind the boxes. He turned to face her.

'Why, little one, I'd clean forgotten you were here. You've been as quiet as a mouse over there. I don't know if you heard any of that, but if you did, excellent. It's important that you know about our friend, Huntsman, because he's a good fellow, a very good fellow. And although he doesn't say it, he's incredibly fond of you—in fact, he has been since the moment he first held you in his arms inside that volcano. He cares about you more than anything else in the world.'

That had been a big learning day for Lily.

Infinitely more fun, however, was the day she learned about the origins of West's plane.

The *Halicarnassus* had long been a source of curiosity to her. From the moment she'd been old enough to comprehend jumbo jets—and how much they cost—it struck her as exceedingly odd that one man could own his very own 747.

'Where did you get your plane?' she asked him at breakfast once.

Others around the table at the time suppressed laughs: Zoe, Stretch and Wizard.

West actually looked a little sheepish. 'Don't tell anyone, but I stole it.'

'You *stole* it? You stole an entire aeroplane! Isn't it wrong to steal?'

'Yes, it is wrong,' Zoe said. 'But Huntsman stole the *Halicarnassus* from a very bad man.'

'Who?'

'A man by the name of Saddam Hussein,' Wizard said. 'The former president of Iraq, a very horrible individual. Huntsman stole it from him back in 1991.'

'Why did you steal Mr Hussein's plane?' Lily asked.

West paused before answering, as if he was choosing his words carefully.

'I was near a place called Basra, and I was in a lot of trouble. And Mr Hussein's plane was the only way for me to get out alive. He kept it there in case it ever became necessary for him to escape his country.' West winked. 'I also knew that he had a lot of other planes scattered all over Iraq for the very same purpose, so I didn't think he'd miss this one.'

'Why do you call it the *Halicarnassus*? Is it named after the Mausoleum that was at Halicarnassus?'

West smiled at her easy grasp of the ancient names. 'I'm not sure, but I think it is. Mr Hussein called it the *Halicarnassus* and I just kept the name because I liked it. I'm not sure why he called it that, but Mr Hussein was a guy who liked to think he was a great Persian ruler, like Mausolus or Nebuchadnezzar. Only he wasn't like them at all. He was just a big bully.'

West turned to Wizard. 'Hey, speaking of the *Halicarnassus*, that reminds me: How is the refit going? Have you attached those Mark 3 retrogrades yet?'

'Almost done,' Wizard answered. 'We've got her weight down by a third, and all eight external retrograde thrusters have been attached and are testing well. As for the Mark 3s, they fit the 747's existing engines beautifully—the balance on the Boeing is really quite exceptional, great for VTOL, if you have the fuel. Sky Monster and I will be doing some testing this Saturday, so wear your earplugs.'

'Will do. Keep me informed.'

Lily didn't know what they were talking about.

Oh, and Lily's interest in ballet continued.

She put on many shows—shows that took place on a little stage with drawable curtains. Each performance was greeted with great applause by the whole team.

At one such show, Lily announced with a flourish that she would attempt to hold a difficult tip-toe pose for a whole minute. She made it to 45 seconds, and was bitterly disappointed.

Everyone applauded anyway.

As families do.

THE BLACK PRIEST OF KABUL

AIRSPACE ABOVE THE ATLANTIC OCEAN
17 MARCH, 2006
3 DAYS BEFORE THE ARRIVAL OF TARTARUS

Twelve hours after its brazen assault on Guantanamo Bay, after lying low in a remote Jamaican Air Force hangar outside Kingston—where it had picked up Wizard, Lily and Horus—the *Halicarnassus*, now refuelled and replenished, soared once again over the Atlantic, heading back toward Europe and Africa, back into the fray.

Once again, everyone sat in the main cabin, arrayed in a wide circle.

The focal point of the circle: Mullah Mustapha Zaeed, the Black Priest of Kabul.

Immediately after their escape from Guantanamo Bay, West had grabbed an AXS-9 digital spectrum analyser—a wand-like device used to sweep a room for bugs—and waved it over Zaeed's body.

Sure enough, at the terrorist's neck, the wand had gone berserk, beeping wildly, indicating that there was indeed a GPS locater microchip buried under Zaeed's skin.

Surgery wasn't necessary. West was able to neutralise the chip with an electromagnetic pulse from a disabling gun, turning the locater chip into a dead piece of plastic.

And so now Zaeed was here, in the main cabin—and while everyone gazed warily at the terrorist, he just stared straight at Lily.

He eyed her the way a hyena eyes an injured baby deer—with hunger, desire, and a kind of stunned disbelief that such a delightful meal could be right here in front of him.

His general appearance was frightening—despite the fact that he had been bathed and was now dressed in clean clothes.

With his shaved head, sharp stubble-covered chin, hollow eyes and wiry physique, he seemed more ghost than man, a walking skeleton. Three years of solitary confinement at Camp Delta will do that to you.

And in the clear light of the cabin, a peculiar feature became apparent: half of Zaeed's left ear, the whole bottom half, the entire lobe, had been *cut off*.

The spell broke, and he scanned West's multinational team.

'Mmm. How interesting, how very interesting,' he said. 'The mice are roaring. Taking on the two lions of the world: Europe and America.'

He looked at Wizard. 'I see Canada. And Ireland,' he nodded at Zoe. 'Fellow scholars of the ancient texts.'

His voice went low as he saw Stretch: 'And I see Israel. Why Katsa Cohen, the master sniper, nice to see you again. The last time we met was in Kandahar, at 2,000 yards. And it was a rare miss on your part.'

Stretch scowled, showing his extreme distaste for Mustapha Zaeed.

Zaeed pointed at his half-ear. 'You were a few inches wide.'

'I won't be next time,' Stretch growled.

'Now, now, Katsa. I am your guest, and a valuable

one at that. After all the trouble you went to to get me, *Jew*'—Zaeed's eyes turned to ice—'you should be more courteous.'

He spun, aiming his wild eyes at Pooh Bear.

'Ah, a good Muslim. You are Sheik Anzar Abbas's son, are you not? The great Captain Rashid Abbas, commander of the elite UAE First Commando Regiment . . .'

'I fear I am not,' Pooh Bear replied. 'Rashid Abbas is my brother. I am *Aziz* Abbas, a humble sergeant and the Sheik's second son.'

'The Sheik is a noble servant of Allah,' Zaeed bowed respectfully. 'I honour you as his kin.'

Finally, Zaeed rounded on West, who sat with Horus on his shoulder.

'And you. John West Jr. *Captain* John West Jr of the Australian SAS. The Huntsman. A name that floats around the Middle East like a wraith. Your feats have become the stuff of legend: your escape from Basra angered Hussein for years, you know. Till the day he was captured, he wanted that plane back. But then you vanished for a very long time. Disappeared off the face of the Earth. Most unusual—'

'Enough,' West said. 'The Wonders: Zeus and Artemis. Where are they?'

'Oh, yes, I am sorry. The Wonders. And Tartarus approaches, too. Mmmm. Forgive me, Captain West, but I haven't yet grasped the basis of your belief that I will even *want* to help you in this cause.'

'The United States of America already has three pieces of the Capstone,' West said simply. 'They are well-equipped and well-informed, and well on their way to securing the entire Capstone. How's that?'

'Good enough,' Zaeed said. 'Who leads the US force? Marshall Judah?'

'Yes.'

'A formidable foe. Clever and cunning. And murderous. Although did you know he has a curious weakness?'

'What?'

'A fear of heights. But I digress. Brief me on your progress so far. You are using the Callimachus Text, I presume. Which means you found the Colossus first? Was it the rightmost pendant?'

'Yes . . . it was,' West said, surprised.

'Mmmm. And then came the Pieces from the Pharos and the Mausoleum, no?'

'How did you know they'd be found in that order?'

Zaeed sighed dramatically. 'This is elementary. The Callimachus Text is written in the Word of Thoth—a most ancient and complicated language. The language itself contains within it seven levels of increasing complexity, dialects, if you will. Your young reader here'—he indicated Lily—'can only read one entry at a time, can't she? This is because each entry in the Callimachus Text is written in an increasingly difficult dialect of the Word of Thoth. The Colossus entry is written in "Thoth I", the easiest dialect of the Word of Thoth. The Pharos Piece is in "Thoth II", slightly harder. The Oracle will ultimately be able to read all seven dialects, but not instantly.'

'You can read the Word of Thoth?' Wizard asked, incredulous.

'I can decipher its first four dialects, yes.'

'But how?'

'I taught myself,' Zaeed said. 'With discipline and patience. Oh, I forget, in the decadent West, *discipline* and *patience* are no longer talents that warrant respect.'

'How did you know the Mausoleum Piece would be entombed with the Pharos Piece?' Zoe asked.

'I have spent the last 30 years acquiring every scroll, carving and document relating to the *Benben* that I could find. Some are famous, like the Callimachus Text, of which I possess a 9th-century copy, others less so—written by humble men who merely wanted to record the marvellous deeds they had done, like constructing great roofs over entire ocean inlets, or carrying marble pillars into the hearts of dormant volcanoes. My collection is vast.'

'The Callimachus Text is unhelpful on the Zeus and Artemis Pieces,' West said. 'Zeus is lost. And we believe Artemis is somewhere in St Peter's Basilica, but we don't know exactly where. Do you know where they are?'

Zaeed's eyes narrowed. 'The passage of time and many wars have scattered these two Pieces, but yes, I believe I do know their resting places.'

Pooh Bear leaned forward. 'If you know so much, why have you yourself not gone in search of these Pieces before?'

'I would have if only I had been able, my Muslim friend,' Zaeed said smoothly. 'But I fear I was not as nimble then as I am now.' As he said this, Zaeed rolled up his right pants-leg, to reveal hideous scarring and fire-melted skin on his lower leg.

'A Soviet fragmentation grenade in Afghanistan in 1987. For many years, I was unable to even walk on it. And a man with limited movement is useless in trap-laden quarries and inlets. While I retrained my withered muscles throughout the '90s, building them up again, I researched all I could about the Capstone. I was actually grooming a team of mujahideen in Afghanistan at the time of the attacks on New York and Washington DC to hunt for the Pieces. But then the September 11 attacks happened and Afghanistan was plunged into chaos. And I was captured by the Americans. But now my leg is strong.'

'The Zeus and Artemis Pieces,' West repeated. 'Where are they?'

Zaeed grinned a sly smile. 'Interestingly, these two Pieces that defy your search are neither hidden nor concealed. Both exist in plain sight—if only one knows where to look. The Artemis Piece, yes, it is indeed in St

Peter's in Rome, in no less than *the most holy place* of the Cult of Amun-Ra. As for the Zeus Piece . . .'

Zaeed leaned back in his chair, recited the appropriate verse from memory:

'No thunderbolts did he wield, no wrath did he bear,
No victory did he achieve.
Indeed, it was only the Victory in his right hand that made him great,
Oh, winged woman, whither didst thou fly?'

Zaeed looked at West. 'It was only *the Victory in his right hand* that made him great.'

West followed his line of reasoning. 'The Statue of Zeus at Olympia was said to hold in his right hand a smaller statue of "Winged Victory": the Greek goddess Nike, a woman with wings coming out of her back, like an angel or the figurehead on the prow of a ship. And since the figure of Zeus was so immense, its statue of Winged Victory was said to be life-sized.'

Zaeed said, 'Correct. And if it was Victory who made him great, we must look not for *Zeus*'s statue, but the statue of Victory. Thus the verse asks: whither did she fly?

'Now, as I'm sure you know, many life-sized statues of Winged Victory have been found around the ancient Greek world. But after a comprehensive study of the works of Pheidias, the sculptor of the statue of Zeus, I have found only one statue of Victory that possesses the features of his superior level of artistry: fine lines, perfect form, and the rare ability to reproduce the appearance of *wet* garments in marble.

'The specimen I have found is the greatest surviving example of Greek sculpture in the world today, yet ironically, Western scholars still assign its construction to an unknown artist. It was found in 1863 by a French archaeologist, Charles Champoiseau—'

'Oh, no way . . .' Wizard gasped in understanding. 'It's not . . .'

Zaeed nodded. 'The very same. Champoiseau found it on the Greek island of Samothrace, and thus the statue now bears that island's name: the Winged Victory of Samothrace.

'It was taken back to France, where its genius was quickly appreciated, whence it was taken to the Louvre. There it has sat to this very day in pride of place on a great landing at the top of the Daru Staircase, underneath a high domed ceiling in the Denon Wing of the Louvre in Paris.'

The *Halicarnassus* sped towards Europe.

It was decided that the team would split into two.

West would lead one sub-team to Paris to go after the Zeus Piece, while Wizard would lead a smaller team to Rome, to chase the Artemis Piece. As for Zaeed, he would stay with Sky Monster on the *Halicarnassus*, bound and secured.

Everyone scattered around the plane, some to rest, others to research, others to just prepare for the missions ahead.

It happened that Pooh Bear found himself preparing his guns near Mustapha Zaeed, still handcuffed to his chair.

'Hello, my brother,' Zaeed whispered. 'May Allah bless and keep you.'

'And you,' Pooh Bear replied, more out of religious habit than because he meant it.

'Your father, the sheik, is a great man,' Zaeed said. 'And a fine Muslim.'

'What do you want?'

'The presence of the Jew concerns me,' Zaeed said simply, nodding at Stretch over on the far side of the main cabin. 'I can understand your father aligning himself with these Westerners for convenience, but I cannot believe he would ally himself with the Jewish State.'

Pooh Bear said, 'The Israelis were not invited to join

this mission. They discovered us somehow—and threatened to reveal our mission unless we allowed them to join it.'

'Is that so? How typical,' Zaeed hissed. 'Then I am doubly glad that you are here, my friend. The second assembling of the Capstone will be one of the greatest moments in all of human history. Before the end, all will show their true colours. When the time comes, Allah's brethren should stand together.'

Pooh Bear just kept his eyes downcast.

In West's office in the rear of the plane, West, Wizard, Zoe and Big Ears were gazing at the brown leatherbound diary West had found inside Hamilcar's Refuge: Hermann Hessler's notebook detailing his search for the Seven Wonders of the Ancient World during World War II.

Translating it from the German, they found several references that they understood:

> **WORD OF THOTH**—MULTIPLE DIALECTS OF INCREASING DIFFICULTY . . . NEED TO LOCATE THE ORACLE FOR PRECISE TRANSLATION . . .
>
> CATHOLIC CHURCH = CULT OF AMUN-RA.
>
> **COLOSSUS: THIRD NECKPIECE.**
>
> **MYSTERIOUS BUILDING EXPEDITION** IN 85 BC.
> - IMHOTEP VI + 10,000 WORKERS;
> - ALL MARCHED WEST TO SECRET LOCATION ON COAST NEAR CARTHAGE;
> - **A WORKER'S PAPYRUS** FOUND AT ROSETTA MENTIONS THE MAN'S PARTICIPATION IN AN

EXTRAORDINARY CONSTRUCTION PROJECT: THE COVERING OF AN ENTIRE COASTAL INLET AND THE FABRICATION OF A SECTION OF COAST.

- THE MEN WHO PLACED **TWO COVERED TREASURES** IN THE INNERMOST HOLY CHAMBER WERE ALL EXECUTED.
- *PHAROS AND MAUSOLEUM PIECES???*

Accompanying these last entries was a teletyped order from Heinrich Himmler himself authorising Hessler to use a U-boat to trawl the entire North African coast of the Mediterranean for the false section of coastline.

There were also some hand-drawn hieroglyphics that Wizard translated aloud:

'THE CHOICE OF MAN

ONLY ONE OF THE TWO RITUALS MAY BE CHOSEN.
ONE BEGETS PEACE,
THE OTHER POWER.
ON THE FINAL DAY,
A CHOICE MUST BE MADE,
A CHOICE MADE IN THE PRESENCE OF RA HIMSELF
THAT WILL DETERMINE THE VERY FATE OF MEN.'

Wizard leaned back. 'It's a reference to the two incantations—the rituals. But only one of them can be performed when the Capstone is placed atop the Great Pyramid.'

They found other references, however, that they did not understand. Like these rather ominous inscriptions:

1ST INSCRIPTION FROM THE TOMB OF IMHOTEP III:

WHAT AN INCREDIBLE STRUCTURE IT WAS,
CONSTRUCTED AS A MIRROR IMAGE,
WHERE BOTH ENTRANCE AND EXIT WERE ALIKE.
IT PAINED ME THAT MY TASK—WHAT WOULD
BECOME MY LIFE'S MASTERWORK—WAS TO CONCEAL
SO MAGNIFICENT A STRUCTURE.
BUT I DID MY DUTY.
WE SEALED THE GREAT ARCHWAY WITH A LANDSLIDE.
AS INSTRUCTED, THE PRIESTS' ENTRANCE REMAINS
OPEN SO THEY MAY TEND THE SHRINES INSIDE—THE
PRIESTS HAVE BEEN INFORMED OF THE ORDER OF THE
SNARES.

2ND INSCRIPTION FROM THE TOMB OF IMHOTEP III:

ONLY THE BRAVEST OF SOULS
SHALL PASS THE WELLS OF THE WINGED LIONS.
BUT BEWARE THE PIT OF NINGIZZIDA,
TO THOSE WHO ENTER THE SERPENT-LORD'S PIT,
I OFFER NO ADVICE BUT THIS: ABANDON ALL HOPE,
FOR THERE IS NO ESCAPE FROM THERE.

WINGED LIONS. COMMON ASSYRIAN STATUE
FOUND IN PERSIA/MESOPOTAMIA.
NINGIZZIDA: ASSYRIAN GOD OF SERPENTS +
SNAKES.
POSSIBLE REF TO THE HG OF BABYLON???

A few pages later there was a pair of scribbled pictures, simply titled 'Safe Routes':

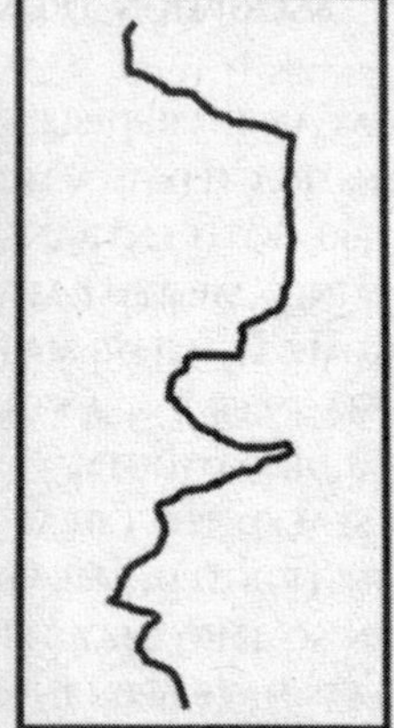

After this there was another translation, which caused Wizard to say, 'Ooh, it's a reference to one of the rituals that must be performed on the final day.'

It read:

THE RITUAL OF POWER

AT THE HIGH ALTAR OF RA,
UNDER THE HEART OF THE SACRIFICIAL ONE
WHO LIES IN THE ARMS OF VENGEFUL ANUBIS,
POUR INTO THE DEATH GOD'S HEART
ONE DEBEN OF YOUR HOMELAND
UTTER THOSE ANCIENT EVIL WORDS
AND ALL EARTHLY POWER SHALL BE YOURS
FOR A THOUSAND YEARS.

'"One deben of your homeland"?' Big Ears frowned. 'What's that supposed to mean?'

Zoe began, 'A deben was an ancient Egyptian unit of measurement: about 100 grams. I imagine it means—'

But suddenly Wizard jumped up and gasped, seeing the next entry. It read:

FROM THE SECRET GOSPEL OF ST MARK

AT DAWN ON THE DAY OF JUDGEMENT,
THAT FINAL HORRIBLE DAY,
AT THE ONLY TEMPLE THAT BEARS BOTH THEIR NAMES,
THREAD THE POWER OF RA THROUGH THE EYES OF GREAT RAMESES'S TOWERING NEEDLES,
FROM THE SECOND OWL ON THE FIRST
TO THE THIRD ON THE SECOND . . .
. . . WHEREBY THE TOMB OF ISKENDER WILL BE REVEALED.
THERE YOU WILL FIND THE FIRST PIECE.

Beneath this entry, Hessler had scrawled:

THE TOMB OF ISKENDER—THE BURIAL PLACE OF ALEXANDER THE GREAT. ALEXANDER WAS BURIED WITH THE FIRST PIECE!

Wizard leaned back, his eyes wide.

'The Secret Gospel of St Mark.' Zoe exchanged a look with West. 'The Heretical Gospel.'

'Explain,' Big Ears said.

West said, 'It's not widely known, but St Mark actually wrote *two* gospels while he was in Egypt. The first gospel is the one we all know, the one in the Bible. The second gospel, however, caused an incredible stir when he produced it, so much so that nearly every copy of it was burned by the early Christian movement. And Mark himself was almost stoned for it.'

'Why?'

Zoe said, 'Because this secret gospel recounted several *other* things Jesus did during his life. Rituals. Incantations. Bizarre episodes. The most infamous of which was the so-called homosexual incident.'

'The *what!*' Big Ears said.

Zoe said, 'An episode in which Jesus went away with a young man and, according to Mark, *initiated* the young man into "the ancient ways". Some sensationalist writers have interpreted this to have been a homosexual experience. Most scholars, however, believe it was a ritual of the Cult of Amun-Ra, which has subsequently been adopted as the initiation rite of the Freemasons, another Sun-worshipping faith to have emerged from ancient Egypt.'

West said, 'Now do you understand why it's called the Heretical Gospel?'

'Yuh-huh,' Big Ears said. 'But wait, the Freemasons. I thought they were *anti*-Catholic.'

'They are,' Zoe said. 'But the Freemasons hate the Catholic Church as only siblings can hate each other. They are like rival brothers, religions born from the same source. Just as Jerusalem is holy to both Judaism and Islam, so too do Catholicism and Freemasonry share a common source. They are simply two faiths born out of the one Mother Faith—Egyptian Sun-worship. They just diverged in their interpretations of this Mother Faith somewhere along the way.'

West patted Big Ears on the shoulder. 'It's complicated, buddy. Think of it this way: America is a Masonic State; Europe is a Catholic State. And now they're both fighting for the greatest prize of their two faiths: the Capstone.'

Big Ears said, 'You say America is a Masonic State. I thought it was overwhelmingly Christian. The Bible Belt and all that.'

Zoe said, 'Just because the *population* is Christian, doesn't mean the *country* is. What is a country anyway? A group of people with a common heritage who band together for reasons of mutual prosperity and security. And that's the key word: *security*. You see, countries have armies; religions don't. And who commands the armed forces of the entity we call "the United States"?'

'The elected president and his advisers.'

'Exactly. So, America's *people* are indeed honest Christians; but America's *leaders* since George Washington have almost exclusively been Freemasons. Washington, Jefferson, Roosevelt, the Bushes. For over 200 years, the Freemasons have used the armed forces of "the United States of America" as their own personal army for their own personal purposes. Hey presto, a religion got itself an army, and the population never even knew.'

West said, 'You can see Masonic worship of the Capstone everywhere in America. Why, over the years, American Freemasons have built replicas of each of the Seven Ancient Wonders.'

'No way . . .'

West counted them off on his fingers: 'The Statue of Liberty, built by the leading French Freemason, Frederic-Auguste Bartholdi, replicates the Colossus of Rhodes almost exactly—she even holds a torch aloft just as the original statue did. The Woolworth Building in New York is disturbingly similar to the Pharos. Fort Knox is built according to the floorplan of the Mausoleum at Halicarnassus. The Statue of Zeus, a great figure seated on a throne, is the Lincoln Memorial. The Temple of Artemis: the Supreme Court.

'The Hanging Gardens of Babylon couldn't be exactly replicated, since no-one knows what they looked like, so a special rambling garden was built and tended in their honour at the White House, first by George Washington, then Thomas Jefferson and later, Franklin Roosevelt. The Catholic president, John F. Kennedy, tried to rip the garden up, but he never managed it entirely. And while he didn't survive, the garden did. It's had many names over the years, but we now call it the Rose Garden.'

Big Ears folded his arms. 'What about the Great Pyramid, then? I don't know of any monumental pyramids in the US.'

'That's true,' West said, 'there are no giant pyramids in America. But when the Egyptians stopped building pyramids, do you know what they started building instead?'

'What?'

'Obelisks. The obelisk became the ultimate symbol of Sun-worship. And America does indeed possess one colossal obelisk: the Washington Monument. Interestingly, it is 555 feet tall. The Great Pyramid is 469 feet tall, 86 feet shorter. But when you take into account the height of the Giza Plateau at the point where the Great Pyramid stands—86 feet—you will discover that the peaks of both structures sit at *the exact same height* above sea-level.'

While this conversation was going on, Wizard was gazing at the text in the notebook.

'The only temple that bears both their names . . .' he mused. Then his eyes lit up. 'It's Luxor. The Temple at Luxor.'

'Oh, yes. Good *thinking*, Max. Good thinking!' Zoe clapped him on the shoulder.

'It would certainly fit . . .' West said.

'What would fit?' Big Ears asked, again not understanding this code they were using.

'The Temple of Amun at Luxor in southern Egypt, more commonly known as the Temple at Luxor,' Zoe said. 'It's one of the biggest tourist attractions in Egypt. The famous one with the giant pylon gateway, the two colossal seated statues of Rameses II, and the lone obelisk out the front. It stands on the east bank of the Nile in Luxor, or—as it used to be called—Thebes.

'The Luxor Temple was built by several older pharaohs, but Rameses II comprehensively rebuilt it and so claimed it as his own. It was also augmented, however, by none other than Alexander the Great. Which is why—'

'—it's the only temple in all of Egypt in which Alexander the Great is recorded *as a pharaoh*,' Wizard said. 'At Luxor alone, Alexander's name is carved in hieroglyphics and enclosed in a ring-like cartouche. *The only temple that bears both their names*: the Luxor Temple is indeed the only temple that bears both the names of Rameses II and Alexander.'

Big Ears said, 'So what about threading *the power of Ra through the eyes of Great Rameses's towering needles*?'

West said, 'Towering needles are usually obelisks. The power of Ra, I'm guessing, is sunlight. Dawn sunlight on Judgement Day: the day of the Tartarus Rotation. This verse is telling us that on the day of the Rotation, the morning Sun will shine through two matching holes in the obelisks to reveal the location of the tomb.'

Big Ears turned to Zoe. 'But I thought you said there's only one obelisk still standing at Luxor.'

Zoe nodded. 'That's right.'

'So we're screwed. Without the two obelisks, we can't

see how the Sun shines through them, so we'll never be able to find Alexander's Tomb.'

'Not exactly,' Wizard said, his eyes gleaming at West and Zoe.

They both smiled back at him.

Only Big Ears didn't get it.

'What? *What?*'

Wizard said, 'The second obelisk from the Temple at Luxor still exists, Big Ears, just not in its original location.'

'So where is it?'

Wizard answered him. 'Like many of the obelisks of ancient Egypt, it was given to a Western nation. Thirteen obelisks went to Rome, taken by the Sun-worshipping Catholic Church. Two went to London and New York—the pair of obelisks known as Cleopatra's Needles. The second obelisk from the Temple of Luxor, however, was given to the French in 1836. It now stands in pride of place in the Place de la Concorde, in the very heart of Paris, about 800 metres from the Louvre.'

'The Zeus Piece *and* the obelisk,' Zoe said. 'Looks like it's going to be double-trouble in Paris.'

West leaned back in his seat.

'Paris,' he said, 'isn't going to know what's hit her.'

FOURTH MISSION THE STATUE OF ZEUS & THE TEMPLE OF ARTEMIS

PARIS–ROME
18 MARCH, 2006
2 DAYS BEFORE TARTARUS

THE PARIS OBELISK

PLACE DE LA CONCORDE, PARIS

THE CHAMPS-ÉLYSÉES
PARIS, FRANCE
18 MARCH, 2006, 11:00 A.M.
2 DAYS BEFORE THE ARRIVAL OF TARTARUS

Jack West Jr sped around the huge multi-laned roundabout that encircled the Arc de Triomphe, whipping through traffic in a rented four-wheel drive SUV.

Lily sat in the passenger seat, while in the back were Pooh Bear, Stretch and Big Ears.

They all sat in tense silence, as one does before an outrageously daring mission deep inside enemy territory.

The heart of Paris is shaped like a Christian cross.

The longer beam of this giant cross is the Champs-Élysées, which travels all the way from the Arc de Triomphe to the Palais du Louvre. The short horizontal transept of the cross ends with the National Assembly at one end and the stunning Church of St Mary Magdalene at the other.

Most important of all is what lies at the junction of these two axes.

There one will find the Place de la Concorde.

Made famous in the French Revolution as the venue for the executions of hundreds of noblemen and women, the Place de la Concorde was the bloody home of the guillotine.

Now, however, in the exact centre of this plaza, in the exact centre of Paris—the very *focal point* of Paris—stands a towering Egyptian obelisk.

The second obelisk from the Temple of Luxor.

Of all the obelisks in the world—whether still in Egypt or not—the Paris Obelisk is unique in one important respect:

The pyramidion at its peak is coated in gold.

Historians love this, because this was how obelisks appeared in ancient Egyptian times: the tiny pyramids on their peaks were coated with electrum, a rare alloy of silver and gold.

Interestingly, however, the golden pyramidion on the Paris Obelisk is only a very recent addition—it was added to the great stone needle in 1998.

'Pooh,' West said as he drove, 'you checked the catacombs?'

'I did. They're clear. The entry gate is under the Charles de Gaulle Bridge and the tunnel runs all the way under the Boulevard Diderot. Lock has been disabled.'

'Stretch. The train?'

'TGV service. Platform 23. Leaves at 12:44 p.m. First stop Dijon.'

'Good.'

As West drove down the Champs-Élysées, he eyed the wide boulevard ahead and beheld the Paris Obelisk, rising above the traffic, easily six storeys tall.

He had climbing gear in his car—ropes, hooks,

pitons, carabiners—ready to scale the great needle and examine its upper reaches. He figured he'd look like just another reckless thrill-seeker and if he was fast enough, he'd be gone before the police arrived. After that, his team would proceed to the Louvre, for the larger, more dangerous mission.

Only then, as he drove closer, the traffic parted—

'Oh, no . . .' West breathed.

The entire lower half of the Obelisk was concealed by scaffolding. There were three storeys of it, plank-like levels shrouded with netting, like the scaffolding on a construction site.

And at the base of this temporary scaffold structure, guarding its only entrance, were six security guards.

A large sign in French and English apologised for the inconvenience as the Obelisk was covered for 'essential cleaning work'.

'They're *cleaning* it,' Stretch scoffed. 'A little convenient, don't you think? Our European rivals are onto this lead.'

'The Heretical Gospel of St Mark is notorious. There are other copies of it around the world,' West said. 'Del Piero would surely have one. He must have already checked and measured the Obelisk and since he can't remove it from here, he's sealed it off, stopping us from doing the same. Which means—damn it—del Piero is one step short of locating Alexander's Tomb and getting the topmost Piece . . .'

West gazed at the scaffolding-enclosed Obelisk, re-thinking, re-planning, adapting.

'This changes things. Everyone. Switch of plans. We're not going to do the Obelisk first anymore. We're going to take the Louvre first, in the way we planned. Then we'll grab a look at the Obelisk on the way out.'

'You have *got* to be kidding,' Stretch said. 'We're going to be running for our lives. Half the *gendarmerie* will be on our asses by then.'

'Confronting the Europeans at the Obelisk now will attract too much attention, Stretch,' West said. 'I was hoping to climb up and down it unnoticed. I can't do that now. But after we do what we plan to do at the Louvre, Paris is going to be in uproar—a state of chaos that'll give us the cover we need to get past those guards at the Obelisk. And now that I think about it, our intended escape vehicle will also come in handy.'

'I don't know about this . . .' Stretch said.

Pooh Bear said, 'What you know or don't know is irrelevant, Israeli. Honestly, your constant doubting grates on me. You'll do as Huntsman says. He is in command here.'

Stretch locked eyes with Pooh Bear, biting his tongue. 'Very well then. I will obey.'

West said, 'Good. The Louvre plan remains the same. Big Ears: you're with Lily and me; we're going in. Pooh, Stretch: get the escape vehicle and make sure you're in position when we jump.'

'Will do, Huntsman,' Pooh Bear nodded.

Twenty minutes later, West, Lily and Big Ears—gunless—strode through the metal detectors at the entrance to the Louvre.

The building's famous glass pyramid soared high above them, bathing the great museum's atrium in brilliant sunshine.

'I think I'm having another Dan Brown moment,' Big Ears said, gazing up at the glass pyramid.

'They didn't do what we're going to do in *The Da Vinci Code*,' West said ominously.

Lily provided the perfect cover; after all, how many snatch-and-grab teams enter a building holding the hand of a small child?

West's cell phone rang.

It was Pooh Bear. '*We have the exit vehicle. Ready when you are.*'

'Give us ten minutes,' West said and hung up.

Eight minutes after that, West and Big Ears were both dressed in the white coveralls of the Louvre's maintenance crew—taken from two unfortunate workers who now lay unconscious in a storeroom in the depths of the museum.

They entered the Denon Wing and ascended the impressive Daru Staircase. The staircase wound back and forth in wide sweeping flights, disappearing and reappearing behind soaring arches, before it revealed, standing proudly on a wide landing . . .

. . . the Winged Victory of Samothrace.

She was, quite simply, breathtaking.

The goddess stood with her chest thrust forward into the wind, her magnificent wings splayed out behind her, her wet tunic pressed against her body, perfectly realised in marble.

Six feet tall and standing on a five-foot-high marble mounting, she towered above the tourists milling around her.

Had her head not been missing, Winged Victory would almost certainly have been as famous as the Venus de Milo—also a resident of the Louvre—for by any measure, the artistry of her carving easily outdid that of the Venus.

The management of the Louvre seemed to recognise this, even if the public did not: Winged Victory stood high up in the building, proudly displayed up on the First Floor, not far from the Mona Lisa, while the Venus stood in confined clutter on an underground level.

The marble mounting on which the great statue stood resembled the pointed prow of a ship, but this had never been a ship.

It had been the armrest of Zeus's throne, the broken-off tip of the armrest.

If you looked closely, you could see Zeus's gigantic marble *thumb* beneath Winged Victory.

The natural conclusion was mind-blowing: if Victory was this big, then the Statue of Zeus—the actual Wonder itself, now vanished from history—must have been absolutely *gigantic.*

Victory's position on the First Floor of the Denon Wing, however, created a problem for West.

As with the other key exhibits in the Louvre, all items on the First Floor were laser-protected: as soon as a painting or sculpture was moved, it triggered an invisible laser, and steel grilles would descend at every nearby doorway, sealing in the thieves.

On the First Floor, however, there was an extra precaution: the Daru Staircase, with all its twists and bends, could be easily sealed off, trapping any would-be thief *up on the First Floor.* You could disturb Victory, but you could never take her anywhere.

Dressed in their maintenance coveralls, West and Big Ears strode up onto the landing and stood before the high statue of Victory.

They proceeded to move some potted trees arrayed around the landing, unnoticed by the light weekday crowd strolling past the statue.

West placed a couple of trees slightly to the left of Victory, while Big Ears placed two of the big pots far out of the way, over by the doorway that led south, toward the side of the Louvre that overlooked the River Seine. Lily stood by this doorway.

No-one noticed them.

They were just workmen going about some unknown but presumably authorised task.

Then West grabbed a rolling 'Repair Work in Progress' screen from a nearby storeroom and placed it in front of Victory, blocking her from view.

He looked at Big Ears, who nodded.

Then Jack West Jr swallowed.

He couldn't believe what he was about to do.

With a deep breath, he stepped up onto the marble podium that was Zeus's armrest and pushed the Winged Victory of Samothrace—a priceless marble carving 2,200 years old—off its mount, to the floor.

No sooner had Victory tilted an inch off her mount than sirens started blaring and red lights started flashing.

Great steel grilles came thundering down in every doorway—*bam!-bam!-bam!-bam!*—sealing off the stairwell and the landing.

All except one doorway.

The southern doorway.

Its grille whizzed down on its runners—

—only to bang to a halt two feet off the ground, stopped by the two solid treepots that Big Ears had placed beneath it moments earlier.

The getaway route.

Victory herself landed in the two potted trees that West had placed to her left, her fall cushioned by them.

West rushed to the upturned statue, and examined her feet, or rather the small cube-shaped marble pedestal on which her feet stood.

He pulled out a big wrench he'd taken from the maintenance room.

'May every archaeologist in the world forgive me,' he whispered as he swung down hard with the wrench.

Crack. Crack. Craaaack.

The tourists on the landing didn't know what was going on. A couple of men stepped forward to investigate the activity behind the screen, but Big Ears blocked their way with a fierce glare.

After West's three heavy blows, the little marble pedestal was no more—but revealed within it was *a perfect trapezoid of solid gold*, maybe eighteen inches to a side.

The Third Piece of the Capstone.

It had been embedded in Victory's marble pedestal.

'Lily!' West called. 'Get a look at this thing! In case we lose it later!'

Lily came over, gazed at the lustrous golden trapezoid, at the mysterious symbols carved into its top side.

'More lines of the two incantations,' she said.

'Good. Now let's go,' West said.

The Piece went into Big Ears's sturdy backpack and, with Lily running in the lead, suddenly they were off, sliding under the propped-open grille that led south.

No sooner were they through than West and Big Ears kicked the pot plants free and the grille slammed fully shut behind them.

Running flat out down a long long corridor, legs pumping, hearts pounding.

Shouts came from behind them—shouts in French, from the museum guards giving chase.

West spoke into his radio mike: 'Pooh Bear! Are you out there?'

'*We're waiting! I hope you use the right window!*'

'We'll find out soon enough!'

The corridor West was running down ended at a dramatic right-hand corner. This corner opened onto a superlong hallway that was actually the extreme southern flank of the Louvre. The hallway's entire left-hand

wall was filled with masterpieces and the occasional high French window looking out over the Seine.

And right then, a second team of armed museum guards were running down it, shouting.

West hurled his huge wrench at the first French window in the hallway, shattering it. Glass sprayed everywhere.

He peered out the window.

To see Pooh Bear staring back at him, level with him, only a few feet away . . .

. . . standing on the open top deck of a double-decker bus!

Only one thing stands between the Louvre and the River Seine: a thin strip of road called the Quai des Tuileries. It is a long riverside roadway that follows the course of the river, variously rising and falling—rising up to bridges and dipping down into tunnels and underpasses.

It was on this road that Pooh Bear's recently-stolen double-decker bus now stood, parked alongside the Palais du Louvre. It was one of those bright red open-topped double-deckers that drive tourists around Paris, London and New York, allowing them to look up and around with ease.

'Well! What are you waiting for!' Pooh Bear yelled. 'Come on!'

'Right!'

West threw Lily across first, then pushed Big Ears with the Piece in his backpack, before finally jumping from the First Floor window onto the double-decker bus—just as the onrushing guards in the hallway started firing at him.

A second after his feet hit the open top deck of the bus, Stretch, in the driver's seat, hit the gas and the bus took off and the chase began.

The big red double-decker bus rocked precariously as Stretch threw it through the midday Paris traffic at speeds it was never meant to reach.

Police sirens could be heard in the distance.

'Go left and left again!' West yelled down. 'Back around the Louvre! Back to the Obelisk!'

The bus took the bends fast, and West came down to look over Stretch's shoulder.

'When we get there, what then?' Stretch asked.

West peered forward—and saw the Obelisk appear beyond the rushing line of trees to their left, its base still shrouded by scaffolding.

'I want you to ram into the scaffolding.'

The double-decker bus screamed onto the Place de la Concorde, almost tipping over with its speed.

The guards at the scaffolding surrounding the Obelisk realised just in time what it was going to do and leapt out of the way, diving clear a moment before the bus slammed into the near corner of the scaffold structure and obliterated a whole chunk of it.

The bus shuddered to a halt—

—and the tiny figure of Jack West could be seen leaping from its open top deck *onto* the second level of the scaffolding with some rope looped over his shoulder and climbing gear in his hands.

Up the scaffolding West ran, until he came to the topmost level and saw the Obelisk itself.

The size of a bell tower, it was totally covered in deeply-engraved hieroglyphics. It soared into the sky high above him.

The hieroglyphs were large and carved in horizontal lines—approximately three glyphs to a line, depicting pharaonic cartouches, images of Osiris, and animals: falcons, wasps and in the second line from the very top, owls.

Using the deeply-carved hieroglyphs as hand- and footholds, West clambered up the ancient Obelisk like a child scampering up a tall tree.

Stretch's voice exploded through his earpiece. '*West! I've got a visual on six police cars approaching fast along the Champs-Élysées!*'

'How far away?'

'*About 90 seconds, if that . . .*'

'Keep me posted. Although somehow I think we're going to have more to worry about than the Paris cops.'

West scaled the great stone needle quickly, climbing higher and higher, until even the big red bus looked tiny beneath him.

He came to the top, more than seventy feet above the ground. The Sun reflecting off the golden pyramidion at its peak was blinding.

He recalled the quote from Hessler's notebook:

> THREAD THE POWER OF RA THROUGH THE EYES OF
> GREAT RAMESES'S TOWERING NEEDLES,
> FROM THE SECOND OWL ON THE FIRST

TO THE THIRD ON THE SECOND . . .
. . . WHEREBY ISKENDER'S FINAL RESTING PLACE WILL BE REVEALED.

'The third owl on the second obelisk,' he said aloud.

Sure enough, on the second line of this obelisk—the second obelisk from Luxor—there were three carved owls standing side-by-side.

And near the head of the third one was a small circle depicting the Sun.

He imagined that very few people in history had actually seen this carving up close, since it was designed to sit so high above the populace—but up close, the carved image of the disc-like Sun looked odd, as if it were not a carved image but rather . . . well . . . a *plug* in the stone.

West grabbed the plug and pulled it free—

—to reveal a horizontal cavity roughly two fingers wide and perfectly round in shape, that bored *right through* the Obelisk.

Like a kid scaling a coconut tree, West clambered around the other side of the Obelisk's peak, where he found and extracted a second matching plug and suddenly, looking through the bore-hole, he could see right through the ancient Obelisk!

'*West! Hurry! The cops are almost here . . .*'

West ignored him, yanked from his jacket two high-tech devices: a laser altimeter, to measure the exact height of the bore-hole, and a digital surveyor's inclinometer, to measure the exact angle of the bore-hole, both vertically and laterally.

With these measurements, he could then go to Luxor in Egypt and recreate this obelisk 'virtually', and thus deduce the location of Alexander the Great's Tomb.

His altimeter beeped. Got the height.

He aimed his inclinometer through the bore-hole. It beeped. Got the angles.

Go!

And he was away, sliding down the Obelisk with his feet splayed wide, like a fireman shooting down a ladder.

His feet hit the scaffolding just as six cop cars screeched to a halt around the perimeter of the Place de la Concorde and disgorged a dozen cap-wearing Parisian cops.

'Stretch! Fire her up! Get moving,' West called as he ran across the top level of the three-storey scaffold structure. 'I'll get there the short way!'

The bus reversed out of the scaffolding, then Stretch grinded the gears and the big red bus lurched forward, just as Jack West took a flying leap off the top level and sailed down through the air . . .

. . . landing with a thump on the top deck of the bus, a second before it sped away toward the River Seine.

From the moment of their daring heist at the Louvre, other forces had been launched into action.

As one would expect, a theft from the Louvre instantly shot across the Paris police airwaves—airwaves that were monitored by other forces of the state.

What Stretch didn't know was that the Paris police had been outranked at the highest levels *and taken off this pursuit.*

The chase would be carried out by the French Army.

Just as West had anticipated.

And so, as the big red double-decker bus shot away from

the Obelisk and its wrecked outer structure, the Parisian police didn't follow. They just maintained their positions around the perimeter of the Place de la Concorde.

Moments later, five green-painted heavily-armed fast-attack reconnaissance vehicles *whooshed* past the cop cars and shot off after the great ungainly bus.

Horns honked and sirens blared as the double-decker bus roared down the Quai des Tuileries on the edge of the River Seine for the second time that day—weaving between the thin daytime traffic, blasting through red lights, causing all manner of havoc.

Behind it were the five French Army recon vehicles.

Each was a compact three-man scout car known as a Panhard VBL. Fitted with a turbo-charged four-wheel-drive diesel engine and a sleek arrow-shaped body, the Panhard was a swift and nimble all-terrain vehicle that looked like an armour-plated version of a sports 4x4.

The Panhards chasing West were fitted with every variety of gun turret: some had long-barrelled 12.7 mm machine guns, others had fearsome-looking TOW missile launchers.

Within moments of the chase beginning, they were all over the speeding bus.

They opened fire, shattering every window on the bus's left-hand side—a second before the bus roared into a tunnel, blocking their angle of fire.

Two of the Army Panhards tried to squeeze past the bus inside the tunnel, but Stretch swerved toward them, ramming them into the wall of the tunnel, grinding them against it.

With nowhere to go, both Panhards skidded and

flipped . . . and rolled . . . tumbling end over end until they crashed to twin halts on their roofs.

On the upper deck, Pooh Bear and West rocked with every swerve, tried to return fire. Pooh spied one of the TOW missile launchers on one Panhard.

'They've got missiles!' he yelled.

West called, 'They won't use them! They can't risk destroying the Piece!'

'*West!*' Stretch's voice came over their radios. '*It's only a matter of time before they barricade off this road! What do we do?*'

'We drive faster!' West replied. 'We have to get to the Charles de Gaulle Bridge—'

Shoom—!

—they blasted out of the tunnel, back into sunlight, just in time to see two French Army helicopters sweep into positions above them.

They were two very different types of chopper: one was a small Gazelle gunship, sleek and fast and bristling with guns and missile pods.

The other was bigger and much scarier: it was a Super Puma troop carrier, the French equivalent of the American Super Stallion. Big and tough, a Super Puma could carry twenty-five fully armed troops.

Which was exactly what this chopper was carrying.

As it flew low over the top of the speeding double-decker bus, along the rising-and-falling roadway on the north bank of the Seine, its side door slid open and drop-ropes were flung from within it—and the French plan became clear.

They were going to storm the bus—the *moving* bus!

At the same moment, three of the pursuing Panhards swept up alongside the bus, surrounding it.

'I think we're screwed already,' Stretch said flatly.

But he yanked on his steering anyway—ramming hard into the Panhard to his right, forcing it clear off the roadway, right *through* the low guard-rail fence . . . where it shot high into the air, wheels spinning, and went crashing down into the river with a gigantic splash.

Up on the top deck, West tried to fire at the hovering Super Puma above him, but a withering volley from the Gazelle gunship forced him to dive for the floor. Every single passenger seat on the top deck of the bus was ripped to shreds by the barrage of bullets.

'Stretch! More swerving, please!' he yelled, but it was too late.

The first two daredevil French paratroopers from the Super Puma landed with twin thumps on the open top deck of the moving double-decker bus only a few feet in front of him.

They saw West instantly, lying in the aisle between the seats: exposed, done for. They whipped up their guns and pulled the trigg—

—just as the floor beneath them erupted with holes, bullet holes from a shocking burst of fire from somewhere *underneath* them.

The two French troopers fell, dead, and a moment later, Pooh Bear's head popped up from the stairwell.

'Did I get them? Did I get them? Are you okay?' he said to West.

'I'm all right,' West said, hurrying down the stairs to the lower deck. 'Come on, we've gotta get to the Charles de Gaulle Bridge before this bus falls apart!'

The rising-and-falling riverside drive that they were speeding along would normally have been a tourist's delight: after leaving the Louvre behind, the roadway swooped by the first of the two islands that lie in the middle of the Seine, the Ile de la Cité. Numerous bridges spanning the river rushed by on the right, giving access to the island.

If West's team continued along the riverside road, they would soon arrive at the Arsenal precinct—the area where the Bastille once stood.

After that came two bridges: the Pont d'Austerlitz and the Pont Charles de Gaulle, the latter of which sat beside the very modern headquarters of the Ministry of Economics, Finances and Industry, which itself sat next-door to the Gare de Lyon, the large train station that serviced south-eastern France with high-speed trains.

The big red tourist bus whipped along the riverside road, weaving through traffic, ramming the pursuing Army cars with wild abandon.

It shot underneath several overpasses and over some raised intersections. At one stage the spectacular Notre Dame Cathedral whizzed by on the right, but this was perhaps the only tourist bus in the world that didn't care for the sight.

As soon as West had abandoned the upper deck of the bus, the French troops on the Super Puma above him went for it in earnest—despite Stretch's best efforts at evasive weaving.

And within a minute, they took it.

First, two troopers landed on the open top deck, whizzing down the drop-ropes suspended from the chopper. They were quickly followed by two more, two more and two more.

The eight French troopers now moved to the rear stairwell of the bus, guns up, preparing to storm the lower deck . . .

. . . just as, downstairs, West called: 'Stretch! They're crawling all over the roof! See that exit ramp up ahead! Roll us over it!'

Immediately ahead of them was another overpass, with an exit ramp rising to meet it on the right-hand side of the riverside drive. A low concrete guard-rail fence separated this ramp from the roadway which continued on underneath the overpass as a tunnel.

'What?' Stretch shouted back.

'Just do it!' West yelled. 'Everybody, grab onto something! Hang on!'

They hit the exit ramp at speed, and rose up it briefly—

—at which moment Stretch yanked *left* on the steering wheel, and the bus lurched leftward, hitting the concrete guard-rail and . . .

. . . tipped over it!

The double-decker bus overbalanced shockingly and rolled *over* the concrete fence, using the fence as a fulcrum. As such, the entire double-decker bus *rolled*, going fully upside-down—off the exit ramp, *back down* onto the roadway proper—where it *slammed* down onto its open-topped roof . . .

. . . crushing all eight of the French troops on it!

But it wasn't done yet.

Since it had tipped over the dividing rail from a considerable height, it still had a lot of sideways momentum.

So the big bus *continued* to roll, bouncing off its now-crushed roof and coming upright once again, commencing on a second roll—only to bang hard against the far wall of the sunken roadway, which had the incredible effect of *righting the bus* and plonking it back on its own wheels, so that now it was travelling once again on the riverside drive and heading into the tunnel having just performed a full 360-degree roll!

Inside the bus, the world rotated crazily, 360 degrees, hurling West's team—Lily included—all around the cabin.

They tumbled and rolled, but they all survived the desperate move.

Indeed, they were all still lying on the floor when West scrambled to his feet and launched into action.

He took the wheel from Stretch as their mangled and dented bus swept out of the tunnel and into the Arsenal district. Having seen what West was prepared to do to anyone who tried to storm his bus from above, the Super Puma just flanked them now, swooping low over the river parallel to the speeding bus.

And just then, the modern glass-and-steel towers of the Economics Ministry came into view up ahead.

'That bridge up ahead is the Pont d'Austerlitz,' Pooh Bear said, peering over West's shoulder. 'The Charles de Gaulle Bridge is the one after it!'

'Gotcha,' West said. 'Tell everybody to get their pony bottles and masks ready, and then get to the doors. Go!'

Pooh Bear gathered everyone together—Lily, Stretch and Big Ears—and they all clambered to the side and rear doors of the bus.

The bus swept past the Pont d'Austerlitz, roaring towards the next bridge: the Pont Charles de Gaulle. Like the Austerlitz before it, the Charles de Gaulle Bridge branched out to the right, stretching over the river; beyond it, the glass towers of the Economics Ministry stabbed into the sky.

The riverside drive rose to meet the Charles de Gaulle Bridge, providing West with a ramp of sorts.

And while every other car in Paris would have slowed as they climbed this exit ramp, West accelerated.

As such, he hit the Charles de Gaulle Bridge at phenomenal speed, whereupon the great battered double-decker tourist bus performed its last earthly feat.

It *exploded* through the low pedestrian fence on the far side of the bridge and shot out into the air above the Seine, flying in a spectacular parabolic arc, its great rectangular mass soaring through the sky, before its nose tipped and it began to fall, and West bailed out of the driver's compartment and the others leapt from the side and rear doors and the big bus slammed into the river.

As the bus hit the surface of the Seine, the four people on its doors went flying to the side of it, also crashing into the water, albeit with smaller splashes.

But to the shock of those in the two pursuing French helicopters, they never surfaced.

Underwater, however, things were happening.

Everyone had survived the deliberate crash, and they regrouped with West, all of them now wearing divers' masks and breathing from pony bottles.

They swam through the murky brown water of the river, converging on the cobblestoned northern wall of the Seine, underneath the Charles de Gaulle Bridge.

Here, embedded in the medieval wall, under the surface of the river, was a rusty old gate that dated back to the 1600s.

The padlock sealing it was new and strong, but a visit earlier that morning by Pooh Bear with a boltcutter had altered it slightly. The padlock hung in place and, to the casual observer, it would have looked intact. But Pooh Bear had cut it cleanly on the rear side, so that now he just pulled it off the rusty gate by hand.

Beyond the gate, a brick-walled passageway disappeared into the murky gloom. The team swam into the passageway—with the last person in the line, Big Ears, closing the underwater gate behind them and snapping a brand-new padlock on it, identical to the one that had been sealing it before.

After about twenty yards, the underwater passageway rose into a tight sewer-like tunnel.

They all stood in the sewer-tunnel, knee-deep in foul-smelling water.

'How very Gothic,' Stretch said, deadpan.

'Christian catacombs from the 17th century,' Pooh Bear said. 'They're all over Paris, over 270 kilometres of tunnels and catacombs. This set of tunnels runs all the way along the Boulevard Diderot. They'll take us past the Economics Ministry, right to the Gare de Lyon.'

West checked his watch.

It was 12:35 p.m.

'Come on,' he said. 'We've got a train to catch.'

The three remaining French Army Panhards descended on the Charles de Gaulle Bridge, disgorging men. The big red bus was still actually half-afloat, but in the process of sinking.

The two choppers patrolled the air above the crash-site, searching, prowling.

Curious Parisians gathered on the bridge to watch.

Extra commando teams were sent into the Ministry complex and also into the Gare d'Austerlitz, the large train station that lay directly across the Charles de Gaulle Bridge, on the southern side of the Seine.

Every train that hadn't yet departed from it was barred from leaving. As a precaution, trains from the Gare de Lyon—further away to the north, but still a possibility—were also grounded.

Indeed, the last train to depart the Gare de Lyon that

day would be the 12:44 TGV express service from Paris to Geneva, first stop Dijon.

An hour later, and now dressed in dry clothes, West and his team disembarked from the train in Dijon, smiling, grinning, elated.

There they boarded a charter flight to Spain, where they would rendezvous with Sky Monster and the *Halicarnassus* and commence their journey back to Kenya.

But their smiles and grins said it all.

After two failed attempts—or three if you counted the Mausoleum Piece—they had finally obtained a Piece of the Capstone.

They were now in a position to bargain.

They were now well and truly in the game.

ST PETER'S BASILICA
VATICAN CITY, ROME
18 MARCH, 2006, 12:45 P.M.
2 DAYS BEFORE THE ARRIVAL OF TARTARUS

At the same time, 2,000 kilometres away in Rome, a long-bearded man wearing the all-black robes of a Catholic priest strode across the wide square in front of St Peter's Basilica, the magnificent domed cathedral designed by Michelangelo, the most holy place of worship in the Roman Catholic Church.

With his long grey beard and stooping walk, Max Epper looked very much the part: an old and wizened priest, perhaps even an Eastern Orthodox one, making a pilgrimage to the Vatican.

With him walked Zoe and Fuzzy, and as they crossed St Peter's Square in the midst of hundreds of tourists, Zoe gazed up at the gigantic stone obelisk that stood proudly in the exact centre of the Square.

'Cult of Amun-Ra,' Wizard said flatly, striding past the towering stone needle.

Zoe turned as she walked, gazing up at this *Egyptian* structure taking pride of place in front of the biggest Catholic church in the world.

She shrugged. 'The Cult of Amun-Ra . . .'

★

They entered the Basilica.

Few man-made structures on earth can match St Peter's Basilica for sheer scale. It is shaped like a giant crucifix—just like the centre of Paris—and its famous dome soars 300 feet above a glistening marble floor. Brilliant shafts of sunlight penetrate its impossibly high windows, as if sent by God himself.

Michelangelo's *Pieta* flanks one side of the main entrance. Giant statues of saints stand in alcoves lining the main hall—St Ignatius, St Francis of Assisi—looming over the faithful.

It is designed to inspire awe.

But the most spectacular section of the great cathedral is to be found at its most holy place, the junction of the cross.

Here you will find the altar of St Peter's, covered by a colossal four-pillared awning made of sturdy iron laced with gold. At the top of each tree-trunk-like pillar, you will find angels leaning outward, blowing trumpets, praising the Lord.

And beneath this awning is the altar.

'It looks so plain,' Fuzzy said, gazing up at it.

He was right. The altar of St Peter's is remarkably plain, just a large oblong block of marble mounted on a raised platform. At the moment, since it wasn't being used, it was covered by a simple red-white-and-gold cloth and some candles. A thick rope suspended from brass poles prevented the public from surmounting it.

'Yes,' Wizard said. 'Considering its importance, it is very plain.'

'It's only important if Zaeed was telling us the truth,' Zoe commented.

Before they had all split up on their separate missions, Zaeed had explained that the Artemis Piece of the

Golden Capstone lay *embedded* in the altar at St Peter's Basilica. The trapezoid, he claimed, had been incorporated face-down in the otherwise solid marble altar—so that its base lay flush with the flat upper surface of the altar. To the uninitiated, it would just look like a square plate of gold on the flat surface, a square plate with a crystal in its centre.

To the initiated, however, it would mean much more.

Wizard stared at the altar. 'I imagine that only a handful of cardinals have ever been allowed to gaze upon the naked surface of this altar. Fewer still would know the true nature of the golden trapezoid embedded in it. All would be very senior, privileged initiates into the true history of the Church.'

'So what do we do?' Zoe asked. 'We can't just pull out a crowbar and prise the trapezoid from the altar in front of all these people.'

'I only need to *look* at it,' Wizard said. 'To memorise the inscription if I can.'

They were surrounded by tourists and uniformed Swiss Guards—and, Wizard guessed, many plainclothed guards, ready to grab anyone who tried to step onto the altar.

Anyone except maybe a doddery old Orthodox priest.

'Run me some interference,' Wizard said. 'Here I go.'

He moved quickly, gazing adoringly up at the awning above the altar, stepping close to the rope, seemingly rapt with wonder.

Then before anyone could stop him, Wizard stepped over the rope and up the steps . . .

. . . and stood behind the altar of St Peter's, running his hands across the flat surface of the big oblong block as if it were made of some holy substance itself.

Plainclothed Swiss Guards appeared at once, emerging from the crowds, converging on the altar.

Standing behind the great oblong block in the exact heart of the Basilica, Wizard swept aside the cloth that covered the altar and beheld its bare upper surface.

What he saw was dazzling.

The flat surface of the altar was made of exquisite white marble, except in its very middle. Here Wizard saw, flush with the flat marble surface, a square-shaped section made of gold.

It was medium-sized, perhaps three feet to each side. And you couldn't tell it was a golden trapezoid, since only its base side was visible. But there in its exact centre was a small diamond-like crystal.

The Artemis Piece.

Wizard saw the inscriptions carved into the surface of the trapezoid:

His wide eyes flashed like camera lenses, attempting to memorise the inscriptions in the short window of time he had—

'Excuse me, Father, but you cannot step up here.' Wizard was yanked away from the altar.

Two Swiss Guards had grabbed him firmly by the arms and were moving him politely but forcibly away.

At the same time another guard redraped the cloth

back over the altar-top, concealing the golden trapezoid—although he seemed to do it merely to restore the order of the altar, not out of any sense that a great secret had been unveiled.

'I-I-I'm s-s-so sorry,' Wizard stammered, feigning senility and offering no resistance. 'I just wanted to f-f-feel the power of my Lord in all h-h-his glory . . .'

The lead guard escorting him off the raised stage assessed him more closely, saw Wizard's earnest eyes, his scraggly beard, his tattered robes, and he softened. 'All right, old man. Get out of here. Just stay behind the rope next time.'

'Th-th-thank you, my son.'

The guard escorted Wizard back to the main doors.

As he walked, Wizard tried to contain his excitement. He had the Artemis inscription burned into his brain—which was the next best thing to getting the Piece itself. Soon, he, Zoe and Fuzzy would be winging their way out of Rome's Leonardo da Vinci International Airport and heading for home.

Flanked by the guards, he stifled the smile that was beginning to spread across his face.

At that very same moment, in a darkened room elsewhere in the Vatican, someone was watching Wizard on a small security monitor.

Francisco del Piero.

'I knew you would come, Max, my old colleague,' del Piero said to the image on the screen. 'That's why I did not remove the Piece from the altar. I knew it would bring you out into the open.'

Del Piero turned to the Vatican Security Chief next to him. 'They'll head for the airport. Follow them, but do not grab them yet. Monitor their radio transmissions. The old man will send a signal soon after he leaves St Peter's to inform his team-mates that he has succeeded in his mission. Let him send his message. *Then* seize him and his accomplices at the airport and bring them to me.'

Minutes later, speeding through the streets of Rome in a rental car, heading for the airport, Wizard sent a short encrypted text-message to Doris in Kenya.

It said:

Mission accomplished.
On our way back now.
Wizard.

Shortly after, his car arrived at the airport and swung into the parking lot—

—just as the air all around it was pierced by sirens and police cars appeared from every side, swooping in on Wizard's car, blocking it, surrounding it.

Wizard, Zoe and Fuzzy could do nothing.

VICTORIA STATION

KENYA

18 MARCH, 2006, 9:45 P.M.

2 DAYS BEFORE THE ARRIVAL OF TARTARUS

In the basement radio room at the farm in Kenya, Doris Epper spoke into her mike: 'That's great news, Huntsman. Wizard is on his way, too. He just text-messaged me a few hours ago. The mission in Rome was a success. He'll be here in the morning. See you in a couple of hours.'

With a spring in her stride, she hurried up the steps to the kitchen. She was relieved that everyone was okay and that their missions had succeeded and she wanted to prepare a nice dinner for when they got back.

She stepped up into the kitchen . . . to find that someone was already there.

'That's wonderful news, Mrs Epper.'

Doris froze.

There before her, sitting casually at her kitchen table, was Marshall Judah. Standing behind him were twelve heavily camouflaged, heavily armed US special forces troops.

Judah's head was bent, his eyes low, his voice laced with menace. 'Take a seat, Doris, and let's wait for them together.'

VICTORIA STATION
KENYA
18 MARCH, 2006, 11:45 P.M.
2 DAYS BEFORE THE ARRIVAL OF TARTARUS

West and his sub-team returned to Kenya.

On the way, they'd stopped in Spain to refuel, at which point Lily had had another breakthrough with the Callimachus Text. She was suddenly able to read the next entry.

'What's it say?' West asked.

'It's about the Hanging Gardens of Babylon,' she said. 'It says:

The Hanging Paradise of Old Babylonia.
March towards the rising Sun,
From the point where the two life-givers become one.
In the shadow of the mountains of Zagros,
Behold the mighty falls fashioned by the Third Great Architect
To conceal the path he hewed
A path that climbs to the entry of the Paradise
That mighty Nebuchadnezzar built for his bride.'

West tousled her hair. 'Nice work, kiddo. Nice work. Wizard's going to be thrilled.'

★

The *Halicarnassus* landed with a roar on Victoria Station's airstrip just before midnight. It was a classic African night—a swollen full moon illuminated the grassy plains like a floodlight, while the low hills loomed, dark teeth against the moonlit sky.

About a kilometre from the runway stood the farmhouse, its windows glowing orange. The emergency signal—the lights on the juniper bush in the front garden—was not on.

Sky Monster swung the plane toward the hangar dug into the hill at the end of the runway. As it taxied slowly, everyone grabbed their gear, preparing to disembark.

None of them could know that as they did so, two hundred pairs of eyes watched them closely.

Turbines whirring, the *Halicarnassus* came to a halt just outside the doorway of the brightly-illuminated hangar.

A flight of airstairs waited for it there, just outside the open doors. And beyond the airstairs, maybe forty yards away, stood a welcoming party of one: Doris, standing by the hangar doors themselves.

It was impossible for those on the plane to know that she was standing there at gunpoint.

The plane stopped alongside the airstairs at the entry to the hangar, its nose section poking into the actual hangar (it had to cool down outside for a few hours before it could be brought fully inside for storage).

As soon as it had stopped, its forward side door was flung open from within and Big Ears and Lily—eager to see Doris and show her the Zeus Piece—dashed out of the plane and scampered down the airstairs. Big Ears wore his backpack, containing the Piece.

Not far behind them came Pooh Bear and Stretch, escorting Zaeed—now flex-cuffed again. They emerged from the plane into the fresh night air, began stepping down the stairs.

Sky Monster and West lingered in the plane—Sky Monster to do a post-flight check; West just to collect all his things: notes, parchments, Hessler's Nazi diary.

It was noisy outside—the *Halicarnassus*'s four massive wing-engines still whirred loudly, winding down.

Big Ears and Lily were halfway to Doris.

'Hey, Doris! We did it!' Lily called over the din, but Doris's usually warm face was stony, cold—as though she knew something that she couldn't disclose.

Then she seemed to regather herself, smiled kindly, and called back: 'Well done, little Eowyn! What a triumphant return. This is all a bit like Gimli returning to Moria, isn't it!'

At Doris's words, Lily slowed her stride.

Then she stopped completely.

Big Ears paused, turned to her. 'What is it?'

Worried, Lily peered fearfully at the dark grassy fields that surrounded the hangar's entrance. Apart from Doris, the area was completely deserted.

'Big Ears, we're in trouble,' she said evenly. 'We have to get back to the plane. This is a trap.'

'How do you know—?'

'Just go! Now!' she said with an authority that belied her age.

And abruptly, she spun, grabbing Big Ears's hand,

and together—still twenty yards from the plane—they bolted back towards the *Halicarnassus*.

No sooner had they moved than all hell broke loose in the hangar.

Every door on every side of the hangar burst open and disgorged dozens of black-clad American troops.

A maintenance door behind Doris was also thrown open and Marshall Judah rushed out of it, accompanied by a CIEF team led by Cal Kallis.

Kallis pushed roughly past Doris and opened fire on the fleeing pair with a god-almighty fury.

When the gunfire started, different people did different things:

West.

He raced to the forward door of the *Halicarnassus*, to see what was going on.

Sky Monster.

He peered out the cockpit windows—to see Lily and Big Ears running together back towards the airstairs, chased by an oncoming swarm of enemy troops.

Zaeed.

He was at the bottom of the airstairs when the gunfire began, flanked by Pooh Bear and Stretch, his hands still flex-cuffed. But his eyes, far from being wild and crazed, were watchful and focused now.

He'd actually just managed to extract a blade hidden in his pants and saw halfway through his flex-cuffs, and was three seconds away from stabbing Stretch between the ribs and commencing his escape when the gunfire had started. At that point, he'd slid the blade back into his pocket and clambered back up the airstairs as they were hammered with bullet impacts.

And Judah.

While his men hurried past Doris, he stopped right in front of her and said, 'I told you, no warnings.'

And then, without the slightest hesitation, he drew a Glock pistol, placed its barrel against her head and fired.

★

West arrived at the forward door just in time to see Doris fall.

'Oh, God, no . . .' he breathed. 'No . . .'

He beheld the rest of the scene in the hangar.

Pandemonium reigned.

A massive American force had emerged from every corner of the hangar. Most of them were on foot, but then West saw three Humvees come blasting out of the grassy fields outside.

The American troops were converging on the big black 747 like an army of ants, their collective movement focused on the two fleeing figures of Big Ears and Lily.

West zeroed in on the running pair.

One thing was clear: they weren't going to make it to the airstairs.

The Americans' angle of fire would cut them off before they got there. And he noted that the Yanks weren't aiming to *kill* them—just stop them from escaping. They knew not to harm Lily.

But Big Ears and Lily did make it to a portable electricity generator wagon just short of the airstairs. The generator wagon was the size of a small trailer. Normally, once the *Halicarnassus* was fully stopped, Sky Monster would get out and attach the generator to it, providing external electrical power. But he hadn't been able to do that yet.

Lily and Big Ears dived behind the generator wagon, and Big Ears immediately opened fire on his closest pursuers, causing them to halt and duck for cover.

So now West stood at the top of the airstairs, while Stretch and Pooh Bear were huddled at the base of those same stairs, ducking gunfire. Zaeed was in the middle, halfway up the steps, getting away from the action.

And Lily and Big Ears lay crouched—cut off, pinned down by enemy fire—a tantalising five yards from the base of the airstairs.

West keyed his radio mike. 'Sky Monster! Fire her up again! We gotta get out of here!'

'*Roger that!*' A moment later the great jet turbines of the 747 roared back to life, the thunderous noise drowning out the sound of gunfire.

'Big Ears!' West called into his mike. 'I hate to do this to you, but you've got to find a way to get Lily back on this plane! *Now!*'

Huddled behind the generator wagon, Big Ears was thinking fast.

Five yards. That was all it was. Five yards.

Only those five yards looked like a mile.

And then suddenly—with a kind of crystal clarity that was new to him—the situation became clear to Big Ears.

No matter what the outcome of this situation, *he was going to die.*

If he ran for the airstairs, he'd be shot for sure—even if they didn't shoot Lily, they'd nail him.

Alternatively, if he and Lily were caught by the Americans, they'd kill him then too.

And with that realisation, he made up his mind.

'Lily,' he said, over the raging din all around them. 'You know something. You've been the best friend I've ever had in my life. You were always way smarter than me, but you always waited for me, were always patient with me. But now I have to do something for you—and you have to let me do it. Just promise me, when the time comes, you do what you were put on this Earth to do. And remember me, the dumb grunt who was your friend. I love you, little one.'

Then he kissed her forehead and, with his MP-5 in one hand, he picked her up with the other, and shielding her with his body . . .

. . . he broke cover . . .

. . . and ran for the airstairs.

The American response was both immediate and vicious.

They opened fire.

Big Ears only needed six steps to make it to the airstairs.

He made four.

Before a crouching US trooper nailed him with a clean shot to the head.

The bullet passed right through Big Ears's skull, exploding out the other side and he fell instantly—crumpling like a marionette whose strings have been cut—falling to his knees midway between the generator wagon and the airstairs, dropping Lily from his lifeless hands.

'No!' Lily screamed in horror. '*Noooo!*'

The Americans charged, moved in on the girl—

—only to be stopped by a curious sight.

At *exactly* the same time, in *exactly* the same way, two figures dived out from the base of the airstairs, each of them holding two MP-5 sub-machine guns, the weapons blazing away in opposite directions as they flew through the air toward Lily.

Pooh Bear and Stretch.

They couldn't have planned the move. There simply hadn't been time. No, they had actually both dived *independently* of each other.

Yet their identical dives had been motivated by the exact same impulse:

To save Lily.

The Arab and the Israeli slid to simultaneous halts alongside Lily, bringing down four Americans each as they did so.

Lily was still kneeling beside Big Ears's body, her cheeks covered in tears.

Still firing repeatedly, Pooh Bear and Stretch each grabbed one of her hands and crouch-ran with her back to the cover of the airstairs.

Up the stairs they stumbled, as the steel side railings of the airstairs were riddled with a thousand dome-shaped bullet impacts.

Off-balance and firing blindly behind them, Pooh Bear and Stretch reached the top of the stairs and flung Lily in through the door, rolling themselves in after her, while above them West jammed the door shut and yelled, 'Sky Monster! *Go! Go! Go!*'

The giant 747 pivoted on the spot, rolling around in a circle until it was re-aimed back up the runway—bullets pinging off its black armoured flanks.

As it completed its circle, it crunched *right over* a US Humvee that got too close, flattening the car.

Then Pooh Bear and Stretch took their seats in the *Halicarnassus*'s wing-mounted gun turrets and let fly with a barrage of tracer fire, annihilating the other two Humvees.

Then Sky Monster punched his thrusters and the big black 747 gathered speed—thundering up the runway, its winglights blazing, chased by jeeps spewing gunfire,

returning tracer bullets from its own turrets—until it hit take-off speed and lifted off into the night sky, escaping from its own supposedly secret base.

A grim silence hung over the main cabin of the *Halicarnassus.*

West held Lily in his lap. She was still sobbing, distraught over the deaths of Big Ears and Doris.

As the jumbo soared into the night sky, heading for nowhere in particular, everyone who had survived the gunbattle in the hangar returned to the main cabin: Pooh Bear, Stretch and Zaeed. Sky Monster stayed in the cockpit, flying manually for the time being.

With Lily in his arms, West's mind raced.

Big Ears was dead. Doris was dead. Their secret hideaway had been exposed. Not to mention the most frustrating fact of all—when he'd been killed, *Big Ears had been carrying the Zeus Piece.*

Shit.

Up until a few minutes ago, they'd actually *succeeded* on this impossible mission. Against all the odds, they had actually obtained a Piece of the Capstone.

And now . . .

Now they had nothing. They'd lost two of their best team-members, lost their base of operations, and lost the one and only Piece they'd ever got.

Hell, West thought, he didn't even know why Lily and Big Ears had suddenly turned and run back to the plane. Gently, he asked Lily.

She sniffed, wiped away her tears.

'Doris gave me a warning. She said our return was like Gimli's return to Moria. In *The Lord of the Rings*, Gimli the dwarf returns to the dwarf mines at Moria, only to find that the mines have been overrun by orcs. Doris was sending me a secret message. She obviously couldn't say anything directly, so she spoke in a code I'd understand. She was saying that the farm had been taken over by our enemies and to get away.'

West was amazed at Lily's quick deduction—and at Doris's selfless sacrifice.

'Nice work, kiddo.' He stroked Lily's hair. 'Nice work.'

It was Pooh Bear who asked what they were all thinking. 'Huntsman. What do we do now?'

'I have to talk to Wizard,' West said, moving to one of the communications consoles.

But just as he reached it, the console—as if by magic—started blinking and beeping.

'It's the video phone . . .' Stretch said. 'An incoming call.'

'It must be Wizard,' Pooh Bear said.

'No,' West said, staring at the console's readout. 'It's coming from Victoria Station.'

West clicked the 'Answer' button and the screen on the console came to life. Filling its frame was the face of . . .

Marshall Judah.

He was sitting at a console inside the hangar back in Kenya, flanked by Kallis and some of his men.

'Greetings, Jack. My, my, wasn't that a narrow escape for you all. Sorry—' he corrected himself—'not exactly *all* of you escaped.'

'What do you want?' West growled.

'Why, Jack. How could I want anything from you? I already have everything you can give me: the Zeus Piece, to add to the three Pieces I already possess. Oh, and I am not sure if you're aware of the fate of your friend Epper in Rome. Seems he's fallen into the hands of our European competitors. I do hope he'll be all right.'

West tried not to let his surprise show. He didn't know that the Europeans had captured Wizard's team.

'Epper's capture,' Judah said, realising with a grin. 'You weren't aware of this.'

Shit.

'Why are you calling us?' West demanded. 'To gloat?'

'To remind you of your status, Jack. Look at you. Look at what you have achieved. Your band of pissant nations shouldn't have tried playing at the grown-ups' table. At every juncture in our parallel missions, I have comprehensively *beaten* you. In the Sudan. In Tunisia. And now here in Kenya. Can't you see? There is nowhere you can go that I cannot follow. There is nowhere *on Earth* you can hide from me, Jack. My scientists are at this very instant about to uncover the location of the Hanging Gardens and, unlike you, we have long been aware of the importance of the Paris Obelisk—and in two days' time, we will use those measurements to reveal the location of Alexander's Tomb in Luxor: the resting place of the final Piece.'

'Are you finished?'

'How about I finish with this: you never had a chance on this mission, Jack. Let me give you a quick lesson in the law of nations: there are big fish and there are little fish. And the big fish eat the little ones. *You came up against a bigger fish*, Jack, and you got eaten. Your mission is over.'

'I'm going to kill you, Judah,' West said flatly. 'For Doris.'

'As if you could, Jack. As if you could.'

With that, Judah cut the signal and West found himself staring at an empty screen.

For a long while, no-one spoke.

West just stared at the blank screen, his teeth grinding.

'Stretch, try and call Wizard,' he said. 'See if Judah was telling the truth.'

Stretch went to the satellite radio console, tried every channel that Wizard, Zoe and Fuzzy could be on. He even tried their cell phones.

He received no reply.

'Nothing,' he said, returning to the group. 'There's no answer from Wizard, Zoe or Fuzzy. They're off the air.'

There was more silence as the full weight of their predicament sank in.

In addition to their terrible losses at Victoria Station, they had now lost three more people—including the one person who had been their greatest source of knowledge on this mission, Wizard.

Stretch said, 'Every move we've made, Judah's known it and followed right behind us. In the Sudan. In Tunisia. Now Kenya.'

'Not exactly,' Pooh Bear said. 'Kenya was different: he got to Kenya *before* we did, not after. He was waiting for us there.' Pooh looked hard at Stretch. 'Somehow he knew about our base.'

Stretch bristled. 'What are you implying? Do you think I informed the Americans?'

Pooh Bear's glare suggested that he was seriously considering this.

Zaeed piped in: 'Unless I'm mistaken, *you* were never invited to join this mission, were you, Israeli? I would say Saladin is perfectly within his rights to question your loyalty.'

'This does not concern you!' Stretch said. 'Bite your tongue, murderer!'

'An Israeli calls me a murderer!' Zaeed stood up. 'Count the innocents *your* country has murdered, you—'

'Quiet!' West called, silencing them.

They all retreated, sat down.

West addressed them. 'The Americans now have four of the seven Pieces of the Capstone. And if they get the Artemis Piece from the Europeans—and we must assume they have a plan to do just that—they'll have five.

'As such, they need only two more Pieces to complete the Tartarus Ritual at the Great Pyramid and rule the world. Now, the two Pieces left to find are those of the Hanging Gardens of Babylon and the Great Pyramid itself—'

Zaeed said, 'You can forget about obtaining the Great Pyramid Piece. It is the First Piece, the most highly-prized, the pyramidal peak of the Capstone itself. It was buried with Alexander the Great and the location of his tomb will only be revealed at dawn on the final day.'

'When the Sun shines through the obelisks at Luxor?' Pooh Bear said.

'Yes.'

'Which leaves us the Hanging Gardens Piece,' West said.

Zaeed said, 'Of all the Wonders, the Hanging Gardens of Babylon have proved to be the most elusive. All of the other Wonders, in one way or another, survived into the modern age. But not the Gardens. They have not been seen since the 5th century BC. Indeed, observers in the ancient world questioned whether they even existed at all. Finding them will be exceedingly difficult.'

West frowned.

Maybe Judah was right.

He honestly didn't know if he could do this.

Not without Wizard. And certainly not when his only companions were a known terrorist, a constantly feuding Arab and Israeli pair, a slightly crazy New Zealand pilot and one little girl.

The thought of Lily made him turn to her.

Her face was still red from crying, dried tear-marks lined her cheeks.

'What do you think?' he asked.

She returned his gaze with bloodshot eyes, and when she spoke, she spoke with a new maturity.

'Before he died, Big Ears made me promise him something. He asked that when the time came, I'd do what I was put on this Earth to do. I don't really know what that is yet, but I don't want to let him down. I want the *chance* to do what I was put on this Earth to do. Give me that chance, sir. Please.'

West nodded slowly.

Then he stood up.

'The way I see it, folks, we have our backs to the wall. We're down on people, on options and on luck, but we're not out of this game. We still have one option left. We find the one remaining Piece of the Capstone still available to us. The Piece hidden in the only Ancient Wonder never to have been found. People, we have to locate the Hanging Gardens of Babylon.'

FIFTH MISSION
THE HANGING GARDENS

IRAQ
19 MARCH, 2006
THE DAY BEFORE TARTARUS

NEBUCHADNEZZAR'S PARADISE

Of all the Seven Wonders of the Ancient World, none retains more mystery than the Hanging Gardens of Babylon.

There is a simple reason for this.

Of all the Wonders, only one has *never* been found: the Hanging Gardens. Not a single trace of them has been unearthed: no foundations, no pillars, not even an aqueduct.

In fact, so elusive have the Gardens been throughout the ages that most historians believe they never even existed at all, but were rather the product of the imaginations of Greek poets.

After all, as Alaa Ashmawy, an expert on the Seven Ancient Wonders from the University of Southern Florida, has pointed out, the Babylonians were very careful record-keepers, and yet their records make *not a single mention* of any Hanging Gardens.

Nor did the chroniclers of Alexander the Great's many visits to Babylon mention any kind of Gardens.

This lack of evidence, however, has not stopped writers throughout the ages from creating all manner of fabulous descriptions of the Gardens. On these facts, all agree:

1. The Gardens were constructed by the great Mesopotamian king, Nebuchadnezzar, around the year 570 BC, in order to please his homesick new wife, who, hailing from Media, was accustomed to more verdant surroundings;

2. They were built to the east of the Euphrates River; and

3. The centrepiece of the Gardens was a shrine devoted to the rare Persian White Desert Rose, a species that has not survived to the present day.

At this point, however, the descriptions vary greatly.

Some historians say the Gardens sat atop a golden ziggurat, its vines and greenery overflowing from the building's tiers. A dozen waterfalls were said to cascade over its edges.

Others say the Gardens dangled from the side of an immense rocky cliff-face—literally earning the name 'hanging'.

One lone scholar has even suggested that the Gardens hung from a gigantic stalactite-like rock formation *inside* a massive cave.

An interesting sidenote, however, applies to the Gardens.

In Greek, the Gardens were described as *kremastos*, a word which has been translated as *hanging*, thus the term 'Hanging Gardens' and the notion of some kind of suspended or raised paradise.

But *kremastos* can be translated another way. It can be translated as *overhanging*.

Which begs the question: is it possible that those ancient Greek poets were perhaps merely describing an

ordinary stone ziggurat whose decorative foliage, left uncut and unkempt, had simply outgrown its tiers and overhung them at the edges? Could this reputed 'Wonder' have really just been very very ordinary?

AIRSPACE OVER SAUDI ARABIA

19 MARCH, 2006, 0300 HOURS

1 DAY BEFORE THE ARRIVAL OF TARTARUS

The *Halicarnassus* shoomed through the night sky.

The big black unregistered 747 zoomed out of Africa on a flight-path that would take it across Saudi Arabia to one of the harshest, wildest and most lawless countries on Earth.

Iraq.

It made one stop on the way.

An important stop in a remote corner of Saudi Arabia.

Hidden among some barren rocky hills was a cluster of small man-made caves, long-abandoned, with flapping rags covering their doorways. A long-disused firing range stood nearby, ravaged by dust and time; discarded ammunition boxes lay everywhere.

It was a former terrorist camp.

Once the home of Mustapha Zaeed—and the resting place of all his notes on the Seven Wonders of the Ancient World.

Covered by West, Stretch and Pooh Bear, the flex-cuffed Zaeed scrambled inside one particular cave where, behind a false wall, he located a large trunk filled with scrolls, tablets, sandstone bricks, gold and bronze ornaments, and literally *dozens* of notebooks.

It also contained within it a beautiful black-jade box no bigger than a shoebox. Before he passed the trunk out to the others, unseen by West's men, Zaeed grabbed the black-jade box, opened it, and gazed for a moment at the fine-grained orange sand inside it. It lay flat, undisturbed for many years. It was so fine it was almost luminous.

He snapped the jade box shut, slipped it back into the trunk, and passed it out to the others.

Then on the way out of the hidden space in the wall, he triggered a small electronic beacon.

Zaeed emerged from behind the false wall and presented the trunk to West. 'My life's work. It will help.'

'It had better,' West said.

They grabbed the trunk, hauled it back to the *Halicarnassus*, and resumed their course for Iraq.

Inside the *Halicarnassus*, West's depleted team went about the task of finding the location of the Hanging Gardens of Babylon.

While West, Pooh Bear and Lily pored over Lily's most recent translation of the Callimachus Text, Zaeed—his flex-cuffs now removed—was on his knees, rummaging through his dusty old trunk.

'You know,' Pooh Bear said, 'it would be nice to have some idea what these Gardens actually looked like.'

West said, 'Most drawings of the Gardens are little more than wild interpretations of vague Greek sources, most of them variations on the classic ziggurat shape. No-one has an actual image of them—'

'Don't speak too soon, Captain West! That may not be so! Here it is!' Zaeed called, pulling a crude rectangle of very ancient cloth from his trunk.

It was about the size of an A4 sheet of paper, rough and rectangular. Its edges were worn, ragged, unsewn, like hessian cloth. Zaeed brought it over to the others.

'It's a draft cloth, a simple device used by ancient kings to keep an eye on the progress of their faraway construction sites. The cloth would be taken by a royal messenger to the worksite, where the messenger then drew the scene. The messenger would then bring the cloth back to the king, thus showing him the progress being made.

'I found this cloth in a pauper's tomb underneath the town of Ash Shatra, in central Iraq—the tomb of a horseman who had died near the town, having been robbed and left for dead by bandits. Although he was buried as a pauper, I believe he was actually a royal messenger returning to New Babylon with a draft cloth of the Hanging Gardens for Nebuchadnezzar. *Behold*, all of you, the only picture, so far as I know, of the Hanging Gardens of Babylon:

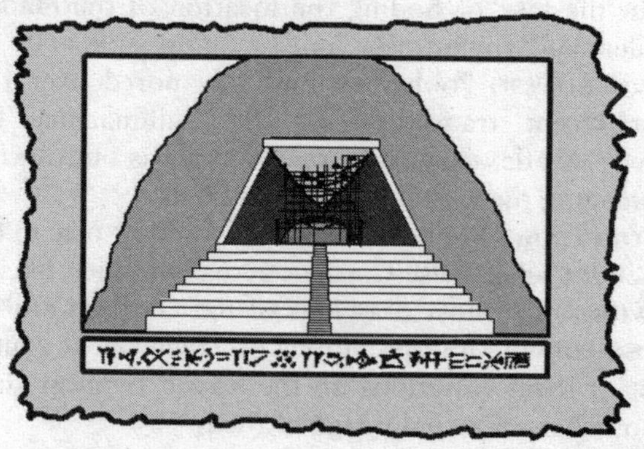

'It looks like an open cave in the mountainside,' West said. 'Only they refined the natural opening into a magnificent arch.'

'What is that upside-down triangle suspended from the ceiling of the cave?' Pooh Bear asked.

'It looks like a gigantic *stalactite* . . .' Stretch said.

West said, 'And that structure on the cave-floor directly beneath it appears to be a ziggurat, encased in a construction mud-mound. You used the mound to build the ziggurat and then you took the mound away after you were finished.'

Zaeed eyed West sideways. 'If that is a full-sized ziggurat, Captain, then that stalactite must be at least *fifteen storeys tall*. It must be immense.'

'What are all those criss-crossing lines covering the two structures?' Lily asked.

'I have long pondered those lines, child,' Zaeed said. 'I believe that they are an ancient form of scaffolding—a multi-levelled temporary structure made of wooden poles used to build the Gardens. Remember, this cloth is a progress report—it depicts the Gardens being built. I therefore surmise that they are a building tool.'

Pooh Bear asked, 'Lily. What does the writing say?'

Zaeed said, 'My brother, this is not written in the language of Thoth. It's just standard cuneiform, written by a messenger for his king—'

'Lily can read cuneiform,' West said. 'Go on, Lily.'

Lily read the text box: 'It says: *Progress report: Construction continuing as scheduled. Nineteen worker deaths. Sixty-two injuries. Losses tolerable.*'

'Losses tolerable,' Stretch repeated. 'Doesn't look like the despots of this region have changed much over the ages.'

★

They returned to Lily's translation of the Callimachus Text's sixth entry:

The Hanging Paradise of Old Babylonia.
March towards the rising Sun,
From the point where the two life-givers become one.
In the shadow of the mountains of Zagros,
Behold the triple falls fashioned by the Third Great Architect
To conceal the path he hewed
That climbs to the Paradise
Which mighty Nebuchadnezzar built for his bride.

'Well, it begins straightforwardly enough,' West said. 'You march due east from the point where the two life-givers become one. "The life-givers" is the name the Mesopotamians gave to the Tigris and Euphrates rivers. This must be a reference to the point where they meet.'

'Baghdad?' Pooh Bear asked. 'It stands at a point of convergence of the Tigris and Euphrates. Isn't it the site of ancient Babylon?'

'Actually, no,' West said. 'Babylon lies underneath the modern-day town of Hilla, to the south of Baghdad. And your theory doesn't strictly obey the verse. The two rivers bend very close to each other at Baghdad, but they don't *become one* there. They actually come together much further south, at the town of Qurna. There they become one big super-river—the Shatt al-Arab—which flows south through Basra before draining into the Persian Gulf.'

Stretch said sourly: 'I can't believe the Americans haven't found the Gardens already. They must have over 150,000 troops in Iraq right now. They could easily have sent huge forces of men to check out every waterfall in the Zagros Mountains due east of Baghdad, Hilla *and* Qurna by now.'

West paused, an idea forming in his mind. 'Unless . . .'

'What?'

'The modern town of Hilla does indeed stand on the ruins of Nebuchadnezzar's Babylon,' he said. 'But now that I look at it closely, our verse does not refer to "Babylon" at all. It mentions the Hanging Paradise of *Old Babylonia*. Old Babylon.'

'Meaning?' Pooh Bear asked.

'Consider this,' West said. 'New York. New England. New Orleans. Today, many cities and regions are named in memory of older places. In some ancient texts, Nebuchadnezzar's Babylon is actually referred to as *New* Babylon. What if the Gardens were *never* in New Babylon, but were, rather, built in an older city also named "Babylon", but built far from the newer city that adopted its name. The *original* Babylon.'

'It would explain why Alexander the Great's biographers never mentioned the Gardens when he passed through Babylon and why no-one has found them near Hilla,' Stretch said. 'They would only have seen New Babylon, not Old Babylon.'

'Two Babylons. Two cities.' Zaeed stroked his sharply-pointed chin. 'This is a good theory . . .'

Then suddenly his eyes lit up. 'Of course! *Of course!* Why didn't I think of it before?'

'What?'

Zaeed dashed to his trunk and scrounged among the notebooks there.

As he did so, he spoke quickly, excitedly. 'If I may take Captain West's theory one step further. Modern logic assumes that the Tigris and the Euphrates follow the *same* courses today that they followed back in 570 BC. They flow down from Turkey, through Iraq, before joining at Qurna in the southern marshlands.

'Now consider this. Mesopotamia is the birthplace of all flood myths. Why, the tale of Noah and his Ark is but a flimsy retelling of the story of Zisudra and his animal-carrying boat. Why is this so? Because Iraq's flood myths stem from *very real* floods: of the Persian Gulf breaking its banks and flooding far inland, ripping apart eroded land formations and, on occasion, *diverting* the courses of the two great rivers of the region, the Tigris and Euphrates. A Westerner named Graham Hancock has written about this very convincingly in a marvellous book called *Underworld*. Ah-ha! Here it is!'

He produced a battered book, opened it to a page containing a map of Iraq. Prominent on the map were the two major rivers, the Tigris and Euphrates, that joined in a V shape in the south of the country:

Zaeed had scribbled the locations of Hilla, Qurna and Basra on the map.

He explained. 'Now. As we continue to do today, people back in ancient times built their towns on the banks of the two great rivers. But when the rivers diverted onto new courses due to flooding, it follows that those same people would have abandoned the old towns and built new ones, the ones we see on the banks of the rivers today.

'Many years ago, in my search for lost documents relating to the Hanging Gardens, I mapped the locations of *abandoned* towns, towns that were once situated on the banks of the rivers, but which, once the rivers diverted, were simply deserted. From these locations, I was able to reconstruct the *former* courses of the two rivers.'

'So where did they converge back then?' West asked.

Zaeed grinned. 'See, *that* was what I did not know—that their *point of convergence* was the all-important factor.'

With a flourish, Zaeed then flipped the page to reveal a *second* map of Iraq, only on this map, an additional dotted V had been drawn directly beneath the present-day one:

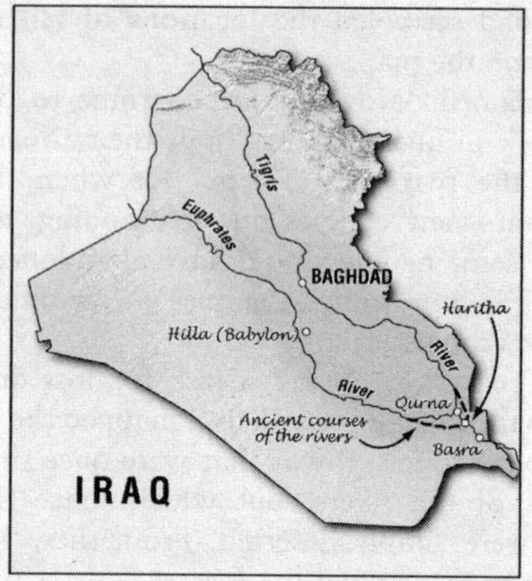

Zaeed pointed at this new river junction—it lay south of Qurna, roughly halfway between it and Basra.

'The rivers,' Zaeed said, 'used to meet here, at the town of Haritha.'

The *Halicarnassus* shot into Iraq, heading for the southern village-town of Haritha.

As it did so, everyone prepared for their arrival—prepping guns, maps, helmets and tunnel gear.

Alone in his office, with Horus perched on his chair-back, West kept one eye on a laptop computer that Wizard had set up soon after their mission in Tunisia had gone to hell.

It was the microwave communications net he had instructed Wizard to create, to scan for any signals emanating from, or coming to, the *Halicarnassus*.

As they crossed the border into Iraq, the laptop pinged.

Someone on board the plane had sent out a homing signal.

HARITHA, IRAQ

19 MARCH, 2006, 0900 HOURS

1 DAY BEFORE THE ARRIVAL OF TARTARUS

To get to Haritha, the *Halicarnassus* had to skirt the port-city, Basra.

As it soared over the outskirts of Basra, Sky Monster's voice came over the PA. '*Hey, Captain West, you better come up here and see this.*'

West went up to the cockpit and peered out the windows.

A long column of heavy-duty vehicles was rumbling out of Basra, heading north toward Haritha.

It was a gigantic convoy. Of American military vehicles.

Troop trucks, engineering vehicles, Humvees, jeeps, motorbikes, plus no fewer than ten Abrams battle tanks and several Black Hawk helicopters, prowling overhead.

In all, it amounted to maybe 5,000 troops.

'How can this be?' Zaeed asked, appearing behind West with Pooh Bear.

'How can they be onto us *again*?' Pooh Bear asked.

West just stared at the convoy, trying not to betray his thoughts: *Who gave us away?*

'Oh, shit!' Sky Monster exclaimed, hearing something through his headphones. 'The Yanks just scrambled fighters from Nasiryah. F-15s. We better find this place fast, Huntsman.'

A few minutes later, they arrived above the dusty town of Haritha, situated on the eastern bank of the Shatt al-Arab River about fifty kilometres north of Basra.

'Okay, Sky Monster, swing us due east,' West said.

Sky Monster banked the *Halicarnassus* above the town, but as he did so, he and West glimpsed the highway coming from the north, from Qurna—

—and on that highway, they saw *another* column of American vehicles.

It was almost identical to the first—lots of troop trucks, Humvees and tanks; and another 5,000 men, at the very least.

West's mind raced.

'Judah must have had people at Qurna, searching for the waterfalls,' he said. 'But Qurna is the wrong junction of the rivers. He was searching too far to the north.'

'And now—*suddenly*—he knows to come south,' Sky Monster said pointedly. 'How about that . . .'

West just tapped him reassuringly on the shoulder. 'East and low, my friend.'

But their position was clear—with a rat in their ranks, they were now caught between *two* converging convoys of overwhelming American firepower.

If they found the Hanging Gardens—which wasn't guaranteed—they'd have to be in and out *fast*.

Within minutes, the jagged peaks of the Zagros Mountains rose up before them, the boundary line between Iraq and Iran.

Numerous small rivers snaked their way through therange's maze-like system of peaks and valleys—

descending to the Shatt al-Arab. Waterfalls could be seen everywhere: tall thin string-like falls, short squat ones, even horseshoe-shaped ones.

There were many double-tiered waterfalls, and several quadruple-tiered falls, but as far as West could tell, there was only one set of *triple*-tiered falls in the area due east of Haritha: an absolutely stunning cascade easily 300 feet from top to bottom, that bounced over two wide rocky ledges, before flowing into a stream that wound down to the mighty al-Arab. These falls lay right at the edge of the mountain range, looking out over the flat marshy plain of southern Iraq.

'That's it,' West said. 'That's them. Sky Monster, bring us down anywhere you can. We drive from here. You take the *Hali* to these co-ordinates and wait for me to call.' He handed Sky Monster a slip of paper.

'Roger that, Huntsman.'

The *Halicarnassus* landed on the flat cracked surface of a lakebed that hadn't seen water in 1,000 years.

No sooner had its wheels touched down than its rear loading ramp dropped open, banging onto the ground, and—*shoom!*—a second four-wheel drive Land Rover came rushing out of the big plane's belly, bouncing down onto the mudplain and speeding off to the east, kicking up a cloud of sand behind it.

For its part, the *Halicarnassus* just powered up again and took off, heading for the secret hangar where Jack West had originally found her fifteen years before.

The Land Rover skidded to a halt before the towering triple-tiered falls. The roar of falling water filled the air.

'Allah have mercy,' Pooh Bear said, gazing up at the falls. At 300 feet, they were the size of a thirty-storey building.

'There!' West called.

A narrow stone path in the rockface led behind the lowest tier of the waterfall.

West hurried along it. The others followed. But when they arrived behind the curtain of falling water, they were confronted by something they hadn't expected.

On every tier of the falls, the water was thrown quite a way out from the cliff-wall, propelled by its rapid speed. This meant that the actual *face* of each tier was largely water-free—except for a layer of moss and a constant trickle of dribbling water. It *also* meant that each cliff-face was *concealed* by the falls themselves.

And behind the curtains of water was a most curious feature.

Cut into the face of each rockwall was a dizzying network of ultra-narrow paths that criss-crossed up them. There were maybe six paths in total, but they wound and intersected in so many ways that the number of permutations they created was huge.

Gazing at the twisting array of pathways on the first cliff-face, West saw with dismay the alarming number of wall-holes and blade-holes that opened onto the paths.

Booby traps.

Zaeed was awed. 'Imhotep III. A genius, he was, but a sinister genius. This is a very rare type of trap system but typical of his flair. There are many paths with deadly snares, but only one of the pathways is safe.'

'How do we know which route is the safe one?' Stretch asked. 'They all seem to intertwine.'

Beside West, Lily was gazing intently at the path system behind the waterfall.

As she looked at it, something clicked in her mind.

'I've seen this before . . .' she said.

She reached into West's backpack and extracted a printout.

It was titled: '*Waterfall Entrance—Refortification by Imhotep III in the time of Ptolemy Soter*'.

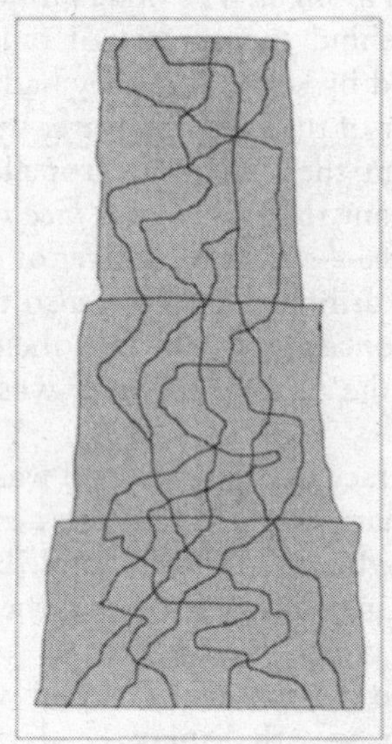

'Well, would you look at that . . .' Stretch said.

The lines on the printed image exactly matched the layout of the pathways on the waterfall.

'But which path is the safe route?' Pooh Bear asked anxiously.

'That I don't know,' Lily said, deflating.

'Wait a second,' West said. 'Maybe you do . . .'

Now he rifled through his pack for a few moments, before he said, 'Got it!'

He pulled from the backpack a tattered brown leatherbound notebook.

The diary of the Nazi archaeologist, Hessler.

'Hessler knew the safe path,' West said, flicking the pages of the diary until he found what he was looking for.

'Here!' He held the diary open, revealing a page they had seen before:

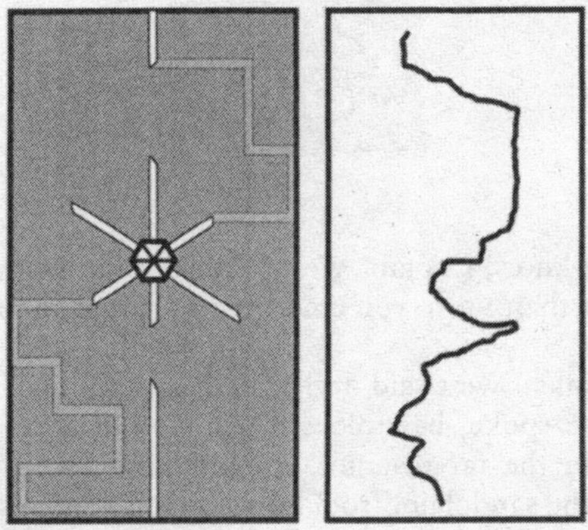

Its title was 'Safe Routes'.

West smiled.

He brought the right-hand image from this page alongside the picture of the waterfall's paths, and everyone else saw it—the right-hand 'Safe Route' matched one of the twisting paths on the waterfall diagram perfectly:

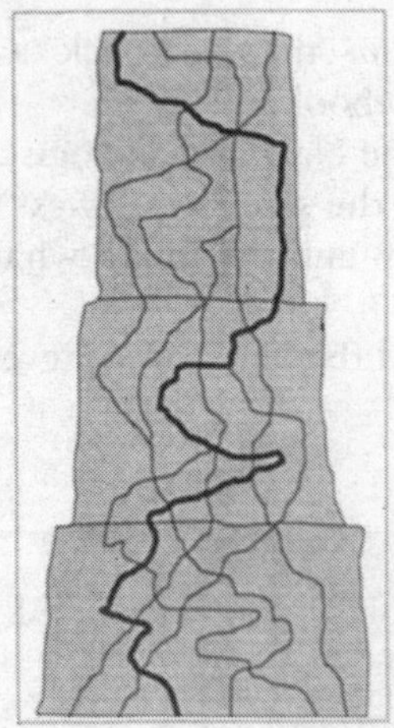

'You know, Captain West,' Zaeed said, 'you're a lot cleverer than I give you credit for. I shall have to watch you.'

'Thanks,' West said dryly.

As he spoke, he stole a glance at the plain behind them. In the far distance, a high dustcloud stretched across the sandplain, from horizon to horizon—a sandstorm, or perhaps something else . . .

The dustcloud of two massive convoys.

'Come on,' he said. 'We don't have much time.'

Up the vertical cliff-wall they went, following the safe path, with the roaring curtain of water falling behind their backs. Diffused sunlight lanced in through falling water, lighting the way.

West climbed in the lead, with Horus in his chest pouch.

Their path twisted and turned, doubling back and

forth as it rose up the cliff-face. It was so narrow that the team could only climb it in single-file, and it was covered in slippery moss, so their progress was slow. That said, without the map, they could never have figured out the safe route up the falls.

At both of the middle ledges in the waterfall, the path burrowed into the rockface as a tunnel—a tunnel that emerged above the ledge, giving access to the next level.

And so after twenty minutes of careful climbing, they reached the top of the third rockface. There, just below the lip of the uppermost ledge of the falls, immediately beneath a stunning translucent veil of fast-flowing water, the path ended . . .

. . . right in front of a third low tunnel—a passageway that bored directly into the cliff-face, disappearing into darkness.

The entrance to this tunnel, however, was different from the lower ones.

It was more ornate, despite the fact it was covered in overgrown green moss.

The tunnel's entry frame—every side covered with hieroglyphs—was beautifully cut into the rockface, in a perfectly square shape. Its smooth walls retained this shape as they receded into blackness.

And on the lintel above the door, partly obscured by trickling water and moss, was a familiar carving:

West smiled at the carved image. 'We're here.'

As West and the others evaluated the tunnel entrance, Pooh Bear followed a short horizontal section of the path that led to the edge of the waterfall.

Leaning out, he peered around the edge of the flowing body of water, looking out at the vast sandplain behind them.

What he saw made his eyes boggle.

He saw the two American convoys—now merged to become one mega-convoy—thundering across the plain, kicking up an immense dustcloud behind them. Choppers hovered above the great column of vehicles, with one dark-painted Black Hawk out in front.

Ten thousand men, *coming right for them*.

'By Allah,' he breathed. 'Er, Huntsman . . .'

West joined him, saw the immense American force, and particularly eyed the dark Black Hawk leading the way.

He frowned.

That chopper actually didn't look . . .

He pursed his lips in thought.

The world was closing in on him, and he was fast running out of options.

'Come on, Pooh,' he said. 'We can't stop now.'

They rejoined the others at the tunnel entrance, where Stretch said, 'If this trap system is anything like the others, there's no way we can get in and out before the Americans arrive.'

'If I may be so bold,' Zaeed said slyly from behind them. 'There *might* in fact be a way . . .'

'What way?' Stretch said suspiciously.

'The Priests' Entrance. The Nazi's diary mentions it,

and I have come across this phrase in my own research. Such an entrance is usually a small one, unadorned, used by the priests of a temple to tend to its shrines even after that temple has been closed off. As a royal retreat, the Gardens almost certainly contained temples in need of tending.'

'A back door,' West said.

'Yes. Which means we can enter through this door and exit out the other end, via the Priests' Entrance.'

'*If* we can find it,' Stretch said.

'If we don't get this Piece,' West said, 'Doris and Big Ears and Noddy will have died for nothing. I'm not going to let that happen. I'm getting this Piece or I'm going to die trying.'

And with that he turned, and gripping Lily's hand, he started for the tunnel behind the waterfall.

Pooh Bear fell into step close beside him, and stole a whisper: 'Huntsman. That lead chopper, the dark Black Hawk out in front of the convoy, did you see it?'

'Yes,' West's eyes remained fixed forward.

'That wasn't an American chopper.'

'I know.'

'Did you recognise the markings? It was—'

'Yes,' West whispered, glancing back at Stretch. 'It was an Israeli chopper. Somehow the Israelis knew our location, and I think I know how. Thing is, it looks like they're trying to get here *ahead* of the Americans.' He threw another deadly look at Stretch. 'Israel always looks after Israel. Come on.'

And with those words, they entered the trap system that guarded the Hanging Gardens of Babylon.

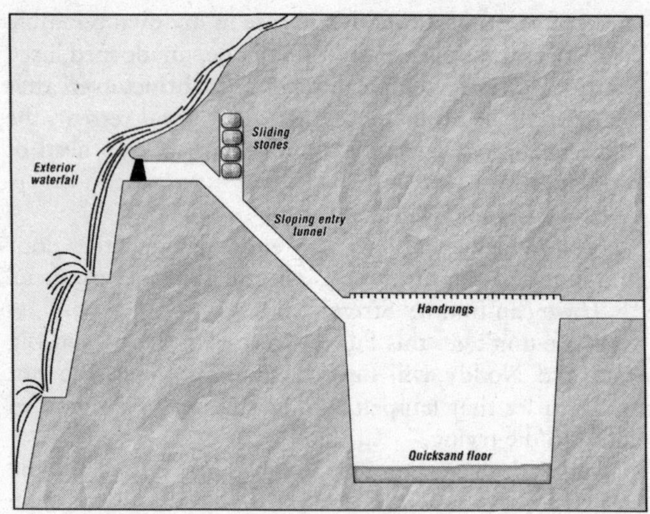

The Entry Tunnel and the Sand Cavern

The flashlight on West's fireman's helmet carved a sabre-like beam through the darkness of the tunnel.

His team followed him, silhouetted by the daylight that penetrated the waterfall behind them. They also wore helmet-lights. Horus flew out in front.

The tunnel was perfectly square in shape, its walls hard, carved from solid rock. And it sloped steadily downward, away from the daylight. Shadowy square recesses were cut into its ceiling, concealing God-only-knew-what. The waterfall behind them roared loudly, a constant *shhh*—

The first trap struck.

With a heart-stopping *boom*, an enormous five-ton dropstone fell out of a recess in the ceiling—just inside the entrance—blocking out the sunlight, filling the entire tunnel!

Then, to their horror, the gradient of the tunnel gave the massive block life.

It immediately started sliding *down* the slope—toward them—forcing West's team forward and downward.

'Move!' West called.

They all started running down the tunnel, away from the great sliding stone, side-stepping warily around all the ceiling holes they had to pass under.

The great stone slid quickly forward, chasing after them, an unstoppable pursuer, driving them toward—

A cliff edge.

Thirty metres down the slope, the tunnel simply ended at a gaping black abyss. The tunnel did not seem to continue in any way beyond this dark void. This, it appeared, was the absolute end of the tunnel.

The stone kept rumbling down the tunnel behind them.

West fired a flare into the dark void—

—to reveal that they were standing at one end of a gigantic subterranean cavern shaped like a giant cube, easily fifty metres long and at least ten storeys high.

Their problem: their tunnel opened onto this cavern right up near the *ceiling*.

The sliding stone kept coming.

Then, by the glow of the hovering flare, West saw *the floor* of the great cavern thirty metres below him.

It was flat and bare, made of sand.

But there was something wrong about it—it was *too* flat, *too* bare.

West kicked a nearby stone off the edge and watched it sail down to the floor of the cavern.

The stone hit the floor.

It didn't bounce.

It just landed with a splonk, *embedding* itself in the goopy sand-like surface. And then it went under, seemingly *swallowed* by the semi-liquid surface.

'Ah-ha, quicksand,' Zaeed said, impressed. 'The *entire* floor is quicksand . . .'

'God, you're just like Max,' West said, snapping round to check on the fast-moving stone behind them—ten metres away and about to force them into the quicksand-filled chamber.

'This trap system doesn't waste any time, does it?'

But then, turning back to the massive square cavern, he saw the answer—a long line of handbars had been dug into its ceiling; a line that ended at a matching tunnel at the opposite end of the cavern, fifty metres away.

Of course, more dark and deadly trap-holes were interspersed between and above the handbars.

'Lily, here. Jump onto my chest, put your hands around my neck,' West said. 'Zaeed. You got any intel on these handbars?'

Zaeed peered back at the sliding stone: 'I found a reference once to something called the High Ceiling of the Sand Cavern. It said, "Walk with your hands but in deference to he who built it, avoid those of its Creator." Imhotep III built this system, so I'd avoid every third handgrip.'

'Good theory,' West said, 'but since I don't trust you, why don't you go first and test it out. Now *move*.'

Zaeed leapt out onto the handrungs, swinging himself along them, avoiding every third one.

Once he'd survived the first few metres, West scooped up Lily. 'Everybody, follow us.'

And so with Lily gripping him around the neck, West reached up and grabbed the first handbar . . .

. . . and swung out over the ten-storey drop to the quicksand floor.

It was an incredible sight: five tiny figures, moving in single-file, all hanging from their hands, swinging fist-over-fist across the ceiling of the immense cube-shaped cavern, their feet dangling ten storeys above the floor.

The last in the line was Pooh Bear, who leapt off the doorway-ledge a bare moment before the five-ton sliding stone came bursting out of the tunnel, filling the entire passage before falling clear out of it!

The huge square stone thundered off the edge . . . and tipped . . . and went sailing down the sheer wall of the cavern before it splashed into the quicksand with a great goopy splat.

Then the stone settled in the quagmire and sank below the surface—grimly, slowly—never to be seen again.

West gripped each handbar firmly, swinging himself and Lily down the length of the cavern. Horus flew alongside them, hovering nearby—seemingly amused at their difficult method of travel.

Following Zaeed, West avoided every third handbar, which was just as well. Zaeed had been right. West tested the ninth handbar and it just fell from its recess, dropping all the way to the deadly floor.

He was halfway across when he heard the voices. Shouts. Coming from the entry tunnel.

The first chopper—the Israeli Black Hawk—must

have dropped its men directly onto the path at the top of the falls.

West reasoned that they were probably commandos from the Sayaret Matkal, the very best of Israel's elite 'Sayaret' or 'reconnaissance' units. The Matkal were crack assassins—ruthlessly efficient killers who, among other things, were widely acknowledged as the best snipers in the world. Stretch's old unit.

Now they were coming in.

Fast.

'Everybody!' West called. 'Get a move on! We're about to have some really nasty company!'

He started double-timing it across the handbars—swinging like a monkey hand-over-hand—high above the deadly floor.

Then suddenly from the entry tunnel there came the familiar heavy *whump* of a sliding stone dropping from the ceiling—followed by shouts and the sound of rapidly running feet.

The Israelis had set off a second sliding stone.

West kept moving across the high cavern, swinging with his hands.

Out in front, Zaeed reached the mouth of the opposite tunnel, swung into it. West followed seconds later, swinging his feet onto solid ground. He turned to help the others—

—only to see a red laser dot appear on his nose . . . a dot that belonged to a sniper rifle in the opposite tunnel, a sniper rifle held by one of the Israeli commandos, bent on one knee.

A voice came over West's radio frequency: '*Stay right where you are, Captain West. Don't move a muscle.*'

The Israeli leader eyed West menacingly.

Stretch made the introductions. 'Captain Jack West Jr . . . this is Major Itzak Meir of the Sayaret Matkal, call-sign: *Avenger*.'

Avenger was a tall man, broadchested, with hard green eyes that were entirely lacking in nuance. For him, black was black, white was white, and Israel always came first.

'The famous Captain West.' Avenger stepped forward, relieving West of his holstered pistol. 'I've never heard of a soldier enduring so much failure, and yet still you keep picking yourself up, dusting yourself off, and coming back for more.'

'It's never over till it's over,' West said.

Avenger turned to Stretch. 'Captain Cohen, congratulations. You have done a fine job on an unusually long mission. Your work has been noted at the highest levels. I apologise for surprising you in this way.'

Stretch said nothing, just bowed his head.

Pooh Bear, however, was livid.

He glared at Stretch. 'Accept my congratulations, too, Israeli. You performed your mission to the letter. You led them to us and you *sold us out* just in time to hand them the last available Piece. I hope you're satisfied.'

Stretch still said nothing.

Lily looked up at him. 'Stretch? Why . . . ?'

West was hardly going to obey—but then, as if it could read his thoughts, the dot shifted slightly . . .

. . . so that it now rested on the back of Lily's head.

'I know what you're thinking, Captain. Don't. Or she dies. Cohen! These handrungs. The safe sequence.'

Right then Stretch landed on the ground beside West. Pooh Bear was still huffing and puffing behind him, crossing the handrungs with difficulty.

Stretch glanced sideways at West as he spoke into his mike: 'Avoid every third rung, Major.'

The Israelis moved quickly, leaping out from the entry tunnel, grasping the handbars, moving across the high ceiling of the cavern.

There were six of them, and they all emerged from the entry tunnel ahead of the sliding stone—it just rumbled out of the tunnel harmlessly behind them, dropping into the quicksand pool.

But they also moved in a brilliantly co-ordinated fashion—so that at any moment, one of them hung one-handed and always had his gun aimed at Lily.

Within a few minutes, they were across the cavern and surrounding West's little team.

Stretch said softly, 'Lily, you have to understand. I didn't—'

Avenger grinned. 'What is this? "Stretch"? Have you been renamed, Cohen? How positively sweet.'

He turned to Pooh Bear. 'Alas, everything you say is true, Arab. The last available Piece is to be ours, one Piece of the Capstone that will give Israel all the leverage it needs over the United States of America. Now, Captain West, if you would be so kind. Lead the way. Take us to this Piece. You work for Israel now.'

But no sooner had these words come out of his mouth than there was a great explosion from somewhere outside.

Everyone spun.

West swapped a glance with Pooh Bear.

They all listened for a moment.

Nothing.

Silence.

And then West realised: silence *was* the problem. He could no longer hear the constant *shhh* of the waterfall up at the entrance to the tunnel system.

The shooshing had stopped.

And the realisation hit.

Judah had just used explosives to divert the waterfall—*the entire waterfall*! He was opening up the entrance for a mass forced entry.

In fact, even in his wildest dreams, West still hadn't fully imagined the scene outside.

The waterfall had indeed been diverted, by a series of expertly-laid demolition charges in the river above it.

Now its triple-tiered rockface, criss-crossed with paths, lay bare and dry, in full view of the world.

But it was the immense military force massing around the base of the dry waterfall that defied imagining.

A multitude of platoons converged on the now tranquil pool at the base of the triple-tiered cliff-face. Tanks and Humvees circled behind them, while Apache and Super Stallion choppers buzzed overhead.

And commanding it all from a mobile command vehicle was Marshall Judah.

He sent his first team in from the air—they went in fast, ziplining down drop-ropes suspended from a hovering Super Stallion direct to the top tier of the dry falls, by-passing the paths.

Guns up and pumped up, they charged inside.

From their position at the far end of the quicksand cavern, West and his new group saw the Americans' red laser-sighting beams lancing out from the entry tunnel, accompanied by fast footsteps.

'American pigs,' Zaeed hissed.

But then suddenly—*whump*—the Americans' footfalls were drowned out by a much louder sound: the deep ominous grinding of a third sliding stone!

Gunfire. The Americans were firing their guns *at* the sliding stone!

Shouts.

Then running—frantic running.

Seconds later, the first desperate American trooper appeared on the ledge on his side of the cube-shaped cavern.

He peered around desperately—looking left and right, up and down—and he saw the quicksand floor far below; then he saw the handrungs in the ceiling. He leapt for them—swung from the first one to the second, grabbed the third—

—which fell out of its recess and sent the hapless commando plummeting ten storeys *straight down*.

The man screamed all the way until—*splat!*—he landed in the gelatinous floor . . . at which point he started screaming in a whole new way.

The screams of a man caught in the grip of a force he cannot resist, a man who knows he is going to die.

His five team-mates arrived at the tunnel's edge just in time to see him get sucked under, his mouth filling with liquid sand. Now trapped on the ledge, they glanced from the deadly handrungs back to the sliding stone, then down to the quicksand.

Two tried the handrungs.

The first man reached the sixth rung—which felled him. The second man just slipped and fell all on his own.

The other three were beaten by the sliding stone.

It burst out of the tunnel behind them like a runaway train and collected them on the way—hurling them all out into the air, sending them sailing in a high curving arc ten storeys down before they all landed together with simultaneous sandy splashes.

As the massive stone itself landed, it smacked one of the American soldiers straight under the surface. The other two bobbed on the gluggy surface for a few seconds before they too were sucked under by the hungry liquid floor.

West and his group saw it all happen.

'That won't happen again,' West said to Avenger. 'Judah sent that team in to die—a junior team without instructions, without warnings. He was just testing the trap system. When he comes in, he won't be so foolish.'

The Israeli major nodded, turned to two of his men. 'Shamburg. Riel. Make a rear-guard post here. Hold them off for as long as you can, then catch up.'

'Sir!'

'Yes, sir!'

Avenger then grabbed Lily from West, held her roughly by the collar. 'Lead the way, Captain.'

★

They hadn't taken ten steps down the next tunnel before they heard gunfire from the two rear-guards.

Sustained gunfire.

More Americans had arrived at the sand cavern—having probably completely disabled the sliding stone mechanism by now.

Two men wouldn't hold them off for long.

The Giant Stairway

After passing through the short tunnel, West led his now-larger group into another cube-shaped chamber—about fifty feet high, wide and long—only this time, his tunnel opened onto the chamber from the *base*, not up near the ceiling.

Before him was a rail-less stone path which hugged the chamber's left-hand wall. A quicksand pool lay to the right, filling the rest of the floor.

The low stone path, however, led to something quite astonishing.

Seven giant stone steps that rose magnificently upward to a doorway cut *into* the ceiling of this chamber. Each step must have been at least seven feet high, and they all bristled with holes and recesses of various shapes and sizes, some of them door-sized, others basketball-sized, every one of them no doubt fitted with deadly snares just waiting to be triggered.

To the left of the giant stairway, flush against it, was the same stone wall that flanked the path. It was also dotted with variously-sized trap-holes. To the right of the stairs, there was nothing but empty air.

The intent was clear: if you were thrown off the stairs, you fell all the way down to the floor, made entirely of quicksand.

'It's the *levels*,' Zaeed realised.

'What?' West said.

'Remember the progress report I found, the sketch of the Gardens under construction. These steps weren't originally steps at all. They were the step-like *levels* that led up to the main archway of the cave. Imhotep III converted them into this ascending stairway trap.'

'Clever.'

Zaeed said, 'If I'm right, the Hanging Gardens of Babylon lie beyond that doorway in the ceiling.'

Avenger pushed West forward—while maintaining his grip on Lily. 'Captain West, please. Time is of the essence. Lead the way.'

West did so, taking on the giant steps.

He encountered traps on nearly every one.

Blasts of quicksand, trapdoors, upward-springing spikes designed to lance through his grasping hands, even a one-ton boulder that rolled suddenly across the fifth step.

But through skill and speed and quick thinking, he got past them all, until finally he stepped up into the opening in the ceiling, emerging on a dark platform which he sensed opened onto a wider, infinitely more vast space. And so he lit a flare and held it aloft and for one brief moment in time, standing alone in the darkness, Jack West Jr beheld a sight no-one had seen for over 2,500 years.

Standing there before him, in all their incredible glory, were the Hanging Gardens of Babylon.

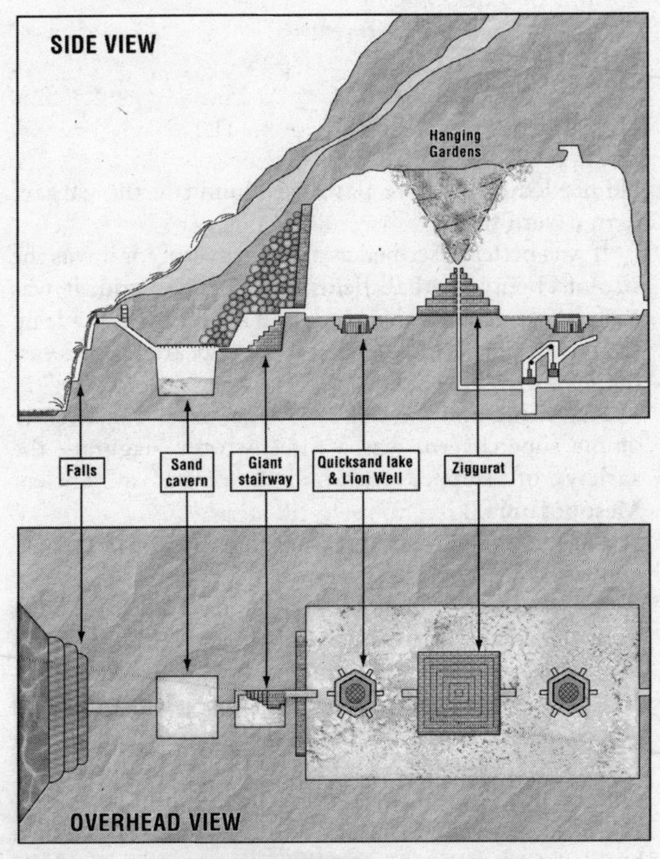

THE HANGING GARDENS OF BABYLON

He needed eight more flares to illuminate the gargantuan cavern fully.

It was better described as a *super*cavern, for it was the size of twenty football fields laid out in a grid. It was perfectly rectangular in shape, and its floor was made up entirely of quicksand—giving it the appearance of a vast flat *lake* of yellow sand.

And rising up from this sand-lake, in the exact centre of the supercavern, was a fifteen-storey ziggurat—the variety of stepped pyramid common in ancient Mesopotamia.

But it was the natural feature that lay above the ziggurat that inspired sheer *wonder*.

An absolutely immense limestone stalactite hung from the ceiling of the cave directly above the ziggurat. It was so huge, its mass so great, it dwarfed the ziggurat. Perhaps 25 storeys tall, it looked like an inverted *mountain* suspended from the ceiling of the supercavern, its pointed tip reaching down to meet the upwardly-pointed peak of the ziggurat on the ground.

But this incredible natural feature had been modified by the hand of man—thus lifting it out of 'incredible' and into the category of 'wondrous'.

A pathway had been hewn into its outer flank—in some sections it was flat and curving, while in others it took the form of short flights of steps. This path spiralled up and around the exterior of the great stalactite, rising ever higher, heading for the ceiling of the cavern.

Dotting this path were nearly a hundred semi-circular archways, each archway containing vines and shrubs and trees and flowers—all of them overgrown to excess, all hanging out and over the edge of the stalactite, dangling precariously 300 feet above the world.

It defied belief.

It was stupendous.

A truly hanging garden.

The Hanging Gardens of Babylon.

As the others joined him, West noticed the wall soaring into the upper reaches of the supercavern immediately above and behind them.

While it was made of densely-packed bricks, West could make out at its edges the traces of another *earlier* structure, a structure that had been trapezoidal in shape and huge—300 feet high—like a giant doorway of some sort that had been filled in with these bricks.

West grabbed Zaeed's sketch from his pocket—the drawing of the great stalactite (shrouded in scaffolding) visible from outside the mountain *through* a window-like trapezoidal archway:

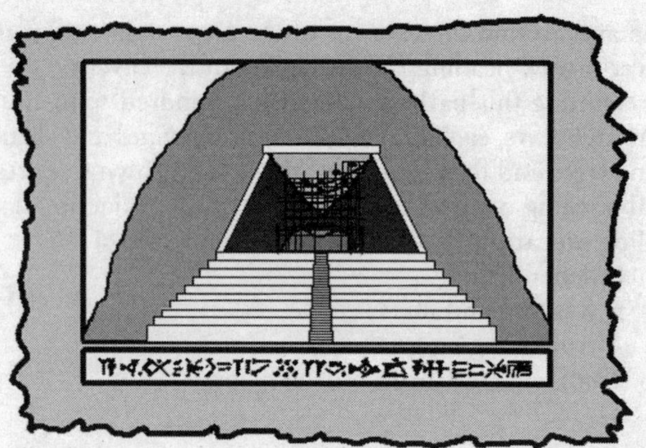

At that moment, he remembered a reference from the Nazi Hessler's diary. He pulled the diary from his jacket pocket and found the page:

1ST INSCRIPTION FROM THE TOMB OF IMHOTEP III:

WHAT AN INCREDIBLE STRUCTURE IT WAS,
CONSTRUCTED AS A MIRROR IMAGE,
WHERE BOTH ENTRANCE AND EXIT WERE ALIKE.
IT PAINED ME THAT MY TASK—WHAT WOULD BE MY LIFE'S MASTERWORK—WAS TO CONCEAL SO MAGNIFICENT A STRUCTURE.
BUT I DID MY DUTY.
WE SEALED THE GREAT ARCHWAY WITH A LANDSLIDE.
AS INSTRUCTED, THE PRIESTS' ENTRANCE REMAINS OPEN SO THEY MAY TEND THE SHRINES INSIDE—THE PRIESTS HAVE BEEN INFORMED OF THE ORDER OF THE SNARES.

'"*We sealed the great archway with a landslide*",'

West read aloud. 'Imhotep bricked up the archway and then triggered a landslide to cover it. But he wasn't done. *Then* he diverts a river outside to cover the whole thing. My God, he was good . . .'

'The Third Great Architect was indeed a master,' Zaeed said, coming alongside West.

Beside them, the others were arriving and taking in the awesome sight.

Lily's mouth hung open.

Stretch's eyes were wide.

Even Avenger was impressed enough to fall silent.

It was Pooh Bear who summed up their mood: 'So this is why they call them *Wonders*.'

But they weren't there yet.

The wide lake of quicksand still lay between them and the ziggurat—the only means of getting up to the Hanging Gardens.

Halfway between them and the ziggurat, seemingly floating on the surface of the sand-lake, there stood a small roofed structure that looked like a gazebo. Made of stone, it was hexagonal in shape and roughly the size of a single-car garage, but it had no walls, just six pillars holding up a heavy-looking stone roof.

A dead-straight path barely an inch above the surface of the lake stretched out from their position directly toward this hexagonal gazebo—only to end abruptly thirty metres short of the structure.

The path re-emerged nearer to the gazebo, its submerged centre section presumably consumed by the quicksand sometime in the distant past.

As West looked more closely, he saw more paths.

Radiating out from the hexagonal sides of the gazebo,

creating a star-shaped pattern, were six stone paths that were also virtually level with the surface of the lake.

Each of these paths also ended abruptly about fifteen metres out from the gazebo.

'How do we get across?' Pooh Bear asked. 'The paths have long been swallowed by the quicksand lake.'

'Can't we just follow the straight path?' Avenger said. 'Surely it continues just beneath the surface.'

'Yes. Let's do exactly that and why don't you lead the way, you stupid fool Israeli,' Zaeed said.

Avenger frowned.

'He means, walk that way if you want to die,' West said. 'It's a trap for the unwary and uninformed. This looks to me like a false-floor trap—the biggest false-floor trap I've ever seen. There must be a safe route just underneath the surface of the lake, but you have to know the route to use it and we don't.'

'I think we do,' a quiet voice said from behind him.

Lily.

Everybody turned to face her.

'We do?' Pooh Bear said.

'Yes,' Lily said. 'It's the second "safe route" that the German man wrote down. The first was the safe pathway up the waterfall. This is the second. That's why he put them together.'

She took Hessler's diary from West and flipped back a couple of pages, to reveal the page they had looked at only half an hour before, entitled 'Safe Routes':

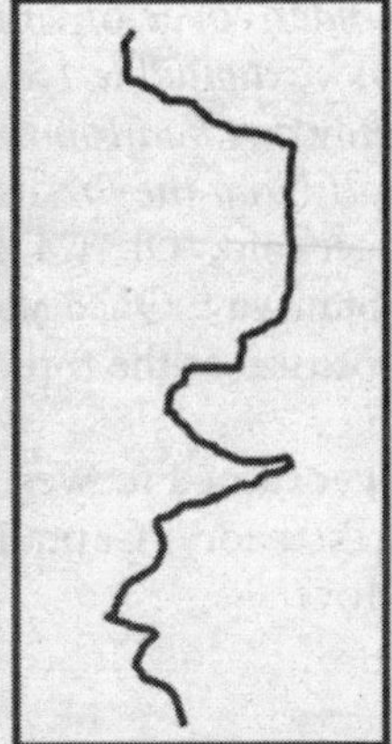

But whereas before they had been looking at the *right*-hand image, now it was the left-hand one that concerned them.

Sure enough, it matched the view before them exactly.

Only it revealed a path hidden beneath the quicksand lake—a circuitous path that skirted the walls of the cavern, crossed through the hexagonal gazebo, and ended at the top of the page, at the base of the ziggurat.

West nodded at Lily, very impressed.

'Nice work, kiddo. Glad we've got someone here who's got their head screwed on right.'

Lily beamed.

Suddenly Avenger's earpiece burst to life and he spun around to see his two rear-guards enter the Giant Stairway cave behind and below them.

'*Sir!*' one of them said over the radio. '*The Americans are crossing the first cavern! There are just too many of them! Under cover of sniper fire, they brought in pontoons and extendable ladders to cross the cavern at its base! They just had too much firepower for us! We had to retreat! Now they're coming!'*

Avenger said, 'Okay. I'll send Weitz back to guide you up the Stairway. Once you're up, set up another rear-guard position at the top. We still need every second we can get.'

Avenger turned to West. 'It's time for you to test your little girl's theory, Captain. I hope for your sake she's right. Move.'

And so following the map, West took a hesitant step off the main path, heading *left*, out over what appeared to be pure quicksand and . . .

. . . his boot landed on solid ground, on an unseen pathway hidden a couple of inches below the oozing surface of the lake.

Lily exhaled in relief.

West tested the lake on either side of the path—and found only inky quicksand of uncertain depth.

'Looks like we found the pathway,' he said.

After a quickly-sketched copy of the safe route was made and left for the rear-guards, the group ventured gingerly out across the sand-lake, led by West.

They followed the map, seemingly walking on water, on nothing but the flat surface of the wide quicksand lake, heading way out to the left, then stepping along the left-hand wall, before cutting back toward the centre of the lake and arriving at the central gazebo.

The Gazebo

The 'gazebo' structure surprised them all.

For, unlike the hidden path, its floor was *not* level with the surface of the lake. It was sunken twelve feet *below* the level of the lake, a stone rim holding back the sea of quicksand around it.

It was also solid as hell—thick-walled and sturdy.

A short and narrow flight of stone steps led down into this pit—which like the gazebo itself was also six-sided, with doors cut into every one of its sides. The structure's thick stone roof loomed over it all, a few feet above the rim, resting on its pillars, like a dark thundercloud just waiting to do its worst.

Curiously, just *inside* the walls of the hexagonal pit, forming a kind of inner wall to the structure, was a cylindrical bronze cage—also twelve feet high, made of imposing vertical bars, and criss-crossing bars across its top.

But while the pit had six doors, the circular cage had only one: which currently opened onto West's entry steps, allowing entry to the pit.

'Ah, a rotating cage . . .' Zaeed said. 'Once you enter the pit, the cage rotates, and you have to pick the correct exit door. But entering the pit will trigger the trap—hence you must survive the trap in order to cross.'

'Like that drowning cage in Tunisia,' Pooh Bear observed.

Last of all, in the exact centre of the pit, mounted on an ornate podium, stood a magnificent statue carved out of black limestone.

It was a statue of a winged lion, depicted on its hind legs in mid-spring, both forepaws raised high, it wings flared out behind it. It stood five feet tall, and its angry eyes were made of dazzling red rubies.

'The Well of the Winged Lion . . .' Zaeed said to West. 'The Nazi knew of this, too.'

They found the applicable page in Hessler's notes:

2ND INSCRIPTION FROM THE TOMB OF IMHOTEP III:

ONLY THE BRAVEST OF SOULS
SHALL PASS THE WELLS OF THE WINGED LIONS.
BUT BEWARE THE PIT OF NINGIZZIDA,
TO THOSE WHO ENTER THE SERPENT-LORD'S PIT,
I OFFER NO ADVICE BUT THIS:
ABANDON ALL HOPE,
FOR THERE IS NO ESCAPE FROM IT.
WINGED LIONS. COMMON ASSYRIAN STATUE
FOUND IN PERSIA/MESOPOTAMIA.
NINGIZZIDA: ASSYRIAN GOD OF SERPENTS +
SNAKES.
POSSIBLE REF TO THE HG OF BABYLON???

'The Nazi was right,' Zaeed said, 'it *was* a reference to the Hanging Gardens—'

Suddenly, a burst of gunfire rang out from the Giant Stairway Cavern behind them.

'*Sir! The first American squad has reached the Stairway!*' the rear-guards reported. '*Holding them off but more are on the way—and we can't hold them back forever.'*

'Delay them as long as you can, Shamburg,' Avenger said. 'We still need the time.'

He turned to West. 'What is this trap?'

West hesitated. 'I think Zaeed is right. The cage moves in a rotating circle, bringing its gate into alignment with the correct exit door of the pit, which according to the map, is that one directly opposite us—'

'Find out,' Avenger said, shoving West forward. 'Schaefer, go with him. Cover him.'

Covered at gunpoint by the Israeli trooper named Schaefer, West stepped cautiously out from his steps, through the cage's gate and onto the sunken floor of the gazebo's pit.

Imhotep's ancient warning about the well repeated over and over in his head: *only the bravest of souls shall pass.*

And then suddenly, four steps in, just as West and his companion stepped out into the centre of the pit beside the statue of the lion, the well's lethal mechanism sprang into action.

What happened next happened very, very fast.

Screeeeech!—with an ear-piercing shriek of metal on metal, the circular cage suddenly started *turning,* revolving laterally within the larger hexagonal pit, thus exposing its lone gate—for brief moments—to all six of the stone doorways surrounding the pit.

But then came the worst part.

Shhhhh!—thick gushing waterfalls of quicksand started *pouring* into the pit from above! Channels in the pit's rim had opened, allowing the quicksand lake above it to invade the pit. The pit began to flood, the quicksand level quickly rising to West's knees . . . and continuing to rise!

And instantly, with the turning of the cage and the influx of quicksand from every side, West lost his bearings.

Which, he realised, was precisely the intent of the trap.

You were *meant* to panic, you were *meant* to be disoriented . . . and so exit via the wrong doorway, where presumably worse things awaited—

His Israeli companion panicked.

As one of the revolving cage's gates came into alignment with one of the pit's stone doorways, the frightened Corporal Schaefer raced through it—

—into a narrow stairway similar to the one they had descended to get into the pit.

Only this narrow stairway went nowhere. It had no stairway.

It was just a tiny space, barely bigger than a coffin standing vertically.

Then, with shocking suddenness, an eight-foot-high bronze plate, fitted with a barred grille at head-height, slid across *into* the doorway behind Schaefer, sealing him inside the narrow space . . . and suddenly a special waterfall of quicksand began to flood into his tight vertical coffin.

As the sand rained down on his head, Schaefer screamed. It only took seconds for his little space to fill, and West watched in horror through the little face-grille as the sand consumed Schaefer, filled his screaming mouth and swallowed him whole.

The screaming stopped.

Now completely alone, West breathed, '*Fuck* me . . .'

The wider pit continued to fill with sticky quicksand—rising past his waist.

And seeing Schaefer die had made him completely lose his bearings. He didn't know which was the right exit door. He was starting to panic himself.

Only the bravest souls . . .

Only the bravest . . .

Don't panic, Jack. For God's sake, don't panic—

And then he heard Lily scream.

He spun, saw her behind the bars of the moving cage—Avenger and the others had retreated back up their entry steps, but Lily was crouched on the stairs, peering through the doorway, trying to see West.

'Daddy . . . no!' Lily yelled.

And suddenly, amid all the mayhem, all the pouring sand and the turning of the cage, time stood still for West.

Daddy?

Did she just say 'Daddy'?

And in that single flashing instant, a wave of adrenaline surged through him—a feeling that he had only ever felt once before, inside that volcano in Uganda, exactly ten years previously, when he had held her in his arms as a crying baby.

I . . . Am . . . Not . . . Going . . . To . . . Die . . .

I am not going to let her down.

Clarity returned.

Only the fucking bravest . . .

And it hit him: *Brave men don't panic. They remain calm in the face of danger.*

Right.

He spun, his mind now hyper-alert, thinking not panicking, no longer rattled by the elaborate deathtrap he found himself in.

No sooner had he done so than the answer came.

In fact, it was Lily's shout that provided the answer.

According to the map, the correct exit door was the one directly opposite *her* door.

Lily, West realised, was his advantage. Most tomb robbers would not leave someone behind in the entry doorway—they'd all walk into the pit together, go for the rubies on the winged lion, trigger the trap and lose their bearings, and then die.

'Don't give up on me, kiddo!' he called. 'I'm not dead yet!'

He started wading powerfully across the pit, past the lion statue, over toward the stone doorway opposite Lily's door. He arrived there as the swirling pool of sand reached his chest.

The cage rotated, bringing its gate into alignment with that door.

Gate and door became one.

West surged through it, pushing through the quicksand, and found himself standing in a tight coffin-sized space just like the one Schaefer had entered—and in a single horrifying instant, he knew that he'd made a terrible, terrible mistake.

No, he hadn't.

It wasn't an enclosed space at all—there was just a sharp right-angled bend in the passageway here, a bend that led to a set of narrow steps which themselves led . . . upward!

West clambered up those steps, out of the deadly pool of quicksand, and emerged in open space, on a low path again, *safely on the other side of the well.*

As he crawled onto the path, he must have depressed a trigger stone that reset the trap, because suddenly the cage rotated back to its original position and the pit drained of quicksand.

Across the top of the well, he could see Avenger.

'You're all going to have to come across!' he called. 'It'll seem disorienting, but I'll stand at the correct door. Just come to me.'

And so the rest of the group all crossed the well safely.

It took two trips, and each time the pit filled with quicksand and its cage revolved dizzyingly, but knowing the correct exit they all just forged across the quicksand and exited the pit before it had even risen to knee-height.

When she emerged out the other side, Lily leapt up into West's arms and hugged him tightly.

'Don't leave me,' she whispered.

He held her firmly. 'No matter how bad it gets, kiddo, I'll never leave you. Always remember that.'

Thus reunited, they pressed on and, following the submerged path on the other side of the gazebo, they arrived at the ziggurat that lay in the very centre of the supercavern.

And there, looming above the ziggurat like some kind of otherworldly spaceship, suspended from the cave's ceiling, impossibly huge, was the great stalactite that was the Hanging Gardens of Babylon.

They climbed the ziggurat quickly.

Very quickly. In fact, there was not a single trap on the structure's ceremonial stairway.

At first, West was surprised by this, but then he realised that this was the first Ancient Wonder they had actually *entered* on this mission.

All of the other Pieces they had encountered so far—those of the Colossus, the Pharos, the Mausoleum, the Statue of Zeus and the Temple of Artemis—had been *removed* from their original structures. They had all been guarded by trap systems built *after* the original structures had been lost or destroyed.

Not so the Gardens.

They alone remained in their original condition. And therefore the Piece they contained also remained *in its original resting place*.

But what West also realised as he climbed the ziggurat was that Imhotep III had shown *respect* for the Wonder he was defending: sure, he had surrounded it with booby traps, but out of deference to its original architect, he hadn't laid any traps on the Wonder itself.

Gunfire continued to ring out from the two Israeli rear-guards stationed on the Giant Stairway, still holding off the American force.

West and his group arrived at the peak of the ziggurat, and found themselves standing seven feet below the jagged point of the stalactite.

It was truly mind-bending to stand beneath such an enormous natural formation. It was just too big, too *immense* to comprehend. It was like standing underneath an ocean liner hanging from its stern, its bow pointed right at your nose.

Directly above them, a tight circular shaft bored up into the tip of the stalactite, driving up into its core.

But there was also a notable feature below them.

The peak of the ziggurat was flat and square—about five by five metres—but taking up nearly all of its floor-space was a wide square hole that disappeared *down* into the ziggurat, into inky darkness.

Ladder handholds ran down into this square well-like shaft, and, of course, the square shaft was perfectly aligned with the round one in the stalactite directly above it.

Zaeed bent to read an inscription on the rim of the ziggurat's square well-shaft.

'It is the Priests' Entrance,' he said to West. They both glanced at Avenger.

The Israeli commander did not seem to recognise the

term—or its importance—and by some unspoken agreement neither Zaeed nor West felt the need to enlighten him.

West, Pooh Bear and Stretch unloaded their caving equipment from their packs and started constructing a large tripod-like ladder over the square shaft.

Within minutes, they had an A-shaped ladder standing astride the square shaft and reaching up to the tip of the stalactite above it.

'Move,' Avenger nudged West forward.

West climbed the ladder, and disappeared up into the bore-hole carved into the great stalactite.

This tight vertical shaft had ladder-like handholds, too, making progress quite easy.

But it wasn't for the claustrophobic. Glistening wetness trickled down its close, tight walls.

Guided by the flashlight on his fireman's helmet, West climbed cautiously upwards until he emerged in a flat man-sized tunnel that led out to the exterior of the stalactite.

There he stepped out onto the path that spiralled up the outside of the Gardens.

By the light of his previously fired flares, he beheld the supercavern from above. The view was breathtaking. He saw the ziggurat far below him, its steps fanning outward, with the quicksand lake all around it, and—in the middle of the lake—the Well of the Winged Lion, with its star-like series of paths radiating out from it.

Interestingly, he saw that the Well had a twin on the *other* side of the ziggurat—complete with an identical semi-submerged path.

He recalled Imhotep III's words: the Gardens had been *constructed as a mirror image, where both entrance and exit were alike.*

There must be another exit out that way, he thought. And now that he thought about it, he realised that Avenger and the Israelis knew of this exit: *that was how they intended to leave all along, without being caught by the Americans.*

So Avenger wasn't entirely ignorant about this place—

'Come on, Captain,' Avenger said, arriving at West's side, rousing him from his thoughts. The rest of his team came up behind him, guiding Lily and Pooh Bear with them. 'You're not done yet.'

West led the group up the path that spiralled around the stalactite.

Everything was moist, all the overgrown foliage was like that found in a rainforest: plants and mosses that needed moisture rather than sunlight to live.

At times the going was difficult, since some of the bushes had grown out and over the path and hung off the edge, out over the drop.

Although it pained him to do it, West hacked through the fabled plants with a machete, to carve the way.

Higher and higher they went, into the upper reaches of the supercavern.

The great quicksand lake and the ziggurat fell further and further away from them. The drop down to the lake was now a clear 400 feet, dizzyingly high.

At one point along the path, they came across a surprising splash of colour: a beautiful cluster of roses. White roses.

'How can they survive here without sunlight?' Pooh Bear asked.

West was thinking the same thing, when he saw the answer: a series of tiny bore-holes cut into the rocky ceiling of the cavern. They were barely a few inches wide, but they seemed to emit *light*—natural light. The little bore-holes must have reached all the way to the surface of the mountain.

West noticed that the roses would catch daylight from some of the holes for a few moments every day—enough to keep them alive and regenerating.

'The Persian White Desert Rose,' he breathed. 'Extinct. Till now.'

'Come on,' Avenger shoved him on, oblivious to the monumental discovery. 'I'll put some of them on your grave.'

They pressed on.

On a couple of occasions the path delved *into* the stalactite—crossing through its core. Whenever it did this, the path met and crossed the claustrophobic vertical bore shaft that West had climbed into at the bottom. The shaft, it seemed, bored all the way up through the great stalactite. On these occasions, the group would just jump across the narrow shaft.

The Catwalk and the Most Holy Shrine

At length, they came to the point where the stalactite met the ceiling of the supercavern.

Here, a rotten wooden catwalk stretched out from the stalactite across the upper surface of the great cave.

The ancient catwalk threaded itself through several U-shaped beams that hung from the ceiling, and it stretched for about fifty metres before it stopped just short of a very large recess in the ceiling.

Handrungs continued from there, heading out across the ceiling and up into the dark recess. To hang from the handrungs meant dangling by your hands high above the quicksand lake 500 feet below.

'This is it,' West said. 'This is where all roads end.'

'Then go,' Avenger said. 'You may even take the Arab

with you—although I shall keep the girl with me as insurance.'

West and Pooh Bear ventured out across the ancient catwalk, high above the supercavern.

The wood creaked beneath their feet. Dust and debris fell off the catwalk's underside, sailing all the way down to the sand-lake. Twice the catwalk lurched suddenly, as if the entire assembly was going to fall.

They reached the end of the catwalk.

'I'll go first,' West said, eyeing the handrungs. 'I'll trail a return rope as I go. If the Piece is up in that recess, we'll need a rope to send it back.'

Pooh Bear nodded. 'I want to kill them all, Huntsman, for holding a gun to her head.'

'Me, too. But we have to stay alive. So long as we're breathing, we'll still have a chance to do exactly that,' West said. 'The key is to stay breathing.'

'Be careful.'

'I'll try, buddy.'

And with that, West grasped the first handrung, and swung out onto it, 500 feet above the world.

Against the spectacular backdrop of the mighty Hanging Gardens, the tiny figure of Jack West Jr swinging hand-over-hand across the rungs in the ceiling of the supercavern looked positively microscopic.

Fluttering near him, watching over him as always, was Horus.

Trailing a 'return rope' from his belt—a rope that went all the way back to Pooh Bear—he came to the large recess in the ceiling.

It was shaped like a trapezoid, with steep inwardly-slanting walls tapering upwards to a point. More hand-rungs ran in a line up the slanting wall—so that it was now like free-climbing up an overhang, with your legs hanging beneath you.

But it was the focal point of the recess—the highest point—that seized West's attention.

It was a square horizontal ledge cut into the rock, about the size of a large refrigerator.

In stark contrast to the rough rocky surface of the rest of the recess, it was ornately decorated—with gold and jewels, making it look like a shrine.

From his current position, West couldn't see inside it. He scaled the handrungs on the near side of the recess, holding his entire body up with only his arms.

He arrived at the ledge, did a strenuous chin-up to raise his head above its rim.

And his eyes widened.

Sitting there before him, mounted proudly inside this exceedingly difficult to reach altar, was a medium-sized golden trapezoid.

The Hanging Gardens Piece.

It was one of the middle Pieces, about the size of a washing basket. Too big for one man to carry by himself. He pulled out his pressure-gun, fired a piton into the rock-wall, looped his rope around it.

'Pooh Bear,' he said into his mike. 'Can you come over here? I need your help. Avenger: send some of your people to the other end of our rope to catch this when we send it back.'

Pooh Bear joined West—after a precarious climb—and together they managed to pull the Piece from its holy alcove and, placing it safely in a pulley-harness that hung from the return rope, they sent it whizzing back down the return rope to the catwalk.

Nestled in its harness, the Piece slid down the length of the rope, arrived back at the catwalk, where Avenger caught it with gleaming greedy eyes.

'*Have you got it?*' West's voice said into his earpiece.

Avenger replied: 'Yes, we have it. Thank you, Captain West, that will be all. Goodbye.'

And with that Avenger cut the return rope at his end and let it swing out over the void.

From his position, West saw the rope go slack, now only hanging from its piton at his end.

'Oh, shit! *Shit!*' he swung past Pooh Bear, moving fast down the handrungs in the slanting wall of the recess, reaching the bottom—the flat ceiling of the supercavern—just in time to see Avenger and his men run to the far end of the catwalk and toss three hand grenades behind them.

The grenades bounced along the rotten wooden catwalk.

And detonated.

The ancient catwalk never stood a chance.

The grenades exploded—and with a pained shrieking, the catwalk fell away from the ceiling . . .

. . . and sailed in a kind of slow motion all the way down to the sand-lake, 500 feet below.

West watched it all the way, knowing exactly what this meant.

With the catwalk gone, he and Pooh Bear had no way to get back to the stalactite.

The horror of their predicament hit home.

Lily and the Piece were in the hands of the escaping Israelis, the Americans were banging on the door, and now . . . *now* he and Pooh were stranded *on the ceiling* of the biggest cave he had ever seen with no way or hope of getting back.

After watching the destruction of the catwalk with grim satisfaction, Avenger scooped up Lily. He turned to head back down the stalactite's spiralling path.

'We won't be needing Captain West or the Arab anymore. Nor—' he drew his pistol—'will we be needing you, Mr Zae—'

But Mustapha Zaeed, his animal instincts ever alert, had already seen what was coming.

By the time Avenger had his pistol drawn, Zaeed had already broken into a run—dashing off down the path and into one of its cross-tunnels.

'He won't get far. Come. Let's get out of here.' With Lily in his grasp, he led his men down the path.

'Huntsman,' Pooh Bear gasped. 'I'm . . . er . . . in some trouble here . . .'

West rushed back—swinging with his hands across the rocky ceiling—to check on Pooh Bear in the recess.

Pooh was heavier than he was, with far less arm-strength. He wouldn't be able to hold himself up for long.

West swung alongside him. 'Hang in there, my friend. No pun intended.' He quickly tied the now loose return rope around and under Pooh's armpits—allowing Pooh Bear to hang from it without effort.

As for himself, West could hang from his mechanical arm longer—but not forever.

'The Israelis?' Pooh Bear asked.

'They destroyed the catwalk. Took the Piece and Lily. We're stranded.'

'If I ever catch him, I'll throttle Stretch,' Pooh Bear said. 'You know, for a moment there I actually thought he might have become one of us. But I was wrong. Dirty betrayer.'

'Pooh, right now, I'd just be happy to get out of here alive.'

The Israeli team charged back down the stalactite, with Lily and the Piece in their possession.

As they reached the tip of the great stalactite, they saw their two rear-guards come running into the super-cavern.

'*Sir! The Americans have breached the Giant Stairway! Repeat: the Americans have breached the Giant Stairway! We couldn't hold them off any longer!*'

'You held them off long enough! We have the girl and we have the Piece,' Avenger replied, grinning. 'Meet us at the ziggurat and proceed to the other side. We're going out that way!'

Stretch ran behind Avenger, saying nothing, his teeth clenched, his eyes vacant and distant, lost in thought.

The Israeli team reached the bottom of the stalactite—just in time to see Zaeed disappear down the square shaft in the top of the ziggurat: the Priests' Entrance.

Avenger didn't care.

Although killing the terrorist would have brought

him much kudos back home, Zaeed wasn't his concern here.

He had to get out.

Only then, as he clambered down the A-frame ladder at the base of the stalactite and stepped down onto the ziggurat, he saw the Americans enter the supercavern.

They came rushing in from the Giant Stairway entrance. But it wasn't the superlarge force of men he was expecting, it was just ten men.

And oddly, they *didn't* venture out across the quicksand lake.

No.

Rather, this small group started free-climbing up the sheer wall *above* that entrance, the wall that had filled in the old Grand Archway.

And there they—

'Oh, no . . .' Avenger breathed.

—started planting explosives, heavy-duty Tritonal 80/20 demolition charges.

The Americans worked fast, laying their charges and then getting the hell out of the way.

The result when it came was as spectacular as it was destructive.

With a colossal series of *booms*, the demolition charges went off.

The rockwall filling up the Grand Archway of the Hanging Gardens of Babylon was ripped apart by twenty simultaneous blasts. Great starbursts of rock sprayed out from it.

But the charges had been directional, forcing the bulk of the debris to be flung toward the outside world. Only a few smaller boulders landed in the quicksand lake.

Giant holes were opened in the rockwall.

Shafts of sunshine blazed in through them.

And daylight flooded into the supercavern for the first time in 2,000 years, illuminating it gloriously—and in the brilliant light of day, the Gardens took on a whole new level of splendour.

Then these many holes collapsed, forming one great 50-metre-wide hole and through this opening, following hard on the heels of the sunlight, came the American helicopters, roaring into the supercavern with a fury.

West couldn't believe what was happening.

First, he'd been left for dead up in the recess by Avenger.

And now he could only watch in stunned awe as the entire cavern beneath him was flooded with light.

Six, then seven, then eight American choppers—Black Hawks and Apaches—banked and buzzed around the immense cavern, hovering above the ancient ziggurat, rising alongside the great stalactite, searching for the enemy, searching for the Piece.

The roar of their rotors in the cavern was deafening, the wind that they generated, swirling.

Then West saw one of the Black Hawks rise up directly beneath him, saw the circular speed-blur of its rotors, and he thought, *If I fell now, at least death would be quick.*

But the Black Hawk hadn't seen him and Pooh Bear—it was peering *at the stalactite*, searching . . .

It moved closer to the stalactite, for a better look, and suddenly it wasn't directly beneath West anymore.

And West saw a way out of his predicament. It was totally crazy, but it might work . . .

He sprang into action.

'Pooh Bear, get a handhold. I need that rope and piton.'

Pooh Bear obliged, grabbed a handrung, while—one-handed—West disengaged the piton and wound in the rope. It was about fifty feet in length.

Then he said, 'Okay, Pooh, now let go of the hand-rung and grab my waist.'

'What!'

'Just do it.'

Pooh Bear did. Now he hung from West . . . as West hung from his superstrong mechanical hand, gripping a handrung.

And then West let go.

They dropped from the ceiling.

Straight down.

They shot like a bullet past the tail of the Black Hawk . . .

. . . and as they did so, West hurled his piton—still attached to the rope—*at* the Black Hawk's landing wheels!

Like a grappling hook, the steel piton looped around the rear landing wheels of the helicopter . . . and caught.

The rope played out before—*snap!*—it went taut and suddenly West and Pooh Bear were *swinging*, suspended from the helicopter's landing gear, swooping in toward the giant stalactite!

The helicopter lurched slightly with their added weight, but it held its hovering position, anchoring their swing.

They swung in a long swooping arc right over to the path on the flank of the stalactite, where West and Pooh Bear dismounted deftly and released the rope, now back in the game.

'Never thought I'd be happy to see Judah arrive,' West said. 'Come on! We've got to save Lily.'

They charged down the path at breakneck speed.

Chaos. Mayhem.

Blazing sunlight.

The roar of helicopters, and now . . .

. . . hundreds of American regular troops flooded in through the newly-opened Grand Arch.

Avenger's Israeli team danced down the far side of the ziggurat and raced out over the quicksand lake on that side. As West had seen before, this side was the mirror image of the entry side: it also featured a concealed path just below the surface with a hexagonal well in its centre.

Avenger's team reached the well, raced down into it in two sub-groups, beheld another statue of a proud winged lion.

Avenger and the two Israelis carrying the Piece went first. The trap sprang into action. Quicksand flooded in. The one-gate cage revolved. But they sloshed through the inky sand and emerged from the other side with little difficulty.

Stretch, the other two Israeli commandos, and Lily went next.

Again the trap initiated. Quicksand poured into the hexagonal well. The cage rotated. They sloshed across it, knee-deep.

And suddenly Lily tripped and fell.

The rising quicksand had caught her feet and she stumbled to all fours with a squeal.

The sand grabbed her, sticky and foul.

She screamed in terror.

Stretch and the other two Israelis spun, saw her struggling. They were almost at the exit doorway and the cage's rotating gate was about to let them out.

Avenger called from the doorway, 'Leave her! We have the Piece! She was only a bonus! It's the Piece that matters, and if we don't get it out, this will all have been for nothing! Move!'

The two commandos with Stretch didn't need to be told twice. They sloshed toward the gate and slipped through it.

Stretch, however, paused.

With quicksand flooding in from every side and the cage turning dizzyingly around him, he looked back at Lily.

The little girl was struggling against the rising quicksand pool, whimpering vainly with the effort. The sand had wrapped itself around her like a constricting snake, it was up to her neck now, consuming her, dragging her under.

'Cohen!' Avenger called. '*Leave her!* That's an order!'

And with a final look at Lily, Stretch made his fateful decision.

Flanked by the flying Horus, West and Pooh Bear were bolting down the spiralling path on the stalactite when suddenly the foliage beside them was ripped apart by helicopter gunfire.

One of the American Apache choppers had swung into a hover right next to them and was now lining them up in its minigun sights!

They dived into a nearby cross-tunnel just as the Apache's six-barrelled minigun whirred to life—and came to the vertical bore-hole that ran up the centre of the rock formation.

'They're *firing* at the Hanging Gardens of Babylon!' Pooh Bear exclaimed. 'Have Americans no respect for history!'

Moments later, they emerged from the same bore-hole at the lowermost tip of the stalactite, having slid all the way down it with their hands and feet braced against its walls.

West jumped down onto the peak of the ziggurat, snapped round to check on the progress of Avenger's fleeing Israeli team.

'Jesus, no . . .' he breathed.

He spied Avenger and four of his men just as they disappeared through an exit tunnel at the far end of the supercavern, having navigated the quicksand lake and the well on that side.

Stretch wasn't with them.

Nor was Lily.

And then West saw the well.

Peering under its canopied stone roof, he could see that the hexagonal well was just then overflowing with quicksand—*completely* filled.

'Oh, no. *No* . . .' West stared at the scene in horror.

Worse still, at that very moment, two American Black Hawk helicopters were landing on the star-shaped paths surrounding the well.

Troops charged out from the choppers, converging on the well from opposite sides.

Marshall Judah himself stepped out of one of the choppers, directing the operation.

'Oh, Lily . . .' West breathed, frozen, stunned.

At the hexagonal well, a CIEF trooper called to Judah: 'Sir, you better come and see this.'

Judah strode to the edge of the well.

And he was surprised by what he saw.

There, pressed *right up* against the roof-bars of the cage inside the well—her face upturned, with only her mouth and nose and eyes protruding above the surface of the quicksand pool that now filled the well, breathing shallowly and desperately, her lips puckered, was Lily.

Judah wondered how on God's Earth she had got into this life-saving position.

The cage—and the well—must have been at least twelve feet deep. Caught in the grip of the sand, she could never have reached up and grabbed the cage's roof-bars and lifted herself out—

There must be someone else in there, he figured. *Holding her up.*

Then Judah saw it.

But only barely, it was so small.

He saw the tip of a *gunbarrel* protruding a centimetre above the surface of the quicksand pool right next to Lily's upturned face. It was the tip of a sniper rifle's gunbarrel—an ultralong Barrett M82A1A sniper rifle.

Only this gunbarrel was not being used for its original purpose.

It was being used as a snorkel by whoever was holding Lily up from below!

It wasn't until he had the well-trap reset and drained of quicksand that Judah fully appreciated the scene underneath Lily.

As the quicksand drained away, he beheld Stretch, standing on top of the statue of the winged lion that itself stood in the centre of the well, his own face upturned, breathing through the barrel of his disassembled Barrett sniper rifle, with Lily balancing on his shoulders in a perfect ballet toe-pose!

Stretch had indeed made his decision.

It would turn out to be a very good one, but for another reason entirely: for Judah would take him and Lily away alive.

Avenger and his team of Israeli commandos would not be so lucky.

For at the secret rear entrance to the Hanging Gardens, an American CIEF squad led by Cal Kallis was waiting for them.

And Kallis had strict orders *not* to be merciful.

Avenger and his Israelis—thinking they had got away with the Piece—emerged from the underground tunnel system to see their extraction helicopter lying nearby, charred and smoking, destroyed, its pilots shot dead.

They also found themselves surrounded by Kallis's team.

The Israelis were quickly disarmed. Then, slowly and deliberately, Cal Kallis executed them all himself—one by one, shooting each man in the head, killing Avenger last of all, smiling meanly the whole time. This was the kind of thing Kallis *enjoyed*.

Then he took the Piece from their dead hands and flew away, leaving the corpses for the desert birds to feast upon.

And so West watched, helpless, as Lily and Stretch were bundled into Judah's helicopter—

—at which moment, a wave of gunfire smacked down all around him, from two Apache attack choppers that appeared suddenly from behind the stalactite.

Horus squawked.

West moved too late.

But Pooh Bear didn't.

And he saved West's life—yanking him out of the line of fire and down into the square-shaped well-shaft of the ziggurat.

Down on the floor of the supercavern, Judah snapped round to see the cause of the commotion.

He glimpsed the two tiny figures of Pooh Bear and West up on the peak of the ziggurat—saw Pooh pull West down into the well-shaft that descended into the ziggurat, the shaft known as the Priests' Entrance.

'Jack . . .' Judah whispered. 'Alas, you've served your purpose. You're no longer a protected species. Time for you to die.'

Judah returned to his heavily-armed Black Hawk, with Stretch and Lily as his captives. The chopper lifted off and zoomed out of the cavern.

It was quickly followed by the other choppers: the

Apaches and the Black Hawks. The American troops covering the liquid floor of the cavern also pulled out, exiting through the blasted-open Great Arch.

Once all his people were out, Judah—still eyeing the top of the ziggurat, the last place he had seen West alive—gave his final order.

'Fire into the stalactite. Bring it down on that ziggurat.'

His pilot hesitated. 'But sir . . . this place is histori—'

'*Fire into the stalactite now or I will have you thrown out of this helicopter.*'

The pilot complied.

Moments later, three Hellfire missiles lanced out from the missile pod of the Black Hawk, their three matching smoketrails spiralling in toward the giant rock formation . . .

. . . and they hit.

Shuddering explosions. Starbursts of rock and foliage.

And then, a momentous groaning sound as—

—the great stalactite slowly peeled off the ceiling of the supercavern, tilting precariously before . . . it fell away from the ceiling.

It sounded like the end of humanity. The sound was deafening.

Great chunks of rock were ripped away from the ceiling as the upside-down mountain fell away from it and crashed down onto the ziggurat.

The tip of the stalactite slammed down against the peak of the ziggurat and the ziggurat—itself the size of a fifteen-storey building—was just *crushed* like an aluminium can, compressed horribly downwards, *totally* destroyed.

Then the great rock formation tipped sideways like a slow-falling tree and splashed down into the quicksand lake on the inner side of the supercavern.

The stalactite hitting the lake had the impact of an aircraft carrier being dropped from a great height into the ocean. An enormous wave of rolling quicksand fanned out from the impact zone, slapping hard against every wall of the supercavern.

Then slowly, very slowly, the stalactite—the fabled Hanging Gardens of Babylon—came to rest, on its side, half-submerged in the wide quicksand lake, just another broken rock formation in a world of broken things.

Thus, the American force left the foothills of the Zagros Mountains with everything they had come for in their grasp: Lily-*and* the Piece.

And somewhere underneath all the wreckage and destruction they left behind—with no possible chance of survival—were Jack West Jr and Pooh Bear.

SIXTH MISSION
ISKENDER'S TOMB

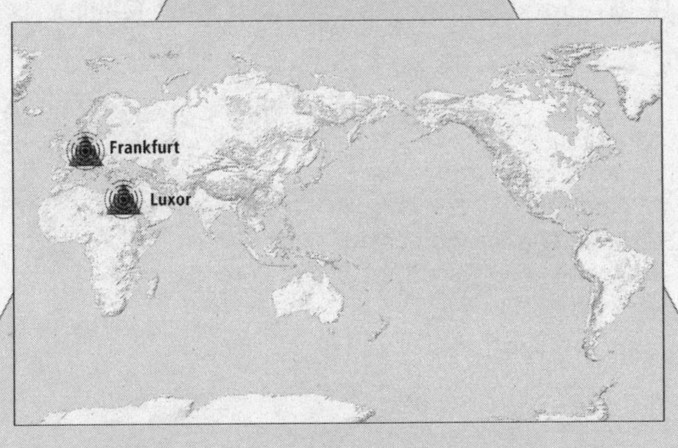

FRANKFURT, GERMANY
LUXOR, EGYPT
19 MARCH, 2006
THE DAY BEFORE TARTARUS

MESSE TOWER

FRANKFURT, GERMANY

19 MARCH, 2006, 1500 HOURS

1 DAY BEFORE THE ARRIVAL OF TARTARUS

At the same time as the Hanging Gardens of Babylon were crashing into oblivion, Wizard, Zoe and Fuzzy were being transported via limousine—under armed guard—from the airfield at Frankfurt Military Base into the city of Frankfurt.

After they'd been captured in Rome, Wizard and his team had been taken by Lear jet to Germany. Having been held overnight at the base on the outskirts of Frankfurt, they were now being taken to the headquarters of the European coalition: the Messe Tower in central Frankfurt.

The Messe Tower is one of the tallest skyscrapers in Europe. It stands fifty storeys high and is known for one singular feature: its peak is a magnificent glass pyramid. More importantly—but far less well-known—this pyramid has been 'sectioned' horizontally just like the Golden Capstone.

But when a pyramid surmounts a shaft-like column like a tower, it becomes something more again: it becomes an obelisk.

The ultimate symbol of Sun-worship.

Conspiracy theories abound that the Messe Tower,

the Canary Wharf Tower in London, and the old World Financial Center in New York—all built in the shape of giant glass obelisks—formed a modern triumvirate of 'super-obelisks' built by the two Sun-worshipping cults: the Catholic Church and the Freemasons.

Wizard thought about these theories as he, Zoe and Fuzzy were brought, handcuffed, to the uppermost floor of the Messe Tower.

They stood inside its spectacular pyramid-shaped pinnacle. Its slanting floor-to-ceiling glass walls revealed a 360-degree view of Frankfurt and its surrounding rivers and forests.

Francisco del Piero was waiting for them.

'Maximilian Epper! My old seminary classmate. Oh, how the Church lost a great mind when it lost you. It's good to see you again, my old friend.'

'I'm not your friend, Francisco. What is this about?'

'*What is this about?* What it's *always* been about, Max: power. The eternal struggle for one man to rule over another. Call it Europe v America. Call it the Church v the Freemasons. It doesn't matter. It is all one and the same. A ceaseless battle for power that has lasted generations, all of it coming to a head tomorrow, at a once-in-5,000-years event, an event which can grant absolute power: the arrival of the Tartarus Sunspot.'

Wizard glanced at Zoe, 'Now you can see why I never went through with becoming a priest.' To del Piero: 'But the Americans have four of the Pieces. You have one, and the last two remain unaccounted for.'

'Max. It is not who holds the Pieces *now* that matters, but who holds them when Tartarus arrives,' del Piero said. 'And we will have all the Pieces soon enough. Thanks to your courageous Captain West, we now know that the Tomb of Alexander lies in Luxor—its location to be revealed by the focused rays of the rising Sun shining through the obelisks at the Luxor Temple. The Americans know this, too.

'But when they arrive at Luxor, we shall be waiting for them. As I say, it is not who holds the Pieces now that matters, but who holds them when Tartarus arrives. *We* shall hold them when Tartarus arrives.'

'We?' Wizard said.

'Oh yes, I don't believe you've met my young friend and greatest ally . . .'

Del Piero stepped aside to reveal a small boy, with dark hair, darker eyes and really dark frowning eyebrows. Just in the way he stood and glared at Wizard, the boy had a disconcerting air of superiority about him.

'Max Epper, meet Alexander, son of the Oracle of Siwa, expert in the Language of Thoth and the vessel of Tartarus.'

'Hello there,' Wizard said.

The boy said nothing.

Del Piero said, 'He has been groomed since the day he was born—'

'The day you stole him from his mother's arms . . .'

'He has been groomed since the day he was born for tomorrow's event. His command of Thoth is unrivalled. His understanding of the ceremony unmatched. This boy was born to rule, and I have personally inculcated in him the mindset of the perfect ruler. He is strong, he is firm, he is wise . . . and he is *uncompromising*, intolerant of the weak and the foolish.'

'I thought all the greatest rulers governed *for* the weak,' Wizard said, 'not over them.'

'Oh, Max, I love your idealism! So noble yet so fundamentally flawed. How about this theory: the strong rule, the weak get ruled over. Some are born to rule;

most are ruled over. After tomorrow, you will be in the latter group.'

Zoe looked at the boy, Alexander. He returned her gaze coldly, without emotion.

'Hey kid,' she said. 'You ever played Splinter Cell in dual-player mode?'

Del Piero frowned, not understanding. But the boy knew what Splinter Cell was.

'It is a game. Games are tools by which we the rulers keep the masses entertained and amused,' the boy replied. 'Games are for fools. I do not play *games*.'

'Is that right? Some games teach us lessons that we can use in our everyday lives,' Zoe said. 'Have you ever thought about that?'

'I do not have an everyday life.'

'You want to know what I learned from playing Splinter Cell in dual-player mode?'

'Enthral me.'

'It's always nice to know someone's watching your back,' Zoe said. 'My question for you, Alexander, is this: when the going gets tough, who's gonna be watching *your* back?' A dismissive nod at del Piero: 'Him?' A disdainful glance at the guards arrayed around the room: 'Them?'

'And who, may I ask, watches your backs?' del Piero shot back.

'Jack West Jr,' Wizard said firmly.

'Hmm, the famous Captain West,' del Piero nodded. 'Although following his exploits in Paris yesterday, I fear you might be a little behind on current events. Your friend, Mr West, turned up in southern Iraq today, where he uncovered no less than the Hanging Gardens of Babylon.'

'Go Jack . . .' Zoe said.

But Wizard frowned. He didn't know about West's last-gasp mission to Iraq—nor was he aware of its origins in the American ambush in Kenya and the loss of the Zeus Piece, Big Ears and Doris.

'I hate to dampen your celebrations, Ms Kissane,' del Piero said, 'but I fear Captain West encountered an American force of nearly 10,000 men in Iraq. What actually happened, I do not know. All I know from our intercepts is that they clashed.'

'And . . .' Wizard couldn't hide his concern.

Del Piero threw Wizard a transcript of a communications intercept—an intercept that was only fifteen minutes old. It read:

TRANS INTERCEPT
SAT BT-1009/03.19.06-1445
A44-TEXT TRANSMISSION
FROM: UNKNOWN SOURCE/AIRBORNE ORIGIN (IRAQ)
TO: UNKNOWN DESTINATION, MARYLAND (USA)

VOICE 1 (JUDAH): Haritha mission is a success. We have the H-G piece in our possession, <u>and the girl</u>. En route to Egypt now. Will arrive Luxor 0200 hours local time, 20 March. Imperative that we be there at dawn to take measurements through the remaining obelisk at Luxor Temple.

VOICE 2 (USA): What of this coalition of small nations? What news of them?

VOICE 1 (JUDAH): Encountered them at the H-G. Met with minimal resistance. West dead. Data from biometric tracer chip in his cerebellum confirms this. Is the next stage ready?

VOICE 2 (USA): It is. The Egyptian Government has been informed of your impending arrival in Luxor. They are being most co-operative, albeit for a price. The platform at Giza has been erected to your specifications and the entire plateau has been closed to the public under the guise of repair work.

VOICE 1 (JUDAH): Thank you. Recommend operation continue from here in utmost secrecy. Have only a small force meet me in Luxor to carry out the mission there: 100 men, no more. We do not want to attract too much attention.

VOICE 2 (USA): It will be done.

Wizard's face fell as he gazed at the terrible words: 'West dead'.

'The Americans have too much confidence,' del Piero said, stepping forward. 'When they arrive in Luxor, their 100-man force will encounter a European force three times that size. You can mourn the loss of Captain West another time, Max, for your part in this drama is not yet done—I still have another use for you.

'It is time for you to join me on the final leg of this

journey, a journey that will end with Alexander fulfilling his destiny. It is time for us to meet this American force in Egypt and steal its Pieces. It is time to go to Luxor.'

THE PRIESTS' ENTRANCE,
HANGING GARDENS OF BABYLON
EAST OF HARITHA, IRAQ
19 MARCH, 2006, 1800 HOURS LOCAL TIME
(1400 HOURS IN FRANKFURT)

1 DAY BEFORE THE ARRIVAL OF TARTARUS

An hour earlier.

As the stalactite containing the Hanging Gardens of Babylon crashed down onto the ziggurat underneath it, down in the tunnels of the Priests' Entrance, Jack West and Pooh Bear were running headlong down a long stone passageway whose roof was *caving-in* close behind them! The collapsing roof seemed to be chasing after them like the chomping jaws of an ever-gaining monster.

As soon as he'd heard the impacts of Judah's missiles hitting the Gardens, West had realised Judah's intention.

'He's trying to crash the Gardens onto us!' he said to Pooh Bear. 'Run! *Run!*'

And so they'd bolted. Fast, with Horus fluttering above them.

Down the vertical shaft of the Priests' Entrance—avoiding some traps along the way—until it had opened onto this horizontal passageway.

Then the stalactite had landed on the ziggurat and the structure had started collapsing behind them—which was how West, Pooh Bear and Horus came to be here now, hurdling traps, running in total desperation from the collapsing ceiling and crushing death.

It was also why they almost ran right into the next trap.

It came upon them with startling suddenness—a narrow but exceedingly deep pit with hard blackstone walls and a quicksand floor. In fact, though much smaller, it was very similar to the first quicksand pit they had traversed earlier: their entrance was right up near the ceiling, opposite a matching exit on the far side; a set of about thirty handrungs joined the two openings.

One big difference, however, was the intricate engravings on the walls of this pit. They were *covered* with images of snakes—and in the very centre of the main wall, one supersized image of a serpent wrapped around a tree.

'Ningizzida, the serpent-god . . .' West said, seeing the serpent image. 'The Pit of Ningizzida . . .'

But then movement caught West's eye and he saw a figure standing in the far exit doorway having just traversed the pit.

The figure turned, saw West, and grinned meanly. It was Mustapha Zaeed.

West glanced from the collapsing tunnel behind him to Zaeed.

'Zaeed! What's the sequence of the handrungs!'

Zaeed eyed West slyly. 'I fear I have run out of advice for you, Captain! But I thank you for breaking me out of Guantanamo Bay. You have enabled me to continue on my quest for the Capstone. Although I will give you one piece of knowledge that I imagine the good Professor Epper neglected to tell you: for Tartarus to be tamed, your girl must be sacrificed. Thank you and goodbye. You are on your own now!'

And with that, the terrorist vanished, disappearing down his passageway, leaving West and Pooh Bear stuck on their ledge, with their collapsing tunnel rushing forward fast!

'Huntsman!' Pooh Bear urged. 'What do we do?'

West spun, saw the collapsing tunnel behind them. It was certain death to stay here.

He turned to see the wide deep pit before him, the Pit of Ningizzida, and a flashing memory raced across his mind, a page from the Nazi diary:

> *BUT BEWARE THE PIT OF NINGIZZIDA,*
> TO THOSE WHO ENTER THE SERPENT-LORD'S PIT,
> I OFFER NO ADVICE BUT THIS:
> ABANDON ALL HOPE,
> FOR THERE IS NO ESCAPE FROM IT.

So it was also certain death to enter the Pit.

Certain death v certain death.

Some choice.

'Screw it,' West said. 'Grab the rungs . . . Go!'

And out they swung, over the deep quicksand pit, *just as* a billowing blast of dust exploded out from the collapsing tunnel behind them.

The eighth handrung broke in West's grasp . . . and he fell.

Pooh Bear avoided it—but the tenth one got him, and he also dropped, down into the quicksand, joining West in the Pit from which there was no escape.

West and Pooh Bear landed in the quicksand with twin goopy splashes.

West made to lie on his back, to spread his body-weight and thus avoid sinking . . . when abruptly, four feet below the surface of the quicksand, his feet struck the bottom.

They could stand in here . . .

So he and Pooh Bear stood, chest-deep in the deep pit.

The walls around them were slick and sheer, made of diorite.

'This isn't so bad . . .' Pooh Bear said. 'I don't see why Imhotep said this was escape-proof—'

It was precisely then that the *ceiling* of the pit—the flat section of stone containing the handrungs—began to *lower*. Its great square bulk fitted the pit's four walls perfectly.

The intention was clear: the lowering ceiling—itself a two-ton slab of stone—pushed you down *into* the quicksand, drowning you.

It was only a lightning-quick swoop from Horus that saved her from the descending ceiling. As the trap sprang into action, she darted like a rocket for the exit tunnel and zoomed into it just as the lowering ceiling rumbled past the tunnel, closing it off.

From her position here, she could see the ceiling's operating mechanism on the *top* side of the descending slab—

the ceiling was suspended from a pair of thick chains which themselves hung out from a wide shaft in the roof. They clanked loudly as they lowered the deadly ceiling.

Just then in the Pit, Pooh Bear spotted movement.

Saw the spotted body of an outrageously enormous python come slithering out of a wall-hole and dive into the quicksand pool!

'Huntsman!'

'I know, there are three more on this side!' He called up at the ceiling: 'Horus! Reset the bucket! Reset the bucket!'

There were three more wall-holes arrayed around the Pit . . . and they too were spewing forth the long speckled bodies of pythons.

'*Ningizzida* . . .' West said, staring at the snakes. 'The Assyrian serpent-god, also known as the God of the Tree of Life: Christianity basically stole him and placed him in the Garden of Eden as the snake who tempts Eve to eat the apple from the tree.'

The ceiling was halfway down and closing fast.

The snakes slithered across the surface of the quicksand pool, moving with intent.

One wrapped itself around West's right leg and reared up around him, jaws bared wide. West, since he had no gun to shoot it with, just jammed an X-bar into its wide-open mouth. The snake froze in confusion, its mouth now held bizarrely open, hyper-extended, with no way of dislodging the X-bar in it. It slithered off West's body, shaking its head violently, disappearing into the sand.

'Horus!' West yelled. 'What are you doing up there?'

Horus zoomed up the chain-shaft, following the ceiling's mighty chains as they stretched upward, bent over a large bronze pulley, and then *descended* back down another wider shaft.

Folding over the pulley, the chains shot down this new shaft, where at their other end they upheld . . . a gigantic clay bucket. It was easily ten feet wide: the world's biggest bucket. And next to it flowed a healthy little waterfall, pouring out of a man-made drain.

Right now, the bucket hung askew, at right-angles, tipped over on some hinges, its open top facing sideways. If it had been sitting in the upright position, it would have *received* the flowing water from the waterfall . . . and filled up . . . and hence via the chains, *hauled up* the movable ceiling in Ningizzida's Pit.

Known as a 'water-based mechanism', this was the standard operating system behind all Egyptian moving-wall traps.

It was an ingenious system devised by the first Imhotep, and was remarkable for its simplicity. All it needed to work were three things: gravity, water . . . and a pulley.

When West had grabbed the wrong handrung, he had triggered a catch which had tipped the (full) bucket.

Now, when *filled* with water, the great bucket perfectly counterbalanced the ceiling slab. But when upturned, the bucket emptied, and thus the ceiling—now outweighing it—lowered.

There was a second trigger stone on the floor of the Pit—the 'reset' switch—which, when eventually hit by the lowering ceiling stone, would right the giant bucket, and allow it to fill again, thus raising the ceiling back to its resting position, ready to strike once again.

As such, there truly was no escape from Ningizzida's Pit. It offered no tricks, no riddles, no secret exits. Once you were in it, you did not leave.

Unless you had a companion like Horus.

Flying fast, Horus swooped up the chain-shaft, past the pulley, and down toward the big clay bucket.

There she landed and hopping around, searched for the reset catch that righted the giant tub.

In the Pit, the ceiling was still lowering fast. It was only seven feet above the surface now and closing quickly.

The pythons circled, moving in on West and Pooh Bear.

Without warning, one dived under the surface—and reappeared slithering up Pooh's body with frightening speed! It constricted violently, trying to crack his spine—just as Pooh Bear swiped hard with his K-Bar knife and the python froze in mid-action. Then its head fell from its body.

The ceiling kept descending.

Five feet.

West was very worried now.

Four feet.

The pythons cut and run—fleeing for their wall-holes, knowing what was about to happen.

Three feet . . .

'*Horus . . . !*' West yelled.

In the bucket-shaft, Horus searched patiently, just as she had been taught.

And she found the reset catch: a little hinged hook that, when released, righted the empty bucket.

Horus bit into the hook with her tiny beak . . .

★

Two feet . . .

West called: 'Horus! Come *on!* You can do this! Just like we practised at home!'

One foot . . .

He and Pooh Bear now had only their upturned faces above the surface of the quicksand.

Six inches . . .

'Take a deep breath, Pooh,' West said.

They both sucked in as much oxygen as they could hold.

In the bucket-shaft, Horus continued to bite at the reset hook. It wouldn't budge.

In the Pit, the lowering ceiling met the surface of the quicksand . . . and touched it, pushing West and Pooh Bear under—

—just as Horus got a good grip on the hook with her beak . . . *and lifted it!*

The response was instantaneous.

With a silent lurch, the great empty bucket rolled upwards on its hinges, offering its open mouth to the cascade of water pouring down above it.

The bucket immediately began to fill with water.

And with the added weight, the great clay bucket now began to *lower* on its chains . . .

. . . which by virtue of the pulley now pulled the ceiling of the Pit upward . . .

★

. . . raising it off the quicksand pool!

West and Pooh Bear burst up from underneath the quicksand, gasping for air.

As the ceiling above them rose, they grabbed the two handrungs nearest the exit-end, and allowed the ceiling to hoist them all the way up the Pit.

Hauled up by its water mechanism, the ceiling slab returned to its original position, and West and Pooh suddenly found themselves hanging in front of the exit tunnel—where Horus now sat proudly, staring triumphantly up at West.

He swung into the tunnel, crouched before her, gave her a much-loved rat treat.

Horus gobbled it up whole.

'Thank you, my friend, nice work,' he said. 'You saved our bacon. Imhotep didn't count on grave-robbers having friends like you. Now let's get the hell out of here.'

Through the Priests' Entrance they bolted—West, Pooh Bear and Horus.

Ten minutes later, they emerged from an inconspicuous cleft in a rocky hillside, a barren desolate hillside that faced onto a barren desolate valley that appeared to have no natural exits. The valley was on the Iranian side of the Hanging Gardens, far from the waterfall entrance on the Iraqi side.

But it was so inhospitable, so bleak, that no human being had had any reason to come here for 2,000 years.

West froze as a thought struck him.

There was no sign of Mustapha Zaeed.

He wondered where Zaeed had got to. Had he at some point on this journey called his terrorist pals and told them to pick him up here?

West thought about that: perhaps Zaeed had triggered a locater signal when they'd stopped by at his old hideout cave in Saudi Arabia. West knew Zaeed had grabbed other things while they were there, including the beautiful black-jade box filled with fine sand.

He considered the rogue signal that he'd picked up on the *Halicarnassus* on the way to Iraq. He'd first believed it had been sent out by Stretch, alerting the Israelis to their location.

But something Avenger had said to Stretch inside the Gardens now made West revise that belief. When he had first appeared, Avenger had said to Stretch: 'I apologise for surprising you in this way.'

Stretch hadn't known of the impending arrival of Avenger's team.

The Israelis had been tracking him *and he hadn't known*. Now West believed that the Israelis had been tracking Stretch from the very start via some other kind of bug—probably a surgically-implanted locater chip that Stretch never knew he'd been carrying.

Granted, the signal from the *Halicarnassus* could also have been sent by Zaeed—alerting his allies to his whereabouts—but West doubted that.

He actually had another theory about that rogue signal, a theory that made him sick to his stomach.

But now, right now, he worried if by breaking Zaeed out of Guantanamo Bay he had unleashed an unspeakable terror on the world.

Zaeed wasn't going to abandon his quest for the Capstone, not when he knew where the final Piece could be found, not when it was this close. The terrorist wasn't out of this race. He would reappear before the end.

West radioed Sky Monster and arranged to rendezvous with the *Halicarnassus* on some flat ground at the far end of the valley, then he and Pooh Bear headed out across the valley on foot.

They never saw the lone figure crouched on the rocky hill high above them watching them as they did so.

Never saw the figure pursue them from a careful distance.

Twenty-five minutes later, West and Pooh Bear, with Horus, strode up the rear loading ramp of the *Halicarnassus*, dirty, bruised and beaten.

Inside the main cabin, West paced, thinking aloud. Pooh Bear and Sky Monster just watched him.

'Every move we've made, Judah's known it ahead of time,' he said. 'We arrived in the Sudan, and he showed up soon after. Tunisia, the same. And in Kenya, hell, he got there *before* we did. He was waiting for us. And now Iraq.'

'It's like he's had a beacon on us all along,' Pooh Bear said. 'A tracing signal.'

West pursed his lips, repeated Judah's taunt from before: '"*There is nowhere you can go that I cannot follow. There is nowhere on this Earth you can hide from me.*" I think he's had a tracking beacon on us all along.'

'What? How? *Who?*'

West looked hard at Pooh Bear.

'Four missing days, Pooh. Four missing days from my life.'

'What are you talking about, Huntsman?' Sky Monster asked.

'Zaeed had a chip in the neck, implanted while he was imprisoned in Cuba, making him forever traceable by the Americans. I can't account for four days of my life,

Pooh, four days *when I was exclusively in American hands*.'

West stood up abruptly and grabbed the AXS-9 digital spectrum analyser—the same bug detector that he had used before to test for the locater chip in Zaeed's neck.

He flicked it on, and fanned it over Pooh's entire body. Nothing. No bugs.

Sky Monster was next. Also nothing. As expected.

West looked at them both . . .

. . . before he turned the wand on himself, running it up his entire body.

Legs: nothing.

Waist: nothing.

Chest: nothing.

Then the spectrum analyser came level with his head, and it started beeping off the charts.

Pooh Bear and Sky Monster gasped, speechless.

West just closed his eyes, cursing himself.

All the time he'd thought there had been a traitor in their midst—in particular, Stretch or Zaeed—but there had been no such traitor.

It had been *him*.

He had been the one leading the Americans to their location every single time.

Four days of his life: those four days he had spent in that American military hospital after his accident in the wargame exercises at Coronado.

Four days during which the Americans had tagged him with a microchip, so that they could keep track of him over the ensuing years.

Why? Who knew—because he had talent, because they wanted to keep track of *everyone*, friend and foe alike.

West couldn't believe it. Australia was a close ally of America's. And this was how the US treated it. America, it seemed, treated its allies no differently than its enemies. No, it was simpler than that: America treated *everyone* outside the US as a potential enemy.

He thought about Judah. Somewhere amid Judah's equipment there was a GPS-equipped computer with a map of the world on it and a little blinking blip that represented Jack West Jr—a blip that had represented him *for nearly 15 years*.

The Americans had known about the safehouse in Kenya since Day One.

Likewise they had known about the mine in the Sudan from the moment he'd got there; it was the same for the Tunisian coast—which only West and Wizard knew about. It also meant that Judah and the Americans would know it was West who had busted Zaeed out of Guantanamo Bay. They wouldn't have liked that.

West strode across the cabin, watched in stunned silence by Pooh and Sky Monster. Over by the rear-most console, he picked up the EMP gun that he had used before to neutralise the locater chip inside Zaeed's neck.

He pointed it at his head like a man about to shoot himself—

—and he pressed the trigger.

At that very moment, inside a US Black Hawk helicopter landing in Basra, a technician at a portable GPS-equipped computer snapped up.

'Colonel Judah, sir! Jack West's locater signal just dropped out.'

'Where was he when the signal disappeared?'

'Judging by the GPS, still in the vicinity of the Hanging Gardens,' the tech said.

Judah smiled. 'That tracer's biometric, grafted onto the living tissue of his brain. If West dies, the tracer chip dies with him. He must have been wounded by the collapse of the ziggurat and held on this long before he died. Rest in peace, Jack . . . never knowing that you led us every step of the fucking way. Fortunately, we don't need you anymore. Kallis. Feed the men, replenish their arms, and set a course for Luxor.'

LUXOR TEMPLE
EAST BANK, LUXOR

HATSHEPSUT'S MORTUARY TEMPLE
WEST BANK, LUXOR

LUXOR INTERNATIONAL AIRPORT
LUXOR, SOUTHERN EGYPT
20 MARCH, 2006, 0200 HOURS
THE DAY OF TARTARUS

In the early hours of the morning on the day the Tartarus Sunspot would turn to face the Earth, three hundred European troops lay in wait around Luxor International Airport, ready to ambush the American force arriving in the southern Egyptian city that night.

Bisected by the River Nile, Luxor is a fairly large town. Heavily dependent on tourism, on its East Bank one will find the Karnak and Luxor temples, two of the most impressive sites in Egypt. The Luxor Temple sits right on the bank of the river, separated from it by a splendid riverside drive called the Corniche.

On the West Bank of Luxor, one will find a cluster of high brown mountains and jagged dry hills that rise up from the desert floor. The very first valley of these dusty hills is the famous Valley of the Kings—the extraordinary collection of deliberately plain tombs that were once filled with all the riches of the pharaohs. It is the home of Tutankhamen's tomb, Rameses the Great's tomb, and hundreds of others. Even today, every few years a new tomb is unearthed.

On this western bank, you will also find one of the most mysterious sites of ancient Egypt: Hatshepsut's

Mortuary Temple, constructed by the brilliant woman pharaoh, Hatshepsut.

Built into a great rocky bay in the mountainside, Hatshepsut's Mortuary Temple is composed of three gigantic colonnaded terraces, all stretching backwards—like three god-sized steps—each flat tier connected to the next by a colossal rampway.

From its dominant position at the base of the cliffs, it stares proudly back at Luxor, facing the rising Sun. The size of three football fields, it is unique in all of Egypt.

It is also notorious.

In November 1997, six Islamist terrorists armed with machine guns massacred 62 tourists in rank cold blood at the site. The terrorists hunted down the unarmed tourists over the course of a terrifying hour, pursuing them through the Temple's colonnades, before committing group suicide themselves.

Luxor is steeped in history, both ancient and reçent.

Luxor's airport, however, is on the eastern bank, and the American planes landed in the darkness, one after the other, their lights blinking—two C-130 Hercules cargo planes, and landing lightly after them, one sleek Lear jet.

It was a small force—just big enough to safely convey the Pieces in its possession but small enough not to attract too much attention—as Marshall Judah had stated in his intercepted transmission.

As usual, the Egyptian Government, desperate for American approval and money, had allowed their entry into the country with not a single question asked.

But the Egyptian Government did *not* know of the 300-strong European force that was at that moment surrounding Luxor's airstrip, aiming their weapons at the arriving Americans.

Father Francisco del Piero sat in a big Toyota Land Cruiser parked just outside the airport, waiting for his French and German troops to make their move. With him were Wizard, Zoe and Fuzzy—handcuffed and immobile, also waiting tensely.

In the Land Cruiser with them was the boy, Alexander, and safely in a large steel trunk, one Piece of the Golden Capstone: the Artemis Piece, recently removed from the main altar of St Peter's Basilica.

On the runway, two desert-camouflaged Humvees sped out from the cargo hold of the first Hercules and skidded to twin halts beside the Lear jet—the jet that held the Pieces.

A line of troopers emerged from the Lear, guarding a smaller group of men who carried among them five Samsonite cases of varying sizes. These men started loading the Samsonite cases onto the rear tray of a third Humvee—a black one—that had just arrived.

The Pieces.

The Europeans sprang their trap—in a kind of surreal unearthly silence.

They leapt from the shadows—French and German commandos—black-clad ghosts wearing night-vision goggles and running with sub-machine guns pressed to their shoulders, the muzzles of those guns spitting forth silenced tongues of deadly fire.

The American troops at the Lear never stood a chance.

They fell in a hail of blood and bullets, dropping to the tarmac. Likewise all the drivers of the Humvees: they were ripped to shreds by the charging French and German commandos.

It was over in minutes.

As various 'Clear!' signals were given, del Piero drove out onto the runway.

He joined the European troops gathered around the black Humvee parked beside the Lear.

With a smile of supreme satisfaction, he strode over to the Humvee's rear tray, opened it, and unclasped the lock on the nearest Samsonite case—

—to discover that it was filled with worthless bricks and a single Post-it note:

Careful, Father del Piero.
Don't let any blood get on you.
Judah.

Del Piero's eyes went wide.

He whirled around—

—just as an absolutely *devastating* burst of co-ordinated sniper fire whistled all around him—sizzling and popping past his ears—and in a single terrifying instant, *every one* of the ten troopers standing around him was hit by separate sniper rounds, their heads all exploding in simultaneous bursts of red, their bodies crumpling like rag dolls.

Only del Piero was unhit. Only he remained standing. The burst of fire had been so well-aimed, so well-co-ordinated that this was clearly deliberate.

Blood, bone and brain matter had sprayed everywhere, splattering all over del Piero's face.

At which moment, the *1,000-strong* American force that had been lying in wait in the mudbrick houses and sewers of Luxor *behind* the European ambush force moved in.

They were merciless, ruthless—as ruthless as the Europeans had been to the Americans. Even those European troops who surrendered were executed where they stood.

None were left alive—except for del Piero and the four other people who were inside his Land Cruiser:

Wizard, Zoe, Fuzzy and the boy, Alexander.

It was at this time that the *real* American air convoy arrived at Luxor.

The first one had been a decoy, its men expendable: live bait to draw out the waiting European force.

Now with the airport secured, Judah arrived in a second Lear jet, flanked by a couple of F-15s and tailed by no less than six massive Hercules cargo planes.

The air convoy landed, one plane after the other, their landing lights blazing through the clear night air.

Judah's Lear swung to a halt beside the first 'decoy' Lear . . .

. . . where del Piero still stood like a thief caught with his hands in the till, covered now by American CIEF troops and surrounded by the bloodied corpses of his own men.

Judah just strolled casually out of his private jet, appraised del Piero coldly, before nodding at the blood on the priest's face.

'Father del Piero. My old teacher. It's good to see you again. You didn't heed my warning. I told you to be careful about the flying blood.'

Del Piero said nothing.

Just then, a figure appeared behind Judah: an old, *old* man, gnarled and hunched. He had a bare blotch-speckled scalp and wore a leather coat and thick Coke-bottle glasses that obscured his evil little eyes.

Judah said, 'Father, I don't believe you've met Hans Koenig. He's been a guest of the United States since 1945 and has been searching for the Capstone for a *very* long time.'

Del Piero gasped, 'Koenig and Hessler. The two Nazi explorers . . .'

'Colonel Judah!' Cal Kallis called from the rear of the Land Cruiser. He stood by the boot of the big four-wheel drive, having opened the steel case there, revealing the Artemis Piece. 'We have the Europeans' Piece. We also have the boy . . . and a couple of West's people.'

Kallis held Alexander out in front of him. His men covered the handcuffed Wizard, Zoe and Fuzzy.

Judah grinned. 'Why, Father del Piero, what possible reason could you have for bringing these good people along on your mission? I imagine it will be exactly the same reason I will keep you with me.'

Del Piero's eyes went wide with fear.

Judah enjoyed it. 'What does the Bible say? Do unto others as you would have them do to you. How ironic.'

He beheld the boy. So did the Nazi, Koenig.

'So this is him. The son of the Oracle. Alexander, I believe,' Judah bowed respectfully. 'My name is Marshall Judah, from the United States of America. It's my honour to make your acquaintance.'

The boy—completely fearlessly—returned his gaze evenly, but said nothing.

Judah said, 'It's also my honour to present to you, for the first time, your sister.'

With that, Judah stepped aside, to reveal, standing shyly behind him, with her legs nervously crossed and her head bowed: Lily.

In the pre-dawn, a dense low mist hung over Luxor.

Through this unnatural haze moved a convoy of heavy vehicles, their headlights casting beams of light.

It was the American force, rushing toward the Luxor Temple.

The Temple sat beside the Nile—with its immense pylon gateway guarded by two colossal statues of Rameses II, seated on identical thrones, and its obelisk standing proudly but alone out in front, its twin long since removed to Paris.

The convoy of US vehicles included Humvees, jeeps, motorcycles, a single Apache helicopter overhead, and in the middle of it all, a long lumbering flat-bed semi-trailer, on which sat a large folded-up crane.

At the Temple, under the glare of floodlights, the Americans raised the mobile crane alongside the still-standing obelisk, in the exact spot where the obelisk's identical twin had once stood.

The crane was a cherry-picker, not unlike those used by electricity workers to fix power lines, with a basket at its summit big enough for three or four men. Judah, Kallis and Koenig were raised up in it.

'Herr Koenig,' Judah said. 'You have your copy of your colleague's diary?'

The old hunched-over Koenig held up his own

secretly-made copy of Hessler's diary. 'As always, Herr Judah,' he hissed.

As they rose up the flank of the existing obelisk, analysing the many hieroglyphs on its sides, Koenig flipped to the relevant page in the diary:

FROM THE SECRET GOSPEL OF ST MARK

AT DAWN ON THE DAY OF JUDGEMENT,
THAT FINAL HORRIBLE DAY,
AT THE ONLY TEMPLE THAT BEARS BOTH THEIR NAMES,
THREAD THE POWER OF RA THROUGH THE EYES OF
GREAT RAMESES'S TOWERING NEEDLES,
FROM THE SECOND OWL ON THE FIRST
TO THE THIRD ON THE SECOND . . .
. . . WHEREBY THE TOMB OF ISKENDER WILL BE REVEALED.
THERE YOU WILL FIND THE FIRST PIECE.

At the summit of the lone obelisk they found three carved owls, seated side-by-side. There, just as West had done on the Paris Obelisk, Judah extracted a little plug-stone from a carving of the Sun above the second owl. He found a second plug on the other side, and removed it too—

—to reveal a bore-hole running horizontally *through* the obelisk, from east to west . . . again, just as West had found in Paris.

Judah then had his crane-basket brought over to where the summit of the *other* obelisk—the one now in Paris—would have stood.

'You have the measurements, Herr Koenig?'

'To the millimetre, Herr Judah.'

And so, using a caesium altimeter and a digital inclinometer to get the angles and the height absolutely cor-

rect, they erected a pipe-like cylinder on a tripod in their basket. They erected it horizontally, angling it according to their measurements, in effect, recreating the bore-hole of the missing obelisk, the bore-hole that would have sat above the third owl on that obelisk.

They had got it just right when the orange rim of the Sun peeked over the eastern horizon and dawn came on the Day of Tartarus.

The *power* of the rising Sun was instantly noticed by all.

On this day, the Day of Tartarus, it was hotter, fiercer. It practically *burned* through the hazy low-hanging mist in dazzling horizontal shafts creating mini-rainbows in the air.

Then it struck the uppermost tip of the obelisk—and the high needle of rock seemed to shine majestically—before the beam of sunlight slowly began to move down the obelisk.

The American force watched it in awe.

From his basket, Judah watched it in triumph.

From his position down in one of the Humvees, Wizard watched it in grim silence.

Then the sunlight struck the bore-hole on the existing obelisk *and shone directly through it* . . .

. . . whence it continued on, shooting right into the pipe on Judah's crane . . .

. . . and suddenly the great shaft of sunlight combined with the unnatural mist to become a tiny laser-like beam of multi-coloured sunlight.

The rainbow-coloured laser beam lanced out from the Temple, shooting in a dead-straight horizontal line *westward*, out across the Nile, out over the fields on the West Bank, out towards . . .

. . . the great bay of brown cliffs that protected and defended the Valley of the Kings.

No.

It was more precise than that.

The beam of light came to rest on the structure built *into* that bay of cliffs—a structure unique in all of Egyptian architecture, featuring two great rampways and three glorious colonnaded tiers.

Hatshepsut's Mortuary Temple.

INSIDE HATSHEPSUT'S MORTUARY TEMPLE
LUXOR, EGYPT
20 MARCH, 2006, 0630 HOURS
THE DAY OF TARTARUS

The Americans made swift progress.

The dazzling beam of sunlight had illuminated a lone archway at the far left of the lowest tier of the great structure.

There a door was found, so well-concealed that it appeared to be part of the wall itself. But above it was a familiar symbol that until today had been attributed little significance:

At the sight of the carving, Marshall Judah's eyes shone with delight.

The Americans were through the door in no time.

Traps awaited them.

A passageway filled with vicious swing-traps—long swing-blades that swooped out of slits in the ceiling and chopped one man's head off.

Then a partially-submerged chamber, the knee-deep water of which concealed leg-chopping blades. Fortunately, from his research, Koenig knew the safe route.

Until Marshall Judah emerged from a stone doorway and stood on a platform that overlooked a gigantic subterranean cavern.

It wasn't as big as the supercavern that contained the Hanging Gardens of Babylon, but what it lost in size, it made up for in artistry.

Every stone wall had been fashioned by human hands. There was not a single rough surface in the place.

It looked like an underground cathedral, with soaring high walls, a curved ceiling, and four immense sacred lakes arrayed in such a fashion that they created a wide raised path in the shape of a giant †. Great pillars of stone held up the superhigh ceiling.

At the junction of the †—the focal point of the great underground hall—was a raised square platform, flanked on all four corners by obelisks. On this high platform lay an ornate glass sarcophagus.

'Ornate' was barely sufficient to describe it.

It was crafted of gold and glass, and it lay underneath a high canopy crafted entirely of gold. The pillars of the canopy were not straight, but rather they rose in a bending, spiralling way, as if they were solidified vines.

'The coffin of Alexander the Great . . .' Koenig breathed.

'It was said to be made of glass,' Wizard confirmed.

'Wait a second. This looks familiar to me . . .' Judah breathed.

Beside him, Francisco del Piero—like the others, his

hands were cuffed—bowed his head in silence, tried to be invisible.

Judah turned to Koenig.

'Take some measurements with the laser surveying equipment. I want to know the length, height and breadth of this hall.'

Koenig did so.

After a minute, he reported: 'It is 192 metres long, and 160 metres wide at the widest point of the tee. Height of the cavern above the central junction is . . . 135 metres.'

Wizard snuffed a laugh.

Koenig turned. 'What is so funny?'

'Let me guess,' Wizard said. 'That canopy over the sarcophagus, the one with the twisted columns, it's 29 metres high.'

Koenig did the computations with his laser surveying gear . . . and turned to Wizard in surprise. 'It is 29 metres in height *exactly*. How could you know this?'

Wizard said, 'Because this cavern has the exact same dimensions as St Peter's Basilica in Rome.'

Judah swung to face del Piero, who shrank even lower, if that was at all possible.

Wizard went on, 'If everything in the Roman Catholic Church is a reinvention of Egyptian Sun-worship, then why should St Peter's be any different? Its dimensions are simply a replication of this sacred place: the resting place of the most prized Piece of the Capstone, the top Piece.'

They proceeded to the great altar at the focal point of the †-shaped hall, where they beheld the gold-and-glass coffin.

Through the glass, they saw only white powdery

dust—the remains of the greatest warrior ever known, the man who had ordered the Pieces of the Capstone to be separated and scattered around the then-known world.

Alexander the Great.

A bronze Macedonian helmet and a lustrous silver sword rested upon the layer of white dust.

And sticking up from the middle of the dust-layer—as if it had once been laid upon the dead man's chest, only to see that chest erode over the course of two millennia—was a tiny apex of gold.

A tip of a small golden pyramid.

The top Piece.

Without preamble, Judah ordered the coffin opened, and four of his men stepped forward, grabbed a corner each.

Del Piero started forward, 'For pity's sake, do take care!'

The men ignored him, removed the glass lid of the coffin roughly.

Judah stepped forward, and with everyone watching tensely, reached in, dipped his fingers into the remains of Alexander the Great, and pulled from them . . .

. . . the top Piece of the Golden Capstone.

Pyramidal in shape, with a base the size of a square paperback book, it radiated power.

More than that.

It radiated a power and an artistry and a *knowledge* beyond anything mankind had ever devised.

It was beyond man, beyond the limits of human knowledge.

The crystal in its peak glittered like a diamond. This

crystal array bored down the spine of the gold mini-pyramid, reappearing at the base.

Judah gazed at it adoringly.

He now held in his possession *all seven* Pieces of the Golden Capstone, something no man had done since Alexander the Great.

He grinned.

'It's time to capture the power of Ra. Tartarus will arrive over Giza at noon. To Giza, and a thousand years of power.'

SEVENTH MISSION
THE GREAT PYRAMID

GIZA, EGYPT
20 MARCH, 2006
THE DAY OF TARTARUS

THE GREAT PYRAMID AT GIZA

It is perhaps the only structure on Earth known by name to every single member of the human race.

The Great Pyramid.

The most common misconception about the Seven Ancient Wonders of the World is that the three pyramids at Giza comprise a single Wonder.

This is not the case.

While Khafre's and Menkaure's additional pyramids are certainly impressive monuments, only one pyramid is known as the *Great* one: that of Khufu (or Cheops, as the Greeks called him). It is this pyramid alone that comprises the Wonder.

In a word, it is breathtaking.

Its dimensions are staggering: 137 metres high, while each of its base sides is 140 metres long. With the addition of its missing Capstone—lost in antiquity—perfect symmetry would be returned and it would once again resume its original height of 140 metres and its intended shape.

It is estimated to weigh over 2 million tons, and yet, despite this unimaginable bulk, it contains within its mass the most intricate and beautiful passageways, all built with an exactness that defies belief.

It has outlasted pharaohs and kings, tribal wars and world wars, earthquakes and sandstorms.

Devotees of the Pyramid swear that it possesses unusual powers: it is said that no bacteria can grow inside the Great Pyramid. It is said that flowers planted inside it grow with unusual vibrancy. It is claimed to heal sufferers of arthritis and cancer.

Whatever one's beliefs, there is something about this man-made mountain that draws people to it, that entrances them. It defies time, it defies imagination. To this day, it is still not known exactly how it was built.

It is the only man-made structure in history to defy the ravages of Nature and Time, and indeed the only one of the Seven Ancient Wonders known to have survived to the present day.

It is a building without equal in all of the world.

THE GREAT PYRAMID
GIZA (ON THE OUTSKIRTS OF CAIRO), EGYPT
20 MARCH, 2006, 1100 HOURS
THE DAY OF TARTARUS

The Great Pyramid of Khufu lorded over outer Cairo, absolutely dominating the landscape around it.

Apartment buildings constructed by men 4,500 years after it had been built looked puny beside it. It stood at the point where the lush river valley of Cairo met the edge of the Western Desert, on a raised section of cliffs called the Giza Plateau.

Beside it stood the pyramids of Khafre and Menkaure—also magnificent, but forever inferior—and before it, crouching, eternally at rest, lay the mysterious Sphinx.

It was almost midday and the Sun was rising to the highpoint of its daily arc. It was hot—very, very hot—even for Cairo: 49 degrees Celsius and rising rapidly.

Reports from around the world had told of oppressively warm weather across the globe: China, India, even Russia—all had recorded unusually high temperatures on this day. Many reported instances of people collapsing in the streets.

Something was wrong.

Something to do with the Sun, the TV commentators said. A sunspot, the meteorologists said.

In the United States, all the morning news shows had made it their story of the day and were looking to the White House, waiting for an address from the President.

But no such address came.

The White House remained mysteriously silent.

In Cairo, the Egyptian Government had been most accommodating to the American force.

The entire Giza Plateau had been closed to civilians and tourists for the day—all its entrances were now guarded by Egyptian troops—and an advance team sent by Judah overnight had been given free rein on the ancient site.

Indeed, while Judah had been at Luxor that morning, his advance team had been working diligently, preparing for his arrival. Their work: an enormous scaffold structure that now shrouded the summit of the Great Pyramid.

It was a huge flat-topped platform, made entirely of wood, three storeys high, and completely enveloping the peak of the pyramid. It looked like a big helicopter landing pad, square in shape, thirty metres long on each side, and its flat open-air roof lay level with the bare summit of the Pyramid. Indeed, the platform had a hole in its exact centre that allowed the peak of the Pyramid to protrude up through it . . . and thus allow Judah to perform his preferred Capstone ritual.

The platform's vertical support struts rested upon the step-like sides of the Pyramid, as did two cranes that rose high into the sky above the platform. Inside the baskets of these cranes were CIEF troops armed with Stinger missiles and anti-aircraft guns.

No-one was going to interrupt this ceremony.

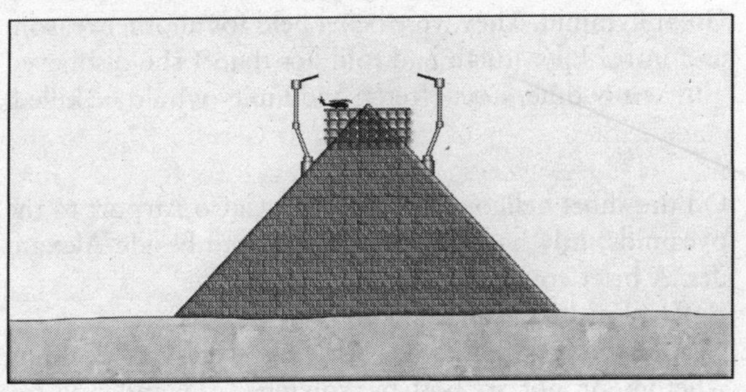

The Great Pyramid on the day of Tartarus

At 11:00 a.m. exactly, Marshall Judah arrived on a CH-53E Super Stallion helicopter, surrounded by twelve CIEF troops led by Cal Kallis, and carrying with him in the back of the chopper *all seven pieces* of the Golden Capstone of the Great Pyramid, ready to be restored to their rightful place.

The Super Stallion swung into a low hover above the platform and in the swirling hurricane of wind it created, the Pieces were unloaded on wheeled trolleys.

Flanked by the heavily armed CIEF commandos, Judah stepped out of the helicopter, leading the two children, Alexander and Lily.

Wizard and del Piero came after them, handcuffed and guarded—brought along by Judah for no other reason, it seemed, than to observe his triumph over them.

Zoe, Fuzzy and Stretch (who had also been reunited with the team when Judah had revealed Lily) were being held in a second helicopter travelling behind the Super Stallion—a Black Hawk—that landed at the base of the

Great Pyramid. They were being held for another reason: to control Lily. Judah had told her that if she disobeyed him at any time, Zoe, Stretch and Fuzzy would be killed.

On the short helicopter flight from Cairo Airport to the pyramids, Lily had found herself seated beside Alexander. A brief conversation had ensued:

'Hi, I'm Lily,' she said.

Alexander gazed at her airily, as if he was deciding whether or not to bother replying. 'Alexander is my name . . . my young sister.'

'*Young*? Come off it. You're only older than me by twenty minutes,' Lily said, laughing.

'Nevertheless, I am still the first-born,' Alexander said. 'To the first go certain privileges. Such as respect.'

'I bet you probably get out of doing your chores sometimes, too,' Lily said.

'What are chores?' the boy asked seriously.

'Chores,' Lily said in disbelief. 'You know, things like cleaning out the horse-pooh in the barn. Washing up the dishes after dinner.'

'I have never cleaned a *dish* in my life. Or a *barn*. Such activities are beneath my station.'

'You've never done any chores!' Lily exclaimed. 'Man, you're lucky! Wow, no chores . . .'

The boy frowned, genuinely curious. 'Why do you do such things? You are high-born. Why would you even *allow* yourself to be dragooned into performing such tasks?'

Lily shrugged. She'd never actually thought about that. 'I guess . . . well . . . while I don't really like doing them, I do my chores to contribute to my family. To be a part of the family. To help out.'

'But you are *better* than they are. Why would you want to help such ordinary people?'

'I like helping them. I . . . I love them.'

'My sister, my sister. We were born to rule these people, not to help them. They are beneath you, they are your inferiors.'

'They're my family,' Lily said firmly.

'To rule is lonely,' Alexander said, as if this was a phrase he had been told a lot and learned by rote. 'I expected you to be stronger, sister.'

Lily said nothing after that, and minutes later, they arrived at the Great Pyramid.

And so it was that at 11:30 a.m. on the Day of Tartarus, thirty minutes before the blazing sunspot rotated in direct alignment with the Pyramid, a ceremony began on the summit of the Great Pyramid at Giza, an ancient ceremony that had not been performed in over 4,500 years.

Standing on the platform, Judah clipped himself to a long safety rope, to take care of his fear of heights.

He gazed at the bare summit of the Great Pyramid, saw the ancient verse carved into it:

Cower in fear, cry in despair,
You wretched mortals
For that which giveth great power
Also takes it away.
For lest the Benben be placed at sacred site
On sacred ground, at sacred height,
Within seven sunsets of the arrival of Ra's Prophet,
At the high-point of the seventh day,
The fires of Ra's implacable Destroyer will devour us all.

Beside this carving, in the exact centre of the bare stone summit, there was a shallow indentation carved in the shape of a person. The 'head' of this person-sized indentation was weathered and worn, but it was clearly that of Anubis, the jackal-headed and much-feared god of the Underworld.

And in the heart of this Anubis indentation—in the *exact* centre of the summit and thus the centre of the entire pyramid—there was a small dish-shaped hole the size of a tennis ball. It looked like a stone crucible.

Judah knew the purpose of the crucible. The Nazi archaeologist, Hessler, had too:

<u>THE RITUAL OF POWER</u>

AT THE HIGH ALTAR OF RA,
UNDER THE HEART OF THE SACRIFICIAL ONE
WHO LIES IN THE ARMS OF VENGEFUL ANUBIS,
POUR INTO THE DEATH GOD'S HEART
ONE DEBEN OF YOUR HOMELAND
UTTER THOSE ANCIENT EVIL WORDS
AND ALL EARTHLY POWER SHALL BE YOURS
FOR A THOUSAND YEARS.

Pour into the Death God's heart
One deben of your homeland . . .

A 'deben' was the ancient Egyptian measure of weight. It equalled 93 grams.

Judah pulled a glass vial from inside his jacket. In it was some amber-coloured soil, soil that had been taken from the Utah desert, deep inside the United States—soil that was unique to the United States of America.

Judah poured exactly 93 grams of the soil into the crucible. One deben.

Eyeing it proudly, he called to his men, 'Gentlemen! Erect the Capstone!'

One Piece after the other, Judah's people began erecting the Golden Capstone.

The largest Piece—the Pharos Piece—went on the bottom and the human-shaped indentation in its golden underside perfectly matched up with the Anubis indentation on the summit of the Pyramid.

The Pyramid's summit was also fitted with a low channel cut into it from one side—since the Capstone lay flat on its peak, this channel provided a tight crawlway that would allow the 'Sacrificial One'—one of the children—to crawl *into* the indentation when the time came.

As each new Piece was laid on it, the Capstone began to take shape.

It was truly magnificent—glittering and powerful—a golden crown to an already stupendous structure.

And of course, the line of crystals running down through the centre of the Capstone pointed directly at the heart of Anubis.

Judah co-ordinated the operation, his eyes wide with delight.

And then the final Piece, the pyramidal top Piece, the Piece he had obtained from Alexander's tomb only that morning went on . . .

. . . and the Capstone was complete for the first time in nearly five millennia.

The Great Pyramid at Giza stood whole once more, as it had originally appeared in 2,566 BC.

It was 11:50 a.m.

Ten minutes till the Tartarus Rotation occurred.

Judah turned to face the two children.

'And so it falls to me to make a historic choice,' he said. 'Which child to sacrifice to the power of the Sun . . .'

'Sacrifice?' Alexander said, frowning. 'What are you talking about?'

'It is what you were born for, young man,' Judah said. 'It is what you were put on this Earth to do.'

'I was put here to rule—' Alexander threw a confused look at del Piero.

'I fear you have been misinformed,' Judah said. 'You were put here to decode the Word of Thoth and then to die for the eternal benefit of Father del Piero and his friends. Although I'm sure they would have worshipped you fervently *after* your death, if that is any consolation. I'm assuming Father del Piero must have failed to mention this.'

Alexander's eyes flashed to del Piero, blazing with fury.

Lily just remained silent, her head bowed.

'So. Who to choose?' Judah mused.

'Her,' Alexander said quickly. 'She didn't even know of her own importance. At least I did.'

Judah grinned at this. 'Is that so?' Then he said, 'No, boy. I like her, because she's quiet. You're not. Which means you're elected.'

And with that, Judah scooped up the boy and thrust him into the tight channel underneath the Capstone, forcing him at gunpoint to crawl through it and lie down inside the arms of Anubis, beneath the fully-built Capstone, his heart directly *underneath* the Capstone's crystal array while also directly *above* the dish-shaped crucible containing the soil of America.

The boy sobbed all the way.

At 11:55, Judah stepped into position.

He held in his hands the ritual of power—which he had taken line-by-line from the surface of each of the Capstone's seven Pieces.

'Everyone, prepare for the ceremony! Five minutes!'

It was then that one of the CIEF spotters in the northern crane spied a tiny black dot high in the eastern sky . . .

It looked like a plane of some sort, approaching fast, *descending*.

A 747 . . . a black one.

The *Halicarnassus*.

The *Halicarnassus* zoomed out of the sky at near-supersonic speed, nose down, wings pinned back, all its guns pointed forward.

Sky Monster was at the helm, yelling, 'Yee-ha! Come and get it, you Yankee motherfuckers! Pooh Bear—you ready to rock'n'roll?'

In the revolving gun turret on top of the plane's left wing, Pooh Bear replied, 'Let's do some damage.'

Sky Monster said, 'Let's hope Wizard's retro system is up to the challenge or else this could be a disaster of gargantuan propor—shit! *Incoming!*'

The Americans had launched two Stinger missiles at the incoming 747.

The missiles streaked upwards from the Great Pyramid, shooming toward the inbound jumbo jet, but Pooh Bear nullified them both—he got one missile to lock onto a chaff bomb, and the other he destroyed with an interceptor missile of his own, a French-made FV-5X Hummingbird, designed by the French in the 1990s for the Iraqi Army, specifically to nullify American Stinger missiles. When West had found the *Halicarnassus*, it had been fitted with ten brand-new Hummingbirds.

The Americans then started firing their anti-aircraft guns from their cranes.

Tracer bullets raced up into the sky—there were so many they *filled* the sky—but Sky Monster banked the *Halicarnassus* brilliantly, avoiding the laser-like streaks while at the same time Pooh Bear returned fire and unleashed a Hellfire air-to-ground missile of his own.

The Hellfire shoomed out from a pod on the *Hali*'s underbelly and spiralled down towards one of the American cranes and—

—*smashed* into it and detonated.

The crane's basket was blasted into a million pieces, its occupants and their weapons vaporised.

Judah and all the others on the platform spun at the nearby explosion.

The other crane continued to fire up at the incoming *Halicarnassus*, unleashing a thousand rounds of AA ammunition and another Stinger missile—which Pooh Bear just blasted out of the sky a moment later.

Then Sky Monster yelled, 'Pooh! *Hang on, buddy!* Here we go!' Then to himself he whispered, 'Please God, Wizard, tell me you got this right . . .'

It was then that, roaring down toward the Giza Plateau like an out-of-control missile, Sky Monster lifted the *Hali*'s nose up slightly and *jammed* all his thrusters back . . . throwing the *Halicarnassus* into a deliberate stall . . . so that now it looked like a stallion rearing up on its hind legs, its nose up, its tail down . . .

. . . at which point, Sky Monster held his breath and punched the *second* collective on his console, a thruster-collective marked: RETROGRADE THRUST SYSTEM.

What happened next startled everyone on the Pyramid's summit—everyone except Wizard.

The *Halicarnassus*—dropping through the sky in a

graceful flat stall, nose up, tail down—emitted a noise deeper and louder than a thousand thunderbooms.

BOOOOOOOOM!

The colossal noise came from the eight Mark 3 Harrier retrograde thrust engines that had been incorporated into its armoured fuselage.

By Wizard.

The result was sensational: the massive all-black *Halicarnassus* stopped in mid-fall, as if it were suspended from giant descender cables, and to the sound of its deafening retrograde thrusters, it swung into a perfect hover, 200 metres off the ground and only *a few hundred yards from the Great Pyramid!*

Sky Monster brought her closer, bringing the big hovering plane's left forward door alongside the platform on the summit of the Pyramid.

It was an absolutely astonishing sight—the massive black jumbo jet, bristling with guns and missile pods, hovering with its nose close to the summit of the Great Pyramid at Giza.

From the platform itself, the *Halicarnassus* loomed large, superhuge, like an angry bird-god descended from Heaven itself to wreak its fury.

The initial spell broken, the surviving American crane swung around to unleash a new burst of AA fire, now from point-blank range.

But Pooh Bear, on the *Hali*'s left wing, was quicker on the draw and also at point-blank range.

He loosed a withering burst of fire—a hyper-fast *barrage* of gunfire—that shook, shattered and blasted apart the crane, turning its occupants into fountains of spraying blood and the crane into Swiss cheese.

On the platform, Judah's eyes boggled.

He checked the Sun, checked his watch: 11:59:29. Thirty seconds.

'Hold them off!' he called to his men. 'Hold them off! We only need *thirty seconds!*'

Consumed with the spectacular arrival of the *Halicarnassus*, Judah never noticed a *second* airborne craft zeroing in on the Pyramid, a very small craft that came zooming in low and fast from the Western Desert.

It was a man, possessed of carbon-fibre wings.

The tiny man-shaped figure soared low over the desert, before at the last second, he rose up swiftly—up the slanting side of the Pyramid as if it were an aerial ramp—and landed with a graceful plonk on the far side of the Capstone, on the side opposite the attention-grabbing *Halicarnassus*.

It was Jack West Jr.

Back from the dead, and pissed as hell.

West landed with his wings outstretched and with two big .45 calibre Desert Eagle pistols in his hands. The instant his feet touched the platform, his guns started blazing, taking down four CIEF troopers with four shots.

Then he punched a release clip on his wing-harness and the carbon-fibre wings fell off his back, freeing him, making him even more deadly.

He ran out onto the platform, guns up.

At the same time, in response to the spectacular arrival of the *Halicarnassus*, four American helicopters lifted off from their positions at the base of the Great Pyramid: three Apache attack birds and the mighty Super Stallion that Judah had used to bring the Pieces to Giza.

A fifth chopper—a Black Hawk—made to follow them, but it seemed to hesitate on the ground as a scuffle occurred inside it.

Then, a few seconds behind the others, it lifted off and headed for the battle going on at the top of the Pyramid.

Pandemonium reigned on the platform.

With the *Halicarnassus* looming alongside it like a ship from outer space, and Pooh Bear blazing away from the plane's powerful left-side gun turret, all the American troops on the platform were either getting shot or diving for cover behind Samsonite crates or the Capstone itself or retreating to the lower levels of the open-sided structure.

In the chaos, Wizard hurled himself on top of Lily to protect her.

Del Piero charged across the platform and slid to the ground beside the little channel, to reach for Alexander, still inside the Capstone.

'Not so fast, Father!' a voice said from behind him. Del Piero turned—

—to find himself staring into the barrel of a Glock pistol held by Marshall Judah.

Bam!

The pistol went off and the priest's brains splattered the golden flank of the Capstone.

With a core group of CIEF men surrounding him, Judah stood before the Capstone—cleverly putting it between him and Pooh Bear's guns—and with a glance at his watch, looked to the sky.

At that moment, the clock struck noon and it happened.

It looked like a laser beam from Heaven.

A dead-straight beam of dazzling white light lanced down from the sky, from the surface of the Sun, and accompanied by a tremendous *boom*, it slammed into the Capstone atop the Great Pyramid.

The Capstone, in reply, *caught* this ray of hyper-intense energy within its crystal array—so that the beam remained in place, giving the impression that the Pyra-

mid was now *connected* to the Sun by this superlong and perfectly straight ray of glowing white energy.

It was a stunning image: the Pyramid—surmounted by the great wooden platform, with the *Halicarnassus* hovering alongside it and with helicopters now buzzing and banking around it—*absorbing* the blazing white beam of pure energy that was shooting down from the sky.

It was incredible, impossible, otherworldly.

But it was also oddly *right*. It was as if this was what the Great Pyramid at Giza, dormant and mysterious for so many centuries, had been designed to do.

The platform was ablaze with light and sound.

Here at the epicentre of the great Sun-ray, the glow was almost blinding. And the noise—it was all-consuming: the colossal boom of the great Sun-ray combined with the roar of the *Halicarnassus*'s retro-thrusters and the turning of its regular engines (which were level with the platform) drowned out all other sound.

And in the midst of all this stood Marshall Judah, before the Capstone. He raised one arm toward the Golden Capstone, palm up, and then in an ancient language not heard in thousands of years, he began to recite an incantation.

The power ritual.

The power ritual was seven lines long.

As Judah began to recite it, several things were happening:

Pooh Bear.

He was waging his own private war with the four American helicopters. He had knocked out one Apache helicopter with gunfire and had just fired a Hellfire missile at the rising Super Stallion. The missile slammed into the front windshield of the Super Stallion just as the big chopper came level with the platform.

The CH-53E exploded in a giant ball of flames—and lurched in mid-air, before it fell, dropping alongside the platform, its swirling rotor blades missing the lower levels of the platform by inches before the whole chopper *smashed* down in a crumpled heap on the sloping southern flank of the Great Pyramid itself.

It now lay at a 52-degree angle—the slope of the Pyramid—at the spot where the platform's struts met the Pyramid, its body crumpled and broken but its rotors still buzzing in blurring circles of motion.

Judah had recited two lines by this time . . .

Pooh Bear swung around in his gun turret and had just zeroed in on the American Black Hawk chopper when—to his surprise—he saw the Black Hawk fire a missile into the back of one of its own Apache attack birds.

It was then that Pooh saw the pilots of the Black Hawk: Zoe and Fuzzy. In the confusion earlier, they'd escaped their bonds, stolen the Black Hawk and leapt into the fray.

But then suddenly a CIEF trooper leapt up onto the *Halicarnassus*'s wing, trying to take out Pooh Bear's turret guerrilla-style. Pooh couldn't turn the turret in time. The man had him, raised his Colt rifle—

Bam!

The CIEF trooper was hit in the back of the head by a long-distance sniper shot, a shot that had been fired by—

—Stretch, sitting in the side door of the stolen Black Hawk, holding a sniper rifle.

Pooh saw the Israeli, alive and with the good guys, and he smiled for the briefest of moments.

Judah had recited four lines . . .

West.

He was waging *his* own private war against the eight men guarding Judah at the Capstone: six CIEF troopers, Koenig and Kallis.

He strode forward, eyes fixed, face set, both of his guns held outstretched in front of him.

The old warrior in Jack West—a warrior Judah had helped create—had returned . . . and he was a mean motherfucker.

West shot four of the troopers—all right between the eyeballs. One shot, one kill.

Another he grabbed from behind, snapping his neck, before using the dead man's body as a shield to receive fire from Cal Kallis while emptying the dead man's M-4 into two others. Then the wily old Nazi, Koenig, lunged at him from the side with a knife, but he received two rounds to the nose for his trouble, the force of the shots sending him flying clear off the platform.

Judah finished the sixth line . . .

'Hold him off!' he called to Kallis as he began the last line.

That left West facing Cal Kallis—who now stood between West and Judah—in the midst of the maelstrom of light, wind and sound.

It was a stand-off from which there could be only one winner.

But there was also one more figure at work in all this.

Beyond the mayhem happening on the platform, unseen by anyone, the exit door above the left wing of the *Halicarnassus* opened and a figure emerged from it, skulking low, moving swiftly, holding something small in his hands.

He scurried out from the doorway and onto the wing. Then he leapt down from the front of the wing onto the wooden platform, heading—again unseen—in the direction of Wizard and Lily.

West and Kallis faced each other.

Then they moved, at exactly the same time, lifting and firing their guns simultaneously, like a pair of wild west gunslingers—

Click! Click!

They were both dry.

'Fuck!' Kallis yelled.

'No . . .' West breathed.

For he knew that it didn't matter now.

Judah also knew. Their eyes met, and West's face fell.

He was too late.

By a bare few seconds—no a bare few *metres*—he was too late.

With a smile of insane delight, by the light of the Tartarus Sunspot on the Day of the Rotation, Marshall Judah uttered the final words of the ritual of power and looked triumphantly to the heavens.

Nothing happened.

Granted, West wasn't sure what *should* have happened. Should the sky darken? Should the Earth shake? Should Judah turn into some giant all-powerful dragon? Should West's gun turn to dust?

Whatever was supposed to happen to show that the United States of America had just earned itself a thousand years of undisputed worldly power, it didn't manifest itself in any visible way.

And then West saw that, indeed, nothing *had* happened.

For there, scuttling on all fours away from the Capstone on the other side of the platform, having crawled over the corpse of the CIEF trooper who was supposed to be guarding the channel that led under the Capstone, was the boy, Alexander.

He hadn't been in the sacrificial spot when Judah had completed the ritual . . .

So the ritual hadn't taken effect.

Judah saw it too and he shouted, 'No! *No!*'

The boy clambered to the edge of the platform, turned back—and seeing del Piero's dead body, he leaned out over the side of the platform, lowering himself down to the level below.

West's view of Alexander disappearing over the edge was cut off by the flash of Cal Kallis's K-Bar knife rushing toward his eyes.

West ducked and the blade went high. He then rose quickly and punched the knife from Kallis's hand before nailing the CIEF trooper square in the nose with the best punch he'd ever thrown with his all-metal left hand—

The blow connected . . .

. . . and had no effect on Kallis at all.

The big CIEF trooper just grinned back at West through bloody teeth.

Then he replied with three *awesome* punches of his own—all vicious, all hard, all to West's face.

Once, twice, three times, each blow sent West staggering backwards.

'You feel that, West! You feel that!' Kallis roared. 'I've been waiting all fucking week for this! But I had to keep you alive, to let you lead us to each site. But not anymore. My boys got your Spanish friend in the Sudan! But I was the one who offed your dumb Irish lad in Kenya! He was still alive after you left, you know—a gurgling bloody mess. I was the one who put a bullet in his brain to finish him off.'

A fourth blow, then a fifth.

On the fifth punch, West's nose broke, exploded with blood, and his boots came to the edge of the platform and he teetered there for a moment, glanced quickly behind him.

Immediately below him, thirty feet down, was the crashed Super Stallion—its still-spinning buzzsaw-like blades *directly* beneath him!

Kallis saw them too. 'But while I enjoyed snuffing out the Irish kid, I'm glad I'm the one who gets to kill *you*. See you in Hell, West!'

And with that, Kallis unleashed the final crushing blow.

Just as West himself lunged desperately forward, his left arm lashing out, extending fast—a final last-gasp all-or-nothing strike.

His blow struck Kallis a nanosecond before Kallis's blow struck him.

Phwack!

Kallis froze in mid-action—

—with West's artificial left fist, his *metal* fist, lodged deep in the centre of his face, having thundered right *through* his nose. The blow had been so powerful, it had *dented* Kallis's nose three inches inward, breaking it in several places. Blood had sprayed everywhere.

Incredibly, Kallis was still conscious, his eyes bulging, his entire body twitching, but his limbs were no longer responding to his brain.

He wouldn't be alive for long.

'This is for Big Ears,' West said, yanking Kallis around and hurling him off the edge of the platform.

Kallis fell—thirty feet, straight down—and in his very last moment of consciousness, he saw, to his horror, the spinning rotor blades of the Super Stallion rush up to meet him . . .

He made to scream, but the shout never came. In a single split second, Cal Kallis was diced into a million bloody pieces.

On the other side of the platform, Wizard had watched in horror as West had fought Kallis.

He wanted to help, but he also didn't want to leave Lily.

But then he saw Jack nail Kallis with his brutal punch, saw the foul explosion of blood from Kallis's face and he suddenly felt like they might just have a chance—

Wizard was struck viciously from behind . . . by the figure who had emerged from the *Halicarnassus*.

He fell, and his world began to darken at the edges.

Oddly, the last thing he heard before he fell into blackness was Lily shouting to someone: 'No! Forget Alexander! Take me instead!'

His face a mess of blood and dust, West rose from the edge of the platform and turned to head back to the Capstone—

—only to find himself staring into the barrel of Marshall Judah's Glock, just as del Piero had. He froze.

'You should be proud, Jack!' Judah called. 'This is all your doing! *You* led us to this juncture! But all the while you were working for me! There is nothing you can think of, nothing you can do, nothing you have, that I do not already possess! Why, I even have your little girl to use for the ritual! Tragically, you won't live to see her fulfil her destiny! Goodbye, Jack!'

Judah tightened his trigger finger . . .

'That's not true!' West shouted above the din. 'I do have one thing you don't have! Something that was once yours!'

'What?'

'Horus!'

At that instant, a blurring flash of brown streaked through the air, cutting across Judah's face, and suddenly Judah screamed, his face spraying blood. He threw his hands to his eyes, still half-holding the gun.

Horus swooped clear of the screaming Judah, clutching something in her talons . . . something white and round and trailing a ragged bloody tail.

It was Judah's entire left eye, including the optic nerve.

Horus had ripped it clean from its socket!

Judah dropped to his knees, wailing, 'My eye! My eye!'

At the same time, with his good eye, he saw the Capstone and yelled with even more anguish: 'Oh, God, no . . . !'

West spun too—and he also saw the nightmare scenario take physical form.

For there, standing at the Capstone, having taken Lily from Wizard and ushered her at gunpoint into the sacrificial cavity in the base of the Capstone *and* having refilled the crucible inside the cavity with exactly one deben of the fine-grained sand from his black-jade box, was Mustapha Zaeed, now reading from Judah's notebook, *performing the ritual of power!*

It was Zaeed who had crept unseen from the wing-door of the *Halicarnassus* earlier, having stowed aboard the plane in Iran after the confrontation at the Hanging Gardens.

It was he who had followed West and Pooh Bear to the rendezvous with Sky Monster and crept aboard the plane through its landing gear, unnoticed—assuming correctly that West would come here to confront the Americans one last time.

Once on board, Zaeed had crept to his old trunk and pulled from it his prized black-jade box, filled with the fine-grained sand, sand that he had kept for so long in his secret cave in Saudi Arabia—sand unique to the Arabian Peninsula, sand that would bring to the Muslim world a thousand years of unchallenged power.

Now, here, on the platform, it was he who had struck Wizard from behind. As he'd done so, he had spotted

Alexander lowering himself over the edge nearby, and he'd been about to grab the boy to perform the ritual, when suddenly Lily had said, 'No! Forget Alexander! Take me instead!'

And so Zaeed had.

Now he only had to utter seven lines.

It took him fifteen seconds.

And there, atop the Great Pyramid at Giza, under the blinding Sun-ray from the Tartarus Sunspot in the roaring wind and the blazing heat, to the horror of everyone else watching powerlessly, Mustapha Zaeed—his voice resonating with evil reverence—uttered the final words of the ritual of power.

This time, West had no doubt that the ritual had been performed correctly.

It sounded like the end of the universe.

Flaring light.

Clashing thunder.

The very Earth shook.

What followed next made man's most spectacular fireworks shows look positively puny.

The dazzling-white beam of light reaching down from the Sun pulsed brilliantly, as if it were doubling in intensity.

An unearthly thunderclap boomed, causing West's ears to ring, and a white-hot ball of superbrilliant energy thundered out of the sky, racing down the length of the vertical beam before rushing headlong *into* the Capstone . . .

. . . where the Capstone received it within its crystal array.

Inside the Golden Capstone, the energy-burst rushed down through its seven layers of crystals—each layer refining the beam into an ever-smaller, ever-more-intense thread of superluminous light.

And then this superthin beam struck Lily in the heart.

The little girl convulsed, hit by the lightbeam. The beam, however, seemed to pass *right through* her chest and strike the soil in the crucible.

With a blinding flash, the soil was instantly transformed to cinders.

Seen from the outside, the Capstone shone with blinding brilliance as it received the energy-burst, before with a terrible *whump*, the white-hot ball disappeared into it, and the phenomenon abruptly ceased and all was quiet, save for a deep humming that came from the Capstone and the drone of the *Halicarnassus*'s engines.

West could only stare at the Capstone, and wonder what had happened to Lily inside it. Could she have survived such a phenomenon? Or had Zaeed been right when he'd said she would die in the ceremony?

Zaeed stood beside the Capstone, his arms raised in triumph, his face upturned to the sky. 'A thousand years! A thousand years of Islamic rule!'

He rounded on West, eyes glowering, hands spread wide.

'The ritual is done, infidel! Which means my people are unconquerable! Invincible! And you—*you*—will be the first to feel my wrath!'

'Is that so?' West said, jamming a new clip into one of his Desert Eagles and aiming it at Zaeed.

'Fire your weapon!' Zaeed taunted him. 'Bullets cannot help you anymore!'

'Fine,' West said.

Bam!—he fired.

The bullet hit Zaeed square in the chest, sending him jolting backwards. Blood sprayed outwards and the terrorist dropped to the ground, to his knees, his face the picture of shock and confusion.

He stared at his wound, then up at West.

'But . . . how . . . ?'

'I knew you were on my plane after the Hanging Gardens,' West said. 'I knew you'd try to stow aboard. How else were you going to get here? You've been chasing this all your life, you weren't going to stay away. So I let you stow aboard.'

'But the sand . . .'

'While you were hiding in the belly of my plane, I took the liberty of changing the sand in your black-jade box,' West said. 'It's not the soil of Arabia anymore. What you put inside the Capstone was the soil of *my* homeland. You just performed the ritual of power for my people, Zaeed, not yours. Thanks.'

Zaeed was thunderstruck. He looked away, considering the consequences. '*Your* soil? But that would mean . . .'

He never finished the sentence, for at that moment life escaped him, and Mustapha Zaeed dropped to the platform, dead.

There came a sudden pained shout—'*WEST!*'—and West spun to see Marshall Judah lunging toward him, blood and flesh dangling from his ripped-open eye socket, and an M-4 assault rifle in his hands, taken from one of his dead CIEF troops.

It was point-blank range.

Judah couldn't miss.

He jammed down on the trigger.

The gun literally exploded in Judah's hands.

It wasn't a misfire, or a jam. It was a total outward

explosion. The gun broke outwards in a hundred pieces and fell crumbling from Judah's hands.

Judah frowned, confused—then he looked up in horror at West and said, 'Oh my God . . . you . . . *you* have the power . . .'

West stepped forward, his eyes deadly. 'Judah, I could forgive you for what you did to me, putting that chip in my head. I could forgive you for the beatings you gave Horus. But there's one thing I cannot forgive: killing Doris Epper. For that you have to pay.'

As he spoke, West picked up the end of Judah's long safety rope, unclipped it from its anchor near the Capstone.

Judah stepped backwards, toward the edge of the platform where the *Halicarnassus*'s wing loomed. He held his hands up. 'Now, Jack. We're both soldiers and sometimes soldiers have to—'

'You executed her. Now I'm going to execute you.'

And West threw his end of the safety rope past Judah . . . into the still-rotating jet engine of the *Halicarnassus* that hovered immediately behind Judah.

Judah spun as the rope flew by him, saw it enter the yawning maw of the engine.

Then he saw the future, saw what would happen next and his one good eye boggled with fear.

He screamed, but his scream was cut short as the enormous turbine swallowed the rope . . . and sucked *the rest of the safety rope* in after it.

Judah was yanked off his feet, doubling over as he was sucked backward through the air. Then he entered the engine and—*thwack-thwack-CHUNK!*—was chewed alive by its hyper-rotating blades.

★

And suddenly the summit of the Great Pyramid was still.

Seeing the awesome blast of light from the Sun and the deaths of their summit team, the American force at the base of the Pyramid fled, leaving West and Wizard up on the platform, alone.

Moments later, Zoe's Black Hawk landed on the platform and Zoe, Fuzzy and Stretch came rushing out of it—at the same time as Pooh Bear leapt onto the platform from the *Halicarnassus*'s wing.

They all arrived on the platform to find West—watched by Wizard—crawling underneath the Capstone to check on Lily.

West bellycrawled through the tight channel carved into the stone beneath the Capstone.

He came to Lily, found her lying motionless inside the human-shaped cavity in the Capstone's lowest Piece. Her eyes were closed. She seemed calm, at peace . . . and not breathing.

'Oh, Lily . . .' West scrambled forward on his elbows, desperate to get to her.

His head came alongside hers. He scanned her face for any movement, any sign of life.

Nothing. She didn't move at all.

He deflated completely, his entire body going limp, his eyes closing in anguish. 'Oh, Lily. I'm sorry. I'm so sorry.'

He bowed his head, tears rolled from the corners of his eyes, and he said, 'I loved you, kiddo.'

And there in the cavity, in the golden glow of the Capstone, lying before the body of the happy little girl he had guarded and raised for ten whole years, Jack West Jr wept.

'I love you, too, Daddy . . .' a soft voice whispered weakly from nearby.

West snapped up, his eyes darting open, to see Lily staring back at him, her head rolled onto its side. Her eyes were milky, dazed.

But she was alive, and smiling at him.

'You're alive . . .' West said, amazed. 'You're alive!'

He scooped her up in his arms and hugged her firmly.

'But how . . . ?' West asked aloud.

'I'll tell you later,' she said. 'Can we please get out of here?'

'You bet,' he breathed. 'You bet.'

Minutes later, the *Halicarnassus* powered up and lifted vertically into the sky, rising on its eight massive retro thrusters.

Once it was high enough, it pivoted in mid-air and allowed itself to drop, nose-down. It fell briefly, plummeting towards the ground, before it engaged its regular engines, using the short vertical fall to get up to flight speed. Its main engines firing, it swung up at the last moment and soared away from the Pyramids on the Giza Plateau.

★

The Great Pyramid was left standing there behind it, with the half-destroyed platform shrouding its summit, and the American helicopters and cranes lying smoking and broken on its flanks. The Egyptian Government that had aided and abetted the American ritual would have to clean it all up.

Importantly, however, the peak of the Pyramid was also once again nine feet shorter than it should have been.

West and his team had taken the Capstone—the entire Capstone—with them.

Inside the main cabin of the *Halicarnassus*, West and the others gathered around Lily, hugging her, kissing her, clapping her on the shoulders.

Pooh Bear embraced her: 'Well done, young one! Well *done*!'

'Thanks for coming back for me, Pooh Bear,' she said.

'I was never going to leave you, young one,' he said.

'Nor was I,' said Stretch, stepping forward.

'Thanks, Stretch. For saving me at the Gardens, for staying with me when you could have gone.'

Stretch nodded silently, to Lily and also to all the others, especially Pooh Bear. 'They don't come often,' he said, 'but every now and then, there come times in your life when you have to choose a side; choose who you are fighting for. I made my choice, Lily, to fight with you. It was a hard choice, but I have no doubt that it was the right one.'

'It was the right one,' Pooh Bear said, clapping a hand onto Stretch's shoulder. 'You are a good man, Israeli . . . I mean, Stretch. I would be honoured to call you my friend.'

'Thank you,' Stretch said with a smile. 'Thank you, *friend.*'

When all the back-slapping was over, West was eager to understand how Lily had survived.

'I went willingly,' she said simply.

'I don't get it,' West said.

Lily grinned, obviously proud of herself. 'It was the inscription cut into the wall of the volcano chamber where I was born. You yourself were studying it one day. It said:

'*Enter the embrace of Anubis willingly, and you shall live beyond the coming of Ra.*

Enter against your will, and your people shall rule for but one eon, but you shall live no more.

Enter not at all, and the world shall be no more.

'Like the Egyptians, we thought it was simply a reference to the god Horus, accepting death and being rewarded for that with some kind of afterlife. But that was wrong. It was meant to apply to me and Alexander—to the Oracles. It's not about accepting *death* willingly. It's about entering the cavity, the embrace of Anubis, willingly.

'If I entered it of my own accord, I would survive. If I went unwillingly, I'd die. But if I didn't go at all, and the ritual was not performed, you would all have died. And I, well, I didn't want to lose my family.'

'Even if that meant giving Zaeed power for all eternity?' Pooh Bear said in disbelief.

Lily turned to him, and her eyes glinted.

'Mr Zaeed was never going to rule,' she said. 'When

he grabbed me, I saw the soil in his jade box.' Lily turned to West. 'It was a kind of soil I'd seen many times before. I've been fascinated with it for a long time. It has been sitting in a glass jar on a shelf in Daddy's study for years. When I saw it in Mr Zaeed's box, I knew exactly what it was, and so I knew I wasn't giving Mr Zaeed any power at all.'

Pooh Bear said, 'Did del Piero know this, too? Is that why he treated Alexander like a little emperor, ready to rule? Did he want Alexander to enter that cavity willingly?'

'I think so,' West said. 'But there was more to it than that. Del Piero was a priest and he thought like a priest. He wanted Alexander to survive the ritual not because he wanted the boy to live and rule, but because he also wanted a *saviour*, a figurehead, a focal point for his new ruling religion. A new Christ figure.'

Through all this, Wizard sat alone in a corner of the cabin, silent, head bent. Zoe sat with him, holding his hand, equally shocked at the death of her brother, Big Ears.

Lily walked over to them, touched their shoulders. 'I'm sorry about Doris, Wizard,' she said with a seriousness that belied her age. 'And Big Ears, too, Zoe.'

Tear-lines streaked down Wizard's face; his eyes were moist and red. It was only on the platform that he had learned of Doris's death at Judah's hands.

'She died saving us,' Lily said. 'Telling us to get away. She gave her life so that we could escape.'

'She was my wife for 45 years,' Wizard said. 'The most wonderful woman I've ever known. She was my life, my family.'

'I'm so sorry,' Lily said.

Then she took his hand and looked deep into his eyes. 'But if you'll take me, I'll be your family now.'

Wizard looked up at her through his wet eyes . . . and he nodded. 'I'd like that, Lily. I'd like that a lot.'

A few hours later, Wizard found West alone in his office at the back of the *Halicarnassus*.

'I have a question for you, Jack,' he said. 'What does all this mean now? We set out to perform the ritual of peace, but now the ritual of power has been initiated—in favour of your country. Can Australians be trusted to possess such power?'

'Max,' West said, 'you know where I'm from. You know what we're like. We're certainly not aggressors or warmongers. And if my people *don't know* they've got this power, then I think this is the best possible outcome—because we're the most unlikely people on Earth to use it.'

Wizard nodded slowly, accepting this.

'I won't let them know if you won't,' West said.

'Deal,' Wizard said. 'Thank you, Jack. Thank you.'

The two men shared a smile.

And with that, the *Halicarnassus* soared into the sky, heading for Kenya, heading for home.

O'SHEA FARM
COUNTY KERRY, IRELAND
9 APRIL, 2006, 1630 HOURS

For the second time in ten years, the lonely old farmhouse on the hilltop overlooking the Atlantic Ocean was host to an important meeting of nations.

A couple of the faces had changed, but the seven original nations represented at the first meeting had not. Plus, there was one extra nation present this time: Israel.

'They're late,' the Arab delegate, Sheik Anzar al Abbas, growled. 'Again.'

The Canadian delegate—again—said, 'They'll be here. They'll be here.'

A door slammed somewhere, and a few moments later, Max T. Epper entered the sitting room.

Jack West, however, was not with him.

But he did have a companion: the little girl.

Lily.

'Where is Captain West?' Abbas demanded.

Wizard bowed respectfully. 'Captain West sends his apologies. Having succeeded on his mission, he assumed you wouldn't mind if he did not attend this meeting. He said he had some things to do, some loose ends to tie up. In the meantime, may I introduce to you all the young lady to whom we owe a profound debt of gratitude. Ladies and gentlemen, meet Lily.'

At length Wizard reported the events of the previous ten years to the delegates of the coalition of small nations.

Of course, they were aware of some elements of his success: the Earth had not been blasted with superheated solar energy; and America had not become invincible—its continued problems imposing law and order in the Middle East showed that. Word had got out about a spectacular battle atop the Great Pyramid, too, but damage to the structure had actually been minimal and the Egyptian Government, ever keen to retain American aid money, had denied the story absolutely.

And so Wizard told the delegates of Lily's upbringing in Kenya, of the chase to locate the seven Pieces of the Capstone, of the inclusion of Mustapha Zaeed in their quest, of their losses—of Noddy, Big Ears and of his own wife, Doris—and of the final confrontation on the summit of the Great Pyramid with the Americans and with Zaeed.

It was only on this last point that Wizard diverged slightly from the truth.

Since it accorded with the state of the world—safe from the power of the Sun, and with no apparent super-powerful ruling nation—he reported that on the summit of the Great Pyramid the ritual of *peace* had been performed, not the ritual of power.

He even informed them of the fate of the boy, Alexander. He had been found after the battle on the Pyramid and placed in the care of some trusted friends of Wizard's, people who would teach him to be a normal boy . . . and who would observe his maturation into adulthood, and keep track of any children he might have later in life.

'And so, ladies and gentlemen, our mission is accomplished,' Wizard concluded. 'This issue need not be addressed for another 4,500 years. At which time, I am pleased to say, it shall fall to someone else to handle.'

The delegates at the meeting rose from their chairs and applauded.

Then, buzzing with excitement, they started congratulating each other and calling home, to relay the excellent news.

Only one of them remained seated.

Sheik Abbas.

'Wizard!' he called above the din. 'You neglected to tell us one thing. Where is the Capstone now?'

All fell silent.

Wizard faced Abbas, eyed him evenly. 'The disposition of the Capstone was one of the loose ends Captain West had to attend to.'

'Where does he intend to hide it?'

Wizard cocked his head to one side. 'Surely, Anzar, the fewer who know the resting place of the Capstone, the better. You have trusted us this far, now trust us one more time.

'But let me assure you of one thing: Captain West has now retired from national service. He does not intend to be found. If you can find him, you can find the Capstone, but I pity the man who is tasked with that hunt.'

This seemed to satisfy Abbas, and the congratulations continued.

The sounds of celebration would echo from the farmhouse deep into the night.

★

The next morning, Wizard and Lily left Ireland.

As they boarded a private plane at Cork International Airport, Lily said, 'Wizard, where did Daddy go?'

'As I said, to tie up some loose ends.'

'What about after that? When he's done, where will he go?'

Wizard eyed her sideways. 'I actually don't know, Lily. Only you know. For all our safety, Jack wouldn't reveal his final destination. But he did tell me that he once gave *you* a riddle which, when solved, would reveal the location of his new home. So now it's all up to you, little one. If you want to find him, you must solve the riddle.'

GREAT SANDY DESERT
NORTH-WESTERN AUSTRALIA
25 APRIL, 2006, 1130 HOURS

The Toyota four-wheel drive zoomed along the empty desert highway.

In the passenger seat, Lily gazed out at the most inhospitable landscape she had ever seen. Wizard drove, with Zoe in the back. Lily shook her head. If there was any place on Earth further from civilisation, she didn't know it.

Dry barren hills stretched away in every direction. Sand crept out onto the desert highway, as if eventually it would consume it.

But it was an odd kind of sand, orange-red in colour, just like the soil that had been in West's jar.

They hadn't seen another car in hours. In fact, the last living thing they'd seen was a big saltwater crocodile basking on a virtually dry riverbank under a bridge they'd crossed a couple of hours ago.

A sign on the bridge had revealed the river to be named, somewhat appropriately, the River Styx, after the river in Hell. A three-way junction a few miles after it offered three options. To the left: Simpson's Crossing, 50 miles; straight: Death Valley, 75 miles; while going right would ultimately take them to a place called Franklin Downs.

'Go straight,' Lily had said. 'Death Valley.'

Now, two hours later, she said, 'It has to be here somewhere . . .'

She checked her riddle:

My new home is home to both tigers and crocodiles.
To find it, pay the boatman, take your chances with the dog and journey
Into the jaws of Death,
Into the mouth of Hell.
There you will find me, protected by a great villain.

Lily said, '"Pay the boatman, take your chances with the dog." In Greek mythology, when you entered the underworld, you first had to cross the River Styx. To do that, you paid the boatman and then took your chances against Cerberus, the dog guarding Hades. We've found the River Styx.'

Wizard and Zoe exchanged looks.

'And Death Valley?' Zoe asked. 'What makes you think that?'

'The next two lines in the riddle, "Into the jaws of Death/Into the mouth of Hell", they're from a poem that Wizard taught me, "The Charge of the Light Brigade". In the poem, the 600 members of the Light Brigade charge into "the Valley of Death". Death Valley.'

Minutes later, a series of low buildings rose out of the heat haze.

The town of Death Valley.

A weatherworn sign at the entry to the town read:

WELCOME TO
DEATH VALLEY
HOME OF THE MIGHTY
DEATH VALLEY TIGERS FOOTBALL TEAM!

'Home to both tigers and crocodiles,' Lily said.

Death Valley turned out to be a ghost town—just a cluster of old wooden shacks and farms with crumbling dirt driveways, long-abandoned.

They drove round for a while.

Lily gazed out the window, her eyes searching for a clue. 'Now we need to find a "great villain" . . . a great villain . . . *There*! Wizard! Stop the car!'

They stopped at the end of an ultralong dirt driveway. It was so long, the farmhouse to which it belonged lay over the horizon.

At the point where the driveway met the road, however, a rusty old mailbox sat on a post. Like many such mailboxes in rural Australia, this one was a home-made work of art.

Constructed of old tractor parts and a rusted oil barrel, it was fashioned in the shape of a mouse . . . complete with ears and whiskers. Only this mouse wore, of all things, a crown.

'A Mouse King . . .' she breathed. '*The* Mouse King. This is it.'

'How do you know?' Zoe asked.

Lily smiled at the in-joke. 'The Mouse King is a great villain. He's the villain in *The Nutcracker Suite*.'

Their car bounced up the dusty dirt driveway. At the very end of the long drive, far from the main road, they found a quiet little farmhouse nestled beneath a low hill, its windmill turning slowly.

A man stood on the front porch, dressed in jeans and a T-shirt, his metal left arm glinting in the sunshine, watching the approaching four-wheel drive.

Jack West Jr.

Lily bounded out of the car and leapt into West's arms.

'You found me,' he said. 'Took you long enough.'

'Where have you been?' Lily asked. 'What were these loose ends you had to tie up for a whole month?'

West grinned. 'Why don't you come and see.'

He led them behind the farmhouse, into an old abandoned mine hidden in the base of the low sandy hill back there.

'Later today, like Imhotep III did at the Hanging Gardens, I'm going to trigger a landslide to cover the entrance to this mine,' he said as they walked, 'so that no-one will ever know that there's a mine here, or what it contains.'

A hundred metres inside the mine, they came to a wide chamber and in the centre of the chamber stood . . .

. . . the Golden Capstone.

Nine feet tall, glittering and golden, and absolutely magnificent.

'Pooh Bear and Stretch helped me get it to Australia. Oh, and Sky Monster, too,' West said. 'But I left them all at the dock in Fremantle. A little later I got them to help me pick up a few other things that we encountered on our adventures. Wizard, I thought you might like to keep one or two.'

Standing in a semi-circle on the far side of the Capstone were several other ancient items.

The Mirror from the Lighthouse at Alexandria.

The Pillar from the Mausoleum at Halicarnassus.

Both last seen in Tunisia, inside Hamilcar's Refuge.

'You didn't get the head of the Colossus of Rhodes?' Wizard asked jokingly.

'I was thinking of going after it in a few months, if you wanted to join me,' West said. 'I could use the help. Oh, and Zoe . . .'

'Yes, Jack . . .'

'I thought you might like a flower, as a token of thanks for your efforts these last ten years.' With a flourish, he whipped something from behind his back and held it out to her.

It was a rose, a white rose of some kind, but one of unusual beauty.

Zoe's eyes widened. 'Where did you find this—?'

'Some gardens I saw once,' West said. 'Alas, they're no longer there. But this variety of rose is really rather resilient, and it's taking in my front garden very well. I expect to develop quite a rosebush. Come on, it's hot, let's head inside and I'll get some drinks.'

And so they left the abandoned mine and went back to the farmhouse, their shoes and boots caked in the unusual orange-red soil.

It was indeed a unique kind of soil, soil rich in iron and nickel, soil that was unique to this area: the north-western corner of what was now the most powerful nation on Earth . . . if only it knew it.

Australia.

ACKNOWLEDGEMENTS

First and foremost, I am indebted to a wonderful non-fiction book called *Secret Chamber* by the Egyptologist Robert Bauval. He's the guy who deduced that the pyramids at Giza are laid out in imitation of the constellation Orion's Belt.

It was from reading *Secret Chamber* that I discovered a Golden Capstone did indeed once sit atop the Great Pyramid at Giza. As an author, it's wonderful when you discover something so big and so cool that it can be the ultimate goal of your story, and when I read about the Golden Capstone, I just leapt up and started dancing around my living room, because I'd found exactly that.

I am often asked 'Where do you get your ideas from?' And this is the answer: I read a lot of non-fiction books, and if you read enough, you find gems like this. As a work on the darker side of ancient Egypt, with interesting sections on the Word of Thoth and the Sphinx, I would thoroughly recommend this book to anyone keen on the subject of ancient Egypt.

On the home front, as always, my wife Natalie was a model of support and encouragement—reading draft after draft, letting me off doing chores around the house, and most of all, happily allowing our honeymoon in Egypt to morph into a quasi-research trip!

Honestly, in Egypt I became one of those tourists who is the first off the bus and the last one back to it, and who pesters the tour guide with all kinds of weird questions. For example, at the Valley of the Kings, I asked, 'Is there a hieroglyph that says "Death to grave robbers?"' (Sure enough, there is, and the image of it in this book is it!) And neither of us will ever forget exploring—on our own—the haunting chambers beneath the 'Red' Pyramid south of Giza by the light of a perilously fading flashlight!

Once again, thanks to everyone at Pan Macmillan for another stellar effort. I've been so fortunate to work with a group of people who can package my work so well (I really love the jacket of this book).

Kudos also to my agents at the William Morris Agency, Suzanne Gluck and Eugenie Furniss—they look after me so well! And they're just from the literary section. That's not even mentioning the cool people in LA (notably Alicia Gordon and Danny Greenberg) doing film things on my behalf.

I'd also like to thank Mr David Epper, who generously supported my favourite charity, the Bullant Charity Challenge, by 'buying' the name of a character in this book at Bullant's annual auction dinner. Thus, his son, Max Epper, is in the book as Professor Max Epper, aka Wizard. Thanks, Dave.

And lastly, to family and friends, once again I pledge my eternal thanks for their support and tolerance. My mum and dad; my brother, Stephen; friends like Bec Wilson, Nik and Simon Kozlina; and, of course, my first 'official' reader, my good friend John Schrooten, who still reads my stuff in the stands at the cricket after all these years. If he starts ignoring the cricket because he's absorbed in the book, then it's a good sign!

Believe me, it's all about encouragement. As I've said in my previous books: *to anyone who knows a writer, never underestimate the power of your encouragement.*

M.R.
Sydney, Australia
October 2005

AN INTERVIEW WITH MATTHEW REILLY

THE WRITING OF *SEVEN ANCIENT WONDERS*

How was the writing of* Seven Ancient Wonders *different from the writing of your other books?

It's funny, but for some reason the writing of this book was a more solitary experience than the others—if anything, it felt a lot like the writing of *Contest*. Perhaps that's because the subject matter of the book, the Seven Wonders of the Ancient World, is *so* ancient, *so* distant, *so* alien to us, that I was creating most of the story from pure imagination (rather than from actual sources—some of the stuff on the Wonders is pretty flimsy). As I did when I created the aliens in *Contest*, I just had to create these mystical places, like the Hanging Gardens of Babylon, for example, from scratch.

What did you try to do differently with this book?

For me, the key difference between *Seven Ancient Wonders* and my previous books is the theme of 'family' in it. The team of international soldiers guarding Lily ultimately becomes a family—complete with grandparents (Doris and Max Epper), squabbling brothers and sisters (Pooh Bear, Stretch, Big Ears, Zoe), and the father-like figure of Jack West.

This was a thematic thing that I started in *Hover Car Racer* and I enjoyed it immensely when I wrote that novel. In the end, when you write an action-thriller novel, you must have characters that you care about, and by creating this quasi-family environment out of a bunch of hard-ass troopers, I felt I'd created a special kind of team that readers would want to cheer for.

I particularly love how Lily renames all the soldiers, changing all their tough-guy call-signs into goofy childish nicknames. Having utilised 'serious' call-signs in the Scarecrow books, I felt it was time to have a bit of fun, and turn this plot device on its head.

Is it true that for this book you created your own language?

I wouldn't go so far as to say that I created a language! What I did do was create an alphabet (not unlike cuneiform) to display the Word of Thoth—but my translation is just from English, not a brand-new language. That would have been way too hard and time-consuming. I'll leave that sort of thing to JRR Tolkien!

It took some time, but it was great fun. I created symbols to match those of our own alphabet, plus rules for proper nouns and special symbols for certain objects (like the Great Pyramid, Alexander the Great and the Sun, for instance). If anyone has the time and the inclination they can translate all the Thoth references in the book back to English, but be careful, as in the novel, it gets harder, as more symbols are used, and sometimes not from left-to-right!

After the book has been out a while, I'll put up the alphabet on my website, so that anyone who's interested can see how it works.

With the exception of Jason Chaser in* Hover Car Racer, Seven Ancient Wonders *sees the introduction of your first Australian action hero. What made you decide to make Jack West Jr an Australian?

It suited the story. Simple as that. I'm often asked why the heroes of my other books are American and the answer is really the same: it suited those stories (it especially suited *Ice Station*).

With *Seven Ancient Wonders*, I wanted the hero specifically *not* to be American. He had to lead this little band of small nations against the combined might of America and Europe. And so I thought of an ex-SAS soldier from Australia. I also knew that the ending of the book required one country to be imbued with the power of Tartarus, and what could be more fun than Australia being the most powerful country on Earth and not knowing it? (I already think that, anyway!)

You mention* The Da Vinci Code *by Dan Brown a couple of times in the novel. Have you read it? Did it influence you?

I have indeed read *The Da Vinci Code* and I enjoyed it thoroughly. I actually read it long before it dominated the bestseller lists—when I was touring with *Scarecrow* in 2003, I would recommend it to anyone who would listen!

That said, *The Da Vinci Code* wasn't really an influence on *Seven Ancient Wonders*. The Indiana Jones movies were probably more of an influence. I wanted to create an Indiana Jones-type story, with booby traps and high adventure, but set in the present day. The reason I mentioned *The Da Vinci Code* in the book was really because that novel is now *so* globally known, if you do write a story about Catholic Church conspiracy theories or one which has a scene set in the Louvre, you should probably make a *Da Vinci Code* joke!

Seven Ancient Wonders *features some pretty dastardly American villains! Is it an anti-American novel?*

I hope it's not interpreted that way. The Americans are just the villains in this book, that's all. They want the power of Tartarus and so they go after it—they just do so a little more ruthlessly than our heroes!

The key to *Seven Ancient Wonders* was that the heroes had to be underdogs, underdogs battling the most powerful nation on Earth, and that at the moment is America. America has more guns, tanks and planes than the next dozen countries combined. For a bunch of little countries to go up against the United States is a big thing, a hard thing. And that, to my mind, makes for an interesting story.

I guess, like many others, I do question the new American 'Imperialism' under George W. Bush, but unlike others I don't dislike America for it. It's a lone superpower in a changed world. It has to figure out how to find its way, just like the rest of us. It will make mistakes. Unfortunately, any mistakes it makes will have a big impact on everyone else on this planet. It will also, it must be said, do much good.

I don't know. I invariably find myself *defending* America when I'm out at dinner with friends. I have many American friends, and I work with some *very* clever New Yorkers and Los Angelinos. Smart people, all of them. I also firmly believe that America is a fantastic social experiment—a land of opportunity, where capitalism is king, and where 280 million people live in relative peace under the rule of law; not a bad achievement at all.

After all that, if some Americans think that just because I made them the villains of this book that I'm anti-American, then what can I do? I'll just have to cop it and know that they're wrong. And hey, the Brits never minded being the villains of *Ice Station*! But then again, I still have not been published in France . . .

Will we see Jack West Jr again?

I think there's a good chance we'll see Jack West in a new book sometime in the future. I enjoyed writing about him and going on this huge adventure with him—and that's the key incentive for me to write about a character a second time. It takes me a year to write a novel, and if I'm going to spend a year with a character, I have to like him or her!

And I do already have an idea of what that adventure could be . . .

You've had a busy year.* Seven Ancient Wonders, Hell Island, *and your movie work on* Contest. *How have you survived it all?

Yes, it has been a busy year! But it's been enormous fun.

I had just finished *Seven Ancient Wonders* when the call came from the Federal Government asking if I would write a brand-new short-novel for their Books Alive campaign. Luckily, I had a new idea sitting in the 'Story Ideas' drawer of my desk ready to go, so I turned around, sat back down and started writing again!

And yes, at that stage, I'd already planned to direct a pilot shoot of *Contest*, so I was in the midst of pre-production when I was polishing both *Hell Island* and *Seven Ancient Wonders*. I'm still not quite sure how I did it, but I figured I could sleep later! Believe me, I'm resting now.

Shane Schofield appeared in the Books Alive edition of **Hell Island. *Will we see the Scarecrow again in a new novel?***

A few things about *Hell Island*, especially since I didn't do an interview like this in the back of that book.

I really enjoyed doing *Hell Island*, and making it a Schofield book. I think it's a pretty kick-ass story—bold, fast and *mean*; and yet still short. It was designed to be a kind of 'side-adventure' for Schofield; a minor mission that occurred in between books (although technically it occurs after the events in *Scarecrow*). You also have to remember that my fans in the US and other countries won't see *Hell Island*, as it was a free book given out in Australia only, which I actually kind of like.

Will he appear again? I reckon so. He's a fun character, who's always getting into trouble, and they're the ones I like to write about. The question is, who do I write about next? Schofield or Jack West?

What is the latest movie news?

Hover Car Racer is still with Disney. Last I heard, Al Gough and Miles Millar were still at work on the screenplay. And, of course, I'm hard at work trying to get *Contest* up and running as a feature film.

I had an awesome time directing the pilot of *Contest* earlier this year, which was the first twelve minutes of the book: this included getting a creature shop to build a fully-articulated Karanadon head and filming it in the stack of the New South Wales State Library. We also filmed in the abandoned train tunnels underneath Sydney, the Royal North Shore Hospital and even in the basement of my house! Ah, movie magic.

So, what's next for Matthew Reilly?

Sleep. Rest. And maybe play a bit of golf. It's been a very busy year and I need to slow down a bit. I'm just going to sit on my couch and read a bunch of non-fiction books! Although if I get *Contest* up and running, then it'll be all systems go and I can sleep next year . . .

Any final words?

As always, I just hope you all enjoyed the book. I had a lot of fun writing this one and I hope you had just as much fun reading it.

M.R.
Sydney, Australia
October 2005